PRAISEWORTHY

Praiseworthy

ALEXIS WRIGHT

SHEFFIELD – LONDON – NEW YORK

First published in 2023 by the Giramondo Publishing Company
This edition published in 2023 by And Other Stories
Sheffield – London – New York
www.andotherstories.org

Published by arrangement with Giramondo Publishing Company

1 3 5 7 9 8 6 4 2

Print ISBN: 9781913505929
eBook ISBN: 9781913505936

Series Cover Design: Elisa von Randow, Alles Blau Studio, Brazil, after
a concept by And Other Stories. Author photo: Vincent Long.

And Other Stories books are printed and bound in the UK on FSC-
certified paper by the CPI Group (UK) Ltd, Croydon. The covers are
of G . F Smith 270gsm Colorplan card – made in the Lake District
at the environmentally friendly James Cropper paper mill – and are
embossed with biodegradable foils from FoilCo, Warrington.

And Other Stories gratefully acknowledges that its work is
supported using public funding by Arts Council England

I am not even dust. I am a dream...
Jorge Luis Borges

Contents

NEW GODS

Kulibibi. Baba yalu kurrkamala, jaja,
(butterflies are flying everywhere)
Waanyi dictionary, 2012

1
Oracle 1...speak.

Beginning with story...

Once upon a fine time for some people in the world, but not so plenteous, nor perfect for others, there lived a culture dreamer obsessing about the era. He was no great dreamer, no greater than the rest of the juggernauts in his heartbroken, storm-country people's humanity. They knew just as much as he did about *surviving* on a daily basis, and about how to make sacrifices of themselves in all the cataclysmic times generated by the mangy dogs who had stolen their traditional land. These people, after the generations of dealing with the land-thief criminals like many others around the world, had turned themselves, not into a tangled web of despair, but into some of the best fighters of all times. They used pure guts for improving life, and said they were in it for the long run. Theirs was a sovereign world view – the main view acceptable to their governing ancestors, a law grown through belief in its own endlessness, and through re-setting the survival barometer from millennia a couple of hundred years ago, by evolving a new gauge – something like a moth's sonar, for only hearing what it wanted to hear. But, to be frank, the facet worked like a shield, for seeing what they wanted to see of the world, or to shut the whole thing out forever. And for deciding whether they wanted to speak at all, for sometimes, this world never spoke for years, then when it did, spoke wreckage words – like a piece of heaven heavy with intent, firing on all cylinders from the sky.

So this dreamer fellow really had some nerve speaking doubt stuff in the God gravitas of these clergy-oriented people, and like, acting as though he was a better type of Jesus, more Messiah than they were themselves, while preaching from the unpopular pulpit of himself out on the street corner every other Sunday in front of all their self-defined denominational churches, and always, like too many times before, asking the same old question: *Hey! Mob! What's the future going to be, whatnot!*

There was not a single soul in Praiseworthy who believed this fellow was real, for asking such a ridiculous question in this day and age, and right in front of the world's greatest human survivors. Weren't they the real business people of all times? Extinction-less tempest people from enduring one million storms, come from the ark of infinity right down to the last baby. They were now forced to speak, and yelled that they knew a thing or two about being trodden upon, and of being more on trend than the rest of humanity about how to look after the future. They would tell you themselves how they had to assert too much nervous-wreck type of anger in their voices: *We studied everything you needed to know about surviving from the biggest library in the world – country.* You only had to take a quick look around Praiseworthy to see all the stories were about surviving. You do not need some redundant bullshit-artist person continually harping on with his eternal question, *You mob ever tried thinking about what the future of the place got to look like?*

The world spins, he was told this fact thing pretty much frankly by the multitudes of insulted people. *It always spins. The world is like a big spin dryer.*

Then this atmospheric pressure blackfella – still acting like God, thinking he was on top of the story universe, in with some fancy contemporary scene – started asking what was the comfort zone, what level, what was living to tell the tale like, of being a survivalist of the situation? He was seeing it all as a hundred per cent thing in the funniness. His stories were too much for a brain, rolling in stitches up there, like he was spinning some ancestor power, and you wanted him to stop telling stories like that, he got no business, but him telling them repeatedly all the same and never stopping, yep, right, like he was the national newspaper, or something called social media cancelling everybody else, and all the while only ever predicting nothing good would come out of a worldwide doom. You got tired of hearing gloominess all the time – with all his remembering of this and that of the twenty-first century hot load in planetary catastrophes of global warming or global viruses, and never tiring of talking about all this stuff, this great mess, while people were saying that they preferred listening to magpies that sung to the moon, and the night-time hopping mouse was having an anxiety attack from hearing this catastrophic stuff, like another dry thunderstorm, when it had to sneak out from beneath some bit of scrubby dry grass where it has a nice hidey-hole thing in the soil, from where it cuts through that spinifex highway along the aeon-old ancestral tracks, hopping along a bit happy, a bit relieved it was still alive and not struck by lightning into a splat while heading way down south, cuts across west this way, east that way, leaving golden moon-shone paw prints behind in the sandy soil, and then what? Well! Hold everything! It too remembers catastrophic times, then quick speed, heads straight back up north, races back over its original tracks to where it had just a moment ago left, and jumps like lightning under the same stump of grass now turned the colour of grey gloom.

Well! One thing! We know all about global warming and deadly viruses. This was what the countrymen repeatedly and exhaustively explained to the zeitgeist Cause Man Steel over and over, that he did not need to lay his life on the line for them, they would take care of business...but, you know what? Cause never liked listening to others. He was saved by his own brain. The old country men and women, totally exasperated, even murderous, wanted him dead. They wanted global warming, wanted the lot, wanted to hasten the thing up, because on Praiseworthy country, people of traditional thought preferred silence and never wanted to speak another word, nor wanted to watch any more stupidity, nor see anything ridiculous, nor think about any of the crazy things other people did with their lives to cause ancestral storms and mayhem. So, they said: *Listen, shit for brains! It never gets lonely and wrathful here, because country here always look after its people, because people here look after their country.*

No matter what you care about in this world, or whether you give two frigs, there will always be times, when nobody will like hearing a scary future thinker's doom stories about the destruction of the globe. They do not want to hear anyone who thinks that humanity is out of sync with the wrathful planet, or someone who called himself a planet fixer *of cataclysmic change*; or, some kind of influencer, likened to one of those modern gods of social media. Nobody wanted to have an anomaly man like this in Praiseworthy. He was told to shut up. Why had they survived since time immemorial? Their ancient law. That's what. This was what took care of business. Not idiots. There were far better oracles than him to listen to who knew white murderers were everywhere, and who could fathom the depth of consequences to the living world from ancestral laws being broken by the destruction of countless sacred ancient law places and culture people across their holy continent since white colonisation. Sure! He was told these things many times, but sadly, their kind of ancient oracle-ising was not in sync with Cause Man Steel's vision of the modern world. They joked about death wishers, laughed themselves silly about having this doom dreamer living illegally among them, but in a nice way, just to show that they thought about the world too, and named him Widespread – for the breadth of his ideas spreading all over the place. Or, they called him Planet – because he was always talking planetary stuff. Or else, they called the weirdo by his real name – Cause Man Steel – cause, cause and effect. He was hard all right, like the power ancestor's essence in Australia's iron ore.

Anyhow! This planet fixer ended up wasting away among the others who did not give a rat's arse about saving a dying world, and in the end, he became as skinny as a rake. He stooped so low from carrying the weight of the entire world on his bony shoulders, that his face was almost touching the ground in front of him, like he was studying the dirt of the planet itself, same as a greedy camp dog sniffing along the ground. Yep! This was the local influencer: a modern god preaching about the planet collapsing. They call this type of person a collapsologist, someone specialising in collapsology – this was what he claimed to be doing, putting himself in front of the collapse – to hold the thing up, as though he was the most knowledgeable wise man around, when everyone else in Praiseworthy already knew the mise en abyme ways of the Earth to the nth degree of each cataclysmic change in either the minuses or pluses of overheating in the twenty-first-century buggered-up world. Yep! Again! Let it be said: this man was a live pulpit, a kind of Marvin Gaye singing about *What's going on* in never-ending parables, as though he was personally responsible for the composition of some big new revolutionary recreation story cycle for the world mind you, even though in normal reality, it was more like driving a petrol-guzzling sedan anyhow over goat's tracks, than walking across the planet as some kind of medieval crusading warrior man from Praiseworthy, like God with the weight of the world strapped over his back.

What's going on?

Wanyinbu-nanja.

What for?

Then, it's like this: in a magical gleaming day of supreme sunshine, something fantastical occurred, which was like a catharsis bingo moment coming on for this one small colonialism-style hot prick of a place on Earth, when Widespread discovered the odyssey plan.

Planet wanted to give his humble culture people the gift of infinity, although they already had the all times surviving stories planted squarely in the culture's soul. Doesn't matter about that. The plan was a real goer, a rhapsody superglued on the door of the main cupboard for ideas in his head, and in a pivotal moment of broadcasting – widespreading the thing – he said, *Listen, my humanity. This is what we gotta do.*

Basically, the plan was for his people to ride straight through the century on the back of the burning planet, and live to tell the tale on the other side. This was what the ancestors had done for countless millennia. Check the facts in the climate change stories they had left behind, which were about how it felt to be a survivor of all times, of being changed, evolved, looking challenge after challenge in the eye, but always surviving in the end.

Then, you know what happened, somebody went and killed Aboriginal Sovereignty, infinity itself.

The story goes...

Hate place was a monument of the moment for some of the poorest people on Earth. A hard bit of magic grown from a corpus of ancient stories that had been scattered into mystery by broken spirits creating hell fires. All those endlessly wandering fragments of ancient words were coming together, and forming the lines of stories entombed in smoke clouds circumnavigating the planet.

Now...A ghostly windstorm from out of nowhere came more frequently, came to this place blowing dry leaves, burnt leaves, ash leaves, and spoke of the tragedies in the epical pyres of life. The wind looked at the remains of life in this place, then blew and blew these fragments away in mountainous serpentine waves that hit the soul world of an even greater local spirit and there, dust, ash, memories written on broken butterfly wings with black soot, all backed up into an ochre-coloured haze that ended up sitting permanently over the flatlands of the *blessed be thou, and more blessed be I.*

This old grief haze cuts a powerful image from forty thousand feet up in the sky where ancestral serpents roamed through the remnants of migrating angels, and you, looking down from the window seat up front of a QF Qantas flight cruising over the northern flat country would see the grand improbabilities. Yes, the supercell anomaly was a miracle on Earth, but not a good one. Sometimes the haze floated, rested on dust-coated leaves, on the rooftops, on every space, house, person, on the dog fur, bird feathers, or else, the thing charged up its weather system into an atmospheric mess of dry electrical storms full of dust. Jundurr! Jundurr! Jundurr! From the sky, you could look down, to see the supercell rotating from where it sat permanently over Praiseworthy, lingering with its belly hovering just centimetres above the ground as though it was resting on a head full of swiftly dit! dit! dit! imaginings. The gravitational force of the slow-moving cloud of haze pushed by the great ancestral government, and held together as though magnetised, hanging like a shadow that made the place perpetually looking sepia, like suppertime.

This was how the dust storm lingered for far too many years, and became a stationary presence, pivoting over the spinifex land of the zeitgeist, where those strugglers of apocalyptic times – the traditional landowners in this isolated place of flatlands – were continuing their long line of imaginings into infinity. Yes, these people might have looked like they were razed-to-the-ground people, yet why would they give up easily, millennia of their ancestors never did, simply because they not only had the will to live, but desired survival over extinction. And now, they were ready and able to gamble any wishful thinking for ridding themselves of the haze scourging the skin, and from touching the skin of their land.

2

Oh! My! Oh! My! Any people could say this was exactly what happens when the world of unreality strikes like a piece of lightning – colliding with misconstrued fact after fact, and forcing country lines apart – bolting this way and that, becoming an entangled knot blurring the light. *Ah! Watch out! Get the hell out of the way!* There were plenty of these uppity upper-class people of Praiseworthy – super people living in the ark with the loudest mouths for saying *that the sun only shone here alone* – while crying out for someone to go out there in the bad lands of the continent, and *get some help from the white government.* They wanted fast help to get rid of the sulky haze which was full of broken ancestors breathing on them with virus air from who knows where else. Stop all this happening – things like that – from that hazard haze parking itself on top of them. Think about it. You expect people to be pretty jacked off in the head with having a haze sit on top of them and weighing down their lives, and this was the reason why lots of the local people were community minded enough to march straight out of their storied-riddled houses to get involved in the campaign to fight the atmosphere. They were not going to be governed by some jacked off spirit acting completely crazy. It reminded them too much of life itself.

One old elder found some inappropriate whitefella music on the Decca label which he used to assimilate into the mind of local thinking about the Anthropocene, the man-made disaster of the world. The locals who knew nothing about European classical music or how it created human heat like global warming, became hooked on what the elder said was Dvorak. Then some other old fella in a suit said that the music was from the New World in his symphony No. 9 in E Minor, Op. 95 and could pacify the gods of the Anthropocene. The music was piped into the haze to speak to its soul in this otherwise weirdo free-for-all feast of peddling stress and anxiety, while trying to coax a deal for blacks from white government sitting pretty thousands of kilometres away, to get it to get up off its arse and do something about cleaning up the air. The sum total of their hymn travelled through the ether, and went onwards into infinity as could only be expected, such was the government's complete incomprehension about Aboriginal humanity.

You could only watch the spectacle of the righteous, sit back and watch the pinging of epical emails that only blazed new and more complicated trails through the existing mazes carved by the loneliest words that ever existed in this world. Many went around screaming at the haze in their distress: *What else could we do?* They sent a common brown butterfly on a journey down south, to flutter four thousand kilometres to the lonely Australian capital Canberra, as their final embassy on the matter. Then they waited, and waited some more, only to see the broken tattered butterfly return the next autumn on a slow breeze with its singed wings. The story went around that the government shot the butterfly with a blowtorch.

After the fateful journey of the butterfly, the luckless people hopped further into the fray, and sent delegations of ghostly haunted-looking people painted in white ash to go tripping down to the country's capital to negotiate on good terms mind you, but that all ended in the toxic wasteland of death threats to the culture if you do not assimilate white, or else. Or else, you would lose count of the many delegations flying off to Canberra to implore politicians across the political spectrum from the extreme Pentecostalist right to every crazed independent governing sector in the country to amend the Australian Constitution to get rid of the haze, and also now, to stop shooting butterflies. Yet still, no assistance came, no aid, no support package like the government gave other people for suffering a heavenly calamity. They all got some handout – everyone, except for the pollution-breathing mob living in the haze that sat over Praiseworthy. The Canberra politicians accused the traditional owners of being deranged, of seeing things that only they could see, a haze. Nobody else saw changes in the climate, nor any unprecedented haze events anywhere else in the land mass of the continent.

The local people followed up with physicality, by having a boxing match with the haze's curse on their kind. The people stood out in the atmosphere punching the curse. Kicked it in the guts. Cursed and swore. But nothing. The story goes that this was when the apparition managed to mutate into its multiaxial position by multiplying itself by two. It ended up infusing some creepy haze spirit into the lungs of the Major Mayor white-influencer thing, who up until then, had always been seen as a normal human being. Suddenly, he was obsessed by whiteness, and lost the natural traditional-owner loving for the red haze colour of the earth of his country. His skin became as white as vanilla ice cream. Then ice cream eroded into sheer translucence, like one of those white plastic shopping bags from the supermarket lost in space. Even his eyeballs had changed colour from naturally brown, to becoming in the end, sheer white. Yep! White eyeballs. He had been turned into a living ghost. It was not the kind of transformation that white people could see. Now, a man like this became known as Ice Pick, a kind of more than albino, who had covered himself from head to toe in a labyrinth of Casper the Ghost tattoos, mermaids and octopuses, but you could still see his power blood coursing under the translucence of a spirit man's skin. And he hid the spook eyes with contact lenses: a couple of bits of pink plastic.

That local magic worked best when Ice Pick practically became supernatural, even if it was just a copycat illusion of a greater-than-usual whiteness, which was to say, more white than white people with added bonus, by actually resembling a lady's doppelganger in the form of a heart-palpitating TV white man from an American western. He had become the go-to strong man of the moment because of his *supernaturalness*. Now, since being turned prematurely white-haired, he believed he had acquired the status of a wisdom man, and was playing with that kind of power in his forty-ish year-old pinhead brain. It was like expecting a Kmart-bought frisbee to fly all the passengers in Praiseworthy as though it were some majestic spirit bird, as though it were the largest and strongest plane on earth carrying hypersonic vehicles to space while everyone cried with happiness at such a feat, when it was not like that at all. Yet, the translucence of more than whiteness had its charm, enough to claim some power status knowledge which was more than Ice Pick could actually handle in his newly acquired improved standing as Major Mayor. He found that he was now everybody's trusted cowboy in the field: the *go-to* spin doctor who was making sure that other people's dreams became aligned with his own more than whiteness style of avariciousness, while he plotted a crazy ton of half-baked dreams to be realised ASAP in Praiseworthy.

Unzipped-lip Ice was making sure that it was everybody's business to have a good straight look at life to come, although not looking too far ahead, not peering through the lens of long-term planetary meltdown, but just enough say, to the next whitefella government election – state or federal, it did not matter which – through the prism of what he thought would happen if Praiseworthy people chose not to act like a pack of compromising lambs to please assimilatory policies of a three-year-term Canberra government.

This was the score, what life had become. A let-down. Weak-spiritedness. Loss of pride. The kind of low self-esteem infinity people felt after choking on too much cursing of the ancestral dust, how decimated it felt to be more acutely attuned – like radar to racism, in a world that fed itself on racism – which panic style led to a traffic jam, realising racism was rampant and entrenched in every thought, and government aid was never going to arrive to northern Aboriginal people, suspected of being terrorists, to purchase enough explosives to blow up the haze. *Not if you do not assimilate and be white*, warned the colossal, over-ventilating, almost breathless Ice Pick, while hyping his assimilating virtuosity like a spirit-dead God man.

Major Mayor was sadly another kind of *be-bop-a-lula* fast-pace mover and shaker in the power and glory. And nope! You could not take any of his preaching seriously – not about one hundred per cent assimilating with white people for the sake of reconciliation. Not even on a bad day, listening to the influencer of the collective consciousness harping his non-denominational new-style scripture from the western world, while pointing an old woman's hunting stick towards a trail of wickedness in the black world. You just do not take someone like that seriously in a palace place like Praiseworthy, which sets a very high standard in its own values, not while he was wearing the wrong thing on his Casper Ghost head, like that Australia Day hat covered in prints of the Australian flag instead of a sacred land rights cap emboldened first class, with the Aboriginal flag. Wrong thing! You were not going to instil Xi Jinping style of consciousness in the soul of your people wearing the wrong cap.

Then, hearing that there were more attacks on its sovereignty – land bulldozed here, mines shafted and blown to smithereens, ancestors falling into the mine pit over there – the old country was awoken, re-awakened, eternal sleep impossible in the anger world. These days, the great thunder fellow was awake all night, all fright, venting his unquenchable anger from point A to point B and so on with a million lashes of lightning flashing from one side of the continent to the other. A mostly dry storm puked a glob of rain that flew straight across the north sky while quickly parting like a curtain around the Praiseworthy haze as if it was evaporating quicker than a spit, split to escape the worst plague on Earth, and then, closing again, flew on with the storm birds, and the seagulls, journeying to the point of exhaustion into the Pacific, or the Indian ocean, without dropping a single drop of rain on the thought land of eternal drought.

They say that year was all the same, a mirage shimmer, just as any other. An endless cycle of replenishing nothing, that went on repeating itself through harsher drought. All the rain, the minuscular drops, was never enough for the leaf litter to become the sodden fancy scene of the golden beetle when it woke from the thunder spirits leaving behind a vapour of moisture while travelling across the ground at night. It was barely enough to fool the golden Christmas beetle crawling out of the underground dry yellow grass country, where along with millions of its civilisation, it came up through the slightly dampened earth to a desolate surface. Underground mud dries and slides off its elytra, the hard protection wings of gold covering its body, as it moves among other golden beetles crawling over every dead leaf on the ground, and up every slender grass stalk. Old beetle spirit now waits on top of a high grass stalk, looks with contemptuous eyes into the red haze of Praiseworthy, crawls back down to the dirt, and begins its work, an awesome task guided by an eternity of law packed in its tiny head.

This was when the golden beetle (*Anoplognathus aureus*) comes around to inspect the country its spirit had continued to build for aeons. The old *aurum* spirit lifts the hard casing to release the soft back wings, then flies from one dry grass stem to another, then up among the trees. It climbs many gum trees until in the light of a full moon, it finds a tree transformed into glistening gold from thousands of other *au* beetles eating among the freshest leaves. A windstorm brings lightning and thunder, and the inspector of country crawls away into the shadows and into the depths of broken bark, where it rumbles around all night as though searching for something among the old cobwebs and discarded wings of insects and dead spiders. It methodically checks each strand of cobweb with its mandible, and prowls the surroundings with its antennae, while feeling everything with its claws. It seems to be imagining the world through the fine old music of the trees sing-talking back and forth while relaying all the storylines, the sounds of infinity reaching through a multitude of tracks over vast distances. It crawls through the leaf litter on the ground, along twigs, turns over soil, moves pebbles around while searching for the tiny devil mob. It finds all of those spirits with antennae that do not stop moving.

All of this checking of country and searching must have taken days for the beetle to crawl along the main road to Praiseworthy at the rate of 2.54 cm a minute, and you know what? It was searching for the brightest light among the illuminated blow-up giant snowmen and fabulous lit reindeers in the town, the security light beaming like the Christmas Star of Bethlehem on the verandah of the Major Mayor's house. This was where the inspector knocked at the door. This was becoming an annual event, claimed Ice Pick, the golden Christmas beetle visiting him at his home to advise him about how to make money. He pointed to the beetle moving down the bitumen street, and told the Praiseworthy world with an air of confidence that far outstretched his ability to make any money at all, that they were looking at his lucky beetle. Whenever he spoke about this fortune-making insect, he chuckled nervously, as though he wanted to believe what he was saying in the old law people meetings so they would stop calling him a fakery, but they continued saying he was full of bullshit.

A belittling in the governing world of country was not pretty for any rhapsodically self-proclaimed king of orators, so the Twitter addict of false news threw more wondrous stories around to all and sundry about the special relationship with his precious golden beetle. No one could own the law beetle. Who could believe him? The elders chuckled to each other through calls with their free mobiles – gifted from international mining companies wanting to dig up their sacred sites – then they chucked the cheap shit into the sea. They were that sick to death of being buzzed by Ice wanting them to tell him the sacred law story about the golden beetle. Instead they kicked dirt into their camp fires, quietened the story fellow, keeping him safe. Said that they were men. Human beings. They abandoned telecommunications altogether, and marched off far away into the bush for a bit of peace and quiet to think straight without any means of communication. Even the tiniest of children knew that this particular gold beetle was no different to thousands of other bush beetles. Why would a beetle be bothered being a destiny adviser to a human being like Ice Pick? *You kids should listen. It came from my traditional country.* Get the picture? The beetle was his totem. The 'real' elders said, *more bullshit.* Golden beetles were crawling everywhere on the bitumen this time of the year. They lived in a beetle-ridden universe during the wet time.

No one appreciated having liars in the pristine, and Praiseworthy people were no exception. They left him to think what he liked about his exceptionalism, and how the pathological dog liar would repent to them. It was not up to them to stop the fantastical junk talk flowing from his mouth like a flooding river, his ignorant interference with a law beetle. You could only speak about the fact in indefinite pronouns, of how somebody's stupid talk was messing with everybody's weather, no rain again, like you had already seen before from a whole string of fortune hunters making a crack, trying to will-up their silly ideas into reality, by saying a spirit ancestor was telling them how to run the universe, when the thing itself was telling them to get back to the traditional country which they knew nothing about, to learn something, and get the ceremonies going for things like the golden beetle law. Ice Pick was no different to any of these idiots, in totally believing that this single little beetle was not only his audacious career advisor that had installed its far superior infinite brain into his brain, but also that the law creature was actually achieving its own gigantic, excessive, and insatiable ambition through him.

Each year, around Christmas time, Ice Pick would capture the beetle after it had followed the distress beacon and crawled onto his verandah, put it in a bottle, and then, bore the life out of it with his lesser vision, the endless talk about how he was building the new Praiseworthy into an all-bustling, all-glitter epoch-making Aboriginal world metropolis – a colossal go-to type of economic powerhouse for trading Aboriginal knowledge in future anthropocentric times that would be on the scale of what? Well! New York. Shanghai. But maybe not Moscow. He stared down the beetle, challenging it to come up with a better plan, to think of a light on the hill, a better brightness in the lighthouse of the developing world. This argy-bargy of *you tell me* between a prized fool and a big law ancestor went on and on, until the beetle gave up, knowing its irenic mission with a fool man had failed again, saw there would be no peace in the near future, flipped over onto its back, and pretended to be dead.

Not long after that, the beetle spirit, fuelled by its own large-scale capacity for hope which turned its golden elytra into glowing russet, thundered off, and returned within country. Another year in an endless cycle of the storyline was lost through miscommunication with a fool who did not know what the story was.

Ice Pick, none the wiser, only grew more confident with the annual visitation of the golden beetle. His gloating became of biblical proportions on and on around the municipality. He claimed to be the head golden beetle man whose totem had walked into town year after year at a specific time – in the middle of the dry storm of another forgotten wet season, to personally advise him about how to build Shanghai out of a dusty haze with his bare hands. *It was bringing me gold, man.* Anyone could do the same, he claimed, if they took notice of the ancestors. The elders watched Ice Pick through all these years, just to see what the fool would do next to make Shanghai out of a haze. *We would like to see that* they said, *and perhaps*, were also, *prepared to wait.* They did this, not because the Major Mayor was potentially a very dangerous man, but because they saw that he had a stupid brain, and people like this would always pick the wrong thing to work on and achieve nothing that would be harmful to the cultural future, and it was harmless to watch a bit of entertainment for free. Yet, he was always on their radar of wondering, a yardstick for estimating what a true hero of the times would not be, even if they could not picture true heroism.

Was Ice the local chief oracle as he claimed to be, already sacred, already holy, the chief Pope-like whip of the multi-denominational churches of all possible persuasions? The elders said no, and called him a robber. They had developed the church proliferation business themselves as their own pet assimilatory project, an extracurricular venture in religious piousness, and were proud to own this façade of modern whiteness, along with all of its superficiality. Or was he just another village idiot who stacked annual general elections in order to be continuously re-elected as the Major Mayor, the biggest loudmouth in town? Or was he just a fool for deliberately not wanting to follow the tiny golden beetle's slow steps back into country, which was, after all, his inheritance, as well as being ancestral law?

It was all cruelty chic, the official stories of the world's struggling people walking the tumbledown life of poverty as they searched for a way to move towards the rich world to ask for a bit of help. But it was the truth that mattered, the hard road towards solving the great mysteries of life's poverty, such as getting the all-powerful, no-action Australian government to come the half mile to help a place like Praiseworthy, to dynamite the haze to kingdom come. One wondered what moved Ice's followers in this type of world. They were full of praise-haste, laughing at the fun of trying to convince the modern-termed *clientele*, meaning the actual residents, to become assimilated as quickly as possible in the cultureless world of the so-called majority. There was no slowing this movement down, or of a chilling out for these praise-haste people. *C'est la guerre*. The upper-class women admirers of Major Mayor Ice Pick – his regalia of Ice Queens – weaponised their emotional lashings to all and sundry about what could be gained from crawling like mangy dogs in full cooperation rather than perpetually feeling ignored in this crawling dog pantomime stage show, which had only made the assimilatory rejects feel more totally cheated and pissed off. They were not buying government magic, and you would never believe how potent a pay-off could be, where the more cash you brought to the scheme, the more you felt tainted, the more, *Ding dong merrily on high In heav'n the bells are ringing…*and why it was so hard to believe in the swinging bells heralding joy to all from far horizons and bringing the magic gift of tapioca symphony officialism over your body and soul. It was not until you saw voiceless people transformed into the most artful orators singing *Gloria Hosanna in excelsis!* that you could believe the story of assimilation rushing straight out of the mouth of the never-ending tidal wave.

While general attitudes were turning sourer and meaner by the minute in the haze's habitable geography of Ice Pick's big camp blame game, and the whole web of the place was becoming thudding heart thicker and bronchial-lunged, the haze monument made a real meal out of this insanity. *What was Ice going to do about our life being mental?* The haze grew denser. Then, everyone started catching the thought of themselves having the albino's disease, and said their hair was turning grey-white. Now with so many grey-haired people feeling that they had grown prematurely old, there was so much more negativity floating in the air about the sight of so much ugly greyness, of becoming Ice Pick lookalikes. He blamed the government for causing his people to go prematurely grey from worry about nothing, except by being down on the government that refused to shift the perpetual haze from their lives.

It got to the point where there was nothing else worth thinking about than counting grey hairs in the hairbrush. This was not the ideal situation. Everything felt like a festering sore under Ice Pick's watch, and the far-removed Australian government for Aboriginal people in Canberra felt sick of being inflicted with that much degree of hate coming their way from these grey-headed people slinging abuse back and forth about an overfed haze they wanted the Australian army to destroy with a bomb. So, the government totally lost it with these first people, and openly persecuted them for being untrainable, and failing every known government program of the last hundred years to teach them how to be assimilated into the Australian way of life. *Hallelujah!* Ice commended the Australian Government for Aboriginal people in the sundry domain, *didn't you know that the government of the country was the boss of Aboriginal people?*

One woeful era followed another, where not much was noticed about the haze growing disproportionately denser in the big stand-off about whether the government was racist, and whether Aboriginal people had failed to assimilate. The government and the Praiseworthy ancients started sending abusive texts to each other and zapping back and forth through the haze by the truck load. The war went on like this for years while the haze settled in, in the endless spite Twittering as the main form of attack, and the Instagramming to each other in capital letter hate words that was way out of control, while both sides were trying to accuse the other for not listening to what they were saying about imploring the government to send the army up north where the most neglected people in the country lived, to choke the guts out of the choking atmosphere, to nuke the haze, or to fucking blow it apart.

All this social media thing of protests, abuse, cancelling threats fell on deaf ears, you know, since the conniving politicians continued through the terms of several prime ministers who did bugger-all about the haze living over the flats in the north. All the complaints of why *I hate the haze* shit-firing into the ether of the government's telephones about what was prejudicial and racial fell quick smart on deaf ears. It was as though there was some kind of conspiracy to keep denying that any extreme weather event was happening in the flatlands, or perhaps, it was not conspiracy, but complacency, easier to ignore agitated bronchial lungs far away, and Aboriginal people making up stories while coughing with bronchiectasis in the airways about an ancestral spirit composed of dust that was gigantic and needed to be blitzed by the armed forces from choking the life out of them. Because why? Weakness! Just like a coup, a take-over of rebels, like blackfellas reaching their zenith, for any Australian government for Aboriginal people conceding to their sovereign rights by even listening to them. Well! Why bother? Who knew where truth lies? But, somehow, it was as though the haze monument, a phenomenal beast in itself, was invisible to outsiders, because even the weather people in this wing-damaged butterfly continent in the southern hemisphere claimed that they never saw a monument of haze on their radar screens, not on their watch.

3

This 'I' thing, or what local people were calling old sulky haze, had become the new normal for the traditional people, who later claimed they had no power to get rid of the haze that they wanted to be lifted off their Australian government for Aboriginal people-created designer town, and who could blame them for acting nervous like Twitter-scape, since they had really tried to turn themselves into white-type superior people. They were letting off steam in trend letters like FOUC to represent the epic edge of oppressiveness, of what it felt like to be a hero ancestral being inside the stifling heat of an enforced assimilatory era that was bent on making them suffer like soft-bellied white people. They had begun dressing up in suits while they walked around in the tropics. Heat was nothing. They were not thinking like their ancestral selves, but more like the swingers of power, the hitters of the Anthropocene, like pseudo-dictators of the speed texting wars, primed up, boiler fires roaring for battle. This daydreaming about defeating the dragon haze, even if it meant complete destruction, could be the armageddon of their traditional flatlands – or in other words, they were having a friggen whale of a time.

The old haze kept on presenting itself atmospherically, claiming ultimate sovereignty of the flatlands, and had grown so exponentially huge that it was sitting on the ground like a fallen angel cut loose from sixty thousand years or something of immemorial time. It felt suffocating to be sat on by a haze, and many people were wearing gas masks and speaking to one another in muffled voices, and the end result was, it was really killing the weeds, the wildlife, and just about everything else of what had once been an aesthetically pleasing environment.

With virtually nothing left in the cupboard to kill except people who somehow still managed to survive and celebrate their infinity, the spirit haze kept on consuming the remaining scraps of life as though it were in a cake shop. The spirit grew fat. And fatter. The bulkiness, like the sky itself, never moved. You could not push the thing away, and like toxicity, it would probably end up staying in the atmosphere for a million years. So much for all the unmeant prayers for peace and goodwill rattling on day and night in the local community's ramshackle faith churches of assorted Christian beliefs, when this country was itself already holy, and not a fool.

All the old people wearing St Vincent de Paul's second-hand suits to make them look assimilatory, friendly and accessible, disguising them from looking like powerful red-ochre law men, now went harking and coughing about how little they could do with an atmospheric ancestor gone roguery because she had become too lonely for her neglectful people. They said what could they do now? It was too late. They had no feather duster big enough to swing about the place, to shoo the sky away, to push her on.

The weather grew enormous, and continued to rage from the mouths of hate-tellers, but none of the people wearing those suits of grey, black, or navy, could keep up with her insatiable appetite for hate, and her complaining with a full mouth in northern dry thunder lingo that she was not going anywhere, while eating more of the type of hate cake that she liked, and acting all sulky, as though she were being deprived of the last cake of its type on Earth. She became more bloated. She was on a sugar high. This ancestral spirit woman was fully fuelled in an all-consuming nasty way of being wired up, while refusing to budge, and she was crying her heart out now, about how, *I-zzed aren't going back to sleep in any old spirit world.*

4

What a boogie-woogie hyped world it had become, to see the red earth-stained clothes swinging about, swish-swashing non-stop, twisting, backfiring the polluted exhaustion into the funnelling gyre sitting stationary over ever greater kilometres of the flat. The spectacle could be seen as plain as day from outer space, and it looked like airborne *anti-miraculousness* – a terrible fetish fallen from heaven. Years went on. The mad dance spun up the highs and lows of the atmospheric pressure, rolling, churning and frothing as it snapped up whatever was left of the country's dried up yellow grasslands, bits of fish-and-chips newspapers, tens of thousands of white plastic shopping bags, the drunks' holy crucifixes spinning through the sucked up rotten stories of the jacked-off and pissed-off in dust, weed, grass, seeds, twigs, and oxygen dragged straight off the baked-hard ravaged moonscape left behind.

Old sulky, oh, loved the theatre of atmospheric soup that was gathered by the bucketload at top speed, where all the cyclically generating hardcore never-ending epics of hatefulness were mashed up in a monstrous fast-paced dance, and just as fantastically, instantaneously almost, spat triumphantly into community operatic wonderment, a march that was reminiscent of the choir of Verdi's *Gloria all'Egitto*, as projectiles of polluted dirt-engrained plastic shards shooting like glistened stars into the hot and sticky humidity of the hazy atmosphere were marching steadfastly into the festering human lungs of the whole song cycle thing, now jammed on repeat cycle, and the traditional owners in their continuous rows, arguing about who the true traditional owner was anymore, could not do a thing about it.

The scenario, now a very stable situation, was potentially ironclad safe. A permanent liquid gold tourist venture. But somehow, the monument did not attract millions of tourists visiting the site, not like the local shire council had anticipated from all the money it had sunk into promoting the uniqueness of the haze ancestor. The council had hoped, and sold their hope in the way that they believed monumental man-made natural wonders of the world could totally possess people, as they were possessed themselves. This was how they framed an open invitation to the world, about how to become possessed, by experiencing the perpetual dust storm they had created without lifting a bloody finger, by being the best haters in the world.

But sadly, the monument failed to move, or move others. It was like a death adder that kept wide-armed anti-guides who could not be bothered about cultural tourism, yelling *stand back you cunts* to shield the few cultural tourists who turned up out of the blue with their fantastic hopes of experiencing pristine culture and a free bottle of spring water in the so-called wilderness of traditional law lands, but were only confronted with pollution in the atmosphere.

The atmospheric so-called glamour haze was so much like the polluted smoke wafting from a rubbish dump that you would never expect it to be a world-famous monument. Well! not yet anyhow, not like rants about other spectacular man-made monuments that had in time become universally liked, even loved by tourists who were not the people who had to make these things with their bare hands. Still, it takes time to be liked. The Pyramids. London Bridge. The Eiffel Tower. Venice in a high tide. The Kremlin. China's modern Belt and Road project. The Silk Road. Taj Mahal. Rome. Bethlehem. A Mercedes-Benz. Their uniqueness was in their possessiveness, to imprison history, which they distil into the stories of those that have been captured.

The haze, seething with humidity, remained disastrous like any festering rubbish at the rubbish dump with black smoke rising in a field of methane, or greenhouse gas, where PM2.5 particulate matter of less than 2.5 microns kept showering a dazzle a minute with minuscule plastic shards and bubbles of toxicity spinning down from the sky, and into the immune system. Those runaround people grew sicker and heavier by the hour but where could they go? They could not be moved from the guts of the atmospheric haze ancestor, and the air, it just became more polluted in this symbiosis of conjoined captivity inside the ancestry world. So much so! It was as though the only power people felt while rushing from one house to another in search of the truth, was to assert themselves in somersaulting and pole-vaulting vernacularism, spreading arguments and fist debates about the actual facts of the never-ending ode they were telling the atmospheric stew to strew.

The ode itself, ended up being an echo-inducing epic poem of stories in the all-twisting, all-turning immersion of limerence, skyrocketing in an out-of-proportion infatuation that would never be consummated. Look though, long enough through the haze, and you will see what became of these lazy people's love of hate. It was the fatal attraction that crashed time and again. The end result of all those epics converging into a single gossipy tale eaten and spat out into the atmosphere as poison.

Oh! But! The gaol cell grew narrower, more cramped and claustrophobic because all the stories were about one man, which felt easier than having to expand one's thinking into creating a whole lot of stories about everybody to feed the insatiable diet of the overgrown formlessness of the bored atmospheric spirit of pollution generating the haze. But how could one person become so worthy of being – the epic? Of being that special? Were the storytellers too lazy these days to look further into the human abyss, or too unimaginative to be bothered to create a more diverse catalogue of stories? Many people were that obsessed with him being the epic, that they said, he was a piece of shit wasting their time and energy.

The vision man was too lackadaisical with his slow symphonic breathing of red dust in and out of his lungs from out there on the flat, the void which he referred to as being the eyesore of the world. This big prick of a fellow, evil through to the core, who was called Planet, or Widespread, or by his real name sometimes, which was Cause Man Steel. Who remembered his real name anyhow? It was not worth remembering. No one wanted to remember his name. They could not be bothered remembering the fellow's name for the way he was buggering up their part of the planet with mad ideas for his global warming business that had nothing to do with them.

Everyone was an angel in Praiseworthy so they say, because if you weren't, it meant your life belonged elsewhere. So! It was really vogue to be one of those angels in rotten times, although this fellow Widespread made the whole angle of being an angel ready to assimilate white look ridiculous, by acting like he was the biggest and only real guardian angel in the ancestral law-bound black man's world. He was just a fake racing with lies. Saying, *Look! I am more angel. I have even more monstrous wings attached to my more Rainbow Serpent country body, and you know what, I smell like my country, not all perfumed up with the foreign stuff of another God's heaven. Smell me.* The smell was breathtaking. He smelt like that old cemetery dirt of the haze hanging over this place, stuck in time, and finding infinite ways of colluding with the stale winds that rose and fell here, but were never taken away.

The more colonialising modern-inclined people liked to call him Omnicide, or Global Warming, but no one cared about the significance of calling other people names. A Praiseworthy man could have a lot of names. So! What? Give it a bit of a hippie name like jet fuel, or stratosphere, but that did not mean someone was really souped up with jet fuel in the stratosphere. Whatever! You could watch this man – Cause, Widespread, Planet – selectively scrutinising his postmodern and recycled world, and saying he had emerged more ancestral from the Dreamtime than even the ancestors, which he always gloated had made him a pre-ancestor. He was always saying things like that, as to why he was way ahead of any of the local flower people hobbled to some new age church mania going on in Praiseworthy. Yes, he exclaimed often, *You can't walk around here without stumbling into a church*. He defined his own eternal spirit as capable of shooting through catastrophes, beginning from when the land was a ball of fire, and his ghost would continue blasting through all future eras into infinity. Why? *Because he was a culture man of all times.* He heard the crying and screaming of every single animal caught in firestorms across the country, and there were several billion of them, like all those thousands of dead koalas scattered through the charred cathedrals of forests, their bodies curled on the ground where they fell, where they had burnt to death, and their spirits breathed new life inside him, giving him the ancestral will, more than willingness, the desire to continue living.

Nah. Don't look away, Widespread tells himself, even as he was right there with the swarming insects being pushed higher into the smoke-filled oxygen-deprived atmosphere and vapouring into nothingness. He was always running with the animals, like the tens of thousands of kangaroos fleeing, and they keep going hour after hour, running and running through fire-loaded winds, until finally in the moment, falling as ashes into the spirit ground. It was the same with those massive floods that created enormous inland seas where old clanspeople hurried him along the changing country because the work of quietening souls was always endless. Planet would always be running, and flying far through the country where spirits lay in the corpses of the dead, and his mind would keep on running until he heard no more screaming, and where finally, he would scream that there could be no more. This Widespread, Planet, or really named Cause Man Steel only knows one thing now. He knows that he cannot stop the chaos of the world always changing. If the only consolation that he offered was that this would be the age of reckoning with the ancestors, then why should he be alive amongst the mourning?

Omnicide! Planet had become locked in some fluey zone of his head which was carrying on about the world committing suicide, and he had decided to act like some freaky doomsayer about the end of the world from man-made global warming, which he called the bloody omnicide – another fancy made-up name for what he claimed was the world killing itself, heading for total extinction, becoming phantasmal. Planet could rip back the bed covers on peace to find some flea omen of his naked truths, and was telling Praiseworthy people – who were convinced of their own exceptionalism and invincibility – that they too were like everyone in the world, were complicit in the upcoming extinction of the human and non-human species. They said, *What are you? God or something?* The man was a solid ratbag of pain in the neck. *A bloody saviour!* He could generate more hate stories in half an hour from a bunch of locals, than any combined humanity of the world could create with all their gossip in a lifetime. He was exactly this: anti-man of the moment. Something white people called a greenie. The real environmentalist. But how would Planet know anything about the real planet? He was not educated. He talked more about how the ancestors felt about being stuffed up by global warming than did any other Aboriginal people. They said he wouldn't know. He blamed the white government for causing the never-ending haze. *Can't you mob feel it is getting hotter?*

Sometimes! He made people who wanted to feel normal, feel threatened instead, of feeling at real risk, of losing a bit of hard-won government largesse. Whatever that was? The pittance! The fight! Was it worth it type of thing? Planet, the outer galaxy, sitting back and smirking at his mob knocking each other out to plant a Mickey Mouse treaty on the table, saying they want a treaty so that they could share in the aftermath, the mess of colonialism and racism, the wholesale disaster of the Anthropocene. He yelled from his bit of a pulpit in the main street, the street with all the multi-denominational churches, *Why you mob negotiating treaties with people who fucked up your land in two centuries flat after our ancestors were able to survive here for millennia?* He ripped the local treaty-mongers, the reconciliation faithful, the recognition front line. *Don't forget Aboriginal sovereignty knowledge when you go running on your bellies – lower than a snake for treaties worth nothing considering the mess here environmentally and so on, you won't have land worth living on unless your treaty agreement ties governments to international enforceable laws against ecocide.* And omnicide? *Yep! Include that word too while you are at it.* Widespread loved saying the words – omnicide, *omnicidalistic* fools. Nobody knew what this omni thing meant to them. Nobody wanted to know about rattling-brain words like cardinal decade, carbon emissions, global warming, rain bombs, biblical floods, El Niño weather phenomena, the Indian Ocean Dipole, doping the atmosphere, cumulonimbus flammagenitus – was that a disease, a virus or weather on steroids? There was plenty of denialism in the talk. And guess what? There was no end of the stories from the small haze-ridden world of Praiseworthy to tell about Widespread Planet's idiotic schemes for surviving the Anthropocene, and other spellbinding facts about how he annoyed the hell out of people from motor mouthing about Aboriginal ingenuity to survive into infinity. Jaws dropped, the ash of good tobacco fell on the pussycats asleep on laps, stone-cold deaf from listening to all that hate.

5

This was not saying that there was anything wrong about being a power schemer, it was just how Planet thought differently, canvassing more widespread than other lesser schemers in Praiseworthy. He hustled too many schemes about what other people should be doing, and said the word *because* too many times. Big deal. You would have thought that there were no other people in Praiseworthy worth bothering about, who knew anything about how to fight their way out of a paper bag. They said, *You think we were born yesterday* type of thing. *Come down with the last shower? Nobody else thought about anything,* and only he knew how to save them from more than two centuries of attempted genocide to wipe their entire culture from the face of the Earth. And of all things, his big current plan was to build an empire that was bigger than the haze: that would blow it clean away.

Though truth being told, it was easy to see why Praiseworthy people thought about being saved by anyone other than themselves, and why they were sniggering that Widespread's ideas were unpalatable, unthinkable, or in other words a piece of shit, since he was always thinking how he knew best in any given situation about survival – like nobody else was interested in thinking about the Indigenous man's preoccupation about surviving on his own country every single day of the last sixty plus millenniums, nor that they did not know that they were already enduring the thing with the big flash name called the Anthropocene – even though they did not know what it was, or could even pronounce the word, or if he had told them that it had something to do with the world ending from man-made overheating of the climate.

We knew what hot was, we told him that. We know all the scientif-y from the ancestors. Everyone in Praiseworthy knew that the haze was making the place feel hotter, but why give a toss about choosing which straw contained universal truth? Widespread was not thinking holocaustic thoughts of a sinking world, or of an actually sunk Venice with tourists wearing goggles while floating on the top of the ocean to peer down into the depths to see those old Venetian buildings, or if they were worrying like everyone else watching the news on TV about sinking islands in the Pacific, or seeing what bleached coral in the Great Barrier Reef looked like from the moon, or imagining the real possibility of destroyed countries and half the world either flooded or being burnt to ashes, nor was he wondering where all those hundreds of millions of new world refugees were going to live, or about places where all the wild animals were moving into the lost cities, and invading apartment blocks, nor thinking anything else catastrophic like wars, and viruses of the future.

There was not a single corpuscle of fatalism running in the blood through his veins. Planet was not worried about whether he was inhaling microscopic slithers of gleaming plastic poison in the atmosphere, or of the world dying soon, because he was thinking the same thing his ancestors were thinking about how to survive the next millennium basically, of how they would continue being the oldest living culture on Earth regardless of everything else being dead. This was the kind of positivism that was hard to beat, unconquerable you could say if you thought about being invincible, and desired to remain so.

Widespread Planet, same person as that piece of work Cause Man Steel, while thinking clear-headed higher rather than thinking low, was confident about how he would survive the climate emergency. He avoided the crowd – which meant humanity – and chose to live as some kind of crepuscular man, moving around the isolated bush by himself in the twilight hours in pursuit of his business venture, to put into action far more grandiose plans about how to make real money. He was not wasting his time as a perpetual trainee on an Australian government handout scheme, for enticing tourists to visit the man-made haze monument hanging over Praiseworthy, which only attracted one or two tourists a month, and usually the kind of eco-tourist from Europe who was scraping the bottom of the barrel for something cheap to do to support tourism in a good eco-friendly way, like for instance, travelling for days on end to the back of beyond in an ageing two-tone beige kombi van chuntering along at sixty k's an hour to see an ancestral haze from the dreaming, that was self-determined to be only worth a gold coin donation to chuck in a tin can at the gate, because everyone else thought differently to the traditional owner of country, thought like a real rationalist believing the phenomenon was not that unusual, that anyone could see a dust storm in this country. And that for what, Cause Man Steel asked himself, to make a couple of coins to see a phenomenon? Aren't worth it. Cheap shit stuff like that was not going to make the kind of money Praiseworthy needed to be able to survive the future. Widespread was more or less shooting for the stars in a real traditional world stuffed with the legends of millennia where his infinity was filled with ever-lasting swarms of brown black-eyed winged emperor moths, although in actual fact, up in the tops of the iconic gum tree of the local legendary stories, these moths had left larvae in plague proportion that were eating all the gum leaves, and stripping the eucalyptus trees bare.

6

Actually, authority to feed the haze was given freely to anyone seriously guzzling themselves up in a self-righteous moral quest of mouthing off about what integrity was, when it came to questions of pristineness in Praiseworthy, where anything was considered honourable enough behaviour, or the scourge for conniving a bit of government money to keep the essential services moving. Begging was not a hard act to perform. The crawlers, if they did not know how to crawl low enough – lower than a snake would – were ordered to be more emotional humdingers about Widespread Planet, legally Cause Man Steel, commonly called nothing but a piece of shit by the Aboriginal sort of albino Major Mayor of the place Ice Pick, who drove around on the top of his game through the baking streets on hot summer days looking triple A in that hot pink Toyota SUV of his covered in bulldust. All that. He was a mayoral megaphone apparatus attached to the roof rack. Screaming like that. Fine enough. The man was only behaving egotistically like any other Aboriginal man would, if he saw himself as a potential prime minister, and was just strutting his stuff of political megaphoning full bore to the all and sundry. Why wouldn't he do that? He was saying something important, about how it was up to everyone around the place to decide how to eclipse, rather than acquit, their debt to God by speaking out about how crisis-prone idiots were burdening the sane world with tears. The Major Mayor liked shouting, and he often shouted at kids walking on the footpath after school finished, how the government would be taking away the community's welfare money because *you kids can't be bothered keeping the place clean.* The cheeky buggers. *You talking to us Ice? Creating uncertainty and whatnot?*

From up high in the Praiseworthy hierarchy at the top end of the town, in an imaginary elevation at least a few bulldozed centimetres above the flatness of the terrain which people like Ice Pick thought of as being higher than anywhere else, there also reigned Ice Pick's queens who each thought that she had the principal prima facie mandate to direct the stories of hate to the haze. Any cute smile from one of these *posh-i-fied* ladies could cause an instant heart-stop. Each diva thought she was the model of assimilation. Each had personally managed her own makeover into a logical localised high class. The stray pussycats uncurled from hours of sleep, and ran faster than their hungry legs could carry them, heading one, two, three, straight down into the flat plains with their shrilled meows fading into the distance, as soon as any of those hot bitches of Ice Pick's posse women were seen dissing the sundry from a distance, and whacking all life with a big fighting stick each carried for personal safety against all the possible enemies shimmering up their way.

The hot days of destroying the last remaining threads of Widespread Planet's personality were like a minefield of frenzied kitsch. The queens hung off every word spoken by Ice Pick as though it was the gospel truth, and then when the community started shouting in a chorus of low whispers here and there about not wanting to hear any more fake news on Praiseworthy's localised social media, the toxicity of hostilities extended far and beyond any person's back, and dug deep into their heart, mind, and spirit. Oh! The way you could see these ladies conjuring Widespread as the anti-deity of Praiseworthy was breathtakingly not great. It was hard news to be caught in the slippage of junk excavated from the dry chalice of the modern Aboriginal epoch.

The Praiseworthy haze could still not be reckoned with, not even from having inflicted upon it the fruits of world humanity for blitzing the shit out of bits of rubbish, or else breaking its heart by serenading it to go away with the music of a gifted mandolin player performing the Bach Sonata No. 1 in B Minor. All this meant nothing to the ancestral haze. The haze was not in the mood for creating miracles like moving its huge weight back into the dream world. It had a real stay-at-home attitude, and this type of music did not convince it, that it should soar off to sit in a plush seat at an opera house in Vienna, or Budapest, or China, France, Indonesia or Spain, or Japan. The haze was not interested in the town's dozens of combined choirs giving it their all night after night with their religious hymns piping through megaphones all along Church Street, the holy place of religious thought, icons and some dubious relics, which was where the holy believers believed that every bit of their prayers went straight into the ears of their guardian angels to come straight down from heaven to fight the haze, to defeat it, push it far out into sea, and send it on a journey into somebody else's hell.

Inside each of the ramshackle churches spreading across the frontline for quelling the bewildering global emergency era, and representing who knows what denomination or religious persuasion, this was where the people of the haze saw power to be gained, and prayed harder. Even though their prayers inspired the need for praying more than the actual doing, they sang faster and prayed harder, and continued praying until their churches collapsed under the weight of the tremendous devotion piling up like rocks on the roof.

The idea of a church being built on a solid foundation was not going to be the reality in a place that was as dirt poor as Praiseworthy. Any slight breeze bowled over the hundred or so flimsy buildings of devotion like a line of dominoes stacked on each side of the street, since these humpy churches were only constructed from leftover things, like bits of old shipping crates, with either a big yellow solar-lit guiding star on top of a long pole protruding from the roof identifying which church it was, or illuminated flags, banners of lantern-lit cod, salmon, saints, angels, despots, or not easily identifiable effigies, or the holy grail, or among other rough drawings of holy symbols, various world deities drawn on pieces of cardboard marked with the name of the big vegetable companies supplying the country's lettuces, cucumbers and tomatoes.

This whole shamble of plagiarised churches was a reality miracle that tumbled and rose, while being held together above the head of the prayers as they rebuilt their falling churches with the fallen bits of rusty sheet iron and cardboard, roughly thrown back together in haste with a hammer and nail under the crucifix nailed on top. The greatest survivor of makeshift ingenuity was the whopping huge cardboard box with Fisher & Paykel refrigerator signs all over the packaging preserved in its original condition long after the thing inside, the big family fridge, had been thrown away in the dump. This cardboard box, now a magnificent cathedral in all its monumental greatness, even if not on the scale of the Sagrada Família, was where some outcast idiot religious leader met with his fellow exiles. Squeezing together, they sat around inside the box with their equally blessed ghetto-blaster streaming from Rome, and after long hours of prayers, there came a time for whistling sighs of exhausted relief at having reached the end of this bit of reality as they knew it, and from this point onwards for at least five minutes, salvation appeared in the form of a miracle where you would see the golden stardust haloing around their heads in the refrigerator box, and this small moment of free imagining was simply what you might call real faith, and nobody else's concern.

Far off in the old gamba grasses rooted decades deep across the plains, insects by the millions droned and deafened all other sounds ahead of Ice Pick's queens feeding their own radio reactive versions of Christian stories to the haze, with enough drama to create hell on Earth. Fire and brimstone tornadoes roared from their mouths and raced through the plains grass searching for heaven, while from the ground, the white-eyed ghost moths' endless drone lifted the ancient spirit women, for it was like hearing the sweetness of a Korean haegeum silk fiddle, or the throat music of the grasslands harmonising along with the Mongolian morin khuur horsehair fiddle, or a great ancient lullaby of an elder calling to country, and losing consciousness to the six o'clock moths swarming, and the ghost butterflies high in the gum trees, and the yellow butterflies fluttering above the grass, and now all moving, journeying forever in the eternal moving upwards above the firestorm and dampening it in the mirage of dense red dust smoke feeding the haze.

Only luckily, the charred and blackened red soil plains lived like ancestors and the humidity rose and became a thick russet fog floating over the ground just before dawn, where everyone had been up early, and were walking around in shorts and thongs. They swung the light from their torches in search of donkeys, and the torch light swirled around the darkened water flats while they followed the Ice Queens through the mud and festering rubbish that had long spoiled the look of the tidy town, and they were all yelling across the streets in a chorus of *git the fuck out, and get to hell youse.* These donkeys knew what was coming with people running left, right and centre, and ducking and weaving and slipping in the mud in this mad chase to get them out of this well-meaning Christian town.

7

Widespread never liked butterflies. Or moths. He takes no notice of any fluttery thing flying around his house, like his gravity-defying butterfly wife. Dance loved creatures of the air. She encouraged moths. Thought moths. Spoke the moths' frequency, a language of millennia which she had learnt in dreams which were only ever about butterflies and moths. The world of the haze became a locked world of lepidoptera that continually fluttered around Dance. She was like a haven for butterflies or moths rising and falling over a world of plastic white lilies, red and pink roses, lilacs, sweet peas, soft pink petals of the peonies, and shimmering blue silk delphiniums covering the dirt mound graves of the beloved, the boundlessly remembered memories of cultural infinity. A plague of white caper butterflies fly like angels high in the air above, as though speaking to one another in ever increasing zigzagging circles, and below, close to the ground, masses of smaller yellow grass butterflies flitter and shimmy in a slight breeze over and through the flowers to ride the currents speaking in the powerful languages emanating from the ground of the cemetery. She was never alone. The haze was full of butterfly spores and frayed transparent wings. A moth took her on journeys whenever she moved away from Praiseworthy, sometimes travelling far inland where you did not hear the incoming tides of the sea, or sometimes seaside, riverside, grassland, plain, and through its law, she became a moth in the sky – grown to a different sightedness in a world askew, and as if in perpetual flight, only desiring movement.

Planet on the other hand preferred a solid and balanced world, one that always remained perfectly still, and stayed in the same place when you put it somewhere. He wished all things to sit permanently in the place where he believed they should sit, just as he admired the stillness of concreteness rather than any movement that created difference, fluidity, flow or attentiveness to changes from either the body, or the mind. You could say that Planet felt the full weight of life like concrete, heaviness that never lightened, as though life really was a piece of concrete. He carried his country-hardened, long thin frame stiffly, and he often walked as though his body was more than it appeared. He was the solid rock-hard weight of country that was also equally lightness, but he had lost this feature of homeland. Talk did not flow easy from Planet. He was not into flippancy, or what was being said without deep thought. It was as though his brain was composed of the heavy inward and durable skid-resistant substance of aggregated concrete. When you get a planet-saver like this – an expert on atmospheric pressure – it was easier for the man to narrow things like the world down to one big vision, to focus on the greatest need, and for this he sang, in slow-like motion, *Good Morning Captain*, Jimmie Rodgers' *Mule Skinner Blues, ha-ha ha-ha ha-ha. I can make any mule listen...*

There were never more than a few moments in Planet's entire life when he felt that he had to think twice about what it meant to be solid because he was too solid to think that way. Solid men have no time to think about whether they are solid or not. He always had the pedal to the metal. *Hey! Hey!*

The very idea of solidity was simply and purely embedded in Widespread's total existence, it had become totally fixed as one of the most solid places on the planet – his own hard heart. Even his dreams were made of solid thoughts. The airy fairy life force would never be able to float in his mind, which was the reason why he was the dead opposite to the floater, the supposed-albino Ice Pick who barely registered on the planet's radar, even though the Major Mayor was always out there on the haze plain for all to see, swinging his weightless hologram effortlessly about like the dial in a compass above Praiseworthy.

The truth of the thing being that the Australian government for Aboriginal peoples had finally caved in about Praiseworthy people up there in the hot sticks worrying about the permanent haze, and had given a grant of a sizeable amount of money to the Major Mayor of Praiseworthy to build a monstrous scarecrow to frighten the haze away. A thirty-plus-metre tall Ice Pick boogie-woogie hologram now swam twenty-four seven across the blue sky like a huge albino killer whale with mouth agape, flung wide open in an all sharp pointy gold-capped teeth-bared full-on attack, as though it was always swallowing the haze. Living with this abomination in the sky made perfect sense to the people of Praiseworthy. Why not? The huge presence of Ice Pick slung up above all else generated a feeling of the purely sensational, and seen as attacking the haze for God sake that felt downright comforting, and befitting, to protect some of the most precious wisdom on the now besieged Earth governed by powerful fascist boys, the uncivilised, who did not know how to grow into men who protected humanity or anything else in the world, and only knew how to play with the aim of destruction on the world stage.

The whole town of Praiseworthy agreed about how they now felt more at ease, were feeling safer, and would say they were less bronchial, and less complaining about suffocating from overexposure to the heating haze that was killing them. All was well. You could read about the benefits of holograms to fight bad climate in any government report about closing the gap with Aboriginal people. You could not please everyone though. The nation's media described the hologram as being a total waste of taxpayer money for whingey Aboriginal people who were allowed to get away with their so-called cultural beliefs about seeing an invisible ancestral haze spirit. Where was the proof that anyone had spirit-induced bronchial lungs? They were still a pack of bronchial sufferers *angst-ing* about healthy country rights, and crying about not being assimilated into the mainstream of the rich Australian fabric. No one liked being a rag, and many also cried that there should be a royal commission to prove that ancestral climate change dust would, or would not, cause bronchiolitis.

On the other hand, and as seen through the eyes of the locals who could not open the door to the future, no miracles were occurring in their lives, not when they had last looked. There was none of the glory-type Aboriginal person that big white government for Aboriginal people had hoped would germinate in the Praiseworthy flatlands from having a hologram of Ice Pick dangling in the skies as a motivation to assimilate and become white. Praiseworthy skin colour stayed, not white. The pigment of colour had not changed to crystal clear white overnight, neither from fright, nor through these small place people of the north believing that they were now breathing calmly like white people did on TV, and feeling that they were becoming assimilated – slowly mind you, though they were not going as far as saying that they were feeling auspiciously prosperous in the same way they would have if they had been the land thieves in the first place, who had stolen somebody else's country, and had left the Indigenous owner for dead.

Inbuilt solidity was only gained through the way it infiltrated Planet's dreams as nightmares – where he felt as though he was unmoveable, as though he had become a lump of wood, a rivergum tree trunk, basalt rock, or concrete – and it was only through his well-honed razor-sharp lens for battling with his fossilised body, that he began to realise how unhinged the climate was becoming by constructing some kind of undiscriminating deathtrap haze. The one thing he hated more than anything else, was entrapment. This was how he came up with a smart idea about how he could construct a door that would take him and his whole imaginary lump of weight into another future. He straightened the spiralling trapdoor, exchanged it for an easy opening door – like a fly door, where you just walked straight through no matter how solid you felt. Planet felt as though he was now more powerful than someone cooped-up, weight-bound, forever trapped in a colossal locked-up haze.

In his heart of hardness, Cause knew what was best, of having to get out of the haze and leave, but also, by having a flyscreen door mentality to placate the mind, he would also, at will, be able to get back inside the guts of the haze. The more he thought about the calamity of the haze entrapment, the more he felt like the world poet Seamus being followed by a dangerous tidal wave wherever he went. Who knew why this Planet was a loner and why he wanted to test the haze, but wasn't it only for the common good of the planet? A man such as Cause Man Steel had no choice but to figure out how to construct, not just a plastic fly door for himself, which he could easily have bought in the virus time of global warming and wars for almost nothing online from Kmart, but a bigger walk-through fly door that would be a plastic monstrosity big enough to free all his country people from wherever they wanted to be freed from a haze. Then, one day he cracked the puzzle when he stared at the haze and the thought occurred to him that the door was a similar type of door to the one his ancestors had built over aeons through their economies. He thought he had just heard poetry, and it felt as though the haze had indeed spoken, if not to him specifically then he was the one who overheard it anyway. The idea was too much. He almost fell flat on his hard face and cracked his skull, such was the revelation about the door of traditional economies that had remained open since the beginning of time, and Planet knew instantly that it was only natural when you thought about it, that all you would need to know to go through the same all times door in the future was what you already knew, and that each time you went through – either to leave, or to return – you took everything, all that knowledge with you.

The dry storm cyclone season arrived in a middle of the night bombardment of tens of thousands of ancestral lightning strikes that went flash-bang, flash-bang, here a boom, there a boom, everywhere a boom-boom, flattening the hologram big time, and destroying it for all times too.

8

Planet hardly believed that he was any sort of genius for working out world matters, but he could not help thinking that if Aboriginal survival since time immemorial had always been about economics, of figuring out how to survive in the circumstances of real time, then why should he not help wonder about how to make money out of the new doom times of global warming. Survival of humanity had always been an economic question, and this was how he came to the realisation that a black man did not have to remain poor. He should take advantage of the new economic circumstances one hundred per cent, in order to continue the long line of cultural existence of changing and being changed by country, even while he perfectly understood that in the full circle of existence, his humanity could end up looking like a single-cell amoeba again, totally unidentifiable to a human despot dictator of the twenty-first century, while bubbling in a stagnant pond of the all times creation ancestor. It would still be all about the economics, of trying to remake the thing again – a creation with higher-standard earthquakes, thunder and lightning, firestorms, volcanoes in rising seas, and tidal waves.

This was how Planet arrived at his economic reckoning that Aboriginal people had always desired surviving – going forth now rather than facing extinction – at every time of their existence as the longest living culture on Earth, and had known out of necessity, like Zen, how to become rationalists, the world's best economists, to survive on the same traditional country for millennia. Imagine that! Think about it, that every one of your relatives since time began had permanently sat down in exactly the same spot on the song line, and had never once said that they had to travel off grid, and never thought of extending the grid to places like New York, or Hong Kong.

Widespread told Dance about his saving-the-world theories, and she sighed loudly, said he was an idiot, and then went around telling everyone in Praiseworthy that her husband was mad. *He thinks he is the demon-queller, like this Japanese Shoki.* She opened her hand for all to see a little spirit man sitting there, a small brass statue of the Japanese protector with a huge sword slung over his back for killing a demon he was searching for under a waterlily leaf. *You know,* she explained, *we once had plenty of those old white government protectors for Aborigines people, and missionaries trying to eradicate black demons from our bodies, and even now, we have many protectors of all kinds saving us from ourselves.* And, flatly, she added, while she felt like speaking to people she normally ignored other than to accuse them of robbing her Native Title land, she was simply inviting the town to visit the cemetery again, to see their lonely families in the graves. And while they were there, she added, they were welcome to see her ugly ghost effigies of the old protectors of Aboriginals in the history of colonialism. Planet thought nothing about a gossipy wife mouthing off. The solid ground that he sought was not made of gossip. She told him to stop thinking altogether, *You only think stupid.* He decided on the spot to stop speaking to her. *Go on then,* she snarled. *How you going to do that?* You could have wars of all shapes and sizes throughout mankind, but a woman like Dance knew how to deal with war as good as she gave. She had spent her married life with Cause Man Steel, by living on the other side of a solid wall constructed from his silence.

His mouth was firmly set like a piece of cement. Concrete words spun and rose from a reactionary heart, hit a teeth wall behind jammed-closed lips, and tumbled down his cement-hard windpipe like pebbles falling back into the gizzard. Still, why speak? Why waste your breath when you know that you were the only person convinced, and damn sure that global warming would become the golden age for the downtrodden black man if he kept his head screwed on right. This was huge stuff. You had to think about it. Think straight about what comes next. Silence had its place, and Widespread knew he was the equaliser. It was his job to suppress all the useless external interference in the Praiseworthy world, and hit the radar quick for dialling up the future. One would guess that Widespread would have likened his style of thinking to speed intellectualism, of roaming high on the human plateau of figuring out what was happening to the world, *devoid-ing himself of unwanted speech-making pushing intellectual reconciliation,* which he saw as *another useless assimilatory push for the traditional owner of country to give up his right to his ancestral lands.* It was no wonder that he had become fixated about the Anthropocene when the concrete solid conglomeration of his inner world asked what that global heating thing was all about. Would it act sane? In the end though, Planet figured out what all the fancy climate change names meant, like unprecedented and exceptionalism, which all in all, meant you are stuffed. All this, in the long run, did not matter to the likes of him, but rather, or obviously, he thought the time of equalising humanity was simply a matter of fate that was literally knocking on his front door. The time bomb ticking at his front door. You could go either way, into the future, or stay behind. In fact, you could safely say that Planet was dead certain of being on the money about the approaching end of a world full of rubbish, by being a seasoned expert on enduring apocalyptic times for his all times culture. It was easy for him to come to the realisation that by utilising other people's rubbish, he could make some money out of it.

This was a man who only had to take a cursory glance into the haze to see what black men endured. There were no rewards here for seeing the obvious. He knew which people on Earth would be facing heatwave after heatwave from sitting up to the eyeballs in the ancestral belly of the haze. And who would have to figure out how they were going to survive? Nobody except themselves. Yep! Planet was in the mood for an epoch-making global warming event. He was fired up to the gills for it. Hey? Think about it? Who else was more equipped in the art of surviving hell than his own mob? This business of endurance? No sweat. Now that he had acquired the right attitude, Widespread put his attention into how he could take the next step into the culture business of surviving by making quite a bit of money, you understand, but only to resurrect and restore the family fortune that was right there in front of him – their vast traditional lands, so to speak.

Sure! It was a feed for the haze. Why not? Make Planet the epical supermarket of hate story. The fat haze loomed heavy with story after story being pumped into the air, taking more oxygen than was necessary from the atmosphere. In these stories, Widespread's feral donkeys became complicated plot lines of everything that had ever gone wrong in Praiseworthy from the beginning of colonial oppression, and the symbol of great fallenness, like an ugly fallen angel looming in minds as big as a cyclone – a hostile hurdy-gurdy bringing everything from thousands of kilometres away roaring in winds that had no place in the world of the haze.

9

Planet had only one thing on his mind, which he called solidarity, of being aligned with millions of other poor people on the planet who depended on forty-two million working donkeys, instead of using a single cent worth of fossil fuel, and had been doing that for thousands of years. He thought if it was good enough for them, then it was good enough for him. Yet he wanted more: prized donkeys. Grey donkeys. Greyer donkeys. Jesus type of grey donkey. A unique silvery grey that he had once seen in a dream.

He sometimes craved for an illusive aluminium kitchen sink-coloured grey donkey that was quite literally one of a kind. A higher-ethereal silver-grey. A tone of grey that was not easy to put a finger on, that was not pigeon grey. Storm-cloud grey. Shale grey. Marsupial grey. Prehistoric dinosaur grey. Or the multiple greyness of say fifteen hundred diamond doves hanging off the weeping stems of a desert oak. Not bushfire smoke grey, where you once saw starlings chasing a swan through the skies. What you needed to do, was think smart in fashionable twenty-first century hues of greyness, and this was the greyness that was mucking up his mind in a search over thousands of square kilometres of plains country, and a long way away, over the mountain tops, and other conciliatory lands. But, like he said, *this was the way that I roll.* He was not interested in any other donkey at all. Not the ones that you could easily get your hands on, like the many millions in the country that were all the wrong colour grey fuzzing into nothingness trhough his mind, nor the strongest donkeys that were the wrong colour yet festered in his brain with complicated dreams of becoming that rich it was not funny, just from creating a sustainable transport industry with feral donkeys for the world to be in the hard century ahead, that would sing the new high praises for donkeys, like Dolly Parton singing, *hey hey, do you want another mule skinner down on your new mud track hey hey.* This was how he intended to make money from global warming, and improve the economy of self-reliance for every man, woman and child in Praiseworthy, who would become millionaires out of donkeys to ride out the overheating in the planet when their country became an inland desert of endless drought in a pandemic festering world. You choose which way to go, where to put your fate in unprecedented global warming. Go for it. You can either decide to assimilate and follow the aimless who are in charge of the world, or try following an unprecedented miracle man's blue-sky vision of saving his people's cultural future with a pack of donkeys.

The plan, as far as Planet was concerned, was to survey the lot – five million feral donkeys on the continent's land mass of 7.7 million square kilometres – muster all the hardiest donkeys in northern Australia that he could find in the bush by using nothing else but his bare hands and a bit of donkey whispering, and gradually, bring the lot to Praiseworthy. But like he said, Planet was not interested in any donkey. He intended to search high and low over the endless thousands of kilometres of open Australian bushland to find a particular type of grey donkey that he had once seen in a dream, the kind of glowing donkey that people would write stories about, like a Jesus donkey, or a donkey the colour of an Apollo spaceship. What he was dreaming about was a really specialised donkey. This donkey was imprinted on his brain. It was the colour of platinum with a patina. It was bedazzled, more flamboyant than say, the acute dullness of cold dishwater greyness, or gun-metal grey, but more an illuminated grey that stood out in the grey hues of the bush, like a grey-white moon-coloured beacon calling him to its spirit. This was about a super donkey beating global warming hands flat. He could see it now, the sun radiating off the platinum donkey's fur. A pure lodestar! What you would need in summers of fifty to sixty plus degrees. A donkey for the hard times that lives off bugger-all. No need for bucketloads of water for these feral donkeys. These buggers could go for days pulling houses across the desert if you wanted, and without them freaking while the old thunder men were throwing spears around in their global warming electrical storms with a million violent lightning strikes jumping straight out from the skies all night long – hit that, fuck that, ripping the freaking lot, trees, the whole darn forest being ripped to threads, piled, and stacked in a single heartbeat. Widespread, while still being an idiot, started speaking like a wise man, announcing, *It was all prophesy man. Someone's got to save humanity. Keep the world going so to speak. Save everything.* This was the message he had seen once while looking up into the sky and had read the billboard which could have been written by a great sky ancestor, or sky writers, a Major Mayor hologram, or he was just seeing things. Initially, he took no notice of skywriters protesting about blackfellas living in a pristine environment which they thought should be devoid of human beings, but then, Cause thought, what if it was a message coming from the highest authority in a real holy place, just for a poor traditional man like himself, and for some unexplainable reason, could only be channelled through the tree huggers? What if the great ancestral serpent was now writing English in the sky, using clouds like white ink? What if the big fella was beating the coloniser at his own game, and was really talking to him in particular, to save his mob?

Widespread was not interested in just looking at a sea of greyness if you could imagine what five million feral donkeys fixated in the head looked like. It meant nothing to him. He could choose any grey donkey of course and he had to, but he kept searching for that long-almost-faded memory of a certain unique strain of greyness – an almost impossible jaguar-grey donkey seen in his dream a long time ago. A dream that had become so diminished amidst the totality of a traditional man's reality, when he was spending crushing years single-handedly chasing thousands of what otherwise turned out to be just normal grey donkeys, roaming anywhere in the vast bush of the country, and becoming grey-blinded by the sight of the wrong grey donkeys separating every which way while bolting through the baking range lands and gullies in every inch of the north that was defended by skin-tearing acacia spirits, spinifex spike warriors, thorn ladies, and swaying spirit grasses lulling with ancient song, willing him further towards the edge of hidden deep crevices in which to fall, and where he might break his neck.

But there was no point in trying to kill the dream. Planet wanted gutsy donkeys with herculean strength, like the war donkeys he had repeatedly watched on TV documentaries and the donkeys of the poor people of the world, carrying a ton of bricks on their backs while stumbling on unsteady legs as they made their way down through crowded streets of ancient cities and villages. Now, while he blindly chased donkeys through thickets and plains country while ignoring the thousands of feral horses or camels trying to follow him home, he only thought of capturing donkeys, and only the ones that he thought were exactly like that true grey colour of platinum that he once believed he saw in a dream. Yep! Mostly, Widespread was wild guessing, since how would he know which donkeys would be capable of carrying the combined household furniture of an entire extended family, or tanks of water, groceries, building material, plus people bloated with junk food. You have to weigh it up. What's plan B? This was why Widespread chased thousands of donkeys, until finally by intuition, he could weigh a donkey's intellectual and physical strength at a glance, even in the scrawniest one living in waterless, overgrazed, clapped-out country. He could tell you its worth simply by sighting a donkey from a mile off and while it was camouflaged in the endless wide-open vista of more than two-metre high spinifex plains across the horizon, and he would know instantly, whether or not it could slog it out day in and day out in temperatures of forty to fifty plus degrees without building up a sweat, transporting a loaded dray over thousands of kilometres, and only living off a bit of drought-dry roadside stubble, and bugger-all water. This was what he called a proper donkey. And he would tell you it was performing at the normal rhythm of the world. Not express mail. That was finished. A relic of the

Anthropocene. And not like long haulage Mack Trucks. What he saw standing in the vista was the future – an engine for surviving the hard times always endured by the invisible peoples of the world, which he explained was the place where you found the true self-reliant man.

Yes, as long as he thought the donkey was capable of being a part of the long haul – like those that had once carried an entire library of books through a Middle Eastern desert, or could carry months of hay to feed a large flock of sheep after scrambling up the sides of steep mountains, or continue ploughing through belly-deep snow, although this was an ideal that would not concern his donkeys in this driest of country, but still, with unprecedented wild weather growing more crazed by the minute, and storming hailstones the size of pigs, or schools of poisonous box jellyfish, Widespread knew you could never tell what was going to happen to the climate anymore, and he could only guess how far his donkeys would take to being besieged by freak geographical and climatic conditions. Nevertheless, if Planet knew one thing alone, it was that he could not really predict the outcome of global warming across the north country routes for his transport conglomerate, except that this whole operation would be challenging, and his life? Well! His life would always be unhinged.

All this homelands man knew was that if he was to build his long-haul transport industry, it had to be led by a super strength donkey. A Godzilla donkey, the type of herculean donkey that the vast majority of the world's population had been using for a thousand years. His major road train transport empire would be driven by these super-charged donkeys that were fit for a super-charged climate. His transport fleet would be thousands of feral working donkeys employed in a self-feeding sustainable network fit to go for the Age of the Precipice. Well! Who else was really planning to replace the collapse of the global transport system? Widespread could feel such a catastrophe happening already even though he was far away from being a major player in the fossil fuel industry. Still, it paid to be ready when you are hanging by your fingernails over the side of the precipice, to be ahead of the plummet, anticipating how to crawl into heaven, and to be ahead of the game by working like a corporate man reaping as much skyrocketing price-hike gold as you could for the survival of your own humanity.

This was the secret. The treasure chest that he kept hidden in his mind. Why would he tell anyone else the secrets to success, if they could not smell the money for themselves? Let this be a reminder to the world, that from now on the smarts will only be on a need-to-know basis about why he was racing around the bush on the smell of an oily rag, being totally selfless, searching for global-warming-resistant donkeys. Why else would a normal ancestral thinking man ever want to get away from Praiseworthy, if it was not for Praiseworthy? How else was the culture going to survive the precipice? Anyway, why would a sane man give away his methodology to even the good wife Dance, the mad wife to go around blasting his business to all and sundry who thought she was only talking to ghosts anyhow? Well! This was not going to happen. His mind was a bank safe. This was where the business world stored trade secrets. In the head. Everything confidential in his brain, not for sharing with a pack of thieves. This was not the Communist Party. A free for all. Giving everything to any lazy bugger vying to become rich without getting their hands dirty in donkey shit, who had not realised the potential of fabulous money just sitting out there, like whorl winds of gold dust in the bloody arid zone; a total dream of a business with free feral donkeys by the millions out there for the taking. Imagine! A donkey could replace Qantas itself and be far more sustainable, then what? Why pay billions of dollars to foreign people for burning every last gasp of fossil fuel from the planet, or letting white mining companies rip up your traditional country and blow your sacred sites apart? Let others dream about donkeys themselves if they wanted, after the deal was done, after Planet had the industry all sewn up. In any case, no other bugger could be bothered finding money to put fuel in a car to chase donkeys around the bush, or worry about the repairs and maintenance of a wreck out in the middle of nowhere. Why did we ever stop using donkeys in the first place? Planet asked the wondering people who strayed from the main camp to sneer at the sight of donkeys penned in the cemetery, or whoever he could pinch from the mainstream for a day, until they were stolen back into the fold of the Major Mayor's dictum of whatever he thought about future truth.

When you looked at what was happening in Planet's mind, of what set him apart from others, and you wondered why he dreamt of becoming so rich it would not be funny, perhaps it was that he owned the strongest beating heart of all, from being fuelled by the haze living inside his blood stream. Who could stop him now? It was just going to be wham, bang, wham all the way, as he assured himself constantly, about collecting his future. Perhaps there was some truth in his side of the story, since he claimed that he could pump more oxygen into that fat brain sitting on top of his starving skin and bone body, that he literally beamed from an aura of self-worthiness. He just saw the path, got on it, and kept walking further into the future than most people, even if he was keeping his greatness at the level of ordinary people.

It was this total self-belief that kept him afloat, that made it possible for him to believe that he could do anything he put his mind to achieving. In another life, if he had been rich white, he could have been a meteorologist, for he could actually sense the nervousness of global warming. It was like being Genghis Khan, or like any man called to greatness. Sometimes though, when a man thinks this big about his humanity as Planet had, it could also pull him down to the ordinary, sink him into nothingness through the envy of others. What helped Planet though, was that he seemed to be completely oblivious to the masses shovelling his name in hate. Hate was not able to spill into his aura. Hate fell like water off a duck's back, for like the man said, he was not born yesterday, but had lived in Praiseworthy his entire life of fifty-two years like a spirit man breathing that old ancestral dust from the earth into his lungs, and what he had was its power travelling in the bloodstream and that gave him the plain old-fashion self-knowledge, that anyone who had his name dragged through the dirt of country as he had knew how to escape the world of the living dead.

While the dust swirled in the haze, Widespread would not mind being ripped off, or knifed in the back, or have his own family slink back in shame from the sight of him smirking around Praiseworthy while publicly mouthing off his capitalist theories about how they should be making some money out of global warming. No one got the itch to join his money theories even though he kept on trying to convince them to act now, that there would be plenty of opportunities waiting for them from the total collapse of the first-world economy with the awakening ancestral spirits creating a global crisis more devastating than the last Ice Age.

It's coming sooner than you think, Cause soberly warned his world swarming in the dust haze. Perhaps he spoke too casually, too much like he was hiding something, and seemed as though he was not really wanting to be taken seriously. This happened all the time when he used his imaginary soapbox to preach his own churchy like thing, to have a yak at the masses whenever he felt in the mood to liven things up, to acquire a few donations, to get the so-called perishers on the Pentecostal Church Street to sign up to his donkey pyramid scheme. *We are already like white government*, they chanted while telling him this was what a deal breaker in Australia should be like. They said they had his measure: *You like the only loan shark on Church Street*. He insulted the intelligence of the complete multiple of religious senses. *Go to hell,* yelled many Christians from the distance while others walked right up to cover the ground at his feet with a pond of spit. *Piss off! Moron!* They paid him with their best wishes, like holy curses falling from the summit: *We hope you die from a very bad disease.* Then, most bade him a farewell: *We all hate you here.* No one could help being the talk of the town: *He's just trying to rip us poor people off by trying to get a few dollars out of our pension money, just to get his stupid business started.* Well! That was true. *You are stealing money from us poor people,* the old ladies complained, and they grabbed hold of their guardian angels, and walked away.

We are going to hex you, Planet.

Saying a lot of prayers for you to stop you doing things like that.

Maybe this is how you make gods.

Even...

A future God.

10

The Major Mayor's town council reached far into its collective non-salubrious mind to find a solution to the hazards of keeping pet feral donkeys in an urbanised zone, to show that they knew how to take charge of the filth and excrement souring the pristineness of the beautiful haze. They needed to set an example, since the federal and state governments for Aboriginal people were shafting feral animals, or feral people of any kind, it was the desirable thing to do, since after all, they did desire to be assimilated. It felt the righteous thing to do, to get rid of Planet and his donkeys. They discussed how to approximate the white masked stuff, the huff and puff of local government, while sitting on white plastic chairs, where they spent most of their lives talking about white matters governing their lives. They took to wearing the white masks of the old colonial protectors of Aborigines to the meetings, in order to create a sense of anonymity. It felt liberating and powerful to be copying the extreme right-wing nationalistic values of the western world, yet at the same time, to remain totally divorced from knowing how it felt to be assimilated. They acted as an angry white masked mob by brandishing fiery flares to wave around in the council building, and yelling slogans for hours on end, such as *Glory for Praiseworthy* and other such wishful thinking, and that there would be no capitulation to impurity, of not being native, to put it on notice about keeping feral donkeys in their town.

There were no apologies from Planet about the town spending hours of their lives having to urgently reassess their complacency towards the keeping of feral pets – puppy dogs everywhere, pussycats galore, pigs under the house, chickens, dingoes, horses, cattle, camels, European and Asian ducks all over the place, migratory birds, foreign butterflies like a plague, cane toads either half-domestic or running wild. The whole lot were feral. All this just to get rid of Widespread's donkeys. Which of their own foreign animals should be able to stay in the pristine ancestral country anywhere on the continent, and which should be crated up in a box and sent back overseas to wherever it had come from, or, should only feral donkeys be targeted and annexed, and eliminated? It was a very hard question. The local magistrate, an old law man, and redundant postman, tried beyond the call of duty to reach an impasse with Planet about which feral animals were acceptable in Praiseworthy, which were non-traditional, which were included because the old pig fellow was his uncle, pussycats were like babies, and camels were more holy, because someone on the council wanted to keep a camel as a pet for the nativity on Church Street at Christmas time. What about dreaming you had a foreign animal for a pet then? Yes, old man, the council said, advise Planet that it was okay to keep invisible feral animals, say if he was dreaming of owning monkeys, deer, rabbits, illegal iguanas, and some migratory birds, just as long as they did not interfere with the Dreaming. Dance stomped down to the gate where the old magistrate was shouting that all feral donkeys had to be culled, and she demanded to know whether her cabbage butterflies swarming in waves of whiteness around the house were free to live in Praiseworthy, and the migratory moths, and some other foreign butterflies, or were they going to be killed too? The old magistrate said he did not know. He did not know the Latin names that Dance continued rattling off from the top of her head. He looked totally confused and said he did not know, but suspected that all feral butterflies and moths would be exterminated by the council with the poisonous spray used to kill cockroaches, and in any case, the edict he was talking about was about killing mangy donkeys, editing them out of the page to keep them out of the story of the pristine. She agreed wholeheartedly, while glaring straight into Planet's face and pointing to all the makeshift donkey pens, snapped matter of fact, *All these dirty donkeys should be cleared out of town.*

The town's officials reached out to Widespread with bucketloads of text messages mentioning their contrivances with fake niceness, then getting down to the tintacks-honest, homegrown-sour and nasty barrel loads of insults cancelling him through their social media accounts. They wanted him dead to the world, and felt nicely vindicated for having ramped up the importance of their new official by-laws about prohibiting all feral donkeys. He ignored them, and in turn, they said *fuck that* – all feral donkeys must die. When good people have bothered to reach out in good spirit, they do not expect insults. Not at all. These were official local government people after all, who had gained their positions with bribe votes. They were almost assimilated, not a bunch of idiots. Who did he think he was?

The long stand-off about feral donkeys polluting the pristine, led to a string of marathon meetings, to nut it out like a bunch of assimilated people about how to implement stiffer by-law penalties about keeping any extra feral animals at all, and with more convoluted forms to fill in to be sweated out and fought over, until greater, more debilitating amendments were devised about prohibiting really feral animals, but not someone's Uncle's old feral pig – Gusto, the pink mud monster under the house – from being included in the cull-by-death law. It was decided that the pig was not really an animal, because it was everybody's cousin, even though it was an atheist.

But! Then when the matter was finally settled about whether any relative could be non-denominational, so-and-so's pet dingo called Aunty was officially excluded from the cull for being too holy, like a dingo saint. Anybody could see for themselves the old dingo aunty going in and out of the churches every day of the week without a shred of bias. That was fine enough, but what should anyone do about pet feral birds roaming free range – walking the street, freely flying in the haze thing – all the free-range poultry running around Praiseworthy, or just some of them, or whether for instance, multi-generational descendants of at least two thirds of Praiseworthy's half-bred feral pussycats could be called domesticated when you would only be able to tell after they had perished from heat stroke when banned to the bush without water on the highway out of town, dumped on the open road in an extreme drought from where the scrawny things had originated. Could any of the supposedly domesticated skin-and-bone horses roaming around wild, the ones that had been fully ordained as spiritual advisers to a newly rushed church dedicated to horses, or any of the loose Brahman x Droughtmaster x feral cattle that would be killers one day. In the righteous piling up of what had to be culled and done away with – stuffed in a sugar bag, or confronted with a sharp knife – the accused feral animals began running around gardens, and were even tidying up the gardens. A great number of pitying exceptions to the rule had to be made in the end by the magistrate senior law man who was too soft about these creatures that did not belong. No one wanted to give up the feral animal load. It was all live and let live. A line in the dirt had to be drawn. There were just too many exceptions to the rule. But this did not extend to Planet's in toto maggoty donkeys which were considered the evil insurrection that they were talking and singing about in church, although again, the edict did not include that old feral donkey named Aunty Polyester that had once wandered into one of Praiseworthy's big churches of its own volition, and was now considered as the true descendent of the donkey that carried Mary in Bethlehem, because it had never been caught with rope, and dragged into Praiseworthy to spread diseases and whatnot, like Planet's donkeys.

Planet was of course a complete moron who failed to complete forms, not even filling in his name on the piece of paper. He chose instead to ignore the mounting efforts by the local council about keeping the type of feral animals clearly outlined on texted official forms created with clear and honest democratic principles. His non-compliance to filling in a simple convoluted form for goodness sake, became a clear indication to the powers that be, that he was never going to abide by any of the rules of domicile – of belonging to the place if you please, so you can see the problem. Widespread had a real problem about reneging responsibility, when he saw that getting rid of the true feral, the cloud haze, had been delegated to a hologram scarecrow while everyone's job became the undoable, to make the undomesticated world go away.

The matter of what was a feral in Praiseworthy became sensational talk for a very long time, and even if nothing else devastating and terrible happened again, the world of a feral would be right up there in the brimming epics of humanity. For the feral story would be hunted and gathered through the all times, and it would be nurtured into the most wondrous epics of what it meant to stay alive as a species of the region. It would be difficult not to see the moral relevance in the feral story. It would live on in every overcrowded poverty house up and down the streets of Praiseworthy, where every person of old culture and story – man, woman and child – lived as a philosopher of all times idealism, purposefulness, dreams and realism, and where, valuing the aesthetics of the fog became less interesting, and the fog more acceptable, as they stopped complaining about whether it would ever go away, while concentrating on the meaning of having anything feral occurring in their lives.

When all the text messages failed to generate any response from Planet, a vast number of summon forms were bundled up, tied with a piece of official shire council string, and delivered to his house. The long-suffering casual postmaster, now continually drawn out of forced redundancy, was given the job of taking a walk down to the cemetery, a twenty-kilometre wide spread of bush land, to hand deliver the tied-up bundle of summonses, which was like handing sticks to that idiot Planet. *And tell him, tell him*, Major Mayor Ice Pick ordered the postman, *that if he refuses to get his ass up to the court house – Where? – That place over there, and on such and such a date for breaching all of these long strings of convoluting by-laws that had confused each of the previous visiting magistrates about all these prohibitions on keeping a feral animal in Praiseworthy by having to re-, and re-reference all these amendments to existing by-laws about the real condition for keeping a feral animal if you had to, and in which case, tell him, that, that was only how you are going to be capable of abiding all the stringent conditions set for keeping anything feral on reasonable and compassionate grounds, and in grounds that were purposefully built to a proper standard to suit all the members of the community, not just a few, not just one person like himself only, and tell him that was the law he could not break, nor any others who were deemed to be idiots, and whose animals the council had deemed by association, were simpletons too.*

The postman, a formidable memory man of country, parroted Ice

Pick's message exactly to Widespread in shorthand: *You hear that?*
Then, while wearing his other metaphorical hat of being the town's
voluntary magistrate, he listened intently while Planet counter-
complained and went off his rocker in an unreal, unjust etc. outburst
of total rage. *This is not a Shakespeare play you know Widespread.*
The strewn summonses flew off in a wind gust, floated with the white
butterflies a thousand feet up in the sky, then fell into the dirt. Planet
looked at that – thought it a miracle, and touched the Buffalo Soldier
t-shirted magistrate, tapping it with his finger while storming words
laced with spit that sprayed across the old man's face about how some
people on the council were keeping feral pigs, and wild pussycats, and
dingoes, a camel, and all that, so what about those people? And he also
announced matter-of-factly just to bring the point home that, *if you
want to see a blackfella in action, then you are looking at him.*

11

Now with many donkeys kept illegally by Widespread down in the
cemetery of Praiseworthy, there was not a real platinum-coloured one
among them. Not a smidgen of a dream donkey with high-achiever
greyness, so that all in all, the quest for making money out of the
precipice seemed to be just an illusion, like the greyness of world peace,
too hard to achieve outside of a dream. But who was thinking about
how to fail in the free-for-all? The dream grey kept being replaced by
hundreds of mistakes of a literal all-sorts grey paintbox. All wrong.
This was what happens when you go chasing a dream, where in the
excitement of the hunt you feel invincible, you become colourblind,
you lose your mind, it is like you would not realise if you were at sea
without a raft, and you start seeing things differently, as though this
wrong thing you were chasing was exactly what you needed. Of all
colours, the shades of greyness were perhaps the most mysterious

and indeterminate. Widespread was already lost in an accumulation of these costly mistakes, always returning to Praiseworthy with the wrong donkey that joined a uniform tidal wave of similar greyness, and it was despairing, to be without a mask-head to pave through the era of the precipice. Plan B was driving him mad.

Yet this total mind-blown idée fixe about the colour of donkeys continued, because Planet believed that he could not begin his business with any flukes of luck, or, economic smarts, until he found some figurehead donkey of the ultimate illusionary grey that so far he had only seen from a distance once in his dreams. Still, he believed such unique grey brightness would be instantly recognisable anywhere once you owned it. He held his belief that he would know it when he saw it, he knew it was out in the bush somewhere, and once it was leading teams of say one hundred, two hundred, or five hundred donkeys all lit with solar energy lights, and brightly painted harnesses of his ancestral creation heroes, like the Hindu trucks of India, this donkey would be like the biggest silvery super lodestar at the lead, and the whole shebang would be all fired up, lit up, and more radiant than anyone had ever seen in the history of all humanity. This was the kind of mythical donkey that was born sacred enough not only to lead across the precipice, but to cast aside all foreign disasters like financial ruin.

Any blue-sky visionary would say the same, that such a sacred animal blessed through time would spearhead the greatest donkey business the world had ever seen in the precipice era of sustainable renewables. A true climate-change donkey, and nothing was going to stop Planet from continuing his search through the vastness of hundreds of thousands of square miles of northern Australia until he found it. If he was delusional or not, that remained to be seen, because this was just the start as far as he was concerned, of achieving, bringing into reality, the biggest transport dream for the world to come, and he would continue on the quest of personally tracking down and sorting through millions of feral donkeys to find the illusionary shiny silver greyness of a long-ago dream when he had glimpsed it standing half hidden in the far distance of a place, that might or might not exist, while it had radiated from the moonlight like literal silver on the top of an imaginary ridge on the horizon.

Planet just knew intuitively, that he would remember the steel-grey colour of millionaires if he saw it hitting him in the eye, yet, so far as anyone knew, he had never seen a millionaire, but so what? It only meant he could never stop searching for the grey associated with the greatest wealth, and that he could never be at home looking at all of the mistaken, not real platinum-coloured donkeys that did not look like Rolls-Royce grey, Jaguar XF Eiger-type grey, or pure chalice-tarnished silver greyness, but were just the plain old HB-lead grey donkeys he already owned. But he was very relaxed about the idea of still not getting the colouring right no matter the cost – not that he had money to spend for hunting donkeys far and wide, knowing all along that he would always be searching for something that might not exist, because what if his vaguely remembered more steel grey donkey did actually appear again in his dreams one night? Why! Well! Why not? Cause Man Steel was a countryman with vast knowledge of country for roaming inside his head, knowing how it looked, its temperament, its desires, its feel, of knowing what was ancestral, spiritual, and real in country. Look outside! His 1970s rust bucket. The thing caked with dry mud. Alaskan frost Falcon sedan looking worse for wear, packed to the gills, ready for speeding off to some exact geographical and spiritually loaded patch of country he had lassoed and wrestled to the ground in his head. Taking charge of the situation. Off again. Travelling across the country to an imaginary scrap of ground he had pinned with a red flag in his head, hunting again for a colour of grey that only a true countryman could see.

This idea of having total commitment to fulfilling his own dream infuriated Dance. Didn't she have a few unfulfilled dreams of her own to chase? Why were her dreams being put on hold? Constantly! She was a born realist too, who knew what it was like to be burdened by an idealistic dreamer of a husband who was always off hunting donkeys, because the responsibility had fallen squarely on her shoulders as the one left to deal with the fallout, the reality of Praiseworthy people hating the dream. This everything or nothing mentality was what she thought was too extreme. Dance lacked desire for being a stand-in for Cause as the social pariah of the community, while being left with an endless stream of abuse about owning illegal donkey pets. The hustling! She could tell you what it was like, as if it was up to her to get rid of Planet's hundreds of donkey pollutants from town. Chase donkeys. Pick up the shit. She ignored both donkeys and the council of the Major Mayor, preferring instead to only listen to butterfly wings flapping against the ground. In her reality of hearing the language of fluttering wings, donkeys and people swirled together in a hate vortex that flew straight into her head and vied to reclaim control over her thoughts. Heaven only knows who knew about her plight. Knew that she did not own any of these donkeys. *Ask Planet?* His donkey business had nothing to do with her. She turned away, turned to the wisdom of moths, of butterflies, while hatching her own plan to escape from the known world. She would risk sanity, future times of calamity, by being taken far away, to live fabulously, flamboyantly lepidoptera-ism, in a poem for a chrysalis hatching into the glory of a simple butterfly.

All this longing that came her way by that redundant postman fellow acting like he was getting on with the job of being a magistrate for removing donkeys from Praiseworthy. His work got nowhere in her brain. Such longings written on scraps of paper by the Major Mayor's shire council dumped at her door was lost in the haze, where, in fact, she had not noticed that hating donkeys had become such a fierce concern, or that this desire to hate donkeys had far exceeded any worry by the general population about the permanent haze, and what it felt like living in a dust fog that had always remained a bone of contention high on the barometer of raising the sweat of intolerance in Praiseworthy. The only thing that inspired her about moving anything was her own desire to move. Well! This was until the desire of donkey hate, replaced hatred of the haze. In some wafted sense of amusement, the donkey hate thing grew legs in her mind, perhaps because it was aligned with the idea of disposal, of getting rid of things, decluttering her personal life, inspiring her to get in the act, of getting rid of donkeys forever. At this point, it had even occurred to Planet, that he was copping a triple whammy of unjustifiable humiliation about his passion to create a dream of bringing his people back to their sovereign position in this country. This new hate was deeply personal, and affected his state of mind. Donkey hate interfered with his will to live. It was polluting the blue-sky vision. He became convinced that he was not only being victimised by a bitter state of affairs because he had always taken sides in who knows how many enemy camps in his Native Title disputed challenges between people, but that now, their hate, total as it was, was pumping his hate. He saw himself not as a person, but transformed into a door of hatred that went wham, flew open, and wham, slammed shut. Widespread challenged the whole town to bring it on, hate for hate. He pivoted hate. Wrapped it. Flung the thing. Sent a hate bundle in all directions. It was a battlefield. Hate flying here, and there. Yep! Let everything be destroyed. The winner to take the flattened moonscape. Who wanted to win anything in this mess? Added to that wellspring of hatefulness, well, there was Dance's overall bitterness to contend with, which left him catastrophically heartbroken, of feeling volcanically betrayed by her joining the world of hating donkeys. Inconsolable became the business of how he felt anyway. In this darkest-of-night emotion of his otherwise positively future-driven estimation of himself, he still found a skerrick of a saintly man inside his heart that was trying to reconcile what had befallen him from having the simple idea of creating an economic dream.

Planet had no idea how it was possible that a man could be deliberately sabotaged by the very people he was trying to save from extinction. How could they not feel what he felt? That they will be tiling over the edge of complete annihilation? Didn't they want to be saved? Viva! Viva, sovereignty! Outlive invaders! Perhaps! It was a saviour thing. Nobody loves a saviour in today's reality. They war against it. They would rather become extinct. Yes, Planet knew it was reasonable to expect that nobody wanted to make even greater sacrifices in their lives by having to put up with the putridness of possibly a thousand interned feral donkeys in Praiseworthy, even if it meant having to put up with a bit of donkey shit to make a bit of money. So, there it was, the heaviest of mind, deeply plagued by a personal trifecta of woe, Planet the ostracised, a broken man walking all the hate vibes in Praiseworthy, punched in the guts by hate each time he stepped out onto a Praiseworthy street.

12

They did not like the idea...*We already business people. We look after the business...every time, all times, big time.* This was the terrible thing about Planet's pyramid scheme, and how he actually saw everyone in the streets dodging him – gliding off like ghosts rhumbaing into the ether from a mile off, or as soon as their eyes caught sight of him. Even his own sons deliberately did the same thing. Each had learnt how to hide in plain sight by sinking inside themselves. Skinny Aboriginal Sovereignty. There he was, seventeen years of age, amateur boxer all rake and bone, whose strength in the ring relied more on nerves of steel and grit, than the power of muscles. He could dance. The old mungkuji countrymen said that this Aboriginal Sovereignty had the ancestors dancing in him. *Country mangayi right inside him, dancing through him. Him true jamba*. It was true that Aboriginal Sovereignty had never stopped dancing, and spent all his time practising his country spirit dance like he was the law personified, the real business. But now, he does not dance so much anymore.

There was something bothering this pride and joy of Praiseworthy wisdom people. Nobody saw what that old red baseball cap hid, that mostly covered his face, the trouble in his eyes. He seemed to have taken his mind a long way from the world of the ancestors he knew through dancing beside them in country. He looked lost, as though he had forgotten where he had left his spirit. These days he walked stooped over so low, his face almost hit the dirt in front of him, and perhaps, he thought that whatever he was looking for could be found in the dirt. Perhaps it was his soul that had been reduced to nothingness, and he expected to find a fragment of whatever it had been that was once easily seen in the world. Perhaps his stolen property was somewhere scattered in bits and pieces that were being carried away on the back of ants escaping down into their world underneath the ground. Widespread watched Aboriginal Sovereignty coming towards him from up the street, walking like a praying mantis, in a slow gait, while staring at the ground. He looked like he was going to trip over himself. He saw clearly, that his son's mind was somewhere else, in some low place that he would never know. The boy may as well be living on another planet. This was the eldest son whom he had personally named, so that the boy would always remember who he was, and that this land under their feet was nobody else's Native Title country, no matter where they had originally come from on the planet. He had to insist on the name, to save his firstborn from being called something stupid that Dance was scratching from the bottom of the barrel of common English names that Australian white people generally called their children. The way she argued about it was as though it was a matter of life and death, and that it was far better to have a common One Australia type of name for her son like Paul, or Pauline if it was a girl, just to prepare tomorrow's Aboriginal children to deal with a life of being ground into the dirt by white people's colonialist privileges, or migrant settlers, or whatever else they wanted to call themselves in contemporary times. You could hear her complaining to this day, who ever thought of calling their child Aboriginal Sovereignty, and not Paul or Pauline.

Planet continued watching his number one son, the boy dragging his face on the ground in defeat, and yet, he did not call him. When Ab.Sov saw his father glaring at him in this early morning deserted street, he quickly readjusted his red mesh back-to-front cap perched like a parrot on the top of his long sea-salt matted brown hair. He pulled the cap lower over his eyes, swung his bony gazelle body dressed in dirty ripped jeans inherited from Vinnies, and his bare chest, into the opposite direction, by sliding his seventeen years of old bones back up the street with his gang of skinny camp dogs following in tow. Planet scowled. He hated that skulk walk. He had a gutful of seeing kids walking their own country like black fugitives, but knew these were the ones who had travelled far in the country of nightmares, and as he intuitively picked all truths from his walk, he knew that this son had slipped beyond his reach. Every intense feature in his face fell into natural scowl lines as his gut churned itself into greater levels of dread that paralysed his soul on the spot. Who knows what grit Planet was made of, historical circumstances, ancestral permeations, he could not move, could not speak to the boy slipping further away from himself. Whatever it was that made him tick with a boundless strength to conquer the worsening circumstances of the black man in the global climate-changed world of his vision, the deep chasm that lay between himself and Aboriginal Sovereignty remained a bridgeless place, never to be crossed.

The desires of the father, apparent in this chance encounter with his eldest son out on the street in the waxing gibbous dawn, not only exposed the unbridgeable space between them, but deformed the mighty challenges of new times where Planet's mind worked to make the world right for his sons. Times that could never straddle the fact that a boy like Aboriginal Sovereignty had walked the distances of old men many times. A vision of surviving was the only reality that ached in Planet's mind, and was what drove his soul. He would never see the police cars roaring through the streets of his son's brain, nor where the deafening sirens roared even louder through thin walls, and open windows in the middle of the night, nor feel how his brain was blasted apart by pistols aimed at his head, nor know the intimate fear of running like dogs accused by the state of being paedophiles.

Tommyhawk! Get here. Planet yelled several times to the tubby little brown-skinned boy with golden curls, the eight-year-old youngest son who ignored anyone who did not address him as a Jedi, or ninja, but he did not look Jedi-like, nor like a ninja, but just a fat boy, a law unto himself, who was following his more superior brother – the song of the country, lightness itself – gliding up the street. Planet watched this other heavy on conscience, no-show, go-slow son, a child so unlike himself, and thought back to how he called it when Tommyhawk was born, as seeing nothing in the baby but a bloody little fascist. *That's right! You I am calling…*nobody was going to fool him by any supposed baby innocence rot either at the birth, or now. His memory of the birth seen again without regret, where he said, *I am not calling him Duruki now. Call him what you like. Just call him some stupid name in English, Tommyhawk. Anything will do.* A man knows how to recognise a shirker: could see what this kid was thinking then, and now, watching Tommyhawk figuring out which way to run, just to weasel out of doing anything like lifting a finger to help his father. *Jigging along over there are you?* The boy's head of sun-tinted brown golden-edged curls bounced around as he crossed the road, and plodded along on the other side of the street deep in thought, his head in the ether universe of global citizens, where else would a sovereign citizen of the world be, or whatever else planet he belonged to, and he passed his father as though the man did not exist. Even if the boy had simply not noticed his father calling him – which was not true, the fact of the matter was that Tommyhawk took no notice of any adults in his world. Like: *You are too real man. Deal with your own world.* Yes, seeing his father anytime was too much reality to deal with at dawn. *Hex! Hex! Be gone folk people.* A citizen of the world only communicated through the world wide web. *Catch the dude on social media if you like. See how that grabs you.*

Fucking Tommyhawk, Planet thought. *Bugger you. Should have let your silly mother name you moron or whatever dumb-arse name she would have dredged up from the ditch of the ugliest baby names in the world.* He wondered why he wanted to call this kid a good solid name from country, like Duruki, which was his real name. Nope, forget it. The kid was not worth it.

These days, and ever since Tommyhawk had hit a jackpot realisation that he was actually escaping the world he lived in by living virtually elsewhere, he only saw what he wanted to see on the streets of Praiseworthy. All he had to do was put his imagination to good use by altering his perception of reality, and hexing that reality right out of any type of existence, and in particular, bending his piss-off feeling about his parents into a knot like a steel pipe for never giving him a thing he ever really wanted in life. Like for instance, he had to get his own brand-new Apple mobile phone and the latest Apple iPad so he could communicate with the real world of social media on the world wide web like any global kid of the new world trying to sort out his own Anthropocene-free future. Shouldn't he belong to a dust-free virtual landscape of a zillion voices streaming zillions of superman thoughts into his head, far more then he could ever possibly manage to decipher in his informationless freefall life? Wasn't it the right of any child on Earth to know everything that was going on through the internet at this moment of time? What was the isolated world of Praiseworthy going to teach him about the future? Mmm! Tommyhawk thought it the greatest crime against humanity, having parents like his, people who were not up to the task of saving the world, who had locked him up in a total brain-dead environment called home. What home? He could feel his life being sucked dry, yet his parents were happy to watch him die of boredom in a stark information-free bubble. In a cemetery. He hated the place. This was his reason for believing that he was adopted, and he had been stolen from his real parents who were smart people of the real world where he truly belonged. A kind of stolen generation in reverse. You know, the little insomniac was deprived from the actual real-time world reaching him, and stimulating his every sense with endless chatter of the vast social media communities. He was convinced that he could no longer feel his heartbeat, that it was slowing down to something like two beats every half hour. In other words, he was dead meat. The only way he could pump the thing up again was to accelerate his mind faster than his desire to know about every thought that existed in the world right up to this minute. Oh! He would make someone pay for the injustice of being deprived of knowledge. Tommyhawk sought no less than revenge by a thousand blows against these kid-napping people who called themselves his parents.

Tommyhawk had no trouble worrying about his conscious thought while traversing this truly dangerous real world he imagined as being fact, not fiction. He now walked with an accelerando consciousness looming with all the Aboriginal paedophile men that could ever possibly exist, and in his understanding of how the world worked, they were everywhere according to the endless social media chat-room theorising about the problem with black people. His anxiety-riddled mind spun like a dog bitten by a flea because he was living in that world the dominant white people were talking about. They had a superior intelligence to the black mind, so how was he going to make himself turn white as...It was a load off, knowing that he was leaving Praiseworthy at least metaphorically if not yet in reality, because Tommyhawk knew it was just a matter of time and he would be gone forever, gone quicker than a scammer, faster than lightning, quicker than the NBN, for he was turning white.

Yet, the eternal question, even for this little boy, was how do you make your dreams come true? So, while his mind was long gone from Praiseworthy and was living not in space, but on the internet, Tommyhawk had begun devising a plan, a checklist of to-dos. Tick box number one. He already felt transformed. What a load off? He was now someone who did not belong in Praiseworthy. But! But, so what? There were questions of authenticity and doubt plaguing his head and bursting out of his ears. *Should I be living here? A thousand times: No! Yes!* The useless friend in his private discussion with himself that could only ever be his own mind was more than useless, a doubter, although a good listener, but ultimately, that engager was giving just one piece of advice – *go for it, stop being as weak as piss, you deserve better, man, no question about it*, and all the while, the mind was having no holidays, it was not a picnic while working at the transformation of the boy into becoming a full-time schemer. Go on. Tick box number two.

A boy's dream was never easy to achieve. It takes time to become an expert plotter of schemes and dreams. It really is a multifaceted task, and now, with so many schemes crashing into each other while spinning around in the Formula 1 Grand Prix mess of his brain mass, his plots merged, began to have no limit, no boundaries, where everything was up for grabs, everything could crash up the boundary walls with multiple injuries, or anything could be achievable. There were no limits to what he could do with a brain anyhow after ticking box number two, and no laws had been ingrained in a mind of someone so young to stop him.

Well! So far so good, the problem was whether he would have the guts to go through with the quickest way he would think of, to make things happen. Because? Because he had to do something to escape the paedophiles that the government said were an infestation in his community, and Tommyhawk thought he was not going to wait about until it was too late. Oh! Do not worry about the mass paedophile situation, even though it was quite true that this little boy Tommyhawk had indoctrinated himself into believing everything he had heard on the powerful news media of Australia, especially black condemnation. He sat around plenty of times while hooked on what was being said in the news, and truly, it was just like watching sport where people keep looking even though the players are getting beaten, and with multiple injured left, right and centre. This was where he became the main spectator of the obsessed, willing the country's politicians to keep saying their racist stuff. He was cheering them on, and praying to God they would keep saying it. Let it get as bad as it can get. *Go on! Keep saying Aboriginal communities are an infestation of predatory paedophiles. I will you to say it.* There were so many triumphs in hearing what he wanted to hear. Goals struck. So much to look forward to if they kept saying he lived in a rotten place. To cut a long story short, racist ridicule was how this little kid was going to make his great escape from the haze of Praiseworthy. He had reached the goalpost where anything was possible, anything was up for grabs, and it was only his impatience with the slow wheels of the country turning his way, that was starting to get the better of him. You could not blame Tommyhawk for his impatience, for children anywhere in the world have been taught that instant gratification is not how it works in the end.

The boy became pathologically addicted to listening to the radio for news about predators but nobody knew what he was doing, and nobody could stop him. Day or night, or whenever he could sneak away to listen to the ABC news without creating any suspicion about what he was doing, he became more fixated to his totally unhinged one-trick-pony mania of teaching himself the ways of an Australian politician. Yes! The white man's government had won his soul. At least this was what he was informing himself, that he had discovered possibility. He had found adventure. Fun. Ambition. No harm in that. He would become the adopted child of a white politician, and learn all their teachings so he could become one of them. It was the way you see. He needed to feel safe. And wouldn't he feel safe living in the big white Parliament House building in the capital of the country, in Canberra? Now, like a frightened little animal, Tommyhawk perfected his escape persona. He listened like a mouse for the slightest sound, for a paedophile coming up behind him. He listened. He waited for more news, and there was plenty of it in the trendy national narratives about paedophiles running amuck on Aboriginal communities in a hundred thousand nights of bedtime stories told by people who were themselves not Aboriginal, and he listened to so many of those voices talking smart, until he was blue in the face from hearing whatever fake news he could hear, or read.

Yes! Tommyhawk grabbed bad news as a gift, and as his own personal mono-minded bonanza that he tightly stitched in his particular goal-driven mind. So, what became of his world? This theatre? Over a complete year he listened to all of the news about how the government and all the white commentators in the country – except those Aboriginal people – were saying how bad Aboriginal communities were to live in because of the paedophiles. It was like hearing the biggest sob story in the country and Tommyhawk loved hearing the stories. There was a total miserere outpouring from all sorts, in the new world psalm of those who were desperately turning themselves blue in the face with worrying about Aboriginal children being attacked by paedophiles and neglected by their parents, and jumping up and down in their tracks, and lurching at one another to be the top dog of all the argy-bargy facts, to dominate the frenzied media about loving Aboriginal children more than their parents loved them.

There was bugger-all need for stitching real facts together in the complete osmosis of Aboriginal men being rampant prowlers of Aboriginal communities to get their molesting hands on the little children. Tommyhawk learnt more from the sport of this media theatre than from anything the school had ever taught him – and that was for sure. Sensationalism was a powerful teacher. The boy felt as though he was hearing gods telling him the truth when he was hearing them on the media, because he believed that only real smart people get to be on the news, and they would know if Aboriginal parents did not love their children, and if Aboriginal men were violent paedophiles. He thought he had cinched his life like a doomed kitten drowning in a bag. Look at that? You could see it anytime of the week on the TV. It was actually true, that he was not loved like the rich white American or Australian kids he watched on TV. The ones who got everything they wanted. They were well and truly loved. Yes, tick another box. Close the gap. Tommyhawk knew he must tell white people that he was not loved by his parents, and he must be taken far away into the white world before he too was molested. He was becoming his own sensational story, and knew that he had found the quickest way to reach the white treasure chest and be set for life, if he could only tell white people what they wanted to hear.

13

You should not blame a little kid like fat boy Tommyhawk Steel for thinking that he had latched onto something great, as though he had been gifted a complete godsend of a revelation about finding the quickest road in the world into becoming assimilated to the level of being rich white, and even aiming higher, as though he was already the prime minister, because he knew that if he played his cards right, he would achieve his goal of being gone from Praiseworthy within a year. Now, he was not leaving to become like some poor white kid living on the edges of civilisation, or like some foolish refugee who risked his life with a people smuggler and thought he was going into the waiting wide open arms of welcoming Australia or anything like that. None of that! The only practical vision he had of himself was not to become like any white person or any colour person whether Asian, African, European, Middle Eastern living in the country, but to become like the richest and most powerful, those who could afford to live in a paradise place that took billions of dollars to build, which looked exactly like Parliament House in Canberra, and in fact, to save the confusion of running to an imperfect perfection, this big white colossal was to be his destination. Achieving the dream was just a matter of time.

You could say that eight-year-old Tommyhawk Steel was already a veteran of planning mega ideas that would not end up becoming mega flops, which could only be expected from being born into the shrill of a nation constantly yelling at the top of its voice about how to fix up the black problem. By the time he reached his eighth year, he had graduated as a student of racism. It was easy for him to believe he was living in a typical Aboriginal community plagued by paedophiles, and being cared for by misopedists, by children-hating parents.

Well! Of course, even if you believed this kid was naïve, and he probably was, but no more so than those being acculturated into thinking that it was only white media-hooked gods who spoke the real truth about saving Aboriginal children. Tommyhawk became convinced that these good white righteous people were speaking to him in particular, and not to other Aboriginal children, because he was special, and this made him most at risk. He believed they were speaking directly to him, and what they were saying ran through his mind in sleepless nights this way and that while he tossed and turned in the heat until he became wholeheartedly convinced that he had not been placed on this Earth to be stuck with dangerous people. Even! Even like his parents. They were a danger to him. That Cause Man Steel person could kill him. And Dance, the moth-er, she only noticed him, took pity when she had mistaken him for a butterfly, or as a cocooned baby being cared for by butterflies flying among the reeds, pandanus fronds, mangrove leaves, drifting in from the sea, like the story of Moses. Hatred was not a word strong enough for how he felt about his parents.

So! Very well then! Tommyhawk's endless deciphering of the barrage of voices on the radio went on through the night and continued as relentlessly as the haze-loving mosquitoes buzzing around him, but neither the activity of squashing blood-bloated mosquitoes to smithereens, or growing his monstrous brain from listening to what was being said on the radio passionately, or indifferently, about the Aboriginal world, was without success. All was gained, and while Tommyhawk had initially wondered why these people were talking the way they did about Aboriginal people like himself, he finally broke the code. He knew the plan as plain as day, that his national Australian government for Aboriginal people was actually speaking directly to him through the voices of random bigots on talkback radio, or in the news, or whatever running commentary he was listening to where anyone was having a good go, giving it all about what they thought of Aboriginal people. This was how he always found the message that the government was trying to get to him. Mostly, it was about how the government was trying to tell him, *You must escape your black parents*, and that was not all. A pretty awful set of scenarios in a very ambitious and elaborate escape plan began building in his head once that first tiny seed of realisation had hit him between his spaced out middle of the night eyeballs. It was up to him now. The government was leaving it up to him to arrange his own escape. But escaping was not a clear-cut path when you were eight, and you hated your parents. Escape was like building a six-lane highway through the middle of the night in a scurry that ran through rapids, hellfire, multiple labyrinths ridden with trip-wired traps, like dealing with one to ten levels of guilt about hate stuff infesting his wafting brain.

Hey! Ho! Instead of seeing plague rats, or mosquito-swarming reality, think of the boy, the truth junkie, who only saw swarming Aboriginal men preying on children at every turn of the mind. Still from thence, to be fair, he had waited a long time for a Qantas jet touchdown on the forlorn red dirt airstrip to pick him up. Half believing it could happen any time, that the Australian government for Aboriginal children was coming to save him, but when the government's army – all loaded with guns, ammunition, missiles and fighter jets dropping bombs – did not turn up in Praiseworthy to save him, instead of accepting his fantasy had defeated him, he decided that the only way he was going to become like a rich white child living in the city of Canberra in Parliament House, was to make the government take him away. All he had to do until that happened was to make sure he did not get molested by paedophiles. All this desire business about escaping was going to take a lot of thought, where every thought had to be funnelled into the right perspective, one of believing that he should not be living where he was not safe, and in his mind, everywhere outside of his mind was not safe if you saw it that way, and this helped him to focus on turning himself into a total wreck.

He needed to become a nut case so he decided never to sleep. He would always be ready just in case a paedophile was coming to get him. He lay stiff as a board, awake half the night, nightmarishly sweating, and tossing and turning through a thousand and one convincing dreams that he was being attacked by bogeymen who all looked like his father, and believing more and more in all likelihood this was going to happen to him, and this went on and on until he was so hyped up, he was not sure if something like this had already happened to him, and he had been killed, or somehow he was already dead but could still feel his thumping heart anyway, because he had reached the stage where he could not stop thinking, and he was doing the same thing over and over, that convinced him he was dead.

At the same time, the boy became totally possessed and secretive about having to guard himself from all adults in Praiseworthy by not trusting anyone, never speaking to anyone, on the lookout every single moment of the day about what was lurking behind him. In other words, the lower he sank, the more Tommyhawk felt as though he was achieving the willpower to carry out his escape plan. He was at the point of no return. Another goal in life. He was ill, really unwell. He had to be totally vigilant just in case his rampant out-of-control imagination grew more uncontrollable chapters of rampant paedophile father rings right in his own home. Tommyhawk felt relieved and less vulnerable awake, more able to guard himself from the eyes of predatory men. What to do now was his concern in a deranged and exhausted over-lived life, life becoming scarier, the home the worst place to be at night.

Tommyhawk became increasingly more watchful, suspicious, and now totally believed his father was like all fathers in his world, who without proof, preyed on little boys. His brother Aboriginal Sovereignty was already being accused by police of being a paedophile. He decided to kill his father after he raped him, because he knew, his father knew, that he had been telling the government lies about what they were doing to him and that he hated his parents for not loving him. Tommyhawk the loner! Eight years what? Gone so quickly in a world where you could spend your entire life speaking to nobody, and avoiding anyone speaking to you. He was set to be his own saviour so to speak. He would protect himself from Aboriginal men hated by the Australian government for Aboriginal people. It was not possible for him to prove his father was part of a big paedophilic ring in a syndicate of silence, like gangs he read about on the internet, but he was sure his father's clandestine gang that he might imagine moving around in the night, involved all the adult men in his community. None! Hear! Could be trusted.

Let's take it for a fact, that Tommyhawk did not love his parents, who through his assessment of them, did not love him either. Well! Not in the way that he saw white television people loving their children in big white family houses in white people's towns. He looked at the white scenario, and asked himself, what was fake? Which was the fake place. Yep! The government true things, not fake news. He reasoned that if he was to be raped by paedophile parents who did not love him, if that was the future, why was he still here if even he could figure out what was going to happen to him. It was difficult for him to understand why the Australian government for Aboriginal people had not taken him to live in one of those white houses if they believed all Aboriginal children were at risk of being attacked by paedophiles. Then, sometimes when he was feeling low because the government had not sent the Qantas jet, he even doubted that those white people's houses ever existed. They were just make-believe, fiction, like a storybook, and nothing more than a pack of lies. How would he know? You could chuck any plot line at the firecracker explosions in his mind, but the bottom-line fall-in-one-place at the end of every story, was his certainty of the government taking the little children away. Then, he realised too, everyone in his world talked about those stories. It happened all the time they said. Nobody could stop the government.

They would take them kids either physically, take them mentally, and take them both ways. Like rape too. Oh! This was when Tommyhawk Steel thought wow, move yourself to the next level! He hit the jackpot of dreams where he would soon be adopted by a white woman. He saw it happening in a delirious dream state. She was his new fixation. This was the golden-hair Minister for Aboriginal Affairs whom he had been watching faithfully on the ABC News, and who with her special powers, reigned from her golden office chair swivelling in the sky above her white palace of federal parliament in Canberra where she lived. Wouldn't any child feel safe living there?

14

Whoa! You? Worth nothing! Come here. Who me? People jumping everywhere from deep sleep out there on the street, where Planet looked like one of those holy pictures with an aura of sunlight captured in the fog-hazed dawn, or like what? That ancestral warrior hero who had risen from the earth, or who equally at the same time, had descended from the heavens like some rattled sky spirit. Maybe he was the haze fighter! Maybe the mighty war angel ancestral one! Quick smart peace shattered when Planet spotted Tommyhawk up in the darkened street, skulking away from him. He screamed at the top of his lungs at the boy slipping out of sight in the low visibility of the haze, yelling for him to *come back this minute*, and help him round up a few donkeys – hidden in the fog, wandering about somewhere up the road.

That kid was a waste. A complete mess. A bloody mongrel. Planet stepped out of his God radiance, and swore laments about how he had to get things done himself, and accused Tommyhawk for being a bloody little fascist until his face turned even darker with an uncontrolled anger. Well! Tommyhawk knew it would not be worth turning back now. Was he going to end up being dead meat on the road just for some putrid donkeys? Hardly. He hoped he would not see his father again for months. This would give him enough time to forget this incident with the paedophiliac so-called father, and the boy yelled back, *Fuck you, man. Go and get your stupid donkeys yourself, you idiot.* Planet began screaming even louder at the top of his lungs, so that the sleeping town could hear his lament, *Is this what a man gets?* The question was repeated before each barrage, lasting ten minutes exactly, about what was wrong with this fascist child born without ears that had nothing to do with him, etc....and etc.... how etc....he could not understand why these things happen to him etc., and ending with a higher, and feverish poor-man pitch, a plea to the wayward child fascist, *couldn't you bloody well act a bit normal for once?* Then! Touché! Just make sure the skulking boy could well and truly hear him as he tore up the street to get away, *Is this what a man gets?* But he leaves the question standing with no answer. He was not going to admit to everyone listening to him out in the street, that he brought this little fascist into the world. Let the world decide. *You be the judge.* How do you father a fascist? Then, the whisked and the shocked sized up in the dawn, and felt a warm current flowing over their skin which they knew was just man wind racing through every hot-aired house in the permanently haze-coated town, where red eyes watch the reddening slack hazy sun rising, bringing soft pink light all around while ears shot alert with empathy to the continuing echo, *Is this what a man gets?* The rest, well that was only diatribe rumbling and waking the town, and it cost too much thought to be bothered with.

There could be no peace found in a dawn dream now. That was all snatched up by the ancestors who could run faster back to the grave with a bundle of stolen dreams than either Planet or anyone else in Praiseworthy could remember what in the hell they had dreamt while asleep, and since the whole town would only be dreaming the same thing as they usually did from Monday to Sunday because they were a community, their dreams were about how to be some angel-like warrior, war-torn, betwixt and between kind of government-preferred pacifist well-meaning Aboriginal, or else, another kind of highly imagined, really deep-rooted ruthless killer warrior destroying themselves, which Planet called *Australian-alities*. Ask yourself, he said, *So! Which am I?*

So, you ask me is this what a man gets? This was the question. A holding pattern of things planted square in the head, instead of thinking general, such as whether there was remotely a hopeful possibility of a great morning-haze lifting, and thinking luxury, hoping something was in the fridge for breakfast. It was not too much to expect, but no, the first thing Praiseworthy people were forced to think about was how Widespread's sick mind always ticked. Why eat? You felt too sick to eat. Hear that? Donkeys! Donkeys! Donkeys! A 360-degree radius of chaotic madness was happening out in the street, heard from every direction. It was those friggen unherdable donkeys with goona–diarrhoea tails running off everywhere, and shit falling off in every direction from that sordid donkey herder. *He can't keep up with them. Those donkeys are too feral. He's bloody well too ancient. Why can't he stop this shit. He's nothing but an idiot.*

Where could a person find any peace in a place like this? How could you eat breakfast when you were caught in a spell being cast over your mind where you were not able to stop funnelling more complaints into the haze than anyone else about how jack sick you were of listening to all the screaming about donkeys going on outside, and forever hearing about the amount of dollars and cents it was costing Planet to be wasting his time rounding up his donkeys because of *all these people's useless complaints* about a bit of donkey shit on the footpath so they could not join his pyramid scheme to employ a bit of help. It was not as if the footpaths of Praiseworthy were anything to write home about, rainy-season potholes everywhere, like deep wells that would kill you if you fell into one. Were donkeys worth more to the future of the place than fixing up the footpath? Shouldn't Cause be trying to spend a fortune on his expensive son's education, *that fat boy, the fascist one slinking off, who wasn't even listening to him*?

The haze swirled into s-bends, and made the whole sunrise madder. It whorled, reigned in, and tightened into a frenzied dance over Praiseworthy, then it exhaled a tinkling shower of vapour, dawn dew droplets dampened the town, settling everywhere, and creating a humidity mingled with slithers of negativity in pre-dawn story mutterings about what had been fed into the metaphorical stomach. Nothing. The humidity grew debilitatingly depressing because Praiseworthy people just felt plain overwhelmed by being surrounded in a continual march of inadequacies. They had no energy to do anything but fret about how they were going to show Planet that they needed to govern what happens to feral donkeys in Praiseworthy, not him, which basically meant that they wanted to make all the donkeys disappear from the Earth! Would you not feel guilty about all the millions of poor people in the world who had no choice other than to depend on donkeys to help them? Who loved donkeys? No. No. Praiseworthy people said that was not true. Praiseworthy people said they knew everything, and that those people should use vehicles to get around like they were using when they could afford petrol. It was easier! Anyone could buy second-hand cars from a shonky car dealer. Pick them up anywhere. We are all modern people now. Even a globalised poor person was living in the twenty-first century world. Praiseworthy was the model for all oppressed people. There was no other place in the world like it.

The haze sighed over this thought. All the old spirits that had gone far away, came back and stayed. The tinkling dew droplets evaporated, the computer technology that was costing the earth, and turning Tommyhawk into a father-hater, rebooted itself, and he wired into the action like some kind of IT whiz-kid for the future world. Heaven help him, but Widespread could not even get the boy who was supposed to be a genius with computers to do what he was told. Generational transfer of knowledge had stopped there. Tommyhawk chose to remain belligerent about how to set up Planet's premier future world business plan with its own hashtag – *#AssToo* – for the Platinum Donkey Pyramid Scheme. This was the only thing he had ever asked a child who ate him out of house and home to do. Create a hashtag – whatever that was – to get people to contribute to his pyramid scheme. Had he ever interfered with anything else in the boy's life?

15

Tommyhawk shot straight from the mighty haze self-generating dry storm thunderclap heard above Praiseworthy, to another kind of thunder in his head. He flipped out big time while running away from his father. He put himself right in the moment – jumping from lightning that scared him out of his wits about a phantom paedophile father. Who knew what to think? *Nobody believes me.* Whack! Lash, lashing out, striking the shape-changing phantom father who could be anywhere, even a lump of grass on the footpath, or a pothole as deep as a well. *Get away from me freak man. Kid molester.* Whack! Whack! *Don't you come anywhere near me.* Tommyhawk spun the tape measure kept in his head, ran it across the ground, checked the distance, ran it again, twenty metres was good, anything less, not so excellent, like floor space was no good neither, never enough floor space for safe sleep, while knowing he had to be on guard at all times just in case rapists turn up, because on and on it went in his mind that Aboriginal communities were full of paedophiles. He worried more about child abuse than the maniac's future ecocidal or omnicidal hashtag *#AssToo*. Frig that. Tommyhawk was past normal. Tommyhawk knew vigilance, to protect himself from what the spirits of the night, the ones that had come back to haunt might bring, by continuously willing his imagination to fuel into crescendo thinking, to take him to the very edge of nightmare where he must find ever newer, more novel ideas of how freaky it was to be living in a community of child abusers when everyone looked normal. He always had to get behind the façade, to see beyond the masks, to see the truth of what the white government for Aboriginal people was saying about his life. You could say some particular evil thinking had overtaken his mind, and that there was no end to this child's thinking and learning from the source, the well of life broadcasting all the rumouring odes of the national narrative, for these were the bedtime stories he listened to in the dead wakeful night, just like every Aboriginal child heard from the uncensored media that never assumed Aboriginal children were listening to all those assumptions about Aboriginal communities.

Tommyhawk's eight-year-old heart had grown like an old man's heart while it swung the tick-tock quicker over the fear spectrum, from not being able to see what was real or false but left by the heartless, to sense the presence of the widespread phantom paedophilic environment of the whole community in which they lived, to the extremely narrow focus of his own father inside the home. One day, people might look over its own man-made wreckage, and say it was a child's imagination that had created one of the biggest epics of this time of climate emergency, but in this stage of his life, he had managed to pack so many lies in his head it could burst open any barrier of truth, fact, or reality. He jumped across an actual fact in the blink of an eye just to make himself sick from uncontrollable thoughts, to vomit on a whim. The trail of the phantasmagorical life on the street continued running off in the dawn. Click of the fingers, and Tommyhawk was right there where he had the ability to control his mind from slipping further into the unreachable, and just catching a glimpse of his father through the haze lit up the neon lights in his brain, unfurling a gigantic banner in red and gold flashing *#ArseToo*.

What if!

The kid took a quick glance over his shoulder, saw his father in the safe distance space, but he was too far off in his crazy world, so he continued flying up the road like a roadrunner with panic attacks. The red alert of virtual reality had kicked his eyes into fright flight, so now he was not sure if he was seeing actual reality or not, but he just knew there were dirty old men swarming all over the street who had made themselves invisible, and he was not sure if these were flies chasing him, or child molesters, but he was running for his life with leaden feet, and his footsteps crushed deeply into the ground that was trying to trip him over, to pull him down into a pothole that was a well. He tried to look down to see where his feet were falling to see what was trying to trip him as he ran, and all he saw were flashing images amassing like pages flicked in a picture book. At first, he could not tell what the pictures were about, but then he realised they were all of the future ass/arse hashtag embarrassing moments yet to come on his social media account. He felt dizzy, and almost lost consciousness with feeling as though he was destined to become world scum banished from having any interaction with normal people on the internet, and his arms frayed as he tried to erase the pictures piling up in front of him like math formulas that showed him only one thing: he was losing the game. He would never escape, and he would die a thousand deaths every minute from knowing how doomed he was, in having to spend the rest of his life in close proximity to a dubious shape-altering father who was a known criminal and paedophile, because he would not be able to keep on creating enough distance, and there would never be enough distance that would take him to a world away from Praiseworthy.

16

In this time of feral donkeys kicking dust into the air to feed to the haze, a league of storytellers gave up their responsibilities for feeding their ancient spell-breaking stories into the atmosphere. Only the ghosts of country sat on the community's white plastic chairs spread about under the *Delonix regia*, where these drought-sickened, thinly laced and sparsely leafed royal poinciana trees clung to life, and shed their leaves on the hazy plains of Praiseworthy.

Widespread's untameable donkeys, unlike the feral poinciana and mango trees, roamed around and were full of scavenging energy. The prize-winning tidy town was looking like a stock camp. Grey all sorts here, there and everywhere, tipping every single overloaded rubbish bin over the prettiness of nanny goat flowering gardens, breaking the limbs of the straggly poinsettia and so on if it was all the same with you – polluting the highly admirable pristineness of Praiseworthy. Indignant men and women with walls stacked with decades of tidy garden prizes ran rampant in self-censored, mopped-out abuse, saying in the remaining scrap of strangled polite language, *Why should donkeys be allowed to take over where decent people live and whatnot?* And, then, cut loose their tongues to uproarious self-righteousness yelled straight across town, followed by a fast train of echoing about what it meant to be residing with these disgusting unkept donkeys. So many families were wronged, and forced to gather as a horde of stomping humans that wore down the buffel grass in a thousand and one story tracks to the Major Mayoral office to make their concerns clearly known – *halla-lu-yah* – and to demand the town be fenced off from the pariah, to ban Planet, the piece of rubbish which they said he was.

In holy gatherings of less outrageous God-fearing folk, they prayed instead for some guardian archangels to be sent by God in war planes to give added value to the ancestors guarding Praiseworthy from donkey filth, if these archangels were not interested in preventing all racism on Earth or something like that, or else, helping the world to prevent a global warming emergency crisis that was likely to create the total destruction of the planet and make their traditional dust-hazed country more stifling unliveable. Twenty degrees hotter than normal. Doesn't matter. They prayed for none of that. They only prayed for more by-laws to be implemented as quickly as possible by the town council to stop all the shouting and arguing about the most extraordinary thing happening in their lives right now with all these hundreds of feral donkeys roaming around town making the place look a bloody mess, making it look how white people stuffed up country. These were the people who sat on the community's white plastic chairs dotted here and there around the flat while yelling across to each other about donkey mess, and the truth was, they had simply forgotten about the omnipresent haze, and with all the prayers of this sort continually remaining unanswered, they demanded to know from the heavens far above the haze, where on earth were angels when you needed them the most.

Some people walked away in a huff after giving up on unserviceable angels whose only presence were images seen on holy cards of old Italian paintings, and they joined the total throng walking away from Planet.

They were led away by upfront women who hated any kind of messiness, and tell you what – there were plenty of ladies like that in Praiseworthy. They would make veiled threats to Planet's face feel like being struck by red hot lava. These queens of the bush told him that they were not going to put up with scum spoiling the natural beauty of these poinciana trees anymore, with donkeys tipping over all the rubbish bins, and while the queens were not interested in slipping over banana peels, they claimed that the poinciana trees were women too that carried sprits of lemurs to Praiseworthy from the other side of the world. *You got to care for those spirits in them trees. Them lemurs were inside the seed that gone into these trees. Kept passing from seed to seed – long time from the original mythical creation creatures that travelled thousands of miles from that other country long ago.* You could never tell the spirit of lemurs were growing in Praiseworthy, but it looked like a joyous thing to see these foreign trees, the old ladies flatly argued, while looking at the tiny dead leaves covering the dirt like little dream hauntings from the old lost bug-eyed ghost lemur – *might be crying to go home.*

Now nobody cared too much about the lemurs which were invisible to everyone else, but they did like the sparse shade as being a valuable commodity in a non-native species like prickly pear bush, or those lovely *chinky* apple trees, and soon enough, everyone resumed telling the stories about scum donkeys polluting the haze. That was Act I. Planet on the other hand, thought all these spirit people were a pack of gossipers spreading hate, and once it was safe to assume that no archangels were coming in fighter jets to kill his donkeys and he did not have to keep looking at the sky, he decided to confront the town. He walked into the story ring of the white plastic chairs where there were only a few old people sitting and thinking about nothing, and he unloaded a mouthful of abuse on all these people by saying – *you know who you are.* They accused him of smelling of donkey goona – *you smell like diarrhoea* – and the storytellers shuffled in their chairs to move away from this hurling of insults back and forth. The audience of one or two elderly ones who had been standing around, or were sitting on the ground trying to listen to the stories about lemurs, scrambled from the so-called stench man too. This was when Planet began smelling himself, under his arms, his clothes, his hands, sniffing himself like a dog. *You think I stink or something?* He attacked in random, shoved his underarm in the face of a bystander. *Sniff this.* Storytellers threw chairs, and Planet threw them back. Soft drink cans became missiles. All the yelling and screaming attracted a dog brawl that had to be broken up by irate people dragging one dog off another by the scruff of the neck in the pile-up. Planet boasted to the world of Praiseworthy about his great sadness of being a dreamer-visionary thing, who was only trying to save people through his entrepreneurship ideas, and while the lament continued – the *Sorry I ever had a thought in my head*, and so forth – he hurried through his extensive oral library while escaping into the supermarket. There, he presented another performance in donkey stench that was an educational lesson about water restrictions and the high cost of soap for the wide-eyed supermarket world watching Widespread running his donkey diarrhoea-smelling hands along the open frozen food fridge, and finally, tossing his old cap into the fridge, his foul-smelling shirt, then trousers and underpants on top of the fresh meat.

There was no happiness in the circus of watching this man run naked beside the women fleeing along the aisles from his sight, while he managed to bundle lettuces, meat, tomatoes under one arm, before he took off each of his thongs caked in donkey shit, and sniffed the smell that he recognised had come from individual donkeys in the dozens of pens and paddocks he had built illegally down at the cemetery spread until that was long destroyed. The lawn cemetery was now a hoof-trodden sacrilegious mess of green manure resembling the surface of Mars. Even the Praiseworthy forced labour, working hard on government schemes designed to train them forever as a way of ripping them off their unemployment entitlements, and with first-class sweat pouring from their bodies as was the usual scheme of things, had flatly refused to work in the cemetery anymore. It was a holy place that had been carefully tended for years with plastic one-litre milk bottles full of water that had been carted in a never-ending cycle of men and women twenty-first-century slaves, to be filled from a tap a mile away through forty, fifty plus Celsius degrees for the

Major Mayor's cold climate annuals, to satisfy the white government funding acquittal form.

The stench of Widespread's donkey shit could be smelt anywhere in Praiseworthy, and this was the reason why it had become an urgent problem to erect a total barrier around the town to keep him out. The stench fence, a kind of new-world medieval battlement, could not come soon enough, and most thought that the entire shire council's essential services budget for the next three hundred years should be redirected to pay for the task of completing the wall inside of twelve months. The whole thing would need to be solidly constructed so that any kind of weasel like Planet would not be able to break through the iron grip protecting everyone from stench, and since these were twenty-first-century thinking people who saw themselves as survivalist humanity on the road to being nearly assimilated into white Australia, they wanted their pen, cage, asylum to resemble the walls of modern times, something clean and crisp and Trump-like, a thirty-foot high steel fence strong enough to keep Mexicans out of the US, and stench out of Praiseworthy, with solar panels lining the top and along the sides of the steel battlement, to collect the full intensity of northern sunshine, to provide free electricity for all, enough to sell across the entire country. Why! It was genius. They would kill two birds with the same stone so to speak, by building their total economy on renewable power far exceeding the ancient western way of dependency on dwindling fossil fuel. But it would cost a lot of money, and even the Major Mayor thing Ice Pick realised that to build any wall, even a metaphorical fence to keep one stinking human banned from entering the real world, was thinking too big, which was never an easy proposition for the black world. So! *Smell it, and get used to it*, Planet yelled while still naked as he stalked up and down the aisles of the supermarket emptying of customers who did not want to be part of the flustering scene of future thinking, nor caught in this fortuitous moment told in the funny stories forever of what it felt like to be trapped by stench.

Planet's thongs flew like skates across the supermarket – *sorry, sorry, sorry* – and those customers in the line of flight ducked as each thong landed in the banana display. *That is what money smells like,* he stormed. His spit flew next, straight into the lettuces, cabbages, carrots and potatoes. *This is what is going to make us rich, not this shit you cannot afford to buy,* he yelled while retrieving his gear from the freezer, and waving it around, before dressing himself in a slow casual way like a man of the century rather than the moment, and then he stalked off, yelling at the top of his voice that Bad Elvis was leaving the building, and on another matter, he would see to it that his fleeing people would one day be recognised as the master race of the future. All they had to do was to pretend they were black. Truth man! Which reality do you want to see the world? *Your assimilation was making you a white primitive.* Case was pulsating, and closed.

Much of the reason why no one in Praiseworthy had contributed a single cent to building the donkey pyramid, to get Widespread's long and debilitating business established once and for all as a serious financial proposition, was not the smell and risk of catching donkey diseases in the cemetery, a place that was now not fit to bury kinfolk anymore, it was simply the poor quality of hatefulness that was being put forward by all the coconuts who could not see the wood for the trees about working their way to freedom through building a close business relationship with God's donkey. This was the guardian angel problem working against poor people like themselves across the world, and the magic moment explanation Widespread felt he had nailed brilliantly in its simplicity.

Perhaps though, he contemplated for a split second or two how badly his body stunk of donkeys. But even if other people were smelling what he smelt, what mattered more to him were far more exorbitant thoughts of how they were not facing up to the fact of how you could spin gold with this smell. It was in the bag in other words, if you realised this was the smell to create the future *ex nihilo*, or the odour of saints, because no colonial government in the world was going to be the saviour of the poor and disaffected Native Title owner, and even if the place was permeated to the high heavens with the stench of donkey piss, truly, that was how true heaven, the obscure roof of security eluding all and sundry, was going to be built.

17

Around and around, and around about, the ghosts of kingdom come were sometimes told to get up from the white plastic chairs framing the distant horizon of forever stories. The disrespect happened when some of those wise ones would sit there for months on end telling epics of infinite dreams – desire, passion, ambition to survive in the stories of all times, and all the other whatnot – before all those stories took a turn for the worse from little whispered somethings coming along and creeping into the ear every now and then, raising doubt about what happened in the first place, which had people of Praiseworthy believing they were becoming contaminated beneficiaries of the planet's psychosis strife – all its hate infiltrating the beloved dust haze. See that haze over there in the horizon? *All that atmospheric stuff that would not disappear?* It was very sad to see the collective wisdom being infiltrated with all those petty jealousies, but who could tell what a haze full of hate really looked like, or wanted from poor people who had inherited their traditional country?

These were the reasons for such fragility thinking when no one person could say what hate looked like anymore, how it blocked the view of the stories of the horizon, nor how it smelt, even though many splendid images were mired from assimilating white thinking about what created wellbeing, and the earthy smell of mist rising from wet season long grass in the early morning smelt nice. How could you tell what the real deal felt like? Was it inhaling briny air rising out of a hazed sea? Who could tell what was lost from the ancient register over there in the flat line? But, but what if, if everyone in Praiseworthy genetically linked to the ancestral country since time immemorial, could smell something foreign like this conglomerate donkey stench ruining Native Title-ness, would this foul air make the country and ancestors sick with madness too?

You want to stop acting stupid. Planet's wife Dance had told him in more than a thousand and one stories about her miserable life in the cemetery. She was not into sharing her life with donkeys. What were these donkeys to her? She had never envisaged them in her life, so why should she share his dreams of building a conglomeration of feral donkeys living in plain view of everywhere she looked. Planet ignored this, since he only saw the perpetual movement of sounds performing the big drama of life with a wife taking him on never-ending journeys through all the unreasonableness of her experiences of living with him. He remained finch-like, fiddling endlessly, side-eyed, staring off into the dance ring of her existence, seeing her prancing around like a boxer. He watched her constantly moving away from the space of those she was speaking to, always creating a safe distance for herself, always obsessing to reach the cleared space and retreat, after delivering her blows left, right, left. He knew the pattern of a woman who had told him that she could feel the vibrations of a distant butterfly fluttering along its looped path from many kilometres away to join its mate, and that these butterfly lovers flew so high that they ended up floating in the infinity of space. She had heard a far-off moth or butterfly splashing into the ocean. Prove it? She said she did not have to prove a darn thing to anybody because she knew what she heard when the migrating white butterflies, and moths too, flew gently into the sea and covered the surface with their transparent wings, but she would prove it anyway, and right at that moment Planet saw some old fisherman – might have been Chinese, Portuguese, or French – whom he had never seen before, standing around in the cemetery calling, *Missus Dance lady, Dance lady, I find this in the sea for you*, and the fisherman smiled calmly as though he had lived to be as old as the universe, while placing a live moth in her hand like it was the most precious jewel – a glistening sun-moth angel with white and brown scale laced wings and said he thought it belonged to her. The old man was still wet from the ocean spray that had rolled into the cemetery, following him from the sea. He looked around, and said he was going back to the sea to catch fish, where he must keep following the rivers of old winds, the birth of new winds, and he would follow the aerial rivers of butterflies to see where they go, and he must chase the great rivers of ocean currents eternally breathing new life into the planet, and the atmospheric rivers bringing the rain, and sail through the dusty rivers of stars in the Milky Way galaxy continuing its infinite journey out into the universe, and he would follow the magnetic rivers forming the stars just to keep fishing, ahoy one, two, three, the fish to feed his country. Dance claimed that foreign fishing men visit her all the time with gifts of butterflies and moths. These were real men. What she was really saying was that Widespread was a limited husband, who not only did not bring a moth as a gift, but whose only odyssey was journeying through the bush to catch donkeys.

The elders of the communal plastic chairs often liked to tell the story of how this Dance had heard two ants arguing for hours over a crumb of bread. They would tell this story of how that wife of Cause Man Steel had listened to the ants fighting on the ground, and how each ant was trying to yell back down into the ant palace, *I am getting it now, won't be long*. It was this continual reading of stories, of fathoming real quests of importance through the interconnectedness of survival simultaneously occurring throughout the cherished lands of traditional country, which mostly intrigued the movers and shakers, the oracles of cultural knowledge and laws exercising the greatest sway over the world of Praiseworthy. On the other hand, this Planet could never reach into the mind of any of the greatest minds of country with his quest for building a pyramid scheme with their loose change, and the more he realised that his vision of a major sustainable transport conglomeration operating at one hundred per cent capacity in the new era and making millions was close to collapsing in a heap before it could begin, the more his mind traipsed through multiple migraines. So acute, and totally exceptional was Dance's ability to govern the world of sounds, she could demand the silence of thousands of caper whites, those *Belenois java* butterflies that were flying up from the mangroves, with some similarly coloured winter butterflies, like those *Delias argenthona*, scarlet jezebels fluttering through their journeying migration around her tin-shed house down in the cemetery. The people of wisdom, all the old mungkuji, claimed that Dance instinctively knew how to measure any sound whatsoever, except apparently, the sound of Planet's enormous herd of noisy donkeys which she had blocked out of hearing. This was the weight of things that fell through the dust-hazed silence like a worthless thud that weighed nothing to Dance's ears in the end.

Dance wondered otherwise, where was the sound of her sons, where had her life gone? She felt her life had ended up in a constant earthquake from Planet's thousand and one intolerances vibrating at an unbearable pitch of dins, of boom, bang, boom like the enormous ancestral world continuously rattling the corrugated walls of her head like a drum. It was a constant headache. She wondered whether there would be enough packets of Panadol in the world to ease the painful crescendos vibrating in her head, with the echoing that charged back and forth down the flat, after barging into one boundary and then back against another. The slightest criticism from her about Planet keeping hundreds of donkeys around the place was all it took to create the ancestor storm, when actually this cemetery was her Native Title not his, and even though he only metaphysically responded to her complaints, if not in reality, but one look from him, even if he was somewhere else a thousand miles away chasing feral donkeys to find his ultimate donkey, would bring on another raging-bull type of headache. This was enough to squash her where she stood on her Native Title land, or anyone else who got in his way on their own country, while he trespassed on what he flatly called his turnout, not hers.

This was the marriage. A conversation ruled by distances, the necessary avoidances which were constantly being reworked without a single word ever spoken to articulate what was wrong in their life together. If in a glance, their eyes locked on the doomed coronae-glowing gloominess of enriched togetherness, each knew the other was speaking of closure, establishing greater permanent distances from the line already drawn in the soil of a marriage worn thin.

Dance was truly as unfazed as Planet was about this end-of-time experience of their life together, while dramatising instead the chest-felt crisis that had fallen at her feet from the *debacle-ising* of her life choices from having to breathe the plague donkey exhalations fouling the pristineness of her right to clean air. This was the dance. A bony bird-like wife racing the sagas around its cage without ever finding a door to freedom. What was the cage? The world. No space on Earth would have been big enough to divide between them, and being conquerless, it felt as though the ancient power of the planet itself suffered egotistical blindness, for having produced the unlucky circumstances of a marriage spiralling downwards into the realm of non-existence, where it was no longer possible to live in a clean world, one without seeing or smelling donkeys, and with the exhaustion of having to push back against the magnitude of empire – the pyramid scheme conglomeration of the feral donkey cabal that Cause was bent on creating around them. The whole business stunk. It reduced her. But who knows, would it do any good arguing with an ancient power while it was vomiting in your face every time it felt in your presence the colonising stench-business of feral donkeys? Who cared if Planet was a donkey whisperer? Dance didn't. *Why you?* she asked him. She wanted to know: *Why pick you instead of someone else to save the world?* She said it straight, *If you actually believe five million feral donkeys across northern Australia are communicating with you, like you were actually the God of the planet, then you are truly mad.*

In Dance's need to live like a beautiful butterfly she was in the wrong little corner of the caged world. This was the trouble. The corner was her Native Title land. There was never silence in the graveyard that the Major Mayor's town council had built without the Native Title holder's permission. She was wrought with the thought of this whole unpleasant incursion. Nothing calmed her down, not in the new age cemetery wired for sound with cables running this way and that for a loudspeaker erected at every gravesite like the whole thing was a drive-in. It brought the Praiseworthy world into the IT age, where they did not even have to visit the foul-smelling cemetery if they did not want to. A loudspeaker for each family of the deceased enabled them to sing remotely anything they liked. The whole thing was a song fest that was not a gracious sound, but not totally ugly in graciousness either. Dance was compelled to listen to the competing songs blaring for prominence from the other loudspeakers all day long, and even into half the night, or another part of the world's daytime if you were beaming in from Europe, or elsewhere faraway on the Earth's longitude of time. Where was the release from all this singing? It was not even enjoyable for dead people to hear badly sung songs of country lasting weeks, sung in Italian or Czech, or someone singing rock'n'roll – every song in the catalogue of Elvis Presley, or the country-and-western hits of Chad Morgan stuck on repeat. There was too much praise for the old people of Praiseworthy, and for distant relatives calling out instructions to Dance like she was the gravekeeper instead of the families, saying why did she not keep people's graves nice and clean, and clean up all the donkey shit that they saw on the webcam.

Dance knew it, and everybody knew that there needed to be a line drawn. There was not a centimetre of her Native Title block shared with other people's dead relatives that was without either spiritual, supernatural, human or non-human sounds. Nobody entered the graveyard anymore, and many said it was a haunted place because it was so noisy. What happened was this: all the dead people's relatives sat on their fold-up chairs on the outside of the fence around the cemetery, where they called out to Dance like she was the staff of their deceased family. She was sick and tired of hearing their lists of orders for her to rearrange the flowers on a grave so that they would not need to enter such a filthy place. It was her job to deliver fruit and vegetables so the deceased people could cook something for themselves, a pot of stew, some rib bones and things like that. Many others just wanted to argue with her about keeping the donkeys off the grave over there. *Woman, you got no shame, you know whose grave that is?*

Oh! So often, relatives were calling from outside of the cemetery for nothing. Dance was not available. She had stalked off over the back fence to follow mangrove butterflies to the swamp country, and while she was there, revenge developed in all their minds over her absence, and in her absence, she developed greater potency in how she too, would have her revenge. In other times, she would remain brooding about the view of her life, but not so in this pining for something missing from her lonely mind, from being hemmed in a cemetery with a litany of invasion from the ghosts of dead people, songs sung blue on the loudspeakers, and being yelled at from fold-up chair relatives, the haze locked in a dome until finally, this woman who adored only silence, exploded with words fired straight, coming at you like long-range missiles of empire building war mongers – R-36M2, LGM-30G Minuteman-III, RS-24 Yars, Dongfeng-41, Trident II – those who wish death on all, exploding all over the place. The thunderclap filled the battered void exponentially with rebound echoing back and forth in the *flash*, flapping, flicking lights, firing across her surveyor mind's theodolite measuring space, measuring the precise boundary to boundary of her tiny whitefella government for Aboriginal people adhocracy settlement of all that had remained from the colonialising theft of her Native Title ancient story interlinked world. Well! This was what happened. The oxygen immediately drained out of the atmosphere. You could not breathe. Nobody could. The whole place became suffocating in an instant. The donkeys stampeded. Snorted. Tried to breathe. Their hearing was sensitive. Spit flew. They ran uncontrollably, gasping at the air. All the ghosts got out of their graves, and began screeching for their relatives to come and collect them in their motor cars. They ran away with the fold-up chairs and picnic tables, and the further faraway relatives turned off their computers, and closed down the webcam. Then, the donkeys went completely crazy and tried to attack the spirits, and this turned everything into another level of lethalness, and with the airlessness that was either real or unreal everything copped the flack, and the whole fright flight went through the roof of the known universe and right out of control, while somewhere in those off-putting moments of a life lived, Dance happened to see the absent husband Planet by chance, while he was walking aimlessly around the cemetery, and she rushed out of her house and challenged him to his face to leave her property for good. She said she would not be sleeping in the same house with anybody dreaming about donkeys anymore, *So you better git. You hear me, Cause?* And, ah! There were many words flowing and being repeated though this far-reaching argument about whose country was whose, that was either familiar, or not, in the dreams of others from faraway lands.

Planet heard these words. But! Who was to care? Unlike Dance's rendering of a sizzling race prompted by Boccherini's *Fandango*, dancing with all the castanets a-click-clicking, he moved purposefully through a thoughtfulness resembling a baroque melody – say *Ciaccona*. His task was to carefully build the crescendos by taking a slow drive through chaos, and so, he went about his business of trying to pacify donkeys, and chase her melodies from one corner to the next. He worked the fence wires methodically, held the line taut in strong hands, and fixed each broken boundary after it fell, and the gate where the mosquitoes fall. There could only be one gate, he muttered as he worked, while brushing off the biting insects – mosquitoes, sandflies, march flies, the constant circling dragonflies that interfered with his work. There would be no other boundary gates, either physical or those metaphorically erupting in his mind. Only these real gates. These were the type of gates that the walking injured needed to go through on the path to the future he was dreaming about. Any silly bugger could understand why you needed a firm gate, a gate that slammed shut behind you, that did not swing in the wind as though it did not know which way to fly. His gate dream resonated with what the Christians believed, that here on Earth, there was only one solid cast-iron gate to reach heaven. Well! Planet had plenty of work to do regardless of how he managed to live in a world of volcanic eruptions. He needed to make a dream out of nothing that showed the enormity of human skills to survive in an avalanche of catastrophes. This was the era man, following in the footsteps of the mighty ancestors who had managed to bring them through the ages to this point of extinction. He was to change all that. He had found his inbuilt desire for surviving the long run, by knowing how to dream for it rather than deliberate about what it was, or might be. What Planet felt about achieving a future home for his kind, and in believing, and desiring to see his humanity in the future even though he would not be there to actually see if they had survived or not, was to rebuild the ancient economy, pump it with much greater scope than ever imagined before in mankind, rather than being in the scrum with all the other haze crazies who thought through heads full of desires, instead of concentrating on the sum of the whole – a chosen dream – if they dreamt of surviving at all.

18

Yet what was the bother about hate, or spite, if you rocked on it? And Widespread! Any kind of snake's venom of hatefulness was only going to fall like water off a duck's back. He was already waiting to fight any god, any logic, strangers, even his own weaknesses, or the spirits imbued in the souls of other countrymen: all those who thought they were God. He was a combatant who was as ready as any other Aboriginal man, woman or child in Praiseworthy to deal with the pervasiveness of deep-rooted hate.

It was a world of full-time irate people who were a bit frightened of Planet, because he was the number one boss man of one of the most powerful spiritual presences in the region. And you know what? The people sitting in the white plastic chairs in the haze knew this was his fault for making the spirit show itself at their meeting, and this bringing up the mighty ancestral being was much, much bigger you know, than any other people's God spirits, such as angels flying in the pale sunlight beaming through clouds above the town, or demons hovering in the darkness and trespassing on Praiseworthy country. The trouble with Widespread was that he had a higher-plane view of the world, where he saw himself looking down from far above where

Praiseworthy people stood. They proclaimed the law edict, and said you could call the haze as embracing obliviousness, or call it what you like, but Planet was a bad embracer. He embraced strife like he was lassoing a donkey, and he eclipsed any other embracer of feral donkeys who could do this without creating strife.

Dance was unconvinced, she knew a thing or two about displacement thinking when it came to her spiritual ideologies, and she accused Planet of squatting foreign feral donkeys on her Native Title land like some sort of hippie shit. She campaigned strong and hard for the municipality to legally get rid of all donkeys for good. And why not? She wanted extreme measures to be taken. Borders closed. Gates closed, not swinging. No more whatnot happening about the place. No more trying to export five million feral donkeys roaming Australia to Praiseworthy. *Take them back to wherever they came from in the first place*, she argued to the Major Mayor's town council, *and get them the hell off my pristine Native Title land*. The municipality bristled, *Her Native Title land?* It was like a snake had appeared out from nowhere, a king brown, a friggen taipan, and snakelike teeth fanged the question, flashed the poison, rattled the big blinking red neon light billboard eyes gleaming with rotating snakes. Dance wanting to get rid of all feral or could-be feral donkeys became the talk of Praiseworthy, because it was a very sensitive issue to talk about who was the sole Native Title holder of the cemetery.

Top-down municipality said they were going to ignore her stupid request because how could you expect them to personally go and round up and export five million donkeys to a foreign country. Nobody wanted a pack of feral donkeys turning up from Australia. *Where are we going to get the resources to do that?* They did not want to. They were too blinded with rage from her claiming everyone else's Native Title rights. Everyone owned the cemetery. Not the squatters with a donkey problem. They could not understand what she wanted them to do about the donkeys. *What? She wants them sent dead or alive?* Who knew: *How were we going to export millions of dead donkeys?* How would you even calculate the cost of exporting foreign donkeys? The question became the main topic of conversation for a very long time, and the worsening of the red dust in the haze dome was temporarily ignored while Praiseworthy tried to work through a rough calculation of ridding Australia of yet another colonialism debacle that ended in the traditional owner having to eliminate millions of feral Jesus donkeys along with myxomatosis rabbits, rats, fire-inferno buffel grass etc. etc. The problem rocketed, became an epicentre of mathematics that was being worked out by the caucusing elders sitting around on the white plastic chairs which they had dragged to the shade as it shifted along the buildings, and from one semi-shady tree to another. *It was too dear. It would take the Australian army to do something like that. Five hundred thousand trucks. Maybe, or maybe more. No buts please, but it would be a very sad day to see all those trucks passing with that many dead donkeys.* They talked about building a massive abattoir as a tourist venture, but decided in the end to put more money into producing another gigantic hologram of Ice Pick to patrol the spreading haze dome. And anyhow, they decided it was just not right to kill a single Jesus donkey, because the bottom line was that nothing was Dance's Native Title land anyhow. The conversation about what to do turned to mass elimination, and they wondered if they wanted to be known as a centre for mass murder, an exterminator of life in the modern world. Would they be able to live with being tagged mass murderers, or being named the Putin people of Praiseworthy? It was decided very quickly down at the town council that defeated the single vote in favour by the Major Mayor, whose vote usually amounted to everything dictatorial, that this was not the look of kindness they were seeking for themselves in their cosmopolitan flight towards a far more lofty form of righteous mindedness, of being actual black humanitarians who thought themselves equal with white people while being assimilated inside the cruel white world. *Just think of five million ghost donkeys coming back to haunt Praiseworthy.* Hey! Hey! Hey! There were no hee-hawings to be heard about this. What was enough? It was not to be reminded of death in the haze that they were sitting in, so the elders went back inside to avoid any more talk about the lovely feral donkeys. They reckoned that all the dead people who were coming to them in their dreams told them that they owned the Native Title law that Dance was claiming anyhow, *that land where they were buried, in the cemetery.* It was their neutral land. It would be easier if she moved. Case closed.

But was the case really closed? The ethics of the thing were malleable in hard times, shifting and shaping what was right, or wrong. *You see!* This was where the problem lay. No one could freely drive down to the cemetery anymore to visit dead people because feral donkeys had assumed the role of the Native Title owner. *They were attacking people that's what, and that Widespread should be locked up himself, for locking up the graveyard and trespassing on sixty-thousand-odd years of law like he was an amoeba, or like a prehistoric low-life that had no idea yet what people's rights were about.*

19

Lording over it all, there was Widespread with his simple mantra, or guiding light. The mantra about anomalies. He often pointed out that anything was possible to the spirit people following him around the cemetery, who were wanting to know when they were going to see their spooked donkey-hating relatives again. That was the mantra. He chose to ignore continuing spirit complaints about not being able to see the fold-up chair people he had forced to sit on the other side of the fence. Instead, he preferred to try to pacify the ghosts by explaining that there was something fundamentally wrong about being oppressed when you were deceased, when you should be having fun, and explained this same anomaly in himself, of how he was overcoming oppression. They said, *We know how we are.* Then, Planet reckoned: *It does not matter if you are saints, or black angels, or whatever spirit realm you are living in now. If you were compliant and pliable enough to meet some high jump to gain a white sense of self-security, or if you were complete mongrel dogs for not cooperating with government programs, you are anomalies from the spirit line.*

Their lives – Widespread pointed out ever so casually to some of the ghosts in his midst who were still following him and arguing the toss about oppression – *were just figures on a sheet of paper. The only value you ever had to white government was in all those statistics about your disadvantage.* This made the graveyard ghosts jump in time with his stick pounding the ground when he told that story of statistics: that his family were statistics, their house was a statistic, this community was a statistic, being dead was a statistic. And the ghosts disappearing back into the ground were pretty pissed off with being slapped around by a stick, and were grumbling about how they were very old people and should not be treated like they were just dirt, and said they hated those donkeys *for trying to kill us. Donkeys should be taken off this country for not knowing the one thousand and one ancient songs for the country like we do, so how are you going to keep the place alive with donkeys with no song?*

All the theorising about statistics had to end, it was the anomaly in the world of the ancestral man, but as Widespread understood his own theories, of foreclosing anomalies, one thing he did not know, was when to end. It was as though thoughts were attached to his feet, and he would continue to walk the talk by listing the names of all those he could remember being buried there as an old so-and-so – who was a paper statistic. Foreclosure perhaps, somehow not complete.

Old wham! Bang! Yep! *You are a statistic*, and names continued to be conjured up and jet streamed into the world of the disenfranchised, further entrenching the reality if only in his own mind, of a new, deeper understanding of the way things were.

You and you, while referring to his elusive sons Aboriginal Sovereignty and Tommyhawk, who were forever slipping further away from his sight, he explained to the phantoms, *Don't be fooled by the false niceties and the pleasantries of people thinking they are doing the right thing for you. You are the expediency for the folly of others, like this graveyard full of our dead people, you exist just for some endless fucking non-compliance to government policies – black statistics, and that is why we are living here in this cemetery so you will always remember that.*

Planet said such ideas did not matter to him though, because he was walking on the metaphorical thin ice of ambition with economic passion growing up from the roots sunk deep into the dirt under his feet, and flowing like a river of life straight through every blood vessel in his body as a matter of fact, and this passion was linked hard straight through to the far away, and to the near, and tied tight into the bolt hole of the ancient lineage of the uber-genius which was the country's brain in his own brain. *It's all of those kind of things*, he explained. *So, don't depend on anyone else while we still have our own guts to get us through.* Keep a lid on. But Widespread kept trying to supersede himself in the ancestral game of survival he was mucking about with, and somehow by instinct, he knew that he was getting there inch by bloody inch, by doing things like an ancestral hero which was in his own spirit, like any of the big bosses of the law story that was contained in, and linked to, all of his imaginings.

Planet did not actually run around the block broadcasting visionary thoughts to the undead masses. He was not their publicity man even if he was trying to save them. You needed to be more circumspect when you have a vision. You need to keep the thing safe, hidden in the back of the cupboard until you can attack by surprise. There was no need for flippancy about being a genius with a plan when you were among people who were not geniuses. You do not want to be forever in the business of regilding the patina of negativity off the golden goose. Any new reality for how the ancestral story would flow into the future was principally about keeping the main plan hidden amongst a plethora of nothing plans, keeping your lips zipped, and acting as though you had no idea what you were talking about. This was the main show, the diversion from seeing where Planet was hidden in the gap – the gap of inequality, that inhospitable void world lying between all others in the dominant society, the world of the poor dispossessed traditional owner of the continent, where you would not see him at all, for he would be just another harmless failure floating around in the ether. If this meant you needed to remain anonymous, unobtainable, mired in the statistical gap, so to speak, then you know what, whatever! Whenever it takes Widespread to clarify his position, it was like gliding unnoticed in the moonlight, which was not so much to do with his family, who refused to listen to any of his monologues about what donkeys would do for them, but to make his point about the beauty of stealth in being an invisible constant presence in the unnamed numbers of the Bureau of Statistics. It was an ingenious plan. Who would think of looking for a dangerous ghost hiding in the statistics? This was the question he frequently asked the non-present Aboriginal Sovereignty especially, the older son, who was too busy to know whatever his father was on about by walking away from him, although Planet did not mind who walked away from him. *That's the way to do it.* He just liked expressing the pure theory of being an anomaly, the invisibility in being anonymous, because this was where to find the focus, from the usually unattainable murky high-plateau moments of life as they currently knew it. *You got to keep under the radar like a graveyard ghost smack in the middle of the low-performance statistic, as you are expected to be in the goals for closing the gap between Aboriginal and non-Aboriginals by the Australian government. That's the way to do it.*

Just walk away, Planet did not mind how he challenged ghosts, or his disappearing-act sons, *I will prove it to you.* He said that he would fight anyone in Praiseworthy with either a couple of words or his bare fists anytime, or with whatever they wanted to name as their fighting stick, number ten boomerang or spears, by announcing that everyone he ever knew was a sycophant, when Tommyhawk had suggested likely contenders that could whip his father's arse clean off the face of the planet.

It was at the family dinner with Johnny Cash rolling, when Planet said he believed that he had flown the starship of ancestral ambition into the ear of his genius youngest son who continued eating as though his father was not there, because he believed he did not have a father. The feeling in the house was strangled by a great sense of breathlessness, of ghosts mingling around the kitchen table and nodding agreement, *true, true,* as Planet spoke on: *I know what I am talking about because you can read any Australian government report you like about the Aboriginal world, and it will tell you that I am a failure, and that is where I want to be, safe from people messing around with my life and making me an even bigger failure than I am already.*

Praiseworthy sighed like an old dog from overhearing what came from Widespread's dinner lips wafting around in the haze. They did not think twice about condemning his manifesto. Who cared about anomalies, or anonymously pushing your hot-air epics preaching failure, hymn-aholic-ing, mongering, hissing, splattering over the ground and freaking out the sly dog grovelling on its cringing belly, as it slid through a landscape of prickles to find somewhere else to hide in the tall grass while yelping a fog of hot wind into the dust haze. In the end though, hierarchy people, and even the people who called themselves nothing, were finished with arguing with an idiot. They were more concerned with keeping a trophy town looking like a trophy town. This was monumental to them, not a pyramid-saving scheme with communist chrematistics, and if that left Cause feeling like he was living the dream by achieving even less human rights for himself by being left out to dry, and being excluded from the official Australian government statistics defining the status quo in the Aboriginal world, then so be it. This was not something they would aspire to for themselves.

Planet's self-inflicted solace as an anomaly in the statistics was a tiresome hindrance in a one-person political stealth campaign of saving morons, and continually reassuring a restless brain on an ongoing basis that he was just doing his job, as he reasoned that in the end the poor would take revenge – probably. *Yippy! Hi! Ay!*

Invasion dreams were big stuff, and plagued heavily on Planet's mind, but most of all, he had one prevailing dream of madness which he never talked about, not even to the ghosts. It was an eternal brooding nightmare that rose from a place where oceans roared. This was when Planet became a long-distance runner of the middle of the night, running from nightly versions of horror to reach safer places he could never find. He was perpetually lost in multiple versions of the same dream, where he became debilitated by a sense of being unable to find where he should be going, and which pushed him further into the anonymous anomaly theories of his perpetual self-arguments about how he was going to break out of a packet of chips so to speak, and fly back to the place of the address he had lost, or the train ticket he could not find, the flight he had missed, in a place with a language he could not speak. He crashed, far from the sight of becoming an overnight success. This looked like the nemesis of not being a multi-millionaire, and honouring his pledge to make all the other poor Praiseworthy *nobodies* into millionaires as well. These were the difficulties. The dream that contained blockages, of concertinaing in the graveyard night like a dial tittering to the bottom of a spinning wheel and never hitting the jackpot, with the chance of flipping instead right off the spectrum of a lot of quick cash, shredded his mind in its own shredder, swung him awake with fists pumping the air to punch his way out of his brain, and disturbed Dance's tranquil butterfly dreams to scream at him for dreaming like a panic-stricken donkey.

But why should a big strong man like Planet tip himself over the edge at night? Somehow, he could not help but fear failure from the moment he drifted off into sleep, while waking again and again throughout the night in the hope of keeping himself awake, knowing that he was too frightened to dream. Then, there he was, like a waiting snake, where he lay stiff as a board for the nightmare to arrive, and he would wake himself in panic, and strike at the unfathomable demons lying ahead setting booby traps to steal his multi-dimensional donkey transport empire that was increasing exponentially, and barrelling out of control from any sense of reality – the few dozen feral donkeys down in the backyard cemetery sleeping on top of people's graves.

Yes, at night, Planet thought he was going mad for nothing in his debilitating journey to success. It was not a smooth ride. Everything fell against him, and as he orbited around the nightmares, he certainly knew it was going to take an angel-type miracle to create one of the biggest Aboriginal-owned donkey transport industries of the kind that this land had never seen before. Nothing was going to save Planet from the enormity of this desire to save his own people. Don't they all say that? You needed to build one big fortress around vision. Treat information as wealth. Something that must be earned and reluctantly given on a need-to-know basis. You have to understand that Planet instinctively understood he was dealing with the ancestor industry. He was connected to the reality of figuring out how to utilise the vast powers the ancestors had given to him through nightmares that were too enormous to grasp, where only through his vigilance to wakefulness, he could release himself from their frightening grip. Planet knew the ancestors were speaking to him from the line into eternity, but this vast ancient library was a nightmare for his brokenness, who was not strong enough to grasp the true meaning of traditional knowledge. Why pick me? How would he learn to rebuild and reform the traditional economies of his people, just as they had learnt to survive since the beginning of time? Yes, he knew this nightmare well. A high level of desire that he could barely comprehend, and he knew there was no point in seeking counsel from loose-lip ghosts covering themselves with sleeping donkeys on their graves. They spoke of the general. Like Dance. Why should he let them manipulate the ancestors by putting silly ideas into people's useless little dreams of surviving the haze?

20

While the haze dome shadowed possibility, life continued to feel as though it was unchanging and glued to the eternal. Then behold! Daylight! The shafts of sunshine slithered down through the haze to wake the butterflies that swarmed into pools of sunlight on the flatlands. Butterflies – all the glasswings, Carpentaria pearl-whites, yellow grass skippers, the cabbage whites and the strikingly marked black-and-white wings of the citrus swallowtail butterflies – were dancing their ceremonies and forming aerial rivers above the leaf-broken, insect-chewed, cobweb-covered dry grass. But the movement of butterflies did not excite Praiseworthy people. They stayed rooted, tethered to the time of the ancestors, their lives in spiritual prayer and devotion. Only their thoughts travelled up into the skies, all the pipe dreams flying far into the cosmos, following the tracks of the old song cycles that they could not follow. Rootedness, that was key, so you can imagine what a sensation was being created in Praiseworthy whenever Widespread disappeared into thin air, and from the combined imaginings he journeyed into the furthest of all faraway places, the Ultima Thule of the world, driven like a wayfarer by devils shoving him and punching him in the back – and making him leave behind his kindred people.

On this, they also thought of another modern idiom, and said old Planet was controlled by a globalised network of mine diggers bent on controlling the independence of Praiseworthy by wanting to come here with cartons of grog, only to rob their traditional secret-legends that told the story of the vast wealth hidden somewhere. But no one could remember the punchline of the stories of where all the gold was anyhow, or was it diamonds, crude oil, rock-solid iron ore, copper or some other mineral? *These donkeys, the ones in the cemetery*, they said, were really disguised international capitalists, and were just pretending to be eating all the grasses, but were really kicking off the topsoil to expose the veins of gold hidden in the ground and whatnot. *And this Planet rot,* he was driving those mine diggers mad from having to put up with him bringing more and more donkeys to add to this donkey plague already living in Praiseworthy.

Yet the real reason Planet kept bringing so many donkeys into town was lost on the crowd. The grand plan was steeped in so many layers of secrecy wrapped tight somewhere deep in his head, that whatever the absolute truth was, it was long gone, lost so to speak, moved off into the hardship of droughts and hotter extended summers of global warming. Only this plague of half-pet donkeys was left to roam the streets, fending for themselves on spoilt rubbish from the wheelie bins, and knowing what it was like to be associated with Planet's complete failure. The vision splendid was not half-tamed feral donkeys dependent on taking direction from the recorded voice of

Hank Williams heard in the distance singing about getting down to the river and feeling so lonesome he could die, as they ran to the river and cried buckets of tears while wallowing in the bloody putrid muddy mess of the town's water supply. That did not bring them closer to fulfilling Planet's dream.

Yep! Each and every one of this grey mass were the plain wrong donkeys, all mistaken identities – not the true grey of his dream donkey. These were just the shabby grey ones that Planet had mistakenly caught over years and years of his journeys, or else, had been rounded up in the middle of the night by a pack of archangels he had bargained with, or in truth, that he had stolen from some southern farmer when he saw a nice-looking grey donkey from the road as he was passing, roaming around a paddock and minding its own business. All these, he took for his unpaid rent from past and continuing atrocities connected with his stolen ancestral land, and if this method failed, he did not mind stealing somebody's pet donkey that he assumed was his because it was supposed to be the colour of his dream.

With only being able to take one donkey passenger in the back seat of his Falcon sedan at a time, Planet would set out on the long arduous journeys back to Praiseworthy. Each an epic pilgrimage that felt like months of slow travel, with either somebody else's pining donkey, or a wild feral donkey turned vicious monster kicking the Falcon to pieces, and screaming all the way. Then finally, in the end, he would be completely jacked off when he saw clearly in the hues of the haze, that each of these journeys had been a failure, and it was finally revealed to him as plain as day, that he had come back with the wrong donkey.

This was the moment of true reality, when all hell broke loose down at the graveyard soon after he arrived back to Praiseworthy with each newly acquired uniquely prized grey donkey, when after idly thinking it could not be true, and then obsessively comparing the donkey with the various shades of mistaken greyness of the rest of his herd, he realised the absolute truth, that the whole exhausting effort lasting several months of hardship to say the least, had been a complete waste of time. This was when he found it hard to relinquish the exhausting effort it had taken a bloody poor man like himself who got no thanks from anyone for having carted another screaming hee-hawing creature in the back of his car day and night for weeks on end. Why hadn't he realised the mistake in the first place? Why was he so colourblind? Couldn't he see the difference in the shade of grey? Was he so gullible and had not learnt a thing in almost twenty years of building the dream? Wasn't he a grown man for goodness sake? Well! He asked all of those questions, and he could not understand what went wrong, and he had to admit that anyone else in their right mind would have been suspicious of how to view greyness, and savvy enough to have realised sooner, quicker, or on the spot, or at a glance even from several kilometres away, that this stupid donkey standing in front of him was not the superior king donkey of all donkeys. It was not as if it was carrying on stupid for weeks trapped in the sedan like it did not have a brain in its head and could not shut the fuck up – for nothing. Perhaps it was trying to tell him something – *I am not the one you want*. This was the gravity of making mistakes with this particular type of vision. The weight was accumulating in his head, and especially when the realisation punched him square in the heart, and he saw again the wrong grey fur, for this was the moment when he saw that the bloody thing was exactly the same grey colour as his other donkeys.

All grey donkeys were good to middling in their greyness, and looked the same, but not if you were building a business model based on the colour of platinum grey, which as it turned out, was perhaps closer to the dense silvery colouring of plutonium, and this was a complete bummer of a realisation if you could not tell the difference between a sea of commonplace grey and the unique, fancy donkey of dreams. It was any wonder Planet felt frustrated. Pissed off. There was no way in the world that he would speak of this incompetence of his brain to decipher shades of grey to Dance's lazy attitude of why bother, each donkey was identical, wasn't it? Why do you want hundreds of grey donkeys, she had already asked him a thousand times, for this lasting mistaken identity. Well! What was the story of redemption?

Planet just remained a stoic and brittle man to the core, and pursued the business of caring for his waste-of-time fake donkey herd. He gave each donkey due diligence while keeping a deep place in his heart to store his pile of hurt, even as he reasoned it was more for the pretence, so as not to look like the complete idiot he thought himself to be. This was the theatre: he had turned himself into an actor of his own drama. And like a proper frustrated mule, he fetched buckets of water from kilometres away for the donkeys, sickle-cut dead buffalo grass by the tonne, carrying sugar bags full of the stuff swung over his sweaty back while he tried to realign his screwed-up mind from going on a killing rampage of every mistaken grey donkey, all the mistaken jacks, the mistaken young jennies, and any burro bebé, and not even that was anywhere near the truth. The man hated being reminded of his failures which were everywhere to be seen, and this was the hard truth about having poor assets when you were trying to create a sustainable economy to take your people into the future. And then there was Dance standing around and watching his every step while grinning from ear to ear as though she was looking at a fool, and dreaming of migration to get the hell out of the place. *Why don't you train those donkeys? Get them to go and fetch the bloody water then? Cut the grass then? What you got them for then?* Planet knew. He knew what she was thinking. He knew her every thought. It made him more determined to be the donkeys' mule. *What are you then, King Mule?* These were the days that were never ending for Planet. *You don't tell me what to do woman,* he hissed under his breath while slapping the mosquitoes attacking his face.

Yet, let it be said once, that Planet remained a very compassionate man. He would never kill a donkey, no not ever, even when he completely lost his block, he got back up again and was still compassionate, just as he could never give up with what the ghosts of the ancestors wanted him to do about saving his people with donkeys. *You gotta save the mob,* they had said, he remembered it clearly, how they were telling him straight through his thoughts. *Don't become some weak thing like that dead white cabbage butterfly lying there on the ground.* One time, they had even told him the dream, how *You gotta become the largest import/export trans-continental transport baron in post-apocalyptic times just like some American blockbuster movie, because in the end, this was hard fact, and it was not going to be a simple dream of you just sitting around on a chair and watching American movies all day, you got to direct it, this was what the dream is about, doing it all yourself.*

Unbelievably, it was a dream come true – the making of the dream part that is – and he believed that the country ancestors kept instructing him about what to do, because they were not telling the Australian government for Aboriginal people how to get some donkeys to save the world and throwing a bit of cash at the dream along the way. The local council certainly were not listening to the ancestral ghosts fanning the haze with their culture stories. They only wanted donkeys to disappear from the face of the Earth. There was not one blood relative who would give him a bit of a hand because they had already decided that they hated having disease donkeys living near them. The entire continent did not care to be surrounded by five million feral donkeys ranging in all sizes, ages and tones of grey, and where some were living in broken-down pens that Cause had built with whatever: bits of rope, bits of second-hand fencing wire and posts collected from the rubbish dump. He had fences everywhere, and fences adorned with kangaroo skins in the process of tanning, to eventually construct an industry of donkey harnesses and whatever whatnot you needed in the business world of a transport industry that ran on donkey fuel, and not gas. The constant stink irked the haze town that had grown to hate donkeys with a vengeance, and that was constantly asking, *Why is he doing this to us?* Nobody was sure that they knew why he was creating such a massive hindrance to poor people like themselves and their need to protect themselves with all of their strength with the officially projected Australian government for Aboriginals' approved plan to be achieved over several generations henceforth probably, possibly, the almost impossibility when you considered the legacy of all government past policy failures in respect of achieving incremental Aboriginal social advancement over endless time into, but not against, white society, which was interpreted to be read, *Why don't you get over your hatred? Start working with white people. Get along with people*, for the plan was a good thing, it was not about over-reaching your own ideas of how Aboriginal people wanted to be human, or wafting yourself into something else, like anarchy, and reclaiming your entire unceded sovereignty over the continent.

But, what can you do? The old ghost ancestor mob had chosen run-down Planet of all people to save the culture, and this was even when they could have chosen Ice Pick who was fat with largesse as the highly influential Major Mayor of Praiseworthy with the ear of the Australian government – big business on his side, and his band of sycophancy woman followers who were going nuts about creating hate laws against donkeys by the bucketload.

The spirits had gone mad instead, and moved into Planet's mind to give him their most glorious dreams about survival like there was no one else good enough to give any hope to the world right now.

And Planet! Well! Lump in throat: he fitted the hope thing like a glove. He understood the times. You would not have to tell him twice that he was a black saviour of the era, that you only get one chance in a lifetime to accomplish some dream of ultimate joy and fulfilment, particularly when he knew it would make him the richest black man in living memory. Yep! He went for it, hook, line and sinker.

He agreed with the ancestral mob. Said, for sure there was absolutely nobody else in Praiseworthy worth giving this mighty dream to. There was no one else on earth he could think of, who would really be able to anticipate what it meant to experience what real splendidness felt like as he did, and was already experiencing even though none of his desires had been realised, and this was the kind of delirium that could push someone to think they needed to own a Zeus-type platinum donkey. Well! Yes, who in Praiseworthy would want to find the right donkey in the holy bush country of the ancestors? There were plenty of little realist voices marching up to his eardrum, and asking normal questions like – *but weren't all grey donkeys grey, Cause?* No, nobody could go worrying about things like that if he were being given a decree by a mighty ancestral being.

21

A magic donkey could rip your heart out and make you go wild, if it knew you had an overwhelming desire to own it, and knew that you would do anything to capture its power. The ghost mob had told him this. He had to be careful. This was the king donkey they had told him about and that you had to be really careful when it turned up in some fable story of long-ago other places in the world. They were telling him how the king of donkeys existed only in their country. *We only heard it was true*, but with all those recurring dreams hitting him in the middle of the night, there was nobody as sleepless as Planet, and having lain there beside Dance and thinking all night, what could he do if he was being chosen by an ancestral creator to be instilled with an atmospheric pressure gauge to read climate change, how would he figure out where this donkey was, on what plains country, or on what string of hillocks, or stringy bark country? Or, where down in the valley, or, where in the middle of a rainbow, or in the middle of the night? Which part of the endless sea of spinifex, or which drought-stricken bone-dry creek bed, or where under a moonlit night, or under the southern cross of which year? Where was the quest to begin, to finally reach the end like some obsessed conqueror? Geography, and the diverse landscape of thousands of kilometres rushed through his head, suddenly zapping a likely spot into focus, then exiting too quickly off the radar before he had a chance to throw a pup dart at the map pinned to his brain, and passing through his head. This was such a vast country. Who had walked over every inch of it? He had great difficulty in deciding where in this enormous continent he would most likely find this magical donkey that was going to make him rich. This was an animal so lustrously silver, it glowed at night in a splendorous platinum grey in Planet's dream like a gelatin silver photograph, the colour of ethereal skies. This was a creature that some might call a wizard, but in the world today you would say it was a chemist, and was capable of mixing in its breath, the trace chemicals captured from the grasslands covering this silver rich country, and exhale a heavenly brilliance upon the night-time land that was like a grey sheen of silvery dullness. It was no wonder that the dream donkey composed in Planet's thoughts as he lay sleepless at night, was beyond comparison with anything else on Earth in terms of greyness.

Planet did not shave in this time of years, and his beard grew longer and greyer, vaster, and bushier, because the one thing that drove him was not vanity, but the higher quest of sheer madness. He had to find this uniquely grey donkey as though this was all he had been born to do. It was so hard to be chosen, to have to undertake a quest like no other, one that had been sent to him as a signal from the vast depths of the country's knowledge, and relayed through its messenger ghosts that had gotten out of their graves in the cemetery where his wrong type of pet donkeys roamed, and where the family lived. It was a kind of angel thing to do, to live in the quest of seeking a shiny grey donkey that kept visiting him for a nanosecond in the pitch darkness at the same time each night, approximately five minutes past three in the morning.

Planet sometimes thought that the donkey was not really the issue, it was the colour that mattered because it meant he would eventually own one of those platinum mines that made more money than one mortal could dream of, but then, while drifting back into sleep, overwhelmed by so much accumulated greyness, he would remember that he was an ordinary Aboriginal man, who was at best just an embassy for his people. He knew that the only way to stop the dream was to find this donkey and save his people from the eternal worries of poverty, even if it was also going to make him the richest Aboriginal man in the world.

Then, he totally collapsed. He was like a dead man in the trance of a sleep so deep nothing else was left in his mind other than a glowing donkey running around in his bedroom, and all around it, a wind roared with what looked like the leaves of the savannah paperbark forests, but were in this dream hundred-dollar bills instead of leaves, or grass, or anything like a windstorm would normally carry across the land, such as thousands of plastic shopping bags that look like a fever of stingrays swirling in the ocean, and this wealthy creature with all of its money flying everywhere kept walking around grabbing money with its mouth which it ate, and would not leave until Planet got out of bed to try to chase it away, to get some peace from dreaming about money. And then again, as he had for many years, he started to get ready, packed up, and there might have been a few IOUs left or not, from what he chucked into his Falcon, and a couple of suspicious spare tyres he remembered were lying around at the back of some other person's place that he would probably have to nick, with other bits and bobs for trapping a donkey, and he was set to go. It was almost dawn when he stood beside the vehicle and looked around. There was nothing more to do as far as he was concerned, and he drove off in the Falcon sedan to chase the dream donkey over thousands of kilometres through arid country, only to find in the end, he was bringing another wrong donkey back to Praiseworthy.

You could say that this was the devil of country. Some powerful trickster like that was not only overtaking Planet's mind, but was controlling his body too by its powerful magic, controlling his heart, beating it quicker, while the sound of its thudding flat feet grew stronger as it ran through the blood stream flooding into his brain, like the thing was running over every kilometre of country, the tens of thousands of kilometres he had ever travelled on his lonely quests.

This was the continuing epic. The unquenchable, incurable disease of desire, of passion to take charge of unconquerable quests that are sometimes laid at the feet of one chosen by the old ancestors. Yet, to be sure, Widespread was up to questing. His mind was capable of racing again and again with each new route he devised in his mind, targeted with a dart, as being the place where the platinum donkey lived. He would actually see it and wonder why he had not thought of going to this way off patch of land before. He could have punched himself for being so stupid, for missing this one place anyone could have realised was where you would find a platinum donkey, for he had passed this exact place of chest-high spinifex so many times in the past and had never bothered to check what was there. Well! Again! Widespread was wide awake now with much to do, too much that had to be achieved with the mental tallying up of his transport industry flicking through his head and resulting in pretty much bugger-all, which was of course the burden of what? Bad vision? There was no time to waste.

22

Who would not want to believe that what the atmospheric pressure man revelled in was his exceptionalism in hazardous times? If you had multipartite alliances like this with yourself, it would be easy to expel the lesser spell of all other praises, and it seemed as though Planet had earplugs jammed in his ears, and he held his nerve while others liked to scream in full off-key crying in his presence, *for whom the bell tolls, it tolls for thee*, which was the only line of Donne known by the people of the haze.

You would need to have a special new God kind of thinking for believing that you were the chosen one. That it was you alone, who was meant to save the world, and who had to find the ultimate grey-coloured donkey roaming about somewhere on this continent of seven thousand, six hundred and ninety-two million square kilometres. You would have to have the capacity to wholly believe you were the luckiest person alive, as Widespread thought himself, to think that only you would find a needle in a haystack, but that was not the end of the story. One thing Planet believed was that it was his skin colouring that was going to better suit the bush in the long run, more than being white rich beyond your wildest dreams. His was the kind of skin for conquering nothing except the desire of survival of his humanity, just like his ancestors had desired survival by cycling infinity in plain sight of death and destruction. Belief in culture survival meant far more to him than being caught up in fiscal policies aimed at leaving the black man dirt poor. The *hey-heyhey-heeeeeeeeeee-he-hee-hee* type of glory day would come for sure. He was the jackpot to get that result, and predestined, he already knew what it was like to own the dream donkey of unproven existence. The man was already powering himself to be magical rich, and even without realising how it was going to happen, and although he was a very practical man in every other sense, he had fathomed from somewhere deep inside that his belief in his own destiny was otherwise to almost every other person, and so he knew he would amaze himself one day by finding that he had suddenly developed that big transport industry for the new age of the fragile planet. It would be a day, he thought, when he saw donkeys rising up in the world and being worth their weight in gold. Already, he was a long way from Praiseworthy on a lonely dirt road, and he saw only the pure vision of being rich from believing in your own doing, and knowing through his very being that his people would never need to worry about being poor again.

The swiftest magical thinking possible kept belting around like balls of dead spinifex in haze dust storms after Planet had left to find the ultimate dream donkey. Fast magic was never going to cut it for the abandoned wife preaching white ideas about going to the bank to get a loan, so they could set up a donkey circus, or something useful with all these donkeys – like normal people would do. The wind blew and he caught the breeze, and old Planet knew her thoughts even though he was miles away on the endless maze of dirt road in the bush where lesser people, people who were not godlike, became trapped and died. He mumbled under his breath about how she should get her head down from the clouds, and stop thinking about bank money. There would be no animal circus in Praiseworthy. The human circus was enough. He wondered if she had ever seen how much money a bank had hidden in its so-called vault. What! Two bob? That was all he had ever seen. Vaults at the back of a bank was movies stuff, what you saw happening in bank robberies on TV. He was convinced that real money was a hoax. There was no money. It was the government's way of controlling poverty Aboriginal people, ruthlessly convincing them to have useless beliefs about banks having money to save them. You had to generate your own money. Otherwise, money never saw the light of day. Money did not hold up the sky on what was left of his traditional land. None, you hear that woman? *Aumpt!* Planet was lost in the maze of being in charge of his own life, and way out there in the bush doing the hard yards to capture the dream donkey, meant that he was not going to run some donkey kind of sideshow just for a bank to make some money out of him. He sneered at the very idea of banks practising black risk, so regardless of where Dance's wishful thinking was leading her, she was alone in that plan about creating a circus in the circus.

What was freedom, but to have the mind adrift? *Yeep! Yeep!* Planet's mind flew around like a dry cyclonic dust storm. It was widespread, and as far and wide in thinking to leave no time for Dance's white-reality thinking. He did not have enough time on this Earth to waste in becoming a perpetual trainee accountant. A black God man was never going to crawl through life for a white hope that one day he might be trusted with a bank loan. His donkey business would work without money – no loan from the bank, no omnicidal-bent government handout with clueless white or black bureaucrats telling him how to do this, or that, with a public noticeboard packed with by-laws that would prevent him from setting up the first real sustainable continent-wide industry for the omnicide times. He kept driving, and mumbling, *Don't need cash to get rich fast in this country.* Would a vast herd of hardworking resilient industrial donkeys need money to eat? Planet did not think so.

Planet had seen the evidence. He had seen it on TV, the tough ancestry donkeys of the subcontinent, Middle Kingdom, Middle East, and Central Europe living rough as guts somewhere in the arid hot lands of these countries. You just had to follow a dream to find them.

And that was what he was doing. It did not matter what language these donkeys understood, he knew all he had to do was speak to the pack in plain old English, and it did not matter if they were of other ancestry, perhaps coming from the ancient Arabic Messiah's donkey, or the sacred Greek donkey of the working god Hephaestos, or from the great travelling white magic donkey of the Chinese Immortal Zhang Guolao, or the descendants from the donkey vehicle of the Hindu goddess Kalaratri, or Epona protector of donkeys, or might be like King Midas who was taught to listen by Apollo. Widespread thought that the ancestors of these feral donkeys might have found, like Agrippa, the ancient Roman, that only donkeys were in the position to receive the divine. These feral donkeys were lucky to be in this country with the best listeners of all things foreign, and perhaps they had already learnt to hear the language of country in which they were roaming about. Planet wondered whether this was the reason why donkeys had thrived here. But whatever it was, he knew they spoke something, and in his dreams, he had already seen that even donkeys got lonely for their true homelands, and all these five million feral donkeys were reaching out, and communicating to each around the world in the middle of the night.

You just had to be able to hear them, and Widespread knew what he was hearing when the platinum donkey had turned up in his dreams on pitch-black nights when the sky was wrapped in a blanket of clouds. You might not be able to see anything on a night like this, but Planet knew the donkey was there. He called it a Zeus-like donkey that came with the thunderclouds of the lightning ancestors, like it was their pet following them around. It was just the normal-size donkey lit up in a sepia-coloured sea of spinifex, or from a thicket of spearwood dancing in a wild wind, and the donkey only stopped when it came alongside his bed, and its head was inches from his own face. Its colouring, a certain silvery hue greyness, almost drove him mad with the need to capture what he had failed to capture, and make him see more clearly, that his total stock of a thousand wrong donkeys, was worth nothing.

While such wild imaginings in his mind about capturing a mythological kind of godlike donkey drove the show, Widespread was certain of some spiritual force continuing to come through the ages to support him to get rich. Who else dreamt about a mountain of money? Endless, fathomless money? Where else would money like this come from, that was not welfare money, or money that came from a bank? He fully realised that there was no one else with the real glint of silvery gold streaks in the eye, that made it possible for him to see the miracles of richness in the form of a midnight gleaming silver-grey donkey in a dream. Only people like himself, with the secret pathways of optical vision, knew how to identify true grey, would see the midnight greyness of multi-millionaires, serious money greyness, such as steel manufacturers, and this had made sense, to change his name to Cause Man Steel, to be in the grey world of shipping magnates, major transport operators, air-force grey, naval-ship grey and so on, and this was the fact about the colouring of haulage that excited aficionados of greyness, as it had appealed to Widespread, where equally he recognised the greyness in the power of oppression, or seen it in the faces of world-worn failed political leaders, or in the wintertime suits of conservative politicians, in the greyness of the ocean churned by supercell cyclones running across northern Australia, and in the rain dripping off the backs of five millions feral donkeys roaming across the land of the ancestral creation beings, of the spirit country.

This was Cause Man Steel as Planet, and as Widespread, the man who cut through the greyness from his hatred of any type of failure, even though he felt it was growing harder to continue wiping himself psychologically after each failed attempt to capture the God donkey. He hated this donkey, and how it had tricked him into wasting his life on that herd of wrong donkeys back in Praiseworthy. He hated his own fallibility, of being left so frustrated from the extreme conditions he had travelled to capture it, and most of all, that he had ended up settling for anything that was second best, or from another trick of the eye, or from another lame excuse of needing to build his herd with anything he could capture with a rope, by falsely hoping he would outwit the power of the God donkey by breeding his own platinum donkey. Hope on hope. Good go. There was such a lot of thought about failure sitting on his brain, his wasting time by continually deceiving himself, by being a captive of his own stupidity.

Sometimes the ocean was nice and calm, and this old man of numerous epic journeys to save the future of his people, would work his brain to avoid another failure to own the God donkey. What was the plan if all plans ended up being the same, even though each had been designed not to waste his time, and had involved the usual format of waiting for the opportunity to check the colour again from a dream, before going out to capture the thing in exactly the same way as before. The waiting for the donkey to reappear in the dream drove him mad, but he had to wait because he could not just go whenever he liked. He needed to be given a map. This was what the donkey in the dream would give him with an indication of where it could be found, to lead Planet straight to it – if he knew the country well enough to know its stories of places – the real map of where to find every ancestral tree and hill in the vastness of old country, for any less knowledge would be useless for finding such an incredible animal with the capacity of making you rich beyond your wildest dreams. If you had nothing, knew nothing, what would this be? Just an ignorant stroll in the so-called wilderness with a stranger that was your own shadow. Planet had long known that he would not be happy just to appreciate the ultimate donkey without owning it, if he could only see it in a dream, as though his dream world was a museum. No! This was not the way it was going to be. This donkey would be a spearhead for the country in uncertain times, a national hero projecting a new future, not owned by government or white money, but as it should be, as Aboriginal private property.

Cause had waited many months of nights before the Zeus-type donkey appeared in an odd dream like a brilliantly bedazzled two-point-five-million-dollar gleaming steel-grey Mercedes, and looked at him from the dove-greyness of the dream country's night-shaded spinifex. Planet had been heartbroken that it would never come back, and believed that he was going to have a heart attack, but in whatever moments it took for him to be compos mentis, Planet pumped enough gas in his body, bolted around the room to try and catch it, switched the light on, and lost the dream. All was not lost though, because Planet, being an expert about all of this country's geographical story lines of creation, pointed to a neon-flashing tiny spot in his brain where he identified the faraway patch of spinifex where Zeus donkey was gazing off in the distance. Do not ask how he knew, but he knew the exact location, and precisely how long the journey would last with his bugger-all resources to get there.

This was the reason why, when Planet left again on this last journey, moving among his donkeys in the night and getting his gear ready, the heaven where the holy lived helped him. Nobody from this point A to wherever he was going, got in his way. The location of an imagined donkey palace was complete in his head, his lucky charm in all of its aesthetics of true grey was already figureheading his long-haul business of several thousand feral donkeys repurposed for the carrying industry in full swing journeys of transporting goods and services across the country. *You got it! We carry it*. He was already dreaming in mottos, in catchy little titles to advertise his vast business with the workings of it, that could make a man's head spin with the motherlode of donkey carriers heading off in every direction, to be caught up with from Aileron to Albury, from Wauchope to Warburton, and all carrying the gold of making his people rich in the new era of heat. So, of course Widespread had to have this only real donkey. Who wouldn't chase the colour of industry, the colour of conglomerates? The colour of fortune-makers that sometimes appear in dreams of a common black man like Widespread, telling him how to get rich. Who wouldn't go chasing a dream that was told in grey?

23

Who knows what Widespread thought while he swung his torchlight around in jerky old-man movements as he moved quickly towards another, and another of his imaginary donkey yards so far away in Praiseworthy, in the middle of the night?

How many more moments of regret would he have to endure as he herded his hundreds of fake donkeys that moved reluctantly towards the open gates where he pushed them out into the darkness of the bush surrounding Praiseworthy? All free to roam in possibly the most dangerous place in the world for donkeys to be while he was away, where he was unable to protect them while questing to find the apotropaic true donkey of billions of poor people in the world, the only kind of donkey a man robbed of his human rights like Planet should own. You should not interrupt Cause Man Steel to his face though, for he was not concerned about flying challenges of the wondrous. It was sometimes best to leave *thy will be done,* and let those hundreds of donkeys wandering around town fend for themselves in a time of general all-out retaliation and retributing by-laws structured about eliminating forever more the donkey matter in Praiseworthy.

Now with all the gates flung open, Widespread continued in his haste in the new land of the platinum donkey, moving without a moment to lose, even though the fleeting image of the land of the giant spinifex that he had caught in the dream was quickly fading in the multiple distractions of what he had to think about to keep a dream eye on his bad herd of wrong donkeys back in Praiseworthy. He kept driving back and forth in nerve-bending journeys in the night while asleep, and to tell you the truth, this was no easy task. This was responsibility. He knew you could not simply disappear into your own fantasy in a reality world of intolerance, but there was nothing he could do to curb his obsession now the prize seemed closer than ever. He had to leave the rest of his life to chance – if his herd of donkeys survived or not in Praiseworthy while he was chasing the vision – even though he knew there was no chance that Dance, or his sons Aboriginal Sovereignty and Tommyhawk, would lift a finger for the enterprise he was building in their name by watering and feeding a few donkeys – that was all he ever expected them to do, he was not asking them to look after the whole bloody world like he tried to do.

Then, strangely, in the nightmare of his long distance to-ing and fro-ing, Planet caught sight of Dance swinging her own torch that lit the wings of hundreds of white terns that looked to him like angels squalling in the winds above her. *You are no angels*, he hissed quietly at the spectacle, while hoping she had not noticed that he was already there, and preparing to leave again. The thought did not cross his mind, that she was far too preoccupied, and had erased his existence from her mind a long time ago.

She was out searching for emperor moths, studying their eagle-eye wings spread out on the surface of night-scented gum leaves spilt over the ground. He flicked his torch light in her direction, once, twice, while hoping for an inkling of recognition of the marriage bond emerging from a small crevice of his conscience – tinged with guilt perhaps, of needing to give her a parting gesture at least, just to let her know he was going now, just in case she might think to remember to keep an eye on their assets, if she did not mind. After all! The thought counted, even if it had no value. This glitter of guilt was instantly dismissed.

See you later. Whatever. He had no time to be bothered about walking around in the dark to catch up with her, just to tell her that he had left, as if she could be bothered...Her torchlight did not falter, or pause, or return a wave, but kept moving further away.

24

In the dawn, the heavy haze falls over the donkey nightmares of Praiseworthy as Widespread's vehicle puffs, crawls into motion, moves slowly while reciting its aubade, through a distant world where the five million feral donkeys lived. The exhaust was moaning with the load, the dozens of red-earth-stained fat plastic containers either filled with water, or somebody else's fuel, a few borrowed spares piled in the back of the vehicle alongside coils of fraying plastic ropes, red-dust-engrained swag, a heavy tangle of roughly rolled wire chucked on top of dozens of steel pickets, and all manner of donkey-catching gear.

In the rear-view mirror, Planet caught sight of himself, the resented view of some person that looked like him who was slipping further away from home. His sight of himself startled him, and he snarled. *Git a grip*. He chose to avert his eyes back to the potholes that were like bomb craters all over the main road. A look out the side window into the aeviternity of the all times brooding over country darkened his thoughts. Of cats now fighting in Praiseworthy. Puppy dogs still sleeping peacefully. Church choirs already humming through the tangled networks of loudspeakers. Nothing was happening rectilinear there. He was moving forwards like he said, changing the landscape of his people's future in his lifetime.

Thongs. What he wore on his feet, would be his only personal item for the trip. Yep! Revved the Falcon further. The ageing engine roared. *Okay! Lets do this*. Planet knew how to talk nice way, or bad way, scold the Falcon, cajole it, or seek the vehicle's advice on direction, instinct, know-how, experience, and its memory of hard roads for spin-outs and blowouts, or where to take the shortcuts, and where to avoid the dead ends. But mostly, Planet cursed the Falcon a thousand times a day for being one of the slowest things you could find on Earth, or for getting another F N blowout in the F N heat stewing his brains into a soufflé at fifty-five-plus Celsius, and he was threatening to set the bloody useless tin bastard of a thing on fire with a can of petrol if it failed to get him through a blanket spinifex landscape stretching over hundreds of kilometres in any direction to the horizon. Then, what to do? The sedan would not make it through miles of pure bulldust while being bogged up to the axles in this mongrel dog of a journey of many weeks. He scraped though. Fixed the junk, and continued through the months ahead to get to the shifty target marked X plastered in his head. The vehicle's original colour was stripped to smithereens from being driven through thousands of kilometres of hard, unfenced scrub. Who could remember its original colour? A colour Planet would not have cared two frigs about, or if the thing he drove was even roadworthy, as the dirty beast, long congealed with red earth sprayed from mud runs, and collecting the dry bulldust in its engine, rattled like a cut snake orchestra of tin cans over yet another northern road.

Sometimes, while driving before dawn, Planet would make the mistake of thinking about Praiseworthy, his mind would wander instead of concentrating on the headlights shining in the darkness ahead on a straight road he had been travelling through, a world of thousands of wallabies and Brahman cattle where any might suddenly stray from a bush on the side of the road straight into the headlights. Distracted, eyes off the vision, he returned to the scene of hearing people in a hurry as the Falcon throws a wheelie out on the street – his parting gesture, more or less, to say goodbye. He was not sure if it was people up there in the headlights, or a wallaby, or cattle rushing across the road to see who was doing wheelies with packs of mad dogs racing alongside trying to bite the tyres with their faces in the dust, barking their heads off while the Falcon continues to speed down the road, hits corrugation, and leaves a trail of dust behind. The thing you would want to see there was Dance's angry face morphing through the windscreen, crazy sprung hair coloured like a flower stuck up from her head, running around on her stick legs after what she called it, *lepidoptera*, and somehow, popping herself back in his thoughts for a moment's worth of self-justification, as he quickly expelled her face, for *not seeing what I am trying to do with my life*. In these memories that make him fume, he swung his head out of the window and shouted to the cattle that they knew nothing: *You hear what I am saying to you?* He hit the brakes, reversed at top speed, remembered shouting out the car window, *Hey! You lot! I am talking to you.* Flatlanders blaring, *If I am gone too long don't forget where you belong.* And someone's kid yelled, *Freak.*

It was somewhere in the flurries, the bits of memory flying like confetti into the headlights further on, where he felt that he should reassemble the shredded paper floating like a pyrrhic victory celebrating the wasting of his life. It is like a vast jigsaw puzzle spread across the country and he becomes totally distracted with the job of re-assembling the *confectum*, the stockpile of floating confetti, until he finds all of the missing pieces to complete each page, and has stacked all of his rejected funding applications to a string of government departments for Aborigine advancement bullshit that had not been interested for one second in helping him to set up his transport industry. The Falcon did not crash, and Widespread regained the focus of becoming a millionaire by making a fortune that was purely and squarely based on the traditional values of desire and ambition that drove his ancestors to survive their times through the principles of their economy. He thought he was wired for surviving through a lens that reached back millennia. Behind him, the ancient dust rose from the road and high into the atmosphere, and up there, flying ahead with the windy bushfire smoke mingling with the starry night, he saw the God donkey in the sky, and escalating the quest towards following the image, he roared into the yonder distance through hissing hymns that could have been Sunday, or could have been Monday, or any other day for what he called hell-obsessives singing Middle Eastern songs when they should be singing their own, and the Falcon left the road and went hurtling through the hurdy-gurdy of grey smoke through the bush. He hits the CD push button. Forgets thinking. Glances over the open vista of gravel and savannah grasslands of the sun-rising voice singing, *Don't let the stars get in your eyes, Don't let the moon break your heart,* while the tyres squealed through the dust. Then he roared off through the morning haze, and far from the sea of white butterflies dazedly falling and rising from fresh donkey manure lying everywhere in thick wads, and the dust trailing around Dance as she stormed back into the house, and he drove at lightning speed, the thoughts crossing his mind, of who neglected whom in the marriage, hearing the car door slam in that dim hazy light of dawn, *You mind telling me who's going to look after all your fucken livestock then – hey?* All these questions he had heard before, *Shh! Stop swearing,* his finger stayed on his lips as he scanned the land, searching for any sign of feral donkeys, his heart pounding, thinking of platinum – trying to recall the finesse, the delicacy of the colouring of a platinum donkey, remembering where he would find it, his heart already shattered into a million rays of joyous streamers celebrating the eventualities of fate, the triumph of finally finding a real masthead for the conglomeration, while knowing at this precise moment, how it would break her heart to see his herd of donkeys going hungry, and without water, which was not much to ask her to do, to care for five hundred donkeys or more while he was away doing this job, but who was counting anyway about what lived in the entangled maze of stinking pens and makeshift shelters of rusted corrugated iron, cardboard, wind-torn plastic, and old worn blue tarps he had constructed across the cemetery.

Why couldn't she see the big dream? A saintly voice jumped in his head, and added: *What was wrong about keeping a few donkeys in the yard?* Freaky questions, questioning the dream, rolled back and forward, thick and fast: *You want to know why? She is just like the rest of them in this country. Who's everyone? Who you talking about? All this country. Too bloody proud for a bit of donkey shit.* There would be no chance of dragging Dance from what he called her nihilistic beliefs about readying her family, improving them, as he had tried to drum into her skull about surviving the new dawning of global warming and whatnot burning the *friggen life out of the world*. Solemn beliefs were not about becoming some half-baked fool. He was not letting her bully him in absentia by mentally divining him to spiral in an eddy of guilt. *You leaving me again are you? Somehow you never get tired of it.* All he was asking her to do was to agree to a simple request of looking after the family business while he was away. Hadn't he always been Aboriginal way, and in addition, for good measure, he added, *Consider those donkeys our family, Dance.*

The far and wide places now flashed through Planet's mind in a fairly tangible way as he remembered the cattle properties where he had stolen all that tangled up fencing wire in the back of the sedan. These were the places where he had pulled out miles of fencing from gibber plains, black-soil plains, mudflats and spinifex flatlands, and hauled the lot around single-handedly over his back in hard toil and toll under scorching heat until his brain fried and gladdened his heart at the marvel of feral donkeys surviving this inland heat exceeding fifty-five degrees Celsius, reaching possibly sixty or seventy degrees in the flash of an eye, in the effects of global warming across the north lands. For there he was, right in the middle of a place for imagining what 158 degrees Fahrenheit would feel like on the skin under the boiling sun, and he rolled and rolled the formula with his tongue around in his mouth: 70°C × 9/5 + 32 = 158°F. Could a man of ancient ties to this country survive in that? He already felt what hell was like in most days of one hundred degrees Fahrenheit plus. What then? And what he was imagining about fossil fuel and other natural resources drying up in twenty, thirty years, when this country was solid heat, was what it would be like – feeling the sweat of his donkey teams against his own skin. He could feel the steady pumping of one hundred donkeys in sweat-laden leather harness driving the transporters, and the ploughing, all breathing the wondrous sounds of animal industry moving through the desert country of the future – carting houses, or a whole town if you wanted, or everything for a bloody supermarket, and he marvelled at the durableness of the donkey, thriving, remaining unaffected by the coming stress of the heat-riven planet. One could only hope, and hope he did, because what else was he to do?

Was this dream holy? Crazy? Stolen business? This was how the Anthropocene business worked. You drive humanity for the survival of the richest, and Widespread was dead-eyed straight about the business between black and white built on theft, and it would only be through continuously readjusting the equity scales with dexterity like he was doing, and finely balancing the bottom line, as he said was necessary in his discussions with the Falcon, how he was putting an Aboriginal man on top for once, by building his own global empire business from other people's rubbish, by taking a few feral donkeys off their hands. The dawn road was nothing suss, it inspired philanthropical thinking in faraway places, and Widespread lead-footed the Falcon because questing burst his energy from the seams, and he was in the mood for grabbing his share of global leadership, by being ten steps ahead of the global meltdown.

He flung a few more thoughts into the flying gravel dust trail while picking up greater speed on the straight, and it felt as though the

Falcon was flying. He wondered if she had heard him loud and clear back there in Praiseworthy – about how he was reminding her of what was important here – or heard him say what he had been saying many times, *We are on the precipice of extinction here. You want to remember this: we will always be the first to go.* Yes, of course he had told her. How many times had he said that nothing was going to help them to prosper from sitting around on a computer. Not when you were falling backwards off the face of a cliff. Couldn't she see it? Well! Maybe she did. Some spirit that looked like her flew into the sedan, and that pissed him right off. *No cliffs around here, Cause.* Her voice swarmed all over his memories. *We only got all flat country here.* And he could feel the big world clock ticking in his head out on this parched road, its hands spinning with winds dryer than the last time he flew down this country in the Falcon, and he takes sly side glances at anything hitting his vision, whether imagined platinum donkey, or returns to the memory of Dance studying stuff about China on the internet day and night like a spy. Someone should watch her. Who else would have thought of China in Praiseworthy? And she turned from the computer, and tells him there were moths flying all over the house and they were all going to live in China, and he thought she was having him on, trying to drive him mad. *Clouds of them!* What for? The world living in China?

Lepidoptera! Planet! Lepid-o-p-tera! It was a rattle on about how he must be going blind if he could only see something the size of a donkey. *The haze must be affecting your eyesight. Everyone knows what moths look like.* The Falcon rattled on, racing faster over the potholed road where hundreds of feral pussycats scooted out of the way from where they were feasting on roadkill – over smashed and mangled lizards, rabbits, marsupial mice, giant grasshoppers, moths and butterflies, whatever had lived a while ago, and while multi-thinking, he was analysing the setbacks he had kept enduring with the conglomerate. He began again with this everlasting problem of Dance who was only interested in other horizons, ones which she thought were the go-to destinations of the future world, which meant she could not form a vision of what was coming up the road, albeit, invisibly from afar. She just could not see it. The spectre of the world he had told her about. Think all ancestral beings. Think of the world as one big spirit travelling so quickly over all distances in its creation of a hotter planet, and if you could not see it, anyone could feel it right now, how it was resting more frequently, and wherever it sat, there would be another massive unprecedented weather event. But! Well! Let it go. *Noli commoveri! Nil desperandum. Viva asinus. #AssToo.* Let it all crash in the gravel out there on the flat. He knew her. Knew that she would starve herself first, before letting any of the donkeys go without food.

25

Rejoice! And forever be the one blissfully swaddled to the country's prosperity, for it was only a black people's moral catastrophe being talked about here, and for this man Cause Man Steel thinking in terms of the faraway, he did not know what the hell his world was coming to.

See over there in the bush? Car parked? The blue-sky man Widespread there. He was still out in the twenty-first century heatwaves of the parched interior landscape, where for months now he had been driving his Falcon in circles like a lunatic. The man had stolen enough petrol from cattle stations and sheep farmers to continue arcing further and further in widening circles of hundreds of kilometres, while crossing state borders this way and that in his quest to capture the ultimate kingmaker donkey.

Nice spirit-laden country though in this sea of grey-green sameness, where Cause was thoroughly absorbed in retracing his grid-like tyre tracks, while peering across the flat spinifex landscape that waved with the breeze and whistled like its ancestral spirit had gone mad in the wind. Where was the million-dollar-making donkey? Where could it be? Planet could never be sure where he had missed seeing the platinum God donkey, so bugger it, he retraced the grid over and over until he was hallucinating. He swung the vehicle off grid. Again. And again. There were so many times now when he had gone into the yellowing spinifex sea, to chase a speck of platinum way off in the distance, that kept morphing into a golden mirage of dust on the horizon. These journeys to find the perfect donkey were no bus ride in the country's theatre of holy places. He was following song paths through ancestral spirit charged saltbush marshes, dry gidgee country, mulga scrub, lightning and thunder worlds, oceans of pale-lemon spinifex plains and ironbark forests. He had continued through these travelling pathways, tracks, roads, spiritual thought maps of millennia until he could go no further, until he started to reimagine, reinterpret, and then even doubt he had taken these journeys, or if he had imagined the numerous sightings of tens of thousands of sites in the song line like a memory man of high ancestral laws. These were the illusionary truths that fired in Planet's brain and bubbled in his self-doubt, wondering whether he really had caught sight of the ghostly silver donkey standing somewhere on some hill that he thought was the colour of stars. Now! Poof! Gone! Nothing remained the same, or had been relegated to over-analysed dreams. Yet, why kill the dream? Planet already felt like a transport baron. His mind rushed with half-imaginings about having money rolling in, and even seeing the road transport rolling down the track. Yes, this was exactly how it would feel to be on the top of the supply and demand transporter industry with the signature king donkey looking exactly like the driver's big silver bulldog masthead on the bonnet of a Mack Truck.

So! On and on in this pilgrimage across his personal mecca of endlessness, in a journeying that had already seen tens of thousands of donkeys of umpteen shades of grey roaming about the bush, grazing like ghosts spotted in the night right across the top end of the country, where of all these thousands which he had discarded for no reason other than not being the right colour, Cause was still to find the right donkey, with the old feral wise donkey he had now taken up as his guide.

Yep! It was always hard to get what you want when you started from scratch with the dream of all dreams. Where you had nothing except the spirits of country illuminating the mind of a seeker who goes too far, where everything appears edgy when you are heading to the end of the unreachable. There was always a toll, and this journey had taken Planet further than he had ever been before, and he had been gone from Praiseworthy for so long that no one thought about him, and he had travelled far with the white birds that flew in great flocks like angels, and he had followed their hypnotic wing beat to off-grid places so far away.

The Falcon was engulfed in another traditional owner's heaven homeland covered in spinifex and heatwaves, and he knew this was where he was destined to find the God donkey to spin his gold. And so, let it be, let it be. Let's suppose in this place of being in the vast aloneness with its ancestors, the whispered words of wisdom had come through the wind in the trees, and the platinum donkey was hidden somewhere in the vista country that could only be found in dreams. The trouble with dream places though, for anyone who was searching for something in such old spirit places, was that all those ancient regimes of landscape might look so much like each other, that unless you knew how to read the subtle variances of the ancient home country through its sacred laws, you would be completely lost. For when you looked at this country in any other way, the whole thing would morph into something else with only a resemblance to Planet's worn dream, for all glimpses of it would seem deceptive, and you would be misled if this country speaks back to tell you that it will always be godless, without gods of any kind.

Well! By now, Planet had seen millions of grey donkeys. Every day he saw donkeys. Donkeys were right throughout this country. Yet he never tired of looking at them, and adding additional hues of grey to his extensive mental tally, in his own virtual memory which was the size of an Oxford dictionary specialising in describing the colour grey. And he saw some good donkeys that would have been excellent additions to his herd back in Praiseworthy. They were strong. Born leaders. Planet was tempted, as he had been on previous trips, but he told himself these were only fake donkeys. Trickery. They were cancelled. He was not settling for anything that was second best even though temptation struck time and again. Sometimes though, he even backtracked to take a second look while questioning his own sanity, reasoning his doubts about whether such a dream donkey existed.

There were other powers being exercised on Planet's mind out there in the old country where the mirages danced if you stayed there long enough like he was doing, min min lights came looking for you, lightning forked across the land in every direction, and his old faded dream had to find new ways of recreating its story in his head. There were many elaborate versions of the dream, which needed to be explored by painting new images of the ever-moving sway of the spinifex grasslands. The story of where to find the best donkey in the world had grown beyond recognition from the original dream when it had appeared on the fateful night of Planet chasing it around his bedroom that had become a vast universe of impossible dimensions. If you looked up as he was now, there were hawks flying in the thermals far above the acacia canopy, circling in the smoky haze where the image of the ultimate donkey appeared, and faraway in the northern sky, the gigantic white balloon of Ice Pick sailed back and forth among the stars while thousands of snowy terns shone as they flew into the rays of light beaming across the night skies of Praiseworthy. He started to believe that this was the exact landscape he was searching for and that perhaps the donkey was in Praiseworthy, one of those fake grey donkeys that Dance was supposed to be looking after. He kicked himself while worship-whispering: *You are here. Not there.* He even remembered some old hippie once telling him to be in the moment. Way out in a sea of inland scrub and spinifex without another soul around, was not the time to be crushed under a tidal wave of bad thoughts about Dance bringing them to their knees on the flagship enterprise. No Sir-ee Bob! He had to keep telling himself not to trust his own mad mind anymore. He did not want to see anything dead, so he pinned a picture of the dream donkey to the big billboard up front and centre in his brain, so he could not see the nightmares of Dance bringing them to the brink of disaster that lurked behind it. He only wanted to see a living God donkey with a silver halo around its head. A donkey that sits in a bank vault on bars of solid gold, where on some days this God donkey was being ridden by a Hindu goddess. He dismissed those other days where it looked worn, like tarnish on the silver chalice of the tabernacle. Or else, his God donkey had once been a scrappy old Sancho Panza kind of donkey before transforming, a force to be reckoned with as it charged through the carnage of war with a frightening sword-slashing Greek god on its back. Eeyore. Benjamin. Oh! Sweet rescued donkey of Swaledale. Then, at other times, the story of the dream donkey was about how it stands listlessly with the pearl-like beads of sweat dripping off its face and trickling into a silvery mercury river flowing over the parched soil. Planet's billboard donkey was a creature of scale, of multiple imaginary possibilities in a journey of extraordinary heatwaves, for each day he vowed to continue to follow the map he had cartographically drawn so finely in his mind with all of his carte blanche hunches of what the God donkey looked like.

The Falcon sedan was seen by a spy satellite, its movement a slow adagio through the dangerous law country of the brigalow where vast herds of kangaroos were rummaging the grasslands in the middle of the night. Some old feral donkey Planet had picked up on the road somewhere, which was advising him on how to get rich, was sleeping across the back seat of the vehicle. It was dreaming old donkey dreams of the good old days when teams of donkeys travelled all over this place. These were fond memories that the donkey had inherited from its ancestors, all those foreign donkeys working overland from colonial times, well over a century ago. The donkey sniffled, took a look out the window, and realised again that it was still in dangerous territory. It wanted to go back home. There were too many rabbits here it whined, and it was allergic to the smell of rabbits. The donkey's nostrils twitched, and it coughed and wheezed continuously to test Planet's patience, and the sedan crawled on dodging and passing tens of thousands of rabbits popping up from burrows that littered this ancient, red-sand country lying under the spinifex and saltbush marshes. Rabbit eyes lit up everywhere like stars, as they stared into the headlights of the Falcon travelling towards them from the south. Multiple sets of eyes followed the lights swinging this way and that to avoid the potholes, as it continued heading north. Dingoes moved away from the approaching lights, while the shocked feral cats did not know what was coming, unsure which way to run, and ended up running straight into the car lights. The old wise donkey pondered the idea of ever finding a platinum donkey and chewed its lips, while sitting placidly in the back seat looking at the passing scenery, and thought, if the vision man wanted to have his vision, let him, but it was getting out of here the first chance it got.

Widespread continued driving through the empty silences of the spiritual domain, overtaken by his thoughts drifting faraway to the lacunose space of the small Aboriginal municipality of Praiseworthy over a thousand kilometres away. Such an ordinary homeland man, a husband and father lost in thought while his wild eyes twitch half-closed, brimming with exhaustion as he falls into a customary fat nightmare. Whoosh the Falcon flew through the brigalow roos bounding away in mobs of hundreds, which Planet only slightly registered as they appeared in front of the headlights – his foot flat on the accelerator, moving at top speed. He was asleep now, and his body weight was flat down on the accelerator in the rush to go home.

This man was stark raving mad as he realised what he was becoming, as he felt the bumps of animals falling on and from the Falcon. You should have heard the stuff coming out of those dirt-engrained lips. He was mouthing off to the wheezing donkey insulting stuff about someone who would not leave his nightmare, a man he hardly ever spoke to: *Your God is on my side more than on your side, and you know what? He's going to get all of you people in the end and murder the bloody lot of you…*this on and so forth, and *may you all rot in hell*, was the sort of thing he was talking about.

So, prison person like, this other person anti-speaking, slings off in the nightmare, but the big lizard at the wheel was incapable of dovish talk at any time, and not now especially, with the Falcon boring across the corrugation. The old donkey panicked, cried in its hee-hawing bark through its snoring nostrils because Planet was preoccupied in a ranting match with the albino-skin Major Mayor Ice Pick of the Praiseworthy shire council, and letting the venom flow too freely in this hell place of his dreams. The car swerved on the loose sand while the songline ancestral travelling women came in the nick of time and kept the vehicle upright. They fly beside the rear wheels. Their hands swooping up sand were stopping whatshisname the big ancestor's world underneath – its name never mentioned for fear of calling him up, and following Cause's crazy path.

26

The starry night twinkled while dust and stones spun through the air as that earth-engrained Falcon sedan roared hell for leather over the gravelly road with its wheels barely hitting the surface. Look! Widespread! Sleep driving! Old Planet, having a hysterical time of it. It was like the dream had stalled in mid-air with the realisation that there would be no peace to be found in running a vast transport industry. It feels like he was in a dust storm, running from a cyclone, hoeing donkey hay day and night to save Aboriginal culture, getting the world moving with donkey road trains a kilometre long running every ten, fifteen, and twenty minutes back and forth over thousands of kilometres of country, moving the goods and services from point A to point B. The dream was a potboiler. A freak-out where he was right there in the middle of the conglomerate working like a systems analyst for industry, dealing with the quarrelling about his direction, ordering people to move faster from sun-up to sun-down, the mantra now being, *this is how it is going to happen*. Widespread suddenly felt alone on this ghost road that nobody cared about, where no one goes, but somehow seemed dangerous, everything in the bush bristling awake with the Falcon speeding through it.

Hey! Man sleeping at the wheel in the dust drive, living the dream among a nightmare mob of ghost women, where old ladies with their savage dogs and feral pussycats kept rising out of the gravel the vehicle hits. They yell out to each other to dig harder while dogs chase and bite the wheels, and the old women were covering the tracks with gravel.

The old back-seat driver donkey could not tolerate this nightmare a moment longer. It did not want to be caught up in a one-on-one monopoly with a madman. Spread out on the back seat, the donkey had been content enough to drift in and out of this world in a belly-up sleep, but now, it looked around real frightened in the darkness, and heard Widespread was still talking to someone who was invisible about self-sufficiency, rednecks and a pear-shaped extinguishing world, and the donkey became bored out of its mind with all the talk coming from the filthy, unshaven and putrid-smelling human foulness that drove the vehicle. Planet continued with the rave about the change needed to help the animals, and about escaping the plague virus once and for all, and the donkey's ears rang with human sounds, and it wondered about Widespread's endless talk about donkeys all day long for hundreds of kilometres of whizzing-by stiff-leafed grey-greenery sprouting from ancestral tree trunks held down by red earth. It surprised the donkey advisor that the man who claimed to have brilliant donkey-detecting eyes from catching so many, had failed to see that there were hundreds camouflaged all over the place behind a bit of scrub, or a lump of spinifex. More than anything else the donkey thought it was trapped, driven by a blind man who did not know what a donkey looked like, even a platinum-coloured God donkey right there – the vision donkey, standing among its ancestors.

The journey of belting through dusty scrub at breakneck speed was taking a sour turn for the wise old donkey. It felt used and unappreciated, as though in its capture it had been reduced to a cheap sidekick in a vicious cycle of thuggery against its own kind. It decided that it did not want anything to do with a global transport industry, or doing government work for millions of Australians, not even the rednecks.

The old Falcon's engine roared and hissed while passing the law country of thousands of countrymen spirits living in this place, and the donkey was glaring up the road lit by the headlights and saw plenty of old people dressed in their best country-and-western clothes that had been buried out there in the homelands, walking through their memories along that road. The Falcon sedan driving straight through what looks like a dense fog of moths, *Hey! Look out. Mad car coming again. Get clean out of the way, move, roos move too. Everything, save yourselves. Kangaroos lying dead now all over the place.* See that frillneck lizard there, those geckos, marsupial furry things just coming out of their burrows to check that the stars don't get in their eyes. Whoosh! Nasty stuff! Straight through the moths. *Can't you look?* Dance yelling. *You got to come home.* She sent the moths. Dead things all over the place. Spirit people scattering in all directions. A lot of bony brindle feral pussycats that had been limping along and sniffing for roadkill baked solid by a blazoned sun drench where only the stench remains for tomorrow's hawks. Same. Off the road others split. They would not stop until they were miles away. The Falcon had its own mind. Heading north. Going home.

The old donkey really panics now, bellowing continuously so that even Widespread notices and turns his head over to the rear seat where the donkey was stampeding and saying, *Do you want ta shut the fuck up?* Widespread did not know what was plaguing the donkey's mind. What was its freedom after all – a bit of hell? Then the local countrymen's spirits checking on country heard Planet calling in his nightmare landscape. What! He was saying no gods knew him. *Me! Look at me,* he raved. *I am properly seraphim from Praiseworthy.* The country men and women were full of wonder at the dictionary words slipping easily off Cause's dream tongue, and flew alongside the Falcon listening for more new words for the country, and hearing him complaining: *I am really pissed off now because this is serious work. Not stupid stuff. That's why all country knows me, knows what I am talking about.* Well! Okay. Might be...

The spirits kind of nodded, and they reckoned that *he might be okay that one – let him through,* and together, the many ancestors holding country up watched what they were calling that *old survival man* spin the loop de loops of spitting gravel in the sky at full speed, while the Falcon was lurching onwards to the north. The dust-encased vehicle looked like a moving big-sky story, while it rocked uncontrollably like it was suffering from delirium tremens, then pelting at top speed, when shit, bang, it hit the dirt, the thing spun, dust flew everywhere, scattering the old stories of country chock-a-block in the middle of the night, and the thing was flung back into the air. The wind increased in speed while the Falcon whooshed through the sky and passed a flying plague of cicadas lit silver by moonlight above the pretty bush of the spiritual danger zone.

27

The Falcon stalled momentarily somewhere way up in the atmosphere, spun out of control, flipped mid-air, and prepared to dive, crash landing where any place was all right in the red sand. And Widespread? He just went with the flow and thought that any place was all right as long as the donkey was by his side. Who was to notice something spectacular like that? Not prison mind. Cause Man Steel just kept screaming wildness in sync with the nightmare, and the donkey woke and bolted upright in the car crashing towards the ground, and in this moment, decided it was going to use its last breaths for one final bit of wisdom for figuring out how to save itself. Those moments felt like forever though, while the old donkey tried to shove itself left, right and centre to rip the spinning car apart. Its hooves kicked the door. Broke the windows. Nothing was happening there in slow motion so it was hard to take in that fast-moving chaos while making a decision, but it managed to kick Widespread multiple times for the mess he had created. The battered animal was desperate to escape, to fall out of the sky as an individual, rather than to its death in some surreal slow-motion turnout of being trapped with an idiot inside a cheap crap vehicle horror show in some low-budget American-style phoney country-and-western action film about space travel. Well! All that jazz, so what? For one thing, because those homeland spirit people had taken over the whole scenario like they would have done in real life anyhow, had handled the lot, managed the theatre, and they held that mud-encased Falcon up in mid-air, while they decided among themselves who was going to drop the bloody poxiest foreign vehicle of all time to kill Widespread straight out dead for being asleep at the wheel, and serves him right. But while the Falcon kept spinning, still out of control, the prison man kept screaming in his nightmare, and it was as though the spirit people in charge of the thing, were trying to decide among themselves who really wanted to be the killer of Cause Man Steel asleep at the wheel. You, no you, wow! What about him, what about me, oh! Which one is going to be the assassin? It was no good trespassing and blaspheming, not without respect on country that only the traditional owner could love. Ring a ding ding, that was the fact thousands of voices were shouting, *You do it*. A big ghost argument broke out that left the Falcon hovering sixty-five feet in the air above the spinifex. *No! You can do it. Whoo! Not me, I am not doing it*. No ghost would grab the keys. Look! He was still sleeping at the wheel, and everyone agreed that they could not hold the vehicle up much longer. Yet it was the law: someone had to teach him a lesson for going about trespassing and blaspheming, and not respecting the country that only the traditional owner could love. Yes! But what about that poor old wise donkey even if it was feral? *You can't kill the donkey too. It was not the donkey's fault.*

Cause was still flying through the silvery dream world that lived in his head, when the Falcon of loose parts landed with a thump – hub caps and bits of caked mud flew everywhere, and the vehicle swerved off the road and continued on its way through the spinifex in the misty moonlight. The prison person's bobbing head continued being dead to the world, and his sleeping foot stayed paralysed like a bit of lead on the accelerator, the engine kept going, and his foot remained flat to the floor. His body was glued by its own weight to the bucket seat of the Falcon, but none of that seemed to matter too much. Cause was being kicked in the head by the old donkey that had not been able to escape as an individual, but he just continued trying to convince the wise donkey about the greatness of being in the transport business, with road haulage costs being minimal etc. as he drove the thing straight through the bush as fast as that old Falcon could muster.

The old donkey put itself out of its misery, bashed its head on the roof of the Falcon, and remained unconscious in the back seat. Cause Man Steel was now a riven man, who felt intuitively that something major was happening – perhaps the global disaster he had been predicting from his study of current affairs programs on TV had already beckoned. The world's fuel crisis was a reality, and he needed to be at the end of his journeying with trainable donkeys led by the platinum spearhead, before his time had even begun.

The Falcon screamed with a rumble of clickety-clack buggered-up parts, and continued, travelling top speed through sacred virgin bush land and in its old stories, which were now ripped to smithereens, before the ancestral world of the place took a hit back. From out of nowhere. Ahead of where the car was heading, a huge ancient tree with a trunk the size of a small mountain stuck out of that flat isolated country of tracks. It looked fine, and as though it had been deliberately placed there to grow hundreds of years ago by someone waiting ever since for this particular crash to happen, and you know what? After a further little while of ripping apart the natural environment – wham! – the Falcon landed with a thud against the tree. The sound of the crash woke the countryside. Birds flew from nowhere and screamed. The night earth thundered with thousands of kangaroos and wallabies belting to the hills. The world fell quiet again. Cause was now parked in an old ancestor's cradle stretching across endless kilometres in this dangerous faraway country, a prohibited sacred place where one of the most powerful ancestors in the whole country was now disturbed and started to act up from the thud of the car being hurled by the sky people down upon its body. The air exploded. Dust everywhere. The ancestral exhalation wheezed away lifetimes of slumber that sounded like millions of tweaking micro bats pulsing through the air, and the vision man Planet dreamt that he was back in a hot holy Praiseworthy night where the haze-laden air carried the brethren singing their collective hymns over the flat plains and in the distance the songs congealed into a single droning of the mighty ancestral serpent that was as long as an underground river stretching far away across the country, breathing from down below the ground where it had slept for an eternity.

28

The slightest unusual movement in this late January night sends atmospheric waves of vibration through the dust, and this brings in the warbling ancestral guardians, coming from all directions on the desert winds. Unconscious man. You better watch out! The seagulls in their thousands were gliding silver on the billowing air waves circling above. Then, as far as the eye could see in the star-brightened night, the spectacle of soft body feathers tossing in the brightness of the fiery rippling winds, fanning the overheating of these powerful storytellers whispering, whistling, growling and squawking in the circling, circling of all life quaking after the sedan crash-landed in a loud thud that woke up the dead.

The prison man's mind mucks up right there and then because of his big social arguments with life. He was unable to think straight about the sight of the Falcon which was not pretty in the bush right now, while the spirit birds continued moving with the wind here, there, and everywhere. The roar of wings flapping wildly, as the birds struggle to escape from the turbulence forged by a flaming bushfire ancestor travelling further off in the distance. Eventually a bird spirit lands, then another, as one by one, they hop around on the still-burning twigs on trees and burnt ground as the smoke drifts after the fires racing away in the tinder-dry spinifex.

A world of warblers alights, and orbits in dizzying rings around the sedan. They know the old donkey in the back seat of the vehicle. They had watched him being smack-banged in the middle of this burnt moonscape. Some of the warblers hop over the Falcon, to check on the donkey. *He's alright. Look at him all injured. Cut and bruised that one. Why he in a motor car?*

Planet had no idea that he was in a crash, which was not unexpected, since the old fool had been more than dead to the world for ages. Well! He was actually comatose, locked in the thought that he was an angel in heaven sent to save the world. He snores deeply, even while being kicked in the head by the berserk old donkey bleeding from gashes here and there, when suddenly the dead radio spooks, comes flat to life with Elvis Presley singing about how he was wising up to angels, *heaven help me*, and the King spoke, screaming angels were really the devil in disguise. Country was not thinking straight after hearing something like this happening where it had known quietness at this time of the evening for tens of thousands of years.

Wait! Country!! Wake up! There is no devil here. This is not devil country. It's other way. Way back. Planet heard some distant whispering of voices filling up the night, trying to wake him, while he missed the massing of white-eyed ghost moths, the *C. delospila* guardians in flight, dancing a silent ceremony that was also like everything else there, as old as the world. The dance was a constant flitting in unison, of togetherness rolling back and forward while crossing their traditional arid story line in a place stretching over kilometres of devil's vine, and from the ground, the ghost moths began to swarm in the tens of thousands around the vehicle. Their language was recorded in the black dotted wings that could be read in the fluttering of this massive song, the sung stories of ancestry, of belonging, of aeons of ancestor travels, until this point of intrusion in the flight path. All language ended with those tattered and singed wings from the pulsing mass of delicate bodies, and thousands of tiny claws fought off others, in the desperation of the whole population of the clan as it was absorbed in the Falcon's headlights. Planet heard the war cries of the dull brown barred-winged castor oil looper moths stampeding in the solid nightmare of battle that began when other white-eyed ghosts turned up to reach far into the headlights, and while he was in his own fight, struggling to crawl back to reason. He cannot breathe without it, not with being in this different country. He worked faster to save himself, to try to think straight, but the radio was pulsing like a heart drumming inside his chest. He heard someone speaking about how another place King fella come here from across another place, now locked himself up inside the engine of the sedan. This spirit bloke, all satin and silk of pearly whiteness, had caught himself up on replay, and seemed to be accusing Planet of being the devil, because he kept jiving about on repeat, saying his sing-song over and over, *you the devil in disguise*. The minute claws of the swarming ghost moths scrape the Falcon's front window, trying to get through glass. The old wisdom donkey really wants out now, and chucks another stampede inside the vehicle. It kicks, snorts, and throws its big body around until it pulverises the interior upholstery, and kicks down one of the rear doors. Then, without another moment to spare, no goodbye and what have you, like thanks for the good times, a mass of bloodied grey fur turned itself right side up, flew out of the Falcon and crash-landed in the dirt, and no sooner, picked itself up, tried to shake off the governance of the dust spirit, the termite kingdom harvesting dead grass twigs, and was flat out gone, disappearing into the spinifex.

How strangely catastrophic Planet felt while hanging upside down at the steering wheel inside the crashed Falcon slammed bum up in that dangerous spirit country. So! Half-conscious, he looked at the reality returning in his brain, and the very first thing he realises is that some of the last petrol on Earth is now pouring on the ground and spreading all over the place. But instead of noticing the raging bushfire brightening the night skies around him and putting one and one together, he wonders whether or not he has gone insane. Why was he unable to link up all the sane bits, like smelling petrol leaking everywhere, and separating the crazy bits of thought about raging bushfires that made no sense, since this was the first time he had heard there was a fire, while the King was still singing on the radio and calling him a devil in disguise? Well! It was what it was, and he seemed to have no thought about losing some precious petrol to a mother of all mothers inferno.

Planet was not carrying a cash register to add up the cost of fuel. Did not need to. What of it, if the world owners of gas want to overcharge him for a few litres of fossil fuel when he of all people knew in his wildest dreams, that a supercharged Aboriginal millionaire created by a God donkey had to be worth far more than all of the world's drying oil wells. Yes, you could say reality had returned to his conscious mind. Planet dug deep. He was in the fathoms of universal consciousness in his regained sanity. Yep! He was there, right back into knowing that he was no better off than a half a billion poor people on Earth who depended on donkeys to get themselves from A to B in whatever was thrown at them – stuck in the middle of a millennial drought, stagnating floods that do not shift, blizzards, plague or pestilence. A donkey, an unrenewable energy source, you weigh it up, and this was what Widespread thought in his fight for consciousness when he landed back in the real world.

While surviving a car crash in the end times out there in a world that was not modern in the sense of New York, Hong Kong or Tokyo, Widespread knew the glory in this country was about enduring its sense of being thousands of years modern, from where would come its own future regardless of insane acts of humanity. This was what being a countryman meant, that he was part of looking after country, if he wanted country to look after him. Now, every part of his body twitched and ached while he jerked himself out of unconsciousness, still trapped upside down in his bucket seat in the Falcon, and he did this slowly, methodically, by calling himself up like he was ASIO, and meticulously reading through the files of the spirit of consciousness that weighed in his soul. Know thy self. One might suppose that it was his natural inclination to study himself, by viewing his dedication to the madness of his big bad *warrakujbu* or *rudda rudda* dream of getting rich quick by having an inexpensive ingenious plan, one that did not cost money, to build the biggest transport conglomerate the world had known, for saving his humanity in the new era. This was what his heart told him, that you had to think short-term plain about what you wanted like white people thought, while never losing sight of knowing that he came from the biggest all times law. The whole thing was continuously being redefined and shaped by the superior levels of ancestral knowledge and its responsibilities for shelving any short-term plainness when it saw it, and by hoisting his ambition higher than even he thought was possible – with the responsibility of course that came with such greatness, from putting countryman's dreams right up there in the realm of the heavens. So, country might have said, why go out with a lasso like some kid cowboy ringer and help yourself to any donkey? That would be far too easy. Far too unambitious and lacking in greatness. Boring and plain in fact. Without real desire to even be alive. Wouldn't it be better, to narrow his search into millions to one, to discover the beholden, a God donkey that was impossible to find anywhere on Earth, let alone in this patch of spinifex ready for the ancestor coming with the open bushfires?

A man could stop killing himself over and over from the sheer boredom of having to put up with plain thinking humbugging his country. So! The triumph! The plan, so huge, so bold, had to be constantly refuelled on panic. He rose, if not from his car seat, in knowing that he would have to implement the plan quicker, even if he crawled on his hands and knees across every piece of spinifex country where the big ancestors were breathing hot winds through the scrub, and the air of the night world carried the slow whining adagios of starving feral cats, while the world of beetles was bristling underneath this bone-dry country and snapping twigs of dried-out spinifex wherever they crawled, and overhead, the never-ending whizzing of the wings of flying ants rising above the bushfire haze chattered about the eternal governance laws of this place.

Woo! Shh! Prison person. Making too much noise. Too many miles to go. Too many days. Shut up please. Be here, the old spirits yelled through his half-dreams, *ancestor coming now full force. He's sick of you.* Unstrapped, power sprung straight out from the ground. Planet felt the sense of a chaotic storm that threw his mind all over the place, and he felt the dust rising in the darkness, and the mellow yellow moon brightened the spinifex landscape right to a faraway horizon. Everything was transforming badly, creating abnormality. The ground was alive with millions of flying ants rising like tiny angels to join the red dust ridden smoke. The air massed with moon-glistened wings in a spectacular serpent-type vortex that swept across the sky, broken and unified by the twisting and turning tendrils, sometimes suddenly dividing off, then finally unexpectedly sweeping back onto itself. The living cloud thickened, and the atmosphere became so dense that it was impossible to see the arid stumpy-grey spinifex. Parts of the serpent snaked in and out through the crashed windows and doors of the vehicle, as the mighty thing continued to climb further into the skies and take a north-easterly direction, en route big time to the haze of Praiseworthy, to be there to cast its shocking eternities, and worsen the mood of Cause Man Steel's people towards this donkey get-rich scheme.

Planet took no particular notice of the ancestral serpent winding its way through the reality of his nightmare. He seemed not to have the least bit of interest in riding the ancestral wave back to Praiseworthy and sneaking a peek at what was going down, of what was unwinding in his story. No, he was not in the mood for shattering teeth stories, but the enormous serpent kilometres in length ripped on through the sedan, and his face and body were continuously pelted by the rapidly moving mass of flying ants until the story crept on its way into the ear of the Praiseworthy God-believers, and words stormed out of its mouth, while speaking like some important figurehead god: *I'm telling you fat bugger-all. YAH USELESS BIT OF LARD.* Country! What was going wrong with this Cause Man Steel? He was not the figurehead of country, nor was he like some ancient god figurehead with flowing white hair and a spear in hand guiding the way of a ship. *We are not ships here for the likes of you.* Planet missed what the world of Praiseworthy was saying about him at this minute, because he was listening to his own thoughts. Wasn't he the man who had no say in anything at all that was going down in the world? Wasn't he just a poverty man with crazy ideas in his head about getting rich in the chaos of a wrecked Falcon, when even the semi-conscious wisdom donkey that was supposed to be his advisor had fled, and the country's big spirit was turning itself mad from inside out? Anyone would have thought he was deaf, or a bigot, and Praiseworthy people who liked to claim to be the collective specialists of bigot behaviour, would say in ping-pong talk that Cause was a bigot, who only pleases himself by bringing other people's dreams down to his low-life level, and this made him not only a bigot, but a bigot with a big mouth, and more ultra-bigoted than even a bigot god – if that was even possible.

29

All the way out there in the red-soil country of the spinifex pigeon, the desert ancestors were carefully inspecting the road less travelled all the way to the full-stop mess of the prang, and they saw Planet dreaming that some business God had actually travelled through the universe to sit beside him. He sees this God of whiteness sitting where the donkey should have been sitting, and he was so pissed off that the apparition was there instead of the donkey, he yelled, *E tinks e's a lard or something. Go on. Git out of my car you animal.* And country saw that Planet had instantly recognised as they had, that it really was the *dee-vil* itself, because even in this faraway country, anyone would recognise the Major Mayor of Praiseworthy.

Now when the apparition refused to move, Planet became unsure if he had really seen the ancestral serpent, or a cloud composed of billions of flying ants that flew like an enormous serpent around the car. Or! Was he really seeing the nemesis Ice, the believed-to-be albino who thought he was Casper the Ghost, Major Mayor thing of Praiseworthy. How did this sellout get here? This power and glory boss of the Aboriginal establishment dressed up in fashion clothes from Sydney. A silver-sequined suit that had swung open the rear door of the Falcon, and jumped into the back seat behind him, while the platinum God donkey, which was essentially the illumination of the ancestral serpent shining on the old grey-coated wisdom donkey, stood outside the vehicle tethered to a piece of rope.

Ice, being the all-knowing populist, quipped to the dazed runaway God creature he had captured for a spirit pet that, *This man is a murderer of all the children in Praiseworthy. Yep! He murders his own children.* It was talk like this that turned the world fiery, and into the flying-ant serpent billowing smoke and flame as it spun itself into fury, and felt like a category five cyclone circling the vehicle. The roaring winds continuing in a deafening din that seemed capable of morphing into other sounds, because Planet felt he was listening to the droll sound of BBC radio English, as the wind matter-of-factly continued through an unseen roll call of the unnamed – *some Aboriginal men who did this, and some Aboriginal men who did that,* you get the general drift, voicing continued condemnation through the decades. For a moment, he felt the same thing that Aboriginal men feel, forever guilty of crimes they had never committed.

Nigga! Get outta of my car, Widespread hissed while untangling himself from his seat, but the Ice Pick spectre continued to echo the radio voices, and then finally, in a voice of exasperation, said that Cause should not call people racist names, *if you don't want to go to hell.*

Ice continued mouthing off like he was the Australian government trying to be mummy and daddy to Aboriginal people, and he went on whinging and whining with his cowering on the ground talk about the third person Cause who should be back in Praiseworthy looking after his children, who maybe did not love them enough or something, and was preventing the whole of Praiseworthy's progress to close the gap, and this was why children were not thriving, and not becoming assimilated into the mainstream.

And so there they were, twisting again like they did last summer, and many other summers, in stereotypical racial arguments that caught hold in household homeland places like Praiseworthy, fighting the multifaceted assimilating war zones that sent Planet's brain screwy. He contorted his lean lanky sprawled body through multiple jerking and lurching actions whilst still trapped in his seatbelt, jumped about, and tried to reach with one arm into the back seat to

160

punch the spectre of the upside-down Ice, when a fabulous miracle happened. Somehow, while Widespread was looking straight through the odd refraction of shards of light in Ice's ghost, he saw something he had never noticed before. He wondered how such a thing could be, how he had never had a real good look at the old wise donkey advisor, and not seen it as plain grey, but as platinum. The old creature, too lazy to move, was the God donkey. He was unable to believe his eyes, but in that instant, he thought again about being deceived, and robbed of his destiny of always searching for a miracle. His hand gripped the steering wheel while the abuse continued with Cause calling Ice numerous names and actions associated with dogs while Ice eloquently described the serious consequences of his failure to be involved with the betterment whole-of-future plan of Praiseworthy humanity to close the gap between black and white as equivalent to being an actual murderer, that he may as well have committed the mass murder of the future itself.

You could see from Planet's point of view, that he needed in the end to seal his lips to the spirit of the thing being conjured by the flying ants crawling in his mouth and down his throat, and trying to choke him while he continued mumbling jack-all about whatever thoughts bubbled from his brain to fire at Ice, so as to avoid the little voice in the back of his head saying he should think about saving himself before he gets thrown in gaol for murdering children. By staying quiet Cause tried to throw Ice off the trail, camouflaging what he was really thinking by burying the real plan deeper in his brain. But his conscience kept betraying him, willing him to break his vow of silence, to argue, *Don't you want to be a multi-millionaire. An Aboriginal millionaire. Tell him the plan.* Cause just sniggered, and sat back to let Ice Pick rave on about how respected he was as the Major Mayor of Praiseworthy, how he knew the way forward for his people better than anyone else in the world, and then he looked at the platinum donkey that had jumped back into the Falcon, and frowned, *What! More donkeys? Why have you got another donkey in your car for Cause?* Ice tried unsuccessfully to push the huge donkey away but it was too strong, and it pinned the Major Mayor to a corner of the back seat. *You have got too many donkeys. They are polluting the whole town. Shit and stuff everywhere. It's illegal. Not right. I will be making by-laws about these donkeys. Get rid of the donkeys, Cause.*

I like 'em, Planet now muttered, *and how are you going to get rid of donkeys anyhow?* The flying ants continued crawling around his face and into his mouth, his nostrils, his ears, trying to find a way inside his head to steal the safe in the back of his brain. *I am shutting up shop Ice so get the hell out of here.* Ice said he was not going anywhere. *I am taking you to court man, number one for killing Praiseworthy children, and number two, to get rid of your donkeys from spreading their diseases to all our vulnerable people.* The mention of court jolted the nightmare. Cause woke up in fright, knowing Ice could shut him down, and the radio burst back into life by suddenly blasting a song Cause could not get out of his brain after hearing Betty McQuade singing, *Leaving on the midnight bus.* His clenched his fists, and the flying ants detoured in the darkness, where air was really like air and not a memory of Ice Pick getting at him no matter how much you punched him away to keep him from interfering with your breathing...

The ghost landscape began clearing beneath the rising swirl of the ancestral being. Cause was still strapped in the driver's seat, slept there right through the night, and finally before dawn, he turned his unshaven dirt-grimed face to look in the eyes of some wished-for dead thing sitting in the back seat, staring at Ice so close, inches from his own face, and said, *Ya think you frighten me, you don't frighten me. F off out of my car will you.*

It was daylight now, and Widespread broke free from his car and looked around at the landscape where the fires had come through and were now far off on the horizon, then he turned back and looked at the car but did not notice the damage – the broken windscreen, doors half off, headlights smashed, the petrified wisdom donkey still sleeping, and he did not remember anything about Ice having been there. He looked at the country, the sea of scrub, the stunted trees as old as the hills, the grasses flowing in waves, the burnt line where the ancestor had travelled, the ants crawling across the ground, and heard not a single sound. He grumbled a bit about not knowing how the fuck he had got there in the first place while reaching into his shirt pocket for a loose Panadol paracetamol he kept for a moment like this, and that he now popped into his mouth for breakfast.

All Cause could hear in the wide openness of bushland was the slow, regular pounding of his solitary thumping heart that began deviating at a killer rate, knowing he had to drive on to Praiseworthy with or without the God donkey, tethered by a long rope to his brain.

The old donkey advisor that looked like the dream of a platinum-coloured God donkey when seen through the icy shards of the ghostly appearance of Ice Pick was still there, sitting in the back of the Falcon, and ready to go, to step up to a hell of an ambiguous plan to save the traditional landowner for the new era of country, by becoming the fabulous masthead of a transport conglomerate of the likes never seen before, and like some pretender, or fake donkey stand-in for being, or not being, a God donkey created by the power of the spirit in country.

Yo! Think properly. Tell it like a normal person. Like somebody learned. Like Desmond Tutu would.

THE CENSER

Don't let the stars get in your eyes, don't let the moon break your heart
Winston L. Moore (Slim Willet) 1952

1

Oracle 2...speak up.

Since he, sometimes called big time...

Aboriginal Sovereignty, named for young hope and all that emotion-laden charged asset language of the modern day – say e bin finished up one time good and proper from the Cause Man Steel family, just like he was some piece of rubbish dump sort of dead discarded thing for all times on the face of the earth. Gone now, from flat out disappearing into the mighty shark-infested ocean of the ancestors – and this same boy one time, causing his people to gulp in the throat, feel badness in the head for a long time, by what he gone done to himself by abbreviating his life span to a complete zero, millivolt, flashgun millisecond, micro scale thing full stop milliwatt, and by where forth, even his seventeen years ended up like some shit piece of holy smoke in the imagination by being snuffed out into nothing by suicide wishing himself to be as dead as a doormat somewhere under the old spirit fog dust covering the sea, and you know what this kind of thing only resulted in? Well! Fool people, it resulted in a proper dead fella the people henceforth say for the northern provincial town of Praiseworthy – right, and in the shock of the terribleness, there was no scrap of fuss.

Nothing made out of this masterpiece thinking. Well! That's right...
Say! Dust lady must have *took* him though...

He was like precipitation, like virga. Like that: gone.

Cloud rain never hitting the ground.

Might be true! Might be too true! This was what the stories said.

What happened to the lungs of country then?

Was it the country's law talking out of the windpipe of those whirlwinds?

So useless brains, what was the cultural comfort in losing Aboriginal Sovereignty?

Marginalised space people can you say something about this?

Go on, take your pick of any empty wide-open field in the brain you want to explore. See what? Empty tin cans. Heinz baked-bean tins. Something like that. Slap on the bottom. Smack! Smack! Search the dirt. Scrape soil aside with your foot.

Look! Did any useless brain cells fall out?

Why fuss? Huh!

No fuss.

This surly widespread dust in the atmosphere that had lain over the country for days on end, on these perfect youth suicidal nights of Praiseworthy, where wind comes in the afternoons, blows the dust out to sea, treading lightly through the water, another child of Praiseworthy was leaving the butterfly country – the land that looks like a big brown damaged-winged *lepidoptera* marooned in flight. He was going to the dream country like those other lost children disappearing over weeks and months, being led away by the hand.

So! What happened? You can ask that question in a thousand different ways. Why? Why? Why? Why was anything gone for all times? *Nah! They don't talk to me.* Immemorial sacredness violated? Nope! Heaven, it collapsed? *Didn't see it myself personally.* What ends, ends. You just don't know? Was there a sharp dip in the astrosphere, the usual sine qua non human condition, in the modern era of the Anthropocene?

The answer? Blanket no. *Couldn't see it myself.*

Of course not. Fools! Nothing was blessed! No promises fulfilled. There were no mass performances of trumpets blaring Te Deums, or drums rolling Handel's royal fireworks with brass wind ensembles, nor anything else magnifying the magnificence of God's will filling up the void.

The ancestral ground around this country moves in its own time.

And out of the normality, of just breathing everyday air and salt flying off the wings of a bird ploughing across the sea where the wind was buffeting this way and that, while the fish fly from the ocean in the tempest of cyclones colliding, or to where people were hiding in fright from unexpected storms, the ancestors turning up to check on their conscience while having a look around at what was going on inside their heads, and refusing to leave. They stay there, sitting around somewhere in the brain – hiding, and telling the same old stories of country – the stories reminding you about me and you, while the old granny lady wind takes the children away.

Someone like that might start telling you stories about what happened to Aboriginal Sovereignty too, of what they noticed about Praiseworthy where so many children were ending it all. What for? The why of those stories? Why the ode was such a mystery? Were those little children frightened of a white world – the only future they could see? Imagining a white people army taking control of their lives? Kids dream, think of being conscripted to fight white people's wars? These were the new legends now. New sagas. What those ancestors asked, what happened to all those spirit children we gave you for country? Everyone in the whole country was asking that, not just those people of Praiseworthy. Where did those children go? Do you think the ancestors will destroy us before they leave too? Look at all these calamities breathing, breathing into the stories connecting country.

Only country trembling, shivering like it was cold, you could feel that. Never stop. Whole country – like, what happened in Praiseworthy.

The ancestors might have to grow up those children themselves. They never let you forget that, those safe-breakers of your soul. Come in, help themselves. Look inside. Examine what you got, like looking in a fridge. This was where they lock memory to your soul. Telling you story after story about what was happening to that kid, country kid, country was like that when it speaks.

Sometimes, you would feel country roaring even on a still day, even in a concrete jungle you hear them telling stories, sometimes like thunder, sometimes just the tree swaying in the wind, sometimes through things you never heard of, or seen before. It was easy to hear them. You might even feel some slight moderating changes in the air as the breezes ripple and flow through your mind, when you could start wondering why the country was pulling all of these punches, coming with old sad stories into your thoughts like this. But don't forget it was like war. A protracted campaign. All quests for decency were like this. Then, country can be kind too, and can make you feel really glad to be alive. But not now while the haze ancestors were talking low after Aboriginal Sovereignty never came back – their voices fading to almost nothing they want to say to you anymore.

2

Something small enough happened though when Aboriginal Sovereignty quit the scene in a blanket of falling dead white butterflies, by walking off completely in a flat sea under a wave of dust and cloud that hovers, never quite falls over the horizon, and covers the moonlight when final steps are taken in the middle of the night.

With this extreme event of a young man, the hope and all that, taking his life in what could have been the holiest of red dust storms that had lasted many decades, nobody could say if this was more of a catastrophe than any other catastrophe, and nobody could say what it was that happened to Aboriginal Sovereignty, or what it meant. If only the country could be read properly as you would see from those old people reading country like they were reading themselves, but country gone completely asleep, covered itself with a haze. The censer was wafting its hazy sacredness, and if you looked over there where the whirling red fog was travelling far out to sea, hitting the far side of the haze dome and returning, you would have seen how it looked around, looked over its shoulder to see if Aboriginal Sovereignty was following and there he was, walking deeper in that glassy flat sea.

About there, in this unusually noisy night where insect hordes screamed the news about Aboriginal Sovereignty from the spear-grass thickets that necked the coastline, if you looked from the reddened dark rouge skies to what caused the squawking flocks of seagulls, the thousands storming in the darkness, and listened to where all those mongrel community dogs were racing up and down through the fogginess of the haze and spreading the news about Aboriginal Sovereignty killing himself by barking uncontrollably at each other and making people, who not long ago had finally been rocked into deep sleep by hours of Christian hymn singers, rip-raw awake and yelling their heads off like a bunch of angry and not very peaceable people, and saying something like, *What! What is all this?* then, *Stop! Stop! Your friggen barking useless pack of other worthless people's mongrel dogs,* and if you had seen that miracle, you might have noticed something else, what must have been the complete assembly of all the schools of trevally in the Northern Arafura Sea leaping from this spot, in and out of the sea, up to the skies as though trying to jump out of boiling water, and seen where these fish were looking over to the back beach in that corpuscle-reddened darkness, to that place in a patch of moonlight shining in that wild spirit mangrove country where those giant moths flutter in a lonely journey in their short life span, and if you followed this fella brown Atlas moth with a snake head at the tip of each brown patterned wing, you would have felt that the *Attacus wardi* had been awakened to the enormity of the all time sadness. This was at one a.m. which was the moth's hour anyway, where they were fluttering about clumsily and slowly in all the breezy pockets, racing through the moonlit haze falling over parched dust-coated vines in the sleeping monsoonal jungle. If you noticed, you would have happened to know that there was only one other human being from this preoccupied hymn-singing turnout who was actually witnessing the suicidal departure of Aboriginal Sovereignty.

3

Way over in the night shadows of mangrove copses, the old grey forest tribe that grew all along the beaches outside of the township of Praiseworthy, just where the spirit of place might lie and be entrenched in the mind of those other fellas, them black, red and white-banded mangrove jezebels always fluttering the yellow spirit of their wings at dusk in their white flower to flower flights, if you had looked carefully enough around there earlier, say at six p.m. for instance before darkness fell, or thought about what was really hiding there with the swamp tiger butterflies off the paperbark country, which was long before the whole thing had happened with Aboriginal Sovereignty, you would have noticed the only witness was being exposed by a flurry of oleander butterflies that betrayed him, those ordinary black-and-white crows that were ascending higher than the mangrove forest hugging the coastline, and leaving earlier than usual, because they had been disturbed by movement in this lonely place before the ghosts turned up. There! That fat little ninja terminator kid who thought he was the assassinator, crawling around in the mud looking for his own demons like that Japanese god Shoki the demon-queller, as though he was trying to expel all the common thereabout head plagues hiding in plain sight that affected his happiness. Watch him! See how he hexes devils at the same time as sneaking around in the mud where the thickening haze was caught up in the arms of the mangroves, where he is half hidden by all those old exposed roots.

You had to look carefully with the deep history eyes to see what those old mangrove trees could tell through their stiff spathulate leaves, and of what else flowed around the aerial roots like spirit fish at high tide, along with the molluscs of periwinkles and mangrove worms burrowing in the saline mudflats, or the long bums and crustaceans, and the hungry mangrove goanna, or what was flushed through fish and the snakes in this place when the tide came in. This was how to read the local story about the terminator – what he came from, by looking through the power moving through this place. It was the kind of power that latches on and tugs like a leech, by drawing you right inside the stillness of the sea of unmoving leaves of the mangrove thicket in the flat breeze, that calls on human souls, calls on the fish, calls on everything in this place while singing those stories in a certain way. This was the way of seeing what was happening over there in the old skeletal city of bones left from pod after pod of whales that had come here throughout times remembered in the stories, to die on this sad graveyard beach amongst these forests of grey mangroves. A feast lasting ages, still celebrated by whistling kites from hundreds of generations ago. Now bones, where sprinkles of worried snow-white albatross butterflies fluttered among scores of mangrove jezebels – the red, yellow and black fellows – in the tropical dry season for butterflies, while ancient dancing feet were trampling to death all the pretty pink flowers of the morning glory vine called in Latin, the *Ipomoea pes-caprae*.

Of course! Those skeletons in the mangroves were holy whales too. Had to be, for they were from ancient law, and spirits returning every year, and again, suiciding in a swarm, just like the white butterflies flying towards their death, off in the sea. Legend law, the big story people told in story after story about how these whales were tossed across the waters of the world like peanuts, and thrown about on the top of mighty waves in the time of cyclones that crawled across the world, and thrown around in the skies by the powerful storming clouds ancestor of this place who then, thinking about giving a big gift story for country, whacked the whales on the sand to die amidst the congestion of stories in this part of the world.

In amongst a thick dark fog buzzing and swarming in the mangroves, sometimes when a cloud moved and the moon and stars shone through, you would just barely see the outline of the little fat boy trying to hide in the bones among the mosquitoes and sandflies. The ninja killer was slapping himself left, right and centre to stop the insects from attacking him and demanding that he get off the beach in the middle of the night. They were telling him as though they were his actual parents, instead of those two in the cemetery, to get home to bed.

So yes, this was Aboriginal Sovereignty (aka Ab.Sov) Steel's younger brother. Tommyhawk! Same one Widespread had refused to call Duruki. Eight years old now. Fat kid. He was prowling around in a real sneaky way, like one of those feral cats you see on the highways sniffing around for roadkill. Those mangy starved things sitting in the dry yellow grass alongside those lonely multinational mining roads crisscrossing over the top of ancient law tracks throughout the interior of the continent. The broken-down pussycats, stilled, with no energy left to hunt their own tucker, and the only bit of movement coming out of them used to draw hot air into half-collapsed lungs while waiting for all of eternity for a middle-of-the-night miner with heavy earth crushing machinery rip roaring over asphalt to splat roadkill in their face.

Anyhow fat chance of seeing the little fat boy for even the seagulls hovering in the fifty-plus-degree Celsius heat of the night and looking like sky church statues cannot see him either. Tommyhawk had no need to give recognition of his proper name anymore. He was no longer to be called Duruki neither. Yo! Yo! Nor would he answer if you called him by his rightful name. You could yell it. Scream it! You could keep calling his legal name in his face forever, but this would be a waste of time, and as though you were talking to someone else, someone who never existed. This kid was too full of his own ignorance, so nobody knew what to call him anymore, if he did not want anyone in Praiseworthy apart from himself to know his new name, saying – as though he was talking to complete strangers – it was none of their business.

The ancestors would have known his new name, and so would the mangrove spirits that knew all the secrets people hid in the mud. The mistletoe and the mistletoe moths in the mangroves knew what to call him because this was where he was always hanging around, hiding and watching the misery of others, like a little academic who thought he knew it all. But who else was extra human or ghost enough in Praiseworthy to start guessing about some foreign secret code name he was now calling himself, like who would want to be called Ninja Assassin? The only trouble with this new name was that it really did describe this dangerous little schemer, or what his father called a fascist.

So forth and so on let's imagine! Say it was true for there he was, loitering in the mangroves like some innocent kid who acted strangely, playing in the mud, *supposed to be*, hiding for hours in those whale skeletons among the swarming ghost butterflies always heading out to sea to die, and instead of being at school, he was watching his big brother Aboriginal Sovereignty taking forever to commit suicide, who was wanting to die like the butterflies, and wasting his time to get out of this world, and this almost bored Tommyhawk to death. The boy, remember, was totally modern. Fast. He fumed under his breath, *Hey! Dude! Can't you move quicker you dumb cunt?*

If only he could march down into the sea and drown his brother himself. After some time, Ab.Sov eventually took another step, to follow the last one an eternity ago. A dead bullock could have moved quicker thought the assassin boy with eyes lolling in his head, impatiently tapping his hands on the side of his legs in a drum roll of wishing to get it over with, and beseeching go, go, behind clenched teeth, like it was an endless mantra screaming in his head, and as though his brain was processing how to project mental telepathy to get the message out there in the sea for Ab.Sov to move it, for not dying quick enough. The fat ninja was now feeling deranged, his head turned screwy, but he was still clever enough not to be seen lurking in the shadows spun by the evening's rouge-coloured clouds crawling across the moonlight.

One hour, two, three, only time would tell if the spirit of *once upon a time Tommyhawk Steel* would still be standing in this same place, where he was counting an infinity of broken ghost butterflies floating in atmospheric rivers stretching through the universe, for right in this moment, this could only be what the count for freedom felt like for the assassin. He tried to project his total strength out to the sea, like he possessed the capacity to become a laser driller firing holes into that skinny rake black back of his older brother, to shake some life into the slow death march of drowning himself in the whispering screams of the slightest sea ripples on the flat ocean calling him to come.

Tommyhawk, although tiring of this business of his brother's death, kept staring into the bony black back – placed a make-believe stethoscope to his soul, and could not take his eyes off Aboriginal

Sovereignty's agony. The day was still baking hot, standing hour after long tedious hour in the mangroves. This was the build-up. Humidity sky high. Sweat poured from every pore of his skin. This was not the reality of a long-held dream in Tommyhawk's calendar, where things happened in supersonic rapid-fire, bang, bang, bang speed, fast, and faster – that sort of way. What he was looking at was an ordeal that was too slow. It had to end. It was a piss off, of having to wait for someone to die. At this point, fat boy felt his own brain was going to explode from the film rolling in his head, of viewing himself in a high-speed mad crazy dash though a frenzy of shark-infested waters where every crocodile in the sea was racing towards him, to tear him apart. As the film rolled on with a boiling sea atmosphere, he stalled, he did not race in the sea to be blood everywhere, even if he was the only survivor – barely alive in the rolling film. But in any case, he also knew if he had to march out there and drown his brother himself, Ab.Sov – being much stronger and older – might instead turn around and see that his own brother was trying to murder him, and just reach out with his bony arms and drown him.

He became so impatient from glaring into Aboriginal Sovereignty's bony back that his brain only saw a dartboard drilled solid with laser-beamed holes created from his own powerful eyesight. Yet, while his sanity was roped to a pendulum swinging one way into dreams of being elsewhere, it would then swing back, returning to the whale bone city, where Tommyhawk zeroed in on Aboriginal Sovereignty's red gauze Raiders cap that he wore back to front, and that seemed to be staring back to land, as though wanting to return to the beach. The swinging mood made the matter worse – of wanting to dream, but of not really knowing what Aboriginal Sovereignty was doing. Tommyhawk began to believe that Ab.Sov was changing his mind, and would not commit suicide after all, he was making up his mind to live while seeing all of those *Belenois java* white ghost butterflies that had flown out into the sea and were flying back, straight into Tommyhawk's face mistaken for land, and were sitting on his face, his eyes, his mouth, on his hair, as though what was being said in the most delicate way, was that perhaps Aboriginal Sovereignty wanted to continue with his useless life. What then for Tommyhawk's own escape plan? There was no plan B. Only a sea of dead butterflies.

Up to now it was all A-plus, with no minuses in sight for Tommyhawk, the Jedi of Praiseworthy, even if he believed it was not possible to stand around for another minute longer waiting for someone to die. He watched the sun creeping lower into the distant horizon of the sea, and one thing he knew for sure, he was not going to stand there in the mud all night inside the whale ghosts, and risk his own life. These whale bones would come alive in the darkness when the tide was in, this was what the old people always told in the culture stories which had a certain plot line about how bored people wandering around with nothing to do had disappeared during the night, and in the listing of all those stories, they talked about the bored people disappearing from the beach, because those whale spirits, they claimed true God, could kill sheer boredom in one minute flat by slapping you into the mud with those bones which were really weapons for pummelling you around like some piece of fish until you were stone-cold dead. This would be the ultimate death came the lesson, if any of the thousand and one ancestors saw you standing around being bored.

Tommyhawk squirmed to his left, then twisted to the right to stay conscious while trying to remember when was the last time he had remained so still since being cocooned in his mother's womb. *What about my brain*, his truly only asset, now exploding from boredom, the only precious tool he owned, apart from the Australian government for Aborigines-gifted iPad, iPhone and top of the class tech, like the new Mac Pro laptop, awarded to any prized closing-the-gap-with-mainstream Aboriginal student in the tropics by the Minister for governing Aboriginal Affairs. His brain was most ultimately worth saving, far more for sure than being wasted by the ultimate dream death of being pummelled by whale bones. His teachers had already told him thousands of times that only his brain would ensure a highly assessable future, to be able to run like a bat out of hell out of the Praiseworthy haze, to be released from its arms wrapped around him and strangling the life out of him with love. Yet, if he thought straight and a bit calmly about having to witness a slow sea death, keep the faith, everything was going to plan.

While the golden emperor moths stirred from countryside to countryside in the mangroves where the phenomenon of old culture was rising, Tommyhawk was beside himself with a paranoid fear of the growing darkness, and itching now to run down the beach, race out into the shallow sea, to really drown that Aboriginal Sovereignty himself. He knew enough about the slow tides in his total of eight years of life though, to know that if he did run into the water after his brother to try to drown him everything could backfire – he could become the target of maneaters, or his own brother would kill him. In a time when everything was ultimate, accessible, of either to be or not to be, he knew he would be deciding not to save himself, and he could ruin the only thing he had spent days waiting to see happen in order to keep being an alive person. No, this was not what a real ninja would do. He knew precisely what an assassin would do because he had studied ninjas on the internet, but he did not have a great comprehension of what it was like being caught like bait in a butterfly net, one that he had devised and woven for himself.

He just willed the dream to go as planned by repeating his *me first* mantra under his breath, *For God's sake hurry up you idiot, you know you don't deserve to live, you paedophile, just get it over and done with.* It was pretty easy really. *I have seen little kids get it over and done with easier than you*. Slap! Slap! Tommyhawk could feel the dampness of his sweaty body that was now becoming mixed with his own blood from the mosquitoes and sandfly hordes he had killed.

He was used to feeling the sticky blood on his hands even if he was too petrified with fear to leave the whale bone palace in the mangroves. Tommyhawk always saw the job through, just like he always did his homework on time. He was not like other kids, and this was why he thought he deserved to live more than others, because in the new order of the real world he was planning to join, only the fittest were going to survive, and this meant getting rich quick, and moving away from Praiseworthy. The haze was already opening its arms, and he sensed the pending freedom of being released from its grip. He had seen other kids commit suicide, and he always stayed and watched, and had never thought of leaving the scene until he was sure they were not coming back. This was how he knew that the quicker you got the job over and done with, the better it was for everyone. Grieve. Sorrow. Not ninja. He was Aboriginal ninja, not nothing, like government action. He liked neat solutions, of what was complete, bereft of emotion, where you cut the losses of war, or plague, or global warming disasters like the most powerful world leaders – the people without friends, and all for which you grieved not. The world he saw was either for the killing, or being a killer, and saved the untidiness of being hamstrung by the weak, of being only half-baked, of only getting things done half-heartedly.

When crunch came to crunch, solid stuff was what Tommyhawk was made of, even if he had to wait until this day was over, or until the end of the next century, or until the last day of life on Earth, when his body had petrified, turned into a stone that would still sit and wait. His mind was now unshakable about such thoughts as could be called up from the click of the fingers, where panicking fear could be nullified and transformed into unexplainable fearlessness. He stood still, in his tidy way of not moving a muscle, his tendency to be tidier than anyone else in the world, while witnessing the action of his set plan, the necessary execution of his brother.

All the mosquitoes in a coastline full of mangrove swamps were driven into whale bone city by the smell of fat boy's blood, and their whining hurried through the muddy landscape to land on his skin. He was covered with thousands of stinging probosces punching his skin, making a feast of his blood, but this was nothing, only his stillness reigned now, because this was what a real assassin would be. A proper ninja. Someone who held the line.

There was no more room for thinking about giving up like a lesser human being, and believing failure was okay. No. The plan was the plan. Aboriginal Sovereignty would actually finish the job off himself as he was just about up to his neck out there in the sea. He was not coming back. Yet Tommyhawk did not turn his back and go home to bed before the job was completed, because he was now steadfast, transformed, had become rock. Aboriginal Sovereignty would die by the weight of this rock tying itself to his feet. Only a distant echo, repeatedly whingeing in the back of Tommyhawk's head, kept going on about what if Ab.Sov did not die this time – *Will you do all this again?* Gee! *That's going to be difficult to have to do it again,* and what would he do if his own life was over once and for all *because you can't get him to die.* No one in their right mind could go through torture like that again. When you decide to kill your brother, then everything has to go according to the plan. There could only be one plan, not two, not three, or countless times to get a plan perfected, to get rid of a cunt. So, the plump little boy waited and felt that he was becoming the bones of whales in the mud of the mangrove forest where mosquitoes lived and feasted on a rock.

4

Bad history! Beware of such history! Everything had a bit of bad history making trouble, where the corduroy lines built by the ages of one's humanity had not realigned, and stayed alienated, like when the old memory people come calling through trees grating in the wind, and when suddenly, the singularity of the cacophony ringing in the bush alive with the sounds of birds, crickets, frogs, suddenly froze, and the *campana* turns, and rings in another direction.

What are you, gossiping woman? Aboriginal Sovereignty had tried to ignore the ravings of Tommyhawk whispering in his ear about all the paedophiles living in Praiseworthy. *No, bro, they are everywhere!* All sexual depravers were out to get him. He wondered how a kid got perverted stuff like that in his head. Aboriginal Sovereignty had wanted him to stop. Stop now. *He is a literal pest, Dad, who should be told straight, to shut the fuck up.* But Tommyhawk was on fire. He raged while following Aboriginal Sovereignty around like a puppy dog. The little boy demanded to know the truth about whether his brother was one of those dirty men, or if their father was one, and if the whole community of old men were *them* paedophiles. *Who? The ancients?* The boy did not hear, but kept naming, and renaming those he suspected, the husbands, the big boys, the list growing longer by the day. *Were they, were they?* Ab.Sov thought Tommyhawk must have named every man in Praiseworthy a paedophile, and yet the boy persisted, he found more and more men to accuse of the most hideous crime against children. *This is what the government is saying. Not me saying it. It was all in the newspapers. I even know the hotline. We got it at school. The number is stuck on the wall. They told us who to call if we are frighten of any man.*

I reckon you are one of those paedophiles. You are? Your girlfriend is underage? She still goes to school. The police will be coming for you, you know?

Where did he get shit in his head? Aboriginal Sovereignty thought that the distorted contents of Tommyhawk's head were self-combusting over the vicinity of his own saneness. *Dad! Dad! You got to get that stupid kid to the hospital. Get his head examined.* The boy felt the rush of his own thoughts spinning on hot coals. *Go on. Dad. Give it to him with both barrels. Go on. Show him who is needing to see a doctor.* Tommyhawk's blood boiled whenever he heard his older brother pimping on him to their father, with the sheer audacity of a paedophile brother thinking he needed a doctor. *Man! It is you who is sick.* Rah! Rah! Rah! When it got to talking about being sick in the head, Tommyhawk neither knew what was in line or out of line anymore, never knew when to stop, just to shut up his face. He kept on taunting, and grabbing half-baked one-liners about living with half live hot ash, the half firestorm dirty stick men were pelting through his brains. *Filthy penises. Stick it anywhere. Into little girls. Sicko.* Tommyhawk could rant on for hours when he was having a fit about the invisible world of paedophilia operating in Praiseworthy.

Aboriginal Sovereignty grew increasingly intolerant of his younger brother and told him to stop at once, said he knew what he was on about, *end it now brother or I will shut you up for good*, but Tommyhawk was gone in his mind, he was full bore, and however his brain worked, it never knew when enough was enough. *You are a sinner person.* He always tipped things over the edge. Ab.Sov warned Tommyhawk a thousand times about going into the no-go zone with him. Nothing would stop him though. *You are sick. Chasing after little girls. Cradle snatcher. How old is she? Mum, how old is that Peter's girl? You know. MARJORIE whatever?*

Dance screamed, *Shut up.*

No, Tommyhawk yelled.

It is none of your business. Leave your brother alone.

Ab.Sov gripped his brother's arm for a moment – that was all it took, then wham, Tommyhawk bit his brother's arm, broke free and was straight out the front door and down the road as fast as those solid little legs would carry him. But all was not lost, Tommyhawk had found the crack to reach through, and he dragged out the map in his mind with the road out of Praiseworthy. He had nailed it. Knew how to get his brother big time. He ran down to his whale spirit in the mangroves, while convincing himself of what he had to do next, to report Aboriginal Sovereignty to the police. He was going to have him arrested and locked away. The power of knowing what he could do to fix his brother for good was almost busting his brain, and forcing him to stop for a minute, to take stock of the situation. *I am going to bust up this family*. He felt an overwhelming sense of relief, of having crossed a threshold of taboo by cancelling it out with another taboo, by actually articulating what needed to happen. He had found the solution to the main obstacles threatening him, which was in the way he saw it, his own life. The opening in this little boy's mind was an enormous revelation.

5

Tommyhawk was right over the edge now. Right over. Yet, even this was not as far as he could go. The little squirt relished the fact that he was intruding into his brother's privacy, making this space his own. His greatest thrill was to push the buttons in his brother's mind that hard, that his life would become a battlefield for the doomed, because Tommyhawk was only after one thing, complete control. The battle escalated. It became an ongoing fight for superiority, although with Tommyhawk, it was a fight to the death, the winner takes all. He wanted nothing less than ownership over his brother's life, where he would decide if his older brother lived, or died. Aboriginal Sovereignty threatened to bash him every time he mentioned white police, and

Tommyhawk inhaled his brother's fear, grew stronger on it, while he constantly used his time in the family home for blowing the hex words *white police* over his hand, and into the air, which was exactly like casting a spell over Aboriginal Sovereignty, who swore that he would kill Tommyhawk for saying that he was going to report him and his parents to the police.

The question of being bashed or not, did not march fright into Tommyhawk's brain to say, *you had better be scared out of your life.* The kid had threats galore constantly shuffling up and down in his brain. Threats only produced some brand-new game-changer plan for this eight-year-old superhero feasting on fear. He was pumping on steroids, fuelling the head machinery and making another and another new idea stick on the wall of his brain. These were the kind of ideas he got off on for festering an unshakable mountain of paranoid fear in believing that his so-called parents were actually abusive kidnappers, and were controlling some kind of hydraulic influencing system that kidnappers build into a kid's brain to brainwash them, to make them too stupid to remember anything. But the thing was, he did remember, he had broken adult power. He knew them for what they were, unloving, just how the white people were saying, that Aboriginal parents were not capable of loving their children. Tommyhawk felt the cold shivers running through his blood every time he thought of his despised, depraved, meaningless life that had no end because he was living with these strangers who kept on saying they were his parents, who were working for a gang of paedophiles from the city who did things like kidnap kids, hide them away, stash them somewhere in a storehouse, like this place where the police would not bother looking, where you could not see anything anyhow, hidden in the haze.

It was no wonder he felt like an alien. In a way, it was easy to figure out the scenario, since anyone could see that he bore no physical resemblance to these sinew and bone strangers who acted as though they were his actual parents. He looked like well-fed white Australians. So, he was dumped then. Kidnapped by a paedophile ring. He had to be saved from people claiming to be his parents who were drugging his meals so he could not think fast enough to save himself from being attacked. Tommyhawk looked at these people whoever they were, who had not even given him a proper home, and the educational stuff required to make a rich modern hero, or a future astronaut destined to explore space to find new super worlds when this one goes belly up, or for becoming any kind of educated president who was not a moron to care for the new world.

Actually, Tommyhawk had madly texted thanks of considerable gratefulness to the Australian government lady for giving him an iPad and his pile of other Apple things so he could protect himself, for giving him Apple technology – the best money could buy. Even a little boy like Tommyhawk, who lived on one of the poorest remote communities in the country, knew what stuff was worth. His feelings of fearfulness morphed into yearning, and before too long he absolutely believed that Aboriginal Sovereignty was more than a paedophile, and not because he had done time in gaol for being one. Tommyhawk had hotmailed the police about how Aboriginal Sovereignty was raping an underage girl. If the police had arrested him, then he must be one. All this, the newer reasons, the newer truths, about why Tommyhawk believed that he was better than Aboriginal Sovereignty, who was always telling him, *It was not going to happen, bro. You will never be better than me.*

6

Tommyhawk Steel kept the big secret locked in his X-ray brain, about how he was going to supersonically shoot himself faster than sound out of Praiseworthy. Nobody would stop him. He would be speeding away that fast, and at that much top speed, he would be like a shooting star inferno propelled twenty times faster than the speed of sound from all the paedophilia infestation he figured surrounded him. Yes, you better believe it, how he was going to be adopted by the number one mother star ship, the Commonwealth Government of Australia. This was the dream, the mission of removing himself from danger. Anyone could see it themselves, how his parents were dangerous, but he saw that the white schoolteachers were dangerous too for ignoring paedophile parents, and this made it hard to say which way a kid like Tommyhawk would aim his wafted brain when the enemy loomed everywhere, and any adult could easily harm him.

He had all the proof in the world that he was living in a dangerous environment if the government of the day was saying *watch out you kids on Aboriginal communities, you is surrounded by infestations of paedophilia*. He packed a bag, was ready to leave instantly, but it was taking ages of waiting for the army that was supposed to have been sent into Aboriginal communities by the government to examine children to see whether they were being abused. He had heard this on the news. The army was coming, and he was eagerly waiting for the war to begin when the trucks loaded with armed soldiers rolled into Praiseworthy to kill paedophiles – shoot them dead, imprison the parents, assassinate or fireball them out of their hiding places, but you know what happened, all the talk of government salvation failed to arrive, and he could see for himself that he was not being saved.

Tommyhawk tried to tell himself not to worry about being a sitting duck, even though the most powerful voice in Australia, the actual federal government, was telling him that he was supposed to be saved from being exposed to a dangerous world. You know, he reasoned, maybe he would survive all that.

Yet, there was too much doubt spinning in the war cabinet of his grey cells, and Tommyhawk knew that he had only been kidding himself, the government of the country knew better than some little kid whether he was safe or not. How existentially, the fog of danger could grow mountainous, even bigger than the bogeyman, and smarter than all baddies combined, but what Tommyhawk was dealing with was invisible, the Australian government did not tell you how to feel when the virus was everywhere and looked the same as everything else, and you could not tell what a paedophile looked like.

He was so desperate to save himself in the national outrage about infestations of paedophiles on Aboriginal communities, that he became obsessive about listening to the national ABC news by stopping whatever he was doing just to hear what was being said about how dangerous it was for Aboriginal children living with paedophiles. He became such a good reader of the news in order to save himself, that he flew to the top of his English class in the school. He craved more news items to read on the internet, just to stay tuned in to the multiple antennae of the information order chatting about Aboriginal children unloved by their parents, and he was jabbing like a ninja for a little bit of this info, and a little bit of that info about the major cartoon heroes on Earth, just to learn how to defend himself. Over many miserable months of wondering whether he was going to be killed by a ring of perverts, he listened to whatever news he could find on his iPad to broaden his thinking about what the brainy superior white people were saying all over the country about why Aboriginal parents did not know how to love their children, like a bedside nursery rhyme. It was like his fairytale horror story, where the word paedophilia laced this and that on the radio talkback shows that rolled on through the many hundreds of times he listened in bed late at night, when unable to sleep past one, two, three, four a.m., until the crack of dawn, because he was too frightened to sleep. But, somehow, in all the actual invisibleness of what was preying on his short life, he had to know what he was dealing with, and what he had to look out for. Instead of it being everything to be afraid of, he had to know precisely what could send him into an immediate panic attack from every pregnant pause, which could be the silence shouting from the sneaky movements through the house in the endless dead of night, or just rusted tin pausing as it cooled from the heat, or the roof creaking, or the endless rustling leaves travelling throughout the cemetery. Any of these indistinguishable sounds could send him off his head through the belief that someone was coming for him as he lay prone in his bed, too petrified to move, too frightened to open his eyes, but he could not tell anyone any of this, or explain what was going through his mind.

Tommyhawk was a wreck in the end. Where could you find the truth? He began to believe that the white people were hiding something from him. They were not even telling him how to identify the Aboriginal people they were talking about who were going to harm him. When. How. Identification. He required names like you see in any TV detective program, and yet, in real life, no one said who they were. How could he tell who to look out for? He felt totally alone, like the orphan he believed himself to be, who did not belong in the world of Aboriginal Sovereignty who was loved by everyone in Praiseworthy, and it was a fact, they only saw themselves in Aboriginal Sovereignty. His wrung-out mind, now suffering long-term sleep deprivation, rattled with his totally angst loathing of whatever genes of humanity he carried in his blood. How could he take it out of his blood? How to drain himself of inferiority? Even if he was not kidnapped and adopted to idiots, it did not leave him any less full of hatred for the many voices jammed in his brain loudspeakering pitch messages to the idiocy that he was nothing, never comprehended what schoolteachers taught, just as nothing would register in an idiot's mind when the army spokespeople talked to his class about stranger danger. Then, a superhero came along – changed the power plug, and before flying off, said those voices he kept in the brain box were wrong. This was when the one neon light idea again lit up in his head: *Get out of Praiseworthy for good in order to save yourself.*

Now, the only thing he really had on his mind, was how not to die? So, he began a life of never being fully awake. In class, looking as though he was still dreaming, his teachers whispered to each other, and blamed his parents for not getting him to bed on time, so he could come to school fully awake. Yet, this near zero-functioning brain managed to excel at top of the class, even if he was just daydreaming about life's riddles, of leaving his kind, of being elsewhere, but not by committing suicide like the kids who were killing themselves. He thought long and hard about what to do if someone made him want to kill himself, how he would defend himself, if he was ninja – game enough to kill an attacker – and if he could stop himself from killing once he got started, and while the imaginings lingered, of how he would kill himself like the other children, of what it felt like to be walking like a zombie through the air with your feet above the ground, until he found a way of committing suicide.

Tommyhawk felt that he did not really feel strong enough about killing himself and becoming another suicide statistic. He saw plenty of faces in his dreams, and had heard the whisperings and wondering about who would go next, and how they would go away. This was how the boy became obsessed with ways of committing suicide, doing all he could to worm his way into the lives of his schoolmates while quietly watching signs of their weaknesses, those he thought might commit suicide, go all the way, until he hit on what pushed them in the end – humiliation, the slightest mishap, a word out of place, a betrayal of their innermost shame. It was revelatory to Tommyhawk, and he had felt like a feather breaking a camel's back, for now he knew exactly when some kid had been pushed too far and their hastiness to be off. To just do it, so very quickly, he followed in the shadows of the night to see how dying was actually done, to know the mechanics of suicide.

Now, while Tommyhawk was plotting how to fly the coup from Praiseworthy, he hatched many plans, each as bright as the previous idea of ascending like a lark, and flying amidst the vastness of possibility. This was the plan, he would tell himself some thousand times a day, and even while pure reason, rational thought, whispered this was not going to work, he would argue back with his stupid common sense, fight it off, expelling it, zap, zap from his brain, *You don't tell me what to do. You and you are not needed here.*

Mostly, they were just thoughts, eventually petering out, the more he realised that nothing was going to work fast enough to get him out of the place, and that he would rather leave in a Qantas flight, like a TV advertisement, than run away into the bush like a feral cat. He had to have a better plan, and the plans grew large and became more extraordinary in how he imagined a way of covering a few thousand kilometres in five or ten minutes to reach the most heavenly palace for a child to live, and the more complex these plans became, the more desperate he felt urged to go.

You could say his mind had already left, and he only lived in daydreams, which is okay, but carrying your body around in the imagination was a true burden that always ended up with his being left behind like some want-a-be, and living in fear of becoming a copycat dirty paedophile like his brother, Aboriginal Sovereignty. Now, whenever he saw his brother, he thought this too could happen to him, as a trajectory which would need to be destroyed, by blowing up any road laden with paedophile poison like a bait in the path leading to his destiny of eventually becoming an all-Australian superhero, long gone from kryptonite paedophile places. He surrounded himself with another thought-bubble survival hex: *I am better than you.*

In the blue-sky imaginary of what the capital of Australia looked like in Tommyhawk's mind, nothing was hazy at all. He had vividly conjured his own storybook where he was the main feature on every page, a child with a happy face living thousands of kilometres away in an outer-space world called Canberra. He saw only a golden goose in the arms of the outer-space child of this super planet that was entirely made of money. Nothing in this world grounded him in the reality of Praiseworthy, for in his future world, it was the exact opposite to any place where poor people lived. Parliament House had the best that money could buy.

Who said money does not grow on trees? Not Tommyhawk. In his storybook, he saw the palace of government surrounded by gardens that extended to every horizon, and he saw with his own eyes the millions of golden leaves falling off trees, so much gold it was just left lying on the ground. There were no camp dogs at Parliament House. No gonorrhoea-tail feral donkeys. No cemeteries, because he heard that Canberra politicians never died. There were no feral cats screaming all night long on a rusty tin roof and vomiting over your paradise. Or frogs. Or a toad wherever you walked. Lizards. Saltwater crocodiles coming up. Snakes. Sharks. Fish. In fact, in his storybook, there was no room for wildlife in paradise, only domestic pets that were not like real dogs, just a poodle here or there that ate money with the politician families, and it must taste good, like drinking liquid gold instead of a plastic bottle filled with creek water.

All this translucency radiating the brightest light on Tommyhawk's perfected world, was like a comfort blanket perpetually skidding over the hazy reality of Praiseworthy. His life stopped, he was now paused, existing only through a mind fast losing control of the off switch to his laser-sharp imagination continually pumping spotlighting beams at warp speed across far too much reality.

Tommyhawk could not stop himself from ventriloquising a popular shock jock's whingeing from his cripple mind on talkback radio, kept on repeat cycle on the boy's iPad for company throughout the night. The little boy too had become a voice of discontent slapping life open or shut like a venetian blind. He was piecing the whole story together, proclaiming his life was a waste of time, and it was often enough for Tommyhawk to cry himself into a stupor after flying into a lonely tantrum over his desperation to immediately start living happily ever after in the capital of Australia. He cried in frustration about the forthcoming mothership of Parliament House that still had not arrived, not giving what he wished for, and then he wished harder that he would be found by the government, so he could become a super breezy rich kid who never had to think this much about reality again.

Sometimes in the mind of the whale skeleton that could wait forever, Tommyhawk reasoned that perhaps the big government people in Canberra were too busy trying to make more money from Aboriginal land to be bothered to come and save him from the paedophiles they kept saying plagued Aboriginal communities. Or, perhaps Parliament House was getting ready to fire at all the baddies with the best superheroes in the world, like ninja warriors ready to fight off anything, even UFOs from outer space. He calculated the cost of all these wars with the baddies, the cost of building the fancy Parliament House where they could plan how to fight the bad people, and the cost of guarding billions stacked to the ceiling from any bad people stealing it, perhaps trillions of dollars. Then, why would the government save him, how would they find him amongst all the Aboriginal children they wanted to save in Australia? But his real family was the Government of Australia, they had to single him out as its first son, and come and find him.

The red fog night searched around town again for the broken-hearted children, those like Aboriginal Sovereignty Steel who felt he could not live when he found out that his girl, the only one for him ever, actually his wife now, had been taken into institutional care by the government of Canberra, and sent away.

You will never see her again he had been told by the police.

Don't you go causing trouble.

You caused enough shame already.

She is not for you.

You will be going away for gaol.

This is Australia law, man.

Everyone had told him that.

He thought life had finished for him.

He had already died.

7

The country's old world reviewed Tommyhawk's plagued young mind, his shifting from ancient to modern, his questioning of realities, the what-ifs and what was really true, his becoming more anxious about the what if of everything going wrong. This was plan A. There was no plan B. Cool heads reigned, but Tommyhawk was too busy thinking about what if his most important plan by far, a potentially pivotal life-changing moment of time for himself, turned AWOL.

What if Aboriginal Sovereignty changed his mind and did not commit suicide? Nothing was a cinch in a world where hardly anything went right. So! Worry! Fret! Worry some more! The little boy kept driving his feet harder into the sand, and consoling himself that they, the government, said he could have something better. *They said all Aboriginal children deserve something better than this. Well! They owe me. And I will get them too if he comes back in.*

Well! Poor little Tommyhawk had mountain ranges of disappointments traversing the geography of his brain, and he was right up there on the highest precipice, dangling from a thread over the jagged edges of the hard rock face with a thousand-metre drop to where Aboriginal Sovereignty was standing in the distance, chest-deep, and not moving.

Look! He was just standing there looking out to sea. There was a red fog that seemed to be trying to lift him out of the water. This did not matter to Tommyhawk. He wanted to know what was stopping his brother, what was he thinking, hadn't he decided to end it all. *Why doesn't he keep his word? You can't even trust him.*

It was not that Tommyhawk cared about what his brother thought about drowning himself because *they, the government,* continued spilling their tidal-wave thoughts through his brain, and he was riding these waves straight to the fairy world of Parliament House, and that was all that mattered. He would never be lonely again while living with smart government people, who he reckoned were right of the moment, and at this moment, he only wished the government's space base would create a freak wave in the Arafura Sea that would whip right around to the coast of Praiseworthy, and wipe Aboriginal Sovereignty straight off his feet, throw him far out to sea, so he would not be able to come back. At this moment, he needed the government to feel sorry for making him wait this long, to conjure their powers of persuasion to order his brother to commit suicide, get it over and done with, so his little brother could have a better life. There was no end to the anxiety fiddling in the child's mind, and palatial whiteness was slipping out of sight, becoming more difficult to locate among those colossal mountain ranges stuffed into his brain – all because of his brother. There was not much shaping his thinking, it was just gossamer, lighter than smoke, hardly weighing anything at all, hard to balance, even by the haze ancestor. Tommyhawk ended up believing in the worst, that the plan had failed, and instead of suicide, Aboriginal Sovereignty would live, and his own life would become impossible.

Ab.Sov, go on. You gotta commit suicide so I can get out of here.

But the golden lady was still not answering his text messages, about how he wanted to become a ward of the state so he could live with her forever, like a prince in Parliament House.

8

Whenever Tommyhawk stood in the last standing skeleton in the whale's graveyard, the calmness of the skeleton resting in perpetuity among the mangrove ancestors would claim his mind. Tommyhawk knew how it felt to have been the whale, and he could feel its enormous strength, its warmth, and he brought it to life again through memories of its life in the ocean.

He would see its journeys in the world's oceans of currents, long flowing rivers under the sea, and the times when the whale swam through mighty storms rolling across the waves. He felt the victory of the many whale wars the creature had fought across the oceans. He experiences riding the storm waves that reach far into the skies, and the journeys far back in time, the dangerous and perilous seas.

Tommyhawk thinks he is the killer whale's ghost. He is the whale's dreaming. A whale leader. An inheritor. Its thought. The boy thinks the law belongs to him. That he is dangerous. When he becomes the whale's ghost, he believes that no one would recognise how the whale had become him, since all that people would see were its bones. Only the spirit ancestors living among the mangroves see, like the emperor moths, the *Syntherata janetta* from the Bombycoid family of Saturniidae encircling the whale. These moths seemed attracted to its bones, flying around the skeleton, thousands fluttering in the humidity, and crushing inwards as they find places to land. The old people still told stories about the Rainbow Serpent, and how the whale skeleton came from a pod of pilot whales tossed up by king waves in the era of colliding cyclones on the shores of Praiseworthy.

In the driest corners of Praiseworthy, the tight-lipped religious oracles sat on high and spoke of these important matters about the Earth. They were generally having a few conversations up there about prolonged droughts in the global era of greenhouse gas emissions, because being surrounded by so much tinderbox-dry bush did not feel like the old days of the last Ice Age when their ancestors lived in a rainforest right where Praiseworthy stood in this now parched environment.

In these continuing conversations lasting the lifetime of many generations of their people, there were the epics about the sea cooling the skin of whales, and the minds of the oracles turned once again, to throw new light on the old mystery of the beaching whales. A strainer shook the knowledge, found grains of new reason explaining why they had neglected the whale skeleton for so long, and yet, it was still sitting intact down in the mangroves like it was alive. Why had it not fallen apart and disintegrated? Someone said it looked as though it was waiting for something to happen.

The new light emerged through the leak that spread through the haze about why the skeleton had not broken apart. This came from one of those oracles who was heard talking in his sleep by his wife. A new story began travelling at lightning speed through every street, and went in and out of every home about why the whale was thrown up like vomit by the sea in a string of old tsunamis that had emptied the ocean's stomach down on the beach with piles of sand, mountains of dead fish, crabs, coconuts and the coconut trees as well. There was whale blubber. Olden-time boats. All of mankind's shitty rubbish, and even now, with the stench rising after storms became too much, the local council would take the big CAT, the Caterpillar D Dozer down onto the beach and doze the stench back into the sea. Yet, the whale graveyard survived desecration, and even though it was clearly seen by the up-and-coming assimilationists as a pure eyesore, no one had the heart to have it destroyed. Others said it never existed in their sight anyhow, so it continued to stand like a monument while the mangrove forest ancestors, growing rich from capturing carbon dioxide from the atmosphere, were quickly expanding through, around and beyond it. The oracles claimed the erect whale skeleton was waiting, perhaps since the last Ice Age, waiting for a time in the twenty-first century to bury its huge spirit into a child's mind.

9

There was only one person who claimed the miracle of realising why the whales had beached, and that was Dance Steel, the mother, when she had been heavily pregnant with Tommyhawk, her second child. The oracles of time had always spoken of the whales as a warning of the coming drought, but Dance said she remembered hearing the sounds of a roaring sea every night while she was carrying Tommyhawk, and she claimed that the whales were calling into the past, and talking to Tommyhawk even before he was born.

Although Dance claimed that she had no idea what the whales were talking about to Tommyhawk either before or after he was born, she said she felt the sea was on fire, and through her dreams, she saw fish throwing themselves out of the sea. Her dreams had been endless, like love letters to the soul of Praiseworthy, and not only that, she flatly refused to budge on what she believed had spoken to her in these dreams. She would keep seeing dead trevally lying in heaps up and down the beach. The oracles explained with much pride of heart that what she actually saw were the marvellous capacities of the powerful CAT bulldozing detritus which made the machinery worth the big-bucks acquisition that Ice Pick had insisted the council buy for this specific task. It was only the dozer working in the moonlight, heaping dead fish, and she was remembering a part of the story about what happened every year in the new era of super cyclones with king waves, and sixty thousand lightning-strike storms that brought the high tides too. Dance disagreed. She could not remember seeing a bulldozer in her dreams doing the job of hundreds of men, by scraping the beach clean of dead fish, and ploughing every single one back into the sea.

Dance hardly believed a word anyone else said in those days, and instead, went rushing down to the beach screaming in her mighty voice capable of echoing far away that she had just seen the end of the world. It was hard to tell whether Dance needed to be restrained from having any close contact with the children of Praiseworthy at that time, or even with the child she was carrying, but then, when you thought more about what she was nutting on about, she had talked about hearing the bones of those whales creaking whenever she passed the whale cemetery as though they were coming back to life again. She said they were coming alive, and had imagined how they would thrash about one day while shifting sand with slow movements of their bodies, and while storms of butterflies flew up from the mangroves to land on the whale bones, helping to push the sand-buried creatures back to sea.

Death finishes up, turned to the past, of what was, that could never be restored. This was what had happened over time when the whales and the people of Praiseworthy never spoke to one another anymore. Nothing existed between people and whales again, and for Dance, lost alone in her dreams of swimming with whales that no longer recognised the voice of a human calling to them, it had triggered a long and terrifying labour through her belief that the whales had come for her baby, and this fuelled her fear that the baby had become a whale, and the birth would kill her.

Dance collapsed, and she became almost demented with the baby kicking and struggling inside her, but refusing to be born. She believed that the baby would die too, after three days had passed before Tommyhawk was born. The baby that Dance believed had been taken from her she said could be traced to man-made global warming, of not knowing how to talk and walk with the planet, but she gets things wrong. Misjudges. Misconstrues. Happened all the time. This was the reason why there were legal restraining orders to stop her entering Praiseworthy these days, keeping her down at the cemetery. So instead of getting it right, she was half right. Right now, it was Aboriginal Sovereignty who was taking a walk through the sea, and as casually, Tommyhawk had thought, as though he was catching a bus out of the place.

10

There were dense clouds of mosquitoes swollen with the blood of the people of Praiseworthy rising up from that long lonely mangrove coastland. The swarms hovered for a moment above the whale bones before joining en masse at whistlestop speed to fly to sea, to where Aboriginal Sovereignty was floating away. You could hear the colossal swarm cloud charging through town to gorge on human blood, before returning momentarily to hover over the whale cemetery, as though seeking an explanation about what was going on, then returning to the ocean in a futile attempt to save Aboriginal Sovereignty. This cycle would be repeated many times in the night of the ancestral world bringing Aboriginal Sovereignty inside the realm of its knowledge.

The incoming tide laps around Tommyhawk's knees. His soul cries for the unreachable distances from deep inside himself: *It should have been me.* But, his brain craves only exciting things, of far more exciting times ahead for himself, all of which lay elsewhere. But where was this dream? Was it disappearing, becoming too hard to grasp, was Tommyhawk losing sight of the dream? How many more times would he have to keep reminding himself that his future was elsewhere, and he was that close to it? *That really, I am the one who should be leaving first.* Tommyhawk felt like screaming out to Aboriginal Sovereignty who was so far away now, to stop impinging on his well-thought-out dream of the fate of two brothers, where one dies and one lives.

He was stealing the show of the person who had dreamt about escaping from Praiseworthy first. *It wasn't fair. It was really unfair. I wanted to go first.*

But, each time, just as he wanted to run down the beach after his brother and maybe try and save him, Tommyhawk mentally kicked his silly little soul for thinking that the sea had more treasure in it than the government in Canberra, and he again inscribed in the biography he was writing about himself in his head, that Aboriginal Sovereignty was just killing himself, he was not really leaving. *He's just the gutless one that's all.* Tommyhawk tried to keep this point firm in his mind. He had to remember that he was the one who always wanted to get out of Praiseworthy – it was his total dream, not his brother's. So why ruin his own chances by intervening with someone else's pre-determined fate? If he saved his brother then he may never get a chance to leave. It was the only thing that Tommyhawk could not understand, why his brother never hated his useless parents enough to leave them, like he did. Why he loved fools? This would remain a mystery to him. Ab.Sov had just never seen it. He never wanted to go anywhere. Never thought of it. Never thought of upsetting the status quo.

Brainless Sov. Why should he be leaving first – just like that, and not even asking Tommyhawk whether he minded or not? So little Tommyhawk punched himself in the face, to punish himself for having such thoughts. *Let him go. He was only killing himself.* Who was a younger brother anyhow? He was not his brother's keeper – was he? It was not up to him to intervene, and make himself look stupid to be out there in the sea swimming like a half-drowned rat. A killer whale would not be calling out to someone to get out of the water while it was making a kill. A killer whale would put himself in the top position. Be an alpha killer. He even thought that he heard Aboriginal Sovereignty telling him – like usual, to stop thinking like a little boy. *All you ever do is think. That's the main problem with you. Always. Your brains will burst eventually. Go home. Get some sleep.* Yes. Ab.Sov would want that. *Cheat his death. Wouldn't he?*

Jellyfish swirl by, and run in circles. Long blades of seagrass float on top of the water. The sandflies of the early hours land on Tommyhawk's skin and nip his back, but he does not feel pain when he is taking the part of the killer whale with its mouth open wide.

What's young Tommyhawk doing over there in the mourning sea? A gathering of seagulls fly in from the sea, and hover over the whale cemetery. One by one, the birds begin to flit, glide across the ghostly presence of the mighty ancestors, and dive low enough to catch a glimpse of the boy with the serious face caught by moonlight. He is watching what they were also watching, then the squadron fly back and forth challenging the boy with fierce eyes, and fly back, circling the big brother moving away, out in the shallow sea.

Look! Look! He had got the suiciding brother believing he was only watching someone fishing over the waves, further out in the ocean while the sky grew louder with bird cries. It was bedlam in the skies with birds calling over one another, their cabal of thousands piercing the howl of the wind buffeting their bird feathers, but such spectacles were ignored by Aboriginal Sovereignty in the sea below. His red-and-white cap sits low on his head, almost covering his eyes, covering his thoughts, covering where he is looking, or what he is looking at. A seagull flies closer. It sees that the boy believes he is in perfect incognito, hidden below the cap's centrepiece of a finely embroidered head of a massive shark, and he is not moving a muscle because he thinks that no one will think he was trying to kill himself. The only movement radiating oddly in the stiff breeze that the bird feels, is the speed of his ticking heart and blood pumping around his body.

That kid Tommyhawk was acting like a piece of stone, his bones rigid, glued to the spot. Not even a brain cell moved with a piece of his thought. His conscience was a void, just an empty space. Nothing in the grey matter was saying, *go save your brother*, or what was totally wrong about watching your brother taking his life. Absolutely! No fricken worries. Tommyhawk just looked as though he was watching some casual act of providence happening in the surf. There was no need to prevent his older brother from further disappearing from sight and never coming back. All he believed was that both he and Aboriginal Sovereignty were doing the right thing about their lives, which meant saying to himself that if anyone wanted to go and kill himself, then let that person go ahead and do it. What his older brother did with his life was none of his business. Aboriginal Sovereignty could look after himself.

There was no denying the fact that sometimes, Tommyhawk felt obliged to un-suppress some of the weaker arguments that barged through his betwixt and between conscience when it showed up in his brain. He was not inhuman. He just knew how to keep a lid on berserk emotion playing tennis with his soul, bashing the ball at some rare spontaneity of guilt frog-leaping out of its house, to force him to feel obligated, to consider the meaning of family relationships, releasing a fusillade of more and more guilt asking – *But isn't he – I mean – isn't Aboriginal Sovereignty your brother? Shouldn't you care about what happens to him?* Whack! Whack! Tommyhawk knew that you had to whack that idea out of your brain if you wanted to rule the cruel world. Tommyhawk was good. One hundred per cent. He knew how to respond to any beckoning guilt screwballing him with its love of failure with a big flat *no*. He had always been quicker to quip off the mark than any procrastinating conscience: *Couldn't Aboriginal Sovereignty take care of himself? No! It didn't look like it.*

You cannot lie about a death wish. Tommyhawk just did not feel as though he should be the one to have to intervene when he saw other kids taking their lives by doing the right thing. Enough! He knew that he was not the son of God. Far from it. He was doing the right thing by looking after himself. He could think of plenty of reasons why he did not want to run home to tell on Aboriginal Sovereignty, and who would he be doing the telling to in any case? He just did not feel like it. This was not his fault. On the contrary, Tommyhawk felt vindicated: he just had to keep on reminding himself it was for the best. Both their lives were on a knife edge, and his depended on not taking his eyes off the scene unfolding on the beach where his brother was now so far away nothing could be done, and all good so far, because he had not returned.

11

The incoming tide had submerged the whale cemetery, and fish swam through the mangroves, the blood-bloated mosquito horde still flew and attacked, but Tommyhawk was on the cusp of success, his wildest dreams were coming true, so he kept his statue-like pose, while continuing his vacant staring over the water.

Yes, yes, the ordeal of Aboriginal Sovereignty dying was almost over. Aboriginal Sovereignty was finishing up after it had taken an eternity for him to find his way out of Praiseworthy for good.

Tommyhawk found himself caught half-submerged in the incoming tide, but he kept calm by reminding himself to keep standing very still now – it would not take much longer for the golden hour, the tide would turn, don't spoil the moment just in case of a dead person coming back to life again. You could not depend on fate which was a slippery beast that could change its mind very quickly, even when a different outcome would seem completely impossible.

Let's say that Aboriginal Sovereignty might have a change of heart. He might panic on his drowning breath and swim back. He was a good swimmer, the best, he could do that. And what if he turned back, and actually saw that his brother was just standing around like the shifty little creep he was, watching him drown himself? Well! Tommyhawk knew exactly what would happen to him. He would be dead meat if his brother discovered him spying on his botched suicide, and feeling peeved by his weak as piss effort to kill himself. This began a whole new scenario unlocking in Tommyhawk's meltdown brain of dreading how all hell was breaking loose, and he could feel his mind racing off and telling his body to run away, or be the dead one instead of his brother.

But what could be worse than getting yourself killed? Tommyhawk already felt fish-dead, dead enough, completely dead from his full-time exhausted effort of keeping himself alive. These were his multiple-choice answers to questions that pinged back and forth over the brain waves in racist Twitter rant about was it worth it, if you is black and all that, if it had to be so hard, if you is black, was it worth it to keep on being alive in a world owned by whites? Yet even ranting racism could not penetrate Tommyhawk's head, because he knew that he would rather die if he had to wait one more time. He could not even begin to imagine what it would be like to have to stand around being as bored to death again, with having to witness another of Aboriginal Sovereignty's suicide attempts. What if, after all this and half-drowning himself with the flooding inward tide and all the other tides that had drowned his brain, what if he changes his mind again, if he had to say again, *Your useless life was not worth living. Be dead. You must be dead. I am so over you, you – paedophile.*

And yet, this eight-year-old kid now eating a bag of chips he was holding above the salty water, was a seasoned witness to a string of kid deaths. You could say he was an expert unbiased observer of this kind of tragedy, kind of like the aspiring first world viewing the third world committing suicide at its expense. The first time he saw a kid die he just felt that somehow this did not happen. It affected him less each time he saw it happen. He could not help it, and he had become fascinated with the idea of some of his friends committing suicide. He wanted to see it happen. Said he would be there. Orchestrated the alibis. *Don't worry bro, I will be there. I will keep you company. I won't tell anybody.*

Perhaps little Tommyhawk truly understood the guiltlessness of obsessive power, and the helplessness of becoming obsessed, or how it feels to be completely driven towards making sure something happened that would make you feel everything that was wrong was actually more or less worthwhile. Tommyhawk's desperation was so freaky, it was at risk of overwhelming him, and he heard nothing trying to temper his lost in action conscience with the many contrary stories he was imagining about how this would be the last time he would get involved in making someone die, or how he would not get involved in something like this again, or that he would never again waste his time standing around in the quicksand of an incoming tide of crocodile-infested mangroves being a suicide witness. He was always shift-changing to deal with the practical, figuring out how to speed up the process of achieving his target to get the death kid over quicker to help build the safe corridor to his own survival. This was a different kind of obsession to how you would feel about taking somebody else's chocolate. In Tommyhawk's mind of seeing himself in the future, it was more like clawing your way towards having the latest next-generation, fastest-on-Earth iPhone/iPad/AirBook/iPod no matter the cost. So once committed to this level of obsession, almost any well-oiled brain system could be trained to reach unparalleled levels of patience to feed the addiction. But his brother's long-winded many suicidal attempts had reached the zenith of an unparalleled virulent force mutating the meaning of loathing and hatred.

Still though, Tommyhawk lied by telling the imagined saltwater crocodiles hunting for murderers while swimming in the mangrove roots of the incoming tide, that he had never actually seen anyone take their own life before, even though he had witnessed quite a number of youth suicides, and you could say he had been implicated, although he only watched, which could have been anyone else watching something bad happening in the world but doing nothing about it. But he did not want to revisit any of those *could have* times right now. He blocked any truth, hid it in the darkness, peering hard at the incoming waves and the wash, where only occasionally in the reflected light of the moon on the water, he caught sight of something in the darkness that he thought was his older brother floating away, and he could not tell if it was Aboriginal Sovereignty or not. All he wished was that Aboriginal Sovereignty would really disappear so that his reality could never be found in any ocean of the world.

Go on! Do it! Do it now! You idiot! he dared himself to think with audacity, but he would not scream at Aboriginal Sovereignty in case he heard himself defiling his own character with the voice of a murderer. *Paedophile!* He kills this too. Words that jump from the brain now suffocate in his mouth. Crushed words, he crinkled them up, and shanghaied the crumpled lumps down in his throat, swallowed down to the garrison languishing in the pit of his stomach. This was where unclaimed words acidified with potato-chip pastings, and nullified screams. No. This child had no time for screaming while he thought about the delicate matter unfolding in the sea's voices of reverence and echoing in the fathoms down to the sea floor. A boy's silence in front of a mighty sea was very important, to remain quiet like an animal hiding, who watched from a distance, and to be wary as he felt the watery ghost arms reaching around mangroves, searching like police hunting murderers.

12

Occasionally, or time and time again, that little brown boy tosses his head of sun-bleached curly hair that generates enough air turbulence to momentarily separate the mosquitoes swarming around him. His impatience takes on new forms of viciousness now because he feels that Aboriginal Sovereignty is still alive even though it is impossible to see where he is in the darkened sea. It had become so late, and he was still forced to wait even though he needed to be in bed at this time of the night. He knew what time it was without checking to see where the stars had moved across the sea, because he knew it was more than half past two in the morning and he does not need stars to tell the time, or have an instinct about what time it was, because he checks his mobile every few minutes, and it tells him the precise time, that it is 2.30 a.m.

If this kid respects anything, it is exactness, quickness, and precision, and the need to have the exact time in his head all the time, even if he was so exhausted from having to watch some arsehole taking all night to commit suicide, because he thought suiciding was boring and this suicide was killing him, and this was not just random boredom because Tommyhawk could have died many times from the sheer boredom of being cooped up in his life, or from continually having to orchestrate each new failed way to escape his life, and the only way he would manage to keep on breathing the one two threes until eternity was by continuously checking what time it was on his mobile, just to keep himself high five awake, to force himself to take the next breath, to save himself from dying from not having the will to breathe, and by reminding himself to take the next breath and the next, through every second all the way through his mundane life, until, well until one day, when his life would suddenly feel like hot burning lights, feel like a bedazzling life which was bigger elsewhere, or bigger than everything under this sky.

His eyelids drooped over those young brown eyes now straining to see the moment that he had been visualising for months, and which should have taken only a few minutes. But he needed to see the end just in spite, to know the ordeal of standing around watching all day had finally ended, even if it only felt like an anticlimax because he could not even think straight in the middle of the night, now that he was fighting himself. But the dreams keep trying to take over his thoughts, and he could see the crocodile police ghosts swimming under the water like scuba divers searching around the mangrove forests for murderers. They are making him feel like a murderer, and he felt those police fingers touching him under the water instead of the incoming tide tossing a million sticks and mangrove pods through the salty waters where he stood, or the crabs and shellfish that have come out of their flooded mud holes, or the incoming schools of fish from the sea dancing with the jellyfish mob, while singing their love song from Handel's love of a tree to the submerged mangrove forest, *per voi resplenda il fato. Tuoni, lampi, e procelle non v'oltraggino mai la cara pace...* No. A boy like Tommyhawk feels truth is very close to him in the early hours of the morning, and he knows that dead police crocodile ghosts still keep their power, keep their guns and batons, and still hunt for Aboriginal boys like him even when they are dead, and he knows that they will use their ghost fingers to drag him under the water where they will lock him up in their ghost gaol deep under the mudflats, drowning him in darkness, to make it look like suicide. You got to watch out for things like the invisible, of what you do not see, of being exposed to ghost police worlds of crocodiles which were far more dangerous to an eight-year-old Aboriginal child than being bailed up by a gang of real live killer saltwater crocodiles crawling over the muddy high tide sea floor in the mangrove forest where you happen to be standing in the middle of the night.

The sea water in this world was very dangerous, and every sense of Tommyhawk's being told him this, that he had to fly out of the place, and he knows this, because all he ever plans is how to get out, but he cannot just fly, not without an expensive ticket on a Qantas flight – and who was going to pay for that to happen? – and the only way to get his ticket was to endure whatever it takes, to stay half-submerged in the tide, until the ultimate decision is made of whether he or Aboriginal Sovereignty had survived. He knows that there can only be one genuine hero. This had to be the ultimate game of exhausting endurance, like a wager or bet made between him and his brother to beat each other to the end, so he must stay awake, stay on guard, survive everything, even ghost police disguised as enormous saltwater crocodiles brushing by his submerged legs in a mangrove forest at high tide. The thrill, its continual warding off, and the resurrecting of its intensity, was all he owned, until Aboriginal Sovereignty's actual final disappearance from the face of the Earth happened, to accept the thrill of a hero no matter what the odds, by being there to see the death wish happen. All this boy could do, was to continue mining for strength from the tremendous storehouse of faith he had in himself, to defeat the total boredom of being a sentry.

Why are you taking so long? Finish it! Finish it! If I ever see your stupid smile again, or have to pretend to love you like a brother...

Across the surging sea, the seagulls squalled triumphantly, screaming as they flew around in circles while heading back and forth, as though they were saying to Tommyhawk, *He is still alive. This is another one of your failed attempts. Idiot! You can't kill Aboriginal Sovereignty, anyone would have told you that, and you are going to have to plan your escape all over again.* The dawn was not far away, and began to lighten the water and this made Tommyhawk almost cry because he knew that he had no endurance for another failed attempt, that this had to be it, or never.

I will kill him myself if he walks back in. I will walk out there and drown him...

But it was finally happening. The months of planning for a new life for himself was on the cusp. The randomness of opportunity, when it finally happened, was unbelievable, even if it felt like an eternity in the happening, where fantastical dreams of living in new worlds could be crushed at every moment. *Whales die slow you know*, when they suicide by throwing themselves out of the water. Yep! Tommyhawk had seen plenty of suicides and normally, he could never believe how fast something like this could happen, how it does not take long, and where one minute, you could be right next to someone and talking to them, and the next thing, they were all action and it was over and done with in a flash.

In a way, Tommyhawk envisaged suiciding as being simple, you decide, you do it, and then it is finished, and a body becomes limp and floats away, facedown in the water. But still, he knew the tricks his brother could play about wanting to kill himself, and then returning like Lazarus from another broached attempt and pretending it was his natural forte, by saying the love of his life was always pulling him back. *Hello! She wasn't even there.*

Yes, Tommyhawk knew that Aboriginal Sovereignty was a trickster who had succeeded in making him stand around in disease-infected mangroves for nothing in the middle of the night. He was probably now ridden with malaria, or Ross River fever, or Murray Valley encephalitis, and standing in mud full of septicaemia melioidosis germs.

Tommyhawk began visualising his body wasting away, becoming diseased, rendering him paralysed. He froze, was unable to move, neither his arms or legs moved, they were now heavy blocks of steel. He panicked, racing questions ran through his head, that he was now practically dead? Aboriginal Sovereignty had killed him. He was the one who had been set up. His own brother was a murderer. He was somewhere out at sea watching, and laughing at him for spying on people.

Tommyhawk said, *Sure*, and managed to believe that being paralysed with fear did not really bother him. You just make yourself pretend dead. That was what ultimate winners would do.

Most of all, Tommyhawk wanted to be the first person to give the news of his brother's death to his True Idol Mother – the patron saint of all Aboriginal children. She was that greatest white lady on Earth with the golden hair who was the boss of Aboriginal people. He had heard that her omnibenevolence radiated like holy-statue rays of sunshine from her head, and that those lightning beams were capable of locating any residual joyful sense left in the world, a rare thing that had remained closeted away in this child's mind, and would allow light to shine upon him. He had colossal pictures of her covering every interior wall of his brain, just so he could always see her secretly in whichever way he looked inside his head. This way, he made sure that her face illuminated his every thought, every sight, so that he would never forget what she looked like. This all-of-brain image of her shone brightly, like a golden angel guardian who watched over him at all times from where she sat on a brain throne while he fought for his life in high-tide mangroves infestations full of ghost police disguised as saltwater crocodiles, knowing that this woman, composed of priceless gold nuggets mined from his own traditional lands, really loved him more than his parents, who were the neglectful and abusive types of people incapable of loving their children that the whole white country were telling him directly in every publicised forum that they could blab on, because they wanted to save him from his own people, just like their leader, the golden white woman who lived at Parliament House in the capital of Australia.

Tommyhawk squirmed to unstiffen his water-clogged body, but he felt confident enough to pre-empt his success, and could not wait to get a message through to the Golden Mother whose presence was exploding in his mind, so he twisted his finger on speed dial to make anonymous calls on his iPhone to Parliament House. He could see her sitting right in front of him in heaven on her swivelling office chair, and handing him even more shiny new iPads, iBooks, iPhones:

all the latest models. He was being lured into heaven, he had already transcended Praiseworthy reality. He felt that he had reached the centre of world power. She had become his Mother. This was the power of the Australian government. This was what big powerful people could do.

These were such extraordinary feelings that ran through his mind and flowed into his body, where he felt adopted by the government lady, and he felt shivery and so excited, that his arms and legs loosened from the tight grip of the mangrove swamp. His fists pumped the mosquito clouds over the whale bones and knocked them flat in the mud. He looked up into the sky and knew he had shown his imagined gold angel that he was a worthy boy. Tommyhawk saw actual transcendence, where the colossal giant of a white lady was bringing her mighty power – the Australian army, and boom, boom, boom, fighting off all the paedophiles waiting around every corner with schemes to injure him. You only had to call her. He could even see the God Government sending her down from wi-fi heaven to save him, and this was why Tommyhawk could firmly believe that his life in Praiseworthy was just about coming to an end, and he wondered what it would be like to live in such a delusional wonderland, and if she would allow him to sit on her swivelling throne...sometimes.

She's going to be very pleased with me now, Tommyhawk knew this, how he had kept himself rigid like a monument throughout the night of drama, while his whole body was eaten by an infestation of disease-ridden mosquitoes and muddy-water viruses now crawling through his blood. He hoped she would not think he was full of disease, and he kept his fingers crossed on his treasured iPhone that she – the gold angel, had – well! sort of – already given him a present. Now her presence was everywhere, and she smelt like the air itself. She was wherever he looked up in the sky, even looming higher than the ancestors, and he tried to anticipate the moment when she would eventually take his call, when he had to call her the Right Honourable, like you were supposed to call a cabinet minister of the Parliament of Australia who says they were governing the traditional owner of country.

He had once asked his teacher: *How do I write to the Minister for Aboriginal Affairs, Miss?* She said to the class that you would start with – Madam, your Right Honourable. He had practised this many times. He scrolled over his text messages. He had texted your Right Honourable hundreds of times to ask her to adopt him, for example, as follows:

ADOPT ME. RIGHT HONOURABLE.

I HATE MY PARENTS.

THEY ARE BOTH REALLY PAEDOPHILES.

I ONLY LOVE YOU.

Just a few words. Short messages were the total gist of the majority of his texts. Always addressed to your Madam, your Right Honourableness. He should remember to address her correctly even when she appeared in his dreams, to be like polite white people with good behaviour, not like his parents, or anyone in Praiseworthy who called people they hated whatever they liked. The Golden Mother would not call him a liar, unlike someone like Aboriginal Sovereignty who had always been accusing him of telling lies.

Tommyhawk sighed, wiped the perspiration from his skin. It had been a hot night, humid in the mangroves, but seeing up high, how her buoyancy caught the light of the moon and glittered through her golden hair as she swivelled in her office chair in the sky while watching over him, he thought that maybe he could text her again right now – even though it was late in Canberra, but he could see her watching him, teleporting herself anytime she liked and seeing everything. It struck him that she was miraculous when he realised that the Golden Mother had real godlike vision to be watching a quarter of a million Aboriginal children all at the same time, and yet there she was, hovering just above the mangrove swamp, while capable of hovering over the entire country. How would he begin, what would he say, how would he make her believe that he was definitely at risk of being abused by Aboriginal parents who did not love their children? An avalanche of words tumbled back and forth, driving him out of his mind. How would he make the important white woman believe him, that he was at risk of being abused by BLACK PEOPLE, the kind of parents the Australian government was saying did not love their children. Then he wrote: SAVE ME! He continued with the text message while busting to pour the entire contents of his head straight to her, and felt he could write to her all night. He wrote her long text messages, telling her stories, making up fairytales, though he had never sent those texts. This was more serious news, like an SOS message. HELP! He only needed to say a few words. HE'S DEAD. How could he just tell her important eminence that Aboriginal Sovereignty had gone, disappeared in the sea, taken his life, it was all over for him? She would not be hearing from that troublemaker anymore. Simply leave it at that? Or, perhaps he could write that her worst enemy – which was what Aboriginal Sovereignty represented – would not be giving her government any more trouble with talk of his buggered-up rights. I KILLED HIM. No, he would not exactly be saying that.

Tommyhawk wanted her to assume, rightly, that he had taken care of the problem, but not that he had actually murdered his brother. This was a white lady guardian angel of children like him. She protected children from killers, from all sorts of people. That was her message right across the country. She was really saying he could trust her. He would have to think carefully about how to frame this text message to her if he wanted her to evacuate him from hell.

This time, he knew for sure, she would arrive personally in an air force jet to take him away from Praiseworthy. Well! It would be dawn soon and the horizon across the sea would look the same as it always looked, and you would not see Aboriginal Sovereignty in any of it. But! Tommyhawk knew what could not be helped, that the only flaw in all this waiting around would be not having the body as evidence. Please make it urgent, he would text her. He would text her again, saying that he wanted to go to Canberra to live with her in the big flash white Parliament House forever. He would text again, saying he wanted her to adopt him. She would agree. She had to. She was his White Mother.

In these early morning hours before daylight, it felt like there was a miracle happening with a white holiness rising from the sea. Tommyhawk continued texting to the vision over the water in the fog, where he could see her swivelling around on her office chair in the brilliantly lit sky palace of Parliament House. She was giving orders on her mobile for the doors to be thrown open for everyone to see her new son, that black kid from Praiseworthy she had rescued from the whale-bone skeletons, where he was standing up to his waist in the sea among the mangroves. The trouble with this vision was that you could never see properly through its blinding brightness. You needed to squint your eyes, peer through the slits of your eyelids to see what was going on in the vision while an imaginary rising sun was striking her worshipped self and radiating off her clouded palace with multiple rays of golden light, so intense in its brightness that the startling light shining from the golden threads of her hair was too strong for Tommyhawk's eyes, or even for the fish to see in total darkness. This was the pity. He was always too far away from visionary distances constructed by his desire. *But I am the special one*, the only child she could possibly see while swinging around on her office chair as she watched over every Aboriginal child in the country.

Honestly, visions these days do not last long, and this vision was shattering for Tommyhawk Steel, who could not believe it when he looked way out to the sea covering the mudflats, and caught a glimpse of the small white thing. Actually, it looked like somebody's stupid dog. His dara. His mungkuji. Bajangu. Kujukuju. What was it doing out there? Bobbing around in the sea like an idiot. Pedro. *I could kill that dog.* But, then, he knows that the dog was already dead. It had died long ago. The whole world of remembering the loss suddenly crashed down again in Tommyhawk's head. His brain flipped right out this time, and he could not help himself from air-freighting his yelling soul message to wherever Aboriginal Sovereignty was drowning, *Save the ghost dog.* He felt robbed, but he had no choice, the finely curated orchestration had shattered through his brain, he felt ad hoc, exposed, shamed. Should he actually scream for the dog to come back? *You are so full of shit.* Call the whole thing off? *Bullshit!* Could he scream to Ab.Sov to go and save his dog. *Arsehole!* Why was Pedro following the suicide person anyway? The dog was already dead. Why was it out in the surf following the non-person? It always liked Ab.Sov more.

Pedro! Pedro! He tried to will the friggen dog to come out of the sea. *If you are my shit dog, then you come back now.* But the more he raged, the more poor Pedro was pulled beneath the surf to drown, although it was dead already and was reappearing from times before like film re-loading, re-playing the re-drowning multiple times and electrifying Tommyhawk's head with too much fury because he felt as though the dog was trying to replace the swivel chair Golden Goddess from her central place in his thinking, turfing the throne and all out of his brain. He weighed it up on the spot, and in an instant, decided that the fake dog ghost was an actual traitor, and poor Tommyhawk's equilibrium was blown up into parts scattered all over the universe like a broken spaceship floating like a pile of junk and sinking away into the loneliest places of his spirit. But, you know, could a fascist let a ghost dog die? He continued to see the distressed dog swimming and sinking under the waves, and bobbing up again somewhere behind the invisible Aboriginal Sovereignty. No, Tommyhawk could not do nothing, his voice failed him, a voice so completely lost it could have been among the space wreckage floating millions of miles above Earth. Who knows why Pedro had to spoil everything? *Well! Bugger you, Pedro. Go then.* Tommyhawk was now the whale. The whale that would attack Pedro. The dog had made its choice.

Pedro, his old dog, that small cute white, must have been an expensive Maltese terrier mixed with some other breed of a thing, what you call a designer dog that his father had stolen from a white family in the city when they were sipping café latte, now following Aboriginal Sovereignty's footprints rather than his own – as though it knew what the end game would be, and had decided, instead of being abandoned by the little traitor, it would rather save Aboriginal Sovereignty from drowning. It had ignored Tommyhawk down on the beach where he was hiding in the whale skeleton, and scampered into the breaking waves instead, preferring to lose its life in a treacherous darkened sea, rather than dog-paddling the high tide in the mangroves.

Tommyhawk stopped feeling like a superhero, but then suddenly, the swivel lady appeared above the whale bones, swinging on her chair, and gazing at his self-pity with indifferent eyes, and he thought what would she think of him now? What would she think, seeing failure? Would she have said that he should have tied up his stupid ghost dog so it could not go wandering around when the deal was being made? He decided to deny everything. He would not say anything about the dog in the ocean looking for Aboriginal Sovereignty and trying to save him. Did he need to tell her that? Would she know already? He usually told her everything. Never lied to the Golden Mother. She knew everything about his life. But she did not need to know this. That was the answer. She did not need to know he had killed the dog. Even though the thought of holding something back from her made him feel as though he had deceived her, he knew she could never know about this. He was not going to text his Golden Mother about losing his dog. It was not even worth it. He would not tell her that his own pretend dog preferred to die with Aboriginal Sovereignty. These thoughts made him feel really angry because he did not need a traitorous scum of a city dog to make him look like some sneaky person you could not trust, even though the dog might have been the only thing in Praiseworthy he cared about, even though he had accidentally killed it, and it was decidedly clear the dog did not love him.

Well! So! It went, disappeared. *Stuff you then, Pedro. Go to hell. I will be all right,* Tommyhawk thought in a laconic voice like his father's, *I wasn't taking you to the new life in Canberra anyhow. You are only one of the halfgreats.* He remembered this was what Aboriginal Sovereignty had once called him. *That's all you will be.* If only he had something to throw at the dog. Now the swivel-throned Golden Hair Mother was appearing in the dust haze above the sea right in front of the mangrove forest, and she was dressed in a business suit that seemed to be made of the bits and pieces of pink-dyed plastic shopping bags that the wind had torn to threads and had ended up being caught somewhere on the thousands of kilometres of fences of the vast cattle properties that closed off the traditional owners' land. Even her golden hair spraying out of her head in thickets of plastic sheen seemed to have the hues of a luscious pretty pinkness.

13

The whale-bone skeletons always lost their dull whiteness of the day when shone upon by the moonlight, and their luminous sheen stood out as a spectacle of remembrance, as though the bones were returning to life, invigorated through dreams of the night long ago in those heaving seas, before they lost life in the strangling air where they had beached. All of them. Those giant bodies watching each other's passing, pacifying each other to the end with talk, filling the air with memories of whale stories.

Tommyhawk had now waited through many sun-baked hours, and through the last sunlight shining through cobwebs laced over trees and across the mud, and the millions of mosquitoes gliding in the air, and then darkness, and all the while, still believing that only the mangrove mosquitoes knew where he was hiding. Yet country sees everything, and the moon shone brighter on Aboriginal Sovereignty standing so far away now in the shallows of the tidal zone.

Out there in the sea, the shiny skin of his back shone brightly like a lantern, and the glow had drawn the long storyline of arriving, the coming of the large *Syntherata melvilla* and *Syntherata janetta*. These were the emperor gum moths that had been gathering for hours like ghosts, and had flown towards the thrumming of bronzewing pigeons through the coastal dust haze after deserting the coastlines of mangroves, the bilkwood *Flindersia* and the billy goat plum *Planchonia careya*. The air grew congested with woven layers in streaks of gold as the serpentine moth trails swarmed far out on the sea towards the shining light of eternity, as though the bat-like moths and the lepidoptera of all kinds were forever bound to protect the life of Aboriginal Sovereignty.

All the dusty gold wings fluttering, and bumping against one another, crafted an illumination of woolly golden scales that glistened on the sea, but Tommyhawk did not see the wondrous golden thundercloud surrounding his brother like he was a saint, and the halo of moonlight shining on him through the cracks of clouds.

The fat boy was busy enough keeping awake. It was difficult to balance standing on one leg, and then switching to the other in the squishing mud with the tide coming into the whale bones. His self-imposed rules of stillness were broken a thousand times already, while his mind wandered off into dream-wishing that he should go home. But he realised that he could not go anywhere before the real deal kicked in and his mind came running right back to where he was standing in ankle-deep mud. His mind should not be tricked into dreaming about being otherwise, or straying from his predestined plan for his new becoming, and this was a reminder for Tommyhawk that Aboriginal Sovereignty would never win this argument.

Why can't you do anything right? Tommyhawk grew more bitter, a bit more pissed off with this long death march out to sea. This ordeal of Aboriginal Sovereignty's suiciding had taken some of the slowest hours on the planet, and the little fat fellow was totally exhausted. He reckoned that Aboriginal Sovereignty was *doing this on purpose.* Tommyhawk's mind was edging on a full-scale eight-year-old tantrum like he would have had at home when he could not get what he wanted. Yo! And, whatever else his mind raced through in the memory bank storing all the bad times you could stuff in an eight-year-old's brain, sought, found, and delivered in a thud of lead on the floor of his brain one after the other in a God audit of the blows to life where distrust constantly hung, stored in the place of not having desires realised. Desire! He was full of desire, his total existence only felt pure desire, a fully directed desire towards his own survival, his complete desire to live, and not just simply to be, but to become far more. What the boy wanted was not a new realisation in the history of humanity, or to be the main tool of human survival for the millennia of Aboriginal existence – for if there was anything that Tommyhawk desired, it was to create a lifelong, rest-of-life exclusion zone from his brother. The question he posed to himself was this: *Did you want to, or not want to be involved with a burden for the rest of your life*, and Tommyhawk could not see himself as a carrier of his brother now, or when he was his brother's age, or even as an old man.

Though Tommyhawk's mind preyed on the need for swift action to seize his own splendid future, it had now taken more than half a day to achieve the death of his old life. Nothing more could happen without his brother committing suicide, and what if Aboriginal Sovereignty did not have any genuine intention at all of going through with his suicide of drowning himself? Perhaps he had no idea about what he really wanted to do? Why was he immune to saltwater crocodiles, sharks, and box jellyfishes tangling their poisonous tentacles around him? This ocean is supposed to be infested with man-eaters. *You won't do it, will you?* There was even another small voice going on about nothing, and saying, *Save him?* Tommyhawk's lips remained sealed. He knew that it would be just like Aboriginal Sovereignty to ruin his plans for a better life if he started calling the police on his mobile to rescue him from the sea and his murdering brother over there in the whale bones, and started aborting the suicide – leaving it for another time, even though he wanted to be dead. *Can't make up your mind. Well! That there was no truer word*, thought Tommyhawk, *You stuffed up your life, don't stuff up mine.*

The boy fiddled, twisted from one muddy mosquito-bitten leg to the other, and was so hopping mad, and still forcing himself to stand there until the bitter end. It seemed like an end of the rope situation, for he could never be sure if Aboriginal Sovereignty already knew he was hiding in the whale bones, and was just mucking around with his mind in this mesmerising circus act of his, enticing him into the sea so he could murder him. If the scales fall anywhere, right now it weighed in Tommyhawk's advantage, for he could never be tricked. He had been tricked this way before with Aboriginal Sovereignty changing his mind, but this time, it had to be it, of continuing to will his brother to end his life so that his own life could start speeding up on the calendar that he had already mapped out for himself, the big secret locked in his head and pushing him forward every waking minute of the day. A desire to get as far away from Praiseworthy now driven by an urgency so relentless and focused, he thought of nothing else, even forgetting to eat sometimes, or to sleep. This was the thing he wanted more than life, what he called his afterlife, and that was to live with his true Mother, the white blonde-hair lady.

In order for this new life to proceed with the big important white lady, he had to be perfectly sure that his big brother killed himself *more properly* this time, not just going on about how he wanted to kill himself, when he only meant half breathing – which was not dead, just like the last time was not dead, and the times before that, when Aboriginal Sovereignty bailed out, had some last-minute change of heart, perhaps remembering some last-minute thing he had to do, and stood in the ocean, showing his true weakness like a gutless wonder that had no ability to make the big decisions, except to keep the choice alive – the either-or of his total lack of resolve. Was this going to be the same scenario? You could see it all happening. Aboriginal Sovereignty would come striding back through the sea with a big smile on his face while acting as though nothing had happened. Not even an apology, just talking stupid, saying he was just out visiting his sea relatives, talking to fish. He was not going to kill himself over his lost girlfriend. He was not that heartbroken after all. She was not worth it. Or, on the other hand, *because she is worth it*. Tommyhawk would have to start all the agonising and insipid whispering all over again, while mimicking an apologetic Australian politician in opposition to the government hell-bent on pushing yes-men to support some of its outlandishly stupid policy decisions. All this was depressing enough, and sapped the boy's enthusiasm to work at achieving his own grand plan aimed at his eventual adoption by the angelic white lady who could not leave him to live with his harmful Aboriginal family. *Go on do it and get it over with. Do it, will you?*

14

There were times when you could see the sickness of conquering floating in the air as a general thing, spreading over a couple of centuries more than any new worldwide virus pandemic. Tommyhawk had told his father about Aboriginal Sovereignty trying to kill himself, as he had always been trying to talk to him about kids committing suicide, and he remembered his father acting as though he had not spoken, as though he had not even heard him speak. The man seemed to be acting as though nothing like that could ever happen to constant sunshine. Cause told the boy to stop telling lies before he killed the little liar in an instant. It felt like a wild wind separating him from his father and forcing Tommyhawk to step back, to get out of the way of an actual murder taking place by this man who he already assumed was capable of murdering him. He watched the back of the tall thin bush man with a mop of greying hair tangled with odd bits of leaves and twigs walking away, and mumbling something into his chin as though he was speaking to his own shadow, *he will get over it.*

The boy back-answered quick smart. He always had to have the last say: *You are not a proper father. You are just an intermediate father.* Well! Cause snapped at that, *What in the bloody hell's name is an intermediary father?* Tommyhawk bit his tongue, *didn't say intermediary moron,* and from blurting out that as far as he was concerned, Cause was always acting like he was overwhelmed by having too many children, whereas in actual truth, he only had these two – and he could not handle two sons whom he hardly had anything to do with.

The question right now in Cause's thoughts was about survival of a black man that came from deep history, and it was about flexibility. Flexibility with reality, and whose flexibility mattered. But what would a little boy like Tommyhawk know about life? *Look and learn boy. How many times have I got to show you how to do something?* The man was wringing his hands. Kid with the mad talk. Follow me. Tommyhawk thought that he was learning enough already about what flexibility meant by watching his older brother's uncertainties. Will I, or won't I? Will I get married, or won't I? Which way? Am I still in love with this one, or that one over there, or neither? Perhaps all ways were better. Or no way. Who could keep up? Aboriginal Sovereignty's life was like a supermarket of choices.

From the time Tommyhawk could put two and two together, he always knew that he was the complete opposite to his drippy brother. The glue was different. He was superglued set to the idea of being a decider, to make, take and defend like his life depended upon how fast decision-maker quick he clicked his fingers. He was wired to the unbendable, on constant repeat cycle about what it meant to decide, and probably, would rather die than bend from his decision. This was how he thought you needed to be hard-nosed, like the government, and what being in power was all about. There was no way he would become like his brother who would always be living in the opposition, who could not make up his mind about anything.

The boy was already a plain little outsider fascist watching Praiseworthy people praising, fawning and admiring the very personification of Ab.Sov's flexibility, and never seeing him for what he was, as an abbreviation of future failure. In fact, Tommyhawk was calling his brother future failure as he stomped around in the mud in the whale bone palace at frigging three in the morning, while demanding to know why an idiot like his brother had ever been named Aboriginal Sovereignty and not himself. It was a complete joke. Ab.Sov was not able to hold his concentration long enough to get a simple job done – like look at the time, and he was still trying to kill himself. The boy was near to tearing his own hair out, those brown curls plastered by perspiration to his scalp, for it was extremely difficult for him to understand why anyone could not just follow through with their own decisions. His thoughts ran through the other kids he had watched on this very same stretch of beach, who had tried to chicken out at the last minute. Who couldn't keep a concrete plan in their head until the end. He blamed the flexibility his father spoke about as being like the wind, and he hated the wind gusts that came and moved in any direction, and he hated everyone in Praiseworthy for lacking in concentration, always being airy-fairy, the prime weakness he would be escaping from, once Aboriginal Sovereignty carked it.

15

Tommyhawk knew at three o'clock in the morning that even though he could not see Aboriginal Sovereignty anymore, his brother was still alive. His brother was messaging him on his mobile. Aboriginal Sovereignty had to be out there in the sea somewhere with his mobile in his hand, which felt absolutely paralogical unreal to Tommyhawk, that his dying brother would be calling people. He checked the messages. Saw hundreds of missed calls. The iPhone froze, unfroze, then froze once more while umpteen messages flashed in. Where could he be, whispering into his mobile while killing himself in the ocean. Why was he texting people? Quickly he looked behind. A slight breeze, the warm breath whistled into his mobile ear. Oh! It was only the hot mobile he felt, but his brother's presence seemed to be close, he knows his brother's presence anywhere, and it was as though they were standing side by side, both watching the death scene. Was Aboriginal Sovereignty standing there, really had he come back? Tommyhawk was petrified, but swung around, looked through the complete circumference of blackness. He could not see the spirit ancestors of Praiseworthy busily moving through one another, going back and forth, fetching up deaths in this night like no other. Left! Right! Front! Back! Pitched black mangroves wrapped up the light and Tommyhawk could hear a lonely repetitiveness in the whispering sneaking up behind him, edging closer, reinventing the sound of country with steady breathing reduced to the minimalism of a last gasping, *help me*. Then, his brother's voice felt as though it was coming from inside his bloodstream, and Tommyhawk did not know how to dislodge the whispered plea coming through his own blood racing to his head.

Nothing escapes the sea's embrace once it has swallowed all life from one's body in distant waters. Its power paralyses, overtakes the movement of limbs or body, you are unable to move freely either towards the sea's infinity to a life beyond death, nor move back, returning from breathlessness. The boy refused to hear repeat-mode brother pleading, playing his song too late, a riff sung blue.

Shut up you. Shut up. Tommyhawk knew about forever, and at least he was truthful about this, he never trusted Aboriginal Sovereignty. *You won't trick me. Get away from me. You. You. Disease. I know you are trying to lure me into the sea.* Tommyhawk sniggered at the sea of heartbreak, a local rallying song, one he championed in his own mind. His brother was always trying to get him to experience country, get used to it, *it's in the blood like*, go out into deeper waters. *Have fun bro.*

The truth was this: Tommyhawk Steel had never truly experienced what the death world was like from outside of a computer around three in the morning. He did not care that there was such a place outside his window where many story worlds interacted more deeply than any one person could ever know. His knowing is of not seeing where he is among the mangroves encasing a city of looming skeletal whale bones that belies an otherworldly legendary, because in the blackness, only a night heron screams its ancient song to another, and it to another along the endless kilometres of mangrove coastline, until the herons all take flight, fly in and out of the eddies cascading through the quivering dance of ghost moths flickering pianissimo in their eternal droning song.

At this point of the night, the boy who thought he was a ninja was drifting into a deep sleep where he met the devil that took over – ordering kicks, a head punch, calling him weak, forcing his eyelids open with its bare hands, to witness the end of time of Aboriginal Sovereignty. All around, the local spirits in the mangrove darkness were massing in flight over the sea dreams of times immemorial, and whenever the moonlight broke through the clouds, Tommyhawk could only glimpse his brother dilly-dallying his death so far away. It hurt him to have to keep this vigil. He became delusional, deciding that he had died and Aboriginal Sovereignty had set him up, and was out in the sea on a vigil, witnessing his death in the mangroves. Tommyhawk started to believe that his brother was making him wait long enough so that he would run into the sea, where he would easily become disoriented in the darkness, as easily as being caught in a ghost net hidden below, and pulled by the currents further out in the sea. His brother's power was overtaking his mind, and Tommyhawk felt that he was collapsing dead in the mud now that every bit of blood in his body had been drained by mosquitoes – yep, all of that. Yet, the small ninja, even on his last blood-drained leg, was able to drag from somewhere in his legacy of crash-hot powerful ancestors who knew how to survive super droughts and ice ages, one last drip of desire to survive, and he was able to hear the rat-a-tat timpani marching his eyes elsewhere, towards the ultimate visualisation of his luxurious mansion home, the safe white parliament palace in Canberra, and he knew this was where he was headed – not in a ghost net like an octopus. He was going to live after this one last ordeal, and he smirked at where he thought Aboriginal Sovereignty was standing in the sea, and he whispered, knowing that his brother heard, *I'm telling you there would be no mucking about if it was me.*

The truth was that no good comes out of government propaganda, indoctrinating the mind of a black kid visiting his nightmares in the mangroves in the deadly night. He was just rolling with the bad times like the devil incarnate, and making spooky stories for the ancestors. A modern power ninja like himself knew the reasons why Aboriginal Sovereignty was not made of the same ancestral stuff that was in the ground all around Praiseworthy, in the food you ate, the water you drank, what you smelt in the air, the same thing that the whole region was famous for, iron ore. Wasn't that why just about everyone in Praiseworthy was solid, and called themselves metal names? *But the baby was crying out there, probably hoping a crocodile wouldn't eat him. Or snakes. Or rats. Where were the sharks anyhow?*

Another thing that kept bewildering the ninja boy was why Aboriginal Sovereignty was the local hero. What did he ever do? Why was he beloved? He was just a criminal. A paedophile. He did not have ninja resilience. Or sovereignty intransigence. Hard to weigh it all up, all of those pivotal questions written on the devil scales. Hey! How come you were treated like a bag of nothing, while your brother was Aboriginal Sovereignty? What makes one better than the other? The question was as inflexible as his not being able to stop the world from falling apart in the middle of the night. It was all about escaping, and focus, and Tommyhawk had the main ingredient, and you know what that was? The resilience for being a survivor, this was the only thing he ever had, mostly learnt from his absent father. But unlike his father, he was saving himself, with a mind that was running like the rings of Saturn slamming all the broken pieces of old moons, comets and asteroids that got in the way.

Even Tommyhawk, or especially Tommyhawk Steel, knew that you needed the resilience of Godzilla to escape paedophile heaven. He knew this while whizzing through eight years of life like a rocket on fire from asking the question, *Dude, who am I?* Unlike, for instance, the mainstream child, he perfectly understood what it meant to be the victim of injustice in the country's historical theft situation. Sweet! He looked at himself, and decided, *Dude, you are the national narrative.* Perhaps he knew this was his time. The glory moment that said to him, *They are talking about you.* He heard the message coming directly to him in endless political diatribes describing his situation on the radio, TV, or on the internet, where all these people were actually talking about him in the singular, and drumming it into his thick head how much he was at risk living in an Aboriginal community. *They are talking about me.* He lived in an Aboriginal community, didn't he? Well! Watch out kid because you are living where all the paedophiles roam. He was not saying anything like that originally, but then, the white people were saying it – like they were speaking directly to him, and saying that he was living in a totally dysfunctional world crawling with paedophiles. Why? Because the Australian government – also, for the Aborigines – had said so. From that moment, when Tommyhawk learnt how to string a few thoughts together about paedophiles attacking Aboriginal children from his addiction to listening to the ABC news, instead of watching the cartoons if he had been normal and had not been born a fascist like his father always claimed he was, he would not stop talking about paedophiles. *I'm a paedophile. You're a paedophile.* He had the radio blasting here, blasting there: Well! That was the news. *This kid is mad*, Aboriginal Sovereignty told his parents. *You got to make him stop saying that.* Yet the whole world was agape on the TV and saying it, and gossiping in an official political government way about plagues of paedophiles rampant in places like Praiseworthy.

Will I get attacked by the paedophiles? Tommyhawk felt he was living in hell. Paedophiles were after Aboriginal children, and so naturally, he believed, *They must be coming for me. I know it.* The radios kept pumping the news that paedophiles were rampant, and all over every square inch of the Aboriginal world. It was as though his brain was being eaten alive by a thought virus, a pandemic, where every Aboriginal child was at risk. He spent every moment of the day trying to escape from the imagined virus snaring him into its grips and finally killing him. He could not get the thought out of his mind that he was an at-risk child. Anyone could see that but who was doing anything about it. He lived in a state of emergency, of total vigilance, of trying to second-guess the invisible paedophiles out to get him. Nowhere felt safe. Hey! What monsters lurked, that created a child's hell *ex nihilo*? Was it done intentionally? What felt definite in Tommyhawk's mind was not infinite time, not far-distant time, but an eight-year-old's heightened imagination for anticipating a very dangerous situation – albeit, one created by the highest authority governing the country – where he felt it was immanently moments before he would be attacked. The only great news came at daybreak when Tommyhawk could not believe he had survived another day, but this only deepened the next item of his apprehension, of having another night to deal with. Another sleepless night, of how to stop suspecting the worst. He was like a rat cornered by cats. How was he going to escape? *You tell me...*

Well! You had to be a superhero writing your own magnum opus about fear. You had to overcook the brain until it fried, until it exploded like an attack weapon, and on this feat alone Tommyhawk spent just about every second, thinking about how to be a human magnum six-shooter, how to keep strengthening the war cabinet living in his brain, to make sure that all the world's paedophiles actually living in Praiseworthy would not get him. But how was he going to know what a paedophile looked like? You got to know what enemies looked like, but how could you tell when the contagion looked like a virus that was invisible to the eye? Suspenseful thinking was killing him, reeking his head with suspicion, and yet it was impossible to tell, so he ended up with the only available solution, that all adults were paedophiles.

And why not? He knew the most important people in the country – the government of Australia supposed to be governing for Aboriginal people as well – were saying his community was crawling with paedophiles so it must be true, so why should he say it was not true, why should he think the government of Australia was wrong? Then it occurred to Tommyhawk that it was not very nice to be looking out for himself all the time, that he had to fight the war himself. If he was living in a war zone, shouldn't a child expect a bit of help? How was a child to protect himself from the world of adults out to harm him?

Right – now! Tommyhawk hit the jackpot. He was planning to get the hell out of any situation where he was the known prey. What he desired most had been ingrained in his world through millennia, and this was his desire to survive. Wasn't he genetically and spiritually wired to fight calamity, ice ages, global warming, any kind of anthropocentric climate change, as well as contagions, viruses or diseases, or anything relating to the above – ditto paedophiles? He was the sum total of twenty-first century thinking, but he also said what the assimilationists wanted from young Indigenous minds. Yep! Exactly that. He was getting right away out of Praiseworthy. Was he dangerous? Anyone would be mad to try stopping him.

What was wrong with that kid? Dance Steel, the moth-er Mother, could not get anywhere near the fire and brimstone mouth of the youngest son. *You keep your distance from me,* he ordered, when he had figured out what a paedophile was. He waved his iPhone at her. *I am going to call the police and tell them all about how you are trying to molest me.* He told her to watch as he measured out an appropriate distance in giant footsteps: two metres from the virus. *Don't come any closer than that, or I will report you to the police.*

His father said that he wanted to flog him for talking to his mother like a fascist, but he was holding his hand because he was a decent man, and because he knew that Tommyhawk was just looking for any excuse to report to white people about his own family. Cause knew what everyone else in the world was saying about paedophilia being rampant in Aboriginal communities. He remembered thinking, *gee that was a sophisticated word* when he first heard about it on the seven o'clock news on the ABC. He thought it had something to do with petrol. They are talking about petrol-sniffing he told Dance while watching the TV from the couch. He had even told Tommyhawk on the spot that he would kill him quick smart if he started sniffing petrol because he was not going to muck around caring for him when doctors tell him he would have to give that new paedophile medicine to him for the rest of his life when he became a vegetable from sniffing petrol. *Don't you go around shaming me, you idiot*, Cause had yelled, and Tommyhawk yelled right back what a paedophile was, *you faggot*, it had nothing to do with petrol. Then, like a gross type of infection had broken out in the world, it was all about paedophile this now, and paedophile that in Cause's argumentative conversations with Tommyhawk, after the boy became obsessed about who was a paedophile, and started accusing his own father of being one too. The shame of it. *Who was touching children then? Where? Where! Who? Who? How could the whole community be paedophiles, if I am not a paedophile, you little know-all?*

Tommyhawk told Aboriginal Sovereignty to social distance himself from him too. He taunted relentlessly, unable to stop obsessing to the family about his paedophile brother. *You sleep with little girls. So, you are nothing but a big paedophile.* Aboriginal Sovereignty thought the kid had gone insane. He was more than an idiot. He had developed a phobia about adults, or everyone in Praiseworthy bigger them himself.

Man, take a look, the little idiot is mad. You should get a doctor to look at him. Time and again, Aboriginal Sovereignty told his father to do something about Tommyhawk, or he swore to God that he would put his hands around the little punk's neck and strangle the living daylight out of the little cunt face himself. Cause walked away. His mind was fully occupied already on how he could make his family's life different, how it did not need to be all this arguing, and how he would show the way to their future by setting an example of himself. He would not explode into a lot of hot air just for the sake of his family and deal with the uncontrollable brat for what? A bit of peace and quiet that consisted of being accused of being some scum thing, violent-violator father, unmanly sort of thing that could not control himself – like he was exactly what white people would have him be, and were begging him to act like an ape, or a primitive caveman from the stone age, like he was an animal. No. Widespread was not having any of what he termed the shambolic race-hate stuff based on white people's perception. This was not how Cause the empire man saw himself. You had to think about yourself as having successful dreams, of having too much money to splash around, of being a big-time provider, to get away from these moments of racialised induced family dramatisation. Vapourise the hate off the radar.

Cause flicked off the well-honed switch involving himself with the run-of-the-mill mindlessness family drama wasting his energy. When he switched off like this, he was like the man in the Bible, a focused man with a plan for saviour-ing a lot of Christian donkeys needing to be fed, handled and whatnot for building the conglomerate model that created x, x, x black millionaires. Well! Put it this way, it would be impossible to count the scoresheets of rich Aboriginal people and it was majestically more special to own this level of accomplished absenteeism, which just meant having the ability to look dismissively at Tommyhawk's latest round of antics, or tantrums, or whatever else the fascist kid's annoying behaviour consisted of, by remarking into his chin, with the coldest, flattest, hardest voice, some general mantra about the hardiness of the local universalism, which was that, *He will get over it in the end.*

16

Everybody got to die. That was a matter of fact. You don't need brains to work that one out. Who was too frightened to die? Nobody in this place. Everyone in the world knew that they were going to die sometime and have their troubles finished with, but Aboriginal Sovereignty was only becoming a young man. New time coming with old time. Why he gone and die for?

The word of all words spread quickly, and it felt as though a secret inquiry was happening about something very serious that had gone wrong in Praiseworthy. Those hundreds of noisy myna birds guarding the place from the rooftops, began hyper-shrilling well before dawn. It felt as though an eternity of fledglings had been lost! The racket never stopped for one moment, while in the darkness the birds jumped about on the ground and through the trees, signalling back and forth the ultimate call in the language for danger that shot across family grounds spreading thousands of kilometres over ancestral country. Oh! Nobody had ever felt such grief of the myna bird's deafening wailing blanket covering the land with echoes in all faraway directions. Then of all things, the haze collapsed in a sigh under its own sorry weight, and nearly suffocated half the town as it squeezed its heavy humidified air through every nostril in Praiseworthy. All the alarm sirens buzzed through its heart as the lungs of the town began to collapse, before the haze managed to drag its haloed dome back up in the atmosphere, and the darkened omnipresence cloud just sat there, as though looking for something while touching into the death sense of all things.

Everyone knew the world had changed by breakfast time. All the sad news was rocketing around town, and pumping that much blood through all those old broken hearts now beating quick time sticks about the insolubility of the mystery. Aboriginal Sovereignty's odd suicide coincided with a dead gum moth's winged eyes staring from the ground in the front of every door, and every place. Then they noticed, when looking out to see whether the favourite view of country was still there, which was generally a relaxing thing to do first thing in the morning before the passion of the day eroded with troubles, the absence in the view signalled that the trouble had already begun. In the omnipresence haziness, it looked like there was an even greater halo sitting over the top of the haze dome squatting over Praiseworthy. There seemed no longer to be a straight view of their world. Haste came next. With no time to waste, everyone who had an iPhone got busy expanding some exposé or other about the density of the haze to any bureaucrat on the Australian Capital Hill etc., about *those things, I ought to tell you, of what I think you ought to know* about those donkeys of Cause Steel causing things like this to happen, in a fervent chat, chat, chat about the inexplicable, of what nobody knew, about yet another mystery to deal with in these times of hardship, when nothing one wished for ever came true.

When phone calls as usual generally failed to change the world order with acts of decency and justice, it left all these local Praiseworthy people running around in circles, and crazy crying. The wrecked world became undone. The debilitating spirit-killing humidity that had been long tolerated, now seemed far too severe to endure. These people became nothing in their minds. They appeared to be like ghosts in the eyes of the myna birds. The long-sustained cooing of the bronzewing pigeon watching from the distance while searching for seed in the stubble grass, only saw the human spirit in a sheen of transparency that it did not like. The bird watched these ashen grey ghost people with bare feet moving through the russet-red-hazed covered landscape. All the mourners were dressed in ash-covered t-shirts and shorts, wearing sunglasses, straw or cloth hats, or their old land rights caps, and had dollops of white sunblock cream smeared over the nose like ceremonial paint, and some of the ladies were carrying fat babies on the hip, while others were kicking the shinbones of the people in front of these processions, and the grasshopper plague jumping out of the way, some to the left, others to the right. And if you looked behind, these people were followed by legends of bare-chested ghost kids in shorts with bare feet scattering in all directions over the countryside, who were yelling *o-ware, we are going to tell on you*. The half-wild ash-covered ghost dogs chased everything in sight. Dead butterflies. Ants. Cause Steel's donkeys hit by cars roaming around looking for donkeys to kill. Along the periphery, colossal numbers of spirit pussycats with kittens went stampeding through the summer dry grass along with the melee, and soon the whole stubble grass plain fell over, and was flattened to the ground.

Run, run on, moving quicker through the steamy haze resting heavy over the spinifex grass, while the ghostly grey people flashed by with odd glimpses of red or ice pink among sprinklings of silver stars, blue unicorns in the snow, and striped PJs. It looked like a stampede of colour hued by ash that was spreading in all directions through the grass and among the riparian jungle of smoggy Praiseworthy. The glue of humanity was becoming unstuck here, breaking loose from a moment of thought that rolled and flew into another level of spirituality from hearing the sound of ancestors crying. All memories were being weighed together in the land of eternal life, then wait a moment, listen?

This was no good neither, when the racket of grey ghosts' panic through the grass woke the spirit country. The lever was pulled. Every resting ancestor that had ever existed on this place was awoken from eternal sleep, rising up from their resting places in country, and assembling their powers in a deep trough forming an atmospheric weather phenomenon in the enormity of its build-up. The denser the air became, the more the country grew hostile, until finally, all the grey ghosts felt this was the end of the world coming in the grass, and they scattered. The place went really haywire after that. The brindle grey pussycats ran for their life from the fright of having their fur coats singed and smoked by the electrified air, and they all but disappeared from the face of the Earth with every dog, brindle, spotted, or one variety of colour, running with shivers down their backs.

Once those spirit storms created out of this freak weather were on the hunt, it was not easy to put them back into their resting places. Their stories were countless, too epical to be recalled right there and then by an inconsequential human mind. The charge in the air was too powerful, and as the almighty creature of electrical storms moved through country a weather system was developing with it, gigantic dark clouds spinning with lightning and thunder like a colossal war taking place through the sky. From every point of the atmosphere, from horizon to horizon, continuous lightning bolts charged across the sky, or struck the ground. A million lightning strikes, mularrijbi, full cheeky – kijibaji – that ploughed in and out of country, struck tree, rock, anywhere, same place bang-bang once, twice, and three times, each lightning bolt ripping a tree trunk straight out of the ground. Trees for kilometres around were ripped apart. The thunder roared like a freight train through every human soul in search of Aboriginal Sovereignty. Soon enough, all the emotion was bolted, superglued together into one big hell of a problem for Praiseworthy. In all of this havoc, it was a dry storm, and not one drop of rain fell from the sky.

Voices, come one at a time – a bit sneaky at first, then becoming more and more brave by the score – and claimed that no blame for Aboriginal Sovereignty leaving their traditional lands could be laid at their feet. Praiseworthy feet were not the feet of community-minded people anymore. They were the pure feet of individuals who were separating themselves from country saturated with cooing bronzewing pigeons repetitively droning ceremonies going on all day throughout the territory. They wanted to break from all of this guttural grief. Life, it was felt, was for moving on. Everyone needed to break free. Break the link to legacy after that freak electrical storm tried to murder everyone in the whole place. Yes, they all needed to assimilate faster now – accelerate the thing to be done with it, by seeing themselves as becoming the more individually oriented people of the current era forced upon them by the mainstream living on the oldest continent in the world of Aboriginal Sovereignty, by resurrecting and dragging the era of the colonialist which should have been long dead, back into the future. *Got all that?* the Major Mayor Ice Pick said. He was now being heard as the one true voice of the higher ground, berating that he had been telling them to assimilate for years, and saying to the ash-covered people he would be teaching them to save themselves by speaking better English in the future like white city people. And Praiseworthy people began noticing the way that they spoke English, and felt self-conscious because they could not hear the white piousness of superiority in their own voices which they felt were inferior, and how they did not sound like a Church bishop asking the brethren, *Why were young people committing suicide here?* They then hardly spoke what they called their backward English anymore, nor would they speak their own language so it would die out forever.

In the best English then, *Why here, and why us, and why not somewhere else where they do not have the same troubles as us?* Every day, these were the inexplicable questions in English that droned on like the pigeon's song everybody wanted to escape from hearing all day. But every person on every street up and down Praiseworthy found that it was not easy to assimilate into white Australia no matter how much you wanted to be reborn white. They simply remained speaking in the same old monotone of the pigeon droning, which was like listening to their own continuous grief.

There was nobody in the world who would be able to deny the fact that Praiseworthy children were disappearing like flies in the eyes of their numb-minded families, and to the point where there was no longer enough despair to go around. There was never any time to recover emotionally from the death of one child, before something else happened, because another, and then another child was gone forever, taken from the midst of a grief yet to be diminished, that would never be extinguished.

What more? More kids dying? While heads were hurting to find more reasons than you could poke a stick at about why Aboriginal Sovereignty committed suicide like all the other children, nothing was resolved. You would hear talk about suicidal thoughts in every house as you walked through every street – about what was the use of anyone living anymore – trilling so loudly over the top of a plague of cicadas shrilling through thousands of kilometres of bushlands in late summer, that you felt as though you were going deaf. It was there, even by the end of the day, when everyone had clearly exhausted themselves from hearing their own echoing voices destroying what it meant to be alive, it remained a mystery about how Aboriginal Sovereignty had disappeared from the face of the earth. Perhaps if you were the kind of person who thought of hope, perhaps then he was only nearly finished, half-finished, and was floating somewhere in the sea, or perhaps, he was an already finished kind of hope, and on the floor of the ocean rolling in the currents. This hope thing was the almost conspiratorial tone of voice in which people began claiming that nothing was a fact yet. Nobody had seen his body dragged out of the sea. Had they? Or, washed up on the beach. True. All that could be said about what was factual or not, was that suicide was a real killer of young people with wrong ideas sitting in their bodies.

Then this big mob of grief-stricken dust-anointed people gazing upwards into the skies with the tears salting around their eyes, these dynasties called out to the greatest non-ecumenical ancestral beings of all in this country to tell them why Aboriginal Sovereignty had gone away, and why no one had seen that shamefaced Aboriginal Sovereignty dead or alive for weeks. They said he better not be dead wherever he had gone. They also said that someone had better find that boy even if he was feeling no good because this was the place where everybody felt no good, so their Aboriginal Sovereignty had better come back.

Praiseworthy wanted the boy to come home, even if white laws thought that paedophilia was rampant in their community, and Australia thought they were all paedophiles. We turned secret people now, they sang to their ancestral creation beings governing the country, even though they said nothing was changed in the all times law, and they only saw themselves as just the ordinary people from each family, camp, or house. They said to the ancestors, *We are asking you because you are more powerful than the boss God of Australian people who wanted to take away Aboriginal Sovereignty, want to kill him dead, break his heart, just because he was a boy believing he was in love.*

In the paedophilia era of belief running through the mind of national Australia, the story was that everywhere you looked in an Aboriginal community you would find a paedophile. Aboriginal people went skyrocketing crazy about this lie, because everyone was starting to believe that they were either a paedophile, or had been a paedophile sometime in their lives. Police came into their homes looking for paedophiles, and the whole town went through each other's homes searching for the paedophiles and could not find any, and being people who could see what was not there, found it very challenging that they could not find a black paedophile. The army came looking for abused children in every house, and the old aunties cried: *Why are you asking me about that? Don't ask me. Shame. Stay right away from this place.*

The whole place burned with heat, and it felt as though there was an invisible fire raging in the haze, while everyone ended up running themselves ragged round the clock to try to sort something out, to help them find Aboriginal Sovereignty. Everyone felt as though they had been changed for the worse and could not understand what was happening to them anymore. Who were they? They did not know, nobody knew. That was except for a few of the upper echelons, the sceptic types, the powerhouse, strung to Ice Pick. He was cool as a cucumber and continued on as usual, making plans about how the brethren should live, drinking an espresso coffee while sitting around in a darkened, freezing air-conditioned clean-air filtered office down at the Praiseworthy shire council. First, he thought, *Every man, woman and child should want Aboriginal Sovereignty to die.* Second: *The take-away line was – why should Aboriginal Sovereignty live on forever?* He thought it was becoming a summer of hell. The heat grew stronger and lasted longer and his gold Christmas beetle looked like it was not coming again this year. The sun poured down every day for months. The hologram of himself had not deterred the dust dome that continued to squat over Praiseworthy. And the record-breaking humidity grounded everything with a mud-coated lethargy that crippled all clear-headed thinking in either an overcrowded house, or in a shack. No one ever imagined it would be like this. *What's that? Where we got to run about solving mysteries while we were already being driven mad in the mystery of this heat?* Well! The whole of Praiseworthy rang one bell of agreement about this. *What do you think we are to be able to fix this?* The Major Mayor said he was not superman – you know. On the other hand, the deadened in the brain people said that nobody could think straight about how Aboriginal Sovereignty became lost somewhere out in the sea at a time when so many other children were committing suicide by drowning in the sea, and nobody knew why. Why they had become adrift! Lost their footing, whatever did that mean?

17

Prayers were on fire, and the ashes fall far and wide across the lands of Aboriginal Sovereignty. The whole place had become giddy in its devotion to off-grid religions, and there were now not many feet planted squarely on the ground that were not willing to hear some kind of angelic message lecturing them about letting bygones be bygones and other stuff about generosity towards the villain, because *the every person* had almost overnight been called upon by the holy, accompanied by harps, organs and violins in either this way, or that foreign belief to create a stampede, in a complete, full on *in toto* race towards accomplishing one's own self-style assimilation – by practising like a rabid trainee in how to become a chosen one. It was profoundly incredulous, and difficult to understand the all-knowing, and the all-grabbing apparatus that came along for the ride, and which generously included visions, such as the plentiful and bountiful appearances of angels flying about the place of the ancestral spirits. Was there a traffic jam in the skies of the spirit war zone? Perhaps, or perhaps everyone just wanted to become a fast-paced prophet – a reincarnation of gabble, the TV preacher, and perhaps temporarily, thought of abandoning the old laws of country. Never mind! These new-style, all-swinging rah-rah churches of Praiseworthy, were very fashionable for the times, and pleasing for any eye to see, the choice of multitude holy places enriching their fabric and even camouflaging the old laws. And then, no one knew for sure how such a terrible thing of losing their Aboriginal Sovereignty in the sea could have happened in the first place, since they had forgotten how something like this had already been happening frequently with the other little children who went into the sea and never returned alive, never came home in time for dinner ever again. They were too caught up in wondering about other things now, like the dazzle of spirit force generated in the multifariousness of so many churches erected around themselves, where every second house had become a place of worship, a temple or shrine to one or another worldwide religious belief.

In the world of the new spellbound, many were hooked on the choral *Gloria in Excelsis Deo* storming the surrounds of this part of the planet, and it was hard to notice the commonplace skies clapping and thundering and lightning as usual in spirit talk about something else. It was exciting to believe that it was only a matter of time before this new communal prayer would be tweaked to perfection, then there would be real miracles happening about the place. The wish was for something small at first – a nightmare-free sleep – and then eventually, if the small wishes came true, the prayer would be built up in a more substantial way, for more focused miracles, such as the miraculous lifting of the haze blocking a clear view of what lay ahead, and to cool their part of the planet substantially, not that they were expecting blizzards, but perhaps less crippling fires, prolonged droughts killing everything, inferno bushfires all over the place, and widespread flooding that does not turn cattle into fish. This would be the end of being barraged with unwanted miracles that smelt like the rot of long-dead fish or feral donkeys infesting the beach. Yes, it was difficult to decide what would be a real miracle when so many miracles were needed. But people had to decide what was most needed in their new religious belief in miracles, where hoping for a wish to come true out of the blue might be granted, from the mere goodness of oneself as a new type of God person.

The sound of multiple bells ringing in the dust-hazed air could be heard through the streets, under the streetlights, and down by the seaside, and so too were the holy men's blessed ghetto-blasters mixing the jive in ministering goings-on through long marathons of preaching. The quick smart became ultra-competitive while rattling their fusible pedagogues with the contemptuous cacology of devotional language. Each tongue bore its rattling on about how their own particular faith church's glory light was blazing more divinely from the will of the Almighty, or the Holy Ghost, in a more holy and legit way than any other fake God person's gammon churchy thing that did not belong in Praiseworthy. These mighty sermons were either praised or damned by a floating congregation spreading itself around like dust and leaf litter in the haze, or by one drop of rain, for that was all you will get from the greatest ancestral creators summoning up a thousand-year drought, and people ran from one church to another while calling for *more miracles!* It was a full focus of vision heavenly storming while whispering devotedly in a bonanza of madness for divine faith to ward off evil from the old fog dust hell in which they all lived, and begging for the return of Aboriginal Sovereignty from the sea.

More and more houses were emptied of their occupants to placate the insatiable demand for churches to administer mass to the masses in their growing desire to be versed in every religion on Earth, and it was not unusual to see these little churches groaning with congregations of a particular devotional deity or belief. And while it remained very popular to create a glut of churches to saturate Praiseworthy with holiness, still more would be erected from bits of scrap timber and any piece of whatnot lying around the place that could be used to build some kind of structure that you could call a church. Oh! Silent night was a thing of the past. Any joy a child had of listening to the sea from a seashell covering the ear was now a thing of the past too, for while the days never ended in hearing the holy toil of bogie clerics sweating it out in the worse-than-drought heat with hammers bashing nails in warlike efforts to out-construct the enemy churches, every other church's fancy makeshift cathedrals housing pulpits were reaching further skyward, and surpassing gravity at twenty or thirty feet high, or even higher just to be closer to heaven, by reaching outside of the haze dome to be surrounded by ethereal clouds, which would be far higher than the high-rise central business district of Hong Kong, but would bring the devotional closer to the source of the holiness of these adopted religions – some that created unimaginable amounts of money from the local black man's land – but if you reached for heaven, you needed to capture this pile of money that should have been yours, so why complain? This flight for building higher than the clouds for church men to find the spirit level was possibly at the altitude of a Qantas Boeing 737 flying at break-speed at about forty-one thousand feet, or whatever it takes to stay that high.

Well! It was not an unremarkable desire – of wanting to reach for heaven where the air was pleasant, with an acuity acquired from having right faith – if you wanted to avoid toppling over, say, on ground baked by the morning sun. This was the reason why, very quickly, everyone thought that they would like to have ultra-extra wishes granted, for them to quickly reach the great heights and leave behind the mess of the overheated world. The question was though, which faith was the best, and where could a church man go to pray higher than the average human ego? How could a person of human weakness be removed from the other weak throng, so to speak, to become ethereal, which was anyone's guess about what was the optimum height of preaching and saving yourself though a heavenly life, one that was far more extraordinary than sweating it out without money to pay for electricity to run the air-conditioner in the orb-like heating facility of global warming over Praiseworthy.

So, it felt wise to be elsewhere, somewhere nice in a temperature-controlled environment granted with extra value, for this heaven had extra dials on the switchboard to suit every wish, including to exile all racist context in this new world. Then being right up there at the height of holy work, you could be clearly seen in the atmosphere like a ghostly angel casting a Mount Sinai type of cool shadow over the haziness from any angle across the flat landscape of Praiseworthy. And you know what, church duty mattered whether of orthodox or unorthodox gods, and Ice Pick, the big God man Major Mayor of Praiseworthy, checked the sound levels regularly for he needed to hear the medley of screaming devoutness at perfect pitch. *Fervour up,* he insisted on his rounds to the Pope-like people of religious all-sorts, *Get that deaf haze to hear the word of Praiseworthy.* There must have been a hundred preachers at this stage, and with more wannabes coming behind to join the megaphoning of daily preaching with battery-charged PA systems connected together through umpteen metres of sun-frayed and half-buggered grey or yellow plastic extension cords plugged into an extravaganza of power boards connected to the mains of a coin-operated – pay as you go – meter box that was hooked up to the mega-rich state's power grid – long resourced from the minerals that came off Aboriginal land for a song, and that guzzled up the pension money hand over fist of poor people @ $20 here, $5 there for an electric bulb to shower a single light for intergenerational families of thirty or more to share, until the money ran out.

Preachiness now claimed the region of the top notch, and with earplugs on, and microphones blasting, dream sermons reached the ad finem right on the stroke of 45C plus – going on to 55C at noon, and a sea of index fingers pointed to the sun as though it was God, while a chain of drawn-out echoes sailed the air mail to the man above to *remove the haze making us vomit, and return Aboriginal Sovereignty to us.*

The will of God was not accepted, and the brethren were not getting over the loss of their own son. Amidst a plethora of preachers, the angry faith seekers eventually lost sight of the promise of paradise, and began arguing among themselves about how to be holy. Thunder roared, and the ten million lightning strikes that filled the skies and struck trees and electricity poles fused all the wiring, and everyone was without any type of power. The church podiums went up in flames while moths and butterflies whizzed wildly through the fiery grass chasing each other in an obstacle course through the masses of churches flying away through the wind, and the arraying splashes of holiness quenched nothing across the vast flatlands, for not one single drop of rain fell on the ground. The haze remained solid in drought, and it did not pay to hear the heated arguments up and down the streets, or along the footpaths, and in the tumbling-down remains of the all-visible makeshift churches that had sprung up like weeds in the front yards. Rocks were thrown about while analysing what had happened to Aboriginal Sovereignty, and where was Cause Steel anyway, *Shouldn't he be here to look for his son, not leaving it all up to people here to do what he should be doing himself instead of chasing donkeys around the countryside?*

The lost sea brethren swayed together teary-choked, and cha-cha'd between all the creeds and dominations – souls were up for grabs, and they went to seances to send another load of messages to Aboriginal Sovereignty, to tell him to return from the dead, for this killer blow was a blow too far. The befuddled asked, *Why would Aboriginal Sovereignty suddenly decide that life was not worth the living, and immediately want to kill himself?* And why disappear without trace, not to be given a proper community burial where everyone could have grieved together over something? His body had to be found, and this was what the brethren wanted the church men to pray for, and for once, to at least try to make people's wishes come true.

18

You want church people burying Aboriginal Sovereignty? You got to be kidding me. Ice Pick, being the Major Mayor with key responsibilities about running the show and orchestrating everybody else's business in the likelihoods from the humane to the economical, thought hard and fast about what to do. No. 1, he pondered about what a normal person wanted when they died. But no. 2, he was not sure whether Aboriginal Sovereignty would want a church burial. Or, even! Even! If he was really dead, since you know he was in trouble with the police people, and perhaps he was just hiding, lying low somewhere out in the sea for instance. He might even return to Praiseworthy waterlogged, or come back looking like a ghost, or perhaps he went to live with all those ghost people dwelling about the place and one of them might come back like a human pretending to be someone else, or he might come back in the form of his totem, which of course, Ice explained, would exclude his own totem, the missing golden Christmas beetle.

Now there were vicious rumours floating though Praiseworthy, even though telling fake stories was against the Major Mayoral *editio princeps*, a book hefty in edicts of legal jargon that had been dragged by the wheelbarrow through the slimmest adit, pumping out his laws into the atmosphere from the gold mine of imaginings from a diehard living in Ice Pick's personal mind, and so, once fired into the open air, contaminated it in perpetuity. Gold! Gold! Gold! This! was gold. That was gold. Well! It was all gold, which Ice claimed originated through a chain of osmosis made of gold connecting the great men of the most powerful countries on the modern Earth, on how to run a place.

Then someone who had an original thought that was unguided, un-coerced, or un-polluted by Ice Pick said, what if someone had actually found the body in the ocean, and had snuck away with it in the middle of the night? That person was shouted down, *You are a stranger to us*. There were too many of these what-ifs in a time of perpetual overpowering grief, and the only way to deal with the ordeal of losing Aboriginal Sovereignty was to build more churches, until there were just too many ramshackle and humpy churches built on stilts where the multi-denominational oracles could look out over the top of the masses, and far over the mudflat horizon, to pluck the angels from the sky that were carrying holy messages of preachiness for the masses, but not for nothing. This was the space. The ocean. This was where the oracles were imaginatively frog-paddling around in the waves to come up with some answers by foreseeing otherworldly things happening, like people stealing bodies. Story emanated everywhere from the countless denominations with pulpits now reaching further up into the sky, and this was where church men sat like lifesavers who saw everywhere, whether seeing or not, the obstacles preventing the recovery of the body. They demanded Ice Pick, as the Major Mayor thing, to launch a full-scale investigation into the reasons why they were being prevented from showering full magnificence in the burying of Aboriginal Sovereignty once and for all. The oracles bemoaned that Ice Pick should be combing the whole sea, sieving and draining the ocean until the body was found, and then Aboriginal Sovereignty should be buried full-stop in the local cemetery in a proper grave, dug six feet deep, and the name never mentioned again.

In the end though, a full-house, mass-oracle-styled consensus was reached. This was achieved only after the haziness of Praiseworthy began to spin uncontrollably in a phenomenal tear-jerker. The high-pitched and totally marvellous operatic performance was beautifully curated and edited, squeezed into a hyperventilating hour, preventing the solemnity of anyone having to be tied up in songs for months. The church men and women said we were modern now, and the urgency of the monumental situation required everything to be assembled in haste, you needed to think like a government trying to cover up the severity of a pandemic being a killer of millions when they said, *You just have to learn to live with it*. And in any case, the leading church men and women were guided by Ice Pick's thought processes, and this was important, otherwise the whole thing would have been strangled to an inch of its life very quickly.

The haste in the haze opera consisted of at least fifty finger-pointing choirs. Not one chorister was able to sing a note of foreign hymns in

247

tune, but they were conscripted nevertheless as volunteers to each of the churches, the ones with plenty of congregation, and the others that were not that popular because of their weirdo beliefs going too far off the scale of normality, and were a bit of a one-horse turnout anyway, and could not be equally represented in a truly democratic manner. So! The choirs sang churchy prayers without any musical finesse and that was fine enough. It was enough that their voices filled the air with a repetitive guttural moaning of great bewilderment and wonder, while accompanying a serious number of ghetto-blasters blasting in sync Vienna Philharmonic orchestral music of a Strauss waltz on the ABC. The epical song prayer could only be translated by the old people as being about beseeching the foreign Lord – not the true creator of their world – to give mercy while they were screaming at the bored-to-the-eyebrows children to behave like normal people, and while elbowing other enthusiasts undeserving of one of the holy seats in the front rows where the elders should sit, to get out of the way from the contaminated singers. You should have heard those plague cicadas humming in the bush for miles around and poisoning the decibel of the foreign music. The tenors went wild. The lyricist who was on a hotline to Ice Pick who stayed at home cross-communicating with the spirit of the golden beetle, was given permission to compose more glorious lines on the spot to be ruined by the untalented throng. Yet the crowd was ecstatic. People flocked to the stage like fans at a rock concert. Everyone wanted to become a tenor with adoring fans, and even Johann Strauss the second may have seen the whole shebang a bit differently too, if he had to compose a waltz for the hell haze created by the Enlightenment, instead of dreaming about how to create a stylistic music inspired by slow-running Blue Danube river-tinkling water type of music.

Then in the stifling heat, the Praiseworthy fiery sopranos, the Ice Queens, frocked in brightly coloured cotton kaftans purchased from free trade shops in Darwin, ran across the stage singing Hell-a-lu-yah here, and Hell-a-lu-yah there. The women sent the whole rowdy spectacle crazy, and the bush world became pyromaniacal. A strange thing happened from the allurement of their pitched crying, and their waving around of dried-up branches or spinifex grass balls of fire in the breeze with live embers flying everywhere. The haze blew apart. Dragon serpents sprouted in the clouds. They flew across the skies with fire-tailed meteor showers trailing behind them. The natural world thought that it was buggered. All the birds and bush animals, insects, dogs, cats, rats and lizards fled for their lives, because sooner than anyone could scream fire, there were wildfires burning uncontrollably all over the place. And! Golly, you know what? A spectacle of fire the like of never seen before was created from pure haze, in this operatic performance of begging somebody or something to return Aboriginal Sovereignty to Praiseworthy.

A kind of shell-shocked awesomeness descended upon the throng. It was the first time they had ever seen fireballs of such velocity and intensity, and they said it felt like the fire era had been fast-tracked on steroids, and had been piled up all together right above them of all people, while they could do nothing but stare upwards in wonder at the haze on fire. Everyone felt the enormousness was too much, and that this total strangler of an opera was far beyond any comprehension, and they were relieved that it finished, and not a moment too soon, for the spirit of the thing was enough to make you jump quick smart out of the way when you saw smoke rising from the ground, and airlessness that made you gasp. Yes, all this. But it was this true type of hype that made the whole town go bananas, of feeling alive and crazy with rhythm, with what felt like having your brain blown apart which was fabulous, for the rapturous thing about being engaged in this new-fangled holy opera business in these local churches, was pure gold, it was a watershed.

It was a blockbuster that sucked the oxygen straight out of the air and starved the brain. This pollution crusher was later talked about for years and remembered to the death by the multitudes who were there, who said it was memorable, but in a belly-up kind of way, and claimed that Cause Man Steel had stolen the show in his asthenia. He was blamed for stealing the body that could not be found. And, they wanted to know how he did that, the trickery, and when would anyone know when they would see Widespread facing the music that they all had to endure. Somehow, it was still a mystery for the righteous people standing on the higher ground where you could reach to the sky and engage the angels to do the specialised investigative work, for fact was fact, candles were lit, lanterns shone, and every piece of artificial illumination was dragged onto the streets of the churches to light up the ash-filled skies spinning with angels for the finale of the reality opera.

Yep! The light shone on the dodgy shark with his get-rich schemes. Who else, it was assumed, would be stupid enough to go wading around a dark stormy sea of sixty thousand lightning strikes in the middle of the night among the man-killer sharks? The spotlight was shining straight on someone thinking he could make some money out of selling the remains of their Aboriginal Sovereignty to a foreign museum, to be displayed in a case with a sign: *Aboriginal Sovereignty: The last of his world*. Did he think he could actually set up his transport conglomerate with that type of money? The people's cash? Nobody thought Cause Man Steel should be spiriting Aboriginal Sovereignty away from others in his community. They did not say he could do that, stealing what was rightfully their right, and robbing the lament from Praiseworthy. You would have thought that a museum would have paid him a lot of money for something so precious and irreplaceable as their Aboriginal Sovereignty. The whole horrible atrocity became the scenario of what went down out there in the sea. The men went back to the sea to bring in the big fish, and there were people that had remembered saying at the time, that when they were under those cyclone clouds and the dry-storming ancestor began howling, it felt like a voice from heaven was saying to them: *All this grief. So much outpourings about the theft of the body of Aboriginal Sovereignty.* The fishermen went into their bundle of churches focused more on the sea, and while watching the swinging of the smoking thurible that was altering their age-old beliefs, wondered whether the fish they caught with their own labour would be enough for men to eat in this day and age. *Was it worth it, I mean, the money he got paid for it?*

19

The heartbroken haze crying for Aboriginal Sovereignty disturbed the hot season butterflies. The jaded wings of the pretty kulibibi were flicking open and shut, fanning in a whiling stillness to cool themselves while clinging to the holy statues in the cemetery. Time passed by slowly like an everlasting raga played to sweeten the prolonged drought sulking in the haze. There, across the cemetery, the butterflies slept on the stiffened leaves of hill-sized oleander hedges, while others hung limply on the ropey vines cultivated along corrugated iron walls, creeping in and out of the windows, and onto the roof of Cause Steel's illegal house, while other small ground butterflies – the grass yellows – were resting in muddy puddles beside the graves.

In a strange awakening of ancestors bristling by, a slight breeze touched this stillness in the country, and touched one by one the hatching of black-and-white winged common crow butterflies on the oleanders, and they began spreading their unstuck wings, and then after a while, were lifting themselves from the silver chrysalis, and took flight. Up into the air, they began dancing their long butterfly ceremony that they had brought with them from ancient times. The air became electrified with the slight approaching sounds of a grasshopper, or the black-dotted and snow-coloured winged white butterfly, and the white-eye ghost butterflies that had left their ant friends caring for their larvae in the spinifex where journeying leaves travelled over the ground in a breeze, and the dry inland lizard's weight snapped a twig, or a sudden whorl of wind lifted the dust from the riparian jungle vines covering the bush country of the coastal pandanus and mangroves. The rustle sent the gathering of migrating caper whites to take flight from the moving leaf litter, and they went fluttering high in the sky where the clouds joined countless other butterflies – the awls, swifts, darters – a mixture of black, white, yellow and tiny brown grass butterflies. More slips of colour were carried away in the flowing dust above the graveyard and joined a sky-borne butterfly kaleidoscope of swirling, dizzy spiralling wings flitting higher into the thermals to join the search of the vast flock of screeching white cockatoos and other birds – myna birds, eagles, ducks, and the bush animals – marsupial mouse, water rat, flying fox, python, gecko, frog and wallaroo, and over there, the fish in the sea, in the search for the lost soul of Aboriginal Sovereignty taken from country.

In their endless chasing after the lost soul of Aboriginal Sovereignty around the souring heatwave inside the haze dome, the butterflies found Dance Steel instead. The ghost moth-er was wearing the drab mothy regalia of blanket grey that she habitually flung around herself. While the butterflies danced in zigzagged rings around her, she stood motionless, where she had remained like a statue in the backyard of her home since the loss of her family, staring at the rusty tin place that Widespread had built smack-bang in the middle of the cemetery that he had claimed was his traditional spirit country, and where he had whacked a Native Title claim over it, and had made sure he excluded the rest of his kindred buried under their feet. Everyone knew that it was sad times. A lot of the old people said they could not wait to die soon enough because of this Native Title stuff-up. *Bring it on*, they said with a general finale humph signalling no more should be said after their last word on this matter. Their wish was only for one thing to happen after they died, to become a wracked soul buried in the contested graveyard to settle the matter of who belonged where, and to enmesh themselves further in one hell of a long death struggle dispute with this cheat fellow trespassing on their spirit home, to make sure there would never be any resolution to the matter for all of eternity for the misery it had caused them in life. Let thy will be done, and make sure they said, that their body was buried in a neat hole, not some slack-arse two-foot hole, but a proper deep six-foot hole in the ground, and they did not care how hard it was to dig a hole like this, because they knew the difficulties of a long war that would last forever, and they ordered, *put me somewhere in the disputed cemetery*, where they would remain forever in close vicinity to the fake Native Title claimant, to be able to jump quicker out of the grave at night without having to walk too far to his humpy thing, without the aid of a walking stick that living people used, so that they would not waste any of the solar energy firing up their haunting the shit out of the stealer of their land, electrocuting him good and proper while he was in his sleep every night for the rest of his life, and, then, when he finally died, the final part of their death wish was that the Native Title thief would be p*ut into a really shallow hole next to mine*, where they would be able to jump right into his grave next to theirs on a nightly basis, to kill him straight out properly over and over and over with all of the weaponry in their stash of cut-throat sharpened axes, spears, fighting sticks and other such-like killer weapons taken to their grave with them, to ensure one thing as a lesson to all hijackers of Native Title, black or white, that this final blow for justice for all, would be done.

The last breath beseeching that their remains be buried lock, stock and barrel, which only accounted for their body as a sovereign citizen right, was catchy, and many who wanted to fast-track the way to the spirit world, could not wait to develop the business interests – shares if you like – against Widespread's sacrilegious donkey transport conglomerate business venture that this global player had established in the graveyard. *We will make it all wreck and ruin for him* was an honourable pledge to be taken to the grave – far cheaper than a bullet, and to face a white court with a murder charge, because in the end it was seriously about jeopardising Widespread's success forever by giving him some justice for his feral animals contaminating a sacred place. *We will be like a gang of ghosts he can't see. We will kill all the grass, the weeds, the lot. Nothing will grow for Widespread. We will turn that place into ground zero. A proper spectacle. Poison the lot.* The donkeys were eating all the artificial flowers that were supposed to be for the deceased people. Donkeys had destroyed all the twinkling solar fairy lights that made night look beautiful for country. Donkeys kept knocking down the crosses that kept the devil away, and were trampling the ornaments in their hee-hawing fights, and what was more, all the trampling around at night in close proximity to personal graves, was disturbing the dead people's right to have eternal peace.

It was strange how great worlds of retribution and revenge were taking place in the everyday world and were never really noticed for what they were, as though they could never be undone, and as though it was an invisible monstrous cruel thing that would be breathed into the lungs of living people. And still, the butterflies' flight continued, though marred and re-synced in the electrified haze around where the statue-stilled Dance Steel stood while waiting for the return of her family, and while the frizz of her greying hair sent shockwaves through the weather system. It was always a splendid thing to be like this, relatively free in the papery thin reaches of thoughts about beauty she might have seen sandwiched in the humid heaviness of problems plaguing the realities of her life. There was a lightness so waferish in her thoughts, that managed to float brilliantly above the mire that abounded in the land of the graveyard, as she kept watching the many-splendoured butterfly ceremonies of jade-edged wings buffeting on the hot thermals. Butterflies always leave, she thought. They flit, dip, rise, while entering and exploring worlds only open to their eyes. She saw the plateauing and rupturing in the dance, where following the movement of air, the whiffs of colour chased away in clouds. They were spell-casters, rapidly disappearing from sight untrained to follow butterflies on these endless flights to who knows where, to the end of a wet, muddy pond, to the mangrove flower close by, or a migration a thousand miles away in a journey so perilous in drought, the great firestorms, or the sudden floodwaters creating a vast inland sea, and she wondered if any would return to the spirit home.

If Dance let her mind spring back to reality, it was in knowing Widespread was never around. He was nowhere in sight on the Steel family's ramshackle headquarters, so why were people blaming him for stealing Aboriginal Sovereignty's body from the face of the Earth? He was not an ocean man. How would he even know where to find somebody in the sea?

So, once her ability to capture small sightings of beauty drifted away, the second important thing imprinted like a daily rallying cry in her brain belted out the question of, *Why me.* It was a simple question. Most other people personally asked why they had been singled out for bad luck sometime in their life, but why was she condemned to be loaded with these two words forever, superglued across her brain? Her eyes followed donkeys everywhere she looked, for it could not be otherwise when she was surrounded by donkeys, hemmed in by them every moment of the day, and while her eyes scanned across the cemetery, she might have wondered how on Earth she had ever got caught up with looking after somebody else's mess in a perpetual battle of flogging a dead horse. The scale of the operation was enormous and out of control, way beyond her understanding and capacity to take on any responsibility for it, and this obvious lack of being superhuman made her feel in jeopardy of being able to handle her life, and unable to comprehend the year in and year out deal of having to defend every square inch of this earth full of graves of people she never knew, and plots for people who would go into their grave carrying their full hatred of her, and wondering why she continued to keep an eye for stealers of her husband's multitude of penned and unpenned roaming donkeys on this tiny bit of land that was not even hers. And she may have thought why she was doing this for donkeys that seemed to loathe her, that instinctively moved away, kept a determined distance from her. Nothing in this life made sense to her. There was no obvious reason why she had to be the protector for his rights to own donkeys on land that was not legally theirs, just because she was there, while he was not.

It was very difficult to defend land that took energy to keep pumping blood through every heartbeat, just to keep mounting a superhuman drive to ward off all challengers whether dead or alive that were bent on evicting her family from the cemetery. If you could do nothing, perhaps it was better to hope for stillness, and in her statue-like pose, she resisted her obsession of counting heartbeats, every donkey heartbeat, years of heartbeats she had wasted on Widespread's follies and promises of colossal wealth while her hands remained empty, and she had never seen even a few coins pass through them.

In the statue-pose, it was an all-out soul-balancing act on a tightrope over the multiple life-destroying precipices into which you could fall in a single day event, and where the total focus of balance became vital and life-saving, just to keep yourself from spinning off the skids. The war against falling was so mighty in her mind, she knew it would only take a momentary lapse of her full attention and concentration to make the difference between saving their old ancient Native Title land from becoming the intended Major Mayor Ice Pick's spy base for a foreign superpower country like the USA, India, or China, or whatever else new scheme of endless possibilities that Widespread had drummed into her mind about what the weaselling scum Ice intended to do *with our land*, to prise it from under their feet. Yes, believe it, great love existed on earth, and a mighty love allowed Cause to indoctrinate Dance into believing that the cemetery was all that existed of their children's homeland and it would remain special, for there was nowhere else on Earth like this place of the dead, *and can't you see*, that all places of paradise no matter how large or small, must be defended with the full-smarts to the end of time. And it really had to be so, for no other place in the world existed when you only had eyes for the homeland.

The battering ram work of taking on all comers that threatened Widespread's past, present, and future land of the great transport conglomeration needed to be left, right and centre of her mind even if it were a distant dream that she did not share. He had forewarned that their marriage was not a job of finesse, or for the faint-hearted, but more primed for a highly argumentative woman, to be willing and able to compete with every other angry soul when it came to the crunch, of having a husband like Widespread and defending his Native Title land. This was the kind of wife who would normally harp on for hours in favour of their defence to own what was rightfully theirs, and if that failed, further expressing herself with physical action, by throwing around her flighty arms to force home her beliefs.

Sometimes though, the theory of a dream became more about the desire of what one ought to be, rather than facing the reality of how anyone could be the wife of a man who was preparing for the collapse of the world through global warming with every inch of his being. Even the butterflies, mesmerised with her attempts to fly from her thoughts, knew where she was headed in the long run. The sun was beating down, and the butterflies copied Dance by sitting majestically like tiny statues on stems of dead grass, and became too paralysed to move. They were enthralled with being dead-like, copying the vibrating sound of her thoughts in their bodies, and returning a thousand renditions of the same continuous ancestor story sung over eternal time down the line to where they now sat in the dead grass, or in the mud, and drunk on their own willowing sounds of songs combining with all song for country.

The breeze turned, and Dance again heard the grieving operas that came from the platforms in the sky where the sermons were held for Aboriginal Sovereignty, and she stood like a ghost with her arms pinned down on her sides, like wings broken out of their chrysalis and still unable to become unstuck, and was unable to say a single word.

Only her thoughts continued to scatter with the bits and pieces of the opera, and were hitting against each other, but nothing made sense, and she thought that she had become mad, and the more she tried to move, the more frightened she became of thoughts clashing and accelerating with the opera, and it was impossible to speak. She felt immovable, like she had become a rock, and could bring no tears to roll from her eyes for Aboriginal Sovereignty. The families of the deceased continued to sit on their collapsible chairs outside the fence of the cemetery, to mourn from a distance because the place was a big pigsty overrun with dangerous feral donkeys, and when these folk saw her staring straight through them and into an unspecified location, they also stared back at her, and yelled from a distance that they were sorry for her loss.

Nobody sitting on the fold-up chairs knew, or understood if she had wanted to say something, and thought that perhaps she wanted to say nothing, because speechlessness was the only raw reality anyone could be expected to endure in the tragedy about losing Aboriginal

Sovereignty. There was nothing that could ever be said about the pain of so great a loss. So, no one bothered to ask her where Aboriginal Sovereignty was buried, and even though they only came to the cemetery to see their relatives, they could not help it if the question was right on the tip of their tongues. They could see she was staring through the bush as though she was watching somewhere else but was unable to reach her moths and butterflies that were being pulled apart by the swirling dust, so they bit their tongues about asking her the question.

20

Up and down the streets the Praiseworthy holy assemblies argued the toss about which preachers were the best in the world, but they did not notice the kaleidoscopic spectacle of broken-winged lepidoptera filling the sky, flying higher into the troposphere. Both phenomena of the spirit were more to do with the strange mourning of Aboriginal Sovereignty's unassimilable mother Dance Steel, than religiousness. Who was she anyhow, to be staring through people and out into space down at the people's cemetery like she was putting herself above others? Never before, or even once, had she tried to act like a team player in this business of Aboriginal Sovereignty like a good Aboriginal citizen who was depending on everyone cheering together for each invented policy initiative by the Australian government for Aboriginal people. She did not know the name of the game. Compromise! Compromiser! You heard a lot of glibber spiel in Praiseworthy. It was good manners to believe what your illegal government for the Aboriginal people thought about Aboriginal people.

They asked only one thing: *Why couldn't she be like us*? Well! One would try to figure the reason why Dance Steel, a woman who had nothing to speak about of herself, would not just accept facts, the home truths like everyone else obsessed by the world of government? They thought if the government of the day was obsessed with saying that Aboriginal people were flawed, then you needed to re-fashion yourself along with each and every government policy to create whatever model of Aboriginal people that Australians would be proud of by their degree of becoming white. But what was wrong with Dance Steel? Why would she not become a team player? She was not cricket. She had no idea what cricket was. This was the reason why she remained a nobody who did not know how to love Aboriginal Sovereignty in the way the government was teaching Praiseworthy to love their children. Now their Aboriginal Sovereignty was gone and it was her fault. She was just an awful woman – a mean cunt of a woman, so they blamed her. And now, nobody knew why the boy suicided because his mummy was just standing around like a statue, looking at the sky. This place retained its drought dryness. The dust haze hung everywhere like it was depressed. Dust stuck on everything. The air smelt of dust, then it was the time of the woeful racket over the death of Aboriginal Sovereignty in drought-stricken bush blooming with cicadas thrilling louder in this time of year.

Sovereignty! Come back my Sovereignty! In so much private grief, the droning mantra involving all of Praiseworthy was sung from sun-up to sun-down, conjuring up memory upon memory through a modern unending song cycle of having lived with Aboriginal Sovereignty, of a time when life was better than this. Around the clock everyone worked hard, and dozens of churches with mini-vans were rostered in a ceaseless concatenation of devotion that was so solid with holiness, you would have thought it was Rome, and the holy drivers were instructed to only pick up members of their specific denomination and drive them down to the cemetery to pray at the fence line, in the hope that their dead relatives might say something to them about how to find Aboriginal Sovereignty again.

So, congrats! Some congregants had made excuses to go and see their dead relatives in the cemetery, without even believing that the dead were going to say something to them. They were happy to test the power of their faith. The cross-infection by religious entryists attempting to infiltrate each other's private new-style churches to destroy the holy inclusivism required by the collectivism of living inside a haze dome, needed to be weeded out. There could not be people coming along and trying to create their own individual entr'acte performances of what it means to be holy in the crisis of coming to terms with the loss of the most loved of all. That required one total holy communion to respond to all catastrophes, which could only be done by the church leaders for the good of all.

You could not have individuals going around saying they were sovereign individuals who were making up their own rules by breaking away from the established churches in a mini-van and acting selfish, by hoping to spot freshly dug earth themselves, or to act secretly, and so were sitting on the fold-up chairs outside of the cemetery, only to pry on that so-called mother, to see if she was still standing around looking like a horrible statue of herself. For of course she was, and that was the reason why you could not have congregants acting suspiciously and concerned with their own self-interest of being there for one thing alone, to pick up clues of where the body of Aboriginal Sovereignty was buried. They all wanted to be the first one to find the body, to return Aboriginal Sovereignty to Praiseworthy. The traitors continued to define the recovery of the body as the terms of their holiness, and the popularity of springboarding individualistic imaginings about Aboriginal Sovereignty's death spread stories quicker over the land than the uncontrollable bushfires down south, up to the north, spreading all over the country by the sixty thousand flashes of lightning dry storm infestations from one summer to the next in this moment of time, when the speedily man-made warming planet went psycho.

The feat was beyond compare. *Al di là del confronto. Incomparabilis!* Aboriginal Sovereignty, who was barely noticed in life, now became praised more than anything else in Praiseworthy, and meant the world to all the arid-zone people of the haze dome. They did not even mind living in a slack shack of government failure if they could recognise Aboriginal Sovereignty as being all things, if only Aboriginal Sovereignty could be returned to them. All they said was that they were through with training to become strong fellas for better futures in the super shire town thing being built shit anyway. It was just a fanfare walk through the haziness of being a common man. They would rather be sovereign people of their own infinite culture. You should have heard the private talk. It was mad.

Copy! Properly *sabi sabi* way quick smart for these were top-shelf people. Copy! Open up thine eyes. No more listening to gammon talk about which way that dead boy was, whose name belong Aboriginal Sovereignty. Along this place, Praiseworthy, that boy Aboriginal Sovereignty was really related to all mother country, he was all the country. The number one stories for all the time – from immemorial times of true ancestral creators of country until now. Even the ghost heron's cry was calling him country like country mob been doing that type of good remembering for many millenniums – forty, fifty, sixty thousand years, or five hundred thousand years, one million, nobody could count that many years, but maybe not too much years to count in this millennium though.

21

All copy, and the running-about people copying, what he up to that Aboriginal Sovereignty Steel to make him want to die? True fella way. Strong sea storm fella way. Big rain excellent fella way. Miracle man way. All way. More capable, more beautiful, far more dazzling smarter, like real smart and, oh! what was funny too – you should have heard him carrying on bang, bang, bang with the joking and making you laugh so hard, and making everyone think more positivity about what makes such a fabulous character that grows more scrumptious on hindsight in Praiseworthy.

Since he been dead though, he heaps more greater praise like a god, much more now than a dog full of ticks, and much more than all those parched-face, bony feral pussycat things running around on the highway that you would not give two frigs about. Those bony things with scabby lice fur thick with mange you see out there in the homelands of what the greenies call the wilderness. See them everywhere running along that bone-dry bitumen, and on the side of all those corrugated roads, which were that hot it got those cats' hard paddy-paws more scorched, and limping along panting fast now, their tongues hanging out and eyes lolling around in their heads while they must have been dreaming about existential roadkill. He was more praised than that, or that dead boy's little millennium brother Tommyhawk, who was the only Praiseworthy baby born in the drought of 2000 that brought all the bad luck to the place. The devil snuck up from hell with that one in his hand, and chucked the bugger clean straight into Praiseworthy, smack into the haze, because no other ghost in hell could stand the sight of him. What's his name, that evil little bugger – Tommyhawk Steel? Cause Steel's youngest son? Son of that Dance moth-er thing who looks like a moth – full troublemaker, and you can underline that with a big black pen marker for emphasis.

They were all a piece of work that Widespread Steel mob – with the exception of Aboriginal Sovereignty because he belonged to country, the others did not. What could anyone do about a stupid little kid like Tommyhawk anyhow. He did not look like country. He looked like he did not have a shred of empathy in his whole body for country. The people of Praiseworthy do not lie. Not about something like that –

like who does or does not look like country – and they do not lie about the lies that little liar could tell in the holy Praiseworthy dust bowl. Rip up to the top of the scales for curse. Tommyhawk! Him government boy! You mob better believe everything you been told, and now you will find out why.

22

See in those clouds! Those were the real thing. Holy mob coming all the time now. Indoctrinators. They have some really good singers. All of them, like some big dust storm fellas flying around country while roaring their heads off in prayer. You can see them everywhere in the sky these days – on aeroplanes flying above the swirling bushfire smoke on the move, one over there in the distance, another coming up behind. Oh! Fucking look harder, further off down the coast. More fire-making mob over there coming up from over the sea. You get some who were like country, but were not. They were just people who did not belong to country who were acting like a pack of God's ghost angels in heaven with their singing about white government values.

You want to know how you can tell that? Books! Big white law books! Look at what they got holding in their hands. The Australian Constitution. Bibles. Government policies. Legislations. The things that do not belong to the real ancestors. The ancestral creators did not carry around a book. The Rainbow Serpent – Boodjamalla Law spilt into everything, and stayed there. Let the white angels read religious monologues mucking around in your brain like a broken record, and convince you to get indoctrinated into assimilation. *You can do it. You can use it.* Singalong way all day, always you can do it, was no wonder Praiseworthy felt like being in a prison run by heaven.

The real indoctrinator, you never seen him. He does not even have to appear in person in Praiseworthy, because he got his appointed

264

angels doing the job for him, and making a big din by singing a bit of this and that over the top of each other – in all these pissy little church mobs' choirs screaming about something or other at the top of their voices – in their gossip songs about how Aboriginal Sovereignty spoiled everything for them.

You know what they say, that only the good die young.

Well! Praiseworthy liked to thank God for taking the good for himself in front of their own eyes, and leaving them rubbish people to deal with – the combustibles with catastrophic vision, like global warming.

Boom! Boom! Boom!

The good get taken.

Shit stays.

23

While Praiseworthy was growing obsessive in whispering private talk about losing Aboriginal Sovereignty, a full-grown man like Cause Man Steel was crying like a baby when he drove back to town with the old platinum donkey in the back seat of the sedan. He had not stopped crying his heart out since that day when, so far away while hunting for a perfect donkey, he had woken up in a cold sweat while exposed in the full heat, and had felt in his bones that Aboriginal Sovereignty had passed away from shame and a broken heart. He had driven home like a bat out of hell, and he would not stop screaming that Aboriginal Sovereignty was just becoming a man. Widespread wept and cried for months. His tears covered the floor, and had to be mopped up and carted away in a bucket, and his tears fell all over town like never-ending rainfall and created flooding gullies and creeks with fish swimming around in the salty waters, and he kept on weeping for his loss.

Then you know what? One day something strange happened in Praiseworthy. It became a place that was so hard-hearted, that you could actually feel the heartbeats clanking like steel because Widespread's continual weeping around the place had made people feel short-tempered. He was not considering their loss too. But on he wept, and he kept reminding everyone in town that he wanted his Aboriginal Sovereignty to come back. *You can't*, people told him, *because he's dead*. It was that plain and simple, and then much later, when everyone in Praiseworthy could not bear the sound of Widespread's wishful, guilt-ridden crying anymore, they knew that Cause Steel's heart was softer than a pussycat, and in the fury of boiling blood pumping through their otherwise more molten steel refinery hearts, in hissy-like nastiness which was fashionable, they told him to get over it like everyone else who had to deal with great loss, even greater loss than his because when you combined it all, he was just one person: *Everyone else had lost Aboriginal Sovereignty for good*.

Praiseworthy people were rather pleased with discovering their new strength of dealing with the profound sense that all had been lost. They were becoming sceptics, and said there was great satisfaction to be found in being nasty to Widespread in the great philosophical thinking going on about how this greatest of loss was really about the building blocks for creating better fate. A signal more or less, to send Cause wherever – to get him to leave their Native Title cemetery while sitting on the other side of the fence on fold-up chairs outside the graveyard, and stewing about how they should be inside the fence tending their ancestors' graves – weeding, and bringing pretty flowers, bunches of gum leaves, and picking off the asbestos flakes that had been floating around in the atmosphere from old crap housing and landing on their family graves, but that was nothing. What really made them fume inside and tremble from head to toe, was to hear Widespread still mouthing off while crying like a sissy. This made you feel sick, because Cause would not stop thinking about wanting Aboriginal Sovereignty to come back, and it looked like he was going to go on about him not being dead forever. Where was the body? And the more this grieving father continued to act badly about the grief of his oldest son suddenly committing suicide after going against Australian law, and seeing how he was building a mountain out of his pain, the more he was shut out and shunned by Praiseworthy with its own mountain of retaliation to sort out against Widespread.

You know what the silo was like? Everything about Cause Steel became an even greater ex nihilo claim about how he was fake. Then, they said to hell with him pretending to be a super leader bent on mad schemes to overthrow local humanity. The ex post facto claims poured in abundance like his tears, where everything became a screaming match about his so called exclusive Native Title claim over the cemetery. The local humanity people were becoming extremists in their vicious lolling-about of ideas of making him feel even more totally ex gratia than ever before. They felt that purposefully shunning his grief was to be executed with gusto, without even a thought. It was just the way it was. The man could scream his lungs out for all they cared. He was like a dead man to them. He was like a dandelion seed floating away in the breeze that no one cared about because he was just one of millions of dandelion seeds floating in the air that no one cared about. He was just another loner who happened to be surrounded by a whole town of gleeful people who always hated his guts in any case, and would never forget how he excluded them in his Native Title fiasco about their cemetery, and somehow or other, ended up having everyone else prove they were the true Native Title owners of the cemetery, all bar of course, Cause Steel.

The word spread about how nobody knew who this Cause Man Steel was anymore. He was history blanked. Cancelled. Nobody knew where he came from. He was a mumu to every house and soul like demons that could not be talked about. Like a true devil. You would not even look at him, never see his spooky white hair, nor catch a glimpse in the corner of your eye of his haunted face unless you wanted your heart broken, and all you could say was, this was a devil who was somewhere he was not supposed to be. He was not in their culture. Not in the long tradition. He was nothing.

Widespread continued speaking the same language as everyone else in Praiseworthy, but they claimed that he had always spoken a different language to the local traditional country of the cemetery. They said he would not be able to communicate with this traditional country. He could not speak it, and how would the spirits even know what he was talking about with talking about Native Title. This was not their language, the spirits of his country were elsewhere, or they had come before time immemorial, or had come after the language of all times for their place. Anyhow. He was just a scam merchant creating his scam scenario like his major transport conglomerate, and if the truth be known, his family had never been anywhere near the cemetery in one hundred thousand years. Where was the proof? He had no family buried in the graveyard. The realisation of what this type of argument meant as a killer of a Native Title claim was rhapsody in motion. Once this great thinking was flowering, the fold-up chair mourners rose with full belief in having never seen any of his family's spirits walking around in Praiseworthy, and this was what they would tell that Native Title judge to prove their counterclaim, the next time they saw the fellow. It was fun to be cruel, to feel full with life, where liveliness had dwindled to almost nothing over two centuries, and to become bloated in the guts with something to think about which was so much better than what anyone else had to say about the matter of being alive. The folded-up chairs people thought you never knew what came tumbling out of the barrel in the mind when you tipped it over. Other than water, other things spilt over the ground too, but who was interested in the spilt water when snakes were slithering around your feet.

Now the thing was, there was nothing much that could be built out of what comes out of an empty barrel, at least nothing that ended up being glorious. So! In short: What do you do with a squatting snake? Wrap it around your brain? This was what happened. With the spreading belief that Widespread's traditional country was elsewhere, and so elsewhere that it was far away and may as well have been in China, this was where the story ended up, not that anyone in Praiseworthy knew a thing about China, or even that Asia was a big country containing several other traditional countries and nationalities, and ruled the sky and the moon too, because this was too hard to conceive when world thought began and ended in Praiseworthy. Now all of a sudden, everyone else with Han blood in their Aboriginal veins thought that, unlike themselves, Widespread was actually Chinese, and not Aboriginal at all. It did not matter that there was total blindness to the considerable mixed-heritage in the racist creepy colonial history of the region. All thought this was okay and were sequaciously pleased, in being prepared to say that Cause Man Steel actually looked like a Chinese person, because an intergenerational string of whitefellas had pointed this out, so it must be. Now even Dance, if not her sons, one assumed being dead, the other being alive somewhere, was not praiseworthy enough for Praiseworthy Native Title holder fact and she belonged in China too, even though not much was known about the world outside of Praiseworthy geography that only included faraway Australia, and American television. Ice Pick came along to talk to the folded-up chair people, the white-plastic chair people, the many denominational churches, and said he was advised by his totem golden beetle, which spoke another language entirely that he would never understand, that the cemetery was his. The oracles of the multiple churches continued to say so much more about who dug the grave holes, and they finally agreed that there would be a grave hole that Ice Pick could have for himself when he died, just like everyone else would be given one, but this was a community thing, and he would have to share the space, with everyone else. Nobody was better than anyone else, and he could not put a Native Title claim over his own hole in the ground even if it was the final resting place for his bones. But why kill the dream of where this story was heading on the likes of Ice Pick? Who cares where he wanted to be buried? Where was Aboriginal Sovereignty buried? So much was being tied up with how the oracles of the churches debated about all the spurious Native Title claims being made over the cemetery, and why the squatters Widespread Steel and his family should return to China, instead of claiming Native Title on country that really belonged to the blood of other people, they were at risk of losing forever any possibility of ever finding the body of Aboriginal Sovereignty – dead or alive.

24

Widespread knew real hate sounded like real estate, and he lived off it. This was his temple where hate sprung up from everywhere in the realm, it rained hate, and you could feel the vibrations of contempt gyrating like snakes radiating around a snake's temple of worship. The popularity he once enjoyed as a loved leader glimmered somewhere in his dreams like a dying star, dimming to less than a speck of dirt on the country's collective conscience.

Cause had become more than an exile, by being shut out in such a way that not even he had been capable of realising what it would be like to come home and feel that his own soul had never existed in this place. All he could remember was that on the day that Aboriginal Sovereignty disappeared in the sea, all the wind in the land had changed direction and flew to the north while picking up dust, dead leaves, sticks and gravel, and all the flying insects. Everything began running to the north, even the feral cats, dingoes, and birds. All instancy was absorbed into the land's mourning, and blown with the wind coming from the south and heading up north to the sea, dust rolling through the roads where Widespread had been sleeping in his car on his mission of capturing a feral donkey more perfectly silver than real platinum. The wildness in the wind was the thing that had ripped Widespread's soul out of his body, and drowned it in the atmosphere of the dust travelling north.

This was the moment when Widespread finally realised that he was no longer related in a place where everything was related. His soul was gone from this land, and he knew that something very strange had happened way back in his journey. He felt lonely in this landscape of quietness that had always felt like his own being. He saw himself back in Praiseworthy living again in his world of donkeys, and this mirror image confused his mind because it was hard to tell which was real, or how he was occupying a memory of where he should be. He knew this was wrong. He could no longer understand why he was away from his home, or why he was in his car, and could not orientate himself. It was as though he had been placed in a nightmare in the middle of the night. He had to go. He repeated the words over and over, as he tried to find a sense of direction, deciding to follow the wind, hoping it would take him home, and stashed in the back seat of the Falcon, an old grey donkey that he had no idea how it got there in the first place, but in this nightmarish state of amnesia, seemed to be like a perfect donkey.

The winds on the way to the north stalled at times, and in the stillness where nothing moved in the landscape, Widespread would begin to remember his life at the cutting edge of the saviour world for pushing his people first over the line in the race to survive the predicament of the crisis, the end-of-world era. Only the bravest of humankind, the people who had nothing to lose and everything to gain, would be able to look at the vastness of the drying land and see the possibility of this eternity, and what he saw was the entire country crisscrossed with short cuts like kangaroo tracks or cattle trails, the quick lines forging the way for his colossal new-age transport empire thriving in a fossil-fuel-deprived world. The whole conglomeration was spectacular. It would not last forever, but it would do for the interim while the real crisis was taking shape. This was what he saw – the medium-term deal, and the sheer energy of seeing himself auto high-tech, the solar pilot orchestrating the country's new transport system, with a widespread donkey-carrying system constantly moving over multifarious routes which were like strands of interlacing ribbons cutting across the burning continent, or like the heavily used international cargo lanes of the global fleet currently turning billions of dollars over throughout the oceans of the world. And he thought about the country he was driving through becoming more desiccated over longer and hotter summers in the bush in the prolonged drought when little could survive – other than donkeys – and he wondered if the heatwaves would ever end, and he realised the pointlessness of hoping for the climate to change. This realisation drove home his need to settle his so-called legitimate claim against Praiseworthy's long-suffering multitudes of conflicting Native Title claims, to prove that he alone had unbroken access to his traditional lands in spite of over two centuries of colonial annihilation, and where the theft of Aboriginal land on a colossal scale from there to kingdom come had left bugger-all of his Native Title land to claim back for all that it was. A ring of steel around his own cemetery was where he must build the high-fangled techno transport conglomeration with pack donkeys to save the fate of his people, or even perhaps, the whole country from that total crisis stage of them having nothing left, not a litre of gas to save themselves.

But nothing is ever easy, is it? And Widespread knew a thing or two about negative charge fallout. The man encountered huge-scale shit everywhere he looked. You know the story about the harder they come, the harder they fall? Questions fermented hex-style out of the bloody ground. The environment turned sour with doomsayers supering up the hype swilling in their brains and spreading rumours, more than you could poke a stick at. There would be no quick run to success in his world, not when achieving was about being weighed on the scale made by the coloniser for weighing the size of failure, and being much more *tant pis* than a real black fellow's vision, and more about the tantalising negative consequences being implanted over the combined brain trust of humanity. You have to expect bombs from any type of fool exploding all over the place. Boom! Boom! Hey! Was Widespread ripping his own poverty-stricken people off? Bring out the froth gatherers, like the floodwaters storming down a dry riverbed spilling over the side bank, or where it sits around until the inconsolable people freak out the place by crying all night about being without hope, for the haze had grown heavier, and it was becoming too much to bear under the oppressive humidity, creating so much anxiety about who had which, any, or no money, or who was the poorest of them all. Or, which people were most ruined by the times? Or, how much was a poor person worth anyhow? Or, who had more money than others? Or, who on Earth created the most wars? And who among them all was the worst person alive today? In the mix of doom, it was difficult to see why Widespread was wanting to take every person's cent to use on his pyramid scheme. What was a pyramid scheme anyway, and why was he calling it his vision, and on a day where so many saw the long-term vision of themselves as sitting on the bottom of a triangle where they were starving, why was Widespread being allowed to sit on top of their combined weight, while throwing their money around for his pet donkeys to eat?

The local world said that the Praiseworthy palace of dreams was being created by one man and was a selfish plan that was never theirs.

It was lessening Ice Pick's rocket-fuelled propulsion to march quicker towards assimilation in the mainstream life of Australia. Most of all, it was thought Widespread was wired with transmitters that were not receiving the correct message, as though he was delusional, and trapped in the bedazzled trance life of an idealist who was bent on one trajectory, to get them lost in a confused trans-everywhere dash for the future with his diarrhoea-tail donkeys. Was that it? The long run? The idealist survival plan? Cleaning the donkey goona? Now, let it be said once and for all, nobody wants to kill the dream, but the whole conglomeration business was stacking them up into living in a total nightmare. This was what the world of Praiseworthy thought, while dreaming of living in a perfect world. It felt as though life was too much with Widespread asking them to give up their dreams. It was almost like asking for their first-born child, asking them to sign up for the pyramid scheme with a few dollars each week from their precious pension money that barely kept them from starving to death. This was asking far more than the cemetery when you thought about it. He was actually stealing their regular heartbeats with debt. Where would they find money to continually feed donkeys? The whole nightmare was making people dream about money all the time, of not having enough, of trying to help an idiot turn zilch into millions, all because he had a hairbrain scheme that he sneaked up to people who never had enough money even to turn the electricity on to look around in the dark.

Now, since he came back pretending to be heartbroken and stuff about losing Aboriginal Sovereignty, who wanted to go down to the cemetery anymore just to sit outside the ring of barbwire fence on a fold-up chair in the sun, getting preached to by Widespread about building their economic independence in the new era? They already had that kind of talk from the Australian government for the Aboriginal people – saying they had to become self-sufficient. They said, the only way you could become self-sufficient would be when you were dead. You did not need another loose cannon talking stupid like the government that had never accomplished anything in the lives of Praiseworthy people. And another thing, wasn't Widespread under investigation by the police about the disappearance of Aboriginal Sovereignty, or something like that?

Tommyhawk hated his father even more than he did before Aboriginal Sovereignty left. His father had blamed him for his brother leaving home. He heard Widespread telling the police that he could not even remember seeing Aboriginal Sovereignty thinking about suicide, or going out to sea to drown himself, or hanging from the tree. Why would he? Tommyhawk thought his father was lying through the teeth to save himself, when he should be killing himself because everyone hated him. His father was like a fool, and Tommyhawk could have told his father that Aboriginal Sovereignty was living out at sea, just out of reach, just out of vision, and told the story of how he could see his brother living on the back of an old sea turtle.

But this truth-telling would never happen since Tommyhawk Steel was not speaking to his father anymore, even though he could have told his father how he saw the huge turtle bobbing in the ocean, and even knew where it was. Liar! He had no idea where it was, but he knew powerful men in the world lied, told fake news, and got away with massacres, butchering, blowing the world apart, destroying everything. He could have said what type of turtle it was: *Chelonia mydas* – a real giant with eyes that could see the clarity of oceans that its kind had mapped over its brain for eternity. He could have put his father at ease, lessened the heartbrokenness, by saying he knew that Aboriginal Sovereignty would always find the biggest and the best in the country, in the skies, in the sea, like he was already inside all of these worlds. He could have said true God he was out in the ocean fishing with that turtle – all was fine, and that was a straight story. Not *liar*. But let the police think what they liked about men like his father – let him figure it out. Tommyhawk knew his father did not know what had happened. He was not there. He was not in the alien place of Tommyhawk's mind. Why would the boy say anything about Aboriginal Sovereignty? Why would he bother? He was long past saying anything to his father about living in a cemetery full of dead people feeling shit about having their peaceful resting place overtaken by thousands of illegal feral donkeys living on top of them. What if these dead people from the time immemorial come for him next? What if they were already making his life hell? What would he know about the retaliation business circling in his mind?

25

You could say Tommyhawk had packed up his childhood innocence in a backpack along with his dreams of leaving home, and like uneaten fruit, it had rotted in the bag. Innocence had become something perishable, while dreams could be controlled and manipulated. In the dream of living in Parliament House, once he had established how to get there, it was just a matter of fact, and Tommyhawk thought he was right on the knocker about ensuring his safety, to survive childhood.

Once people talk, you get it. There was always a chain of constancy, but sometimes the flow bolts off and never returns, and what you are left with is a kink in the chain creating a humanoid, a freak waft replica of human behaviour, such as that sly little Tommyhawk acting incognito, like a cruel trick of nature, believing that he would not be seen by the everywhere eyes of community already jumping on to the fact of how good they were in recognising befuddlement when they saw it, and were already zeroing in on this runt kid with one big mouth attached to his troublesome mind, more than any other kid about the place.

In this time of no more Aboriginal Sovereignty, Cause felt as though the house suffered from a beehive hysteria that perpetually flared up over any little thing, and he could only look down on it from his lofty height close to where the spiders were running, across the cobwebbed highways floating from the ceiling of the house. While he had always chosen to hear the flat rhythms of the world, he now chose to hear whatever was going on in the family, to hear what motormouth had to say, the runt who always had to have the last word, even after being told to shut the fuck up a thousand times. Yet, what could you say? Whatever was heard from being up there in the ceiling, no one would be spared from what spewed out of Tommyhawk's mouth about the world in which he was living like a misfit. The kid was a complete knockout. Cause thought he had become some kind of moron banging on about technology all the time, about his brand-new iPhone, iPad, iBook, iWatch, the complete Apple combo the boy claimed he had won from the government for being top of his school's curriculum, which he said was super easy if you aligned to the government's point of view about Aboriginals to gain a bit of empathy for yourself. That was pretty simple for any idiot in the world to do what he did. If you were an empathy freak all you had to do was add up the masses: the most people likely to give you empathy. Check the figures – black or white. You just needed to know how the government for Aboriginal people thought about Aboriginals, and the most important thing, know that everything led to the government's power to intervene into Aboriginal lives for the good of Australia. Tommyhawk said this worked like electricity. You stop the power of rogue circuits. Yep! Tommyhawk thought he was invincible, like a ninja, winning everything hands down – Mathematics – tick, English – tick, Human Society and Personal Development – tick, tick whatever, you name it, won it just by expressing his raw opinions with a few oddball equations about living in a world of shit.

Now Widespread was not thinking with envy in his mind about how smart and superior his child's fascist brain was, compared to his own. He only thought plain and simple, that the kid was humiliating him. What? Again? Tommyhawk was really on his soapbox, continuing his usual diatribe about how he must have been an orphan. Outside the dogs were barking. Donkeys were carrying on with the hee-haws. The pussycats screeched. Cause weighed in with his version of the orphan story which he wanted to believe had happened. *Yes. That's right. Your mother found you under a frog so that is why you have such a big mouth. That was what your big brother said, remember.* Cause smiled, although he could not believe some of the stupid things that came out of the boy's mouth about how he thought all men living in Praiseworthy were the government's paedophiles and no children should be living there. *Where do you get ideas like that?*

I knew the moment it happened, Cause said to his wife Dance while trying to catch her attention – another of his life's ambitions, to get her attention long enough to speak while she was continuously in flight. He had become the watcher of a wife who was already a whorl wind even in the most restricted of spaces – in the pokey kitchen, or anywhere else in the cemetery house – and he wondered whether she might become catastrophic like a storm he once saw that spun into a cyclonic mad woman that left a trail of destruction from the sea to where it had become a thousand-kilometre sandstorm he remembered long afterwards as being just like Dance. *Stay still!* He was totally distracted with sinister thoughts jumping about in his head while watching her running around, and trying to catch her attention so he could talk about the evil and sinister thoughts going through his head. But if you were to hear someone speaking from his head somewhere up in the ceiling, he would have to be quick enough to articulate the goods from his brain, so why did she have to run around endlessly looking for things that they did not need on the table when all he wanted to speak about were the evil and sinister things that were bothering him? *What's the hurry? We are only having dinner.* This business of where to find what was evil and sinister lurking in his head could take five minutes, or five hours, or he could grow old from having dinner for all he cared. She said, *You look as though you are being chased around by some wild devil dog.* Now his stomach was swirling into a tighter knot for he did not know what to say, so he said that he was finished with dinner. He no longer felt hungry. *Forget it. Anyone would think we were trying to eat dinner on a footpath in the middle of a city.*

Dance picked up the pace in her speed to be gone elsewhere, and she had blocked out particular words from her hearing, anything that sounded like, *Will you stop for a moment while I am talking to you?* She did not say that she was too preoccupied to hear a man speak. The skinny rake of a woman just continued moving, spinning from one moment to the next, almost fleeing from too much thought, and while running left, right and centre around the table of the very small kitchen and serving the dinner, it seemed like a miracle more or less that equal proportions were dolloped on each of their two plates. Then, barely sitting down herself to eat, moments later she was up and out of her chair like a rocket shot into space, and the table was quickly cleared because she felt Cause had finished eating anyway, whether he thought that he had or not. Then she was gone, and had simply disappeared.

Only her physical movements could be heard leaving the house. She was somewhere in the cemetery where the birds had fallen silent and closed their eyes to avoid being disturbed by whatever she was doing, sweeping the leaves, the invisibility of tidying up nothing, washing, hanging up, picking up, throwing out, bringing in, carting this or lifting that, watering donkeys, putting stuff away.

There were soundless insects spinning themselves into oblivion from being caught in her turbulence. Cause had tried to keep up, to keep following her no matter what she did while talking, yak, yak, yak in free thought to explain the vagaries of life happening from her not teaching Tommyhawk how to hold his tongue. She told Cause there was no explanation needed – that she was not interested in his evil and sinister thoughts, because she already knew where the boy had picked up his loose tongue. But what the heck? Why spoil Cause's dream about who was responsible for what their life had become? She had made her bed long ago, and it would stay that way.

Whatever the problem was that struck her mind about how to be a devoted wife, Dance allowed Widespread to continue with his case: this was a free world. Everything was a matter of your degree of tolerance. He had always claimed that people had a right to speak about the ills of the world in this cemetery. Well! Go ahead, she thought, open wide those locked rooms of imagining where the overgrown gardens were dust-laden, and make of it whatever you like. This did not mean she was not listening, or had not heard his exposé on matters affecting his dignity and human rights, his Aboriginal rights, his actual ability to be a man which, as she saw it, was his business. She continued moving hornet-like, without interfering with a single word, or waiting for his voice to hit any of the right frequencies for a woman who was more tuned to listening to the language spoken by moths. His theories flew helter-skelter around the cemetery for insects on the buzz to snipe at and catch as he followed her, and the same theories were heard by the wind that brought the clouds back for the bewildered Praiseworthy to see that it was raining again on the cemetery while everywhere else had remained dry, and again were heard as dry reverb by rain-soaked donkeys with big heads about becoming the prime carriers in a conglomerate transport business for the new world.

While Dance was attending to the chores of running whatever it was she said was life after all, she never listened for the spirits of the ancients challenging Widespread with their knowledge of time immemorial, and who were helping him he said to squash each of the new forms of being denigrated and denied, and which he had explained many times to Dance, were about systematically losing his rights. He said, *I am talking about Praiseworthy*. Where else, she thought, since he had never lived anywhere else. Words like Emergency. Army. Protecting kids like Tommyhawk from his own parents. She heard that. *I am being accused of child molesting and being a paedophile. The government is accusing Aboriginal men of all sorts of decrepit evil and sinister things.* She wondered who he was talking about, who was this someone who was so poisoned he had become totally paranoid. What felt strange to her in all this evil and sinister talk, was how ugly Cause had looked when he kept talking about how the government was out to get him. The more she tried to figure out what he was saying about what was making him go silly in the mind, the more reasonable life seemed to her. Had they not both led the same life? Why say these stupid things, taboo things, how could the Australian government for Aboriginal people be in his head all the time, particularly when she had not seen any government in her life. What government? she asked with a couple of clothes pegs in her mouth, and a bundle of clothes in her arms. Their life was nowhere near the government. She had not seen any Australian government in the moths and butterflies all around the mangroves and estuaries, or in the monsoon forests, or in the rift valleys and deltas, or around the sand on the beach that slipped in and out of the sea.

There was no need to spell it out, but Widespread gave his usual pledge, from the all life from the ancestral to the modern epicleses of the multitudes of Praiseworthy churches, and from the ancestral beings that do not sell out to the Australian government for Aboriginal people. Oh! Do not worry. The ancestral creation beings knew all about the Australian government, for country never abandoned its people in the long stretch of time from and to infinity. He beckoned to the blue-sky dreaming that he wanted to make it clear that he was not saying how his donkey business was going to be a raving success even if it was a great idea. He just knew what to do – that was all, and all it was about was saving his own kind by giving them more economic independence than they could ever dream of having in their lives. More even than what was actually needed. Yes, cheers. There was no doubt that his plan would make his people rich, or richer in any possible future scenario of a clapped-out world. And you know what? The failed government would be dead. Well! That was what he said in the kilometres of foot traffic following Dance around the cemetery, and she was wondering what these rich people would look like in the super-heated waves of an even hotter world.

We will be staying put right here in this cemetery of our Native Title land with those donkeys worth a lot of money, Cause said while feeling pretty good about himself, and he would be building an effective argument to put before the courts, which was the normal scheme of chopping wood for practice that a black man had to do against *the government wanting to bring Aboriginal men down, now labelling us criminal paedophiles to justify taking our land rights. Same story,* he said confidently, *but we will never leave.*

This was the high horse.

Even while we cannot achieve our dreams, or our vision yet, we will. Or, even if we are not doing enough for our children, or we are not loving them enough or something like that in the eyes of what the Australian government for Aboriginal people wanted to keep saying about us, we will never leave. We will be on this land forever, because this is their conspiracy theory – to make us leave here. They do this just to get us off our people's coffin-choked land.

Can you tell me why government wants to own this place? Dance spoke in what she thought was her charming self-talk, and as if trying to conceal her deceitfulness about the place being a joke, and while taking stock of the view. A precision view of a tired-looking house they had both constructed out of sheer determination to claim what was rightfully theirs. The dream of so long ago built with all shapes and sizes of other people's abandoned old chipboard walls nailed together with corrugated iron that had seen better days over a century of its life, and asbestos fibro sheets that had been lying around on the ground for years. The whole lot covered with the bits of ageing plastic shower curtains fluttering in the breeze like a carnival of faded colours. Then, she inhaled the stench of one thousand donkeys soaked with five minutes of rain and jammed into the cemetery, and she said nothing.

Cause too, glanced back over his shoulder towards the house, and stood there staring into an undefinable distance where he expected to see Tommyhawk the assimilationist fascist, and finally he said in a low grunt, *This child of ours has become a total running motormouth on the subject of sexual abuse of all Praiseworthy children, of paedophilia, and all sorts of mumbo-jumbo innuendo. Dance. Listen. Haven't you heard all the foul stuff that comes out of his mouth? I am telling you, he has froth in his mouth while he is saying what he says. Well! He did not learn anything like that here. Not in my house. You should know where he is learning things like that?* He would have preferred her to reply, to show some solidarity as a parent of her mongrel child, that what he was saying was correct, and was the truest thing he knew, *that their child was learning white shit at school.*

That was it. Cause had pleasingly named the cause of the problem plaguing their lives. He nailed it. So! He returned to an old story, wound it up, hit play, and started the spruik all over again. *Didn't I warn you? Didn't I tell you on several occasions you got to watch out for the fascist? I know what these assimilationists smell like: it comes from all the dirt and shit they claw through to get in with the Australian government, by thinking they are going to get something by turning asbestos white. You can smell an assimilationist a hundred miles away. I told you right there and then on the day he was born, as soon as I saw him, I said watch out for this one. He was going to turn up with a tribe of white pussycats. Ghost cats that looked like abstract art painted by that foreign artist fellow Picasso. White cats hiding under stuff around here and watching over the fascist.*

You are freaking mad. That was what Dance said. *How can a baby be an assimilationist fascist?* She did not say anything about never seeing the ghost white cat tribe, just in case it really existed, and she did not want to appear to be lacking spirituality by not seeing invisibility.

Only for my eyes, lady. Only my eyes. I don't even remember how many times I have had to keep telling your deaf ears, it feels like I am in a time warp. How many years has it been? All these years I have been talking myself hoarse, and you know what you got to realise, he is not even grown up yet. Eight years of age still. Well! They own his brain now.

What! The ghost cats?

Don't be bloody stupid. I warned you there was going to be a problem with this boy getting himself indoctrinated by the Australian government. Well! They got him already. He's assimilated. Wasn't immune enough. Couldn't resist it. He couldn't even hold out until he was a man or something before running off to be white. He ran to them willingly while he was still a little kid.

Widespread told Dance he was just speaking plain. *One tells a wife and hopes she hears the thing she is being told to hear. What can you expect if the kid is forced to have the education of an assimilationist? See the result? He laps anything up that white people tell him. Now he hates his parents. He only loves the government.*

Dance asked Widespread how that could be true. *How would you know?* She had frequently asked him to explain some idiotic corpus delicti stuff that he was telling her with his superior tone of voice, and speaking as though every word was general world knowledge that only she failed to understand. Yet she would be curious enough to continue exploring his mad mind when she thought his thinking had become so outrageous that even she agreed with the rest of the town saying that he should be locked up. Well! The cemetery was a small world, and Dance wanted to see what she was missing in life from not worrying all the time like he was about every single thing that was happening in their world.

Sometime, whenever she felt in the right frame of mind, she thought it might be interesting to see how he would explain the crime of the century to her yet again, of just how he thought Tommyhawk was capable of not loving his parents completely and wholeheartedly like any other child of Praiseworthy. Other people might say *whatever,* but much ground was covered in journeys taken by Dance into the wilderness of her life, sometimes to view the fountain of grief, or the quiet open plains-like rationale of doubting whatever crawled out from the dense, fast-growing thickets of mad ideas that came out of her husband's brain. *You are an idiot,* she flatly rebuked him. *How could any kid be so simple-minded and prone to assimilatory ideals, that he only wanted to love the Australian government and not his own parents?*

What? Cause asked. *The news hurts your ears? Anti-government ideas are not your preferred viewing platform.* Widespread just grinned. He loved the self-righteous. There was nothing like boosting one's social role in life by convincing others to get on the same page. Now he saw himself as being on a winning streak, because Dance kept insisting that only an idiot would think he could stop a child from having an education that was approved by the government for all Australian children. She gave Widespread one of her steely glares, called him mad because he was acting like some tragic person again, like someone who thought he was better than the government. As a matter of fact, she claimed, her son must go to school. *Its compulsory. You can't stop it. It is the law. You can't break the law. It is illegal to stop kids from going to school.*

One thing Cause hated, was to be called mad. This was where he drew the line in the sand. Dance stopped her own deranged state of chasing whatever she was doing, stood still for one moment, then she crossed the line, and said flatly, *Tommyhawk loves school. He was top of his class. He is a very bright boy. You should be proud of him.*

Dance moved onwards, moving so light and with her regular rhythm of footsteps falling onto the ground in the same tracks where she had walked so many times, it looked as though she was flying like her effigy puppets of the most hated, that danced in the flames of her bonfires. She was in the world of her own silences while emptying, flinging around, and filling dozens of buckets with water for the donkeys from a hose connected to the water tank on the back of a truck. Ordinarily, she would have flung the effigies out of sight, but now, with donkeys crawling all over the cemetery, she had lost the battle of being some sort of domestic queen whitewashing herself with the fascinating minutiae of home life. Her narrative was different, as she toiled with the seeking, and the feeding, the watering, and the cleaning, the gates open, gates closed management for interconnected, interlocked families of the all-visible, and all-invisible, array of the multitudes.

The battle for keeping domesticity vastness in order was her world, since the sense of regulated bliss lived elsewhere. Her home improvement consisted of the numerous gigantic hate effigies that secretly turned up around their domestic space, and whenever Cause noticed these ugly puppets – a replica of the people Dance hated – he thought there were little devils in the bush dumping this unhuman ugliness at his door. He could barely stand the sight of these puppet sculptures and chose to look away, to not see what he did not wish to see anymore. Who wanted to see the closed-winged dead things like enormous bats painted moth-grey with stitched lips, with no ears, and having the same haunting peregrine eyes that stared straight through one's soul and into the vast distances beyond? The donkeys feared the ugliness, and steered off into the furthest space in the cemetery. The number of effigies increased as Dance would decorate her world with them. She hung them on nails all over the walls of the house, and she hooked the ugly people puppets to the water tank, or draped them over tombstone crosses, while others were left on the sharp ends of dead branches of trees, waiting for their fate, the general bonfire. Widespread, struggling to keep up with the pace of his wife, continued trying to communicate from the growing distances between what each chose to see, to convince her of his unrequited love song of saving their culture, by saying to her, *You must be blind.* Well! That did not convince her at all. Dance just dropped the high-pressure hose that danced all over the ground with water pelting in every direction like the fandango, and slowly walked towards Widespread. She stopped exactly five centimetres from his face where she whispered so low he had to strain to hear her say, *He will grow out of it.* And he did not realise, that they were still talking about Tommyhawk, and not his general overall vision of saving the future.

Stolen him, he muttered into his chin, remembering the thread of the earlier conversation, but only the mosquitoes cared about what he said while sinking their probosces into his arm and drawing blood from the saviour into their bellies, and wondering why he was telling them to listen to the radio. *You want to listen to the ABC news on the radio. It's in the national news, you know.* Dance's mind was now somewhere else entirely, and so far down the road heading away from the cemetery, speeding away through the swarming mosquitoes and the old fraying wing feathers of migrating swallows diving through the air above the graves, and even the murmuring of her thoughts were gone, departed, far off and could only be seen as a magnificent storm aura spreading through the atmosphere in its twisting and bending speed, puncturing the air with enough force that its vibrations reach back to the cemetery, trips mosquitoes, disorients the swallows' flight over the graves, and sends them crashing to the ground. While she does not notice the vibration destroying the swallows, she searches for the rare mangrove moths flying unnoticed above her head, and dizzy with her smell, sweeter than mangrove blossoms, they cling to her back.

In the stilled mangroves, she talked to the forest of moths too deaf to hear her talking whispery-like, like a moth, and only hearing blasting from the cemetery Widespread's radio world that he had refused to switch off, since they lost Aboriginal Sovereignty. Even the insects had grown accustomed to the sound of the chattering classes on repeat, booming across the graves and down to the mangrove forests, speed-talking about all the paedophiles rampant in Aboriginal communities, where those Aboriginal parents did not love their children, and all Aboriginal men were violent. And the chorus – wait for it – *why should they have special rights?*

But while the insects paid no attention to the news of the nation, Dance spoke in whispers: *I told him that dead people do not want to hear that kind of news.*

And the insect world droned on and on right across the landscape as though they were not interested in the news of the national broadcaster.

Yep! Widespread, why were you spreading the news of the world like anyone was interested. Hey! She yelled back to the cemetery up the road, *Why do you have to be the spreader of the fucking news?*

He yelled back from the cemetery, down to the mangroves: *A poster boy. That's what he is.*

A prize-catch for the government, wouldn't you say?

He is their mantra now.

We are all preachers here by the way…And yep! Fuck your stupid domestic bliss stuff too, for all I care.

MOTH OPERA

Es gibt unendlich viel Hoffnung, nur nicht für uns
(There is an infinite amount of hope, but not for us)
Franz Kafka

Es gibt Unendlichkeit, nur nicht für uns
(There is infinity, but not for us)
László Krasznahorkai

1.
Oracle 3...speak like a wise man.

Though to be fair to the world, the people named for new times had ancestry grown in the winds of the jet stream, or blizzards, tornadoes, zephyr wind, sharqi, simoom, sarma, sukhovey, trade winds, aajej, haboob, cyclones, or from anywhere on Earth who come to the wirriwiji homelands. Zephaniah, Jolene, Roy, Ford, Holden, Toyota, SUV, 4WD. Caterpillar Dump Truck. Priest. Holy men. Bujimala. Sheet iron. Scrap Metal. Birch trees, larches, pine forests rising over the land of the gum tree continent. Yukal. Jangu. Waterless rivers. Bone-dry tributaries. Endless blue skies. Haunt seeker. Jazz. Rock-e-roll. Lovers. Country and western. Killers. Outback. Whatever made the reading of a heartbroken planet. The thing crippled by barbarian situations under the safety net of nuclear threats, not called a war, for obliterating other people's land and future in what is called a modern century. A heart broken by the virus let loose worldwide and killing six million people in two years. Or was it the long cry for the overheated world racing towards its death rattle while the ocean tides running with salt-laden sea water continue to turn back and forth in an epic being written while the world's combined humanity could not find within itself, the common sense to hold back the hastening tide of its own destruction.

Would the death of Aboriginal Sovereignty eventually mean something, or nothing at all?

The local Praiseworthy people bustling with thongs through the red earth, gathered around Church Street, where they shouted suspicions and accusations about the continuing disappearance of Aboriginal Sovereignty, while posing a very modern style of academic questioning about whether Aboriginal Sovereignty could really be dead. *You saw the body then?* Nobody had seen the body. *Say something. You got a voice.* A voice though, was not like it was in the old ways. His spirit never came into it.

The slim pickings of actual evidence to prove anything at all in this very secretive social dominion of the multiple churches, did not get far. There were hitches. All kinds of unscrupulous sceptics in the haziness of such a place, even without counting the modern-day holy people, and even though you could not point a finger at one person in particular, all kinds were laying on the table what they called their legitimate claims of having actually witnessed the leaving of the miraculous from their souls when they had lost their Aboriginal Sovereignty. *I saw what happened with my own eyes and I am telling you it was a freak wave that took my soul.* Ah! A ghost tsunami? Or, a thunderous man with a bag full of lightning? Or, was it a giant octopus with arms for stealing stray souls? Or, was it a young black-and-white domestic drake with a golden crown, whose very own soul was a pearl lodged in its gizzard? Or, did the tsunami wave look like an open-mouthed snake that snapped your soul right out of your heart? And, they talked about other freaky stuff, like seeing some little fat kid – they did not want to name who they thought it was – but they had seen him running amuck down at the whale skeleton graveyard in the middle of the night. The search for evidence to find the guilty was overwhelmingly endless for the haze world, which was coming from a bottomless font of philosophical thought. With old-world thinking you have to reach down into the depths of time to raise it to the surface, and compete with the faster-than-thought new world twaddle dazzle skimming across the skin of the spirit. Well! Shit was happening in the first world, where the many religious denominations were bursting with pride in their newly acquired popularity to help find what happened to Aboriginal Sovereignty. The heads of churches strutted around – a messiah here, a pope there, bishop, or prophet – and paraded their most pious parishioners up front like it was a competition in truth-telling without any justice, and such as it was, the whole fiasco kept flowing in the mystery, just like the haze continued to pile up the shedding dust falling over everything.

What came next was the explanation through a miracle competition, where each of the churches upped the ante by claiming that their really top-order people were actually living saints with the sight capacity of 360-degree-focusing eyeballs inside their head. They said that these people had been gifted from God to have his special eyesight in Praiseworthy. Who knew why? Perhaps because this God was too busy to look upon Praiseworthy. This eyesight was described by the holy men as being like two lighthouse beams swinging forward and backward for capturing whatever in peripheral vision. Who could doubt the holy? These special law people with new world order powers for extra miraculousness, and who were so holy you had to believe that they could see further than forever, to see everything that ever existed, and even the stuff that had never happened. Listen! You should not try to fool these people of Praiseworthy, even with the holy. They were too up there, far closer to the sky heaven than ordinary people, because they grabbed all the churches that could ever exist, as well as some newly formed local churches of their own, and all this holiness alongside the most powerful holy law of all, Aboriginal law. This made the haze place the holiest piece of real estate on the planet. More holy than Rome. You could say it felt like being in a Hollywood movie about God while you were hearing what the eyeballing people – who were like movie stars – were prophesising in some lingo down to the crowd gathering about to see these eye angels making miraculous things happen in the sea during the night. But between the open sea and themselves perched up in the church towers, they had overlooked what the little fat kid was doing in the whale cemetery. Perhaps their eyes only focused on the miraculous, rather than a child, like Tommyhawk. But news of the miraculous was a much better peace of mind any day of the week, than watching the episodes of a crime series happening under your nose while you were sitting on a couch. It was considered a good thing that a place like Praiseworthy had its own peripheral holy eyes watching from the corrugated tin floor watchtower verandah jutting out from each of their multi-denominational churches, since you never know what it meant by being extra holy, if it was simply hedging a safer bet for power-adding to some of the wrecked sacredness about the place. A bidding war developed between the all-eye competitors, about who was creating pictures for the feeble-minded who had no imagination at all for imagining what could have happened to Aboriginal Sovereignty.

No fairytales existed once upon this land, but you would be spellbound by seeing so much wonder lust floating in the dust when Aboriginal Sovereignty disappeared, and this was exactly what those special eye-balling people saw, the ones whose 360 eyes were capable of looking backward, and forward in time. They would see clearly what dust was doing to a human soul in the cruel modernity for the Aboriginal people of the haze country, like the elders posing as church leaders, writing with their eyes in a new time ledger book titled *The Losing of Aboriginal Sovereignty*. It was a handy comparison to use against country steeped in deep time – the old ledger of Aboriginal law stacked in the ancient libraries of country which those elders drew upon with every breath, and archived in their mind. What happened in the war of the two ledgers, could only be described as a nightmarish fantasy, watching the super-eyed people now presently stationed up on the church towers where they could closely watch the changes in the atmosphere, and shouting down the shore! The endless shouting. The vexed climate change catastrophe shouting the highest, and unfolding bang, bang, bang – right as a matter of fact in front of their eyes. You could call the eyes what you will, catastrophists or realists, but these 360-vision people were the first to see a super storm coming, the super cyclones approaching from far across the sea, saw where those super bushfires might spring up from a slender stem of the driest grass to tear the country apart down the road. And somehow, those eyeballs – the planetary guards living permanently on those half-falling-down rusty corrugated iron verandahs hanging out of the church towers – were not keeping up with the toll of realities since the disappearance of their Aboriginal Sovereignty.

These eye people had no time to think about the death toll, nor the case of one individual going missing among many, like for instance, Aboriginal Sovereignty. They were already doing triple-shift time by taking turns to consult the heaven in country where the ancestral spirits slept, and where they confronted the impossibility of understanding the infinite mysteries of all times. This was a different matter than counting a few hundred cattle racing through the chase into the stockyard. The stockyard of the planet required much greater accuracy, only gained from nuanced thought through the ages, and reconciling one's time with the ancient stories. It was far beyond the means of these holy people to keep up with the colossal number of losses on

Earth. For instance, it would make you wonder what those powerful creation spirits of the all times thought of the growing extinction of species after species across the planet – or, were they already saying it, in the almighty flood over there, or that catastrophic fire.

Yet, what can you say? Hard to read country? The eyes were quite incandescent about insisting that only a high level of gut proof was good enough to challenge any police law test insisting on factual evidence, such as producing the body of the dead, when it was plain to see that it was impossible to find a body in a sea that hides what it takes, which should make this the end of the matter, and that being that. Only the slenderest possibility of life, mostly more about Aboriginal Sovereignty's spiritual being, would remain somewhere out in the sea, and all over Praiseworthy, so they said, for sure: *He's here.*

Some said that Aboriginal Sovereignty's spirit would always remain in country in spite of the continuing dust haze perched over the land. Well, it continued to look pretty much the same if you give or take life being a degree or more hotter this way or that on the scale of global warming, and if you turned a blind eye to what else was dying pretty fast here and there. The realists said that they were too busy putting out the daily bushfires rather than concentrating on approaching infernos. Yet, there were so many people still standing around waiting for police proof to happen, because this was the type of waiting you expected from something official, which was what they normally did anyhow – wait, no matter what the time was in an emergency.

2

Oh! What a feeling to be Toyota-less, and living forever in the familiar, a new-age ghost place of broken-down brittle single-mindedness. A mashing of waves-on-waves place ripe with old-age payback and washout recrimination. This was where time was stalling, not moved on at all, since the proof of evidence was still lacking with no body of Aboriginal Sovereignty being found.

A new scheme was introduced to the shire, cleverly designed to close the gap about this mystery. This scheme was tasked with the responsibility of choosing the official hand-picked searchers for Major Mayor Ice Pick's Praiseworthy shire council forward planning committee – for creating a golden future in the best Aboriginal Tidy Town on Earth. Anyone who thought of becoming a voluntary official searcher had to prove that they were extremely keen to close all the gaping holes between black and white people, because right now, closing the gap was the trendiest language of government policy between Australia and the Aboriginal world, and many of the locals wanted to close the gap with all of their heart. They were dead keen to create whatever splendid golden era they could that would put them on par with white people, but most of all, to demonstrate their loyalty to the Mayoral Gap Closer. These official close-the-gap searchers went door to door, with a trick questionnaire in their hands and a biro, to gather evidence leading to the discovery of what happened to their Aboriginal Sovereignty.

All these eager householders wanting to help, along with their families from whatever church they belonged to, or how they were placed on the ladder of succeeding into assimilatory ideals of One Australia, were expected to pass in extreme quick time with a clock banging out the seconds, a tricky test gap-closer form that had been adapted from the one used for granting Australian citizenship to foreigners who could not speak English. They needed to be able to swear their allegiance to Praiseworthy by answering these simple questions based on the dominant white people's common bonds and values to Australia, such as knowing what a real kangaroo was called. *Oh! That's easy. We know that! Marraji! Badakalinya! Ngangulbuwarra! Bidirrika! Wadarr!*

Wrong, you people. Now people in every country in the world knew what a kangaroo was, but here in Praiseworthy, these original people of this part of the continent failed to answer this first basic question correctly. Forget about the rest. You could not tell them to stop talking about how the kangaroo was really sacred, or how it was one of the biggest ancestor spirit beings, or how it was more their relative than anybody else's, and then, some people even ran away and hid, because by law, they never talked about this animal. *Yo! Come back here. No! No! Think man! The word begins with the letter M, think of a word beginning with M. K is only for Kangaroo. It is a–ha, what starts with M then? You are wrong. M is for morons like you grovellers. Marraji! Marraji! That's wrong – stop saying that! You got to stop thinking about song line, and talk English. Marraji does not even sound anything like MARSUPIAL. How are you going to stop being un-Australian, and be MATES regardless of any old background? Forget your background reaching back forever on the same inch of ground, or being Ice Pick's friend if you cannot think in a common freedom denominator of speech language, where M stands for MATE, and it also means M for MARSUPIAL, which is what you say whenever you see a kangaroo? Yes! Say you can see a marsupial then you might say like some afterthought, Marraji. And that is how you got to think no matter if it is really Marraji, or if it is a picture of a Marraji, or just a cheap tourist souvenir statue of a Marraji, or a kid's fluffy toy of a Murraji. That was not correct. M stands for MARSUPIAL. What you got to do is stop thinking in blackness, and start thinking in white wash, where we are all one people, one country, even if we think we are desert people, saltwater, freshwater, hill-country, or forest people whatever, where anywhere is blackfella homeland, not what was called – Outback, and where the big law MARSUPIAL lived and covered all that ground.*

Why would anyone want to keep remembering what an official M stood for when you were living colonial history? If you were the recipient? You were the prized fool caught in the Australian government for the Aboriginal people's half-hearted, hideous, slack-arsed epoch-making golden-era fantasies. A dream world that had never arrived? A circus that came and went – and came again and again, yet never closed the gaping hole of inequality between black and white. You would be mad to say you wanted to be thrown into a chasm of the gap reaching right down to the centre of the Earth without anyone standing up there on the edge holding a lifeline to pull you out when you got sick of the fire in hell. Everyone knew how little thought shifted from one golden era of chasm building to the next. This was the panorama. The overall view in the haze dome – for all to see with trachoma eyes while living in those cheap dilapidating health-hazard heat traps that continued to be built by dollar-skimping bureaucratic decisions. Like, who gave a frig about global warming and climate change? It was just about enough for any hot-box recipient trying to survive the largesse by the literal skin of their teeth, while continually falling further into the chasm where they saw themselves in the faux-mirror walls of the sheer descent, struggling tooth and nail to cling to the slippery side of their complete drop into hell.

While in the front of every hazy dust-clouded house, a street sign was erected that read: *Have you lot seen Aboriginal Sovereignty anywhere? Think where he might have gone?* These were the two questions now popping, and being inserted in every conversation like a chant – to go with the rest of having saga lives.

This search for Aboriginal Sovereignty was, according to the Major Mayor, a call to arms, not a call to shame, and of asking people to go back inside their brain for one moment, and come up with some answers. He wanted them to get some smart results. It was like he had not spoken, and Ice Pick was deadly furious about the lack of action to deal with what he called a gross crime, because he wanted to be seen more like a Major Mayor in the style of a modern dictator out to rule the entire world and feared by all, and he demanded loyalty of the troops, his yes people, to be either plastered to his side like the Casper the Ghost multitudes tattooed over his entire body – or, be non-existent, his enemy for life. The mystery of what happened to Aboriginal Sovereignty had become the size of a flood in Ice's brain, and the flood needed to be quelled, to be done with, so Praiseworthy could move on in its chase for a golden era of assimilation, with or without having their Aboriginal Sovereignty returned to them. Either way it did not matter to Ice Pick, who tried to act nicely about the whole thing, by demanding the whole town go out and find someone who knew what happened. The whole town became so afraid of losing their homes when Ice Pick began threatening eviction notices for not working hard enough to find the answers. He called them a bunch of slackers, armchair sitcom detectives wearing outback cowboy cattle stomper ringer hats while attempting an esprit de corps to overturn him, and also, by being in an active spy racket which was too busy protecting all of the murderers, kidnappers, and kidnapping rings running rampant across Praiseworthy. He proclaimed to those in the know, his various golden-era committees, that someone had better dream of an answer soon. The rush was on. All the hundreds of church services were rushed, to finish before dust. Alarm clocks were set to ring on the stroke of nightfall. This was when all the residents of Praiseworthy rushed off to bed, just so they had longer nights for dreaming about the questions of perpetual colonial occupancy. And now there was an added pressure, of finding the answers for the Major Mayor who had turned into a dictator based on his knowledge of the greatest dictators of the world, so he would not throw them out of their houses.

It was only in dreams where you could hear the spookiness of dust storm particles scraping in the night winds, in answer to the questions you had been asking yourself. The dreamers of the town tried not to be spooked by the exhilarated devil magic joking with them to be a doll and fess up to the crime, if they had killed their Aboriginal Sovereignty or not. The night itself became a fearful interrogator without relief, and this created great mental tiredness among the sleeping people of Praiseworthy who felt verbally bashed, as though they were being terrorised by the night trying to separate them from the living world. The dreamers said it was like being captured in a barren desert, and all they saw there were devils fly about like spinifex balls coming at them in a storm of grass seeds, twigs, and sand grit blowing with so much velocity towards the lonely walker lost in the streets of the nightmare, they could only feel the sorrowful pain of having their face shredded by this wildness, and to tell the truth, by the open-mouth plastic shopping bags flapping along the boundary fence screaming some kind of ordinary English, and accusing you of knowing about what happened to Aboriginal Sovereignty.

The Major Mayor was not in the least bit sympathetic about kaleidoscopic sufferers of useless dreams for not coming up with clues about the disappearance of Aboriginal Sovereignty. *You are all a bunch of gutless wonders,* he cried, *you can't even dream properly.* So, he berated them frequently about what they did about white plastic shopping bag rubbish devils haunting them, *Did you fight them? Tell me you knocked their guts out? Destroy those plastic shopping bags?* And when they said, *We were too spooked to walk up to the fence line, and punch those plastic bag devils in their mongrel pollution-creating gaping mouths, and yank them off the barbwire fence,* he said, *Tell me you are kidding me.* The general consensus of the spooked dreamers was that they no longer knew what to think, even though they wished they had the guts to make some smart-arse comment back to the plastic bag ghosts with the big mouths in those dreams, but they subsequently thought that would only be making some useless esprit de l'escalier quip to what was after all, just a piece of flapping plastic. It was not a bad dream anymore they told Ice Pick, who still thought they were demented. But he had to believe that they had already moved on in their thoughts, just like the plastic bags of nightmares went back to the real-life daytime world where the reality was. All the plastic shopping bags stuck along the boundary fences were still flapping about, and did not look as though they were mouthing off and accusing people of killing Aboriginal Sovereignty.

If all the hazy-minded dreamers were feeling guilt-ridden for the crimes of the world, they had no idea about how to save themselves from the irk of Ice Pick, the Major Mayoral Gap Closer. The investigation crawled to a halt. Nothing happened. The churches went back to singing hymns. The old people sat around on the white plastic chairs. The search to find out what had happened to their Aboriginal Sovereignty had become a very dire situation. The whole tribe had become so dream-wary, they said, in a forsaken state, that they were no longer able to dream at all. What could you do, if you felt more dead than alive? The old people sitting on the white plastic chairs said they were, under those circumstances, feeling too incapacitated to be seeking the true path to the golden era by fast-pacing the heart in a broken-down car chuntering and spewing black exhaust to victory down the road towards white assimilation without having Aboriginal Sovereignty by their side. Though let it be said, that while they were feeling distraught, the un-dreamers managed to form a secret pact behind the backs of the official golden-era searchers of Ice Pick's closing-the-gap committees. Even though the poor tribespeople would remain more bone-weary than at any other time in the long-suffering assimilation era that had gone on for too long, they were far from losing their way through the never-ending nightmare webs of colonisation. Instead, they were hopeful that their total silence on anything to do with their Aboriginal Sovereignty would stall Ice Pick from calling in the white state police force to arrest everybody for crimes that they were only half sure – more or less – that they had not committed. Who among them could decide, if they loved their children enough? They were told that only the Australian government for the Aboriginal people had the answer for that. They were not even sure if their children loved the Australian government enough either? Who knew? Nobody could know more than white people about what was best for Aboriginal people. The only problem was the questions plaguing on about who was going to close the big wide gap of inequality if Ice Pick had the whole town arrested for murder? Would the actual statistical gap become wider? Would a wider gap affect their chance of winning the Australian government for Aboriginal people's Aboriginal tidy town of the year competition again, which seemed likely if the whole town had been arrested, and were rotting in gaol for the rest of their lives? There were other gaps too. How would you fill the gap of having no Aboriginal Sovereignty?

Then the view from the white plastic chairs decided: *When you is in hell, who desires joy for goodness sake?* The only joy to be found in these days for the traumatised, lip-sealed homeland people, was in going behind the backs of the official search by saying nothing, and by creating a new fiction about the warped dreadfulness to be endured from not helping anyone achieve a golden era. All the old grannies and granddaddies, uncles and aunties, those big law bosses of country sitting on the white plastic chairs out in the open under the sun, were still being treated like they did not exist to anyone else, as if they were only an apparition, a doppelganger of themselves. This was where the matter rested, although nothing really rests while Ice Pick is in pursuit of the golden era.

Bang! Bang! Banging. On it went for hours, through the streets of Praiseworthy. The loud knocking on the door of each house continued with greater vigour of intent as the official search party carried on from door to door, in a roll call for implementing personal injury as the searchers went on their merry way. Firstly, the house people hid in their houses, did not answer the knock, although uselessly trying not to be seen hiding behind their own ghosts. *You! Open that bloody door.* No door barely opened. The search party could hardly see a pair of eyeballs staring out from the dark gloom when first light crept into house number eighty-nine so far in a raid that had continued hours before, to first dawn. At this house, the same story continued to be played out. The family hid somewhere, anywhere they could in the house, their faces and bodies frozen like statues under the table; a woman with a sharp knife hid behind a couch, men with clenched fists waited, while the old people lay flat on their faces on the floor in case the house would also be peppered with bullets. A stand-off went on until the door of house number eighty-nine was finally half opened, or knocked down by one or another of the search party with a big crowbar, or kajala – hunting stick – and hesitantly, families filed outside in the yard to be quickly drenched with the dust that the haze ancestor was blowing around, while being threatened by the yes-people search party that the whole household was being arrested on the spot, and would be locked up forever until they died, or at least, until they started to act more mainstream like civilised people, like real Australians, instead of constantly being un-Australian by closing their doors to visitors – *us, your own relatives, or everybody and sundry just because you felt like it – like you are a pack of individuals,* and, *what's this catchy banging the door shut syndrome mentality you people got in your head anyhow like you are a plaguing bonus to the rest of Australia turning their backs on the refugees, the outsider, the boat people, then you listen here, this thing, the thing we are talking about, is not going to happen in Praiseworthy where us people share by the rules of ancient law, where we squashed selfishness into a tiny ant-sized pulp,* and, *why we kick our door open to every blood relative-ancestral law.* You could feel the sudden whoosh of hot air rushing right through the situation at this point, and it left you feeling breathless from hearing how a pack of dogs was insinuating that you had locked your door from these thugs calling themselves relatives, which meant that they were saying *you had become that assimilated, you were dirty*. The whole surprise business about you having a locked door flew fever pitch, when every householder retrospectively started ripping their front door off the hinges, chucked the symbol of assimilation into the street, set fire to the thing and stomped on it with thong-feet until it was nothing but ash, while simultaneously, a sophisticated arguable point of contention fevered into a fight of relatives winding through the streets of domicile like the woken great ancestral serpent had taken flight in the thunderous carrying-on about who were the biggest door-closing losers in the country, was it black or white, and the householders said it was not Praiseworthy people who only closed their doors to traitors.

Let me tell you something…what happened then, was that the whole shebang of churchy leaders appeared from out of nowhere and they ran here, and there, all frocked up in their black or white cassocks, kissing the little children, or offering blessings, or forgiveness, and writhing for peace with a capital PLEASE. A volley of bibles or crosses were held high like they were calling for God to come down and cast a miracle that would bring ultimate peace to world humanity. Sadly, this beckoning to the God only added more fuel to the injury fire from church people accusing the fighters of acting like uncivilised activists, and doing nothing to implement Praiseworthy's important forward plan, the whole complete merry-go-round, for reorienting its multiple compasses towards the golden mecca. There was no compass in this mess. The dust ancestor had confused the compass. The compass was limbo-ing between what was law, and what was lore. There was no *Jack being nimble, Jack being quick, or going under a limbo stick*. The official search party left. The clock ticked on while more confusion was created in the messy debate about reorientating compasses, and whether Aboriginal Sovereignty had finally committed suicide, after he had walked off into the sea like a lot of other kids who had quietly slipped away, and maybe it was too late to hope that he could ever be found.

3

What happened was that Tommyhawk had disappeared too. He melted into the shadows of the haze, and from a safe distance, followed the forward planning searchers in the raids of the long nights. If the search parties felt a sense of something small following them in the early morning hours after hearing the sudden sharp snap of a twig on the ground, or the cry of a startled willy wagtail, or the slight rustling of branches, it was thought that the old freaky dog was following them. Not a real dog. Nor feral, or a non-feral spirit, or non-spirit animal looking like a dog that was breaking the by-laws banning them from the face of Praiseworthy, or that had something to do with any other by-law of at least a thousand amendments about keeping an illegal *haunter* dog, or vermin, any non-spirit savage pack of dogs biting humans or non-humans, or roaming about in packs, or creating dog fights and barking all night, or letting real children roam around town at two a.m. when they should be in bed asleep at home, ditto, ditto, all scrawny cats, fat rats, lazy lizards, bush pigs, cockroaches, fowl, ducks, cicadas, frogs and any real, or invisible, or plastic snakes of all kinds crawling all around the place, or whatever class of animal became included in the miscellaneous section banning white animals etc, and the paedophiles. Smoky haze! Why would any potentially first-class Aboriginal citizen in the hard era want to mention to anyone that a spirit dog was following them? You think they wanted to be seen as untrainable? Too mind-crippled that they would never be assimilated, like a hypersonic nuclear missile being fired into the white world?

You cannot go around saying you saw dog ghosts, dead spirit dogs, or anything to do with the ancestral realm concerning a dog. You would not want to be seen dead talking about what was now called something meaningless, like lore. It would be murder to talk about the diminished property of your Aboriginal Sovereign Law. Wouldn't you rather believe that you belonged to the new sophisticated idiom of modern people spiralling out of control in their self-made doomed world? They just said that the town was being haunted by a pack of cancelling-culture mongrels, and some real dogs too, down on Viper Street.

So, with this said and done, the boy could not help feeling that the whole search thing for Aboriginal Sovereignty was stupid, by watching the way adults were carrying on – the wailing, the never-ending miserableness as though it was the end of the world, and as though all their gods had deserted them, seeing the spectacular seriousness of their unending relish for searching, and of turning the whole place upside down. But, why? What did they expect to find? The scriptures? The scriptures were everywhere in this country. Tommyhawk knew this, and that his big brother had meant absolutely nothing to any of these so-called progressives, these hierarchy upper-tier climbers, arching ever higher than the church towers of Praiseworthy reaching for heaven. Yes, they were going all the way to heaven, but he remained far behind them, far out of sight – but in plain sight anyhow, hidden by the haze.

Why were they acting like it was big tragedy now? He could have told them, and he had, that Aboriginal Sovereignty was dead. Tommyhawk had sent an anonymous text message from his secret iPhone card, the spare one he had prepared for spreading the news to all the power people whose numbers he had copied from the Praiseworthy Essential Services list, the church leaders, the forward planning hotline, emergency services, triple-O, the Federal Minister of Police. This was the pack of what he called *dumbos* that he knew would do nothing, and he thought that was the great thing, for they would be dangerous if they actually achieved anything. Now, while he enjoyed mimicking the search huddle exploring ideas of how to elicit information from the next householders they would be raiding and leaving injured, and requiring hospitalisation, he repeatedly squeaked the set-piece diatribe, *Have you seen Aboriginal Sovereignty anywhere?*

These people meant nothing to him, or to anyone else as far as he could observe, and he wanted them to waste their time. It suited him that they would never know that he existed, and while standing in the early morning dewiness, he wondered how many adults had ever noticed him. Very few, he realised, perhaps none had known who he was, when he had already made a terrible impact on the world of Praiseworthy – the life possibilities of the future – and he wondered how he could possibly be so totally ignored, that he had never stood out for all to recognise that something special existed inside his soul, nor seen the sign sent repeatedly by a wise elder that could not have been clearer, the hauling of a spear for all to see, over and over ploughing into the ground before this kid's feet, that differentiated him from anything else that had ever happened in their existence. Yet, there was some pleasure for him to gain in settling the hugeness of what he had done, in the safety of his own mind. He revelled in the powerfulness of his non-existence in the gravity of the continuing sadness, which would continue for eternity for children gone forever. Yet at least for now, he nestled in the certainty that no one would come looking for him as a multiple murderer of children believed to have taken their own lives, and no one would realise his betrayal of Aboriginal Sovereignty to the police. The search parties would never be looking for him in the way that they were poking under every rock for a bit of slime, never comprehending what evidence it was that they searched for while interrogating the town to find Aboriginal Sovereignty. No, they were not interested in the child who believed he was not meant to be dead, who needed to be more alive than he was already.

One might wonder about the life force working in the invisible world of Tommyhawk's consciousness, if it felt dreadful to be in this place, and askew to be a dweller in the world of shadows, but the truth was, Tommyhawk could not find it in himself to fling a single shred of joyfulness into his pile of quests for achieving greatness. You see, while being a smart little boy whose only desire was to live like a rich kid in Parliament House for the rest of his life, he now began examining the world of his invisibility to all the adults living in the vicinity of his current address. If you slung in the questionable parents with those searching for Aboriginal Sovereignty, he knew that if he actually stepped out of the bushes right now, and marched off down into the sea to kill himself in front of the whole town, who would make a fuss of him? There would be no search parties like this dumb arse one making a big fuss about finding Aboriginal Sovereignty, running like there was no tomorrow, to find a dead paedophile, an escaped criminal. The complete idiot! If it was doing his head in for one minute, who knows what it was like to keep on watching these idiots running around and acting like they were the only ones caring about the most stupid person on earth who had, through his own volition, made a choice, decided for himself, and said he was going off to be with some legendary sea lady – his girlfriend, whose view of home was totally everywhere. Would Aboriginal Sovereignty have known that hers was a powerful view that was eternally alive, uniquely tied to all times, that travelled far beyond any human capacity to see the interconnectedness of all life, in spirit, and in all things, from the highest point in the furthest mountain range and everything in between, to reach the deepest point in the faraway seas?

Well! Whatever! You won't find him, and in needing his own small comfort from the risk of having Aboriginal Sovereignty's ghost jump out of the sea and into his head, and saying things, Tommyhawk pulled his iPhone out from the side pocket of his shorts, and with his hand tightly holding its case, he felt reassured. The technology of powerfulness gave him strength. It replaced his faith in his own heartbeat. The warmth of the metal extracted from the ancestral world, protecting him from harm, the lifeline pulsing to another world, pumping him with life, the energy and so on, shielded him from haze-borne diseases, and contagion viruses like his brother. Most of all, the iPhone was the treasured gift from the Australian government Golden Mother of Aboriginal children. He flicked it on. He noticed that the battery was almost dead. His stomach churned. A fear ball the size of a dog shot with lightning speed right up into his mouth. Tommyhawk suddenly forgot his invisibility as he felt the shadows like a giant stage curtain being ripped open and exposing him to the whole world as its single most wanted fugitive who had murdered his brother Aboriginal Sovereignty, the loved one. The little boy felt as though he was going to die. He could not breathe, and in his panic, he thought of what he would do, would he call out to someone to save him, but no voice came from his mouth, and he knew then, that the ghost of Aboriginal Sovereignty had come back to get him, and his brother was calling from way out there in the sea with his voice snaking its way to the open stage of the parted billowing blood-red curtain, and saying in his ear, *Come on, bro. We got to go back to the sea lady. Quickly, come with me now.* Tommyhawk limply shook his head, would not speak, and only thought, *You are mad. I am not going anywhere with you.*

The boy listened to all of the heavy-duty argumentative whisperings being carried so lightly, as though it weighed nothing, flowing through the stilled night air from the human huddle of the forward planning search parties. All the true hunters and gatherers were arguing about which type of evidence they were actually looking for – was it mental, were they searching for a pack of lies, or were they trying to root out deceptive facial expressions from people they had always known, or for any new bodily signs of their obvious guilt? Were they just going for the physical evidence, since they were always failing to find the actual body, and perhaps it could never be found and they were wasting their time trying to find a body wherever they searched? Or were they just searching for anything at all, which meant they did not know what they were looking for? All the while, they were meditating upon the force of power bestowed upon them to solve the disappearance of Aboriginal Sovereignty, and again as in times before, understanding the appropriate use of excessive power to extract a good level of truth in a confession by anticipating everyone was guilty, they were all trying to hide something they knew about their missing Aboriginal Sovereignty. Perhaps it was Tommyhawk's young age, but he could not figure out what they had decided while now finishing off their pre-dawn scheming about which set of doors would be knocked on in the next search throughout Praiseworthy's upper and lower echelons and the expanding municipality, where the harassment plan would be waved in the faces of the entire household from the oldest to the foetus in the mother's womb, and pets including dogs, poultry, cats, wallabies, kangaroos, snakes and so on, now being ordered to get outside immediately, and stand there in the storming dust to wait, while their house was ripped apart floorboard by floorboard, wall by wall, roof sheeting iron by sheeting iron until a thorough search had been completed to find – out of respect, *you know who,* without mentioning the name of the deceased person.

4

Don't you know Ab.Sov is gone really, like really forever? He's finished! Cancelled! Dissed the man right off! Postponed him! Aborted him! Pow-ed him! Disappeared him! Ex-ed him! Nuked him! Done him! Nullified the dude! Eliminated him! Vapoured him! Deleted the story man! Obliterated the page. Stoked him laissez vibrer-like, fading him into stoke-less. Well! Revoke-d him! Like! It was lights rights off! The atrocity witness Tommyhawk the fascist, continuing to itch and shuffle from one foot to the other like a hider, was ripping in his best hip-hop beat in some overgrown laissez-faire oleander bushes, composing in his fast-paced muttering a string of lyricism for his impromptu all that jazz composition along the traditional lines already established in his heart for ridding the place of rubbish, and with the yawn of a child who felt the passage to infinity was passing too slowly for him. *This was because you were stupid Ab.Sov – you decided you wanted to die and it is your fault*, and Tommyhawk thought for a second, then backed up his call to close the curtains on the drama, *I glad you did it Sov*. There was nothing much else happening out on the street. The monotony of the action he was witnessing did not stretch the boy's mind any further. He was growing more fidgety. It felt a bit passé to see nothing else surpassing the destruction of multiple homes and families by the forward planning searchers undertaking their job description in a satisfactory manner, and producing zilch worth of evidence to prove Aboriginal Sovereignty had been murdered. The cute little boy with the gold curls could feel glad about that, and he quickly tapped another text message and flicked it off to the Minister for Aboriginal People's office in Canberra. Just short: CALL ME. Then, he waited a second, to imagine she would already have his message in her hand. Again, there was no reply. He had to believe in the slippery road, that something terrible was happening in Parliament House – you had to believe in something for having hope in the worst of crises.

He chose not to feel rejected at all, but to imagine that the Golden Hair Mother was not swivelling on her office chair in a cloud at this moment, but was struggling to find where her mobile was in her handbag after the accident in her government vehicle, which would have been when she had heard the ping, and she would have wanted to answer a desperate message for help from one of her Aboriginal children living in a dangerous situation in an Aboriginal community with Aboriginal parents who did not love their children, but she could not text back, it was simply impossible. Her motorcade was being blown up at that moment by terrorists as it had been in all of those other times he had imagined why she had not texted back, and the huge impact of these repeated explosions had prevented her from actually remembering where her handbag had fallen in the shock of the accident, when her government vehicle was travelling on the same route as all the other accidents, a route she had taken thousands of times from a café in Manuka to Capital Hill, and the vehicle had flipped several times mid-air, and very sadly after that as he had imagined many other times when the handbag and all of its contents had fallen everywhere and there was no hope of finding her mobile phone with his number, she had fallen to ill fate by being kidnapped in a helicopter full with terrorists. Yes, there was always a good reason she had not texted back, when the tantrum subsided, and hope was restored and joined the great reservoirs of hopefulness that claimed their space in his mind. It did not matter that a reply had not come in an instant, nor a reply to any of his previous messages requesting to be adopted by the beautiful white lady so he could live like a rich white kid in the palace of Parliament House. But! Hope could be problematic. There was little room left to stuff any more fat hope into the kid's eight-year-old brain. He was overconfident that she was connected to him through a number punched into his government iPhone. With his mobile in his hand, it felt as good as a hug, not that he wanted anyone to cuddle him. He was not a baby. But he felt her closeness as though her very being came through his hand holding the shiny new mobile and it excited him to know that his life was soon going to feel safer than anyone else's in Praiseworthy, because he was linked that closely to the Australian government it was not funny. He was in the moment, a thumb press away from feeling, touching, and owning real glory. Pow! Pow! The boy punched the awesomeness of this big government of Australia dream world into the air. *You are the best you, government! Go. You. White people.*

Everything was pure screeching drama, a real-life mayhem, and in this melodrama of the town ripping itself apart to find Aboriginal Sovereignty, young Tommyhawk Steel was awe-struck by all the intricacies of life and how fully and truly wonderful it was, to feel wide awake. The sun was high, the roaring furnace heat bellowed directly into the haze dome as though its focus was just to hit this small place on Earth, and it seemed to be casting its worst possible spell to quell the forward planning searchers. Instead of the ancestral spirits from the clear blue skies casting the searchers into pillars of salt, statues of rocks, or a pile of ashes, its intent was far, far more virulent, with the sheer heat radiating into the humidity of the haze, destroying their ability to hold their precious weaponry of incriminating notepads, pencils to write lies, bibles for blasphemy, and batons to injure and kill.

No one owns the opera. Not when they have been thrown into the gutter. If marauders owned every scene, every score, and could prove their superiority while blasting themselves non-stop through the streets of a Praiseworthy of heightened suspicion, the town would turn on one another one hundred per cent in memories unearthed, and the contents of minds would be re-sorted, rearranged like beds, tables, cupboards, television screens, clothes, the t-shirts, shorts and thongs strewn out on the road.

There was nothing that could possibly have escaped the desperately searching eyes of the marauders and now others quickly formed cohorts that were spruiking allegiance to assimilatory practices just to be momentarily spared, and in the hope of dashing in and out of trashed belongings to save the only photo the family had ever owned of a treasured grandma, or a sacred object passed down the generations from cherished ancestors, or the only proper good tea flask in the whole town, or the slain family pet. *No way! Leave it! Leave it! Get back, right back. All this stuff is police evidence now.* There was nothing that was likely to be missed by a marauder whose whole heart and soul was possessed by some spooky white operatic dream about needing to have total ownership of the whole Earth one stood on, while forensically searching every single piece of evidence scattered on the ground, right down to the sub-normal level of ripping apart packets of cigarettes to see whether Aboriginal Sovereignty's body had been hidden inside a roll-up, or down-sized to fit into a match box, or whether, as rumoured, he might be inside one of the unlit Redheads spilt over the ground. Marauders liked being possessed by demons, and asking the demons if they were checking these matches properly, just to make sure nobody was tricking them in a cunning way of concealing a body, by magic turning of Aboriginal Sovereignty into a little matchstick. In the climate of the humid haze, there was nothing worse than having a demon working for the Major Mayor Ice Pick telling you how to do your voluntary unpaid job properly, and how they hated what you were doing anyway. Tommyhawk remembered his brother once calling the town the Opera House of old operas. Not European opera. Not Chinese opera. Not Phantom of the Opera. Not a soap opera. Tommyhawk watched the yelling and screaming of people being attacked by the forward planning marauders, which was basically about broken human rights and broken bones, as fights continued to break out all over town. He heard once more, how Aboriginal Sovereignty once described Praiseworthy opera: *The only thing different, we have high opera, a more theatrical theatre, more like one act continuing into infinity with innumerable scenes in the universal theatre. You are just a small scene bro in the beautiful bigger picture, remember that.*

The boy thought that the scenes unfolding in the streets were not really being orchestrated by the marauders as such, but by puppets repetitively acting out historical moments where each new master of the time pulled the strings in this age-old open-wound theatre. It was a theatre that burnt the ground in the soul where the ghosts kept rising up out of the ashes. So! There it was, this unrest of high drama paralysing Tommyhawk Steel with its mesmerising rapture that froze him to the spot where he stood. He was unable to untangle himself from those operatic flashback renderings tumbling lightly through his mind, that to his mother Dance might have felt like spinifex butterflies massing, or sandhoppers with half-open wings slowly fanning while resting on the ground, daydreaming across reality and not noticing the people walking over them.

The reality, and this was the absolute clincher of the thing about losing Aboriginal Sovereignty to sea life, was how the scale of the whole thing was changing the local world. The local mob, exhausted from turning this way and that to suit numerous official search parties which were totally hopeless at finding anything, was beginning to turn away from the sour feeling of existing in lives where nothing else happened to them, because now, they were acting more like they were pushing into some kind of immaculate reincarnation, they were becoming something far more splendorous in a strange and crazy way. It was as though country believed that they had to cook grief into the size of a hysterical cyclonic spin-dryer to help them see that the atmospheric ancestral serpent creator consisted of their entire world, if they were going to bring their Aboriginal Sovereignty back. They sought a grief that was so monstrous, that it would become a soul beacon glowing like a huge firefly star flashing over the seas, showing the way to bring Aboriginal Sovereignty back without even needing to do another single thing, like, having to physically go out in the sea to find him.

5

All the ghost pigeons moan sad songs in the mangroves of this mournful country – there was mourning all around, while the normally grief-stricken were overcoming themselves with an everywhere sense of tremendous loss, the weight of which was plain and simple too much for anyone to bear. The kinspeople were cutting the excess sadness loose, letting the hurt fall where it may amongst the zealotry of grief scrambling about crooked and random in complete mayhem and bedlam amongst the sovereign country of Praiseworthy. And tell you what, this was like shovelling every bit of grief into some fat devil's cement mixer churning full bore, until the load grew that heavy, it spurted the contaminated wreckage back into the atmosphere. Sometimes, grief can be too much, when it overwhelms the phenomena of the time with all its heavy-coated pieces of sadness scrambling back into the brain magnet of the personalised life like a roll your own, rolling up in the gut pain pressure cooker, then spits out in that cyclic gloom, the solidified ball of grief sinking deeper into the weft of dust particles woven like a heavy web in the haze. Call it grief ramped to the hilt. But, in knowing too, that it would be grief alone, not your physical effort, that would eventually find Aboriginal Sovereignty on a rolling wave in a sea precisely imagined. This was the magnetic power of grief, for no clansperson thought there would be any other power in the world that would bring him back to Praiseworthy. They knew you would only bring Aboriginal Sovereignty back through the miracle dreamt, where wave after wave of their eternal tides of grief would end up plonking Aboriginal Sovereignty right back in the midst of the breathing heart and soul of the traditional country. If only you could hope enough through grief, and hope for more, hope in the higher realm, and keep on hoping for the entire world to change its shape by tilting towards Praiseworthy – and the only way to do this, of making hope work for you, was by drowning yourself many fathoms deep in hope, and this was precisely to live through right hope, without lifting a finger to pull the country apart with your bare hands, or by dredging the entire Pacific Ocean to find your Aboriginal Sovereignty. Sure! Why not ask for too much hope? This would have to be a type of hope that required a real mob of country who had suffered so much grief there was nothing else left but hope, and from knowing that through your eternal grief you would have nothing to lose, and right hope would come straight, and it alone would bring your Aboriginal Sovereignty back. Yes, they knew there was no sense in hoping to achieve anything through searching the ocean with your bare hands, for you needed to do something better than that, and the searchers of Aboriginal Sovereignty were thinking about this different type of real hopefulness, one that creates blazing mega-stars brightening the skies, the beaming brightness that belongs in the realm of gigantism, of infinity itself, that needed to be over-imagined, and overgrown with its own natural sense of finding what you longed for, of what truly belonged to your world, not elsewhere. You would need to get rid of any trace of memory where you could not see hope, where all you saw was that broken skinny boy who thought he would become a professional boxer one day, before he punched reality too hard and he ended up with so much hurt from the enduring, all he could do was to hold his gloved hands tight and guarded against his body in defence against his eternity of racial pain, before he had walked off into the sea in the middle of the night.

Yet even though Aboriginal Sovereignty was no longer standing around in full view of the place, being dead and all that, his importance became totally off the planet. He had become the all spiritual universal, ancestor-charged, and he was searched after and seen everywhere in the country's omnifarious ghosts, right down to the last ancestral microbe, and even sighted in spirit ants – *yep honest to God I saw him there*. You get a clear view of nothing in the barrenness of country without Aboriginal Sovereignty, for once he leaves he goes anywhere, and for all you know, he could travel far into the air you were sucking into your lungs, for this was where he likes to hunt down stupid dreams, and leave a big placard behind with the words *empty skull* written on it. Yep! Aboriginal Sovereignty likes you to spend the rest of your life questioning what you thought life was all about.

Now that Aboriginal Sovereignty was way out of control, there were kinspeople saying they could not drive a car anymore. They would not be able to control the steering wheel. Aboriginal Sovereignty would make them have an accident. The sea was going mad, roaring all day and night with sixty thousand lightning bolts in every dry storm, and flip-flopping the country with fiery tornadoes, monstrous things like this happening, for Aboriginal Sovereignty was in another realm now, like he was all grown up and dead. Why would he even want to support his stupid father's donkey and son business now? Nope! His hallelujah was not going to point any beacon of shiny light on anyone's future.

Tommyhawk was always kept in the moment by hanging around in the vicinity of the search parties, the in-crowd, listening to their private discussions, or keeping just far enough out of sight while hiding with his big radar ears hearing the secret talk about the importance of Aboriginal Sovereignty. Or he was covering his ears from the yelling about the pestilence of nuisance donkeys littering up and down the streets that anyone could see in broad daylight, or even lit by the moon in the middle of the night. Well! You had to be deaf not to hear, for it was like the kinfolk had big powerful Yamaha amplifiers running direct from their brains and out of their mouths whenever they wanted to talk about donkeys. Sometimes Tommyhawk never heard anything for there were no new ideas flowing fast about how the official searchers were planning to bring the pure essence of Aboriginal Sovereignty back onto country. This was when the talk became so boring for the boy from hearing the same monotonous thoughts of what to do, which felt to him as though all he heard were so many empty superman dreams spoken in meek voices by people who did not have any skills between them for dreams that they would never fulfil. In the end, Tommyhawk felt as though he could not tell the difference between hearing these same monotonous voices, or listening to a plague of grasshoppers obsessed with a single blade of grass in the greatest grasslands on the planet.

Yet Tommyhawk would never stop himself from needing to know what was going on in other people's conversations, to see whether they were talking about him – at last, since he thought it was very obvious and anyone should be able to see that he was the murderer of Aboriginal Sovereignty, and he just kept cranking the philosophical opera his mind was staging, with Aboriginal Sovereignty enjoying his role as the dead director who was out for revenge, to get the fat little brother as a murderer by killing him slowly, to drive him to his own death with a gangbuster cast of totally unsophisticated and unskilled actors without any inkling of clicking castanets between them to create a bit of excitement while for endless hours they stumbled around the stage with boring continuous monologues spoken to each other that when you thought they would stop never ended, and he could barely manage to shut out the dullness, the extreme tedium of having Aboriginal Sovereignty boring him out of his mind any further. He knew, that if he actually closed the show down, dead Aboriginal Sovereignty would scheme behind his back, and would kill him, if for one second he lost sight of his own battle to escape. You needed to dare to dream at all times, and poor little Tommyhawk's head shook involuntarily by this stage of the game of trying to release the toxicity of his brother's death roving in his head, and his eyes rolled from the continuous pervasive moment of the common man's theatre for the masses scheming to murder him. No, Tommyhawk had no wish to begin another campaign for freedom from half-murdering himself, not when he had come this far with his toxic brain that was so far gone from normality it was capable of desensitising anything that interfered with the excitement of his anticipation of becoming white, in his exile to the white people's Parliament House palace of complete luxury made off the backs of the traditional owner sufferings. Parliament House would become his monument which would beat the scales off of his vision, of having to remove himself from this world.

Then something better happened, and Tommyhawk clapped his hands with sensational joy, for you know what? Just in the nick of time, some big luck thing coming through the time immemorial jumped into the big brother's premeditated suicide drama designed to pay back the little brother from murdering him. This happened when the major recurring thought of big ego, momentarily lost in action in Tommyhawk's head, flew into focus as a colossal mega-hawk, a prehistoric monster that was hovering full of chastisement with its bulging eyes, and with its huge wings flapping oxygen like a Woolworth's air-conditioner down in the frozen goods lane, and demanded he get his stupid act together, strengthen up his head and think straight. He mounted up immediately, and was again riding high on his golden gilt mane and flowing-tail black horse built like a frigate and the fastest thing on Earth. The thing was set aside for only a complete ninja to ride as it galloped around in the imaginary carousel lit by colourful lights, that Tommyhawk had personally constructed in his imagination of the magically rich world of the Parliament House palace, and while riding this most dangerous black steed named Destroyer, he could once again see with perfect vision, where lay the true reality of his perfect dream life. This sweaty-head little kid knew that you could not afford to have a failing imagination if you were a black boy, not even temporarily, never one moment of hesitation in believing step by step what would happen next in the grand scheme of your plan to save yourself for a glorious new childhood. Yes, he felt he was the total winner about that, his identity war, and he was truly beating Aboriginal Sovereignty hands down by fetching up his so-called ninja powers for eliminating the endless threats going bang, bang, gangbusters, from preventing his dreams from coming true. It was always a total war, and the boy pushed ahead like he had jumped from the ditches, and was already flying Qantas like a piece of war machinery that was destroying the mediocre killer drama, and the whole sick and sorry trail of far-reaching consequences that were coming to a head, to prevent him from enduring the final moments of being in his ancestral world, before he would be long gone forever from the scene. Anyone could have a few bad-thought moments, and you would have to expect to have some of these little smart boy Tommyhawk thoughts while being on a solo journey towards an immensely great life, and he had to keep promising himself that this radically amazing life to where he was heading would be better off for him in the future. This would be a time when he was not worrying anymore about crap stuff from dealing with a revengeful Aboriginal Sovereignty, who was probably feeling sorry for himself for snuffing out his own life, and maybe the ancestor world was getting cranky about Aboriginal Sovereignty ending it all. No one say you could do that, so he assumed this was what the ancestors who were fighting the angels believed too. Tommyhawk put aside all of these deep thoughts. He just set his sights on controlling the box office in his brain, where he began banning ghosts. He relegated the endless monologues to an underground cellar in the left field of his skull, and bolted the door. He kicked out the death-rattling ghost pigeons, sacked the bad actors, and began acting like one of those millionaire laid-back black artist dingo types, moulding his personal future into a piece of cake.

Well! Take a load off that since no one was going to stop Tommyhawk Steel from concentrating on the task of saving himself from paedophiles, even if he had never seen one in Praiseworthy, but no matter, he was no angel either, and he just sweated some more, tossed the curls, and drove home the fearfulness narrative, hammering the shivery scary-cat squealing right back down into the poisonous box-jellyfish belly of reality in his own life or death situation. His imagination greatly improved. He swung himself off the carousel turning out of control at top speed when he saw a bigger frigate in his head, where he was doing luxury in the hula aisle, or drinking coke in an economy class seat of a Qantas flight flying in a direct line above the overgrazed drought country of the north coast right down to Canberra. *I gotta go now*, he tapped his hands in a quickening rhythm against his thighs, and repeated the end-of-time mantra over and over in his head. *You gotta get me out of here.* He had to put a hand over his mouth, because he wanted the screams of Dave Clark Five's *Glad All Over* to pump the beat two thousand miles away and right into the ears of the superhero types of white people in Canberra – the boom, boom, big-mouth no-action politicians – to come now and save him for Christ's sake. *Now.* It thrilled him to know that he did not belong with the boring people that Aboriginal Sovereignty had put in the brain stage to drive him into killing himself. He felt right on course, living only temporary in Praiseworthy with these black people who he thought were never related to him anyhow, and apparently he had only landed in this place accidentally, like he had been adopted, or had fallen from the sky like a gift from God. This boy whoever he was, the fascist, who was never spoken about in Praiseworthy because he was some kind of bad luck jinx thing, was sure that he belonged in Canberra with the white people, and it felt like a truly magical turnout moment was flowering in his mind like a springtime tulip of another world, and the flower was bravely navigating each hazard of local tropical storms and cyclonic winds with a sharp turn this way or that just in the nick of time, while saving itself from being pummelled to death by the natural forces of the home country, and he got that high just from thinking that those white people with sacks of money who ruled Australia were a more powerful type of people any day of the week, than his Aboriginal people who ruled country with their own laws. He was thrilled with being in the fairytale, and the spell was turning his every thought on his journey in the clouds to the great world of Australian power.

Tommyhawk looked around and sighed that he was still listening to the searchers. He heard more storming arguments about what to do to save Aboriginal Sovereignty killing the dream like an axe chopping the exile's head off whatever, so he sent another SOS message, another ten times or maybe more with his thumb shooting bullets of words into the airways, while ejecting Aboriginal Sovereignty's ghost fingers from hopelessly trying to find a way to get into his skull. His head tingled, and he tried to wipe the dust off the iPhone with his dirty t-shirt so he could look at the big picture of a killer whale on the screen saver.

While wiping the front of his shirt over the sweat running through the dust on his face, he saw the iPhone was nearly flat, and this really frightened him. He ran off, and snuck into the back of a house where he heard one of the numerous denominationals screaming strings of abusiveness through his Fu Manchu moustache to the forward planner authorities about not wanting to be a searcher. He had already found his own god and did not need to be searching for anything else. The other searchers were accusing the stray dominical of harbouring a murderer on the run if he was not prepared to put any physical labour into finding Aboriginal Sovereignty. Why would I do that? the dominical demanded. Tommyhawk heard some more screaming, and it sounded like people were fighting, so he quickly found a socket in the wall to connect the iPhone for a few desperate minutes, before someone charged up with fight caught him in the house, and called the police to interrogate him for stealing electricity. What if they broke him, forced him to talk about what he had done – to say that he was a murderer before he could be taken into proper care, to live at Parliament House?

The iPhone was taking an eternity to charge on the slow-use electricity supplier's low-voltage pay-as-you-use card paid by pension money and slotted into the meter box for all the family to use until it cashed out, and he prayed for the federal government's golden-hair guardian angel, the saint Mother Holy Minister in charge of all Aboriginal children to hover above him in this moment of great peril, and to prevent him from being caught by marauding black people. And all the while, he cursed her because his stupid parents refused to live in the twenty-first century, and had cut the power off to the house so he could not use any of their precious electricity. He was being forced to live in a primitive house of mantras, like, *Our people survived thousands of years without electricity. Our people survived for thousands of years before there were any telephones. Or Coke. Or hamburgers. Can you imagine what that must have been like?* His father, Cause Man Steel, had a mantra a day about what people were doing for thousands of years before today. *Oh! Was that so,* replied the moth-er, in total adoration of the ridiculous as far as Tommyhawk was concerned. He had switched off years ago from listening to them, and pretended to be stone-deaf whenever he was in hearing range, but their mantras about the use of electricity were glued in his eardrums from the time he was born, and even now, while being forced to steal electricity from people fighting like a pack of hyenas over who was wasting too much electricity to find Aboriginal Sovereignty, he could hear his father mantra-ing about how their people had been happy without living with expensive electricity thousands of years ago, as if he would know, as if he had been there thousands of years ago talking about saving power. He wanted to kill these parents who had never left the Holocene, or any other time, when they could have used a bit of electricity to help kill dinosaurs or to keep themselves warm in the ice ages of time immemorial. This was the reason why he had to sneak around just to charge up his technology. *White Lady! Please, please,* Tommyhawk was desperately waiting out the agonising slow minutes – trying to get going, trying to hurry it up, to get the hell out of the house before some crazy dominical person with a mad face came back inside and caught him in the act of stealing electricity. A troubling new thought started tumbling with all the other freaky thoughts that the head ninja was trying to fight off. Now he thought someone else was sneaking around the house all this time and speaking to him and it sounded like Aboriginal Sovereignty, and he thought about the possibility, *What if Ab.Sov was not dead? What if he was just half-dead?*

What do ye reckon happened to ya brother? Hey? What if it was a dominical person's deceased granny talking? Tommyhawk rips the iPhone cord out of the electricity plug in the kitchen, and shoots through the back door. He left like a ninja, lightning speed itself, and was gone.

It turned out that not one person in town had personally seen Aboriginal Sovereignty since he was locked up, and had escaped from custody over the so-called rape of a minor, which had made him not only a statewide, but a nationwide criminal in the world of government Indigenous policy on paedophiles, though not necessarily so for the local people. They were up in arms, throwing plenty of weight around for the cause, and demanding with placards, *We know Aboriginal Sovereignty here. You can't lock up Aboriginal Sovereignty.* The word goes that he had run off, or more likely, with the tremendous power of Aboriginal Sovereignty, that he had literally walked free through the brick walls of the gaol.

You could ask questions about whether Aboriginal Sovereignty should have been locked up period, but the local people were told by the forward planning committee searchers that they thought that these airs and graces of Praiseworthy were just thinking sarcastically again. They were always knifing the government, always knifing police, and knifing white people in the back for practice, for making their lives shit. But do not fret about this, the forward planners said, they would continue scouring the country for months and years if they had to, since the Australian government for Indigenous policies would pay their salaries to find one of the country's most accused persons in the infestation of paedophile cockroaches living on Aboriginal communities and preying on Aboriginal children. The henchmen barked at the local mindset, that their search would go on forever until they found Aboriginal Sovereignty's murdered body, even if it cost the government sixty million dollars that could have been used to fix up the entire stock of substandard houses being rented to the locals, and that was the wonder of the thing, the fairytale magic of compliance, and a wonder why more kids were not running away with dust sweat running down their brows, and getting murdered. The hostile ladies fanning themselves sophistically with a bit of broken-off cardboard box, stood at their doors to talk officially about substandard worlds being stuck on their pristine land. Some fat anger spilt from their mouths about this continuing colonial state of affairs, and how it felt with colonial substandardness sticking to the skin of this ancient place by having a load of government crawlers working around the place, for a few dollars betrayal cost less than a beggar holding out his arm for someone to spit on it.

This dust place felt like an oven, it was already a prison, so don't worry about arresting Aboriginal Sovereignty. It was these houses that were the real killer. Fix that first. And no jobs. Bad health. What school? And roads that were a proper mess. Nothing to buy at the store. It was too expensive for anyone to eat. All that kind of thing needed to be arrested. Stand up to the bullies. That was why kids disappear. The big powerful ladies continued fanning themselves at a hundred miles an hour to cool off the heat of the moment, but too many memories of their time with white power was like a huge bonfire surging from the heart, and pumping the flames out the door of their big mouths. The brain lights flashed and said more and more, *and don't forget all the hungry children.* You could call it abusing the enjoyment of white power, or call it what you like, but the forward planners felt that they were working in very poor conditions while being expected to be involved in the greatest rescue mission of the century. They did not mind being attacked, no one minded being attacked by relatives be they humans, dogs, roosters, big pigs, nor being treated like a bunch of idiots by the big fanning women, but it was difficult to think properly about rescuing while being the target of a tirade about the poor state of vegetables being sold at the grocery store as well. How could you search for Aboriginal Sovereignty when you have a bunch of big women law bosses demanding to know, *Why weren't there any fresh vegetables to make a stew for the kids? Why do you forward planners keep putting the prices up all the time? We can't afford to buy anything. No wonder Aboriginal Sovereignty ran off. You can't make them stay. No good sending him off to gaol for nothing. And you think the government wants to educate us. Educate themselves first! How would white politicians know how to run this country? You think we can't see? We see this whole country inside out, and their stupid education can't educate their own kids, let alone these kids who won't go to a foreign white school, and they are cutting our pension off for that, for not making our kids put up with white rubbish, so you stop them doing that, or we will go out and kill the government ourselves without even stepping a foot off our traditional lands, so you may as well hear the truth you stupid government lovers.*

Well! It might be the same old, same old...but Tommyhawk was racing away from the set-piece drama about the everlasting war, and skitter-scattering with his iPod jammed halfway down his eardrums belting jazz, so if he was lucky, only a few thoughts would be heard by his mind. The fanning ladies who had done a fair bit of soul-searching themselves while out hunting for the feral kittens trying to catch moths around the beacon lights at the airport, and goanna for a proper healthy meal, were lately hearing themselves yelling continuously over everyone else in the public meetings of the forward planning committee. They were beseeching the searchers to go right out there to the aerodrome beyond the town, and find that fat fella forlorn boy whatshisname sitting alone where the moth-eating pussycats lived around that beacon light. *Who you talking about, old women?* They said, *Widespread's son, the fascist brother of that good one we lost.* They said, *He said that he was waiting for the Minister of Aboriginal Affairs to arrive. He said,* they said, *she was flying through the dust storm in her big flash Qantas jet,* and they said, *He was singing some old pop songs.* The women jumped up and did the twist to demonstrate that he was listening to Chubby Checker, but only twisting sad way because they were mumbling like he was when he was twisting in the dust. All the old straight-thinking ladies could do was just pretend to be like someone who was not thinking straight. They were not fools. Yep! And they were singing, while twisting, *And I'm feelin' boom boom glad all over, glad all over...*Well! They made everybody laugh, but they got real cranky about being laughed at, and said, *We will fight you until you get some respect. This was not supposed to be funny. We were just showing you something serious, so you could use your imagination properly. So! Stupid people, I would not laugh if I were you, not if you don't want to be knocked out like a goanna with this kajala splitting your empty head open so everyone could see how brainless you are.* The point was, the old ladies claimed, *He was believing that he was some famous rock'n'roll artiste. We told him straight like we are telling you so you know, we don't want any roll'n'roll people living here. And we did not know the Minister of Aboriginal Affairs was coming here...It was not right her coming here all dolled up and not telling us she's coming,* *not giving us a bit of notice to clean up this dust, to make it get out.*

Days of longing marched through seasons in an endless all-souls' day procession, and the Praiseworthy council's forward planning searchers spent a lot of the essential services money for mending potholed roads, fixing the dwindling water supply, replacing decrepit housing, and dust patrol, etc., on meetings focusing on how to find Aboriginal Sovereignty without stepping into the life-threatening shark-infested ocean. Nor would the search parties journey down to the drought-dried aerodrome to walk among the scary pussycat kittens feasting on the soul of a little fascist.

Tommyhawk was running in the spooky place with the feral cats and meowing kittens, and they all rolled together in the dust ancestor incubator covering the claypan airstrip. And there, somewhere in the solid part of his brain where he hoarded an ocean of rubbish that had outgrown his head, his soul had drowned. Yep! Gone. Soulless! And the little boy was calling aimlessly into the sky: *You're mine.* This was the big picture that others failed to see, where he stared continuously at the blonde lady swivelling on her office chair in the sky while his third-generation AirPods axe-thumped Dave Clark Five thoughts metrically looped on some magnetised repeat chain plugged in his eardrums to pump the rhythms of the bloodlines in and out of his skull, which he sang off-key to the sky lady, *You say that you love me all of the time.* This was where the old ladies with bulging eyes liked to hunt. They were long accustomed to finding and rooting out pussycats infringing the feral animal by-laws by breeding thousands of kittens each calendar year for nothing. They were also watching the tubby little boy. Their eyes were peeled and in awe of some strange enchantment looping through their own heads about what was wrong with Tommyhawk. They stood from afar, keeping their distance by a space of at least one hundred yards, for they too were afraid to go any closer to a fascist catastrophe that they agreed was far too enormous for their considerable powers. No, you *don't poke with fascists,* if you do not want to feel the consequences. You could only watch him running and rolling on the dirt airstrip like he was trying to disguise himself, and by thinking he was becoming the actual dust spirit that Aboriginal Sovereignty's heartbroken ghost roaming in from the sea would never see, *until the end of time...*

6

Stoic does what stoic say, and this was because Praiseworthy folk had not appeared from out of nowhere like other people, or as though their backbone had only evolved two minutes ago, or even from two hundred years of unjust colonialism being rolled out by lopsided fate to belt the poor buggers living on Earth. No. Their stoicism was entrenched in the ancient ties that bind everything together in country. This type of binding was calculated and tightly wound into each and every backbone, gut, head, heart of the kin throng through legacy of long endurance as country, people, tree, plant, animal all the one thing fighting and surviving together as one big family related to each other through respect. This was what true stoicism was about, what it looked like, what made sense of real solid people. Nothing was half-baked. All this weight carried from the back tracks of memory right down into the bone of those big epic stories of how their world had survived to this day, where many others had perished in the greatest calamities. This was what Praiseworthy was all about, solid people stories. Well! Mostly, for everyone in this place, give or take a real smart schemer or two. And it had to be so in any new story of reaching further into infinity, to find the mysterious truths of a blackfella's life that kept walking to kingdom come, either lightly with grace in their agility, or heavily, by crushing the last microbes existing underneath the trudge of footsteps following those who came before in thousands of years of ancestors walking the same ground of this place, and further onwards, by those who will come later. They will go far down to the tidal line wherever that may end up from either a rising or withdrawing sea, and they would continue the mourning ritual to Aboriginal Sovereignty in front of a flat encroaching sea steeped with its eerie deafening murmur, and hear the whining hum of spirits crowding in a clear blue sky. They will see what the sea has to say, and there will be such forlornness across the faces of these kinspeople in this continuous everlasting moment. They had no other choice than to remain this local, and they had no other choice but to join the useless voluntary forward planning search party. The houses and churches with the hundreds of makeshift lookouts reaching into the skies were abandoned, left to the crippled dogs. There was no one watching the aloneness moored in this vast geography, from where it was perched on the slightest whisper elevating over the flatlands to distant horizons looking like an Aventine relic of other greatest times. The awesome silence continued to reign under the wild weather sweeping high in the skies, where the dust touched every corner of this world, colliding, before dropping into the haze.

Looking at the sea was not the same anymore. The sea felt different without Aboriginal Sovereignty, and this eventually led to a lot of discussion by the forward planners about the strange heaviness they saw in the colour of the sea. Although these busy official people never looked frequently at the sea, or at all, or could not remember when they had last looked at the sea that was right beside them, they were fast to agree that this was a new sea and it looked haunted to them. A decision was made, and it was decided that the colour of the sea had turned into the truest grief grey that they, or anyone, had ever seen before in this part of the country. It was not fun to believe in such a thing as a dead sea, but nobody wanted to go out in a speedboat and be like one of those colonial explorers searching for ghostly seas to invade, to see whether it was alive, or not. They instead insisted that they wanted to leave the mysterious ghost sea alone, and simply agree that the sea's greyness was the true colour of a ghost.

This was a clarifying moment, for now the forward planners realised that they were looking not at a real sea, but a replacement sea. Their sea had been replaced by a ghost sea. Then the thought arose that if people saw a ghost sea, were they ghosts too, since nobody who was alive, would ever expect to see such a sea. So were they themselves already dead and their spirits existing in a ghost world called Praiseworthy? Had they died but had not travelled over the ghost sea of the departed because they had forgotten their culture, and what did that mean to anyone? Everything they saw now looked like a ghost. These were frightening questions for forward planners in charge of searching, particularly for their Aboriginal Sovereignty. They became paralysed with fear of the grey spirit sea that seemed to remain flat as a tack, and that you could hear throughout the night murmuring like a normal sea. Yet, while agreeing that they had never seen such an enormous ghost in their lives, they also did not want to be possessed by a threatening sea spirit, and this became the point d'appui question framed with genuine poignancy that spread with lightning speed up and down Churchy Street, and then along the beach frontage. It was like a new morning had come at last, where everyone felt united even if they were only ghosts and not really alive, but at least they were linked together against the sea through having their mind on the job of reconnecting the power of country back into their soul. It was like they were liberated from deathly exhaustion, and were again linked with the infinity of all times, and deadly serious about keeping this unique unified moment alive, by focusing on how to liberate themselves from the vengeful ghost sea that refused to return Aboriginal Sovereignty, or the normality of its real colour.

In a different kettle of fish...

Down on the beach, shimmering in the hot reddened dust-storm haze, the old power ladies were assembling and fanning a bit of cool breeze on themselves with either some big jungle tree leaf, or the waxy Palm Sunday frond from the palm trees growing down Church Street, or the pandan leaf frond of the pandanus tree, depending on what was handy, since all were their relations anyhow. Others, though, preferred brightly coloured fans painted with pictures of blue or pink oriental birds, or goldfish with long opaque fantails trailing behind them like smoke, or white fluffy cats, or pink peonies. All the old wisdom women came down to the foreshore of the ghost sea to fish, and were flicking their lines to catch sardines, while bringing the sea's storytelling job into their minds. Together, the women sent off long piercing primordial yelps that sliced the moment and went volleying through the ages, to call up the spirits of all times, to say what their eyes had seen in the sea.

In the humming of the low voices, while these old ladies were conversing with each other, telling stories of the Earth that would make you cry forever and be grateful to have lived, the sea family ancestors arrived. The old ladies' eyes never strayed for a moment from watching the changes in the sea as the journeying relations were arriving, tired, wretched, and weary from listening to the faraway endless song of the grieving ocean. *Santo! Santo! —— San-to!* The ladies with the busy fans glared further out to sea, to where a low moon sat on the horizon. They saw the dust of the ancestral heavens with the shining stars, and could tell you there were no white angels ascending, or descending into the russet haze. There were only the spirits from the aeons so far off left out there to watch, when the old ladies heard the sea unlatch its soul. They felt that a dragon snake had reached from the bottom of its being, and had gone through theirs instantaneously in a spiritual symbiosis bringing all country and sea souls together, and all the families of the planet to swarm among them. The old ladies were shaking with fear in their thongs as they felt the sensation of the country quaking in the sand from the crowding of these holiest of ancestors, utilising the essence of their power in an act of harmonising with the sound of the sea's cathedral, from where miraculous waves rolled and crashed, while above, from between the drifting clouds, came the sacred rhythm of a vast ancestral droning of kulurrungu, or yidaki. These were the sounds of infinity made from this Earth, reverberating with more power than any man-made sound of this world in a spiritual act that far surpassed the smaller glory of hearing multiple Fender Stratocasters of the local rock'n'roll bands amplifying across Praiseworthy throughout the night the praises from the vast array of churches. The women felt they were witnessing a thousand miracles happening at once from all these old *'lations* ghosts pouring into their soul, and even as they were forced to fan themselves faster and faster with all the country hot air emanating from this greatest of miracles, they could still say what these spirit-charged relatives were wearing on this day of pure reckoning to create a new form of beginning, which would be the era's genesis for the oldest place in the world. The old ladies said that the spirit ghosts were wearing the country of lands and seas, the places once ripped from under their feet, and many of these poor souls were carrying the spirit of millions of dead peace doves, and many others the truth of their spirit animals, the energy of all places, held tightly against their skin, and some looked like an all-silver Saint Jimi Hendrix coming in from the sea, flowing in brightly coloured embroidered satins and silks.

Yes, see, sea, our Aboriginal Sovereignty was in a little bit of trouble. The voices of the old ladies were cutting across the heralding of new beginnings that the sea was offering, and the chorus cried out in unison along the beach in an attempt to make its voices louder than the sea while singing, *Well! Sea! Him in really big trouble.* Then, a strong-voiced soprano amongst them, the highest coloratura with well over 1000 Hz in operatic range, began crying out in her new bel canto style of English lingo singing which sounded exactly like she was channelling to the sea a free TV advertisement for the government. Her hemispheric slogan for this part of the world spread through the atmosphere like a violent national newspaper yelling, *Stop the violence*, and on she sang, *The little children are sacred*. Her voice rang through the universe in a wailing song about how the settler government policemen were chasing her Aboriginal Sovereignty like a pack of wild dogs. The chorus women responded, *He did no wrong*, while a battalion of those old fanning lady sopranos began pushing and shoving with histrionic yelling to reclaim leadership of the song from the angel exterminator coloratura through piercing yelp-whistling, and their voices were altering range, and leaping high over one another to achieve the loudest pitch capable of travelling through the air and far across the sea, before any other bell-crier in the vicinity of the amplified rock'n'roll churches had the opportunity to push their lower point of view across the flat. The opera was so great, that the old fanning ladies shoved any other anti-black liturgy down the neck of the sea in a purposeful dialogue about how the empty heart of the white settler government of Australia from Canberra was chasing it, to lock up Aboriginal men. Then, they turned to all the anonymous policemen that had been residing as invaders in their own heart for ages, and chorused, *I hope you are listening to this too*.

Sea! The chorus, harmonising perfectly, rose further up into the breeze wafting across the stilled shocked sea, in a murmur, *Don't cry for Aboriginal Sovereignty. Give him back*.

Then Praiseworthy was left dead on its feet with incandescently white-hot fevering as the sea turned greyer and higher, which must have meant something, that they were wrong, their soul was not right. There were people doing the vogue thing, megaphone blasting their thinking for country, instead of country thinking for itself. They were hanging back in the mangroves, the deniers of any wrongdoing, to spy on the old fanning-lady opera, and slung back, *Wrong! Sea! We live by the new white law. It stronger, and those police want to lock up that Aboriginal Sovereignty. You bring him back here. That boy was the principal bogeyman of little girls. We need him locked up for good, and throw away the key. See, sea, all of Australia was calling for evil black men to be put away behind bars.*

White Australia was a black devil, the old fanning-lady sopranos yelled back in tandem, with words riffing and volleying over the surface of the sea. You could say it in a flash, that their Aboriginal Sovereignty had become the epitome of dust ugliness for the whole country. *We are telling you that. He is not a dirty man. Go on! Sea. You give him to us. Sea cannot arrest. Let him go free.*

Perhaps it was the way that the sea ancestor was rolling, but it had a way of speaking bluntly in an almost silent language heard very clearly by the pandanus tree, the palm tree, the fig tree, and along the mangroves, and those leaf-fanning old ladies who were now all ears, listening to how the sea whines rhythms with the words that came naturally from their mouths from hours on end. These have become almost melodies made with fragments of thoughts – *skinny boy* – *miserable face boy* – the sounds of these five words continuing on, having grown heavier and larger, and rising like a heavy fog from off the waters to saturate thinking, of how a story about police, government and the media could create a monster out of a bony kid who had been born with nothing, but with everything to love and live for, in the eternity of the world.

Now the women were asking themselves the same question, blaming themselves for the death of Aboriginal Sovereignty, while mistrusting their own conscience to understand what truth was like, because they no longer knew what truth was if they ever did, for they lived in the mind of country, and it would be hard to recognise the truth of others, even if they fell over it. All they felt that they could fall back on was the ideal of justification, in a world of liars calling themselves rulers not only of humanity, but of all life, and of all places.

You all know why? And what for? For marrying his underage sweetheart, now properly deceased. Cannot mention her name. She was now letters, M.P. The schoolgirl. Weren't they in love? The sea gulped this question along thousands of kilometres of coastline for anyone to know this story, and this made the local people feel much shame from having to swallow the sea ancestor's question. The drama unfolding in the sea air left the beach people feeling unbearably heavy, almost as though they felt unable to breathe. They looked at each other with fear as along the beach the country felt as though the sea was draining the oxygen out of the air. Now the old women lay in a heap on the beach struggling for air to pass through their nostrils and into their lungs. They were there on the sand dying together, suffocated in memories of culture overflowing in their minds while at the same time forced to ask the aeons of country's law whether this marriage was the right way.

Then, in the long enough, the women were saved, not by their husbands who were locked in the same fate, but by the sand releasing them. They were able to rise from the sand after answering the sea country's questions about those two children now lost, who had been promised to each other. Nothing was wrong about that. It was just like everyone had known, but had been locked up in the brain by the stories of powerful people like the police, the government, and the media. *All us old ladies were that age when we had married. Nobody said anything about it. It was our law. It was not like now, and their marriage being against the law of white government.*

Everyone in Praiseworthy knew what had really happened. The old women knew that the young girl had chased him, and they knew she was doing the right thing. She wanted to take her husband straight away. Weren't they always going to be married someday anyway? It was the thing the teenage girl said, of how those other girls were chasing him. And if this was true, if the older girls were chasing him, saying he was a warrior, a true lover man, saying she was a child, still underage, and saying that they were all in love with him, and the girl knew that in no time flat one of them would have got pregnant, wanted to marry him for themselves, and that would have been that. Bad marriage. He would have been long gone by the time she turned the legal age of eighteen by white law. She would lose him. Anyone could see it. What of her future? What if anyone would steal him away from her even though he was her promised husband? More bastard country. Then what? Would she have to end up in a bad marriage? Look at all of the bad marriages, lose count, more happening all the time, no worry about right marriage for building strong future or anything like that, just making more bad country. Those old women of wisdom knew that those two loved each other and were already married.

He was facing rape charges now you know, for raping a minor – that Aboriginal Sovereignty, and you know how long you get for raping a child? Read the news. It was in the newspapers all over the country that were making sure that no paedophile ever walked free in Praiseworthy.

7

You better get out there and find him, came the order to Praiseworthy – although the message was more politely disguised in the usual threatening policy language that was blasted across the news media in times of worsening global crisis with very freaky out-of-proportion weather, illness, wars and refugees. The island mentality persisted on the continent, staying local, to take up the baton and microscopically focus on a single homegrown anti-black issue. So even though the nation that had stolen seven and a half million square kilometres of the Aboriginal landmass, the total continent, it claimed to be sick of young Aboriginal kids suiciding to get out of reality, by going home to the ancestors.

Tommyhawk had been watching from the aerodrome while texting his furious SOSs to his Golden Hair Mother to hurry up and come quickly in a Qantas plane, to collect him from hell. He wanted to start living in Parliament House ASAP – please your highness, to be in the only place on Earth where the government cared about Aboriginal children, so SOS please and thank you, because he feared for his life in Praiseworthy, SOS plus, plus, plus, please, and he lay on the ground with the bulldust swirling around him as an infrequent flight landed, dropped off its cargo, and took off down the red-earth airstrip. He had even texted the police. There it was in lights as he scrolled back a few months earlier, ABORIGINAL SOVEREIGNTY IS A PAEDOPHILE. HE IS SLEEPING WITH AN UNDERAGE GIRL. The police cars sped by, and drove by, day and night up and down the dirt airstrip. Tommyhawk could not be sure whether Aboriginal Sovereignty had really committed suicide, or not, and does not even want to retrace what happened on the night that his brother had walked out to sea. Somehow though in Tommyhawk's mind, it felt that his brother might not have died, and that only he was the one who was going to die in the end.

He saw the relentless rallying of police in their search through every inch of Praiseworthy, but totally ignoring the dust boy playing with the feral pussycats on the airstrip as they pursued their endless chase for a ghost, while searching through all the cupboards and behind every door for that paedophile called Aboriginal Sovereignty, and gathering in the tiny gaol cell an overcrowding of illusionary or real paedophiles arrested for causing children to suicide, and who may, or may not be the true suspect, or a person of national interest.

Much time passed while Tommyhawk watched the radius of the crime scene grow with no stone left unturned in the hunt to find Aboriginal Sovereignty. The boy seemed to have a knack for invisibility in clear slight as he stood behind people being hunted by the police around the aerodrome, and the hunted were running everywhere and being captured, and manhandled, and Tommyhawk watched the many on-the-spot interrogations, where the apprehended were pretending that they either did not know who his brother was, or had never known anyone named Aboriginal Sovereignty, and did not believe in Aboriginal Sovereignty because that would be against the Australian state, and they said that they only believed in assimilation – in becoming white as quick as possible, and were belted by the police for insulting white people by thinking that black paedophiles like themselves could ever become white people. The more they were intimidated by the police, the more the apprehended would pretend not to know what was happening, when weeks ago everyone had known how the police had rocked up and dragged Aboriginal Sovereignty across the schoolyard. A teacher woman ran after the police, while trying to drag Aboriginal Sovereignty back, and demanded to know why he was being arrested. *He was at school*, she challenged. *You should not be coming here. Stop this stupidity.* The police pushed her aside. *Better get back lady or you will get hurt. We know what we are doing.* She protested, *But this boy is a star. A star pupil.* About a dozen police stood between her and Aboriginal Sovereignty. She was told, *Stand back! Stand back! This is police work. Stop obstructing the work of the police.* The woman teacher called out to others to help her save her star pupil who belonged to her, not the police. She said she was not going to have all of her work destroyed by some ruthless police, and they said, *We are warning you lady. You will be out of this place in a minute. It only takes one phone call to your department and you will be out on the next plane.* She persisted: *You can't just come barging in and arresting schoolboys.* So did the police: *He's a man.* Can't you see he is just a boy? *He is seventeen.* But he had just turned seventeen. *Get out of the way this is police business.* The teacher puts herself in front of Aboriginal Sovereignty. She shuffles to keep the policemen away from her student by transforming herself into a human shield, and becomes a non-combatant jumping from the left, jumping to the right, and who was calling herself a woman of peace, and now, she will fight with her fists against ten policemen. *I thought you teachers were supposed to be smart. Can't you understand English, the part which says the law is the law and you don't interfere with police business.*

The local police force said they could arrest him when he was seventeen if they wanted to enforce the law, and in this case there was no choice. They had to. The government makes the law not schoolteachers, the lady schoolteacher was told as she was pushed aside. As she got to her feet and re-formed the human shield, the policeman in charge of the bust spat into her face, and called her a stupid bitch, before he pushed her aside again with full force. He proclaimed that the law was not going to be left to a bunch of schoolboys thinking they can do what they like. The teacher yelled from the floor, *Are we talking singular, or plural? Are you arresting all the boys?*

The lady teacher got to her feet to stand between her pupil and the police once again, and again, while she was thrown back on to the floor by the police chief, while the other police took a lesson in watch and learn. He told her to remember that the government makes the law, not schoolteachers. That child abuse on Aboriginal communities had to stop. That means the law applied to everyone. No exception. This was what the government wants to stamp out. What the media wanted to stamp out. The opposition. All Australians. Only a bleeding-heart schoolteacher now decides how to run the country.

The police chief started to feel a bit suspicious of this left-wing schoolteacher from the city and wanted to lock her up too. Did she support paedophiles? If she did, it was the duty of the police to report her to the Minister of Education because (a) she was breaking the law, and (b) she was harbouring a person of interest, who had broken the law. You will go to gaol for that. He abused a child. She was fifteen. The teacher retorted: *Nearly sixteen. Sixteen now. The police should leave them alone.* But the police in the school room do not do that. These police carry out the law of the law enforcers, enforcing the law of the government. The OIC, a big man who does not care for this nuisance wasting his time now asked: *Don't you teach this in school? What exactly do you teach here? Don't you teach what the government wants you to teach, that the police will stop this paedophilia happening all around Aboriginal communities for once and for all. We will not have any paedophiles here if the government says there are, and we are saying this boy is one.*

All Aboriginal communities they said.

Don't call us paedophiles.

We are men.

Well! We are women too.

And Aboriginal Sovereignty was a man.

He was just a boy.

Going to school.

She was just a little girl.

They loved each other.

They were getting married anyway.

What was the point of calling it a crime?

You people stop talking because it is too late now.

Look down at the sea about what was real here.

Anno Domini Nostri Jesu Christi.

How shall we overcome.

8

In a long weave spell of rainless nights, when only the waft of night-mares drifted in Praiseworthy's dry-season dust bowl, a superhero cop arrived on the scene. He came to find Aboriginal Sovereignty too. But he was far better than the ordinary police. He was a multiplier. An investigator. One who specialised in the policing of blood lines. A refined skill, which was most popular in the colonialised mind of the era. But he was even more – we are talking about an organiser. One who specialised in categories, and assigned boxes where his client criminal belonged based on the degree of crimeless purity, or the impure blood of crime. This fellow, whose name sounded more like a business proposition, was called Maximum Security Service. He was the ultra-modern cop analyst of one of the world's greatest slave-master nations. Perhaps he had a sickness in the head, but he enjoyed being slicker than others, by setting and capturing a criminal type of person in unescapable traps while conducting his work as a chief investigator of petty and major crime – well, let's not beat around the bush, all crime amongst the originals. This was a man who was like an industrial zone. He embodied the dirty work, felt invigorated by endless sacrifice as anyone would, if you saw the possibility of blood-linked crime as being off the scale of normality. This was the chief blood-line crime-stopper Ice Pick said he was talking about, who was on call night and day as the real identifier of the racial make-up in the blood lines of whoever his chosen people happened to be at the moment, to sort the chaff from the wheat so to speak, or to sort out the rotten apples in Praiseworthy. Well! It was all quick smart, when Praiseworthy ended up with the superhero cop by special request of the Major Mayor who claimed that they needed this expert quester in the brain work, the someone who was not anybody, who was extremely knowledgeable about what ran in the genes of the original people in the zone, what was in the make-up of their race, where the impurities originated and propagated like a pandemic, and hence and so forth, where their race had ended up on the law of averages with the greater killers, biggest infringers, most uncontrollable rage, a plethora of thieves with more wandering fingers, and an overpopulation of habitual liars who could not keep their trap shut. Ice Pick announced the coming of the new order over the stringed loudspeakers throughout Praiseworthy, and said that he was welcoming the super cop whose total world was a sphere of passionate investigation into racial purity, who would be examining in the finest detail the minutest intricacies of the genes of the Praiseworthy race, searching endlessly for all the impurities in the weave of heritage found in the genetic make-up of every man, woman and child that he would entrap in the cop's human laboratory, a zoological garden exclusively dedicated to the study of his newly adopted domain, and where in the final analysis, the lives and future of his chosen ones would remain forever branded in order of criminal tendencies, and frozen in time. What Maximum Security Service hated most of all, was the drop-stitch; the ugly flaw in the weave, spoiling the fabric of human antiquity in what he deemed was once a one hundred per cent pure-bred Aborigine. This fellow's quest was for godhood-derived purity, a divine quest to be the biggest know-all and saviour of Aboriginal knowledge in his chosen people. In this particular type of godhood, he needed to hold more weight than anyone else in an Australian court of law concerning Aboriginal rights, and more weight than Aboriginal people's knowledge of themselves.

Once the big yellow-haired God man masquerading as a superhero cop had heard the news that the natives were stirring over their loss of Aboriginal Sovereignty up in Praiseworthy, he had jumped straight into his Avis rent-a-car like one of his Viking ancestors would have jumped into his warship and headed for the battlefield. He drove non-stop on the long road north, days of travel on teeth-shattering corrugation that had made his teeth grow crooked, and bulldust-choked roads of the short cut similar to Aboriginal roads anywhere, to find out what the Aboriginal Sovereignty nonsense was about. Someone high up in the state government Aborigines Department had rung him in the dead of night, and said he had to make this Aboriginal Sovereignty business go away, or the government would be cactus in the next election. The government was not really interested in kids suiciding, don't worry about that, just get this business about Aboriginal Sovereignty out of their minds.

Then, finally, the superhero cop, or God cop font of Aboriginal knowledge arrived on the scene filthy, since he had stopped bathing altogether as soon as he had left his clean city, to show he was in solidarity to the hilt with his mob who for some reason or another, had never bothered to clean themselves. He filled his lungs enthusiastically with the hazy red dust piled in the Praiseworthy dome. He had a hard look around at the haze, and thought he had hit the mecca of the modern Aboriginal world with all of its criminality elements ripe for the picking. The sum total of knowledge about Aboriginal people was right in front of him, and he showered his newly chosen people with his deepest affection, and absolute concern for their welfare while sussing out the scene, plucking tweezer-like any evidence about whether Aboriginal Sovereignty was really Aboriginal Sovereignty for this place, or not Aboriginal Sovereignty at all, and getting to the point where no Aboriginal Sovereignty ever existed in this place. But the showering of fake affection was not easy, when the targeted people were full of distrust for super cops. He turned a blind eye to the trust problem about a cop poking at what Aboriginal Sovereignty was in Praiseworthy, whether it existed, and let the old tick-tock in his heart waver this way and that in a continual dissection in his head about who belonged on the top of the pile of racial worthiness here, and who among them would not matter in the lofty and aloof anthropological ladder of theory planted in his purely analytical brain.

This disappearance of Aboriginal Sovereignty was always going to be a job for a super cop academic who was not a crime-buster like a normal policeman, who would have dived into the ocean in a deep-dive suit and remained there under water, until Aboriginal Sovereignty was found. No. This was another level. This was a deal-breaker situation. A head-cracker. To make mess disappear. He had already captured the scenario of dragging out all the Native Title court proceedings over the haze dome for a couple of decades if he had to, just to safeguard the rights of the people he deemed as being the purest and truest, and he would stick it up any counterview of hallucinating Native Title pretenders like Cause Man Steel opposing his ideology of what black purity was, if they were of the mind to challenge the superiority of his arguments. He had the arsenal, a backyard-rat nous for the courtroom, and could Chubby Checker twist his way out of a paper bag on one foot while dishing up multi-fold counterarguments to outfox any other trifle intergenerational consequence evidence rising from the ashes of hope, which he would consign back to the smoke-pile – more there to suffocate the planet. Yes, Maximum thought he was in Praiseworthy to stay for some time to sort out this Aboriginal Sovereignty business.

There would be plenty of arguments about who had Aboriginal Sovereignty of course, and that was the beauty of the grandest argument about ownership of the country. There was no other place in the world where people had to argue as much as those people up there in Praiseworthy about losing their Aboriginal Sovereignty, in the one last question mark left standing like some lone soldier on the battlefield blasted to smithereens. His only motivation was to preserve his turf of expert knowledge about what constituted purer than purity in his Aboriginal people, and hence, Aboriginal Sovereignty. Maximum superhero cop-God had his legacy to preserve, to make sure his theory of purity would remain intact forever more, regardless of what was actually happening in reality, and making the quests for Aboriginal Sovereignty to die in the ditch.

Yet, things were not proceeding well for Maximum Security's percolating brain with the continuous sirens beseeching the return of Aboriginal Sovereignty, and amplified Mayoral announcements screeching in his head. It was difficult to think straight, and he was highly challenged by the accumulating theses in his mind competing with the pace of change in Praiseworthy, with everyone either laughing or crying universality for all things, all spirits internationally, instead of just keeping themselves pure with their own local spirits, as if spirits never travelled, and these dilemmas kept challenging him every time he looked outside his door. Take for instance, the plague of feral donkeys now grown into a swarm, and living in Praiseworthy like a traditional owner. What did donkeys have to do with a claim for Aboriginal Sovereignty? No wonder no one could figure out who had, or did not have, Aboriginal Sovereignty. Then, there were those invasive church steeples which were a total offence blocking the pristine view to the clear open cultural horizon. How could they see the ancestral realm with churches blocking the view? There was no way he could work out what was driving these ancient place-rooted spiritual people to bring all of the foreign religions into the place. Good modern, or bad modern. What kind of modern thought was driving such madness to destroy purity? He had long wondered how ideas of native aestheticism were deteriorating in the modern Aboriginal mind. What native asceticism could be found in such ugliness?

The corruption drove him crazy, and he had to break into the nexus of evil, to save these people from themselves. He would dissect the diseased parts of the communal brain under a microscope, to discover how they had become obsessed with fantastical corrupt stories about the disappearance of Aboriginal Sovereignty from their lives. He would discover why the old ladies with the plant leaf fans were always looking at the sea. He would try to understand the improbable, of how you could lose your Aboriginal Sovereignty in the ocean like people kept telling him, and if this idea was a different form of sovereignty that was unchallengeable to the sovereignty of the state? The industrial-estate mind of the hero cop was losing the way to frame the question about ancient land ownership being converted into sea ownership, or if this had always been owned by the same ancient sovereignty, or by a Johnny-come-lately sovereignty, and could you do that, and he began questioning whether this or anything even was real Aboriginal Sovereignty, or did it include the universal timeless nature of having overall sovereignty? Let it be said that there were sleepless-night equations of highly speculative theories, and finding real Aboriginal Sovereignty remained an illusion to the task that would have to be hunted down to find the persons who were putting such dangerous ideas into the heads of his chosen people in the first place, and he hated having to do his, to add one more problem to the mountain range of problems affecting his idea of discovering a dream civilisation. It was unquestionable, that the nature of being a superhero copper was an unbearable weight, a felt burden of broken purity that rocked inside the squealing siren brain going wee-ho, and Maximum Security Service held his head in his hands as he tried to work out the way in his search for enlightenment in this new Aboriginal world going haywire, but the more he tried to control the wee-ho mess, the more it felt like an electrical storm was taking place in his head alone, and not in the mind of his people who were either laughing or crying over what he called spilt milk. This was where the sixty thousand lightning-strike storms pummelled, and where all thunder reverberated, and the head din sent shockwave after wave around the far reaches of his wee-ho-ing malfunctioning industrial-zone brain, and sent the God skull into a permanent sideway tilt.

9

While the brain world of the cop-God descended further down the corridor of hell by the hour, and into a masterclass of physiological darkness, his mind was also becoming something else, where he thought the view was beautiful, and far more destabilising in reality than a screaming siren. This was when the industrial zone super cop hero believed his ears were on fire, and he rode with a Mack Truck called *Gift Rapper* speeding through his head, which was able to shake his brain into a more tangled mess of corrugated nightmares about the whereabouts of real Aboriginal Sovereignty. There was only one trouble though with riding with the Mack Truck roaring over corrugation. The roar rattled in his eardrums, and drowned out the sirens calling for Aboriginal Sovereignty to come home, but the injury in the soft tissue of his brain felt like a tanker of water that was being dangerously shaken into a full-blown tidal wave in another sixty thousand lightning-strike dry storm.

The super cop was losing his cool to nearly one hundred per cent, and perhaps, he no longer considered himself to be a hero, but none of this insecurity was helping him to think straight about anything as audacious as unpicking messy flaws in the racial fabric ruining everlasting purity. The view of Churchy Street continued to change sharply, with more monstrous steeples and hazardous lookouts to the sea growing in the endless search for Aboriginal Sovereignty. The donkey plague continued fouling the pristine purity of the landscape. Widespread was away searching for ultimate donkeys. And there was still some weird local Praiseworthy push for Aboriginal Sovereignty having precedence over the modern cross-cultural reconciliation that was thrilling the nation.

Look! Maximum Security tried to understand the how come – that half of his brain had been rewired by the modern bastardy of this corrupted ancestral-laden landscape. He knew his head was being done in, had been invaded by the gross impurities he saw on a daily basis, but he would not leave the challenge of analysing his chosen ones who were nothing but a disappointment to his excellent mind. He was really finished on the intellectual rubbish heap of being the highest know-all about the Aboriginal race, and what was the most dismal realisation of all, he understood how all out he was of designing proper racial category boxes to capture the extent of the polluted genetic messiness, for he could not find a pure thought anywhere in his brain to capture the racial purity in this place, not while the bizarre screeching siren sounding for Aboriginal Sovereignty to come back made it impossible for him to hear his own thoughts. The super cop might have simply been missing the beat, the best part of his life, having his superior intelligence shanghaied into the existential minds of children who the government said were not loved by their parents. He would have run over hot coals with bare feet if he had heard anyone ringing alarm bells all over the place about their dangerous existence. Anyone would do that – try to be a saviour – but he could not hear a thing happening anywhere on Earth anymore because of the siren blasting non-stop, and being rendered totally non-sensical, he never heard what drove the suicidal thoughts in the innocent, because he was never anywhere near these children.

In the end, the super cop non-hero never left his so-called camp, the place where he was squatting in a broken-down official government house at the abandoned end of Church Street. This yellow-haired fellow would lie in his scruffy swag bed on the cement floor from morning to night like he was eighty instead of forty, like some type of dishevelled no angel in the fairy ring of sunbeams showering rays of golden light on decades of dust floating in the room. Each night, while either drifting in and out of fitful sleep, or twisting and turning as the spiders spun more labyrinths of cobwebs around the room, and unable to sleep, his body jittered from the light of the night sirens piercing the skies, that threw the spotlight right over his bed before moving on, and it felt as though the moving light was running away with his brain. These were the hours of flickering old broken newsreel images of bombing raids passing through his thoughts, but there was nothing good that came out of sirens making your head spin. It could make you feel as though you had not slept for a thousand years, and drained of his senses, he had no idea what he was doing as he walked through the dust-coated floor with his bare feet while his head spun. He wished he was somewhere else, on parade, collecting more medals for his brave work in racial categorisation. His hands moved over his bare chest, and even though he could not hear the tinkling, it was comforting to feel that he was still wearing his bucketload of bravery medals – all invisible, they had not been stolen, and he had not been murdered, or beaten up, for saving these poor Praiseworthy Aboriginal people from harming themselves.

The wailing waaa...continued, the more so on his shock-absorber wrecked body, and although he did not have great strength he drove the Avis rent-a-car around town adorned with umpteen bravery medals on his chest, accidentally ran over a cat, and did not notice a dozen dogs biting his tyres as he drove, while trying to remember where the forward planning searchers were hiding from him, or where he should search for them. He tried Church Street first, to ply them away from praying, by telling them they had a very serious job to do for the country as crime eradicators in their work in Aboriginal affairs. Their main job was to stop singing hymns and to close the gap of racial impurities by clearing the place of the genetically mixed-up thoughts of traitors. But he did not talk theorising to their face, instead he wanted his people to understand him on their terms, so he ordered: *First of all, you have got to find all those radicals pushing this Aboriginal Sovereignty business. Squeeze them out. Poke a stick down the holes where they are hiding, and pull them out like a goanna.* Most of all, while he was using up his budget on the Avis rent-a-car that he was driving into the ground, he wanted them to focus on their race, and to stop bothering about paedophilia, and children suiciding etc.

The waaa-aaaa...continued busting the sound barrier in his head and he felt more crazy, even though he was blasting everyone in sight for not doing their job quicker or smarter so he could leave this racial impure place once and for all, and the shrill waaa-ing continued to burst the water tank in his head, and this was happening even quicker he thought, as he was trying to talk some sense into the forward planning meeting on the futility of continuing their search for Aboriginal Sovereignty.

Yet things in his brain did not improve. No one would own up to being interested in having Aboriginal Sovereignty returned to them. They said that no one was in love with something like that. *We don't want that kind of love. It was illegal. We only want to build better church steeples. Better look-outs, to keep good Christian practices for making a stronger God capable of resisting temptation while we search for Aboriginal Sovereignty.*

Even with his head done in, Maximum Security Service was still a clever man, and he soon realised that the unstoppable brain siren had not only invaded his mind, but the sound was shredding his brain to pieces. The siren was using its own cruel logic to whip his thoughts into a frenzy, to push him beyond his capacity. Was he paranoid to think that this world was falling apart with racial impurity, and the void that was left was waiting for him like his grave, burying him forever in this place of racial impurities? For he could do nothing more, than to go with an organised plan, because that was what he would do, that was the job of a hero super cop like himself. All he had to do was to look like he was up to the job by driving very slowly up and down Church Street hour after hour, and be on the lookout for insurgencies sneaking around the crumbling-down makeshift towering church spires yelling for their Aboriginal Sovereignty to come back. The car barely moved, would crawl by the churches so he could have a good look at who was doing all the praying for Aboriginal Sovereignty, and see the siren alarmist eyes staring back at the wound-down driver's side window. He felt as though he was watching devils, instead of seeing ordinary Praiseworthy people coming and going from their churches. But God man knew what criminalised people were capable of doing, his mind had not been minced that long ago, and he thought if the sum total of his knowledge about humanity added up to anything, it was about killing off the weak, with a real knife, or a metaphorical backstabbing cleaver.

Whenever he reached the end of Churchy Street or whatever it was called, he always needed to drive back for a second look at some suspicious piece of work, back the car up, crawl past for a better look at some old man or woman acting all Aboriginal Sovereignty like they thought themselves high and mighty, as though they owned the whole country, while hiding their insurrection behind faith. This Avis rent-a-car made people feel angrier towards white people, and they grabbed the shoes from their feet, stomped through the red dirt and, while aiming high, threw at the hire car their broken thongs, dust-engrained R.M. Williams boots, or sneakers that had seen better days. They aimed for a bullseye, to hit him smack on the head through the car window. When he could not find the capacity to explain what an insurrectionist was, they forgot the teachings of any compassionate God, and threatened to belt him with real law. *You should leave this town now,* he was told. *We do not want any white men here like you.*

The Praiseworthy Golden Era Forward Planning Authority's search for Aboriginal Sovereignty had fallen into a total loss about what to do after Aboriginal Sovereignty went missing, and now relied on Maximum Security Service to solve all mysteries associated with the crime. *We give all power to you,* they said, while they themselves would just sit back inside somewhere, and oversee his superior knowledge in anthropology with his government paid job as a professional. They wanted him to immerse himself in all the suicidal thoughts of their affairs that would not be silenced, not even by the fear ringing in his ears.

It would be a grand affair – his job. So instead of their feeling bad all the time, his job would be this, to be continuously heartbroken, to be sick and tired of kids taking their lives, and to try to ignore all those church people assembling themselves around them. Deal with their problems. Fix everything. The forward planners set out their terms of reference. For a start, they wanted him to cease hibernating in his sunbeam room showering golden light on the floating dust – stop saying he was burnt out, start finding a bit of empathy for other people, and eliminate all fearfulness from their lives, not only in themselves as the forward planning searchers, but, to truly feel what poor people's fear was like when he slept like a baby at night. The manifesto of the job description was put to him orally, and they waited for him to memorise what had been said word for word, until he was able to repeat his duties to them, so that they knew he understood what they wanted, instead of him going around half-cocked with his racist theories. They also wanted him to experience total fear as they did, but when they described the magnitude of this fear on a scale of nightmares, they demanded that he know the combined fear of billions of the poorest people in the world. They asked him if he knew what this felt like, of how the have-nots dotted all around the planet experienced loss of destiny and their Aboriginal Sovereignty. Could he imagine the unimaginable scale of loss as they did and he thought he had, did he know the loss of all the millions of children enduring endless wars, forced migration, homelessness, famine, drought, greenhouse gas emissions, firestorms and rising seas, their future robbed? Did he know how to stop these things happening, because this was what a government employee should know how to stop, otherwise he was just swindling poor people like them by being paid on false pretences to drive that flash Avis rent-a-car around their community for nothing.

Every day the flag prayers for hope faded in the wind until they were blown away on the highest mountains of another world, and this was when the superhero cop rose to the challenge set by the forward plan searchers. He went in search of the hope they required. He developed a dot-point action plan which was designed for a vision which was different to his heart's cry for eradicating impurity from the racial mix to re-achieve purity in the turnout. Got rid of that. This was a head vision for eliminating all fear through some watch-this-space mindfulness activities that would be held throughout the Praiseworthy world until the proper results were achieved. The plan was a healthy-living scenario, something that was aimed at being reconciled to the status quo, of being without any Aboriginal Sovereignty, instead of people organising insurrections in the guise of the multiple twisted theories for radical uprisings going on in the denominational churches. The perfection of the vision was that once the breathtaking painful task of mindfulness was accomplished by these local people overcoming their long-held pain and continuing war against having their country stolen from them, he would begin the overachieving business of his growing list of desires to rid all fear from Praiseworthy. But, first things first. He organised a proper, fully weaponised search party to round up all the potential soldiers in a war-weary people who had been fighting over their Aboriginal Sovereignty for over two centuries, and he did this by using all of the power necessary for a super cop. He used a lot of force, cajolery, callously pissing the people off, coercion, the compulsion of a loaded gun, whatever power he thought would help him to rope in every able person in Praiseworthy to become a soldier in his army. His will to succeed in the war for hope became a carte blanche force exercised in what was officially tagged a state of emergency of unprecedented disasters affecting this particular humanity, and that with one exemption, excused the people overseeing the maximum power bestowed on this war thing. The most powerful in the Mayoral assembly of Ice Pick, had said that they had no wish to participate in an idiot cop's war games, and got on with their lives.

But here is the thing, Ice Pick told the super cop, a bit of war did not matter much to him. It did not bother him in the least what wars had to be fought to execute a vision of hope, as long as the cop won the war in the end. He claimed with confidence that any war would certainly help him meet the overall vision of his people's haste to assimilation with the broader Australian community. He wiped his hands clean of the super cop plan, turned a blind eye to the stupidity of this city copper's vision of ridding the world of fear, and continued on with his own more important dream of achieving the much-coveted national reconciliation for all across the land, one that had the entire population of twenty-six million mixed-race people being a friend to one another about the continuing injustices of Aboriginal land theft, denial of property rights, and ongoing oppression. His dream was too bent on achieving assimilation as quickly as possible by forgetting the past to be worried about a local war about hopefulness. *Oh! Just let bygones be bygones. Why can't we all be just Australians*, he had already announced many times in his broadcasts. Of course everyone had a dream of hope, so he continued on with his own super hope that there would only be a singular breed of people in Australia who were called Australian, and he continued promoting the one-breed policy by schmoozing in-sync rich people, the golden beetle of culture, his powerful Ice-breaker women, and feeding his hatefulness for donkeys to his greater hatred of Cause Man Steel whom he accused of murdering and hiding the body of Aboriginal Sovereignty.

The superhero cop man ordered whoever turned up in his office to fight the war, to show him how they had the guts and wits about them for solving a crisis on the spot, to demonstrate in five seconds how they would not be killed on the battlefield. Did the people of the hunt, the survivors of the oldest living culture in the world, fight back, yes, they did. They were imbued with the intellectual wisdom of the hunt to survive honed through the ages to outlast time in a caring relationship with their traditional homelands. As a result of the cop ordering them around, the office was flattened, destroyed by the powerful ancestral intelligence, the customary weapon of culture. Bullets too. Physicality. Pain. Memories. The holding on of Aboriginal Sovereignty. He drilled these soldiers about how to find the perpetrators, the leaders of the multiple insurrections hanging about the place. The downcast eyes swung around the crowded sealed-lip room from one to another, and said nothing. He would stand in the middle of the room, and wait for the action to begin, to see who would let the cat out of the bag so to speak, by their various acts of betrayal.

The pain of unadorned truth screaming from the white demountable industrial building that now became the larger office of the war for hope, showed absolutely no sign of being anything like a showcase for the hefty local importance of running a modern Aboriginal world like Praiseworthy. Every day, more and more wheezing soldiers of the people were squeezed into the confined space of the conference room to stare at a big fat ginger cat snoring as it lay fast asleep in the middle of the long conference table through hours of verbal torture, and remained oblivious to the screaming arguments taking place all around it about how to win a war.

There were more and more people arriving to see what the noise was all about, and they were mingling in the hallways, banging on doors, and lounging around in some of the other buildings. They wanted to be soldiers of hope too if they could help create so much excitement in their lives. Many others chose to sit in their cars parked around the shire council offices, and back along the streets. These people communicated with each other by banging on their car horns, or through their mobile phones. They wondered if they would be better off creating another army, to defeat the hopeless armed forces arguing with each other and destroying the town's assets.

With a high-pitched megaphone that hardly reached over the noise of the arguments and blasting car horns, Maximum Security Service tried to influence his mandatory volunteers with the God-man plan. But he was defying the odds as far as Ice Pick and his few trusted allies were concerned, who thought he had no idea how to control the army for hope. Maximum Security, they agreed, was like the ginger cat. He did seem to be oblivious to mob noise, and of course he was deaf. He was deaf to all. All he heard was the on-going search siren wailing over the sound of his own thoughts. He was deranged, but you had to put the whole thing into perspective. And the thing was, more people began to listen to the strange way the God man cop was speaking to them, meekly whispering – as though he were the child – instead of the usual way he spoke to them, as if they were his children. Then people started ambling towards him, closing in around him like a hug, and urging him to speak more. They started to listen, and were eagerly welcoming him into their embrace, to hear more about what really happened in the super cop's nightmares.

The more people heard about this strange wandering nightmare happening on their traditional country, the quicker they tried to squeeze themselves into the stifling overcrowded board room where the ginger cat slept on the table. The story of derangement was progressing with so much power that everyone wanted to believe in the story about how to make a superhero cop with a shirt full of medals feel deranged. The story became so powerful, the whole town grew silent. No rooster crowed. No donkey brayed. No dogs barked. The winds left. And no bird sang. Every living creature in

Praiseworthy remained silent so it could hear the whispering story of the God man who had gone deranged on country. You could say that this was a nightmare on the loose with the story travelling from mouth to mouth, and different mouths recalling bits and pieces of the far-fetched and complicated never-ending story, and adding more flavour, or stitching in a few lies and half-truths, as the story snaked along while being retold, from one place to the next. What became frightening most of all, was that the story started to be elaborated way out of proportion in each retelling, and any or all the doubtful parts were being replaced with a black man's proper thinking for a real story, rather than feeling they had to continue suffering the white God man's unfathomable anthropological story about himself, which they did not want to understand. The remaking of the story continued with questions about the faults of the original story, such as whether anyone should be listening to this tainted story at all, or should be amazed by something like a wailing siren that had never been dreamt about before in Praiseworthy, or whether it might be vitally important to watch the lie words tumbling out of the mouth of an outsider professional liar about what happened to him in the ghost hour when they were worried about how Aboriginal Sovereignty had disappeared for all times by floating away over the seagrass. Watch those last words. Was this a message? And why were the sirens wailing? Who should have heard? Then they thought this was all about sliding further away from the realm of ancient storytelling, and the great original storytellers began to believe that somewhere in the unlatched ocean, something was telling them the real story, of how Aboriginal Sovereignty was still floating over the grass meadows, still alive, and it felt as though he was not lost anymore. He had only gone to the sea.

Yet, wouldn't you know it. There always has to be one lone-shark loudmouth who was wanting to break the nexus of a conciliatory moment, who could not get the picture of waving fields of seagrass serenity, and just had to insert a piece of his mind into the picture by yelling at the top of his voice, *I seen someone lost in a kelp forest once, saw it on TV*. Everyone wanted to know exactly where the police chief's deranged mind thought Aboriginal Sovereignty was floating in the sea, just so that they knew where to go and find him. The trouble with this wanting to know the answers all the time was that Maximum Security, who was in charge of surmising because that was his job, now thought he was being challenged by an insurrectionary breakaway army. A discussion broke out between the God man and the kelp-shouter, that became a contest about who was the brain's trust for the place of the dust haze, with each shouting, and not hearing the other person speaking. *We don't have any kelp here. I was not talking about here. Anyone seen any kelp here? You are not listening to me. No! We have never seen any kelp whatsoever here. What does kelp look like, does it look like seagrass? Nobody knows what kelp looks like.* Now everyone in the so-called dangerous army felt that the super cop thought that they were stupid people who did not know what kelp looked like. He was accused of not knowing anything at all if he thought that sophisticated people who had come from the longest surviving culture in the world did not know what kelp looked like. At this point of the discussion, Maximum Security began to sulk, and threatened to resign from his position of whatever it was he was supposed to be doing to quell their *que sera sera* insurrections with a vision of hope. *We were only asking about kelp...No need for getting hot under the collar. Idiot!*

Then, Maximum Security thing began realising that there was something wrong about his story of sirens belting in his ear, it was a fatal flaw in his character by saying he was deranged. He began to realise that his ears could never be as important as the story of kelp. His hero with the medals standing was quickly descending on a slippery slope, so he replied to this pack of naysayers that would never be capable of being an army, that really, *Aboriginal Sovereignty could be anywhere.* Kelp itself was not a great mystery – it could be found floating anywhere in the ocean. But what was more ginormous, more herculean-ly fantastical and stupid in the blue-sky thinking he was witnessing about the place, was how some people were content still to continue to hide their longing for Aboriginal Sovereignty in their head.

Insult silence felt like the sun had fallen down, or that no old elder's arm could reach up and push it back into the sky. *But!* The cop man must continue, by saying that everyone should go and re-read their own country again. *You tell me where in the country it says anything about having Aboriginal Sovereignty? You are thinking wrong way. Read the newspapers if you don't believe me. Think about it.* This was definitely the wrong thing to say in front of the old wisdom people of country, and the sensation of culpability travelling in the heat waves passing over the sleeping cat on the table, nearly knocked the Viking off his feet. He felt giddy with vertigo. He lost his grip, his head spun with the rustle of children moving quickly, each taking turns to ring the warning sirens so loudly, it felt the siren was inside his brain, and as he looked around the room, he could see that everyone else was either deaf, or prone not to hear anything, other than the sound of their own voices.

The meeting of discontent continued, and the curled cat slept on while the failed army men and women who now despised the God man more than they hated colonisation, wanted to know what he was going to do about the big haze circling the town, and took turns in telling a thousand woeful tales about Widespread Planet's donkeys ruining their hope to live in a nicer place.

Maximum Security replied matter-of-factly in the way of his blue-sky thoughts, by saying that he thought the weather was acting a bit crazy. What was beautiful one day, felt terrible the next. Many sniped along the lines of saying how would he know anything, and he said, *I am just telling you what I see, and I don't care what any of you assimilated people want to believe in. Don't bother losing sleep over what I think, or threatening me with alienation for spoiling your half-baked dreams.* He needed to calm down, so he stopped throwing around condescending thoughts to his fieldwork people, and re-wrapped himself in the decorations of complacent practicality as an emergency strategy to move on. All the same, he thought that he had it worked out. This was brainpower to kill off any more silly talk about needing to find their Aboriginal Sovereignty. His face remained flexed in a contortion of muscles, but underneath it all, he tried to relax his siren-shrilled brain. He listened hard to hear his people. He wrote notes in his little notebook while staring around at his clientele spinning stories of disbelief while he kept a loaded rifle by his side like a policeman, and a pistol in the holster across his chest like a gunslinger, and while holding his breath, he tried on every occasion he could to catch the humanity in what audibility he caught from countless voices lying to him at the same time. There were those that were telling him that he was not from there, so he should shut up and listen. Those that were saying anything could have happened to their Aboriginal Sovereignty for all he knew. Those saying he knew nothing about their history. And others saying what they saw floating in the sea, which was maybe just kelp, or perhaps it was Aboriginal Sovereignty, or an unlatched sea might show the seagrass meadow, that was not kelp, but nobody had ever seen anything like this in the sea before that was full of glorious greatness as their Aboriginal Sovereignty. Maximum Security felt a bit trigger happy with his disordered siren-ringing brain, and he asked if the ocean flinging itself apart was like the story of the Book of Exodus, or was it like seeing a wild woman waving her hair over the ocean...

You shut up about her, you can't talk about that one.

10

So! You are saying it was pitch black as – in the nightmare? Black as. Darker than multiple cumulonimbus clouds. Saw them. Thousands of storm-maddened seagulls darting in the pudder wudder, flying through the plunder of thunder, through the bolting lightning forking in a sixty thousand lightning-strike storm. All dead really. Being slung about in the wind, and *I am telling you a fact now, that I saw Aboriginal Sovereignty down there, floating facedown in that grass.*

The outsider, the super cop with the medals on his chest, was big-noting himself about the law of the atmosphere like he was more gigapascal smarter than anyone else. The old people holding all the laws of atmospheric air pressure, and knowing theirs was a relationship of perfected symbiosis, had no time to argue with this fool, so whenever he talked to them, they did not listen to him. Ditto. He never heard a word of what they said either. All the misunderstandings flourished in either the stories they made up about him for a laugh, or the stories he made up about them to put cash in his pocket.

Anyway, they told him they owned the haze in all its manifestations through their traditional law title for this sphere of country from long before kingdom come, and all this was theirs all the way to heaven and hell...and more, *cuius est solum eius est usque ad coelum et ad inferos.*

While Maximum Security lay with plaguing thoughts of failure and alone late at night in the swirling dust storm of his cobwebbed room, the spiders flecked in the floating dust particles, and flew neck and neck in crosshatched flight paths on their gossamer silken strands. As the night deepened, the nightmares worsened, and he thought how easy it would be in those vague moments in drifting sleep, if he could move around in his nightmares to find agitators pushing for the return of their Aboriginal Sovereignty. If only it could be that easy, to identify who they were, crush their insurrection, destroy their coups for all time, but this was not to be. Not in his dreams, where he saw something else altogether different in a blank grey canvas nightmare where he would begin to distinguish the enormity of what lay behind the vagueness of a multitude of components forming the uniformity of greyness, and through nights of continuing nightmare, began to realise there was a world of children moving across the greyness towards the sea, and committing suicide in Praiseworthy. He saw many children spilling through his dream as they passed in loaded lorries through his room, where all he could do was look up, and watch their white ghostly faces staring blankly ahead as they passed. The lorries moved further away, out of reach across the border of dreams in a procession without end, while he remained cemented to the ground, motionless in his dream, as though paralysed in its sea, its sky, and unable to follow where they were going. It was through these nightmares, the ones with children that felt so real, where he felt that he could almost reach out and feel the pain of each child moving towards the end of their life, while being unable to prevent what was happening to them. The return from sleep to be awake was another form of paranoid hell, of knowing that he had not done more, and of being too frightened to sleep, to be forced to look again at the ash-white ghostly trucks rumbling along a spirit road in his own mind, passing right through him, and moving out of reach, beyond the back of his nightmares, and being unable to call, or do anything to bring them back.

Maximum wanted to give the impression to the old wise people attending his war cabinet of pretend soldiers, that he was handling these nightmares with a powerful intuition, one in which he believed that Praiseworthy children were living in a divided world that was insane, and were being put at risk. He felt lost, knew he was sinking into the ghost world, and wondered what normality was anymore, and was it this? A job like his would have to be done properly, and when he spoke to his Canberra bosses who believed he was off the planet with hoodoo, the only thing they could full-heartedly agree with was his analysis of his deteriorating mental health, and focus on killing bush-worshipping blacks tweeting hourly images of their symbol of Aboriginal Sovereignty and their ancestral cloud of dust before the federal elections.

The local forward planning authority were good people. They searched through the abyss for the white ghost lorries with all the kids, speeding away from the scene, driving along the beach through the sand and leaving no tyre marks. Then, these authority people wondered why Maximum Security could not see Aboriginal Sovereignty on any of those lorries passing through to the world beyond thought.

Some believed that the ghost lorries that Maximum Security saw were actually those big trucks of the international mining companies, that were being used all over the world to dig up the First Peoples' land. What happened to mining trucks? They die. Then these ghost lorries continued to cart what they had destroyed – *future, life*. The realisation stirred yearnings in dreams about all the dead mining trucks coming back to Praiseworthy as ghosts, and bringing Indigenous babies. Bringing them here. Sorry camps sprung up all along the beach, and perpetual wailing could be heard even far out at sea.

In the council of sorry business, the kidnapping story grew, but Maximum Security and his silly dreams were left out of the picture. In fact, he was confined to his cobweb room by the insurgent army, and treated like a reviewer of a picture show that was considered fakery, and of no value.

Only local people could complete this story.

Strange miracles continued. Clouds of white butterflies swarmed across the traditional domain. *Belenois java* or the commonly named caper whites. These kulibibi had flown hundreds of kilometres from the grasslands with the dancing brolgas, the kudaiku, snakes, lizards, and across the hills of the time immemorial locked in their genesis. This migration of sorry business finally flew into Praiseworthy one day, and the butterflies returning from the far-off country began invading every space. It was as though they were searching for Aboriginal Sovereignty too, and in this search, were trying to pick up on the true scent of a widespread, deep-engrained guilt. Many landed, country greeted, and all surfaces became a swarming of antennae a-shiver, like fearfulness. So many white butterflies tasted human skin while searching the content of a person's soul with the chemical receptors of their probosces busy, analysing guilt. Then, finally, in a storm flurry of fluttering wings, the ceremony alighted into the haze, flew over the salt pans, over the mangroves, and far away into the sea. No one had ever seen a butterfly suicide before. Now, it seemed as though all the butterflies in the world were dying in the quickness of this procession, while the sea looked as though it was covered by fog from the continued massing of whiteness in the dust-hazed skies, with the butterfly migration continuing to arrive from where, no one knew. There were large flocks of seagulls dancing over the foggy water and above, in the fog, while the tides that followed gleamed with white wings being washed up all along the beach, or taken back to sea. Along the beach, white wings lay like a map of a newly formed spirit country in a geography of mountainous flotsam lying over the sand, and changing its contours from low tide right up to the high tide mark. Ghost butterflies came by at night and flew along their spirit lands formed on the beach, and finally, around Praiseworthy.

The whole town went down to the beach to see this miracle of the butterfly spirit taking shape on their country. The old people carefully studied the shifting nature of the butterfly maps, forming and being washed away, and were careful not to stand on any of the dead creatures with sea-washed wings that lay all over the sand. The miracle on the beach, the enormous tomb, became a holy place of spiritual significance. A sacred site. The butterfly spirits were growing into a big story in the world of timeless Aboriginal Sovereignty, and as the corpses faded into invisibility, it would be sacrilege to stand on these sacred butterfly spirits that held the story of people's souls drowned by the sea. This was not to be spoken of again, except by the old wise people, after they had seen the God cop trampling the sand, creating sinkhole craters into the sacred geography. While staring out to sea to figure out what was going on through the sirens wee-bazz-ing warnings in his brain, the super cop kept worrying about the children of the world suiciding in ripped sacred lands, and did not hear the ceremony happening all around in the stillness of forever times where he stood.

He thought the butterflies migrating to the sea was only a natural phenomenon. A bumper season of butterflies that fly into the sea all the time. It was not unprecedented. Or, an act of misplaced faith. It was Mother Nature. It was even God's will. In the end, he decided it was all of these things. The old people, feeling his soul's propensity for broken elasticity, felt he was too negatively geared for their liking. Their sense of prophecy had stretched through the ages. They could not understand who he was. Their truth came from their own intuitiveness of built knowledge stretched from time immemorial.

And they watched the intuitiveness of his hardworking negativity as he stared at the sea, the waiting for the waters to part, the retrospective revelation, or insight. They realised that he knew nothing about Aboriginal Sovereignty from the day he was born, when they had seen the baby with their own eyes, and had ever since sung the old songs through the air about what he had meant to country. And sometimes, when they thought of Aboriginal Sovereignty, they even sang country-and-western songs to remind themselves, *Not to let the stars get in their eyes or let the moon break your heart*. This, they knew always, that something would happen to this baby before too long, but he would never be taken from them. *Ah! That Aboriginal Sovereignty. Too hard to even think about him sometimes.*

GODDESS OF SCALES

I bequeath nothingness to no one.
Jorge Luis Borges

1

Oracle 4...speak true.

Listen! Unravel the mystery death thing correctly. Look proper way. Carefully. See detail, if you want to see properly. Go back to the night Aboriginal Sovereignty walked into the sea...Wade through the blindness of no one noticing a fascist call centre operating in the mangroves, but never mind that. You need to find witnesses. The little trainee gangster kids less than three feet tall, all the toddlers in their wet Kimbies and Huggies diapers down there on the beach running free in the rapturous ancestral world, out in the night playing with the country spirits living in their minds with the kind-hearted wise old fellow elders walking forever on the sand with their packs of ghost puppy dogs and their pet baby kangaroos, and carrying around plenty of old ghost pussycats, with hundreds more spooky feral cats running around their feet, and on those really old bony people's shoulders the pet white cockatoos danced, and those black ones with the red tail feathers talked with much ado about this country, and up above all this rapture of place going on, frenzied seagulls by the thousands massing over the moonlit inky sea when those mad parents had stomped down to the beach in the middle of the night after receiving an anonymous phone call.

Only minutes before, the caller, sounding like some ancient world kid disguising whoever he was by talking in a muffled voice, had

called the lot – every mobile phone in Praiseworthy – and he was
threatening to give the mobile numbers, Gmail addresses, and social
media accounts of *you paedophile parents,* to the Parliament House
chief whip cruelty police station cop up on the top of Capital Hill
in Canberra, *for nah gettin your mongrel kids ta bed early, like the
Australian government said you were supposed ta.* The muffled-voice
kid was talking like he was some kind of trained parrot with a lot of
nerve to be quoting vital confidential harassing sections for dealing
with non-compliant Aboriginal parents in breach of the government's
legislation for any emergency, or non-emergency, or for any reason at
all requiring a fistful of Intervention into their lives to stop whatever
the government did not want Aboriginal people to do. With mobiles
jammed hard against the ear, the parents kept listening to the freaky
rage muffler who called them in the middle of the night, and were
pissed off with being placed in a frightening fairytale nightmare about
how a wicked white government stepmother would bake them all in
a pie up there in Canberra, and on his voice flew, wafting about this
section, and that section of some political on-trend Commonwealth of
Australia Act about dealing with so-called abusive Aboriginal parents
this, and this article or whatever, and that, about Aboriginal child
injury-protection measures against really nutty murdering parents
who happen to be Aboriginal. You could tell these parents could
see the kid was a government-spruiker-muffler who was a genius in
reciting the ins and outs of many racist legislations. He knew the lot,
and the parents decided to run in fear to the seaside with their mobile
still glued hard to the ear, for they had now realised that they were
listening to a government-indoctrinated robotic type of kid fascist,
and probably the only one of its kind in the entire country who could
quote at this pacy rate, all those unfathomable miscellaneous articles,
parts, and subsections of government law to do with downgrading
the lives of Aboriginal people, and making their lives feel worse.

Those parents knew exactly what the muffled kid was talking about, and wished they had a real kid like that in Praiseworthy, instead of those mongrel toddlers sneaking down to the beach when they should be in bed dreaming how to become smart. And they thought of themselves, while thinking who among them had not been born without an in-depth historical knowledge of government legislations about Aboriginal people fog-horned into their own brain at birth, and it ran like thick mud in the blood, and kept troubling their heartbeat. They would have been able to figure all this rot stuff out in their sleep, in an instant, about what the full extent of the ramifications of the fuzz meant in a piece of legislation for dealing with their matters: *It's always the parents who get the blame.* Yes, of course they knew with an appropriate high level of fear for such an occasion like this, and had known what every inch of the historic paper trail was for any law connecting bad white government to their lives. Even if they were half-dead, they knew what to fear, but even so, these fathom experts for figuring out the nuances of government language, for being the infinite translators of completely useless government claptrap, definitely understood the gravity of the muffled child prodigy regaling his knowledge about the newly reinstalled old mission-day laws of the 1950s aimed at making these twenty-first century modern Aboriginal people less of a black disease for white people. *Why couldn't the prodigy kid be a famous piano player like Chopin, instead of being a prolific reciter of government crap?* But! To tell you the truth, they knew you had to run faster than hell with fear written across your face when you were Aboriginal parents, just to prove you loved your children more than white people saying you did not love your children enough, like they loved their children.

The parents with a mobile pasted against their ears ran harder and faster in their mind, far quicker than their feet, as the muffled kid ramped up the prodigal pimp thing, by cutting loose that he was going to dob them all in to the government, *all youse child sexual abusers – I know who you are*, when suddenly, the mobile call went – tang! bang! Like! Like retaliation, like the battery went flat, like someone had hung up, and the house lights flicked on quick smart, and the noise of doors slamming could be heard several blocks away, which announced that things were being lashed out about who was to blame for their culturally independent-minded toddlers running amuck, going AWOL on the beach, this late at night. There were a number of outstanding matters being discussed between husband and wife that were on their minds for a moment like this, for suddenly being awakened by a fascist kid calling in the middle of the night, with stuff crashing against walls. Walls punched! Floors thumped! The town became a stampede of feet stomping up and down on the wooden floors of practically all the homes, tumbling in a domino slide while off in the distance you could hear another mobile phone ringing, and then another across town, and others too, the house next door, or another up the street, followed by switched-on house lights, doors slamming, and things banging, words that did not tremble while being fired full of force, as well as objects being lashed about in angry noise, spreading from house to house.

Next, almost at the exact same moment, the whole town was lit up and the town's horizon was perfectly joined with the Milky Way. It was at three minutes past three o'clock in the morning when the angry parents had checked every room in their home to see which kid was in bed, and which was not, after receiving their own personal threatening phone call from the muffled-voice kid. Those who were quick enough, before the kid deemed a wasted prodigy had a chance to lay out his final fracking king hit in the ear by hanging up on them, had a nanosecond chance to double-threaten the kid in screams heard within the town boundary, and further on, spinning deep in the riparian water jungle bush where the ancestor mob and the snake crowd were trying to continue their deep sleep. Yep! Those quick-enough parents told that kid trying to blackmail bully them, that they would hunt him down: *You better believe it.* The whole place would be cleared out until every vicious little bastard with a mobile phone was caught. Those parents who were the quickest of all at four minutes past three in the morning, did not even need to speak into a phone. Their threats could be heard right across town as they breathed. Others did not need a mobile phone. They just yelled threats of murdering through an open window, *and we don't care if you are dead or alive after we finish with you...arsehole.* There were other parents that had become further deranged on the spot, and had managed to think quicker on their feet by sending a verbal thought-volley quicker than social media, before the kid had a chance to hang up on them. All he would have to do was interpret the deeply snorted breathing that threatened, *Don't think you can hide from me. There is nowhere to hide twerps in this town.* Then, almost simultaneously at precisely four and a half minutes past three in the morning, front doors were slamming bang, bang, bang, and the town's parents moved off together into the shadows as they set out on a mission to find the kid causing them trouble, silently promising themselves that the first thing they would do once they caught this government fascist, would be to ban nuisance callers by smashing all mobile phones making calls to them in the middle of the night.

All along the lonely tracks, through the tufted grass plains country which belonged to the ancient creatures of the night, the parents jostled in a march to the beach in search of the kid with the mobile phone. All the little wannabe wallabies scrambled right out of the way of the crossfire moment, first in fright, then they fled as quick as they could hop far away through the corridors in the billowing tuft grasses, escaping from the bellowing voices berating toddler children hidden somewhere in the darkness, and on the voices that flew in the wind, heard the demented parents demanding to know which kid had the nerve to call anyone in the middle of the night.

A few dozen toddlers were quickly found and searched for a mobile phone by parents who had eyes like owls for seeing if any of their children had hidden anything in the grassy hidey-holes of this particular pitch-black paradise. The whole parade was soon frog-marching back home, but in the end, the crying babies too sleepy to walk had to be carried. In the morning, all of Praiseworthy took part in the interrogation of why culturally independent toddler kids in nappies were being allowed to act on their own free will in the middle of the night. The toddlers cried because they had only learnt to speak minimal English, and could not find the words to articulate how they felt about Australian laws, and were still unable to discuss at length what government legislation meant to them, even though these racist laws were an inheritance tainted intergenerationally in their blood. There were many questions thrown at the parents for acting like sovereign people who did not feel like providing answers about this crippling part of their sphere of existence, even under threats of their own survival. They just snapped disdainfully: *You know what? We can't live in this situation.* The police were not interested in parents seeking answers about a mobile phone-calling muffled-voice kid prodigy calling them in the middle of the night because as far as they were concerned, Aboriginal people were not smart enough to produce a prodigy. This understanding would not go into any official police report meant for travelling up every tier of government, that had to be written and analysed in terms of the Emergency Act for Intervening more greatly into the lives of Aboriginal people.

Once the super cop had arrived on the scene to save the world, he too was a regime man who liked urgent meetings of what he described as the collective brain trust of neglectful hostile Aboriginal parents. To demonstrate this point, he threw a box of white and black rattles over the floor to see whether they landed in one nice heap together as though colourblind, or had remained colour-segregated. This began the ordeal that he said would take hours of total absorption in brutal self-analysis, where the super cop anthropologist kept insisting that every bad parent should bare their soul completely to him – tell him why they did not love their children like white people loved theirs. This, he pleaded, was the only way he could establish what type of parents they really were, and to be able to kick a few black rattles towards the white rattles. There was no choice about non-segregation, he said, while acknowledging the fact that the race of black rattles to the white world was a slow affair, but he continued by saying this was the wonderment of the beauty and craziness of non-compliance in the scattering of toy rattles. Whatever! It did not matter, for wherever the rattles landed, he was obliged to tell the government why the equity gap could not be closed in Praiseworthy, it was about their continued non-compliance, which was like the random spread of these rattles on the floor. He continued the analysis with a matter-of-fact face, by saying he had no choice but to tell the truth, for the government needed to know why its legislation for Aboriginal people was not working at the grassroots level. And why, he insisted, the closing-the-gap laws between black and white were always failing in Praiseworthy, and not only that, the gap was actually becoming wider, and becoming the bloody Grand Canyon of chasms, and what was more – *like*, the whole place was becoming an expanding sinkhole for crying out loud.

You are not the boss of here, clapped the united thunderclap of country.

Of course, big fellow government putting on fake compassion about the Aboriginal un-white moral crisis was just another meaningless quasi-winter type of intervention, and now even packaged with this super cop to implement by crawling lower than a snake to enforce something called legalese on the black crowd. The lot, bundled up as a done deal, and imposed upon the eager-for-change forward planning committee by the government insisting on perpetual training of homegrown specialists like these, was the hope for enacting the government's law for every special emergency closing-the-gap situation known to mankind for saving Aboriginal toddlers in a Kimbies or Huggies diaper from unloving parents. The breadth of fakery knows no bounds, for all things needed to be changed in the view it seemed, and with the view being so multifariously rattled, you never knew where to begin, and this was how it was for the nation's most righteous super cop as he continued on his beat to close down the gap forever, so there would only be one white Australia, that did not look like some humpy country that was all over the shop on the colour spectrum.

The meeting did not go well. You could not get the truth out of those street-type culturally independent kid toddlers who were preoccupied with trying to rip off their disposable nappy, or crying, or screaming, and not talking properly, and generally acting tough, as though they just wanted to be totally one with country by running amuck on the beach in the middle of the night.

Say you were sorry that you were not interested in closing the gap you naughty kids, and leave those disposable diapers on. Say that closing the gap was the net to catch all Aboriginal people so they can be saved. Say you wanted to become quick smart white and leave those diapers on, and stop wanting to go native.

The whole fiasco became a bedlam of loss in the brains trust, for those toddlers looked too radical for anyone to take on, and could not be disciplined since they preferred kind old spirit elders, to living parents. They cried non-stop, complained about headaches, and crawled all over the floor, deliberately scattering the assimilated rattles as though they wanted the white rattles to start becoming black, rather than the other way around.

You kids stop throwing those white rattles out the door right now!

Then those staunchest of women, all the young mothers, and the seriously powerful senior law women of country, the mothers of many children, grandmothers and the like, great-grandmothers who were sitting around looking hostile, after having had to bother themselves to come to another of the super cop's meetings to explain themselves as being worthy of assimilation, now had the difficult task of trying to capture the rampaging toddlers to demonstrate the nurturing skills they had learnt from mandatory closing-the-gap classes, a special examination class which was now being held in this emergency in front of the super cop to anthropologically analyse their motherhood. It was an exercise in abysmal failure. The toddlers could not be captured or cajoled, and the babies simply chose to stay in their soiled diapers forever. This meant that the super cop could not decide what was learnt about how to change a baby's nappy after these ladies had received lesson after lesson at great cost from an eighteen-year-old white sociology student called Betsy, who – in her not cheap role of saving black people – was living high on the power of what she called her white supremacy work experience stint in an Aboriginal community.

Then through the fifteen-foot-high cyclone fencing to keep out the unwilling, the riffraff, the agitators, the hard to train, the unassimilated morons etc., in marched the schoolchildren with their thongs flapping loudly and raising the dust on the floorboards of the modern purpose-built training complex for the emergency intervention into the sixty thousand year plus cultural history of Aboriginal survival to assimilate them into white people. Well! The war had been long and had taken a multi-purpose, multi-pronged and multi-layered heavy toll, and who could say how much longer it would all go on in a global emergency future where the poor people continued to suffer, but never mind, the spotlessly clean schoolchildren kicked aside the unassimilated rattles scattered over the floor, and sidestepped the mad smelly toddlers scooting in every direction with mothers in pursuit, and formed a neat parade to express their gratefulness in being excused from school where they might be learning how to win the war, to spend the day being interrogated by a cop. They were each able to speak personally into a megaphone, to say that they were not calling their parents paedophiles like the national media was saying they were anyhow. *So,* super cop said could each say after him, *You had only been out playing football on the beach, and had not realised that it was the middle of the night?* Each child refused to tell this lie, and was forced to stand with the megaphone until each word of what the cop wanted them to say could be dragged out of their mouths.

The air foul to breathe, quickly grew thicker with hostilities, while parents were forced to listen to these kids plying sympathy out of the theory cop anthropologist, who simultaneously was parting with his expert opinion about rehabilitating unloved children to the forward planning authority searching how to achieve rapid assimilation. The toddler babies said they were too scared to go back home on the dark tracks from the beach where devils were lurking to kidnap them. Who told you that? Our mummy and daddy, sir. And yet, strangely, the cry-babies would not stop talking when they were called little liars. More information flowed. Each toddler chucked a tantrum about how they kept seeing bad people in this ugly purpose-built asylum – *What kind? What kind?* The toddlers took turns at the megaphone and cried, child molesters, murderers of children, and plenty of paedophiles. The super cop anthropologist, also practically social worker, was almost overjoyed, and immediately jumped to conclusions from seeing a vast thicket of reasons lurking in front of him, where he saw the toddlers hiding from their parents on the beach, and started surmising that these babies were not only late going home from the beach in the middle of the night, they were not even intending to go home. Well!

Wipe the hands of that, for one thing led to the other, and a little ringleader toddler stepped up to the megaphone, and said, *Yep, that's right. We were not going home.*

All the parents called the little fellow a liar, lying through his baby teeth, and claimed that all these toddlers were naughty children who should be dealt with most severely by the super cop anthropologist, until they learnt to tell the truth, and the cop stood his ground, and said he was not going to punish babies.

The parents called this lunacy sideshow a load of rot run by toads, and said they were sick of things, like, *you idiots acting like a pack of cringing dogs.*

The forward planning thinkers formed a justice system right on the spot, and said they thought it was not bias when a mob of parents turned their focus on the *cringing dogs*, by accusing them of showing a little bit of empathy towards the toddlers, just – *to prove their overwhelming love for the little children.* The meeting totally lost it. The church leaders were called in to mediate in a holy way that took hours to bring up what was holy with a smoking censer. The forward planners asked why they had to suffer these false aspersions when after all, all they were trying to do was to work hard on an important job like closing the gap as volunteers, and further blamed these parents for neglecting their children.

The little children began screaming for some café food – a fizzy drink, and a falafel salad – in exactly the same way that they had seen white children chucking a tantrum for food on TV advertisements, only these toddlers cried more fiercely that they needed a doctor because they were starving with nothing to eat in this purpose-built asylum. The little jerks became paralysed from totally losing it when offered turtle eggs to eat, and cooked freshly caught fish served on a plate. They ended up lying on the floor as stiff as a board, unable to move either leg to walk, or to lift up an arm. They could still use their tongues, so they began whingeing and blaming the angry parents for turning them into stone statues. This was amazing enough, but then, a strange breeze full of dust suddenly came up the street from out of nowhere on this breezeless day in the haze, and the dusty current flew into the meeting, and slammed the door behind it. The breeze continued flowing over the children pinned to the floor by their own tantrum paralysis, and then, it picked up speed. The parents felt as though they were being slapped by grit as the flooding air grew stronger and out of control. The cyclonic wind, still confined inside the purpose-built training centre for assimilation, now picked up the rattles, threw the white rattles back into the box marked white rattles, and the black rattles back into the box marked for the black ones. As though this tempest wind had miracle hands, it closed the boxes, taped them with sticky tape, and then this monstrous 250-km-per-hour bedlam wind picked up the cardboard boxes like a rugby player, knocked down the door on the way out, and roughly flung the boxes onto the dirt outside where an old man was sitting on the ground. He did not need to look up about any of this power, but continued to scratch the dirt with a stick, and the dust blew away, and faded into the bush.

The wild little toddlers were fessing up to nothing, and were unable to move their tongues even though they wanted to rat on each other for the crime of not being in bed asleep at the allotted time of closing the gap which was five p.m., to be fresh in the morning, to be able to jump this way and that through the atmospheric hoop of lies, to gain a few smidgens of truth. Now, the little toddler spies, seeing the old man outside thinking about them, were too petrified to lie on the floor like statues, and jumped into the lap of their parents, because a bogeyman might come and cast a spell on them. Hours passed, and they still would not move away from their mother's apron strings, so now with nothing else to say that could set them free, the toddlers started claiming to have seen things that they should not have seen. *What was that child,* asked the super cop. The most articulate toddlers had seen the sea woman turning into a cloud of seagulls and swimming with hammerhead sharks, then flying around on top of the water and kicking saltwater crocodiles in the guts.

Their parents thinking which way, half believed the stories because there was a powerful sea woman who had been living in the sea around these parts for thousands of years, and she was more real and alive than the glut of paedophiles that the Australian government and the national media were saying they were seeing in the Aboriginal world because they believed all black men were predators and abusers.

Things were being weighed in the dust particles that the old man threw from the ground, and now, the Praiseworthy parents were just relieved that their toddlers in either Kimbies or Huggies diapers were safe from the sea lady's power which was far more real, than believing what the land thieves were saying about them.

The smart little toddlers were saying that they were not stupid, and were telling the truth so the old man would stop making them feel like they had been turned into stone statues. They now claimed to know what suicide was – *we seen it happening all the time here. We know what was going on, when we see someone walking off into the sea in the middle of the night and not coming back – you call that suicide.*

You want to stop your lying, you kids.

We big now. We've seen it happening plenty of times.

Enough of that talk. You kids are only babies and should stop lying.

The toddlers said that they were even thinking about suiciding themselves to get out of this purpose-build hell for assimilation.

We will do it if you stop us playing with our old people down on the beach at night, and the toddlers added anyhow, *Aboriginal Sovereignty was not coming back to you mob.*

The parents of several of these youngsters wanted questions to be answered there and then: *Tell us you did not have anything to do with that? You tell us right now! Tell us you never pushed him in the ocean, did you? We don't want any murderers in our families.*

We good children. Tommyhawk – he there. Saw him. He shouldn't have told...

The big ears super cop instantly became another kind when he thought he had heard criminal evidence for the first time since he had arrived in Praiseworthy. He turned whiter, as though in shock. He looked like a white monster experiencing full wrath against Aboriginal people while moving slow-motion towards the toddlers. Then, just as suddenly, as though reacting to the rampaging of a white monster, the confined space of the purpose-built training centre became another thing altogether. The atmosphere inside the building turned into a bulletproof viper's nest of poison when the public good that was happening nice and polite up to this point, turned into full-throttled ugliness of the type you would not want to encounter. All those sour faces converged angrily, *accensi ira concitant se in hostem*, and like an illusion, the phenomenon hurled together into a totally tangled but unified crazed ancestral being lunging in every direction at a simple enemy, the shocked super cop.

Full rage followed.

The government's trainee parents shielded the toddlers behind their bodies, and the women closed the open spaces with roared hoarse-voiced rhythms pumping for battle, and thumped their chests, and the volleying primordial whistling blew the top off the building while they were screaming that these children were just trying to bring attention to themselves. *Get away, cop. You stop right there you loose cannon of the government! Don't listen to these cry-babies.* Blood shook. The entire radius of country gathered its belongings into a monstrous powerhouse that was at once almighty, real and final, and pulsing hammerlike, it was like the sky had fallen down on the relevance of the frightened cop and pushed him out of sight. As the haze of dust rose in the building, the people of country continued volleying, *Can't you see, these little babies are just squirming their way out of trouble.* Well! Sure! All was indignant. The toddlers cried like innocent babies while hiding behind their parents and tugging and biting their legs, which forced the parents to cry with raw emotion from seeing themselves being forced into a deadly seriousness, now of wanting to kill anyone who came near their babies. It was a real mayhem situation in a long day of quivering the spears, without saying anything about the bigger story curdling in niggled thoughts travelling through the stick the old man was using to draw all the facts on the ground.

2

Way, way out in the sacred world of rolling waves where the ghost spirits of the ocean sometimes sung like Perry Como to the galaxies, *don't let the stars get in your eyes,* you could listen to the sea singing back, *don't let the moon break your heart,* and the moon taking its turn, and singing, *there are too many splendid moons,* and in the splendour of stars you could hear the whole ancestor country chorusing, *there are too many stars so remember you are mine.*

Then one day, after a thousand nights of ordinariness where nothing sang, the sea lady from the beginning of time was somehow changing the movements of ocean streams. She had turned from swimming deep in the sea in her dance with hammerhead sharks and scaring away sacred crocodiles, and come to the surface to glare at the stains in the timelessness of what had been ordinary. This happened when the old lady had been listening to a dumped boyfriend wafting into her ears the same country-and-western song about the stars that he was playing on sky radio. She focused her gaze elsewhere, towards other incongruities happening around her body which she saw in the moonlight hitting the watery surface, and lighting up the silver rippling from the wake of the grief-stricken Aboriginal Sovereignty Steel.

This was when she saw the boy's waterlogged body floating alone out there in the sea. Just occasionally, the old sea lady could still manage to hear him fretting as he was dying, almost dead, and moaning about something that he had left behind. The old sea ancestor wondered about the trail of glittering light, and she softly asked, *What was that? What could it be?* The sea quickly became disturbed over too many miles, across too many stars, from too many nights of the moon, and from too many days of being alone. The sea woman rose up in the wailing winds, to search for what it could be, that the boy had left behind.

In the ordinary ebb and flow now grown into howling winds and roaring seas stretching from ocean to ocean, the old sea lady asked the fishes and the ghost of fishes in all the magic of the tides, and while searching through the sea river currents, to find what it could be that was worrying young Aboriginal Sovereignty Steel: *What thing had he left behind that was stopping him from dying.* Finally, though, in a world where all times seemed like nothing at all, it had probably only taken a half an hour for an answer to be found. The busyness sea itself rose, spilling Aboriginal Sovereignty over the waves, and heard him whispering: *You know what? It was the bloody Basics Card.* You know, the silly white man government's tool of the twenty-first century for cruel means to suppress any real sense of sovereignty out of Aboriginal people. Yep! The oppression tool, all rolled up with land thief in a bloody Basics Card. *Are you sure about that, sure that was what you will need for an eternity, in the infinity of your all times?* the busyness sea asked. Why was this boy of sovereignty thinking about racism when he could have been imagining the joy of death, or another joy, the hopefulness of his sovereignty in country?

But! Hey no. Aboriginal Sovereignty was more worried about what would happen to his independence, about his bit of welfare entitlement, his social benefit under Australian law, even when he was dead. How was he going to feed himself if he lost his Basics Card. Worrying! Was this all he could inherit in the twenty-first century? Worrying about not having any money because he had forgotten to bring his Basics Card on his suicide, after he had been floating out there in the sea for days. The government was not worrying about eternity. It only worried about getting rolled in the next election after a four-year trip of further disempowering the sovereign peoples. Luckily, the sea lady chased away the hammerhead sharks all day long, kicked the man-eating crocodiles in the guts every five minutes, blew away another ten thousand Portuguese man-of-war in a sea plagued by these creatures this time of the year, and gathered up the deadly sea snakes and threw them to the other side of the world to think about how to behave while swimming back home, while the Aboriginal Sovereignty kid was worrying about not being able to buy a packet of chip potatoes at wherever he thought he was going, if he did not have his stupid white government's Basics Card.

In the faraway sea under a clear blue-sky day, while the boy was being kept afloat by the old sea lady throwing her weight around with whatever was deadly confronting in the busyness sea, and also busily calming whatever while she was deciding on what to do with him fretting in an ocean now heaving with his heartbrokenness way out there, all consciousness slid through schools of trevally, more than any fisherman had ever seen. What might have seemed calming to the fish one moment, had become a fretting place, of worrying about how to get past a bigger weather system developing underneath, in the deeper waters of this world. Now it seemed that the whole sea was fretting about how Aboriginal Sovereignty could use a bit of money tied up in a piece of plastic on the things he wanted but could not buy in the sea, and which was not on the government's prescribed list of what he was allowed to purchase with his money. And somehow, he never saw himself dying in the middle of the ocean, or panicking from knowing he was lost from the land, but just sliding from one thing to another. Where was little creep Tommyhawk anyhow?

Aboriginal Sovereignty grew weaker. He struggled to focus on anything at all in the watery world that had taken hold of his life, and once this had happened, his wish for a piece of government plastic to spend in the sea lost its grip, fell from his head, and was quickly fading away. The currents took him too far away to the deeper sea world where there could be no fighting to take flight but it did not matter, he did not feel he had a struggle against the waters of his homeland. And yes, although assuming he felt sorry about his predicament of being too far away from his parents' home in the cemetery to ever be able to return, let's say he used what was left of his capacity to think about one of the great mysteries in his life, of how to create a pipe dream like his father's grandiose donkey transport conglomerate in the emergency of global warming, and perhaps with his last thought, he felt sorry that he had not made a will for his Basics Card that would buy a few stars for the dream.

3

The sea lady was not interested in Basics Cards. What use was another piece of plastic to her? The ocean was trashed with plastic. Untold billions of plastic bottles, and the rest of the many trillion bits and bobs floated into the centuries to come by winds, currents and waves, and journeying towards one of the many rubbish dumps, creating their own thousand-kilometre circling mass, gyres like giant weeping sores festering the ancestral planet in the centre of the ocean basins.

The local fishing people of Praiseworthy were returning home at the end of the day after another endless search to find Aboriginal Sovereignty. Each day, they would leave at dawn, and come back at dusk to pull the aluminium motorboats up on the sand, while the hunting dogs that had gone on these journeys would refuse to leave the boats and would sit there and howl for having failed again, and had to be forced away from the sea as they tried to swim off to continue with the hunt. Then, as the fishing men gathered together to talk about the fruitless day on the sea and walk home, they ignored dozens of large blue-and-white government signs that had sprung up and down the Praiseworthy beach that were an Australian Government Initiative Warning for proscribed areas where no liquor, or pornography, or paedophiles were allowed, and described in large lettering what the penalties were, such as the max being $74,800 or gaol, or $22,000 max or gaol, and to call 1800 333 995 (24 hours/7 days) for information (and hopefully, to make complaints).

The searchers of the sea who preferred not to see signs polluting the pristine beach of considerable ancestral consequential powers, were now bone-weary from searching for the body of Aboriginal Sovereignty in a heaving sea that had refused to help any human being today, yesterday, or the day before that. These were mostly old fishing people who had been roped in as a search party to find bodies in the ocean, who said they only knew where to find any fish whatsoever in ancestral waters, not bodies, and refused to work for any Australian government symbolism. Now, to prove a point, they avoided seeing English language signs as they walked with their heads staring down on the ground.

These were ocean-hardened people of country, not forensic scientists, or the police. They were always at sea, and had never bothered to learn how to read English, and often claimed there was no need to understand English to belong to their world. They walked along the beach of the ancient homeland in thongs making a squishy sound on the watery beach, or quietly barefooted, while trying to draw in deep breaths of the saltiness of the sea that would tell them every single time that this was the peace of mind they needed to know about, the important punchline in their lives, not government signage. Yes, even the sound of the sea could not corrupt the thoughts being aired by the fishing people on reckoning to each other about how they were not going to waste a second of their eyesight on rubbish stuff like proclaimed area signs from the government, and how they would rather have their tongue cut out of their head with blunt scissors than speak in that weak Australian language of signs. You could see, so it was said about the days of searching for Aboriginal Sovereignty, that these fishing people never spoke a word that was not for this place, that sounded like death walking around in their mouth. All that was fine about not speaking this or that, but they had to admit that they were being poisoned in English. These old coughing men would punch their own chest to listen to the wheezing echoing in the lungs, to announce, *Here! This is where all that stuff goes.* Any fool knew the sea air was not the same sea air it used to be. This sea air would make anyone feel sick, and these real scientists believed that there was only one thing causing their bodies to rot: they were being infested with microparticles of racism, which were just like any other microparticles encountered in the plastic hazes the size of a thousand kilometres circling in the sea, and floating in the dusty haze dome over Praiseworthy. The diagnosis: all racism.

So there was talk of starting another war in the language of the sea country gently moving out beyond the horizon, and it too never saw the proscribed area warning signs where the fishing men walked while feeling unhindered by the ring of steel signs cemented metres deep, and mere metres apart along the beach, and, continuing on around the circumference of Praiseworthy like numbers on a giant clock, until joining back at the beach again. The old men and women eternally searching for the return of Aboriginal Sovereignty were *bequeathed to nothingness*, other than to a consciousness of interconnectedness where relatives were all life, and further related to ancestral creators, and further related back into deep time, and across all country places of land, sea, and skies.

It was in this time of government signs that the old fishing people who had been trying to find Aboriginal Sovereignty started believing that there was a funny thing happening, for even though they never looked at government signage, they claimed that they had never seen a dust particle from the haze settling on any of these government signs, and they proclaimed, *this meant something was very strange about all these signs being dumped in sacred country*. They noticed the smallest things about country anyway, and now saw how the storming seagulls following them home from the sea – as seagulls had done since time immemorial just to catch fish heads or fish guts thrown back into the sea – were also behaving strangely. Seagulls normally liked to sit anywhere, but had never once landed on any of these signs to fan their wings while facing the sea breeze, nor had a single lizard, ant, or any other animal like a snake bothered twisting itself around a government signpost, or had sought shelter in the shade of a sign.

She can't read English either, some countrymen reasoned, referring to the sea lady now becalmed, who had not bothered explaining why any Australian government sign was important either, not to any part of this country place of Praiseworthy. She had simply moved her magnificence away from the becalmed sea, and the fishing men walking home from the sea, and on the tides turning, and flown inland, low across the ground through threads of ancient cobwebs lying across the powerful boundaries of the ancestral creators.

The sea woman exercised law differently, sometimes quietly, and it felt as though the old mermaid never had, and no longer existed. A pack of ghost dogs ran up and down the beach looking for the ancestors. The grey spectres barked and barked at the puppetry of the signs erected for one act alone, capturing the souls of the free fishing men, the now proscribed people who no longer went fishing at all, after being turned into corpse hunters, who walked home without the fish haul, attacked by the growing numbers of hungry storming seagulls flying madly about overhead. The atmosphere grew congested with questions created from the open wound in the soul of the corpse hunters, who were now openly, and annoyingly criticising the missing parents. Why weren't these parents going out in the dangerous sea journeys? Shouldn't they be searching for their boy along with everyone else? Did they think they were better than the people who needed to catch fish to feed their families? Did anyone have the right to be different to themselves? Every day, while the corpse hunters were losing the rhythm of fishing people, they thought it was the parents who needed to be searching for their son, instead of not lifting a finger to help the people who should be fishing for a job. Why couldn't the actual parents be out scanning the sea like everyone else working side by side on the occasion of this sad time? The walk home from the sea grew heavier with the weight of failure. No one could eat the fish from the deep sea. The corpse hunters cried that they were carrying the weight of the sea woman hitching a ride on their shoulders. She was sitting there with her full weight. Her long trailing ghost net embedded with cockle shells, jellyfish, crabs and sea stuff crushed the cobweb world covering the ground, and altered the many intricacies of gossamer shaping the ancestral map. The talking increased. What about the horrible nightmares the corpse searchers were having about what was lying out in the sea for them to find one day when they were just simple people trying to catch fish. The atmosphere grew darker out where the storming seagulls flew after the fishing folk, who knew how to see where a fish might be in the swell, but could not find their Aboriginal Sovereignty. There was a shift in the mood, and the fishing men turned corpse hunters now talked about how they wanted to punish these parents, make them pay for this nightmare of having to trudge home without success every day, and having no time to fish. They wanted these parents to feel what it was like to fail, by taking away their identity like their identity as fishing people had been taken from them. They were now only referred to as being corpse people. So why shouldn't those parents lose everything they stood for too. The walk home from the sea with the heavy sea lady hitching a ride on their shoulders crippled the souls of these old fishing men and they thought that locking away those parents for good would be too good for such useless people.

Then, one day in this story of the unsuccessful quest to find the son, the sun faded from the sky when the old sea lady began breathing spectacularly like a gale force wind, and her ghostly high atmospheric pressure breath filled the region, and while she flew, her perspiration fell like a fine sea spray that rolled off the waves. She picked up speed. A quick succession of darkened storm clouds rolled into a low trough, bringing the birds – brolgas, ducks, bush turkeys, and seagulls – flying alongside her for company. The spectre of darkening storm clouds roamed far in the land and far away in the sea. Seagulls dwarfed in the skies, and the heavy clouds crawled almost on their belly as they passed over the proscribed people walking home on the beach, inking the waters where schools of hammerhead sharks shook with a glimmer of fright before scattering and diving deeper to slink off on the sea floor covered with meadows of rolling seagrass where they hid. Further away, white masses of sea birds swooped upon the sea snakes hissing along the top of the waves and in the surf. The old woman had a hint of a smile on her face as she roared down from the clouds, and in her speed she kicked the crocodiles swimming too near Aboriginal Sovereignty and sent them flying to the mangroves down the coast where she had seen them a month before.

Through the clouds, the moon shone on the body being carried far away in a glistening stream on the backs of ocean fish, the enormous school of silvery trevally that had lived in these waters since who knows when, and were ancient carriers of human souls taken away by the sea.

The whispering fish know about meshing, crisscrossing and the entanglement of storylines carrying all things into a home that was as expansively universal, as the world. Their fins were pumping and propelling a flying silvery creature composed from the sheer vastness of their numbers through the water beneath, and that carried the boy above the water. In this spirit world, a full silver moon reflected its light on the flurries of air he drew into his lungs, that keeps him breathing, while being barely alive.

All these images were real, and could have been captured on the latest space technology imitating a god's eye for peering into these eruptive waters spreading across the top of the continent. Or, could have been easily picked up on a radar, and watched by the checkers of countries in the region of Asia, and by those powerful people on earth who were using satellite images in their surveillance of fishes and the nautical activities of boat peoples, border intrusions, and so forth.

These spies, watchers of the sea, may have seen the blurred shadow of Aboriginal Sovereignty floating in a rippling sea off what they thought were the un-sovereign borders of traditional land, and may have thought nothing of seeing what they believed to be a traumatised boat person. Easy to watch, while infra-red lungs breathed in the froth and bubble of what happens. Drownings. Ghosts. Remains. Things you see on the radar, the human business end of political bargaining over the harmlessness of the forsaken, were not the colossal ramifications reshaping the ancient story in country. You could not see that so easily on the radar.

4

Death was not cut and dry, nor do these out-of-the-blue things only happen to Aboriginal peoples – a wheel spinning repetitively – nothing to be done about it, nothing to stop it happening no matter what you threw at it – and so, *salutare*, in glory they will go...*En their medh riki fara...*

This was a midnight voice calling out for honesty, a stranger peeling back the layers of truth to examine what held a place like Praiseworthy together. So! Even though there were many people out searching in the sea, when walking along the beach these people of sobriety stood in front of the government's Proscribed Area signs along the beach, and felt like they were the accused of murdering their own culture. They besought the sea in its own language, to give Aboriginal Sovereignty back to them, and even after all this time of searching futilely, kept wishing with all of their hearts, that this would not be another suicide. The waves rolled, and would continue to roll, while they waited. The fishing people calculated the tides, while silently surmising about what really happened amongst the heavy harvest of their theories, possibilities, probabilities, and waited, for the body to roll in, and although nothing was said openly right away, none could stop wondering about the missing parents – these anti-Praiseworthy people. Yep! This Cause Steel, who thought he was the main traditional owner, who could not prove his Native Title at all, not like they could. Well! It was a show. A radiating fever like ultraviolet waves on the beach. They saw it themselves: *You see those rays coming off those government signs? It's poisoning our brain cells.* Who knew, and perhaps they were over-preaching the solemnity of the reason they were feeling no good, but they thought all eyes should be scanning the sea to way yonder, and back, not just their own eyes.

The people were curious, and sometimes asked between themselves, what kind of father was Cause Man Steel really? Why wasn't he on the policy radar, doing his bit to close the gap thing between Aboriginal people, and the rest of Australia? He should have been the first one, not they, who needed to be out here on the beach standing in front of those signs emanating poisonous radiation, and also proving, like they were, that he was not like other Aboriginal men the government and the media were accusing of not loving their children. Well! He should be there, if he claimed to be like everyone else, standing side by side like a real man, and involved in the search. Many of the corpse hunters texted each other when they saw he was not on the beach again like they were, preparing to be like a real man ready for the war of fighting the entire ocean to bring Aboriginal Sovereignty home. They wanted to know from whoever was in charge of this war thing, to find out when the father would be coming down to the beach like everyone else? Find out what was wrong with that murderer? It might be all right for someone to be antisocial if they liked, but they should be helping the main people like themselves facing a killer sea wanting to keep Aboriginal Sovereignty for itself. He should be helping to fight this great war of the all times, here and now.

The intermittent screeching of the collective town crier, the alarmist of country trying to find a corpse, went on and on from the sea to the beaches, from the bush to the home, into mobiles, along Church Street, and into the ears of all things, *We have lost our Aboriginal Sovereignty*. The search grew into an overwhelming deep grief that sent twangs of shivers shingling up and down the back, and the mourning ceremonies were activated in clouds of smoke on the beaches, but the oldest spirit world was continually interrupted by the simple human conscience of the time: *Which side are you on?* A Christian force beaming from Church Street ascended onto its throne perched in the psyche to decree that everyone was a church leader, yes, yes, while trying to mitigate its songs to the old songs of country.

A choir of gospel songs began rising magnificently into the rolling clouds. Then, thunder roared, while forks of lightning went bang, bang, bang and hit every single one of the signs around the periphery of Praiseworthy, like a circle of firecrackers lit up on a cake. This was strangely miraculous for sure, since what took place was shocking, so instantaneously powerful, in reducing those metal signs into little blobs of molten scrap metal on the ground. Well! The corpse hunters and the fanning beach ladies said so, and felt fortunate enough that they were not hurt in the unspeakable holy fracture of country raising its awesome irk. They considered it a joy to have not been struck by the enormousness of the lightning ancestral being, so the loudest town crier shouted, *So two more times please*. The clouds grew heavier, and the fishing people began singing like they were channelling Pete Seeger, singing *We shall overcome someday*, and about giving peace a chance, then got on with the old ceremonies.

Thank you. Thank you. Deep heart, someday we shall overcome, and live in peace, and it was to be expected, to have grief as enormous as the ancestral lightning screeching amongst the crowd on the beach. The stricken had become more stricken since there had been a string of suicides by the young people, but somehow, again and again, calmness was regained, and once again, hand in hand like a bunch of black flower people, their dry eyes stared out to sea to find the son of all. They needed to have at least sighted the corpse once to make hope keep breathing in his body returned to them from the ancestral spirits.

5

The trouble of hearing donkey noise was not the number one choice for anyone wishing only for a bit of respect, like wanting some peace and quiet in their lives while they were trying to hear the tinkling of water falling from Aboriginal Sovereignty, the moment he walked out of the sea on an incoming tide.

*You know…*these sad old ladies said with mad voices while furiously waving the pandanus fronds, *These are not holy donkeys.*

Not Corpus Christi donkeys.

Not Palm Sunday donkeys neither.

They are the wrong colour donkeys anyway.

These are Jaguar colour for carrying rich people around.

Not like real holy grey carrying Christ.

The old women were completely pissed off that they were being tricked by the colour of donkeys that were supposed to be actual machinery, and did not look like, nor sound like expensive machinery to them, for instance, the sound of a naval frigate or aircraft carrier cruising around out in the ocean, or an air force fighter jet landing on the deck, were they themselves in such a reality, were they earning the salary of a fighter pilot. These people who had already suffered majorly and substantially said they were exhausted from hearing the constant braying of freaky coloured donkeys they did not like. They did not care how fucking valuable this fake machine was, or if it was the machinery for the prized new world transport conglomeration of the heart's desire, it just looked like donkey all-sorts to them – the ones that were nearly the colour of platinum, or the not-so-prized ones, or the plain wrong ones, or even the most special and rarest ones. Whatever! They were all fakes, delusional versions of a single platinum magical millionaire-making donkey that did not exist, and did not even look like machinery to them. So. What? They hardly cared less, even if all these wrong donkeys had personally taken Planet years of crawling around in every bit of spirit-charged spinifex-ridden bush containing the most sacred songlines running through the arid middle lands of the continent. Any donkey was a donkey of this stupid man's illusion of the type of machine he had in his mind, pursuing whatever relentlessly, bloodied and possessed through landscapes covered with the sharpest spinifex known to mankind, that tore most of the skin off his entire body.

In the hunt for an elusive creature of someone else's beautiful imagination, to find the most silver ghost donkey that ever existed, everyone in Praiseworthy knew it did not exist. It was neither real, nor spirit. Widespread was actually looking for a creature of myth, one capable of creating magic, of fulfilling every wish, and never gave up hoping to turn his donkey business into gold.

Now Widespread was still nowhere in sight of the mourning dust haze of Praiseworthy. He had either slipped in and gone, or had disappeared from sight, not hearing the beseeching of the town criers searching for him to help in the search for his son, nor did he hear the women with fans on the beach, or the fishing people consigned as corpse hunters roped into a sea search as volunteers who hated searching for corpses of other people's children. It was rumoured by the dream travellers that he was still at least a thousand kilometres away, and was heading home with the mask-head, actually a very old platinum donkey. It was a slow journey in a vehicle, a broken-down piece of machinery worth nothing that only crawled, stalled, and clapped out under the weight of carrying his heavy nightmarish premonitions, while trying to contain a struggling donkey that had messed up its platinum quality fur coat, and was still pining to be taken back to his home. This did not feel like gold, nor like a world of millionaires, and there was no gold being made yet in any of this high almighty business venture of sustainable magnificence in the fast-approaching new era of global warming.

All was not well either, down in the cemetery of Widespread's dwindling Native Title estate. He had been away so long, many thought he had died after bringing all these donkeys into the place, and they said, *you don't mourn people like that.* Don't worry about him. He had gone and died, and left them to find his son's body.

There was a whole lot of neglect going on down at the cemetery. No one bothered to close the gate anymore – the boys were gone, and Dance only cared about searching for lepidoptera dancing over the bushland, and she literally could not see the fast-breeding thousands of feral donkeys standing all around her. Well! The donkeys escaped, and were migrating to the beaches of Praiseworthy as though it was a luxury tourist resort with free food, and soon enough, there were hundreds of hungry, gangly and distressed-looking donkeys galloping towards the searchers who were looking to find the real one, but who only saw instead various shades of grey donkeys, or some white ones, brown, brindle, black, yellow ones charging towards them, blind with hunger from the scent of food, melting ice creams, corn beef sandwiches, minty lollies, cough drops, Coca-Cola, and other fizzy drinks, not to mention gallons of tea sweetened with condensed milk and sugar, cooked chickens, hot dogs in a bit of bread, sausages from the community barbecues and truckloads of food for all the involuntary search parties, paid with money siphoned from the council's essential services budget from the government's closing-the-gap vision of assimilation, but which the mob thought was for creating equity in building roads, like the ones in white towns, and providing services like education, sewerage etc. that were on par with the rest of the country's towns and cities. Nah! Really! The old fanning ladies who were being run down by stampeding donkeys thought it really did not matter what colour these animals were, since they all looked the same to people who hated donkeys. Same wise, in a time of flux, the hordes of wild donkeys did not care who was on the beach. The hordes stormed, knocking people over like sticks. They went crazy. There were packs of donkeys all over the place rearing up on hind legs like they were dreaming of being high-ho silver, or they were kicking out their back legs, and rolling in the sand in the middle of the involuntary lady searchers fanning themselves while trying to stare out into the hazy sea at sunset, annoyed with being lumbered with two jobs. Wasn't it enough that they were trying to measure the density of the thickening haze of global warming which was what they were supposed to do in their real job as elders, but now they also had to scan the ocean twice, not only to measure the density of the haze, but also to search for a cripple-head God boy dripping water as he rose from the sea. The donkeys attacked the fishing people who were totally pissed off with being involuntary corpse hunters forced to travel in ever-widening grids further out in the ocean to find Aboriginal Sovereignty, and who were now just trying to walk home and have a sleep before returning again to the sea, but had to fight their way through thousands of donkeys trying to mangle their bones. There was no end to the troubles, for the donkeys were attacking the gangs of toddlers in diapers trying to kill these animals indiscriminately with sticks, and as the hordes of donkeys and dogs fought one another, the oblivious children playing rounders on the beach and having a good old time were also attacked. The all-out attack continued for hours with no side giving an inch of ground while everything that got in each other's way was destroyed by donkeys, people, children and dogs flying all over the place.

There was not one among the big old ladies fanning themselves, the corpse hunters, the old people sitting on the white plastic chairs, others on the fold-up chairs outside the cemetery because they were too afraid of donkeys to go inside the cemetery yard, and the church people building more churches on Church Street, who were not carrying an injury caused by a donkey which was either physical or psychological, or both, and who thought it was a beat-all disgusting act of Widespread's, to abandon his feral donkeys in Praiseworthy. They claimed over and over that he had no business dumping his donkeys on the people who truly belonged to Praiseworthy to have to worry about in their time of much life hassle, and how they cried with injuries and worrying, that as far as the eye could see, vast herds were now invading the tribal Native Title land, the holiest of law places of the all times. Everywhere you looked, you could see these dirty creatures wandering freely over the pristine ancestral beach. There was no end to the trouble and the worrying, since there was no one either official or stupid, like the Major Mayoral thing Ice Pick who was too worried about whether his golden Christmas beetle would bother turning up this year, nor were the lackeys like the forward planners bothering to iron their mustering gear like civilised people, and saddle up on a real horse to round up these savage donkeys by whatever means, and export the buggers to some place on Earth that wanted to purchase packs of untrainable, savage donkeys that broke your arm or bit you on the leg or rolled all over you, just for the hell of it. There were some people who said they clearly remembered a time when Planet said he was going to let these donkeys go loose like this, to let them roam free-range, to let them rip up the countryside, the country that was not his in the first place, just like the cemetery on the edge of the town where he was squatting by saying it was his Native Title right. Now, it appeared, he had probably died in his own country which was elsewhere, and had left his mad donkeys on this country that was not his.

Now look at this. Shit everywhere, and it had gone on for too long. These were really mad types of donkeys, and the whole town thought they remembered Widespread saying that they were not feral donkeys. They could not tell what he had been collecting, for if all these thousands of donkeys were pet donkeys, why were they destroying the town like a pack of wild animals? These feral donkeys had no respect for Native Title land, or anything sacred. These were bad donkeys. *We want to win here.* No one should be bringing feral animals to Praiseworthy. How many times had they told him this, that Praiseworthy was a tidy town, that people in this place win major prizes for tidiness by picking up more rubbish than anyone else in Australia, and had raked up every single leaf that fell on the ground – things like that. People here do not want a place that looked dirty. This was the cleanest place of all. Now there was donkey shit everywhere in a place that had no history with donkeys in any time of the human experience. This Widespread, they added, must have been from somewhere else, some foreign country for instance, for he was not like themselves in any respect, so he must have come from somewhere else, where the local people have donkeys living with them. They wondered if he might actually be Greek, Italian, Portuguese, Indonesian, Chinese, Filipino, Arab, other people with donkey traditions, people with donkeys from countries they had seen countless fleeting times on TV, and actually, that was why he could not be a Native Title holder over the cemetery.

This chorus up and down the streets rifting night and day said Widespread was a bad man, and it was a genuine prophesy of theirs to say the writing was on the wall for these donkeys in the not-too-distant future while Planet was behaving like some excessive remote-areas Belshazzar opera person around Praiseworthy. The various search parties could not wait for him to come back dead or alive, and in fact, they were hoping he had not died somewhere in the desert, so he could come back and see what his vermin donkeys had destroyed on Praiseworthy territory, land that was not his law country, and even if it was, he had no right to destroy what he was supposed to look after. They could not wait for him to return, so they could tell him to get out, to go away and leave them alone. Let's just say that Cause Man Steel, the un-emanator of the assimilatory times, was under the pump because he was an irritant of the pristine being raked and scrubbed for white trophy tidiness, and he was therefore a habitual nuisance like his noxious un-Australian donkeys. He was not anyone's choice of what was real, for not manning up to reality in the world of practical existence by perpetual compromise.

6

The nuisance bugger donkeys of the fabled transport conglomerate continued to create hindrances for the searchers while the owner remained nowhere in sight. Either dead or alive, he was not putting in the hard yards as they were, to find the dead son. Everyone now realised that these donkeys were really wild animals. They attacked everyone. They were untameable. Anyone in their right mind could see that they were not domestic animals that you would use for a proper haulage conglomeration placed in the pointy end of the business and financial world. These were wild animals. That smelt. None smelt like money.

In the world of Praiseworthy with glory walls practically in every home resembling a sacred temple covered with intergenerational prize ribbons, trophies, worn-out ringer boots, akubra hats celebrating the world's greatest cattle musterers, bull-riders, fastest lassoing champions in the hemisphere, and several silver mines worth of belt buckles engraved with renowned buck jumping horses of the dry country impersonating Godzilla on the rampage, the home representing more prizes for major feats of excellence per population than anywhere else in the world, there was not one person who chucked a saddle on any of those so-called pet donkeys, to get it to go somewhere you wanted it to go. They figured that riding a donkey was absolutely incomprehensible. Who wanted to ride a wild donkey fouling the pristine beach to the extent that you could no longer walk on it, would you call that a class act?

While it was being left to everyone in Praiseworthy, the people who already had the job of being a volunteer wisdom person, watchtower or beach sentry, or corpse finder in the open sea, they also had to stare down the barrel of pollution on pristine beaches, to look at the vast foulness like an environmentalist, and do the actual sums of what they called donkey arithmetic, to work out the cost of cleaning and scrubbing each grain of sand, to restore the place to something that looked a bit nice. Well! Everyone ended up arguing the toss about scrappy scrub donkeys that had never carried a real thing in their lives, and could not see it themselves, how donkeys were going to replace container ships in the congested shipping lanes in the Kowloon Peninsula off the South China Sea with about twenty-five thousand tons on board. Or, how a donkey could become the fuel economy's next-gen 770-horsepower refrigerated semitrailer hitting melted tar while overloaded with more than seventy tons of vegetables or anything else. You needed to see something real like steel in a conglomerate transport business bounding through the globalised world. Real business. Not gammon stuff. Anyone, even an idiot, would be able to see that Widespread's filthy donkeys would not know how to help the Australian economy, and would not even be interested in a looming global warming situation for *us hereabout original peoples. No way! Anyone could see these donkeys were not going to make any kind of impression on Wall Street, not even in a hundred per cent hundred-year prospect of peak global warming happening everywhere.* So! This is what happened. The official searchers here, there, and everywhere still surviving somehow on some new-fangled version of a government perpetual training scheme designed to magically teach them the non-existent value of white social responsibility, were all together, staring at the dung beetles getting rich on donkey droppings that covered the beach more than the sand did, and they tried really hard to mentally improve upon the reality of the arithmetic, to work out how they could make a few dollars out of transporting a box of tomatoes from A to B on one of these ugly creatures polluting the paradise of the pristine ancestral beach frontage, and how they might turn a meagre return from the box of overheated rotting tomatoes into a fortune, or at least a going concern, before Widespread took the opportunity, if he ever returned to Praiseworthy and started to claim back any of these straying donkeys. Who, they claimed, even on this beach, wanted to be a squanderer of opportunity when it was supposed to come knocking, or to ever let a chance go by?

These people had enough powerful notions thrown at them about how they could get rich fast, if only they took the opportunity. Yet, the idea of becoming rich when you were dirt poor could grow into a mountain of wishing in the mind, that would in the end be all you could think about, and why you would begin believing in fallacies. Now the way popped in the brain like osmosis, and the searchers thought that perhaps they really did know more about donkeys than Widespread, since, well, you only had to look at their knowledge of livestock which was practically in the blood, and it felt as though they were the greatest in the world in knowing how to work livestock while communing with the pride-of-place intergenerational devotional wall of fame, the trophy paraphernalia and so forth and you know, *So what if Planet says he's a donkey whisperer, he's a bloody donkey whisperer my foot!* What was really going on with this donkey conglomerate anyhow, when anyone could see that these scungy animals had come straight out of the desert where they had been living for more than a century. Just because they could survive out there in the wild and in the baking heat which *had mutated and improved the genes*, and looked like Rastafarians with dreadlocks, did not mean Planet knew more than they did about donkeys. The searchers reached for the real, and they believed that these donkeys had recreated themselves in country that had already reached the peak of the climate emergency forecast. Widespread had plagued the place with freak donkeys with fur that looked all weird and silvery like platinum and weak from global warming, and were what you might call – *half albino*.

But: *Who were they to say anything?* They were only people who had been forcibly recruited to be corpse searchers on an enforced volunteering government training scheme to help them to become socially responsible. Yet, this feel-good stuff was not sustaining their inner soul, and they thought further about the numerous instances of hindrance from these donkeys interfering with their need to have a totally clear access and view of the sea, and talked further between themselves about how Cause Man Steel was only obsessed with donkeys, and would not have any idea about how to start a transport conglomerate. What was really bothering their minds, was how they needed to see mythical supernatural donkeys gifted to them from the God of the multiple denominational churches, and so they prayed for real donkeys, something with more oomph, looking like they had the power of the ancestral creators of country, and death to ferals. How would you expect Widespread to develop a powerful wall against fear, like wildfire? Fire that produces its own tornadoes of lightning and thunder, and fire clouds raining live embers in howling winds all over the country? These were in the old stories raiding the nightmares. How was he going to develop a world-standard conglomerate transport system to drive right through all those mega-fires in the Pyrocene age of global warming? You needed superhero donkeys belting through the era for something like that.

The donkeys did not get it: why the involuntary volunteer searchers were always screaming at them, *Shoo! Get out of the way.* The pack became indignant, stood in the way of the search parties moving in a line along the beach while prodding the sand with sticks in search of foul play, any evidence at all that could be linked to the disappearance of their Aboriginal Sovereignty. All the old volunteer ladies fanning themselves on the beach kept yelling to the God cop anthropologist that there were too many donkeys obstructing their view of the sea, but he pretended that he could not hear them by writing notes in his notepad with a sharpened 2B lead pencil.

With no one believing that feral donkeys had the right to exist in this space, there was a stand-off between a fuming and hot-tempered people with no time for intruders, and this large pack of hungry donkeys that had grown to like sea breezes and wanted the space to continue moving around on the beach. The anthropologist cop soon became bored with the eye-balling because he did not know what was going on about belonging, and he soon left the heat of the sun to go and do another report to the government about how a bunch of agitators were protesting on the beach over the loss of their Aboriginal Sovereignty. These were not like the 'real' Aboriginal people he used to know, he wrote with a flourish in the stylised, dot-point report, not like the ones he knew years ago, who never complained about the government, like these modernised whingers about human rights.

This was when one of the searchers was fuming about the state of the world to the point that blood literally bled in his eyes and sped in an agitated whirlpool of anger throughout his body. He cast away the devotional belief of all the churches believing in one God and said he did not want to sing any more hymns to make things feel better in his head for a few fleeting moments. He was very pumped up. His body shook. He pranced over the beach like he wanted war, and wanted the thing with the donkeys to be finished with once and for all. He walked up to the donkeys packed in a huddle a couple of hundred metres down the beach, yelling bitter words about how he felt about life, and waving around the long hunting stick he held in his hands. In this full threatening gesture of anticipated battle, he aimed to cast the first blow. He swung the stick with full force haphazardly in front of these animals that refused to move, or acknowledge he existed, before a sharp crack echoed back along the beach when a donkey was struck on the head.

This war man chased the stunned donkey, nearly killed it – the almost perfect platinum pole star of the proposed transport conglomerate. He was bent on attacking it, storming after the striking ice greyness through the stampeding pack, and the more the stunned creature ran frantically in circles of fear, the angrier became the attacker, because he could not understand why in hell it would not just run back to wherever it came from, like for instance, back to friggen Widespread's place. The attack turned into some kind of sport running red-hot with targeting and hitting the injured donkey, while he lashed out on any other donkey that got between the one that he was now determined to kill.

This bleeding donkey, in shock, punctured skin all over its body, with fear in its eyes, began attacking and biting the person with the stick, and this escalated into a fight in the sand flying sky-high between the stick-yielding man at one end, and the donkey that had grabbed the stick and was holding it firmly between its teeth. The great tug-a-war turned into a marathon that was watched by both humans and donkeys to see which would win possession of the stick, but neither would relent in a storm of kicking, punching and biting while sand flew with skin, fur and blood.

The mass of startled, open-mouth donkeys braying loudly and locked in nervous twitching panic bolted in a heaven-like stampede – not of angels, but of donkeys, dogs and people. The old women yelled and shook their fans. In the mayhem, the toddlers and children cursed and attacked both donkeys and people with their pocketknives as they weaved in and out through the searchers. The children were kicked by the frightened animals lashing out in this war, and they retaliated by yelling and swearing about being hurt. Parents threw sticks, stones and buckets of sand at the fattest donkeys – dozens of pregnant jennies – trying to hit them in the eye. Many were bitten on the neck or arm, or kicked, as the donkeys reared up to fight back while being prodded with sticks, shovels or walking sticks, or pounded with stones by people trying to move everything off the beach.

7

The major transport conglomeration, its so-forth beautiful vision of resilience in a hot as hell new world, and as a monumental cause in the hope of saving his people for the new era which had driven Cause Man Steel to the edge of insanity, was already heading for ruin. This new God-hero Widespread, who had been suddenly driven by a premonition that he had to race back to Praiseworthy, did not realise that he was being locked out of this reality of the show on the beach. He was still far away, further west, and south in latitude, caught in another ancestral country – thousands of kilometres away, while fixing his broken-down Falcon in the bush lands, and trying to convince the perfect platinum donkey to forget its sulkiness about being captured, and instead, be more cooperative about becoming a world-famous mask-head, almost one of the senior angels, a seraph for driving a sustainable, high-edge unpolluting business venture of purity into the new future. *What could be more worthy than heading the world's first sustainable transport conglomerate? You were doing nothing out here.* He pattered on about his worthy vision of the life fantastic – of how to do it when they were all living in hell, while he was still figuring out how to reassemble the contents of a useless motor engine scattered on the ground all over the bush, and he further challenged the feral creature by asking it, *What else were you planning to do in this heat?* Both man and donkey looked around at the scorching heat somewhere near fifty degrees in the middle of the day, canvassed the mirages up the road, drew into their soul the wilting hard leather-like leaves of the flora, and Widespread challenged the donkey to step up to the fact of global warming. *Well, it's going to be like this, you need to be a bloody good warrior when it becomes hotter than this in the future. So, my friend, you may as well be doing something useful with your life and your future generations. You will either be just baking like everything else around here while it gets even hotter than this, or you start doing something about it. Which hellhole do you want? Even king donkeys like you have got to step up, just like everything else, if you are going to have a snowflake chance of surviving on a burning planet.*

But remember, and there was paramount remembrance about what was happening in the fight for the beach, that it was a total bedlam of misunderstanding from day one about what these donkeys were doing in Praiseworthy in a fight of one man with everyone else.

Now, it was plainly obvious that this donkey enterprise would have to end.

Many of the beach people were knocked over in the fracas. Sandstorms flew up from the dry beach. All the donkeys that were almost the colour of platinum were gone, and some were among the hundreds of donkeys struggling far out in the sea. Tempers were raw. Injured people were screaming. Others were yelling for people to save the donkeys. Others were yelling for more blood.

Those who noticed the struggle of at least a hundred light-colour donkeys half-drifting, half-swimming far out in the massive blueness of the sea where it meets the sky, perhaps thought that these animals were doomed. It may have crossed their minds that these donkeys drifting further away, were either losing the will to live, or were lost or disoriented from never before experiencing an escape from horror in a blind run through the sea, or were just too terrified to swim back to the beach. And then, as the people on the beach were preoccupied with censuring themselves with the perpetual immediacy of danger approaching their lives, they turned their backs while juggling a lifetime of mixed emotions, and perhaps in the seesaw, were pleased one minute to see this view in the sea, while feeling mortified the next.

They may have imagined the animals coming back, floating on the incoming tide either dead or alive, while holding Widespread to account in their chastising minds for being the owner of these donkeys who had not yet witnessed the end of their ordeal. Perhaps, in a truly long sigh of resignation for preserving their integrity to fight another day in the long struggle of life, each had showered themselves with a winnable diamond-cut finality fetched up from the surface of their souls, this small thought resembling a kernel of generosity from experience, a well-crafted inherent knowledge that all good things must come to an end.

We will wrap one of these rotting stinking carcasses around his neck when he gets back.

The super people saw new times with a contemporary, flexible agenda, which Ice Pick said was how to manage the moment of perpetual change for the better, *which meant accepting the fact that when you are in mean times you got to conserve your energies to do one or two things, those most concerning your own needs: You don't have to see everything with a tear in your eye.* A dying donkey was just a conservation of energy, another evil preventing rapid progress in the theory of *We shall overcome,* in a newly acquired conservatism on the road to freedom.

What if Planet valued these donkeys, they would make him pay for this bloodbath on the beach. The old ladies called the faraway police of Parliament House on their mobile phones to fly up to this Praiseworthy beach right now, and shoot all these donkeys suffering in the sea, and along their beach frontage, blocking the view of their search for Aboriginal Sovereignty.

409

8

Far, far away, and far from where the solid core thinking of Praiseworthy was heading with vendettas and so forth, Cause Man Steel was assembling hundreds of engine parts for the broken-down Falcon, walking around with his rubber-thong feet in the prickles. And, perhaps through enough bad feelings, and curses, and his premonitions about nasty stuff reaching him from thousands of miles away, he felt the need for individualising his weird obsession about achieving Aboriginal self-sufficiency, to recoup like a last will and testament to himself, where his type of economic independency was heading, of reassuring himself in his righteous getting crazy rich vision through his totally unbendable singular focus, that he was dead right. He was right to believe in a dream by spending decades to acquire a unique millionaire-producing donkey the colour of platinum which was worth more than gold, even if he had only once seen it in a dream. You had to trust luck. Really trust a particular type of magic he knew existed in his ancestral orbit, that was as far removed as you could get from hexed lingering-death government schemes for covering the inequity gap with whiteness as far as the eye could see – and so on and so forth, because he knew what real luck was, and he said it now, *You got to fuck that lingering death into nothingness.*

How would the government know anything about the Aboriginal predicament?

At this stage of luckless journeying, his fat head was only capable of spinning its own golden threads of vision that were, *at best, better than all the rest. Just follow me,* he cried aloud like a prophet from the peak of a desert sand dune to the faraway people, and by assuming that the whole of Praiseworthy was hanging out to hear what he had to say, like a magic man with great powers whose words floated far away with the ancestors over country of the song lines, he telepathically chucked them the goods, by giving them a thought or two about having faith in a better fate, which was what he was thinking about while reconstructing the empty cavity of the Falcon's wrecked engine, and he said more matter-a-factually, far more than any time he had spoken about anything in the past, *I will show you a way where you will not have to speak to white people again.* The thought struck gold big time with such a fantastical idea in a place where there was no spanner in the works of his brain, and he felt great for being on the way about this, about being nearly at the boundary gate, where you just had to figure out how to open the padlock, to be on track with achieving his simple, blue-sky vision. So, wanting to be clear, he went on explaining the flight from oppression, his rags to riches deal: *You got to control the carting and transport industry of Australia. If you can cart what you need, and you can transport yourself for nothing, then you will be a free man,* he claimed. *You owned your destiny because,* he said while teleporting into the fray, *whatever else you need in life will follow you, if you can carry your own load. This was how our people lived in the past and survived. This is how we will do it again. Fossil fuel is not going to last forever. Mate! We are blessed that some of those old pioneer buggers of colonisation left us the gift of these five million feral donkeys. Well! At least it is something, after they took just about everything else, let's show the buggers that we will rule this place again from their waste.*

Donkeys, the gloater cried to all and sundry in a voice capable of travelling several hours and days, through heat-shimmering mirages, dust storms, electrical tempests, into the swamps, bushfires, floods over the plains country, through earthquakes, and other global catastrophes, before reaching over the old rooftops, crawling around multiple rickety church steeples, and seeping into the broken temples of the mind with a word or a sentence either deleted or lost by the weather editor, until finally, all that was left to hear was a clear half sentence checked into one's thoughts, and they did not know what this incomplete sentence meant, what was *the new economic order*?

411

What was the new economic order? The half thought was a complete puzzle for the searchers down on the beach while pondering the shire council bulldozer's flattened sand monument dedicated to their massacre of donkeys. All they remembered Cause saying from his soapbox days, was something about how it would take a hundred years to complete a blue-sky vision, *a hundred years to build perhaps, but you know what, you are the ones who will scoop the future trifecta, because not only you, but your heirs will be in the hot seat. They will inherit the future of mankind.* He had wired that news too, via an old megaphone hanging off the side window of his vehicle as he drove up and down Church Street spruiking his views like a politician. Widespread knew the sums, and it was all plus, plus, plus without any hesitation, or subtraction of hope while he was saying, *You know what idiots? I am going to unshackle the Aboriginal person. You want to know how? Brainwave, pure and simple brainpower, doesn't cost a dollar, and you know what, you will get it for free from me.*

Where was the spirit of all things, was it lost? Did it exist at all? Or was it, too, searching for Aboriginal Sovereignty? Time was passing quickly for a man building a dream far away in the desert country while the body searchers keep searching the sea for a corpse, and the old ladies on the beach keep looking sideways out to the sea, and becoming far more occupied with collecting incriminating evidence. All day long they tackled the hate barnacles attacking their mind while trying to keep an eye on the sea, and taking selfies of themselves beside marauding diseased donkeys running up and down and past them on the beach in plague proportions right in front of their eyes. Or else, they pressed their mobile phone hard against the ear to beg the capital of Australia's police to drive about three thousand kilometres to the haze dome, to make donkeys disappear with a bullet.

The search parties wanted to take the matrices out of finding Aboriginal Sovereignty, to lessen the complexities of being an involuntary searcher under their intergenerational circumstances, to be without thought, or to concentrate all thought on the search. They no longer wanted to be forced to live with the painful views in life, either from feral animals proliferating in the world, or hearing the views of a bad person far away fixing his broken-down vehicle on some unused bush highway. They wanted action against this proliferator for living illegally down in the cemetery, squatting on land that was not his to squat on with hundreds of donkeys slumming around in umpteen humpy pens thrown together with rubbish and tied up with rusty wire. All this got in the way of a clear mind, that should be thinking with respect about where dead people should be buried. The action corpse hunters who were out searching for bodies in the sea, should not have to be searching for a final resting place when they already had a cemetery. It was their right to be entitled to a peaceful eternity of independence that was not in existence when alive, to finally turn the lights off, and lose themselves in the quicksand of eternal peace, and not to have to worry about a dead feral donkey being buried in the hole where you should be buried.

Ode to glory in the haze, the citadel of the high ground knowing no bounds, where the steeple people, right down to the old granny lifesavers on the beach, knew the cost of their freedom was too much. They knew the kind of freedom that Widespread was talking about. The thought of too much freedom could make you go mad when the proliferator went over the place in your head, and made you act like a dingo. His slung-shot freedom messages using his ancient telegraphy powers were deleted from the brain. He was not going to control this mob, like other people who sent emails to your brain even though they were miles away.

The whole world of Praiseworthy knew he was tampering with their minds with his messages, and trying to make a pack of whingers out of good involuntary lifesavers battling saltwater crocodiles, sharks, box jellyfish, snakes and whatnot to find their Aboriginal Sovereignty, and forcing them to be reskilled again as failed volunteer search parties whose only task was to recover the bodies of children floating in the sea when these kids learnt the future in a few weeks at school. The warp thing about Widespread's travelling messages, was that he pushed the local brain trust in an instant too far, into pure hatred towards whatever he was visioning – like this last-straw donkey business, that had left them fighting for their culture down on the beach that used to look like a million dollars and could have been a popular tourist venture, but you know what? It was pristine-less, and no longer spotless by any stretch of the imagination.

There was just never any respect, none of this in the mind of an involuntary corpse searcher, for his mind was an on-the-ropes respect-free zone, because he was too livid gone, and sour he could not be himself, a true fishing man throwing nets in the estuaries for mangrove jack, free to dream about as much fish as he liked, like an ancient fishing man far out at sea in a place of his choice, and bringing home proudly a haul that could break your back, or dreaming about fish like a proper God man, or seriously like the Greek god of dreams, Morpheus – the swan-winged one of the thousand sons of sleep – Somnus. The suicide retrieval business was not for them. They were not into being involuntary volunteers upsetting the great serpent frightener of men, or whatever else huge was out there squatting in the sea, or worrying about who was squatting illegally in the question mark Native Title quest cemetery, or why the parents were sitting around at home eating another packet of gingernut biscuits with a cup of tea, and not searching for their own lost children with funeral eyes like they were themselves. Ordinary fishing men should not be asked to do this kind of no-statement work for nothing. This was really a police job, but, where were the gutless police? The devoted got down on their knees, and it was a total all-out frenzy of praying along Church Street in forty-six degrees Celsius out in the midday sun, or at least fifty-four degrees in any tin shed holy place of the denominational churches – if there was room to squeeze in another of the devotees, for there were always too many holy people trying to squeeze inside an oven that was called a church, and needing to yell over one another their own unique story about bad donkeys to the burning-ear God. And they repeated what the number one holy smoke God fellow had proclaimed in a pamphlet showered into the dreams of Praiseworthy: *Let us pray. Pray for the decent thing. Let us pray that we will be able to destroy all these dangerous donkeys as quickly as possible before they kill everyone every now and again. Let us pray that proper police will come here soon and knock sense into Cause Man Steel and drag him down to the beach at gunpoint to collect his poisonous cut-snake donkeys, then let's hope the police make him clean up this guts-all-over-the-place mess of the pristine ancestral beach frontage, make him real sorry for himself, make him shake like a rattle snake with fear, and bulldoze his eye-ore house into the ground, pour a forty-four-gallon drum of petrol on it and burn this rot, then make him go away. Let us pray this will be done, and that only we true people, will get a Native Title determination from the Australian government telling us we own our ancestral land, and not him, or a donkey, not that these were proper God-carrying donkeys anyway glory be, Amen.*

9

So that was what it was all about. No one would be helping Cause Man Steel after his slaughterhouse-mayhem donkeys transformed the pristine beach by turning it into a major crime zone. And the searchers grumbled, *this is how he pays us back for helping him. Looking for his kid. We had told him straight a long time ago, that we did not want an international transport conglomerate set up here in Praiseworthy, not his type of bodgie bogan type of peasant people turnout with donkeys.*

As the seasons shifted from summer to winter and back again, the jamming of electromagnetic frequencies also increased through the extraordinarily high number of simultaneous mobile calls being made from the terrible-looking beach to the nation's capital police by the involuntary search parties suffering flashbacks of the major crime. They screamed into their mobiles: *Morons! Look at the satellite images from before the crime, and now, where we look like aliens living on Mars. What are we going to do with the shocked sky, flat and drained of life? The brokenness of the ancient rhythm of the sand – all scattered over the broken beach. The universe of sand-dwelling tiny micro-creatures and the crab spirits strewn on the surface and desiccated by the sun. And in the swish-swash, clusters of unconscious sardines tossing in the surf. How would you feel about that? We cannot even feel the ancient pristineness in this killing field anymore.* The collective voice of the little people of Praiseworthy orbited across the biosphere, and demanded to know from the faraway police, the enforcers of law from thousands of miles away, what their human rights were worth from roughly zero, to one hundred per cent. *Why did we have to lie on the beach wounded for days like we were the donkeys in this war zone while requiring medical help to arrive to wrap bandages around the wounded? What was that worth? Zero, or one hundred per cent, you get what we are talking about?* They demanded to know what they were actually worth, whether they were worth nothing, or eighteen per cent, or forty-seven per cent, or one hundred per cent, such as a Commonwealth of Australia politician that makes these laws for crushing Aboriginal people.

The fear of more violence spreading on the beach escalated in the minds of the battle-weary, and soon began skyrocketing right out of proportion against what the rest of the poor world knew as the gentle beast of burden, the donkey that carried Mary through the streets of Bethlehem. The expensive government medical staff barricaded themselves inside their locked gated compound in Praiseworthy and issued a proclamation saying that they were not going to treat diseased donkeys, or people fighting on the beach. They stayed in their cyclone-proof fenced compound, behind a three-and-a-half-metre-tall cement wall around the hospital grounds annexed by state laws from traditional Aboriginal lands, and handed medicine out to the sick people through a hole in the wall, otherwise kept locked by a tiny window hatch. Ditto, the local police officers who hid in their compound on land long ago excised by state laws too, and would not come out to enforce the law, because they feared for their life. SOS rocks were thrown on the roofs of the hospital, nurses' quarters, the police station, but it was evident that neither nurses nor police were taking any requests to attend the crime scene of an escalating calamity created by the perpetual troublemaker Cause Man Steel.

The terrified donkeys not only continued attacking people on the beach, but were now up and down Church Street tearing apart the multi-denominational holy places. The church people became blinded by fear and rage, and were fighting one another, while with untreated injuries or not, the involuntary searchers continued fighting the predators. Donkeys were kicked, pulled to the ground, tackled, and half-strangled until luckily, by sheer brute force generated from the fear of being killed, they managed to escape, regroup, and gallop in a headstrong way, back down the beach, to again charge at the corpse searchers trying to inch their way towards the safety of the sea. All through this scene of sand flying and screaming donkeys attacking the yelling wild crowds armed with pandanus fronds, shovels, hunting sticks and crowbars, you could hear people cursing donkey devils, donkey shit, but from time to time, there was a pause, the almost tranquil calm of a flat sea singing as it gurgled across the sand, while the people of Praiseworthy waited in vain for the police to come with guns, and the medical people to bring bandages and a needle and thread to stitch up their open wounds.

Well! Nothing. No police came. No field hospital. The senior police in Canberra said, *Good, go pull the other leg* in a text message that was sent back down the barrel of nuisance calls about donkeys mucking up the pristine sand while fighting with human beings. The local police behind the barricades claimed that they were laying charges against the people who had burgled Cause Man Steel's home and let those donkeys loose in the first place. The police claimed that they knew who the trespassers were, because they had received very interesting anonymous phone calls, which were all from the same muffled voice broken up by the sound of waves crushing on the beach. This was the tip-off. *We have names*, the police texted the *villainy* people to desist from texting, *Or! Else! What? You can expect heavy fines* for *trespassing by text on police property*.

The involuntary people texted the police back: *Idiots!* There was a lot of verbal damage in the exchange about who was who on someone else's property, and the police texted back. *Theft of property. Stealing donkeys.*

Hey! Brain trust!

Why would anybody want to steal feral donkeys from the bush full with millions of them?

Have a look at this.

Blood! See f-n blood pouring from my arm.

The thing must be broken.

See my fingers. This one is dangling. They are all dangling. All of my fingers are f-n broken.

F-n donkey kicked me in the face.

Some old lady over there, she is unconscious. She's been well and truly kicked in the head.

All of my ribs are gone.

That bloody donkey tried to chew my leg off before I killed it.

The old pandanus-frond-fanning ladies were photographing selfies of themselves with injuries, and they too texted the police who still were not flying in from Canberra with a shipping container full of dynamite to blow up every donkey on the beach. The next text they sent screamed: *Who is going to pay for all of this damage to our pristineness we are looking at? We are going to sue you cops for compensation.* They themselves, as old women, did not have that kind of money to spend on repatriating beach pollution. Their money was locked up in a government Basics Card, which meant that every cent was controlled by the government. The real people were screaming around on the beach about how debts for repatriating a war zone could last forever, and they really hated Cause for not setting up a proper worldwide money-spinning transport conglomerate, the biggest shipping container company in the world. They blamed him that there were no rich Praiseworthy Aboriginal people as he promised there would be, and how they would be the captains of the transport industry controlling what was to come – things like worldwide pollution, now hitting home with colossal unprecedented weather events – and looking at this destroyed ancestral beach that could have been a luxury beach resort, they now felt certain, that even the great sacred ancestral being had well and truly risen, flown off, and look, probably would not return any day in this millennium. This did not make the real people happy. They just wanted to be rich enough to deal with the future by buying some justice, or silence, on their own cultural terms.

Now, the way things happened, it was these involuntary searchers who were losing the battle for the beach. They were too used to dealing with killers, colonisers, land thieves, human rights abusers, or poisonous snakes, global viruses, spiders, mosquitoes, flies, and unprecedented catastrophes of global warming. They had never had to fight a donkey human killer. The old ladies said they would not be waving a palm frond for any of these savage donkeys next Palm Sunday mass. They would not be cutting any fronds from the foreign palm tree. The involuntary corpse searchers as well as the pandanus-fanning old lady coast watchers of the ocean thought it was impossible for good cultural people like themselves to fathom what was holy about a donkey that wanted to kill them, or how you could put these murdering feral donkeys to good use in a global transport industry.

The thing was, the beach had its own thoughts of manufacturing reality, where the more the searchers raced over the sand and struggled to grip the edge of the sea by their fingernails to save themselves from being mauled by mad donkeys, the more it felt as though there were other donkeys on the overhead flight path of a Qantas Airbus 380, jumping into the sky from the height of thirty-five thousand feet, and falling with their full weight on top of what was left of the shattered beach. The fatigued corpse searchers wanted it on notice that they had been forced to do this terrible job, and were now placed in jeopardy, seeing for themselves what it felt like to be rained on by donkeys falling from the sky, since the old fan-waving law women had gone home to cook fish soup. Where was the God anthropologist cop – well, he was useless. He was gone without recording a scrap of evidence of this theft of the ancestral land by a pack of donkeys. But, as the cop said, he couldn't handle the job. It was too violent. He was so disgusted with seeing the violence of human beings fighting donkeys, that he had gone back to his university down south, to write a sizeable book about everything he knew about anti-violence, whatever he could think about, and to prove it was a higher virtue that was only possible for white people's minds, to conquer the sensitivities of being civilised. For he would say, Aboriginal people's minds were too ancient, and incapable of reaching the hefty heights of a sophisticated modern civilisation, since they were basically inferior to the white race's own superior inferiority and greater abstract cruelty for destroying the entire world.

The remaining searchers who were still capable of standing and fighting on for their lives, deeply felt the pain of abandonment, but nevertheless, they felt as though they were involved in some magical mighty curse battle that had suddenly befallen on their cultural domain because they had lost their Aboriginal Sovereignty. Even when beaten, they took heart, and the involuntary searchers picked themselves up time and again from the sand littered with injured and broken body parts, to challenge the jinx of this nightmarish reality, to be there in the last almighty stand, ahead of being driven into the sea by donkeys.

10

And what about that Tommyhawk? The other kind. It felt as though Planet could catch elsewhere in a single breath, and bring the boy's spirit to this place where he was stuck with the broken-down Falcon he had crashed, and his magical whingeing donkey. The boy's rapid breathing felt so close, close enough to catch, while standing so far away, and Planet paused, felt his lungs constrict, and a sudden pain ripped through his heart. He instantly knew the boy was frightened, probably up to no good again, and he had to take a deep breath while thinking about this mischievous younger son, the born fascist, who was useless to him.

The moment passed, and he looked around the spinifex plains deep in a dangerous spirit world where he was ensnared until the Falcon would be ready to go, when magic had taken place through his bare hands, and that load of rust would shoot like a bat out of hell, and he would be gone from the never-ending spirit songs whispering around him, that he felt were flowing across the atmosphere, when he was labouring with this crapped-out engine of the Falcon disassembled into dozens of oily parts, which were still a mystery even to the spirit world staring at the tremendous puzzle of damage spread over the ground. While growing more unsure of knowing where he was, as though this country was trying to disorient him, pulling him in the undertow of its power, Widespread of all people seemed to have lost the plot, because he began to believe he had been in this place for a very long time, longer than he had imagined, and now, though becoming further disoriented by the very thought of his fascist son, suddenly no longer knew where he was, and he felt the urge to run, to escape, it was like pure rage whistling in his head. Widespread had always sped through this country, never stopped even for a piss, but now, he had no idea where he was in the vastness of wind singing through waves of spinifex that reached far away in every horizon. His total being, sunk in an aloneness that he had never before experienced, lost in flashes of imagining, aching to destroy this mystery dragging him into a sink well of himself, suddenly feeling as though he was already back in Praiseworthy, and while staring out to sea, and wondering why Aboriginal Sovereignty was not coming home, realising he wasn't at home at all. His mind had only flipped out, blanked before he realised the heavy reality of where he was. Disoriented, shocked, he spun around and found himself on the plains of spinifex, and saw the parts of the vehicle all over the ground. He had forgotten what he was doing. It was as though a door had slammed shut on the powerful vision of a future that had always held him, even if it remained so far removed from the reality of where he happened to be.

Seeing nothing but everything existing across the plains of spinifex reaching further away in either direction, he felt the wildness of this strange country of wind ancestors blowing their travelling waves onward, towards many homelands, and he wondered why he was in this strange country, someone else's country. He could feel the pulse of the wind flowing across the waves of yellow, knew it was pushing his soul, quickening his heart, and this movement of country unnerved him, and he kept asking himself, when he realised the situation he was in: *What the fuck's name am I doing here?*

The sound of his own heart beating with the whooshing of rolling waves of spinifex was unnerving him, and he kept spinning around, certain of a presence in the wind that stood directly behind him, and he called to the fascist, *Is that you Tommyhawk?* And as he would often step back, move away from the crashed Falcon, he felt the flow of the country's breath moving over the back of his neck. And then, nothing, all movement stopped, and old Planet would growl at the ghosts, *Get the fuck lost.* As the sun rose higher in the sky, and the remains of the previous night's dew dried, spinifex butterflies flew everywhere. Flies rose, and settled. Ants travelled over the ground, over the disassembled parts of the sedan, and crawled up along the slender spinifex stems flowing in waves to where the gossamer was flying in the air, laden with travelling spiders. Then the stillness arrived, and nothing else moved except sweat, and the tremendous thumping of earthly quietness. Widespread felt laden with the weight of not understanding why he wasn't already at home. What was he doing in this place with a donkey of an unusually grey colouring that would not stop staring at him, and was crying out to its own destiny?

In his battle with spirit country tangling him in the stillness of its ancient world, and paralysing him with bewildering thoughts that held him in its grip and prevented him from leaving, he became more imprisoned in this world where nothing moved except for the wind ancestor bringing a feed of the atmosphere to the spinifex, and where only ants tilled the ground while forever moving through the yellowness in the clockwork rhythm of winds dying down. While he searched the landscape to find its potency, a thought convinced him that this country would kill him, and it left him intoxicated with a heightened awareness of pending doom. He sensed he was being dragged into the dangerous infinity of summertime wind, calling up a dry-storm lightning strike that would race through the spinifex in firestorms, sending ash particulates higher into the atmosphere, while leaving behind a totally blackened landscape transformed into ash.

Only a big god of country would know Cause Man Steel had no idea what he was thinking about anymore while he raged with a spinifex fire exploding sky-high through his head, every time he thought about Tommyhawk. *You see the way the fascist was behaving? Well! Have you?* He spoke forcefully into Dance's face, even though he could see that she was too busy with chasing moths around the house, or whatever else she liked to do. He was standing right in front of her, but she ignored him, and he could not believe she could not see him. But, she could not see, she was in a snowstorm of moths, so he answered himself, *You just go on, but I bet you anything you like, he never learnt whatever he kept in his head from me. I never taught the little freak not to respect his father, and one day I will promise you this, I am going to teach that fascist kid a lesson he will never forget about lying to people.* Dance could not see Planet through the storming moths even if she had felt his presence. Her eyes were elsewhere, mesmerised, moving with the flurrying moths and capturing all the rapture of the moment she could squeeze into her head while pushing him back to the crashed site of the Falcon, and telling him to leave the kid alone.

Planet's sulking mind tramped back into that distant spinifex country, to stay with the platinum donkey, to make sure it would not leave him, but all he saw out there was Tommyhawk in his imagination – squealing about being hurt, and threatening to tell the police. Planet was quick, stitched the defence, already rehearsing what he would say, *I never touched him.* Hell! Was that all? Give a man a break: *Nobody could even look at that kid.* He had to keep reminding himself that he was not in Praiseworthy at this moment, *So! How could I be bashing a bloody cheeky fascist? I told you*, he was muttering as though speaking to phantom police as he kept on walking through the plateau of endless spinifex to find the donkey that had taken off, while knowing he should not have taken his thoughts away from the sneaky thing, but he could not help feeling the police were already touching him, and his speech was in the flow of such a moment of claiming innocence to power that was not on his side, *I never touched him*, and you could never be sure if this was just a thought, or a defence mechanism for just another endless conversation he was having with no one.

Well! What if the kid was totally assimilated as far as a man like Widespread was concerned, and he had told Dance this many times – *who cares hey?* She had no idea what he was talking about. Her mind had departed the vicinity long ago, and was dwelling in another country entirely, where the likes of Widespread hardly featured at all. In her mind, he was a foreigner lost in thoughts of being elsewhere, an anchorite in his cocoon of rusted spare parts, like a solitary bag moth that travels in its silken home spun with piles of sticks it drags along behind itself, lobbing like a stranger in and out of an imaginary sometimes world. If he knew this, he also knew it was like flinging oneself down into a well of dreams, to drown there, if you wanted to wait around forever while trying to capture enough interest from others about your dreams to save a complicated world, an ascetic life, which to her mind meant that nobody would ever want to know what you were on about.

In the end, Cause chose wife avoidance, and while disappearing off her radar, and without a thought about coming back again to check on his married life, he was able to solve the jigsaw of the crashed Falcon. He began reassembling the motor parts back into the vehicle, and knew he would continue with the job, even if it took forever to get back on this loneliest of roads again. He kicked-started the engine a thousand times, until he heard its sick rumbling, which felt as though the entire vision of the transport conglomeration had shot through his veins and back into his brain, and the thing, mighty in itself, was breathing more vision, it was becoming greater, and not only that, its life would grow. The vision grew more splendiferous by the minute, and it did not matter to him if he knew the reality of where he was heading once the Falcon was back on the road, once he recaptured the reluctant mask-head platinum donkey again, and they would drive off in a storm of hope to build the unforgettable dream. Sure! He was no match for the government policies for Aboriginal people which were the stagnant swamplands in his brain. Sons? He already knew Tommyhawk was no use to any good vision where trust was required since the day he was born, but no matter! Aboriginal Sovereignty would lead culture to eternity. There would be no problem about re-signing himself up again to the worst of what could happen to him, for he knew, being behind the eight ball was not going to destroy what he had in his mind, the abundance of hope in what kept him alive. No one would have to fling themselves down into a cavernous pit at the bottom of the stairs to understand his language of economic independence, translatable to anyone on Earth: a thing that covered the whole vast vista of all that has been, and all that will come to be.

11

The compression in the cylinder head of the vehicle kicked in because it knew it had its part to play in the big vision even if it was only machinery, motivated by Cause's brain turbocharging and belting around the bush in his head to check with the big checker running the universe into overdrive, about how the eventualities of the future era might pan out. He could not help himself. Widespread had to go tramping around in his brain every second of his life like a rabbit poacher, to find out where all the traps were set to ensnarl his vision and make mincemeat out of it. Vision like this was a precious commodity, and a man of vision had to be ready to go out and conquer the threats, throw explosives down rabbit warrens, blast the lot, ply traps open, until he just about killed himself with making sure that no threat had been left on the gold-clad road of clear vision, for this was what having a vision was like, dealing with freaks getting to the vision traps before you, and turning dreams into a quagmire. But the trouble with having an army of thoughts out searching for traps, you start to remember too many things that will convince you that you have yet another trap to eliminate, and this was what was happening even though he was thousands of miles away from Praiseworthy, because he had always known that Tommyhawk was a threat to the new era of the culture's survival. What to do? The troubles playing on Widespread's mind were endlessly unfathomable, as he worked methodically on the engine of the Falcon, and tried to ignore those faraway words in the back of the mind whistling in the wind through endless waves of spinifex. *You touch me, and I will tell the government all about you.* Tommyhawk pointed to his bloody government iPhone, and all his other iWhatnot information gadgetry that he reckoned the government gave him to protect himself against family violence, *and you abusive fathers*, and Widespread could hear the God anthropologist policeman saying that Aboriginal men were inherently violent – they were natural killers. Who knows who else the kid was talking to, or texting right this minute, or what he was reading, for who knew where his mind was, or what he was up to.

Planet smiled. The pistons were not choking from the herculean strength and endurance it had taken to hear the motor running normally again. If this spinifex country thought he was less a man from seeing his son as worthless, with the jubilant Falcon purring to go, he felt pleased in remembering the look on Tommyhawk's face when he had the electricity cut off to the house. *See who you can iPhone now? Go on texter, text someone then. What? You got no power. Did the government forgot to give you free electricity with your computer and mobile phone? Well! See who pays for the power. Text them to pay for it. Remember who puts the food into your mouth? It's not government.* He would teach the little fascist a lesson if he ever heard Tommyhawk call his brother disgusting names, and call him a paedophile. He had asked Dance, what kind of talk was that? Where did he learn talk like that? He had told the woman who bred a fascist that the kid would be the death of him, and he could see him now, running off into the bush across from the cemetery, leaving him to stand around with the crucifixes by himself, while she, the mother, yelled from inside the house, *you leave him alone, or I will call the government myself to take you away.*

A get-rich-quick scheme was the simpler answer to the woes. Money was the answer to all this, as he had said time and again, even if his soapbox spruiking was as slippery as an eel, or his imaginary supersonic weaponry for destroying enemies of the vision was non-existent, or his goals were grey-coloured like the old donkey he now pushed back into the Falcon. It was deal or no deal, and a lucky thing that the magical creature of long-known self-preserving adaptabilities to preserve its species, hardly minded at all about getting itself out of the spinifex and going for a drive, for as quick as a flash, the donkey seemed to have reduced the size of its body to mould itself back into the confined space of the rear seat of the Falcon, and its face looked as though its vision of itself as a platinum donkey mask-head for the transport conglomeration of the petroleum-dead era, instead of a jaguar, or a pit bull on a Mack Truck, was simply meant to be.

The sedan was now heading in the general direction of Praiseworthy which was possibly some thousands of miles away, but Widespread suddenly felt uncomfortable with his imaginary angel wings folded flat behind his back against the driver's seat. There was something wrong about the senior angel wings he needed to implement a grand vision with the force of a god. He had not noticed that he had been dragging these oily grease-stained feathers around for days in the spinifex and wind while fixing the engine. He looked back at the silvery-grey coat of the donkey sleeping in the rear seat, and noticed that the sublimity of having wings now tattered and knotted with twigs, grass, and sharp thorns, was totally impractical for these desert environments. Widespread had gifted his prized companion a set of glorious wings as well for its new role as the spearhead of the grandest transport conglomeration ever known to mankind. Now he frowned at the rumpled, tangled feathers wrapped around the old donkey's body. The donkey had slept anywhere on the prickle-covered ground, having lost its patience with standing alert permanently like it was meant to be a pristine dreaming angel of this continent. This was not what the donkey thought was meant to be. It needed its hooves to break desert rocks, and to tear the ground apart in search of a herb, but the spearhead that Widespread had in mind was a glistening angel-winged creature of blinding titanium that was ten times faster than speed as it flashed brilliantly across the atmosphere. What he was expecting the old donkey to do, was to fly jaguar-like like a platinum hypersonic missile straight into the future. This was the type of donkey he thought he had found.

All the stars looked down at the car lights of the vehicle driving through spirit country at an incredible speed on an almost invisible, overgrown back-country spinifex track while following a storm of migratory caper butterflies in the moonlight. Widespread wiled away the time on this spirit journey of returning home, by reminding himself and the ageing platinum donkey that they both were on a winner here, even though the old donkey was still querulous and ungrateful about being captured, and doubted whether it was up to spearheading a long haul road train like a Mack Truck for the rest of its life because it would destroy him, and while the idea of being hypersonic was out of the question, it wondered whether Widespread could find some alternative natural resources to destroy and leave it alone, so it could retain what was left of its donkey powers for a retirement with the rest of its Equidae family.

Widespread said *don't be stupid*. He told the sour-face donkey that he had studied everything anyone needed to know about transportation, and he knew all about the donkey business by watching forty-four million donkeys work as beasts of burden in all the poor countries in the world on the Discovery Channel. The donkey said he was mad, but Widespread said he was not just making up a vision for saving his people in the new era without checking the facts. He said it was not just the make-up of the animal that had nailed it for him, but the donkey's sturdiness, its strength and ability to endure harsh conditions like a local native animal, but the difference of course, which was better, was that you could not convince a native animal to carry your stuff for you. So quit complaining, donkey. Think about it. Widespread did not accept the donkey's reasoning about not having supersonic missile power. He told it to have some belief in itself, that it should not think in fractions, but in the vision headed by a platinum donkey which was so magical, they both had a fine pair of invisible God wings with enough power to fly barge after container barge down the Huangpu river in Shanghai, or anywhere else in the world, in a fraction of the time it was taking now in the global challenges of climate change, viruses and wars. *Just say*, he challenged the donkey continuing to tell him he was madder than a cut snake, *that we could manage to beat humanity at its own game? You got to think like a game changer, that was the way to do it.*

The Falcon's reconditioned miracle engine rumbled, and it crawled over the gibber rock terrain in a wild blizzard of butterfly whiteness, and Planet kept on explaining the business to the platinum donkey in so many hours of words which, in summary, were about the suitability of donkeys from the point of view of overall global convenience. He prophesised the new world in the sucked-dry fossil-fuel-depleted world, where *all the eyes of the world will be looking at you donkeys. They will be looking at your sustainability rather than having to search the entire world for some rusty spare parts for heavy transporters, cargo ships, road trains and things like that. Anyone with half a brain would see that you mob of dry country donkeys will flourish like sacred animals in time to come because you will only require the most minimalist of care, so what do you say about that?*

You could storm a religious heaven and beat the door down for holy answers, but this sacred continent was created by the greatest ancestral beings of time immemorial, and as remembered through religious laws, had left a labyrinth of crisscrossing tracks over the entire land. Planet knew the powerfulness of this law, but he could barely comprehend how he was being entwined in the awakening of an ancestral realm while in a long storming cloud of ghost butterflies, captured in its thrilling serpentine snake road meandering across arid country through swathes of spinifex grasslands, the acacia, mulga, turpentine, to the black soil plains, the claypans and onwards to the coastal savannah through a riparian vine country of insects, to travel over the beaches, before finally, heading to sea. He was being steered on the path of this ancient journeying of story that would eventually end in the sea, after it reached far across the land. His eyes concentrated on the whiteness that had marked his course for he was not able to deviate from the travelling cloud of butterflies, nor stop the Falcon from continuing with the spirit journey, and nervously, he kept the conversation moving while talking shit about changing the world order of the underdog. He asked the donkey if it minded being *a minimalist creature,* and tried to reassure his surly business partner that *donkeys were supposed to be smart, and easy to get on with. Don't know what happened to you. Even I know how a donkey is supposed to act. But, hey! Why should I talk? I suppose you just don't know how to act properly if you can't watch how your homeland donkeys act on the Discovery Channel. Anyhow, just try to get with the picture about surviving for the new world. Act brave and unnerved like donkeys do in wartime while walking through the massacres and the bombed-out craters and carting the injured to field hospitals, since this is how you are going to have to act in the many wars created by mankind with their escalating global problems, and look, you've got to admit it, you donkeys would be excellent in these hot wars that will last centuries.*

Anyway, Planet warned the sour-face donkey, *we will have to be ready for war – just in case, to be ferrying supplies, and bringing road-train hospitals to carry the injured over rough terrain etc. And the only animal* he knew of that would be uncomplaining *as they moved amongst the dead or dying in a battlefield while bombs were falling all around them in the sometime future, would be, you – donkeys. Well! Even donkeys, like men, have to make hard decisions in life,* and so, *having a broken-down Falcon sedan in the middle of the desert was okay if you were making your own future for free. What could be better than scouring the spirit country for free in the good days, but keeping an eye on the abyss ahead? You needed to be able to view the world through your own eyes as a feral donkey captured in the chasm of a big dream, as being an offset to a near distant, totally altered world.* He wanted the donkey to try to make the quantum leap, to place itself into a global future, and Planet kept explaining the facts of life until he was blue in the face to the ancient platinum donkey over the slow journey of following the ghost butterflies across country. But, of course, Widespread did not mind refining the countless equations running around in his head, which were totally about how a dirt-poor man like himself could in his lifetime, *a lifetime that coincided with the clamorous death of the known world*, make himself a very rich man. This would be a time he explained, when donkeys were the name of the game. Where anyone could make a quid. It only required a bit of imagination to see how you could roll with the doom. In fact, he would be helping all other living beings to survive. The conglomerate would be owned by the feral donkeys, even more than he would own the business. All the feral donkeys had to do, was agree to work with human beings – to pull the load so to speak, as much as he had to work to establish sustainability for both species in a heating world. And on Planet went, trumpeting the dream about how the feral donkey species would be helping to create a new economy for millions of poor people across the world, which collectively meant donkeys were already worth billions of dollars, it was just that nobody realised the potential of the new era – yet.

So, was Planet any better off than any other poor bugger on the face of the planet right now? He did not think so. *Imagine the scenarios when the world's financial markets are collapsing,* and it was not that he had much to do with global monetary funds, *but anyone would know what happens in a world crisis. The Arabs stop selling oil – then, there is no more oil anywhere on the planet,* and very soon he told the donkey, *You have to be ready for when millions of people could not afford to run a car anymore, or fly around the world on Qantas jets because it would be more expensive than in a pandemic to fly anywhere, and the rich people will want to become like most blackfellas and try to steal our ideas for surviving, but if you play your cards right and close to your chest about what you are doing, and you are able to adapt, you are going to be one hell of a rich donkey so don't go ringing up anyone about your plans. Keep it tight. Tell no one, and I should not even be telling you this but I am bored just sitting here. Look! It will be like this: you won't have to walk around in the desert looking for a blade of grass anymore. People will be shoving a mountain of straw at you every time you open your gob.* Cause said he was waiting for this time, anticipating almost every breathing moment for when this new hard-up world would emerge. *Believe me,* he continued, *I have been listening to the business reports on the ABC radio for years, and on ABC TV,* and he had been doing this long before he had the electricity cut off to teach the fascist Tommyhawk a lesson in budgeting, and fiscal control. *But! Who cares? Having no power, excluding the use of electricity in the house was not a problem,* not for an entrammelled man like himself, who had to break free of the shackling, and teach himself how to become *the acute business man that I am today.*

The donkey was lulled into a deep sleep from listening to the groaning vehicle singing its song while Widespread harped on about the precarious state of the planet. Then it began twitching through its cantankerous dreams of the finances involved in running an international transport conglomeration in the new times, and wondering how many donkeys the operation would entail, and did it actually want to be involved with so much drama so late in its life. The journey was long and slow, with the serpentine butterfly cloud only moving about eight kilometres an hour, and occasionally, when Widespread thought that the donkey might be in a rare good mood for hearing more about its role in the International Monetary Fund, he would speak either at length about the state of the world's dwindling finances as a result of global warming calamities, or how Dance would refuse to acknowledge the world's deepening financial crisis, because she thought it was not money they were actually going to miss when she did not even have twenty dollars to buy food, and he would have to tell her to just stop thinking about herself for a minute, and start thinking about everyone else. In these tales of *how are we going to survive,* when he had spent decades in analysing the collapse of the world's banks, he could not believe she did not seem to care in the slightest that he was putting himself up to be the man in the era, to save everything. And he told the donkey a personal observation that he had not told anyone else, that she was just not interested in planning for the collapse of the world, at least, not for a world with him in it. She could not see his donkey franchise spreading across the country, nor that their lives would probably become international, equating to rock stardom.

He told the business partner another thing as well. He was figuring out how to stake a Native Title property right claim over the ownership of the country's five million donkeys, which kind of made sense to him, and he thought that should have been enough to inspire the donkey's brain about dollars and cents; but he could not inspire financial world imagination in its mind. Perhaps it was because Cause was the type of man who was not a cowboy – *that was what we did when we were young fellas*, he told people who said *Praiseworthy was horse country. We don't want feral animals here.*

There was no money in horses, he remembered slinging back in the deep gravelly voice he said he would preserve for a town full of idiots. *There was no money in cattle neither,* he sniped at the ancient ringer tribesmen who were still trying to re-ignite their youth as slaves to white cattle men thieving their traditional lands. He had said the idea was simple for anyone thinking about becoming a property developer. All they had to do was think of feral donkeys as property development. They would be in the box seat, reap the benefits. What could be simpler than that? He told the business manager they would not be asking the Australian government for money so they would not be getting hand-outs, nor would he be going to the bank for a loan either, because he would be remaining a free man, *and, you my Equus asinus, would remain a free burro – an ass, so to speak.* It was all about investing in the future, and he spoke of being in a time of total independence as though twenty golden trumpets were blaring behind him, and he kept challenging the donkey to do the same, to build this ring of fire business up from the ground around itself, to cover itself in the glorious flames of burning money, or else, he would do it alone if he had to. He did not know what the donkey wanted for its part in the vision, but he claimed that the only thing he wanted in return was that his people backed him with flames in their own hearts that matched his own, for he had found the perfect donkey to make the fire wild, to send the flames higher so that heaven could see that the black man of this continent was a free man and not only that, the best man, but sadly, he said, he could not walk away when the only acknowledgement he got for having kept this prolonged vision alive, was a garden-hose dousing of this almost-built heaven in his heart, his proud dreams, his pride.

And the old business partner donkey dreamt on, as Widespread described how Dance was not listening to him anyhow because she knew what he was talking about was not going to be like Jetstar, Virgin, or, or dare to say it, a national carrier, like Qantas. *You know my friend, I told her, You just had to use your imagination about this. Aboriginal people were not going to survive the twenty-first century when the world's economy and all the rest of it collapses with an airline company. Man! I mean donkey, I told her once and told her again, stop thinking piecemeal, incremental change, the language of government's closing-the-gap policies between Aboriginal people – the have-nots on their own land, and the non-Aboriginal people.*

I told her to at least try to imagine people with donkey carts, you see them all the time on the Discovery Channel, remember, I told her, stacked with hay? I had pointed to the bloody TV screen, and said, See how much those donkeys could carry? Carts loaded with produce. Carts loaded with bricks. Carrying anything. Poor people all over the world use donkeys and we have got five million of the buggers here.

The donkey dreamt of Dance's voice whaling through the long winding snake dance of the butterfly song line travelling across country, and it could hear her telling Widespread that there was no hay in Praiseworthy. *We have got no hay to feed donkeys. You noticed that? The vista remained spinifex,* and she said, *the only dream was for a new car to drive from square a, to square b.* Then, while long gone from being in his sphere of influence, and having her own *crise de nerfs* moment about their personal financial situation which was far worse than what the World Bank had to worry about, you could feel that she was having a complete nervous breakdown. *You can forget about the world financial disasters. Forget about donkeys. Begin with something simple, like a reliable car,* she said that was what she wanted most of all. *Let's be like other people getting ahead around here, who are not interested in the world economy. We will still be poor no matter what happens in the world and you can't get more poorer than that,* and that she claimed was her personal, long-range vision.

She did not say that her sights were unable to lift off China, an imagined other ancestral land, where clouds were made of butterflies gathering precipitation from the humid fabric of the day, and where she saw jewel-coloured wings flitting in bamboo forests, and over the sun-glistening watery terraces snaking across the hillsides woven through emerald-green grasslands, rice paddies, and green-leafed vegetables, all of which felt far away, the distances inconceivable from Praiseworthy. Was she being called to another homeland, this world unknown to her, and what for? The question ranged deep in her psyche. Where was the origin of the strength of her wonderings? Was it from being pushed to China, by her own people telling her to stop claiming other people's Native Title land? *You take your family away from here, you are really Chinese, not Aboriginal. Go somewhere else, back to where you come from, go back to China.* And the strength grew from wondering how to understand the infinite stories, the collected and integrated texts that made up the battle for precedence in a soul.

12

What will they eat? These donkeys? She asks too many questions of a spectre travelling with the lightness of dust. Her eyes rolling all the while, staring beyond the presence of Widespread standing right there in front of her. Whether ghost, magic transporter man, or alive, he remained dead to her. She pushes past the levitating spectre, to breathe in the cemetery, its sparse landscape of billowing yellow grasses, the many giant lopsided plank crucifixes, wind-strewn plastic flowers, all of which were beginning to annoy her. She tries not to notice the grey mass of the levitator, another piece of madness that interrupts her China plans, but she continues asking the same question to the absent husband who keeps sending his spirit back from wherever he was, only to remind her to look after his donkeys.

There seems to be a lot more diseased and half-crazed donkeys living on the grounds of the cemetery since yesterday, and she screams *that there is no room for more animals. Haven't you got enough?* Where was the *we* in this folly, and how was she going to feed all these donkeys on this dry, bleached-out country stretching as far as the eye could see. *What was the use of putting donkeys on any of it?* She flung her arm across the open view a bit too triumphantly, to where patchy dead grass chewed and scratched level with exposed roots would not even feed a few cattle. She picked up the dirt like an old seasoned pastoralist of the cattle industry, and invited the levitating self-transporter to look at this rubbish, although she called it *shit anyway. See this? This is parched. That's parched.* She walked around while kicking at the dust with her red-thong foot, and claimed *you have ruined the ancestry, these donkeys eat everything, even this shit.*

In those wild carried-away dreams of emigration, Dance had already moved the true Native Title family to the other homeland – the unknown China – and out of racist Australia. She said they were leaving the time immemorial. Moving into a new sunrise. Getting away from the down the road, downward spiral of government largesse aimed at keeping a beggar a beggar, and she told the levitator to pack his bag for China: *We're moving. This whole racist thing is costing us mob too much.* When the *going to China* rumour spread, the weight of community sentiment agreed with her. *Yep! Pack your bag and go to China. We don't want any Aboriginal Chinamen-looking people here, and you look a bit Chinese to me.* So of course one day, a brilliant idea jumped right into her head when she heard of China becoming the greatest country on Earth where phenomenal levels of poverty had been crushed, and she had thought, *Why not? We'll go. Take me. Perhaps they should go and live in China.* She thought it might even be a bit of a change. See what the soul thought. And suddenly, her soul said it actually felt lighter, and yes, why not emigrate, and forget the historic racial profiling of her family that was killing their soul. What would it be like – you know, not to be like a dog feeling the hatred of racial differences for the rest of your life? What would it feel like, not to feel like a cringing dog, and being re-educated like a human being who was valued enough to be submerged in Chinese characteristics that had already been defined for your mind, without having to do a stuff-up job of having to define yourself among other stuffed-up people, and she thought it would be a blessing to be profiled for constant surveillance which might give you a sense of security instead of living with intergenerational insecurities as a dispossessed person, and to let the government decide what you should think so you would not have to bother wondering about what the wonderment of being was, and not be bothered to be eternally imagining your exceptionalism to all else, but a single conjoined human organism of billions. She wanted to know what such a lightness of being like this would feel like over an eternity, where you did not have to think too hard again, and she began to ache for such an invisibility, where you would not be insulted to your face because you did not exist. Which was worse, she did not know. *You really look Chinese. You must be Chinese.* She imagined being lost among a billion people of similar appearance, and wondered what that would feel like? She would save her family from a Sino-Aboriginal heritage that was considered to be a far worse crime in Praiseworthy, albeit a sentiment copied from the majority of the population, and a far greater crime than an Anglo-Aboriginal heritage in quests of Native Title over the cemetery.

The trouble with the China dream was that Dance had no idea about how to unlock the secrets of history. The obscure Chinese ancestor of long ago left no trace in Australia of his ancestral homeland in China. This lack of foresight was a real hindrance for any of his descendants to the end of time to work through to find his ancient family home. She created hypothesis after hypothesis of wondering what this ancestor's intentional sneakiness was all about. Why was he blending in with the native flora and fauna like he was hiding in the land of the Rainbow Serpent, and in the end, not leaving a trace of himself in this country, except his genes. These were matters that really hindered her arrangements for migrating to her imagined butterfly-jewelled paradisal elsewhere, where she could see the tepid sky growing heavy with butterfly clouds that eventually became an atmospheric river sitting above the land for months, in the season of typhoons. She received no reply to her daily pestering, the haranguing applications to the Chinese government pleading for asylum – for her family to be saved from racist propaganda that was killing her culture, and pleading for refugee status in the land of the long-ago ancestor whose name she did not know. Well! Not to worry! She was totally ignored by China, even though she generously included plenty of complimentary flourishes in her applications, where she also remembered to mention a wish to live like those landless ancestors in overcrowded stilt-house cities perched above the sea water, or on a city of old decrepit boats stacked side by side along the Pearl River Delta, so that she could experience what it was like to live among the largest number of species of butterflies anywhere in the world. No one in Beijing knew what the foreigner was talking about by romanticising over a world that no longer existed in the genius of modern China. But, somehow, it never occurred to Dance to dampen her enthusiasm about migrating to the other homeland, even though the Chinese government had yet to answer a single email enquiry, along with the applications for permanent residency as a returning national.

Listen to me? she pleaded to the Chinese Embassy in Canberra. *Do you know where such and such place was in China?* Another Chinese place name smashed, crumpled, destroyed by the mispronouncer, another name pronounced like nothing else heard on Earth, and spelt in the dialect of the worst Aboriginal pidgin English from the Praiseworthy region. She flipped off that many emails to China with hypothetical villages with unpronounceable names that were so way out there, they were totally bewildering to the homeland bureau in Beijing. The secret surveillance facility for the study of foreign languages and behaviours that might threaten past, present or future China, did not have a clue what this foreign woman was on about. They wanted her to stop stalking China. Stop invading their national idiom. The emails ended up in a large dossier marked *serial stalker*, and were passed on to a string of security hypothesisers to find these mystery villages that were hiding in plain sight among more than six hundred thousand villages across the national register.

No one in the echelons of apparatchiks wanted to go looking for some old culture village while constructing modern China in record time, and they wondered if such a stupid distraction would end up taking an entire army to keep up with the serial stalker's surmising in her emails about wondrous hypothetical villages secretly ensconcing some of her blood relatives in China. The mysterious Chinese ancestor of well over one hundred years ago was officially hypothesised to have been some kind of spy of the time with a long-range vision, who had created an opportunist world of espionage against China through his future descendants hidden in a secretly formed village that kept falling off the radar. Why was this ignorant foreign woman opening up her can of worms by poring through a vast list of Chinese ancestral villages on the internet in incalculable hours – the generations of thousands of years just to re-tie a family knot created in the Australian gold rush? No one in China could say why she was uselessly leaving no stone unturned to drag up what had long ago been given the final flick.

Any of the names she had found on the internet and mispronounced matter-of-factly to Cause to instil a piece of Chinese information in his brain, proved that their family had a more than casual connection to China. But Cause had a dead brain for anything to do with Chinese ancestral homes. All he wanted to know about was Chinese donkeys. *What do tha use em for? They only got about six million left from killing them and selling the skins*. He added up the figures of about forty-two million donkeys already working in developing countries across the world, and he wondered if there was an international donkey transport conglomeration being forecast for China's Belt and Road Initiative that would outcompete his own initiative, and how he would harness more from Australia's five million feral donkeys. And, while he ate another cold pie, while espousing about the numbers of donkeys in the world, she said that the consumer price index would be naming a fridge after his big mouth one day.

Most of all, he wondered why nobody else had thought about the economics of donkeys in the heating planet, and had said he was searching for a platinum donkey to lead his transport conglomeration. *Do you know how much platinum is worth on the market today? It's worth more than gold*. He told Dance that what was happening in his dreams, was that he could see how magnificently the extensive signage for the donkey business would blot any other Praiseworthy reality. In fact, the signage would bulldoze what was real today into oblivion, and the power of the signage would grow his super herd of platinum-coloured donkeys bigger and stronger, more than anything else ever seen on the planet in the transport industry. The signage itself, singed by hot-iron branding, would be perfectly read on the rump of five million feral donkeys, THE REAL PLATINUM DONKEY TRANSPORT CONGLOMERATION. All major stuff, that would be truly seen and highlighted like a gold texta from outer space, and you know what? This gigantic placard branded on each donkey would look like it was printed by an enormous angel, and to complete the picture of how to be successful the whole operation would even be read by aliens flaring strategically across the world in hyper-solar-charged night brightness like the stars, and still be possible to be seen by a fool, even if the planet was totally covered by blizzards. Why planetary success would be so good, he told Dance, was because his signs for the future could be read in four easy words: transport, independence, rich, freedom. It was all in a dream, he explained while expanding on whatever the original dream had been, in a place of middle of the night madness where he saw how all his people could be free people, more free than they were already, with a plus-plus added bonus – of being richer but good rich which was possible if you worked with feral donkeys, and in any case, everything would be platinum rich, and have the benefit of a whole vision, like this – although he was only revealing a slice of the dream cake, for the whole thing could never be really and truly shared with anyone else in Praiseworthy, because the depth of it would blow your mind away. He was very sorry, but said the real details of the major operation would always be locked up in his head like a secret. Nobody could be given the true secret of economic self-reliance, which he said would be the platinum number one rule for maintaining Aboriginal sovereignty in the new age.

Anyway, while he could read the lay of the land, Dance was caught in a whorl of encumbrances of her own making, when in fact she should be listening to him explaining over and over until he was blue in the face, how to achieve the self-reliance of economic independence. He told her once, and he told her again, their world must remain surrounded by donkeys to visually demonstrate the world of economic progress, and this was the reason why he wanted her to build more enclosures while he was away, to contain his growing herd which would never be too much. Enclosures! That too, would demonstrate real economic progress, that the things don't run around freely, gates left open and donkeys roaming all over the place. This was not the way true discipline worked. She told him he was stupid. *Can't you see fouling up the place feral donkeys are the reason why the police force are always looking for you with intervention orders to stop you talking about this nonsense to decent people. You'll get locked up soon. They don't like people like us talking about money. Makes them frighten like they might have to fight us fair and square about who owns this country. See! You want to stop talking about Aboriginal economic independence. Your so-called people are not interested in how feral donkeys are worth millions of dollars when anyone can see they are worth nothing. So stop making wars with your own people. Talk this poison talk stuff somewhere else. Take it up to the Mars men and see if they can be bothered reading signs from humanity, a species not worth knowing about.*

But if others lacked vision for the cause this never stopped Planet in his tracks for a second, and he made up for his people's combined total lack of vision for a transport conglomerate by spending every single minute in the day tackling wild donkeys to the ground to prove his point – which was this, that nothing would stop him from keeping his eye on the prize while calculating how much money a wrestled to the ground donkey could make, adding up the figures while lying spread-eagled over the top of a panting donkey pinned to the dirt, which mind you, was the closest you would get to seeing the dollars and cents falling from the ceiling in his mind, which was far more than he actually had in his pocket. He believed that if anyone else had the mind to be a genius, then they too would see real money in the bush, by having a casual look around, and being prepared to have a shot and build a global transport conglomeration from scratch, just by wrestling as many feral donkeys as you could find with your bare hands. But, sometimes, it took more than genius to wrestle a donkey. It also took panache to do something greatly, to do it beyond one's own meagre capacity, and doing it before somebody else jumped in and stole the thought, and became ridiculously rich by using your original idea. This was the thing about vision, it never hides in the scrub, never hides from view, for it sits like a piece of sunshine for anyone to grab and be ahead of the game, to get yourself into the main frame before the oil reserves dried up and most of the Earth became an unbearable zone of hot wars. Nevertheless, Widespread also believed that fretting was pure hindrance for the visionary, because when you were having a flamboyant fight with a bad-tempered feral donkey, the scale of the thing meant you had to be in the moment, to be in the spirit of place, and to believe you had the ability to pace around in the vastness forever to find what you were looking for, and to believe you had won the battle, before it had even begun.

This was how to do it. You sourced where to find feral donkeys, and you got out there alone – somewhere in the bush of the spirit world – and up for a fight with your bare hands. But! Where were the takers? Who wanted to queue up to beat around the bush, and acquire some rough experience in empire building? *Nobody could see the vision Cause*, Dance explained the clear reality of what seemed less than perfect to her, and she plainly made it clear about how she was struggling with every idea of having any vision, when all she saw around the yard were a pack of recalcitrant untrainable donkeys trying to escape from her, running off ten, twenty, thirty kilometres away in the bush, where she had to footwalk like a cattle dog, to chase them back to the cemetery again. She did not have time to be his roped-in visionary who was left to chase donkeys around the flat, to cart mountains of grass and tree branches around on her back daily, just to feed his increasing herd of livestock, while he was away catching even more donkeys, driving around in his vehicle like some black kind of pastoralist.

Even thousands of miles away from Praiseworthy, he still heard her voice whistling in, questioning and trembling like a tempest, everywhere ethereal, wrapped in the sky – all possible in the unexpected power of country, and there in a single tiny flower miraculously growing in the sparseness of an inferno-cleared ground, and there soaring – a single bird flying overhead, and there, her presence mist, moisture, wind, as expected as the morning stars that hung over his shoulder.

There would be many donkeys to bury when Planet reached Praiseworthy. He had been away for weeks, months – existing on next to nothing, while travelling the hundreds of kilometres at no greater than butterfly speed, after searching for the mythical platinum donkey he had finally found, the old one in the back seat. While he travelled the distances and years to this point, he had always believed such a donkey actually existed, and although he barely remembered the original dream creature, he was certain it looked a lot differently than reality, a lot younger, stronger, better looking, and like a real pride mask-head of such silvery-grey blinding brilliance that possibly did not belong to this world, which of course would have adorned it with otherworldliness powers of the kind that would make it capable of leading a global transport conglomeration comprising of countless thousands of donkeys. Widespread had to accept this version of reality, since he had practically used up his eyesight on seemingly endless journeys throughout the entire song lines of the country in search for this unique creature. And Widespread himself would agree with this logic of what really happened, since plenty of his epic journeys had turned sour, and were now the legendary focus of a thousand and one tales of his being thwarted by his own visionary search for the true colour of platinum. And apart for those numerous false true donkeys he had hunted down in bush journeys that turned sour, he had to bargain with idiots – more feral types than you could imagine – to acquire many extra donkeys at about a dollar a head by refusing to pay a cent more than his bargain basement profit margin, and while always imagining in a good way, that one's haggling, bargaining, paying less, and sometimes getting an animal for free, or in foal, would all lead to the prospect of a truer platinum hue to increase the much-desired ancestral type power required for his growing donkey empire.

Widespread's premonition of unprecedented loss felt more powerful than he could control. His mind moved minus, minus, minus in the ghostly plains of spinifex that had existed in this place since time began, and he ended up losing all sense of where he was, or where he was heading while the Falcon drove on, journeying in the cocoon cloud of the spirit butterflies travelling north. Was this homesickness? Was it something in the mind he had never before experienced, of feeling totally lost in the ghost country of the homelands? Yet, in the absence of knowing, the feeling of having lost something dear would often create a state of panic in his mind. He would be overcome with an ever-deepening sense of sadness and foreboding, that in this crippling state of his mind, could only be explained as having lost the only thing of value to his vision, and that was the platinum donkey. He could not explain it in any other way had he felt the old donkey would die before he reached his destination, and it felt as though he was dying in himself from thoughts about what he would do if it died, what it would mean to the dream, for where on Earth would he ever find another platinum donkey like this one. And he thought more in terms of subtraction, of another minus, for what if it was already dead, and he had only found a ghost donkey, for the reality of the question was, why was he looking for a platinum donkey which was the colour of ghosts in the first place, when this might be the colour of any old donkey whose fur was greying with age? Each moment like this felt closer to his own death, and of feeling as though the ground was opening up, and swallowing the only donkey on Earth he needed, of burying him forever too, for he may as well be dead. He began weeping over its death even as he would pathetically keep checking and feeling the air it drew in and out of its nostrils on the back of his neck, and he could see that the rare, money-making lucky donkey had not taken its eyes off his back, and had not robbed him of the future, as the maker of progeny, of the rarest herd of platinum donkeys.

When you looked closer, you would see that it was only his grease-engrained hat that looked like giving a sense of sanity to cling to while passing in this dangerous country. He continuously shook the grease-and-dirt-engrained hat while flies buzzed in the slow-moving vehicle, brushing back his own oil-laden greying hair, as his mind wavered off into some mesmerising dream of appeasing itself with thoughts of failure in the swarming whiteness spread across the endlessness of spinifex country. He lost track of time, and sometimes wondered whether he had been driving in circles, and the circles became endless and felt as though, he had always driven in circles. He saw Dance in the distance walking through the spinifex, and he knew at once that this meant she was not feeding his donkeys, and he watched her – knew what she was like, totally ignoring the starving herd, and blissed out in this snake country, while she moved with the butterfly haze leading her astray. She continued walking through the spinifex covering the red earth, as he became locked in a fear that there were snakes coiled under each passing clump of these yellowing balls of needle plants nearly as tall as Dance, and yet, she continued to stay ahead of him in snake country dreaming, a cabaret of snakes, where she did not seem to notice any of the power he felt while watching her from far away, moving more swiftly then he was, and finally, she simply faded away.

The Ford Falcon passes over a rise, and another rise through sand dunes, while the fabled donkey of his fortune in the back seat does not take its eyes off his back. Planet knows a thing or two about donkeys, and fully comprehends how it was trying to unnerve him to spook him into letting it go free. But Widespread just thinks that the donkey does not really know him. He will never let it go free, and so he tries to call Tommyhawk on his flat mobile just to see what was going on, if everything was alright at home, but of course, the kid never answers because the little fascist was spoilt to the core by his mother. He lays the thought aside from the catastrophe of life, and he still could not work out the reason why the bloody government would want to give Tommyhawk an iPhone, or a computer, or an iPad, even though he heard the echoing of the child's voice in his mind, *These are going to be my weapons against thugs like you, ya old paedophile.*

Huh! Well! Cause has never worried before about snakes, but right now, while in the wonderment of thinking about the government dishing out free computer stuff to his son to disrespect the parent, he also began to dwell on poisonous snakes. There were snakes all over the place, that leapt into the vehicle from the dense spinifex plains forest, and while he pumped the accelerator to the floor it made no difference to the five kilometres, or butterfly speed, that the Falcon travelled on its own volition, the snakes lunged into the open windows and attacked the donkey. The shock of the situation trapped in his imaginings of possible scenarios that would destroy the only platinum dream donkey by transforming it into a huddle of snakes in his elusive wavering from reality had now gone completely overboard, but he felt nothing except his grip on the steering wheel, and he knew it was now or never if he was to be the saviour of the situation dragging him beyond his control, and he did not loosen his grip until he reached the edge where this country would release him from the *longue durée* of its infinity, and let him continue through the lines of the law to reach his homeland.

13

One wonders why people say things about someone else, whether the person is there or not.

Cause! Yep! Away again. Always out of town. He likes being elsewhere. In the bush somewhere big-noting himself, but nowhere near Praiseworthy of course. Good then. Let him stay there forever. Let him rot in hell. Let him never come back. We all hate that person anyhow. Held up our Native Title settlement for years with that fake claim about his old Daddies and Mummies, and making meeting after meeting with the government tribunal. We never want to see him again.

Call me shit. Why not?

Couldn't give a shit what you call me, understand?

Widespread never cared whether he lived or died in Praiseworthy, and when he had eventually returned to find his life upended, transformed into a major crime scene, had wished he was already dead and had never returned, for at the end of the day, he may as well be dead, and he wondered why he was still alive. Why should he live instead of Aboriginal Sovereignty? Why live in this endless mess of life that seemed unconquerable, knowing his world would never recover? He of course knew the reason for being alive was to despise himself, and no one would do this better than the man himself. No other person could use every breath of air being drawn into their lungs to better curse the shallowness left in the faint echo of himself that kept on reminding him that he had a business to build. What a laugh?

A fool's vision! Who was he, trying to do the work of a god? He sometimes thought about his former self, who had once or twice said he had thought of dying somewhere out in a sacred place where only the local spirit creation beings were living, and that, even if he was a man who felt as though he had died with some desperate idea of conquering life with death in his mind, he always remembered one thing in the end, that he had work to do, and that was enough, and what kept him going, kept him alive. At every stage of disassembling and rebuilding the vehicle destroyed from the crash in the place where only spinifex grew, he felt the spirits of that country were forcing him to live on and on like he would never die, and even more than this, the spirits of that place were conquering the sabotaging platinum donkey mask-head for his transport conglomeration from escaping back into the bush. They were encased in this world for a long time, but, he knew finally that he was unable to conquer death with the life of his child while he had been thousands of miles away from any other human being and even though he had chosen to take death, while the spirit ghosts kept giving him life to overcome his own fragility, to bring him back to face death all over again.

Move! Will you? What could you do with a man devoid of the will to live, who had a business to build to get his people through the next thousand years, so that they could continue their time immemorial journey to infinity? You could leave him to waste all that oxygen pumping into his lungs for nothing, or someone could start making sure the bloody country would always be there for the spirit of Aboriginal Sovereignty to continue living in this place. Widespread knew that some God making money was not going to do it. God knows there were enough praying for sackloads of money in Praiseworthy, but you know what he saw in the infinite haze parking itself across the traditional homeland? He saw that there was no God on Earth setting up a Reserve Bank in Praiseworthy, not while the most powerful ancestral beings that had made the country in the first place were not into making money for any predestined fate of these times. It was imported gods that made money for Australia to think about making a mess of the future, but well, Aboriginal people needed to think about how to make a bypass through the mess, to reach their own future.

And so, this flat man wrung dry of tears, the bloke who wanted to be dead by pumping his grief, and stuffing it into his lungs, fuelled himself on the fact that when you have no money as a black man living in an Australian democracy, then living on country felt only ethereal, like the stuff of unfulfilled dreams, and the only dream coming for Widespread while feeling like he had no life, and letting these dead thoughts roll over and over in his mind, was that he had forgotten about the script, and the script of the country was about the infinite timelessness of the ancestral will to survive into eternity. The script was written in country, and in the skies by endless thunder read in the light of sixty thousand lightning strikes, which was enough to make you forget any of your vague useless dreams that were less than a flick of time, and you would remember where you belonged in the moment of time immemorial, the care and responsibility for good country being greater than creating a world of infinite grieving, and this was how to control the future when you cared about the great powerful beings warning you deep down in your soul to keep on script, and that you better learn how to let those big creators rest easy in the places of their creation. Don't let them start wandering around and feeling lonely, to wake up and come looking for the people who neglected the world, and in their powerfulness to create, use the very same power to destroy all things.

But what could a man do about that young brat of his, Tommyhawk? A real creepy fascist kid! This boy who thought his father was a piece of rubbish? How would this dead meat father, the man ripped of emotion from head to toe, feel about the loss of Aboriginal Sovereignty, and being left with a sneaky kid like that? Did some relic of love swathe across his shattered mind, smother the smelting ashes in his memory of the repressive younger son, the fault-finder, the one educated by the government to evolve into a new organism, an arch-conservative white man in a black skin? Where was the thrilling in the heart the greatest, or where hardest to digest, or else, what was the point of dealing with uncomfortable pictures? Who cared if the man would never fathom to this day the story about how Dance had sung naming in his head when the top son was born, forever harping on, *What about Peter, Paul*, etc., nice names? *Why couldn't you have called him something properly normal, and fitting in with our colonisation, our subjugation, you can still be powerful by just fitting in with the status quo by being called a name like, racist, or why not a worthless name like haulage cart, cartage, carrier? Or, why not flip to the other side with something saintly, a bit biblical. Aloysius was good. Solomon. Something like Bartholomew. Like Moses. Forecaster. Truest Formula. Or even Babylon. Nice Praiseworthy names from a church. Bible names. Or, just plain Donny Cat? Fuck! A prophecy name so he would live forever, Tithonus? Better than an I wish you were dead name, because that's what people in this country will be saying about a name like what you are saying, you know.*

Widespread had said he wanted to remain being a proud man, by saying the words of his own choice, whenever he felt like it. He did not have to become a heretic, like some black man addicted to the Australian way of life if he did not want to, and anyhow, he asked, where was the insult in saying the only words that he loved to say and mattered most to him, to feel how smoothly these words rolled over his tongue. He was talking about the only two words relevant to his existence, Aboriginal Sovereignty. He remembered saying something significant to Dance about how his firstborn would fully capture true ownership of country, and this would be a source of pride in his every thought until the day he died. *Then you know what happened,* he told Dance, *the ancestors had actually rung me up while I was at the supermarket down the street, and buying a packet of cigarettes – look at this mobile phone here – you can see their number, and what they told me all rapturously and blessed, was this, Call him Aboriginal Sovereignty. And you know what, I rung them back while I was having the smoke, and you know what I said – why not?* And Dance, she only asked one question about the ancestor's mobile, which was about what the ring tone sounded like? She just could not get her head around the idea of what a deep-time ring tone would sound like. *And, it was a funny thing,* he said, while explaining the phenomenon of receiving a phone call from beyond belief, how these big conversations with the ancestors of thousands of years ago could actually be understood by a language-contaminated human being of today, even though mind you, those old ancestors spoke pure deep-time lingo from this place which had come a long way before modern pidgin English, like how these white people spoke in Australia while thinking their speech was the height of world sophistication, and had insisted on teaching the real people, but still, you could feel those old people fixing your brain with thoughts too big to decipher properly, because what they had to say, had to come through eternity to get here, imagine that, and weep, because you needed to have a mighty big brain to deal with a challenging message from the ancestral telling you to go and pick up your firstborn, and take him outside into the starry and holy night, and hold him up for his old kinspeople to see from the Milky Way, and say, *Here is your Aboriginal Sovereignty.*

SITTING IN THE BONES

if we fail to plan, we plan to fail
Henry Puna, Prime Minister of the Cook Islands speaking to the
Nansen Initiative on Disaster-induced Cross-border Displacement,
2013

1

Oracle 5...Eh! Where that moth woman? Dance! The Moth...er?

Everywhere, the world was moving quicker into a crescendo of the
confused, but up there in Praiseworthy, there were plenty of slower
words being said sad on the beach by old ashen-skin spirit people
walking up and down several kilometres of sand in an never-ending
search through the haze, while hoping to find the absent ghost spirit
of Aboriginal Sovereignty, and all awhile, jointly wailing, screaming
really, saying things like, *You had to ask yourself: what world did the
moth-er think she lived in?*

And, again, and again, through these ancient coastal laneways
running through the sands, and into the sea far away of calm and
storm, the old ghostly kinspeople moved steadily through seasons of
bristling air thick with thistle and seed among butterflies, dust spores
flying high and low in the haze, searching under every grain of sand
where the caper white butterflies or *Belenois aurota* were ending
another migration while straining to fly that last short distance into
the sea, with practically destroyed wings now almost denuded of the
dust scales that had once formed perfectly intricate art deco patterns
of white drop feathers encased by thick black lines. Earlier, the
migration had flown through an infestation of spinifex sand-skipper

butterfly, the low flying *Proeidosa polysema*, which moved quickly with wings of silken dark brown infused with white patches, as their compound eyes watched in every direction in search for the flowers of stringybark, bloodwood, ironbark, the curly spinifex growing on land covered with the soft grassy spinifex *Triodia pungens*, amidst monsoon vines covering woodland trees of the savannah. There were many other local butterflies troubling Dance's cabbage white butterflies, her precious *Pieris rapae* massing through the streets, and streaming down on the beach in silky strings, in search of anything rotting in its dying leaf heart carcass.

Those were the days, and the old people hummed in a dizzying talkfest about the songs of the ages being a marvellous balance of infinite existence that they described in one movement after another, even while they too were rummaging through the contemporary view of momentary existence devoured by the quickness of change happening through every second of life in this known world. And, these old ghosts well knew the gigantic ghost clocks of the all times covering the ancient land, and could see how this clockwork too was being transformed. Through having to search perpetually for something wavering off the radar, the spectrum of belonging to all existence, these old people had to find the essence of maintaining the learnt stability that had come through the all times – until now – to bring it back before it was too late, before it was lost forever, while being unable to stop dead time from progressing forward into new time, to be killed before it had a chance to live inside infinity. And so, they kept pushing back against these unknowns of time, to again be without any specific time, belonging only to the infinite existence of the world, and the finite possibility of being without change in the changing of every moment.

Help us find our Aboriginal Sovereignty. Some of the old ashen people, now walking among the scores of able-bodied voluntary searchers, were talking back to the ghost butterflies floating through the hazy breeze laden with lepidopteran dust, and out there, carpeting the sea. The searchers did not see anyone talking to the butterflies, and did not pay respect to the old people. They were far too busy being without shame, the empty container itself in the soul, while throwing around the dirt, all those bad feelings towards the mother. Yet, even though the ashen bodies of the spirits were walking about invisibly in the midday sun, the effervescence of the timeless aura was there, translucently reaching out on the beach, the thing itself finding and strangling the wrath, and eventually endowing the voluntary forward planning searchers with a slight soberness, where they surprised themselves with feeling a bit guilty, less hateful, and losing the vindictiveness pounding the drums in their minds. Still, you could not help feeling alone, even in a throng of foot-thong people, and that was how the voluntary searchers felt, doing the hard-yard work for nothing while being exposed to sixty thousand lightning-strike storms. The size of the voluntary search party, now comprising hundreds of people roped in for nothing by the super shire council mayoral outfit of Ice Queens ruling the roost, were ordered to continue to comb the entire over-trodden beach for the ten thousandth time, and search until they found a clue of what had happened to their missing Aboriginal Sovereignty. In the growing vengefulness of having to search for a needle in a haystack without payment, the searchers realised that they were being forcefully hypnotised, and were now even meditating like yoga people. They had been involuntarily zombified which made them feel all airy-fairy, to the point of feeling that they needed to be more careful about talking haphazardly, *like fools – you fools*, in front of the unseen, for they felt the presence of the old people breathing on their backs, as well as looking over their shoulders, staring into their faces, and standing on their toes unless they changed their tone of voice into something that sounded nice. *We should be able to look around this*

457

beach and see her here with us voluntary searchers, they agreed. *She should not be hiding from people with butterfly eyes. Well! You know what? Why didn't she come straight down here on the beach where everyone else is doing the hard work for all the people of this country – out in the heat searching for her son, while also being attacked by injury donkeys, where everyone will be waking up and finding themselves either dead in a hospital bed after this, or immobilised? Didn't she love her children like everyone else here?*

There was nobody worrying about what that fascist kid Tommyhawk was doing, while he was skulking around like a mangy dog in the bareness of the caterpillar-stripped landscape, where a gravel airstrip had been cut through the middle of this vegetation chewed-up wasteland. The kid stood out like the eyesore he was, while trying not to be seen, but was seen clearly anyhow, by the hawk-eyed voluntary searchers staring up at this airstrip on the higher ground, from down where they were on the beach. They saw this weirdo, even though they did not wish to see him at all. His world, wherever that was, was neither immaculate, nor even the immediate business of ordinary voluntarily people searching for their lost sovereignty. What for? Well! They should have been applying their full-strength vision concentration to see what lay far off – like, for instance, the body of Aboriginal Sovereignty – by looking binocularly far away, at eye level. There was no need for wavering by swirling around 180 degrees to look at what was behind you, and also, upwards. You were not searching for angels, saints, fascists, spirits in the sky, or big-sky vision. This was not where you looked to find your suicidal Aboriginal Sovereignty. But, these straying sea-eye searchers, who had only ever felt compelled to look outwards to the sea, now seemed driven to look multifaceted upwards and backwards like a compound-eyed butterfly or plague fly, like they were God dreamers. It was simple glare, they said, that had latched their eyes on a stray sun gleam, and they saw plenty of the eyesore talking on his incredibly must-have sun-glistening iPhone, which was an envious thing for any poor people dazzling from afar, and provoking silent jealousy of what it would feel like, to have a piece of government-owned polished stainless steel glued to your ear. They could see how the fascist looked as though he was already elsewhere, and his addictive nervous pacing back and forth along the airstrip, and they too began to replicate his pacing, and being transported to some classy world of the fast lane where you robot-walked in moon boots for the rest of your life, and you were not just replicating a marooned fascist on a lonely airstrip running through the mulga in a pair of broken thongs. The voluntary searchers who had never before wished to be elsewhere in their lives except being on country now felt their time immemorial beings jeopardised, by knowing this kind of little fascist was not dreaming ancient homeland dreams, and this made them feel as though their sanity was being stolen, and that they too had been placed in some jeopardy departure lounge of a busy international terminal, the sub-normal monstrosity of unnaturalness that they had never before managed to imagine in their holy-place mind, and all this foreign mind-transporting stuff happened just by watching the way the kid was prancing around like a caged animal in their arid-zone airstrip cut through stripped land, where even they, who had never been to a city, were now impatiently pacing while channelling anyone for the sake of just saying hello, and checking for non-existent incoming and outgoing flights bundled in the blue sky, and expecting a call from somebody calling the scenario glistening in a sunray, and, *Oh! My God, it was not even the Mother, moth-er, or the White Mother calling.*

When Tommyhawk heard the spilt-guts laughter, and caught sight of the frenzied mimickers pacing off, like they were challenging each other in rows of line dance down on the beach, he felt caught in the burn, and drawn into this larger moment igniting into an uncontrollable wildfire as people yelled to each other, to him, to anyone, and his face winced in disgust. He spun on his heels, and took flight. He fled from the airstrip, ran for his life, and never stopped running until he had raced through the streets of Praiseworthy, pulled his mind back from the beach, re-packaged his scary-cat headspace into a suitcase that he dumped back into his re-ordered brain, fired up the telepathic power of his every thought to auto-kill the cheer of leery child abusers photocopying the impatient trademark pacing style of a chosen one legislated by the God government to act elite, and real nervy, until safely removed from the dangerous Aboriginal world. And, so, remembering he was already transformed into a rich white child inside a dark skin, who knew he was destined elsewhere, and even though he was waiting for the miracle to happen, know this, he was already living with the Whitest Mother of all Aboriginal children in Australia in the one and only spectacular $1.1 billion-dollar taxpayer-paid whitest shiny palace down in Canberra, instead of living in a government-designed tin shed erected as an endless emergency shelter for Aboriginal people to dwell in for the rest of their lives.

He crept through the mangroves where the voluntary search party was busy staring upwards through the gloaming of the twilight haze, searching to see the fascist on the barren airstrip. Silently, he moves into the ribcage of the whale bones where he instantly becomes as formless as the spinifex butterflies flittering through the skeleton, and amassed, asleep on the mud humming with mosquitoes. He becomes the whale ghost sitting in the bones where he would not be seen. The Golden Hair Mother had still not called her Aboriginal child. But, looking up into the sky above the sea, there she was swivelling in her office chair on the clouds, and seeing her busy working, he noticed her power cord was plugged into the power supply of heaven. This was a revelation in itself to Tommyhawk about powerfulness, and he knew for sure this was a complete step up from stealing pre-paid electricity meter vouchers to charge his iPhone. Well! Anyhow, he realised that her job in the Australian government was not easy, if she was to save all Aboriginal children from their parents. Why? He can imagine, and he imagines the difficulty of implementing so many inquiries to develop the necessary exhaustive formulas for determining which Aboriginal child of hundreds of thousands, was most in need, and which then, should be removed first to close the gaping hole of inequality, with the relative safety of white children. But, wasn't he living in the most fear as a narrative fascist coming from a rampage happening right next to you? Wouldn't that make you the most vulnerable? Didn't this put you on top of the list? Why could she still not see that he must live in her beautiful parliament house?

While having to sit like he did not exist in the whale skeleton as the line dancers were exhausting their frenzy nearby, he thought if she was a real mother of all Aboriginal children, she should be able to see her children, and it was not right that he had to become invisible to save himself. He looked at the lady in the sky who was not offering assurance to anyone, and it was a complete quandary that when he tried to call, she kept staring into space, and neglected to answer his calls. He kept posing the question, of why he still had not heard from the big important white lady in Canberra who was sitting up there in front of him like a golden-hair angel in the sky. Where was her power? How did she look after all of the hundreds of thousands of Aboriginal children simultaneously, and instantly, if she was their true mother? But somehow, even that did not matter much if you had to depend on how well you could become invisible, even in the middle of a hostile line dance. He was already highly practised in safeguarding his invisibility and doing alright for a fascist. He had mastered how to keep the world at bay, but he really needed to be waiting at the airstrip for he expected there would be no advanced warning about when the army would actually turn up, flying in to remove this top-of-the-list Aboriginal child from immediate threatened danger. He slipped through the paces of how this eternity of waiting for help would turn out while rolling the iPhone in his fingers and checking for the text from the swivelling chair sky lady that a secretive almighty white government air force stealth B-2 Spirit bomber was on the way, and he had to be waiting by the airstrip if he wanted to be saved, because the stealth bomber would only make a quick landing to pick up the cargo – one threatened Aboriginal child, and rapidly take off – zoom, zoom – before the line-dancing locals rioted, and damaged the stealth with flying rocks, hunting sticks, strangeness and the like.

With nothing else left to do except maintain invisibility at all times, Tommyhawk tried to believe he was safe, while slipping into another bout of despondency, where he continued questioning the absence of anything at all being done about removing him from harm foreshadowed – once it dawned on the searchers that he had murdered Aboriginal Sovereignty. His father would kill him first, then throw what was left of his carcass to the extinction makers. But! Hadn't he told the White Mother everything the government wanted to hear about child abuse and why he had to be taken away to live with her? *She'll call. She'll call.* He argues against his own doubts, and all his hopes rest on repeating his own mantra: *I am her witness. She will save me.*

What if there was nothing more left than a mantra to vanquish his foreshadowed foe as it turned out to be, and the foe was enormous, and encompassing the entire world and spilt out of the planet like rays of capillaries dangling in space? Tommyhawk Steel did the only thing possible for an Aboriginal child who thought a great deal about his particular circumstances. He rebuilt a stronger escape plan to get down to Canberra in a hurry. He pushed aside the dense fabric of doubt in his brain about the seemingly failed rescue mission, and he imagined a humungous piece of burnt-out flatland in his head that far exceeded the unlikely idea of the national flagship landing in the night, or a stealth jet. Neither could land on a broken-down Aboriginal community's airstrip bulldozed through the scrub for an emergency landing by the Royal Flying Doctor Service. Instead, he blooms with a bouquet of larger empowerment in the middle of a rocket-fired flattened landscape. He felt calm while strapped inside a superpower's designed rocket sneakily trucked into Praiseworthy by order of the White Mother. He knows that such an awesome lady, who owned hundreds of thousands of Aboriginal children, was powerful enough to arrange world peace if it was in her mind to do such a thing, but he also knows even as an eight-year-old child, that peace was not on the mind of any political manoeuvring bent on secrecy, and the spirit of stealth. He closed his eyes for the countdown, and he continued to feel calm in the overpowering exhilaration as the rocket fires up for the take-off, and he remained calm while feeling himself being launched straight out of the whale skeleton at about five miles a second, then being hurled through space, and arriving down in Canberra in a nanosecond as the latest saved Aboriginal child freed from savages, and the welcome symphony orchestra played the Stars and Stripes Forever, as he was being marched into the White Palace.

2

There are always two sides of a story. Say for instance, just for the sake of looking at the larger picture and fiddling around with the facts, let's say, you were that blonde-haired White God Government Mother of a quarter of a million unloved Aboriginal children scattered across the country, when all these little jewels were put into your care. How were you going to save them? Who from? And how in the heck are you going to look after them? If you are the saviour, how are you going to remove all these children from their unloving parents and families by being everywhere at once in the entire land mass of 7.692 million square kilometres of the Australian continent? Was it even possible to be White God Government Mother simultaneously in every Aboriginal home like a picture of Chairman Mao, or Stalin, or of the Australian Constitution? How will you keep up with the Act? Remember! That Speedy Gonzales was only a comic, make-believe, not reality. Only the powerful people of country are able to be in all places simultaneously. It was a quandary to be the mother of the multitudes. It just cannot be done, even if you send the entire Australian army in to pick up all these children, and even with wasting billions of dollars in trying to reshape a world that was not yours to shape with long-term goals for closing the gap of inequities, it cannot be done.

You better believe that it was not just Tommyhawk Steel who felt special. Lots of Praiseworthy children had deep matters of concern festering in their minds. The compass is what it is. You don't inherit the oldest surviving culture in the world for nothing, not without developing a bit of devotion to the interconnectedness of your world – even though you were being taught nothing but human specialism in the classroom. Yet surely, wasn't this a totally urgent hour of need for a kid like Tommyhawk? Yes, there he was, roaming up and down the dust-laden airstrip while anxiously peering into the empty sky, and telling himself, *Well fuck her – a million times*. She could have at least texted back to one of his multitudinous SOS messages, especially while Tommyhawk was dealing with the frightening experience of being spooked by Aboriginal Sovereignty as a persistent memory. He could be seen flashing like a life-size ornament all over the airstrip. The object glowed with golden beams of stardust, and Tommyhawk thought the aura had been caught in the barbwire glare of the scorching sun belting on the airstrip, and it was not pretty to experience having a spook looking in your face, like a blowtorch. No Aboriginal ancestral hero staring at his murderer need to look like that.

There were too many revelations happening down on the search beach of Praiseworthy, and Tommyhawk eventually lost all sense of checking in with reality, for now he was blinded by the blowtorch aura, he could only see ghostly forms that might have been reality, or actually ghosts. He still had not been saved by the sunshine halo gleaming Blonde Hair White Mother swivelling on her office chair in the sky, but then he saw another ghost when he heard it yelping. It was his dog Pedro. The thing had returned one more time from the sea as a dog ghost. He saw its incandescent white fur looking spooky – shimmering in a mirage on the beach – but the dog ghost blazed with white-hot temper from the cosmic dimensions of its sufferings in the sea world where it had experienced hell while trying to prevent Aboriginal Sovereignty from drowning. The dog said it was only born to chase down rats, and never thought of itself as being a winner of the bigger battles in life it had endured to save the mightiest power of the all times, which was Aboriginal Sovereignty. Far from revealing if Aboriginal Sovereignty was dead or alive, this story of tragic experiences was not to be celebrated as a victory, or of winning the war, the dog ghost said, but it also said that it would never do a dog smile again. And, even while Tommyhawk stared down onto the abyss beach from where the airstrip abruptly ended on the edge of a cliff above the beach, he knew the dog had changed forever, as though its memory of happiness had been wiped clean out of its head.

He watched the little ghost dog spin around through its madness of trying to shake off whatever demon had wrestled with its fight to reach the beach, and as the dog flew around the sand and cut through flights of white butterflies, Tommyhawk could see it was dragging something it had brought in from the surf. This was when the jackhammer thought thumped in his heart, *Why come back?* The thought really annoyed Tommyhawk, even though he had severed all his emotional attachment to the dog after it had decided to run off into the sea in the first place, to follow Aboriginal Sovereignty's walk towards suicide.

Anyhow, let the mind games run wild, and Tommyhawk ran the imaginary machine to flush out the pictures of the future, where he could not see himself with an old camp dog ghost following him around in Parliament House. And the future kept pumping the flow of possibilities on that lonely airstrip while he was waiting to be saved, and he stopped at the thought of whether Apple Inc would in time, invent an iDog for Aboriginal kids, to help them become assimilated into white culture more quickly, or else, leave holograms behind on the empty homelands of Aboriginal children playing with real dogs. Tommyhawk thought he would ask the White Mother for a designer dog although he had never actually seen one, but he thought as he watched Pedro's demented ghost spinning in the sand, that a designer dog would have to be a better dog any day than some mongrel dog like this, that his own father had stolen, and given to him as a pet.

Then, after looking out to sea where a plane would take off, and wishing he could fly, Tommyhawk looked down from the pancake ridge at the end of the airstrip where he could see the ghost dog, and yep, it was still yelping around the voluntary searchers staring at it, and you know what, he saw the ghost dog actually dragging his brother's old sun-bleached t-shirt, the one he recognised at once, with ABORIGINAL SOVEREIGNTY inscribed in big black lettering across the back that – hello, the thing in its mouth was ripped to threads.

When finally, many hours later, the dog had finished racing and spinning in circling yelps, it yelped its one last sad story which was about trying to bring home some of its sanity – yep! Yelping to prove something, that the old rag had brought old Pedro's sanity back home. This unmoored the voluntary searchers who were bent on retrieving the first piece of evidence of their missing Aboriginal Sovereignty. There were searchers all over the beach screaming at Pedro, *Bring it to me,* until finally, after the endless chasing and manoeuvring around the flying grains of sand, the dance was done. The dog ghost sat staring at the sand-engrained wet mangled cloth with its bared teeth that looked like they had come out of a shark's mouth.

Tommyhawk focused in on the insinuating rag on the sand until finally, he believed, felt certain, that when you really thought about it, you could say it looked as though the t-shirt had been ripped off Ab.Sov's back by a crazy shark pack – honestly, he thought, even every man-eating crocodile jazzing up in a death crawl – truly. These thoughts were not good, were paralysing his mind, but he knew it was Ab.Sov's own fault, he wanted to die, *and that brother, was your idea, not mine. Let me hear you say I had nothing to do with it. Say, you were the weakest, always were. Blame yourself for what you did, not me – yep.* He kicked the cloth out of his mind – one, two, three, and many more times – sent the thing flying, while the spinifex butterflies flew after it floating in the sea and brought it back, and dumped it in front of the ghost dog. A thousand times he called the dog to go away, but it did not move while sitting there looking at the rag on the sand.

3

We never seen her. While the time immemorial geniuses mathematically absorbed more of the greatness of ancestral infinity, they calculated in precisely half a second flat, that nobody had seen Dance, moth-er Mother, in non-specific ages they described as, ever. This inability to see her, added more layers to the haze legend about people becoming miraculously lost in the fleetingness of human existence. It was just part of the wondrous supernatural phenomenon of forever, if only it were true, for the fact of the matter was that she, and her entire family, were somehow disappearing into the faraway. Nothing to regale about that, or to distract oneself from any of the multifarious realities of wasting time on self-absorption by constructing your own major construction site of bugger-all consequence in the mind – when the old minds had already been there long ago, constructing the road to the all times. Leave it to them. They erect the barriers, the invisible steel around the minds of their people that was capable of shutting out the dark clouds of the twenty-first century as though it was just another breath in time. Leave it to them to break from the pestilences of the past in reshaping new eternities in existence.

On the other hand, whilst being personally rearranged by the here-and-now government to take yet another detour into their policy world of mayhem, which was all you could say of a sad and sorry time for the whole of Praiseworthy while pining for the return of their Aboriginal Sovereignty, a fool had found in the toolbox of oppression a cruel tool to use upon themselves. There was always a fool, and Praiseworthy people said *yes, yes, yes, park that on us. We'll have some of that kind of crazy assimilatory measures if you think us poor people are helping the government to make up their mind to chuck us a few dollars*. They let the fool in their head pin on every door their own locally designed restraining order against themselves – like those prohibition signs being used by the police across the beach, and so the nailing went on. The designer notice – bang, bang, bang – was nailed on every gate of the locality, flown from flagpoles, or tossed on the dirt for a downcast eye to see on the spot, and from stopping the word thing from being blown away in the trade winds, by chucking one of those old mission days white painted rocks on top, an artefact, a left reminder of even greater oppression, to hold strong words down. A government interpreter who was not cheap went around each house to translate what the flapping notice proclaimed into standard English – from rampaged white supremacy diction, into something all-encompassing, like this: *Nobody knock here*. This saved a lot of trouble of saying the notice applied to multifarious peddlers of government hype, typed in fat print to include pissheads, pornos, paedophiles, perverts, dopeheads and drug lords with laundry bags. But the thing about the designer signs was the tendency for flexibility, interchangeableness, like graffitied legislation continually being amended. The plural *persons* was scratched out, until a singular person remained on the censored signs. A local who was powerful enough to write something epical in a single word – lead-handed, and grave heart – wrote DANCE with mega-sized texta in a snake-track scrawl like a single Chinese shan shui brushstroke painting reminiscent of an ominous mountain range where fireflies lit up the darkness with their dance.

But! This was not an ordinary dull piece of paper after it had been written on by the power of country, the wisdom of the ages, the Pope et cetera and so forth of the north. The message was everlasting, indelible, a change-shifter, a heightener of emotion for creating such an exalté atmosphere of everlasting Aboriginal Sovereignty in the brain it would be stuck there forever. This was what happened far away from all else not worth knowing where the world was full wondrous, and all the more reason to celebrate with solid prayers to *get up, stand up and show up*, roared exaltedly by the faithful of the tabernacle down in Church Street. This was the news of country. Paper signs combusted, caught fire and exploded. Little fires sprung up from these bits of elder-altered paper where the notices were nailed bang, bang on doors, gates, fences, or had been whooshed, chucked under a mission rock painted holy white. Moths rose, and poured into the flames. The paper messages manifested into an unstoppable petrolhead pyromaniac and no one could pull themselves back from the fire head's irresistible powers for smelling like exploding petrol driving along like a racing car through the streets of Praiseworthy while shovelling the petulance hiding in the dust into its souped-up fiery spirit that continued flying off in x, y, and z directions of multiple ancestral pathways that led farther away, and into the sky. Oh! jubilant ember-lit atmosphere, the congregations grew far too excited while linking together in arm-intertwining connectedness to sing *Shall we gather at the river where the bright angel feet have trod*, and so forth. The prayers continued far into the future, and this sign-burning devotion was like a hex that kept Dance from knocking on other people's front doors. She kept her distance, almost, as though being unable to penetrate the ferocity of the petrolhead's power to fire up a piece of paper.

Wide and far, this real sovereign owner mob got smarter, and were emphatically certain that Praiseworthy did not need a police presence which was invisible to them, not if a policeman was actually doing his job by being embodied in a piece of paper, and could actually, without being anywhere in sight, and sitting over three thousand clicks away down in Canberra, while disguising himself as a piece of paper, construct invisible twenty foot walls around their highfaluting residences that were capable of stopping the cemetery woman from coming around and making an utter nuisance of herself. They said it was good that her heavy arguments of all and sundry had been silenced. They took great pleasure in knowing that her mad mixed-up voice could not penetrate the invisible barrier of inextinguishable gasoline fieriness that now oozed from those notices nailed to the front door, gatepost, fence, and under the mission rock boundary. This was the beauty of living in a furnace while feeling the overpowering heat of radiating fangs jumping to the other side of the road where she was forced to stand out of the way of becoming inflamed like an Olympic torch, while she remained shouting her loose-tongue abuse about suffering Native Title cruelty at the hands of *common people*. The hiding policeman in the exploding paper was too strong for her. Nobody could hear her vile voice anymore. Instead, they were happy sitting around on upturned kerosene tins watching TV in the lounge room in the poverty-stricken sovereign owner of the continent's supposed to be rightful legal home, each an overcrowded boxed oven built on the cheap side from a government loan that even twenty generations of their families would be paying off forever, and long after the house itself had collapsed to the ground. You only had to hear the crackle of a bushfire running over the sacred lands from a long way off, and you would have to ask yourself, *What was that big magnas hissing taipan Dance saying now*?

But you do not knock a miracle, not in this most awesome of outcomes, where you would never have dared to believe that one day you would not have to hear her treasonous voice belting on again about rightful legal people, and robbers of Native Title. Their voices stayed on the main holler line – *We are sick of her.* Of course they were, and would tell you themselves she could get stuffed for jeopardising their Native Title claim, that falsifier of legitimate claims, asking the big stealer Australian government to recognise her above all others as the Native Title owner of the cemetery land. Liar! Anyway, those who were silenced, were history. They were the vanquished.

The volunteer search party of fan-waving ladies, fishermen forced to give up fishing to search the entire sea for bodies, the throngs of people on the beach who desired to become godlike searchers, all had one thing in common, they wanted Dance to stay right off the beach, and mind her own business. They would rather be dead than have her helping them, even though they liked to go on about how she was nowhere in sight in the search for their Aboriginal Sovereignty. There was always a second story, the one underneath the mask when chewing the fat in the greater story, taking form through zigzagging across memory in the cliques, gatherings, campfire discussions, and kitchen caucuses critiquing legitimate problems of how neither she, nor Cause, those other kinds, were even from Praiseworthy. *You know what? She was from China.* In the echoing of what was contaminating the strain of the bloodlines, you could hear the seashell wail of the sea reminiscing how she should take her family, and go back to China where she belonged.

What do you do with questionable questions, the ones newly written in the bloodstream? Let the belongings spill across the floor? Create a win-win spin for assimilationists on the march one way or the other towards treason to the ancestors – not even hers, betraying their traditional country – not hers? For who was she anyhow? In any case... She was not even one of their types, and for some strange reason, it was determined by someone whose word spread like truth, or fun, or ancestry, ancestry hidden, ancestry all or nothing, or for some strange reason, she had come from some other species, the inferior subspecies that had escaped from a bottomless well of evolution. Who was right about throwbacks? Who had come first, who had come later, and who were not really the time immemorial people who were descended from the ancestral creations?

On the red hazed beach of the futile search, down there among the white butterflies killing themselves in the act of mass suicide which might have been over the sadness of losing Aboriginal Sovereignty, all of this did not matter to the locals of Praiseworthy continuing the extensive search to find their infinity more as an obligation, rather than from the desire of recovering human remains amongst dead butterflies. They just felt glad with what they had written about Dance Steel's treachery on the census form to the Australian government, which was in short, about her attempt to overthrow the natural order of things. They had all copied the same message written in simple white-people language which seemed to be a perfect solution to find a quick way of destroying Dance, instead of unpacking the interconnected intricacies of the time immemorial language of high culture. Such an undertaking would be like turning the life of your mind into a quarry, and jackhammering your soul into a million little pieces. You would have to sort out into which pile of incomprehension you would categorise your infinity, before you could pick a single box out of time immemorial to be translated into common English.

But believing white government required your art form was meaningless. The trick was, how to get meaning into the heads of these people. Ah! What for? So, Praiseworthy people just wrote: *Dance Steel had lost her way*. Fine! Who was Dance Steel? *She was caught up with the butterflies*. This final statement confused the distinct mind-field of the policemen who were asked to *go figure* that big black woman of wasted fury up there in Praiseworthy tangled up in butterflies. The message was police code language for drug-smuggling activity by this Dance Steel's relatives in Asia, who were butterflies.

4

Over in the distant grasslands where Dance was searching for Planet's disappearing donkeys, she had not known whether she belonged to a dream or not, while walking through a swarming carpet of small yellow grass butterflies preforming their story for this place inches above the ground and bringing it to life. In the distance, and far as the eye could see, the country shimmered in a vast single yellowness of rhythmic waves of dance. The sameness of the breathing land grew more dizzying the longer you looked at the lemony country leaping to life, and Dance continued walking slowly through the narrow path the butterflies cleared as they flew apart in front of her, and closed again, back into the vast singular movement, as she walked on ground that was no longer solid. The land was alive, and breathing as a spiritual organism, disconcerting to walk on, and in this sparse yellow spectacle consuming all horizons, all direction was removed. What remained was the bleak beauty of a great ancestor joined only by the intensity of blue sky. Without knowing where to turn and to stop falling apart, Dance kept her eyes downcast, and tried to distract herself from the power of country in ritual, while humming *Eurema smilax*, slowly rolling the scientific Latin name of the tiny yellow butterflies of country in her mouth. She had never seen these common butterflies massing on this scale before. In these grasslands, it was thought, these butterflies came back to the ancestors, and they were multiplying in tens of millions while reliving an eternal memory in a lemon-dancing haze becoming the ancestral serpent's gigantic body, stretching over the land and passing through her, crossing into faraway horizons.

This mesmerising yellow sea continued radiating outwards in waves, spilling over the ground and drawing Dance further into its enchantment, hypnotising her in its story-making ceremonies of enrapturing country, and she sleepwalked further into its strangeness, where now, all low landmark tracks and footprints were blanketed by the vastness of this oceanic serpentine yellow. In following this ancient map of a single ancestral being, there was no freshly spun silken spider thread powerful enough to draw her back into the tracks of contemporaneity, and the more her transfixed eyes stared into its eternity, the more she became disoriented in the vast scale of the grassland country's stories, and the more frightening this power place felt to her. With no lifeline to stop the catastrophic sense of fear that falls like quicksilver down her throat and churns through her stomach, as though the fear itself was being chased by ghosts, before racing back up to her throat, she tries to force this overwhelming fear to subside, not to reach into her mind and spin out, and she would collapse under the pressure of the passing ancestral serpent. Who would find her body dissolved in the dirt? What would happen to her as she became soil passing through the atmosphere of the haze? She felt a weakness in herself, of failing to place herself back in the world, as her mind spun with half-formed thoughts of becoming lost forever, of being absorbed in the overwhelming stillness of the sky, of being inseparable from any other particle of dust on the ground, of never being found, for she had become nothing.

A place lost? Earth? Dance continued, cautiously trying to find her way through the yellow fog of butterflies, and without having any true idea of where she was heading, except for being vaguely aware of one familiar sound in each heavy step as it hits the ground, that made sense to take the next step. The yellow ground ripples with waves while alternating through new and deeply unfathomable changes, through all the known spatial realities that lull her ahead, onwards, taking her further inside the ancestral map. But while trying to break free of the yellow flood, she knew nothing would ever be the same again in her life, even as she tried to recapture and to hold together the broken shards of scattered images from her memory's fleetingly integrated random moments, which in themselves were not enough to capture the wholeness of a single momentary truth from what was ever real on this grassland, or to lay out the way back into her knowledge of homeland.

Dance continued moving through the flow of the country's awakening and fought to resist it, with her own sense of her willpower over the overwhelming aliveness of the ancestral world, by swerving her mind away from the direction in which the mighty yellow ancestral being moved. Each time she resisted the onward flow of the shape-shifting land, only to be smothered by the single movement of countless millions of yellow butterflies, she would be forced back into an unreliable focus – no matter how incomplete and vaguely comprehensible. She pulled the dry monsoon forest butterflies and moths into the single delicate caterpillar thread in the flood of life that had always drawn her home. She gathered up those spirits, a flood of wind-broken winged butterflies which were held in place for the moment into a rainstorm dillybag, before being erased in the moving life of the woken ancestor.

In her attempt to evade the grip of the ancestral serpent's body spread across the land, she stirred and reanimated the monochrome yellow flow through thoughts which ran with a gathering of much-loved butterflies, an assemblage of fleeting colours spilt in dizzy flights against the blinding blueness of the sky. Then the single pearly whiteness of the common butterfly called *Elodina* captured in memory splashed over the yellow flowing through the blue sky, before soon adding the snowiness of the rarely seen migrant white albatross – *Appias*. Latin names spilt through the ancestral awakening, and her mind's eye travelled the firm and rapid flight of the black pencil-lined wings of the white *Belenois java* butterfly, the evening brown *Melanitis leda*, and the large yellow grass *Eurema hecabe*. These were only some of the butterflies living within the geographical range caught by the vast shadow vibrating like an earthquake rippling across the homelands.

Dance throws more imaginings of country into the ancestral flood. She recreates and jumbles the diversity of the homeland. She casts the luminous riparian vine thickets laden with numerous species of storm-broken-wing butterflies and moths, the ghosts that fall over the vast landscape. Her mind races quickly through the catalogue of lightning, the sixty thousand lightning strike storms that gel together, stories of flight that ended with turmoiled wings. She throws faith from the mandala of her imaginings that, seen from the distance, fall like handfuls of ash. These were the black and white spotted common crow butterflies the Latin expert knew as the *Euploea corinna* species. All these butterflies floated and spun into a silent screeching of hot air in this atmospheric flooding, with more country butterflies thrown into the reimagining, the amalgamation of returning vision to the faithfulness of homeland. The sky is stirred by the orange lesser wanderer – *Danaus petilia* – and the swamp mangrove tiger-coloured *Danaus affinis*. The spinifex grasslands re-emerge with the travelling of the white-eye ghost butterfly, an old spirit that shows itself in the world with snowy-fringed heavily scaled wings, that flies its ancient routes, reminiscent of Hitofude-ryuu style flight lines, along delicate parasitic vines meandering their serpentine pathways over the spinifex. This old ghost is commonly called the spotted dusky-blue, and somehow someone came along with a Latin name in this ancient world and called it *Candalides delospila*. She found other butterflies perched on the memory lines of country, where each had momentarily formed its place in a scatter map before slipping back off into nothingness. Yet they had lived long enough to be defined in the country of hot dry winds blowing in from the coast that had sucked their dust scales into the hazy darkened sky, before settling down on the grasslands by the morning, and on the waxy opened pores of the tiny tough leaves of the hot country's mangroves.

In this bedazzlement of ceremony, the dust gathers higher into the atmosphere and blocks out the overall sense of single movements across the ground. The sun penetrates the haze like a torchlight, flashing over the large brown emperor gum moth *Syntherata melvilla* flying across low distant stars to another caterpillar-leaf-eaten eucalypt, and the light passes by, catches the velvety brown hues of the clumsy flying multicoloured Atlas moth with a serpent's head and body drawn on the tip of each wing that catches the glow of moonlight. She watches the single mouthless *Attacus wardi*, the largest moth she had found floundering in flight around the cemetery at night, flying from grave to grave every night in its short life of a few weeks, before it died on the same old lady's grave where the others had fallen. Her mind turns elsewhere, always falling onto a plain unadorned recollection of what contained love, hope, joy, sustenance, gutted joylessness, broken-heartedness. It was something, all she had recently left behind sitting on the empty kitchen table in the empty cemetery house, the food that would be waiting for Aboriginal Sovereignty when he returned. Or? Now unsure who she had left in her inheritance, she saw the fading image of abandonment left for

Tommyhawk, or for Widespread, in a place where someone would need to return to one day.

Only the starkness of a white whale skeleton rising up from its nest among the yellow dust-covered mangroves on the beach was seen by the sea's ancestral eyes in this place, though the old whale would never be visible to those other spirits living in the Milky Way universe of the celestial equator, where the serpent bearer *serpentrius* gripped in both hands the death of deaths.

Where was she? What do we say? What do we want?

We want the moth-er Mother?

We want the Mother.

What she doing that idle woman?

The great throng, gathering in a spellbinding politically charged upset protest movement from the capital cities of the 1970s, were travelling from near and far by the busload to become voluntary searchers on the beaches of Praiseworthy. All had only one aim in mind, and that was to find their Aboriginal Sovereignty. You can imagine that it was an ordeal, continual struggle to regain Aboriginal Sovereignty from becoming an all-round total disappointment for the world-weary thousands of Indigenous rights voluntary searchers who could not see the mother of Aboriginal Sovereignty being staunch like themselves. They chanted, *where is the mother of Aboriginal Sovereignty? Why was she hiding among the yellow-winged mangrove jezebels flying from the monsoon vine thickets and storming into the mangroves?* Meanwhile, the shadow of the yellow haze carrying its treasure of broken-winged butterflies higher in the atmosphere darkened the beaches when it picked up the collective thoughts of Praiseworthy. These worries! They were slung straight up into space, and what was now orbiting in the galaxy was about Dance, the moth-er Mother, what was she doing? Shouldn't she be helping to raise good Australian children that stayed alive, and not dead ones for other people to come to the end of the world to find floating around in the sea? *I mean, do you know how big this sea is?* It was no wonder giant death adders were being thrown at Praiseworthy from the serpent bearer up in the celestial equator when the whole universe was being earbashed about how their Aboriginal Sovereignty had gone off the rails, with so much talking up big by the mother about being traditional, while at the same time, the father with the mass of donkeys was banging on about how you needed to be the era's most ruthless entrepreneurial money-grabber.

She was making evil, effigy devils. Who were those devils anyway? All this, and more, was happening inside the illegal house of modern Praiseworthy's Native Title cemetery. Oh! The world had changed when these thousands of volunteer beach searchers said that they had seen some eerie things in their dreams – spirit mob, disguised as something else, appearing like giant puppetry, but equally, looking like her – Dance – the woman they had never seen, a Chinese spy person moving around that hearsay full-of-moths house, sending her weirdo signals in their dreams. It was purely the vision bro, in every house you saw them images – hundreds of moths clinging to the ceiling, crawling up the walls – kulibibi fellows everywhere, like dikili. Saw there also! Giant-sized ghost gum moths, flying, twisting, hula-hooping like nobody's business in the whirly wind cemetery of that big junba – ceremony mob. Kabarrbarrijbi. All types of mumu now, dancing and twisting about, jiving it up while even singing like Sam Cooke down in his Harlem heaven – *Bring him on home...Repeating that phrase over and over, singing it like a thousand times – like they was saying it to us – who you? Get out of the way for they would bring Aboriginal Sovereignty home themselves, and even like we were the strangers here in our own country. That's right. Mumu wild party, looking like they hated us. Yep! What was being said was the truth! There in the middle of a real dark night, there were things you shouldn't be able to see in pitch blackness rocking and rolling, but they just looked like plain mongrels shining like fluoro, or phosphoresceence. Some even looked like cringing crap dogs sneaking around where they shouldn't be, singing you know, singing dog language – Hello! Hello! – actually saying hello to us, instead of barking woof woof and tearing our guts out, but we just plain cut-snaked it out of those dreams after that. We refuse to have dreams in Praiseworthy.*

These searcher people who were sneaking around the cemetery in the night needed to be cross-examined by the pious churchy crowd who were asking if it was not copies of Dance dancing, that had made the horde of searchers star-crossed lovers of hers in their repeat-mode mind, *and all that you were seeing was just some other kind of illusion like these donkeys here pissing on us?*

No! No! The horde searcher people said how amazing it was to see rhythm ghost ceremonials, for you had to see it to believe how it felt like *a hot breeze had hit your skin each time those ghosts swung past you, but we were too frightened, and so we ran away in those dreams. But before we took off in our ideal dream car, we heard things too. There was wild talk blasting from the radio – real ghosts talking in the proper sense.*

Chinese, but nobody else living was in that radio, we swear true God. You can tell...

They – searcher people from all over the place – said exactly the same thing to each of the elder congregations of the hundred churches, that she – Dance – had stuffed her illegal house with effigies, and you should have seen it, more-than-life-sized puppets disguised as beautiful Asian spy butterflies instead of our spies, which was treason of their traditional law. These butterfly-lover souls were not their homeland ancestral spirits of lepidoptera. They were *hudie* in Chinese, or, *ho diep, pattampoochi, ya-a, nabi, titili, chocho,* or *kupukupu*. Those moth puppets were in the yard too, with real moths, and it was eerie to look at this new ceremony for who knows what it meant for country seeing this stuff?

The horde searcher gang marched in protest to the cemetery that night to find out why Cause and Dance were not helping on the beach with their search for their Aboriginal rights, but nobody was home in that illegal house full with those heebie-jeebies. *Nah! We could not get out of there fast enough.*

What Dance saw was something that nobody else could, and this continued to flummox the broader collectivism of the haze gaze. The woman was watching butterflies and moths swarming over the cemetery, over Praiseworthy – feasting on mangoes rotting on the trees, and flitting unnoticed over the searchers down on the beach. She never heard the searchers calling all over the cemetery, and then yelling, *Anyone at home.* She was listening to the world of hundreds of species of butterflies and moths, the butterfly country that existed in all of its fullness, if only in her mind. The world she looked at, or only wanted to see these days, was butterflies, and this was where she lived, even as she continued to live through an obligatory dialogue either with, or about, her children, and in any case, all of which could singularly be interpreted into something or other, like this: *Tommyhawk, you get yourself down to that school in Praiseworthy and show those white teachers who's got the better brains.* Or, saying to Aboriginal Sovereignty, *You stay right away from those white government crawlers for your own good, good boy, listen to what I am telling you – you should be listening to me and listening to your father. Why don't you listen to us?* Widespread contributed nothing to the talking on how to make normal human beings from sprog. It was left up to Dance to unpack the whinge, the commentary, the dialogue, the undisciplined conscience of landscape rattling away with itself, while otherwise preoccupied, until the family left the house totally confused, left to pursue the different routes of their own making – Widespread to his great vision of building a world-class donkey transport conglomerate, Aboriginal Sovereignty in search of never-ending love, Tommyhawk in his wish to leave the vicinity of the homeland for good, and she being left to pursue her vision of searching for butterflies.

This Dance was so far away in thoughts about how her family would ever survive the realities of their time, that she never saw or heard those who had been sent to fetch her to search for Aboriginal Sovereignty. You could not hear people screaming if your world was locked by thoughts that told who she was: *My name is Dance Steel. I have nothing to do with these people. My name is Dance Steel, and this is my traditional land and fuck these people who have told me to keep out of their town. My name is Dance Steel, and I never walk where I see these despicable people on the land of my children, and I do not walk on their land that should be somewhere else.* It was easy for Dance never to recognise other people, because she walked where others could not walk on the Dreaming track of moths and butterflies. She only thought of their resting places, which were her responsibility because no one else was looking after their spirit country.

Who looked more Chinese here? She was the first to scoff about who was who, with a toss of her white hair matching the colour of the mass migration of white butterflies landing in the sea, twinkling with light, faded to gum-moth bronze at sunset, before finally reverting to a red silvery tinge like a mangrove jack. She gave as good as she got while chucking around a few of her own ideas about what she called the Praiseworthy look, which she scaled in whiteness, Chinese or Aboriginal. The blend of common colonialism, even though nobody admitted ever having heard of her relatives, all her aunties and uncles, and old grandfathers, but never mind any of that, because she could easily claim the lands of Praiseworthy just as good as anyone else under the circumstances of white law-making compromised rights.

So she challenged back that everyone else belonged elsewhere – were not of the same blood as her butterfly song line, and even if they were Aboriginal, she could not recognise any of them as being Aboriginal people of Praiseworthy.

It was difficult to lure a mangrove jack, and even more impossible to drag the world of the ancestral out of its country by acts of hostility, insult and criticism. Look again! Even the resolute husband – Cause – was told time and again that he was illegally squatting on other people's cemetery and decimating traditional country, knowledge, law, culture, and society. But he was deaf too. He did not speak the same English language as other people. *You were excluded man.* People told him to his face, and letters from the Native Title bureau presented him with the judgement itself, which if you took all the fine print away, just said: *You were not blessed.* Haze people wanted him to stop lying about being the most important traditional landowner of Praiseworthy, and that he too, should move back to his own country, wherever such a place existed, because they did not know any foreign countries themselves. *Take all those donkeys and your mad wife.* But Cause just replied, *You know what? I am the Dreaming. I am the air around here. My Aboriginal Sovereignty is the lungs of this place. Get out of my way. I got a fucking business to run.*

What you talking about? Yap! Yo! We talking too – about getting rid of donkeys even if they got a cross of Jesus on the back. That's foreign business. Not for this place. We are modern twenty-first century Australian people here moving up in the world. We are not into the exporting and importing business like salespeople. We are only into becoming the Global North, and not importing anything that's going to make us look like even poorer cousins of the Global South than we are already. Exporting means minerals, pastoralism – cattle, sheep, barramundi. We are not importing anything, and especially not any donkeys that are going to make us look like the majority of the world

– like millions of poor foreign peoples from Asia, or those poor buggers, the vast majority in Europe walking around with donkeys to help them carry their load and whatnot, or South America, Africa, or the Mediterranean, or the Middle East.

5

You can tell...

The old country wrapped kinfolk like Dance Steel in its living being. Yo! Yo! You could reckon that it would be a miracle on Earth all right, to be able to see who she truly was inside the stories of country stretching into infinity, and you would never know whether she really lived in the stillness shrouding the land, or see her there, on the summer leaf that barely moves for decades, or if she was in the monstrous display of the sixty thousand lightning strikes fury of a top country storm lighting up the night. No, without imagining, you would not see her at all, just as you would not find the moth cooling itself under the brittle bark of those solemn white gum trees lining the ancient kinspeople's river. To be able to see the country in her properly, you would need the eyes of the ancestors, the ghosts, and the spirits of this place. Those that have appeared right in front of your eyes and you did not see them, and they saw nothing of you, not in their reasoning reaching far beyond the capacity of human vision, which sees only itself in memory, but never the reality, never the unconquerable breadth of ancestral knowledge.

Nobody had seen this woman beyond the grey questions of government-contrived politics, although you might have briefly seen her through imagining yourself as being elsewhere, up on a higher plane than Qantas, and have dared to feel what it would be like to look far down from up in the stars of the heavenly dome, and just for a while concentrated on the idea of migrating elsewhere, like the fallen from their homeland taking a chance on the rough seas you see heaving below, and then know how she might have felt like a butterfly taking the left turn of life, the orange and black patterned wing wanderer, or the white and black winged caper white, migrating through the hazards of faraway majestical spirit tracks to end up dying in this sea, or else, the migrant butterfly that comes and goes across the rolling ocean of the northern sea while travelling in the wind above this living ancestor, flowing on its endless journey. Who knew how a spirit mapped the migrations of fate, while Dance secretly broadcast the absolute certainty of her migration to all and sundry, of how she could not wait for the day to come when she won back legal title for her ancestral land after more than a century of hardships, of how this day could not come more quickly, and the very first thing she would do when she clutched the title of her land in her hand, would be to demand the removal of all those illegal carcasses of people she did not know, who should not have been buried on her land. This was how time stood still in the endless struggle of getting nowhere, in the lifetime wasted in all that drive and effort to keep up the bravura while the struggle goes on and on in the war without end, until all that was left of the lonely spirit, which was almost nothing at all, was an ability to see there a tiny road running off to the left. How had she missed it before, you would not have seen it at all if it was not for the reminiscences of faintly amplified voices popping up from memory to point the way – to take that road over there, and get out as quick as you can while you have the chance. This Dance, well, the dance of the times was called calamity, of never knowing whether she would ever feel safe on her land, but there was this road to another heritage.

Turning away from the floating spider-web district spun over the ceiling, Dance began searching thousands of social media networks. Where were the people smugglers on the dark web who, while dropping off boat people in Australia, might be interested in taking her family to China? She set up a Twitter account called @CheapAsPossible. Illegal people smuggler wanted for some poor Aboriginal boat people, she messaged. Pick up Praiseworthy beach ideally. Destination China. Boat smugglers people with leaky boat need not apply. Small modern-day people ark was essential for four Aboriginal people leaving country. Never to return. Don't need US C-17 Globemaster military transporter. Only genuine people smugglers need respond with non-government references, e.g. positive emojis e.g.: 👍 👍 👍.

There are always plans far too grand for all manner of people, and far too long the distance to accomplish, but not for Dance. She had dispensed with the unfortunate stockpile of her life, and now thought of nothing else except how to achieve her ultimate dream, which in a nutshell, was to remove any further interference to whatever fortunate moments of good luck she had left in her life. Dance offered a favourable description about the type of people smuggler she was seeking to take her sacred family to the new world of the greatest power on Earth. She racked her brain over how to construct the plan on the cheap, before providing the type of blurb for scouring the globe in her search of a creepy shyster. She searched to find an apt description of a low-life from the back cover of a huge book by a great poet. She then wrote on her Twitter account a message, addressed to @CheapIllegalPeopleSmuggler etc., the following statement: *Wanted people smuggler whose presence on Earth reasserted itself at a deeper level to boat people who were surprised to find themselves more chastened, more astonished, more humble*, although retrospectively, and still and nevertheless, she seriously thought that even this description might not necessarily include all of the qualities of the good human being she was truly searching for in a modern-day, hardcore people smuggler.

The living serpent of country crossed many, many tracks while following maps of its creations, and had somehow felt the urge to create the world anew while listening to Dance harp on in country, of her desire to be gone henceforth, and to travel as far away as she could get from this Praiseworthy world. You know what, she had the audacity to preach to country instead of praising its eternal gloriness – in spite of the troubles, *the place is dispensable*. Whatever! The creator of country too could move, and it began moving across the broader world in search for that ideal people smuggler that was going to take it for a ride. The melodies of travelling thoughts that Dance heard coming from the ancestral serpent's wide journeying broadened her perspective of what it meant to be in eternal movement, of travelling henceforth and so on, and she felt the infinite flow of this ancestry transforming beyond the cemetery, she felt the enormity of the long serpentine movement rushing headfirst through the ocean, the weight of country itself striking upwards, taking to the skies like a flash of lightning that crosses and re-circles the globe in repeat-mode of returning and departing, like a big hoon doing a U-ey, or a burnout of the world out on the flat.

The circumnavigational spirit quickly became a globetrotter hyped on its own kind of steroid ancestral powers, and Dance grew accustomed to the giddiness of the ancestor's spin-out view of the world happening in a flash, yet she was unable to stop the ride, to slow down and gain any reasonable perspective on her direction. She just grew increasingly more determined to keep on with the search to find the faraway visionary homeland – the China of a historical ancestor. She was becoming the China that was. Her imaginings, now unleashed upon the world, grew greater and the whole thing in her mind became inexhaustible in its demands, and in particular, that she, just a poverty woman who had never travelled from her homeland, had to reach further into the unknowable, be off the radar of the planet, all elsewhere, and sundries. She became sleep-depraved. She could no longer describe where she was in the all place, or where she was going in a monochrome world. Having lost her sense of direction, she could no longer describe how to get to the end of the road let alone to China. How would her family ever reach the new life? But, anyway, and nevertheless, all her unrequited dreams were of being elsewhere in the monochrome, which was still further than could be imaged, and she abandoned her struggles in Praiseworthy. Why worry about winning back her Native Title when she could explore the total planet on the internet? This was the superglue place to be, expanding her brain until it burst with chasing an illusion, and a ridgy-didge boat smuggler.

A sharp turn of events stuffed the lot, and threw the superglue up into the air when the nothingness in her soul became lost in its own void. Nevertheless, she hit the alarm clock and checked in with reality, where she conceded that a seeker of old culture needed to know much more about how to find the fieriest people smuggler to trust the precious cargo of her family. She required a true ferryman who treated people decently while transporting them to the brave new world of the heavenly kingdom. But the grandest of ancestral creators that normally lived in Praiseworthy, had not paused once in its mad tempest of rupture, havoc, and upheaval in its journeys around the planet to find the truest shepherd to take the family of Aboriginal Sovereignty into a new world. And then, guess what, it saw the internet! The ancestral being drew breath, paused, and you could tell it was loving the technology of the slack road. It saw beauty in this type of journeying without physical effort of continual effrontery to create vast new story lines for extending its law over all the broken planetary domain, and it would not stop pushing Dance forward in its quest to claim all ancestries, and link them all to the country's ancestral domain through virtual technology.

While the mighty live ancestor of country held Dance in an endless quest of creating tracks for the new era with modern modes of transport through flights of technology, she was in a complete frazzle from being mentally used by country to link the world together with Praiseworthy, when she really wanted to be uprooted, and plunked elsewhere in the unknown world. She wrapped her head around China, and became far too engrossed with surfing the internet to find an illegal people smuggler who wasn't a thief or an idiot, and who had never heard of the great horde of voluntary searchers down on the beach of Praiseworthy combing every grain of sand to find a trace of their Aboriginal Sovereignty. Neither she nor any people smuggler heard the noisy search people frantically calling at her door, *Anyone home?* She did not notice the salty-air-encrusted beachcombers walking through the house among the scary lungkaji policeman moth puppets that they had mistakenly thought to be Chinese spies. Strangely, she did not feel the persecution of what she called a living hell pressing against her skin, while she was too busy complaining about the cost of people smugglers these days, who thought poor Aboriginal people were millionaires by demanding thousands of US dollars paid up front, just to bring their leaky boat off the coast of Praiseworthy.

A humid eeriness saturated the internal world of the house that was enough to make your blood curdle, and this was a feeling, the searchers said, that they were being caged inside of Dance's mind. They had panicked. Cried. Screeched that loudly, they had frightened each other, and in this bedlam of screeching in each other's ears, had felt what it was like to be trapped forever in the slut woman's mind. The cold shivers were racing down their backs when they realised there was a very huge presence in the house that felt like the greatest power of country. The thing was suffocating them, they could not breathe, and its sheer bulk was blocking them from getting out of the door. And so, they said, they never had a chance to see if anyone was home other than evil, because the whole thing did not matter anymore to them. They would rather forget about feeling weird, and do all the searching for Aboriginal Sovereignty themselves, rather than being captured inside the slut's house.

Yet, in her solitude of escapism dreams, nothing was going to plan for Dance. No illegal people smuggler stepped forward. It seemed that China was not on their agenda, not the drop-off point for the world's rejected peoples. She had lost count of the number of times that she had applied for her family to be repatriated to the Republic of China, by filling in what she believed were online repatriation or asylum-seeker forms without understanding a word of Chinese, and probably not even contemplating whether she had confused the Chinese immigration officials with all the wrong answers. The cost of muddling anybody's brain cells was not her responsibility. She never received a reply. But the hopeful asylee Dance was made of much stronger ideals than nationalistic idealism and what Chinese characteristics were required to be a resident of China. Such stuff was out of the question for one of the traditional homeland who was versed in not giving up anything easily right to the struggle of the last breath. She decided to write back to the silent Chinese officials a ream of reasons why her family should be accepted as genuine Aboriginal refugees from Australia.

If you want the truth, I will tell you the truth for this was how it went...

She wrote about fearing for her family's safety by living in a ransacked homeland where they were racially persecuted by all and sundry, either consciously or non-consciously for being part Chinese. On the other side of her genetic make-up argument, she described how she was the small grey moth that flew through the sandstorm of donkeys and searchers attacking each other on the beach, and far out to sea where it hovered when it saw Aboriginal Sovereignty at war in a watery, aqua-blue sea. He was in an epic struggle with the mighty ancestral sea woman, now caught in her massive swirls, and she was pulling him further down into the depths of the sandstorm on the

490

turgent ocean floor. She, the moth-er moth, had watched the struggle down in the depths, until suddenly Aboriginal Sovereignty released himself from the water's embrace. And in one rapid movement, he shot to the surface, then skyward up from the sea while water drops billowed behind him like a sunshower, and he met the moth eye to eye, and she saw his grinning face as he reached with an outstretched arm to grab the moth in his hand, before diving back into the water like a silvery-scaled fish.

The moth returned again and again to the dance of the water dragging Aboriginal Sovereignty to the bottom of the sea with the fish, crabs, and the seaweed caught in the tumbling whorl pool, and again, the moth dragged him back to the surface. She was the respite until his downward fall, diving again, and again, the struggle back from the bottom of the ocean. This was the dance: a grey twist of clouds opening the rays of sunlight that caught the rainbow colours of the ancestral serpent's breath as it sprayed through the storyline of the time never-ending laws. This too, was her dance, the dance of the moth.

6

You can't actually hear ghosts talking on the radio. Bulwa! Kadajala! But bogey radio men were speaking in Chinese on the beach. Everyone was talking about these radio ghosts. Ghosts of the blood. In local blood. The ghosts of all sorts were in the head and there, sitting around and speaking through the radio, getting in the back of real smart minds, talking nothing but trash. All that type of bullshit talk going on. Wakada-wakada. Mungkuji then. The ghosts created plenty of heated arguments, and the voluntary searchers – the inside people, and outside people – were arguing among themselves about who should be the top boss of the search party. Should it be the modern-thinking people to say which way to look, or homeland people who let ghosts tell them what to do on country? Nobody could say how some Chinese ghosts showing up might talk politics on Australian radio, and then they argued about whether anyone in Praiseworthy would know if their ghosts were also talking in Chinese, even if they did not even know a single word of Chinese themselves?

Jidimbi what I am telling you is true, and if you don't believe me well bugger off the lot of you.

Choke on it.

Well! A modern-era person asked, *What time did you hear the Chinese ghost?*

Doesn't matter.

Let's make a note about this, build a thesis palace, so we can think about the significance of who was telling these lies later on in the middle of the next century.

One of the startled searchers who had fled the slack evil bulk blocking the cemetery, remembered hearing water splashing around in that house like a huge fish trapped in an aquarium. Or in a bowl of water. It might have been Dance taking a bath, but it sounded like evil splashing that was nothing like the sound of her, for she was worse than evil. She hides by making herself look inconspicuous like grey moths blending into the environment, such as those gum moths sitting on a piece of bark over there in the eucalyptus trees where the river flows, that cannot be seen easily, that seemed to be invisible to the eye. A mother should be the first person to be seen down on the beach helping to find Aboriginal Sovereignty. She needs to be totally visible, seen clearly as the most bereaved, and leading the grieving throngs to some kind of salvatory hope. Why doesn't anyone keep to the script? If she could sling a donkey halfway down the flat, or smash it against the walls of Parliament House in Canberra, if she chose to do something about feral donkeys, then she should be there on the beach with the rest of the modern-day ark humanity of

Praiseworthy. Was she inhuman? Gone white? Why couldn't anyone save on scoring the counterpoint? All the truth and justice about their missing Aboriginal Sovereignty will be dealt with soon enough in a courthouse, but let's not act classless like a cultureless throng down on the open beach. This was not Surfers Paradise. The great influx of Aboriginal Sovereignty protest searchers were justified in feeling fatigued and annoyed from looking at the same fruitless flat sea, but like the homeland people of Praiseworthy – the voluntary search parties of fanning ladies and fishing men – they felt it was important to keep on being hopeful by watching out for a good time whenever that might be, or to keep a hopeful thought in mind for seeing a particular type of frothiness on the beach the elders were talking about, and that may or may not have anything to do with finding Aboriginal Sovereignty. Or else, another divine ray of light would spill across the sea from the setting sun and like a miracle, light up the glowing body of the miraculous of the all times, and in spite of enduring the atrocious absence of parents, all these contrapuntal contra mundum voluntary searchers knew deeply in their heart, that their demand to have Aboriginal Sovereignty returned to them would go on forever – if necessary.

7

But these mementos of the great throng of voluntary searchers were hung out to dry with everything else – dust falling off birds' feathers, fish remains, insects, the windswept leaf and the animal that shook its fur, relations, and ghosts. Nothing easily put aside while speaking about what one knew when the weight of knowing the era was too much. A number of children had committed suicide right where the searchers now stood. Their little ghosts were everywhere, and it was unsettling the haunted beach. Even fish stayed away from the sorry

493

place. It felt like a massacre was still happening right here, and when you thought about it, it was.

All the sad thoughts of children rose up from the sand, grabbed you by the ankles, climbed up and jumped into the brain and talked to your mind about those four teenage girls who had committed suicide together, and saying, *You should not be down here on the beach talking about this. You saw girls running around on the beach when there was a waning moon. You felt for them closely. Off to a party, they sang. Migrating like swallows. Drown themselves. Hard to forget that! Then that little boy. Nice kid. He was always on the beach fishing and fishing, loved that fishing. Twelve. Another boy. Eleven. One fish totem. Another family lost a girl. All copycats, all same way. Then there was another girl. She was at a good boarding school down south. Prestigious. How lucky was that? Able to go to an expensive college, all expenses paid by the government's closing-the-gap scheme? She should have been happy? Then another kid the other day. Children going down like flies. All the boarding school children had to be brought home to keep them safe with their own parents. And still, more children. Nothing stopping them. It was like a pied piper thing, somebody's spirit coming up from the sea at night and talking rubbish to those children. Everyone saying this was another stolen generation, and no one knew the real cause of it, but Cause Steel did not make a lot of friends either when he kept saying it was Praiseworthy's own fault for being a bunch of Australian government lackeys, paid to keep their mouths shut, and not standing up for their rights.*

There was a suicide pact of ten schoolchildren but someone saved them that time. No one remembered if it was Cause Man Steel who had actually stopped the kids in time. He was out at night, down on this same beach where he had set up his own one-man night patrol with a high-beam light spinning from the top of his sedan, watching what the kids were doing in the middle of the night. This was the first time he had been accused by the shire council of being a prowler, a peeping tom. Forgot all about that time. Forget it happened. It was funny how the negative part of the mind started jumping ahead of itself in the twenty-first century, and spoke out of turn. But no one wanted to forget that old Gerry and the Pacemakers song *You'll Never Walk Alone*, playing at those funerals for children. Those thoughts were as pungent as the saltiness in the humidity, at the end of a storm...walk on in the sunset-lit sand, eyes scanning the sky where the gilded sprays rolled and sparkled off the top of waves. It was as though the children had no idea why they were deciding to leave Praiseworthy once and for all, and had left as simply as walking into the sea, and as though they were off to a party, some community incentive disco turnout to attract youth. Perhaps what becomes of memory was stilted, not the whole of reality, and what was more disturbing, the sensitivity of childhood was lost to the tighter government controls over the freedom of the Aboriginal world to define its own future. Put very simply, those children had felt the pointlessness of the new era, that there was no future. Whatever the reason, there had been no new reality dawning as far as they were concerned.

And all those mothers of the ghost children were not like Dance. They were not hiding. They were visible in their grief. And they were not like a bird that had never insulted this community. A starling singing sweetly. As the hours passed, the shadows grew longer and the whispering came closer to cover Dance in malice, speculating that maybe Dance had migrated, like a moth, and this was the reason why she was not part of the search. Or that maybe she had died, or something else had happened that prevented her from walking down to the beach like other people to volunteer her services to find Aboriginal Sovereignty.

And where was Tommyhawk? Why hadn't anybody seen the younger brother who had the misfortune to be born into a dysfunctional family? Everyone began asking if anyone had seen Tommyhawk around. Nobody had seen him, although they did not expect a fascist would commit suicide.

8

Who's this Tommyhawk? The Minister for Aboriginal Affairs was beginning to feel a bit nervy about all those weird tweets on her gold-class mobile being sent, she said, from this Tommyhawk. *Look here, this someone named Tommyhawk.* His umpteen bucketloads of texts continually appearing on her golden image. What were all these numerous text messages about? Click delete. Chuck another, click delete. She was sick of deleting messages from this same person. She should not be receiving so many unsolicited text messages. Who gave the stalker her personal mobile number anyhow? *I don't owe somebody called Tommyhawk.* Why was she being harassed? Pestered? Did anyone know how many Aboriginal people loved their minister across the country? And why did this person Tommyhawk seem to know her every movement? Could you believe this? He wanted her to adopt him. *I can tell you now that is not going to happen. I don't want to be loaded with a black child with problems.* But! Wait! He kept calling her White Mother. If she could just feel...something? There was something special about this type of adoration that buoyed her, took her up into another level of the stratosphere, and reinforced in her mind the concreteness of her government's racist policies being a real blast for Aboriginal children. She was after all, the federal government's White Mother for Aboriginal children. Then bingo, she thought more about a win-win situation, like a what – exploiter, or a reaper? Why not make something of the crop? Perhaps, she could adopt this Tommyhawk, send the RAAF bomber up north to pick him up, have her staff check him out first? See if he was the real deal.

Not just a set-up. Not an activist. Healthy! Was not going to lumber her with a crippled mind? Questions kept coming thick and fast at Parliament House. She somewhat explained how to go about the new situation, *See if the kid was not too fucked up. Don't consult anyone with legit standing in the community who claimed any authority while accusing us of nigger farming. Just get the gossip. Consult the idiots.* She was already visualising her future self, parading her Aboriginal child, the last of his tribe, across all factions of parliament, just to demonstrate how far she was prepared to go to facilitate the success of her government's emergency interventionist policies into the lives of Aboriginal people living on wretched communities across northern Australia. One success at a time. Clink! Clink! Costs a billion dollars.

9

A dust storm continued blowing in varying degrees of velocity each day as it normally did to stir up the haze dome and rattle the forty cents donation tin hanging on a gate. It was time for the windswept swallows to return home with tattered and vane-broken wing feathers from another long migratory flight. Through the storm, the swallows managed to sing a few terrific tunes while gliding in the dust that followed the traffic roaring through the streets of Praiseworthy as though there was nothing much else to do in this world.

There were still no Canberra-like stirrings to Verdi's beckoning of *Go, thought, on the wings of gold, Va, pensiero, sull'ali dorate.* Aren't no government jet plane being fuelled up and firing to go at the capital city's airport, to be seen at whatever angle the Golden Hair White Mother was going to acquire her policy-showcase black child to the public cries that it (the fascist) be inserted centre-stage in the Coat of Arms – equally between the kangaroo and the emu, hammered and screwed above the door of the Commonwealth of Australia's white palatial Parliament House. But she was on the job, even if losing the battle on behalf of Aboriginal people. She was demanding Cabinet, or what she called Cactus, release no less than an RAAF fighter jet for the greatest rescue mission on Earth, to save an Aboriginal child from cultural extinction in his northern homeland. What she was planning was beyond the pale. A step too far. She would educate the child in his culture. The Cabinet solidly argued that it was ludicrous to think the Aboriginal Affairs Ministry could use an RAAF fighter jet for the use of an Aboriginal, and that, when viewed with the greatest of margins on the other hand of politics, she was creating another stolen generation. Her colleagues were just not into a rescue operation on enemy territory like this inside domestic borders. They were not into kidnapping an Aboriginal child or greater acts of domestic terrorism, and then – think about this – collectively raising such an Aboriginal child in Parliament House was like ceding sovereignty of their own home and country, for what, or what next? The Cabinet demanded that the current Minister for Aboriginal Affairs' acts of sedition cease immediately, and she renege from the dangerous path of reckless dreamy idealism, one that was bent on destroying the total fabric of the country.

On the other hand, Aboriginal Sovereignty Steel's suicide way up there in the woop-woop haze dome country of the other kind – where the black fellows lived – was recorded for posterity in the overall figure in a category in the census – the way the bleak spirit maintained its distances, and could if required, fetch up the anomaly to slightly brush against, for a moment, the lonely complacency of the illegal nation-state's soul.

10

While Aboriginal Sovereignty Steel's body rolled in a pelagic swirl of currents, normality was resuming in Praiseworthy with every man, woman and child required by the Major Mayoral thing, the albino Ice Pick, to throw themselves back into the forward plan. There was no time to waste with what was done. Not here. Not in this place busy with putting everything right in an eternity of bad things that had happened to the people. What was still fresh on the mind of Ice Pick's mayor business of another view of the world, was how he had spent considerable time putting the whole town – young and old, babies and all – through a five-year agreement with the government by wheeling and dealing, and selling their soul and so forth, by forcing through their collective mind a totally compromised reimagining of themselves through a new retina, the one that turned a blind eye. So! Let's rejoice, and do it. It was out with the old, and in with the new, for there was real metamorphism whiffing in the air to change the butterfly continent's 'free country' personality into something else, in becoming a little master of their own region with locked doors to outsiders, and without a care in the world for those who fall by the wayside, like the old and the weak, ensuring self-preservation in the era of building crisis, and from the calamity of having idiots in charge of a global wreckage company that was rifting along like a bunch of idiots while in charge of the world's demolition from a deadly pandemic, and climate change. There was, of course, always another view of the world as a fanatical continuing paradise.

Heaven forbid, Ice Pick warned, if anyone had niggling thoughts creeping around the left-hand corner of the wall in the back of their mind every now and again. What more was there to say, if you ended up having a shitload of a bomb explode in the thought-nigglers for continuing to talk about their Aboriginal Sovereignty? Who cared what rubbish truck exposé of a colossal mess of bad thoughts they were dumping in front of the forward plan for closing all gaps in that old pipe dream of living in a fully assimilated world? You could not have ordinary people letting their stray thoughts from left field stuffing up the instrument to move into the assimilated future where you neither saw black nor white but only greyness, which was the forward plan. Nor could you let thought-nigglers do the questioning about what was normal for normal people going about their business in a world full of chasms too wide to jump, or asking themselves questions about what they thought was happening to the body of Aboriginal Sovereignty, who had been floating around at sea for a good amount of time now. Well then, no, you couldn't have these things stuffing up the future of the twenty-first century. So, listen! Ice drove around to his Ice Queens to explain *this was what was going to happen – better thinking,* which was a stupid thought since great thoughts were not even going to rise to the surface. But he knew if anyone else was given a chance to have a thought, the forward plan would be a total ruin. Tinged! Shanghaied to hell! Pinged straight into a sick gut swilling up to the eyeballs with semi-digested grease-laden dinners, a packet of crisps, a can of Coca-Cola, a packet of Minties, a Freddo frog, coalesced with a packet of smokes.

Ice knew that it was only in his dreams where the other people's bad dreams of dumping on the forward plan needed to be resolved. He knew that it was somewhere in his dreams of the middle of a night, where he needed to sit on guard on a fold-up camp chair, and wait for traitors to show up. You would catch them sneaking around, dragging their free minds behind them, stirring up their stray thoughts, pondering about whether they chose life or death, or muttering about the fate of the dead boy's body. Was he swimming with a school of silvery trevally fish? Was he living with the hammerhead sharks? Was his spirit alarmed at the touch of a fish's mouth nibbling his skin, or a shark gnawing on his rib cage where the great flocks of sea birds were splashing in and out of the sea? These were the self-glorifying thoughts he always had to push away, and those simple thoughts that a fish spirit swimming in the sky at night might point them to the final discovery of their Aboriginal Sovereignty, and let all hell loose on the forward plan, if they waited around long enough on the beach to see what would happen, instead of safely dreaming about nothing in their beds as soon as night fell over the soul of Praiseworthy.

These were times long ago, and new times for the nature of grieving. Everything was changing, and Ice Pick knew this. What pleased him was how the forward plan had been set in concrete. Nothing should crack it, for it covered all of the main contingencies, such as how much scope should anyone have to behave like an idiot when there was a future to plan? And this was why the thing foreshadowed how much more you should grieve over a broken heart than the next person, how to strike the right balance about grief? Or, how much of eternity could a people spend crying about themselves? What could you do with so much grief anyway? What else was in the engine room? Well! Do not worry. It was all in the forward plan, which was like a war plan, the hated plan. The thing with Ice was, he could not stop wondering how anyone these days could find the time for pondering loss, or for idly staring at the old sea to see if they could find the floating bodies of children when they had nothing left in the tank for any more sorrow? Not that this was the time for minding other people's business, when they were thinking about becoming non-aligned individuals, champion separatists without a cashed-up plan to pay for the revolution against a Commonwealth government-imposed nonsense plan of closing the gap to waste your life fighting about the frig all thing of it. This forward plan was the work of a far bigger champion than ordinary people. You needed a fool for the grieving business, like Cause Man Steel. He liked wasting his time by being different to everyone else. Or, his wife Dance, lost on moths. Or, the lost child, sitting in the dark place wherever Tommyhawk the fascist hid. The forward plan only had one purpose, to move the entire Aboriginal world of grief into white prosperity.

11

Ice Pick said he was sick of all this beachcombing stuff, and put a stop to the grief scene by permanently closing the beach. He sucked up some air, and shot down to the beach himself, acting all huffy and puffy, to announce the lock-out – everyone to get off the beach. Hammered the banned signs, sweated, ate some peanuts, drank a bottle of soft drink to clear his lungs, and then held up the forward plan to the illiterate beach squatters and said, *Read this, and stop grieving will you.* The voluntary searchers shed thousands of tears of protest, would not stop crying, swearing true God that they saw enraged smoke palls shooting out of his pink nostrils, and that his pink eyes had grown pinker, and it got to the point where it looked as though his eyeballs were about to explode in the sun, even though it was only sunrise at five minutes past six in the morning. They thought about this, and realised that it must have been his body radiating such enormous amounts of static electricity, even his natural white hair looked like it was being frazzled in a microwave set to cook a roast.

See this? Ice screamed to be heard over the sound of the lolling sea slurping onto the beach. He needed everyone to hear him speak clearly like an accountant about the piece of flapping paper he was holding up in the sea breeze. *See this piece of paper? That's me, you lot, what you are looking at. No not this piece of crap. You are looking at the bodily incarnate of this piece of paper. I am the Commonwealth Government of Australia's forward plan for Praiseworthy. This is what gives us our power. Figures. Multiplication. Not division. Not subtraction. Economics. Mathematics. Equations. Me! I am your multiplicator. I am this paper. No. I am not paper. I am this piece of paper. The proper power paper! Not grief. Grief isn't power. So! Go home you people and get back to working with reality.*

He had some lackeys use a bit of speed anger, like a whip cracking, to hand out copies of himself in the form of the forward plan.

Hurry up. Give 'em all a copy. Everything that breathes. He ploughed his newest expensive four-wheel-drive work vehicle through the sand behind the beachcombers trying to leave the beach with his hand flat on the horn to stir up a bit of energy in the place, to get everyone moving quicker off the banned beach, instead of dilly-dallying and moaning about having a heavy heart. *My heart is heavier than yours*, he challenged with pink eyes rolling in disgust. *What do you think having power to bring the forward plan into reality is all about – nothing, like its weight is worthless, it means nothing?* He felt as though he was choking on all the words racing to be said of what he thought all his people should know about, what the weight of this power felt like when it came with the ultimate responsibility to carry out the power of the Australian government, which felt so powerful indeed that it was like being bulldozed into the ground. No one believed him at all, for the weight they carried, even if it was made from fish and chips, felt heavier than the weight of the albino, but Ice's sermon about what the heavy weight of everyone else felt like while being carried on one's own bent back continued. The weight left the beach. There was no one left but still, Ice's words about carrying all the weight could never stop. Even the empty beach should know the weight he felt about having to question the old law business of country while all this sorry stuff was taking up so much time and making the weight heavier to carry since all the work of the era had been left entirely to him to complete. *Why me?* The heaviest heart of all in the place had not asked to be the saviour.

What Ice Pick wanted to be placed in his head, was a simple answer to his questions. He wanted somebody to tell him how come he had been relegated to be the solo think tank for everyone else? Why did he have to be the one with the hard story to tell about how he was being left high and dry to carry the load, while everybody else had decided to be a beachcomber? Why was it left to him to ask *how come you people can't help yourselves by getting hysterical and mindless about keeping your 'old world thinking' of being here forever and never giving up a thing? Put yourself in my shoes. Think real fucking hard about my responsibilities as your Major Mayor working my guts out to shape your acceptance by white Australia so we can at last all become one people under one Australian law.* It was a more major pity that he had foot-in-mouth disease, and was prone to dropping the clanger. *You know what? Assimilation will be good for you.* It was such a terrible disease, an awful contaminating virus of a thing that just would not go away. So, anyway, he created another simile as a tool of explanation to the constituency. He explained it simply, like this: *You know, when you see this piece of paper looking at you, can you say your law is the best, when all you will really be seeing is me looking at you, not just a piece of paper looking at you, because believe me, I made this paper into the very likeness of myself, but also remember too, I am not just a piece of paper, and a piece of paper is not me neither. Get that into your brain cells?*

This was how the old people were always saying that country gets lonely without its people. The sea, while looking from afar, saw the banned beach of this solemn and lonely place where even the mud crabs were gone to try their luck elsewhere, leaving behind all their ancestral ghosts of countless millennia to be born over and over in the wrong time. The sea sighed, turned its back and continued to withdraw further away from the expansion of mudflats. And you would swear the flattened sea looked like plains of glass. Then the sea swell spilt another way to the other side of the world, so this place could forever haunt itself in loneliness. And without even knowing why this was happening, unhappy ghosts flew through the gaping hole misery had made in the sky. Now, it was left to the ghost crabs to spring up from their bone-dry holes to cradle hot sand with their claws, to sprint off, back down another hole, disappearing from the glare by clawing into the soft wetness far beneath the surface, where they waited in hope, for an incoming tide. Only these spirits of country – flies, darting blue butterflies, seagulls hovering above the death-scene beach, their eyes searching for scraps of food – were the witnesses left of the death of the human soul. It had been the end of the slow death show when the people of the sea had turned away, slowly walked back to their homes, and returned to work on the forward plan. From this point on, they would strive to meet the expectation of having their lives prescribed by a set of statistics so that middle-class Canberra bureaucrats advising progress to the government for closing the statistical gap in equity, could prove that equality could be achieved through assimilating black into white culture.

At each end of town, the old country men and women returned to achieving paper goals that were and that weren't turning them into white octopuses. They knew this was not right. They also knew there should not be any margin for error in modern thinking for becoming white people, and they should not be striving to become a living treasure like an octopus of the ocean with a truly remarkable mind for understanding the fathoms. But, here they were, balancing the pretence, acting like a bunch of pseudo-modern thinkers, trending in tangents, bending the mind until it became half-baked, having a boogie-woogie whale of a time with their life tied up in a million knots to untie while carrying on, staying afloat, sometimes even having a fun win in the future decades of being in the war of the everlasting and doomed forward plan.

Now, while the dust floated more thickly in the haze dome, who had time anymore to understand eternal love, how it was created in the all times of this place? How could such a love be measured against those whose longest memory was inconsequentially shallow in comparison, and unable to recall the depth of a single dream, let alone infinity, of love created since time immemorial?

12

In the picture-book world being hotly imagined upstairs by the God government for Praiseworthy, where there were many bewildering holy pictures hanging on the wall to bewitch the soul, it was the beguiled local economists of the all times who were bothering about adding up and subtracting the nuances of eternity, albeit the forward plan. While ducking and weaving around the political sensitivities, and doing a bit of the basic cha-cha grovelling with the talk, they were just asking the simple question: *You know something Ice, what was going to happen on the scale of our ancient ceteris paribus, and all other things being considered equal in our all times, if you put too much into the light of the white right, what do you think it is actually going to cost us mob to get a coin-operated bit of electricity from the white heaven?*

Finally, they asked: *If Aboriginal Sovereignty was dead in this place, what was his death all about?* Wasn't it a privilege to be alive in the all times? They were remembering when they were custodians to the waves thundering onto the beach. Seagulls screeching in the white spray. Winds howling. And when the custodians screamed over the roar of the sea to be heard, and were demanding a Native Title court case to settle the matter, that paradise on Earth was theirs. But wasn't heaven better? they were asked. Or, would they be better off being a pack of sinners? Why should they follow the forward plan? they had asked the judge. They wanted to fight the stormy seas instead of packing their life in somebody else's plan, and demanded Aboriginal Sovereignty be given back to them. There were old people sitting around on the white plastic chairs again instead of searching the beach, who were that wild in the head, they said that if anyone came near them with another forward plan to turn them into a bunch of white octopi, they would fight it with anything, bomb it, poison it, knife it with broken glass bottles, but they weren't going to love it. No. They were not going to love anything they hated. Nor would they sleep again, or eat neither, until they reinstalled the economies of their own sovereign future by bringing the forebears of Aboriginal Sovereignty back on watch for this place.

Then it was strange, a fluttering ribbon of thought blew itself into a gale-force wind as it went through the gate in the brain which started everyone off with accusing Sovereignty Steel's father, Cause Man Steel, of murder. The man killed his son. Ice Pick choked on the madness happening while he watched Praiseworthy throwing the baby out with the bathwater so to speak, and he lamented how the forward plan was destroyed by Widespread. But, and nevertheless, someone had to be the killer, and the people who had gone totally warrakujbu crazy said quite logically, that there was no one else in Praiseworthy who was a killer. They had never seen any killers before. So! Who did it? Cause Steel killed his son. The black father killer, the John Howard image imprinted on the brain of the Australian citizenry. So why not see the phenomenon of the black killer father right under your own nose, the maddest village fool said, right in Praiseworthy?

Mayday! Mayday! Will anyone think in terms of millennia? Ripped out the lot. This scene was terrible. There were no good pictures left in the picture book. Well! You could not leave thousands of years of violent fathers there to look at. The picture must be changed. The Praiseworthy council's Ice Queens seized the day and sticky-taped the forward plan back together quicker than you could wink, because there was a killer in their midst. A plethora of Aboriginal men's conferences were being funded by the Commonwealth left, right and centre for the haze dome to be free of terror, so that all the local Aboriginal men from four years old to ninety-four, could face up to themselves, to understand why they were so vile and violent. Everything called social welfare was being thrown at the problem of tribalism, and amply reflected upon, even though in the end, as it was in the beginning, everyone knew there could only be one killer father who killed Aboriginal Sovereignty, and it was not them. A pack of old white professional anthropologists, social workers, criminal lawyers, store managers, nurses, priests, teachers, police, doctors, judges, journalists, motor mechanics, builders, road builders, casual labourers and office workers who had been studying every breath of Praiseworthy people for years and missing the light shining on their egos, were called back to town by the Major Mayor, so Ice Pick could ask them what it meant to be a violent Aboriginal man, which he was sure he was not, so he would not know what it was like to be violent, but he wanted them to tell him about other Aboriginal men, the ones they thought they knew better than themselves. Look! He did not know which ones. Do you think a Major Mayor has eyes at the back of his head? How could he see who was hiding under the radar, like Planet? There was a white-out as one by one, each of the professionals stepped up to the podium on Church Street to speak their take on the new trend dialogue about violence as recorded through their eyes while taking care of their Aboriginal people, to help prove that Cause Man Steel was the most violent man on the planet.

The defeated from imaginary kingdoms who rushed back to Praiseworthy to share their accumulated pain of wanting was impressive, mighty, and endless. The gravy train, more lucrative than pots of gold, looked broken. It was a circus. These people were a total mess. All of them, irredeemably broken. They carried mountainous internal gripes. Gaping wounds more open and salted than the Dead Sea. They were the beaten. But play on. And it was game on, for this gathering wanted to get to the root cause of this father violence theory rampant in Aboriginal culture. Let's root out evil. Destroy that violence. Let's attack the devil. Get this Widespread murderer who killed our Aboriginal Sovereignty. Say, he had just lost it, or say he was just an ape-man who killed everything in sight. But, hold on. Hush now.

Listen! You could not move for the decrepit old professionals with plenty to say rushing into the shire council building, and wanting to get to the stage first, to be the first to get everything off their chest, to spew as much misery as possible. It was like a rugby scrum with a lot of pushing and shoving to take charge of the podium, to grasp the microphone and enthusiastically screech at fever pitch their bulging bags of woes, and to take the most time to offload their life of suffering carried silently for decades, before leaving on the charter flights at the end of the day to get out of the place as quickly as humanly possible. But what can you say about truth telling? It had to be done? Firstly, there was the pain of years, the burnout from the broken wing nation, the years of suffering silently, now returned to the village square like flowing lava, to rant to their favourite black people compelled to sit through hours, excruciating hours, of long-winded analysis about themselves, explained through treasures of thought patterns gained from the sacred anthropological shrines from Stanner to Lévi-Strauss. You could cut the air with a knife, for who at the source of so much anxiety wanted to hear how they were not the type of people that the professional helper had hoped their black people would become? Nobody felt happy about the fact that they had not somehow overcome crippling poverty, that they had not shone like a beacon of hope in total despair, or were not the joy of the professional helper while still living as oppressed and robbed people. Nobody felt thrilled about this truth finding at all, while wanting to kill somebody there and then, enthusiastically, and at fever pitch.

After the exodus of white suffering from black hands, what remained in Praiseworthy were not only the general nightmares, but a more terrible feral-themed nightmare. Everyone was having them. These nightmares were mixed with the most tragic loss of a joyful soul, and being left with murderers. The bed where one slept became a feared place, a dungeon, it was hell on Earth. Sleep was the most unpleasant time of all for you could grow very tired of journeying to frightening places of the soul. You knew this would be the place you visited if you succumbed, after falling exhausted into the dreaded world of sleep. You knew where that went. So! There you were with your last thought of being carried into the recurring dream of separation from your homeland. How many different dreams can you have of becoming lost? Countless it seemed for Praiseworthy. These were the dreams floating in the night air. Was it the ancestors calling you to find your way back to the spirit land? It was no pleasure being lost in those unknown alien worlds and to encounter unparalleled terror. You were no warrior equipped to fight nightmares of the spirit. Nor a way-finder to joyfulness. Praiseworthy became this dreamscape. The place where the soul-dead always became lost, and were forever alone. Well! Nobody on Earth wanted to be lost in such a nightmare. Or, to be lying sleepless in the dead of night, waiting to find another way to become lost. Who would even care for a wink of that type of sleep, to lie in wait until the time came again, when you confronted what it felt like to be totally lost, and then, while stuck in the groove, only to hear some murderer type go plap, plap, plapping with his thongs hitting the gravel sideways in a cloud-covered starless night, where the other thing you would hear in the haze spirit dancing was yourself whispering stress stuff, like: *Shh! Listen! That's the murderer.*

This was exactly the type of idiot sound that Cause Man Steel made wherever he walked. He always walked as though he did not know how to wear thongs properly. This was when everybody realised that this was the sound made by a murderer, exactly the same sound that Widespread made while he was chasing his feral animals around the place late at night. So, of course, it did not take long to figure this out. They were the world's wisest people who knew how to put two and two together, and realised he was the devil murderer walking stupid in contemporary thongs.

Yep! There were many types of devils that knew their way to Praiseworthy, and all this questionable nocturnal behaviour of the thong man, was raising many questions and answers. There were dozens of people rushing and dodging devils in the middle of the night to get to the Major Mayor Ice Pick's major palatial house, the only house with fancy this and that, a good door, and a swimming pool. Instead of staying in their beds like proper citizens who were almost taking the road to assimilation into the white mainstream, they had felt the urge to ask Ice at two o'clock in the morning, how to go on living like this while a murderer was running loose in their lost soul? And, in the glow of moonlight in the hazy gloom, Ice's snowiness sheened back at the sleepwalkers like a vanilla ice cream ghost when he appeared on his porch to confront these constituents who claimed to be lost in a nightmare.

Ice ordered the night walkers to go home – to leave his property immediately – but they never left. They continued to sleep where they stood at the mayoral palatial front door, even though their eyes were wide open and looked frightened while the froth dribbled from their pretty wide-awake-looking mouths, vengefully spilling out the total content of what it was like to have a crippled soul – if they were really asleep, for there should be the sounds of some snoring at least from their apparently sleeping mouths, not one hundred per cent wide-open and invigorated with a terribleness that felt like thousands of spears striking Ice in that lump of clear ice pumping in his chest. This whole shattering effect of ice being split was now escalating the nightmare to fever point, where it could reach into the uncalled-for effrontery that immobilised Ice Pick on the spot. He felt as though he had been impaled on what was supposed to be his own private front door. He struggled to free himself from being hooked in space, so he could stand up straight on the ground like a real man dealing with people pretending to be walking in their sleep, so that they could dump him with a tidal wave of demented words, as though he was the public rubbish bin where you threw sticky ice cream wrappers, empty packets of chips and things like that. How many times in a day did he have to think how he could be the best mayor in the world when there were people trying to destroy him in their sleep, and all because they had failed to dream properly. Ice took his only chance at surviving other people's nightmares, by grabbing what he could from reality. He ordered his ears to only listen for hooting owls but these were silent, or seagulls squawking but none were making a sound, and he listened for barking dogs somewhere down in Church Street and other places where the nightmares were so thick that nobody heard the dogs barking outside. In this, he was victorious, and how victoriously good victory felt, to be able to ignore the sleepwalkers' complaints as he grabbed his own mind from trying to fly off with the fairies. His head rang his mantra bell, which was, *We never used to have any murderers here*. And Ice did not mind the fact, that he would have to spend the remainder of many nights listening to bizarre stories of how the haze dome was making murderers on an epical scale. He liked the main game of this developing narrative being continuously repeated and redefined, while travelling through every sequence of DNA in generations to come, and he travelled with the catastrophism that the Anthropocene haze feasted upon, and blamed it all on the murdering Widespread's donkeys.

Fancy that!

The Christmas beetle lifted its wing out of its gold case, and flew away to get some decent sleep elsewhere than at the dimly lit door.

By day the world would be seen differently, when the whole infrastructure of Church Street once again became mobilised in wide-awake prayers of the *Glory be*, to fight against bare-faced murderers of individuals, murderers of Aboriginal Sovereignty, and world murderers. They too, decided to storm the Major Mayor Ice

Pick's house so their complaints could be heard in broad daylight, that there was no future, no new era, because there were not enough Aboriginal men's sheds in Praiseworthy for all the violent men in the world to hammer some wood together to make something look nice, instead of being hands-on violent criminal kinds, and not enough steel gaols in Praiseworthy to lock up murderers, and not enough healing courses to let bygones be bygones, and not enough anthropologists to wrap up the Native Title arguments before they were murdered by their enemies.

Even Ice knew what it was like to run through – what he called – his superior mind, a few thoughts about how easy it would be to take another position, as some of the people of Praiseworthy had in the past, in the days when they had never thought of themselves as being used as a sideshow expo of violence for a desperate big government's stab at politics. But those times were a faraway memory when you knew there was another option to suit the times, like pointing the dead-easy finger at your nearest and dearest. Well! Why not? Someone had to be the scapegoat in the unsettled colonial crime involving an entire population of millions of people. And all you had to do was give it up to the donkey trapper wherever he was, the felon last seen roaming around some overgrown landscape infested with millions of fireflies where he was slowly retracing his way home with that old platinum donkey that he had spent years trying to capture. A creature so worm-riddled and life-worn that had anyhow fulfilled the impossible dream of being the prerequisite mainstay of the overall visionary transport conglomeration for the new era, simply by looking like a gleaming stainless-steel kitchen sink scrubbed cleaned with Jif.

Ice knew the scene and what happened when you thought enough about the scale of cataclysm that sat in the gut, like those in the tide of building full-bodied accusations about their favourite subject, the guilty murderer. These people of the old times were experts in finding a murderer of anything in the world, and if you truly thought about it like Ice did, anyone could see that Widespread personified everything that was manifestly out of control, right up to the level of the planet being murdered by his type of humanity. This was the type of guilt you carefully poked at the end of a long stick. The only way to catch the killer of their Aboriginal Sovereignty since the police were not locking up that real murderer.

13

Ah! The soft and dreamy moths flying far away, followed the moon running through the gleaming stars above the eternal haze of Praiseworthy. The moth-er Mother sat at home late, balancing the heart-stir see-sawing between the very best of Ben E. King, and the latest claptrap about Aboriginal people on the radio. The moths on the walls soaked up the art, the stuff she had pasted throughout the house in multiple layering consisting not of red roses *I beg your pardon*, but entirely of newspaper clippings Widespread had collected ad nauseam about the Australian government's racist intervention policies to control the lives of Aboriginal people. Perhaps moths kept up with the news of their countrymen too, by flying into the house to study the archive of hell.

We will make sure these atrocities will be remembered *for a thousand years*, Cause told his family whenever he shone his Eveready torch over the complete walls of remembrance throughout their Native Title cemetery home. He waved the torch around like it was a wandering moth, and said that he wanted to be constantly reminded about what the national cheer squads in the media were saying about his people. *Remember to have recriminations*, he warned his young sons about their future before they even knew what a future was, and while running his fingers over the juiciest pieces of outright racist slander, he whispered in a low murmur, reminding them about their responsibilities in the future world. *Here listen. Pay attention, and remember you will be living in a time when all the food you will have left to eat every day, if you are lucky, will be a few grasshoppers starving in the dust, that's if you can catch them, while you are living up to your eyeballs in a goanna carcass global warming famine catastrophe like you can't even imagine, just like the countless other millions, and I mean millions, of other poor people in the world with no fauna and flora, like the people in Madagascar are already doing, who did bugger-all to create global warming. Remember you are no different to any of the poor people on Earth and this is the reason why you have to be extra careful, always vigilant, never lose track of the bigger picture or the long view of where you are going if you want to survive.*

Don't waste your time sweating on the small things for nothing, but don't forget about the recriminations, and justice for the poor.

The speech would become quite emotional, and Planet just thinking about the future planet, would be enough to activate the power within, and it was the kind of power that would make a dam burst from an unprecedented mega-flooding, or an electrical storm massive bushfire event, when he became an overexcited colossal, a giant of a man made from a skinny ageing man who frightened the sons who still had not learnt how to talk properly when he jumped up from his chair at the kitchen table, and went searching the wallpaper with the torch again, hopping from one article to another, to find a few words that especially made his heart burn volcanically, spewing a river of lava from his mouth that made him look like a devil to his wee sons learning how to keep stoking the fire, until it grew into something resembling hellfire and brimstone while he continued on, vaguely remembering what was stored in the enormous vault containing his collected thoughts on the subtle differences in the world of racism against all Indigenous peoples, but then deciding it made no difference, a racist was a racist, and all racists were equally bad, and none were to be forgiven for destroying the planet.

He was proud that there was a black question mark hanging above their house, and pleased that he was against the stereotypical age-old dogma of *lest we forget*. There would be no forgetting in his house, he whispered to the sons now transfixed, almost hypnotised by the wavering torchlight beaming over the walls glued together by news clippings on one particular subject, racism on a grand scale. The man thought he was the world expert on the language of war, and was not interested in growing red roses, cabbages, or food for his donkeys, while telling the startled Dance that he was free-range, like a chook.

All was good and proper in the household that hated racism, and each time Dance caught another incessant broadcast of her favourite topic to fire up the anger for a good fight with the radio broadcaster some several thousands of miles away, she would eventually switch off her own internal nervous breakdown antennae that were looking pretty buggered up these days, and blocking out her imaginative world where all the racists lived, she would calmly continue counting the moths which had arrived like a storm to read the walls dedicated to memorialising racism. The whole house blazed with golden orange-wing moths flying straight to the flickering electric light bulb, the *Syntherata janetta,* and *Opodiphthera eucalypti,* pretty moths swarming in from the mangroves. The house was stirred by the pronounced eyes on the wings that seemed to be seeing what was really inside the feast of thoughts brewing on the walls in fine print. Dance moved carefully through the mass gathering of moths while trying not to injure any of the fluttering creatures pasting themselves to the newspaper walls with the thousands of pulsing wings that made the air swim in a dance.

Dance looked at the wall of moths, and just thought all this reality was happening elsewhere. This was not her news. But being left alone in the house, Dance repeatedly turned the radio on and off beside her, then turned it on again, exactly on the hour, to see if there was any news about her missing son. She sat still in the 1960s blue lounge chair that swallowed up her small frame, while not noticing how the house was swarming with moths. The daddy-long-leg spiders crawled out from under the cracks, to create vast webs over the newspaper walls to capture the moths. She continued listening to the hourly news throughout the night, while hoping she had not missed an important snippet of news about Aboriginal Sovereignty in another racist diatribe about an up-crippled-creek Aboriginal world, just so that she would remember exactly how Aboriginal Sovereignty always came home. She knew this news going around Praiseworthy about his death would make him laugh, but then, when the newsreader finished, she rose from the nest of blue vinyl, and switched the radio off. In her quest to ensure complete accuracy with what her memory was telling her, she repeated the newsreader's text word for word in her mind, and this was what she was doing in the silent kitchen – a place of worn, subdued brown dust-stained dullness where dull-coloured moths were clinging to the walls until, sensing the first hazy glow of sunrise, and following one another, they flew en masse from the house, leaving it empty at dawn.

She did not know why her eldest son had fallen in love with that girl who was his promise wife. She is only fifteen, *I told him*, and he being two years older – *you should have known better*. Why did they have to fall madly in love with each other now, and not wait until they were older? Aboriginal Sovereignty was oblivious to the lectures Cause gave the family at mealtimes about what was written on the wallpaper about Aboriginal paedophiles. He just would not see it. He was not a paedophile. Could not believe it. *Have you learnt nothing about what you needed to do to be assimilated into the mainstream world of Australia?*

No! Aboriginal Sovereignty just did not want to hear anything different to what he thought about who he was. *Stop preaching to us, Dad,* that was what he said. *Let's eat some food in peace for a change.* The boy was full of his own magic. Dance thought he flew, he moved too quickly, all you had to do was turn your back for a moment, and whoosh, gone. She smelt him now, the smell of him always lingered.

Why? Inseparable? Aboriginal Sovereignty and the girl could not be parted, so the old people agreed to leave them alone, because you know what? The schoolgirl did not want the older girls to take him. She saw them flirting with him all the time. They were doing things that schoolgirls were not supposed to know about. She went after him. Shadowed him. Would not let him out of her sight. She was his responsibility. He gave in. They were already married, and look that was it then, and even then, you could see that one day they were going to be the future of Praiseworthy. They would make things work. Leave them alone and they will be alright. Everyone said that. The old people sitting on the white plastic chairs nodded their heads in agreement. The multi-denominational wholeheartedly agreed in sermon upon sermon, *They were meant for one another those two,* and whenever anyone else happened to see those two kids together, well that was what they said too, *and that was that.* Dance remembered what people had said before her boy was accused by the police who came to their door with government orders about stopping anyone from interfering with underage children. Where was Cause? He should have been home. Why was he never there to deal with the racists?

14

What the hell! And it was a matter of hell, when the truth struck home the moment Widespread rushed through the door of the family home while screaming that he was the only man left standing on the planet who was the true law boss for this place. Now, he claimed, he arrives home and sees what is happening, there was a new law calling itself the big Silence Dreaming, and he wanted to know why this story was sitting on top of his ancestral estate.

Even though this might have been some crazy news for all, Dance wanted to know what he was doing by bursting in on the widow woman of the world's worst family who had no husband, no children, and if this was a hoax, just to cover up his guilty conscience for never being where he ought to have been in the hour of life or death of Aboriginal Sovereignty. He was dead to her. She was a widow now. Let the weight of the world fall on his back, instead of hers for a change. She had already slipped into her widow clothes of vile veiled grey to greet him at the door, when she had heard he was back. Well! It was not difficult to hear of his return. She heard the whole town screaming in the distance. They were yelling news about losing Aboriginal Sovereignty, all the voluntary workers who were now redundant and spitting about being banned from the beach, were banging iron bars across the broken-down Ford driving through Praiseworthy with a startled and frightened kitchen-sink-colour donkey stampeding in the passenger seat, staring with fearful watery eyes at the humanity eyeballing it with wild eyes and trying to pull it out of the vehicle, while Widespread was freaking out and driving like a maniac when he saw the ghosts of people he knew – all his old family mob, waving to him from the deserted beach.

It means, I am the father of Aboriginal Sovereignty, Planet roared in hoarse-throated, guttural grief when he brushed past Dance in a stampede through the house. She stood back, and watched him behave like he was an animal destined never to rise from its rage of raw screaming that poured into the home. Dance walked away in disgust. She couldn't decide whether to be shocked by the rawness, hearing him trying to strangle his lungs to the point when finally all that was left of his grief was a belated pall of silence that now seemed out of place, a shock to witness, since the season of grief had already long passed in the spiritual law of responsibility and observances. And here among the dead, she had to continue to be responsible for life, not just of her own, but of others around her.

What had he witnessed here? Should she feel anger? Seeing him like this, intruding upon the greater silence that had fallen, and now governed the house since Aboriginal Sovereignty went missing. It was this sound of nothingness that slapped her in the face while she watched the rush of soundless words pouring from a mouth still imbued with memories of the summer angels in themselves, the everlasting glue which lay at the very core of the emotional tug that kept her spellbound. Yet she had known what it felt like to be scourged by the heat of frenzied ancestors, those ensnarled in her conscience ever since the suicide of Aboriginal Sovereignty. *He's gone. Gone, I am telling you. Something happened to Aboriginal Sovereignty. He disappeared. People are saying it was the old fellow. The sea.* She glanced sideways at the ground. *He rose up – just like that, and took him. I had to identify his clothes. It was his, his, I said, but the police kept me there all day long, asking the same question. Was this his? His? His t-shirt? I guess so. I think it was his. How would I know? They asked me that over and over. I thought I knew, and I said yes. Then I wasn't sure, and I said no. Then I ended up with no idea whose bloody t-shirt it was. It could have been anyone's. I don't know what clothes he wore. I never looked at what he was wearing like I was a snake looking at him. I am a man, he would tell me. They did not believe a thing I said.*

Well! Where is he? Who? Your son. You know who? Then these stupid people wanted to know what I did with the body. They interrogated me. The police. A million questions. All like that. Like, I had done it. Can you believe it? They thought I had killed my own son. You killed him, they said that because someone told them I must have, so it must be true

then, and I said who told them lies about us, why would I want to kill
my son, what for? They made me feel like a piece of rubbish. Less than
rubbish. How did I do it? Look at me! Am I rubbish? Do you think I am
rubbish? Something just dragged out of the rubbish dump? Maybe you
were talking to the police. You are always talking to people. Can't keep
your mouth shut. Now we have really lost him this time.

Again, he thought, what had he witnessed here of what Dance did not
say in the hours that followed his return home? He was doing what
he normally did to continue destiny, to continue living until the end,
when he was dead. He takes care of the practical realities of life. He
must care for this life, the one from which Dance had already departed.
He did know where she was in the scheme of things. He spends most
of the night housing the platinum donkey amidst the destruction
of his vision, and wonders what else he could have said, when there
was nothing to be said. What becomes of the future? How could he
describe a visionless future? She had not said that she didn't have the
ability to hear humanity anymore, could no longer listen to any of its
joys, laughter, sorrow, sadness, the hopelessness of those trapped like
prisoners in a long war of invisibility in their realities.

A soul simply disappeared. A soul refused to hear what another
person said for the rest of eternity. Was this a loss? Would it seem
insane even, if the world could no longer hear a sound falling within
the range of a human voice, losing whatever this voice had to say in
its fading away from country, mountains, rivers, the trees, plants,
animals living in holes, sea, bush, the plains country, or in other
words, from where human speech was becoming too low to be heard,
inaudible to anything else existing on the planet. Neither Dance nor
Widespread could say if this was the case for the other. Any soul could
lose its ability to hear the drama of human life in another, and it felt
to Dance as though she had lost her soul on that day of the police

interrogation. What she did not say, what was left of herself, the lonely shield, guarding emptiness, nothingness.

She did not say, and it was not important for her to say what could be heard of joy, since joyfulness was hardly the remembered realm in the greater marriage, and what weighed and balanced, she knew, was only her personal opinion. It was not important enough for her to say what joy was found elsewhere, the faraway higher range of sound frequencies heard by moths. Nor would she say what else she knew of the marriage, since if butterflies wished to communicate it in their flight, or in the trail of life's minutiae, it was already spoken through the ancient spiritual law of country since the beginning of time. And she did not say that moths lived in far more heavily populated and experienced worlds, even if at a gentler moving pace in the hectic road of survival.

Shh! Why listen to Dance speak in this day and age? She could not say, but felt it would be far more important to be tuned elsewhere, listening to the higher frequencies of a moth communicating at say 300 kilohertz, instead of the human range of fifteen kilohertz. She could say what a moth sang, while listening to their ghost ceremonies of journeying from the time plants began flowering millions of years ago. What she was listening to, was the changing eras of old ceremonies of flight dancing, where the prophesies were continually guiding their survival into the future changes of country.

When darkness fell, she slipped away through the donkey yards, and almost flew, away she went on another of her solitary journeys, to a faraway vine forest to find the gathering of millions of moths in flight, flying together, or separately, from one vine-entangled ancient eucalyptus, rivergum or paperbark, to the next. This was where the large brown-winged emperor gum tree moth was nestling under the bark, not far from where it had broken out of the cocoon it had lived in for a decade, lovingly cradled in the breath of old gum trees, and perhaps sensing something else, the travelling song humming across the country, of newly hatched ghost moths that had left behind vast fields of thousands of empty pupae shells protruding from the ground before flying across the starry sky canopy in a single ceremony. There, once back on the ground while resting their wings, whispering about being *Noctuidae*, of the smorgasbord of colour and patterns on each other's wings, and reading the story board of evolution in the orange, yellow, mauve in the old lady moths' night-raiding, nibbling on overripe fruit, for the granny's cloak moths could be seen flying in circles against the counter-clockwise flight of the four o'clock moths, and so many others that looked like flying leaf-litter landing in the dusty, ancient tangling of drooping vines, where vibrating wings were whispering through the moonlight hours.

15

A raid on the house.

Sirens rang in the sky.

Those local ancestral angels singing *weee-wooo*.

Where would Widespread find Aboriginal Sovereignty?

Who was to say?

The moth-er had left behind a total house rage. Cause could not break enough stuff. He would force Dance to feel what he felt, because he never saw what she felt. Yes, perhaps he thought about making her feel more pain, a greater raging than his, far more then he felt possible of unequalled, unsurpassable grief. So, he went on breaking stuff and smashing whatever was in sight, upturned the furniture and guess what? Nope, Aboriginal Sovereignty was not there. He bashed the walls down, the shrine of racism, and again, found nothing, because nothing as huge as worldwide racism hid in the cracks of timber, or under sheets of iron. He broke every piece of furniture in the search of his home, smashed it to bits, not just to find their lost lives, or memories, or just to bring back another time, but for something else, the brokenness circling in the crush of what was already broken, crippled, and undefendable, himself.

And then, suddenly he stopped the wrecking, as though he stood in the open space, and remembered something. If it was a reprieve for the wrecked house, a disaster zone, the sight of it caused him not to groan in pain, or laugh with relief, but only to fall silent. He noticed Dance. She was still standing in the same place, where a wall had stood for years and had always looked the same until minutes ago, and still, he had not realised that she no longer needed a wall to protect her, if she fell, if she became caught in his war with the world to find his son. What else was missing, because Cause did remember something, perhaps what he had really been searching for, and then he grabbed it in his fist, the passing thought of what had happened earlier while he was walking home, after the police had finished interrogating him about where he had been all these months, and if he had done something to Aboriginal Sovereignty.

He remembered warning Dance about what he had heard on the way home, of how it seemed as though someone was actually trying to give him a message from the dead world, almost like a God man was wanting to give him the answer, giving him a gut feeling blackfella way, by pointing him in the right direction so to speak. *You know who that was? It was Elvis Presley himself, a god from our times. You want to know what he was singing? He was singing, 'Devil in Disguise'. You want to know what I thought when I heard that? Tommyhawk? Where is the fascist? I am not saying anything, but I think I will kill him when I see him, I will not be able to help myself. Should have done it the day he was born. You should have done it. Keep him away from me from now on Dance, or I think I will murder him because I will only be seeing the devil there in front of me. He's all yours now.*

Whoosh! More wind blew, or, it was like that, felt from the flutter of a moth. How sweet it would be, if one could read a story written on the wings of that moth stirring the breeze while flying in the moonlight. Dance said nothing about the lost home while reading the unfathomable or innumerable messages held in the billions of microscopic scales stacked like sets of roof tiles on the wings of the moth. She watched this flight of the immeasurable, of a holy epistle, a moth's map of time, reading the text through the light waves hitting and bouncing off the ridges, ditches, the rivers and crossings contained in each scale. Country always tells its people that there are endless ways of reading its world, depending on whether you are a moth, a butterfly, a dragonfly, a mountain chain, the sea, a river, moon, or stars, or the atmosphere itself. The story was always about sanctity, the sacredness of country.

Dance sat prone-like in the rubble, a statue on her throne, the old blue vinyl lounge chair, where she could still clearly see the sanctuary of her world, as she had surveyed her home countless times. She saw through the house, dwarfed by the scheme of how her life was being played out, and continued her gaze across the open space outside the missing windows, taking away all that was familiar of the world of her husband's grand schemes. It was way past that now. The space collapsed, blurring time into nothingness. She looked further into the stillness in the evening glow of the cemetery's flat lands, glimmering with large crucifixes, statues of broken-winged angels, the Virgin Mary, mounds of freshly dug graves, plastic flowers, tinsel and Christmas decorations lit by scores of flickering solar-powered white lights. While in this flicker of hauling up from the depth a life's baggage to the surface, the stuff of what had already passed by, she saw in a metaphorical sense, that the crumbling roof had long ago collapsed and killed both Cause and herself. She reviewed the scene repeating itself, and in that instance, saw how they were already dead, dead to each other, dead to themselves. They were already dust swirling in the haze tower, the dome growing denser and higher into the atmosphere. Beyond this, she saw oblivion, no obstacles in the path to the horizon, and this was where she caught a movement that violated the sacredness of this quiet moment of contemplation. It was just a flash, something moved, but still enough to know who it was running helter-skelter in the hazy gleaming far away captured by the full moon. The other son. The younger brother. Tommyhawk Steel running for his eight-year-old life right across the empty space.

What are we going to do with him gone? She knew this was what Cause meant to say, when he suddenly came into the room that no longer existed, and stood voiceless before her. Her view of Tommyhawk was now blocked, and she sunk further into the sea-coloured vinyl lounge while his brokenness burst from utter silence into a sixty thousand lightning-strike storm of thunderclaps spoken by the ancestors, and she watched him planting his accumulated grief in the raw tilling of the outpouring, sees him drag from his gut each fat seed, drop it with a bang, and cover it with his foot, to let it grow in the muddy open trench. Bang: *It should have been me.* Bang: *How can I go on now?* Bang, bang: *Nothing to live for.* Et cetera: *I can't cope without our Aboriginal Sovereignty. I want to go back up there and kill all those bastard cops. I want to kill everybody. You watch me.* He finally stopped, turned, left the house, went into the cemetery, and desecrated graves, hauled up the holy paraphernalia of statues and crucifixes, the plastic flowers and fairy lights, the bones too if he could have dug deep enough while busy hurling the lot across the dry earth, and he kept on hurling until all of his grief left his body, when it jumped to the other side of the fence.

The puzzled donkey stock – the hundreds of what had been similar-looking silvery-grey donkeys, all that were left and mostly injured by fighting with the people of Praiseworthy on the beach, now looking like the colour of old stained kitchen sinks – ran around the cemetery in a braying racket. This song went on for hours in some kind of ceremony from God knows where, while Dance captured them and locked them away in their pens. The old platinum donkey lay flat on the ground fast asleep with a smile on its lips.

After his regard was shown in the wielding of a crowbar, Widespread retreated into his silent dreaming, the faraway place in his brain where he created the hard yards. And it was hard hearing the silence of the Australian bushland in the summer time broken by a crowbar, when nothing much created sounds except the piercing cry of a bird, or the call of an animal, or the sound of a snapping twig, and it was much the same around Praiseworthy, where people only spoke in whispering now that their Aboriginal Sovereignty was gone, while saying, *Great news, the murderer is back.*

This was how great news spread, while people in Praiseworthy went about their business of discussing among themselves about what had to be done to finalise the death now that Cause Man Steel, the killer father, had returned. It felt as though the news itself had created days of suffocation by heavy humidity, when the whole town said it could not breathe, all the oxygen had been sucked right out of the air from the precise moment of the return of the killer in the midst of all the better people, when Praiseworthy felt obliged to pronounce that Aboriginal Sovereignty Steel was officially dead.

It was hard to catch your breath in the stultifying haze dome. Wherever you turned, you would see people gasping for the same bit of oxygen. Children collapsed in the classroom, out on the streets, down on the beaches, dazed and lost in the airless bush, panicking parents slouching around on foot breathless, or driving up and down looking for kids to apply mouth-to-mouth resuscitation to. That was the trouble with global warming already striking one of the world's all times people's hottest place. There was big-time panic. There was mayhem, and all the conjuring to bring back the dead could not be conquered by the obsessed in either liturgy, or lethargy. In this catastrophe-collapsing world, even the birds struggled to stay in the air. You had to watch out for the bigger birds, lungs saturated with dust like vacuum bags, dropping out of the sky like bombs. Breathless, the little birds began to fly lower until they could only make it to a few centimetres above the ground, disturbing the dust with their wing beats. This was serious business for the world of the creators of country, when you saw rats gnawing the hard earth trying to draw air, and the old bush animals slinking belly to the ground, breathing the dust, futilely searching for a hole in which to bury themselves.

When it got to this, there was barely a soul in Praiseworthy who could breathe properly for the prescribed minute of official silence in remembrance of Aboriginal Sovereignty. Everyone choked instead, in a day of particularly heavy dust clouding the atmosphere in the haze dome. The ancient people looked at the dust being pumped out of the guts of country, and said this was happening because the haze was crying, and this was the most unnerving thing of all for them to see in their old age, not good at all to see the spirit of country shedding tears of dust. This type of grieving for Aboriginal Sovereignty was becoming worse, with tons of dust generated on a daily basis from the skin of the ancestral settling on the skin of the living. But this trifle was not going to stop the obsession with the mourning business firing on and on in a vapoury plume signifying the enormous, unprecedented nature of the greatest loss, the loss of morality, the words left after the loss of futility.

Everyone was going to die – right, sometime, and Planet, after turning his back to all else, told the platinum donkey, *At least you are not dead.* He ordered the donkey to get up from the ground and stop acting depressed, and to start acting like the mask-head of a transport conglomerate. He needed it to stand up straight, with alacrity, and act like a leader that knew how to trudge onwards and forever more, through the era of the burning planet.

But, first of all, Widespread said, *I am going to help you to steal back your conscience*, just as he claimed to have stolen his black conscience back from being the property of the Commonwealth Government. He told the donkey it had better get ready for plenty of action with its new status of belonging to his Native Title country. Widespread said he was going to dream it into his traditional country. *You are going to be inside Aboriginal law. I am putting you there. Same thing, for all you donkeys. You are going to be sitting beside my story. My law. Yep! I am changing all your foreign ceremony, the lot, since anyhow, the universal story will end up where it began, with Aboriginal law. I am doing it. Putting an end to the past couple of centuries of you mob of donkeys being treated like an outsider, or a pest, and being treated as though you are nothing more than some unwanted feral creature that don't belong on this land. Who's to say*, Widespread claimed, while the seriousness on his face deepened its sun lines into a network of north country rivers as he reflected on his power to reorder the all times, *Yep! Who is to say that you are the invader, when the real invaders brought you mob here in the first place like slaves, and against your will?*

The sun kept shining more brightly and all the land grew hotter without any human abatement to lessen the overheating world, and in the sun's constant attempts to penetrate the dust haze with even greater heatwaves laced with lightning and thunder, the platinum donkey eventually rose from the inferno of baking ground. It raised itself, stood upright and straight, and demonstrated with a strut and a fast gallop around the cemetery, that it was full of enthusiasm for Widespread's plan of incorporating all feral donkeys into his laws for the transport conglomerate. After hours of shaking off the dust, the donkey was full of a silvery sheen, a picture of Hollywood glory that demonstrated the kind of herculean confidence required for saving the world of Widespread's vision from going under, for it was ready to hit the road running. Its inquisitiveness had gotten the better of its own inherent incapacity for success. What you were looking at now was a donkey of the type of resilience that could match anything an overheated world threw at it, without any human intervention, because it knew in its total being that it was capable of surviving by itself thank you very much in the roughest conditions – extreme heat, bugger-all food, and barely a drop of water. Done that! It had already built itself to be ready for global warming as though it had predicted this would happen, and because it knew what man was, a useless denying destroyer of all that was good in the world. Who knows why it would actually want to know more about the bravery of black consciousness by agreeing to become a mask-head beast of burden for a transport conglomeration run by a nut-case human like Widespread?

But the clapped-out old donkey was rejuvenated, and you could say it had been reborn, for it looked as though the ancestors had come along and groomed it into absolute rocket-ship metallic condition. It shone like newly minted silver. You could have fired it to Mars, or any of the planets. It looked out of place in the decrepit donkey stables in the cemetery and should have been stabled on a rocket launch pad at Cape Canaveral if you looked at the way it stood fit and ready to prance at the world with flaring nostrils in readiness to fight the climate war, and too eager in its stance of biting at the bit to be ahead of everything else in its path of flight. Perhaps it had hung around with Planet too long on those isolated dirt roads of the back and beyond, and the way this donkey fellow was acting was all show, this king for wars had lost its natural wisdom, but these were the times of climate emergency, of facing up to being in the era of uncertainty, for the donkey kind to take over the fightback operations of the vision to survive, since it was still smart enough to know that it could trust someone like Widespread only so far. Yet the donkey's curiosity knew no bounds, and it wanted

Widespread to speak more about breaking shackles with the false narratives of either the real gods or the fake gods. Detail. Detail. Planet complained that the donkey was up itself. How could you tell which was which if some gods looked like black people, and some were white, or brown-skinned, or some were complete animals, and others had almost zero appearance in those multiple gyrating hula-hooping waves of hallucination.

The platinum donkey grew more shiny silver, and now it took on the colour of a faraway star, and all it wanted to see was the faceless imitation gods that infested the Commonwealth Government that Widespread himself had said thought they were the only gods on Earth. So! What else was fake, and where was real? Its inquisitive energy grew further away from the fakery, and into an inquisition about what was actually holy on Earth. Which of these multiple gods had made the donkey a beast of burden for its saviour? How would you ask something of a god? Demur! A flower is a god? A sick baby animal is a messiah? A huge storm cell, swirling crazily in the upper atmospheric of heaven, was a god too. Air is a god. Dust. Haze. All gods. The silver donkey now behaved like it was more than a native research animal, but a messiah among messiahs of ancient law and story, and of being country – a messiah of its own domain. Naturally, it wanted Widespread to show it some of those Commonwealth Government plans for eradicating feral donkeys with bullets shot from high-powered rifles from helicopters flying over the inland, or by more powerful means of eradication by sterilisation. This messiah did not like the plan of pretend gods with those false narratives to squash other stronger or lesser narratives, and it said so. It wanted its job of being mask-head to the transport conglomerate to be bigger than a Commonwealth government – that was only an elusive thing – and would be aiming to reinstall an Earth Government for the caretakers of the great creators of country, that was the real

531

narrative the donkey hawked like a proper countryman, the story of Aboriginal Sovereignty.

The donkey, built like a thousand battleships, asked if pretend gods would be exposed by the real gods of the Earth Government, which was the Earth itself? Would those ancestral creation spirits of country change the planetary era from one thing to another? Or was it already happening when living spiritual beings flung themselves with purpose and intent across a forest of giant mountain trees and broke them apart like match sticks? Or, when seas roar? Or, rain stopped? Or, floods destroyed entire countries? What happens when ancestors re-create? How do you become trained to imagine the powerfulness of other living beings, and to read the many depths of history in the ancestral stories? These were the many questions that the platinum donkey had to ask Planet, before dignifying its glossy platinum-ness as the ultimate mask-head of a global warming era conglomerate transport industry.

16

But...

While hearts were pounding to say, *please, please say that Aboriginal Sovereignty is not dead, tell me it is not true,* the drumbeat was not answered, the conch shell call went unheard, the travelling ancestors returned empty-handed.

A waning moon still hangs overtime in the middle of the day.

Scores of stars fall from the sky each night.

Take it away, take this grief of the people away.

Nobody wanted to touch that limp t-shirt dragged in from the sea.

Aboriginal Sovereignty's poor limp body, all seventeen years in the making, a man in the eyes of his law frankly speaking, could easily have been pulled out of the faraway ocean directly north of

Praiseworthy, and flicked onto a cargo ship travelling on a busy international shipping lane.

Did the sky ancestors wait while hovering in the heavy clouds far at sea, and see the many failed attempts of the fishing men throwing themselves into heaving waves with recklessness and shocked minds to retrieve the body before it disappeared altogether?

These old ghostly-looking fishing men who belonged to the sea country, were following a glimpse, which they spoke about endlessly to remind each other of what was seen in a momentary glance hours before. They had been doing this for hours, busily casting nets in the shallows, searching where nothing greater than an unexpected translucence had last been seen floating beyond the breakwaters. They were looking for another glimpse of waterlogged skin, knew it was human skin, and trained their eyes to catch the translucence the colour of mother of pearl, thinking that perhaps they were longing the wrong way to find a glimpse of life that wanted to belong in the wondrous sea country of silver fish, making itself impossible to distinguish in the dazzling multitudinous iridescence of rolling waves heaving with tiny pearly shells.

Only the t-shirt, a relic too sacred for normal mortals to touch, remained on the beach where it was guarded by the ancestors. The proof of death, the white sodden rag, lay forever in a clump on the sand. It was washed over by the incoming tide that brought more sand, shells, and seaweed to burrow in its folds, while on the outgoing tide, the sand crabs came by to pluck off the colonising microscopic life, and set to work reorganising the structural fabric of the little temple the sea had built in the sand.

The humidifying stillness in the air would only be broken with the unrestrained screaming and yelling all along the prohibited beach that poured from cars driving away at breakneck from the changing spooky scene of the crab-altered t-shirt relic seen from a distance, through binoculars, to see what was happening to this most precious sacred site. A pitying grief also came from deep within the lungs of the nostalgic people longing to go to the prohibited beach, who happened to be walking by to see what had changed to the t-shirt clumped with sand, and when they saw that it had moved closer, towards Praiseworthy, they ran off, hobbling with their pile of grief, or they ran down the footpath screaming – *get away from me* – and brought this never-ending grief news back to every home in the community.

These tender memories of Aboriginal Sovereignty's new life as a t-shirt spread like fast wind throughout the super shire of Praiseworthy, and nobody knew what to make of a sacred site moving closer towards them, and what would happen if the wet season came again, what would spring out of the ground in the sun shining through the haze.

Then, those fishing men who had thrown themselves at the waves with their lines of nets in the open water, said that they saw tears as he slipped away from their arms, reaching to grab his body in the boiling water.

It was claimed he had been crying, because they could still feel the moisture of Sovereignty's tears on their skin, long after their bodies had dried.

17

What did it matter who thought what? The people of Praiseworthy were generally straight-talking people, who spoke to one another at the rat-a-tat-tat breakneck speed of the local vocal music. It was all the way with one hundred per cent honesty, and for good measure, heart-raising thumping with five thousand per cent emotion. While others may have thought silence spoke louder than words, there were many in this world who could go on about something bothering their mind for days, and then, when they created a human earthquake, shake the life out of the culture, and not shut up about having to bury the t-shirt without a body.

These memorials grew into a symphony of raw grief endlessly poured into dozens of microphones electrified with kilometres of power cords tangled like snakes throughout Church Street, and amplified to the max through tinny triple-bass loudspeakers. This song ceremony went on for days and the pervasiveness of the loud humming sound with the drumming of pigeons engulfed the environment, and penetrated the soul of everything, where even the ants, birds, fish, beetles, butterflies, lizards, a stray dog, a pussycat, a passing cloud, and even a single breeze, lay down on the spot as though paralysed by the loss that could not be overcome in the crying land.

These Aboriginal Sovereignty people refused to talk about anything else, and throughout the accusing dramatisations, and name-calling about those murdering parents living illegally down at the cemetery, they spared no English syllable in the one-dimensional positioning of blame a long way from themselves. No spanner in the works here. Nothing was going to shift the direction of their precious thoughts, even though, everyone knew Aboriginal Sovereignty had died of a broken heart – *that's what happened*.

That was what had killed him.

Yo! If you looked around the big-ticket underbelly of shrilly-dilly blame-calling, nothing seemed to be how it looked, and only a foolish person would believe that Praiseworthy was a place for making jokes that you did not take seriously. For one thing, look at the renewal. The results already in. A forward plan doing its job. This town was practically brand new, a model, a reconciliation wonder, built into a modern-thinking people's ark for carrying the all times over the proverbial waves, the tsunamis, through the mud of a receding sea, a desert, or rising seas travelling a thousand kilometres inland. The ark would do its job, and carry you into the era. It was the glory of the vision. The thing that equals paradise. This was what Ice said. He had always claimed the dream was *an ark, a floating dream – freed of tragedies, sailing over the top, cannon-balling bad things until they were dead meat, like what you do if you bring a cat, feral donkey, or feral anything like thought into the place because what you do, you kill it so you don't have any problems*. Ice stacked this louder word with a superior communication system well-strung and multiplied through Praiseworthy for mantra-ing: *You need to score. Forget all this major grieving. Grab life like it was your one last chance for escaping over the rippling waters infinitely catching the oratories in their eddies, get on this ark, start paddling the rapids gathering thoughts in the flow, navigate yourself through the sovereign brain estuaries flooding the mind of country. Forget the endless memorial, the nexus in the head, this never-to-be-settled-ever-in-many-lifetimes type of disagreement, stop saying we are never forgetting this century, or the last, or the one before that.*

Ice Pick was just like any other dictator in the world who liked to control people. But Praiseworthy people said he might be of use if his heat was freaky red. Phenomenal. Madder than white heat. A Fahrenheit furnace-blower. Even the engine of his latest four-wheel-drive vehicle disrespected him, and overheated whenever his burning body of white anger sat in it, when he took the memory of the golden beetle, as he often did, while driving around, to watch the minutiae of the now daily processions carrying the faithful heading north, making their way to the banned beach in cars or on foot, and with them, carrying mail-order bunches of brightly coloured plastic lilies, lilacs, sweet peas, roses, religious statues, solar lights and solar-powered candles for the imaginary grave of Aboriginal Sovereignty's t-shirt, the stuff that had arrived in big cardboard boxes on the freight plane or a barge, then lay around for days at the post office like wasted lazy dollars, waiting to be picked up from the floor, and in the meanwhile, had ended up clogging the corridor of the nerve centre of the ark, the mighty flash and not cheap administration offices, where people like Ice kept tripping over the stuff parked in the hallway, in what should have been a nice salubrious walk to get into his flatly controlled fifteen degrees Celsius cost-a-fortune air-conditioned Major Mayoral council office.

You can't knock any of these eventualities that could siphon off a bit of luck, but this Ice Pick was a magnanimous mayor of officially recognised major capacities. The pink man did not worry much about tripping over a pile of cardboard boxes containing a few plastic flowers. He had bigger worries on his mind in the role of his life, of being the major influencer of the place. This was how he preferred to see himself. Like? Someone who did not complain about tripping over anything, like a clumsy idiot who did not know where he was going.

All Ice Pick hoped for, was that he could keep the sharks out of reach of the tidal wave place in his mind where the secrets of his success rolled, stacked, and fell in the surf, and were taken back to sea. The last thing he wanted in a place full of probers, the ten-seconds boners of fish slapping the fillets onto the scales to see how much juice they had actually scored, or the unofficial world record holders of butchering cattle quicker than any other people on Earth, these people now, to start shining the light too closely into where he was coming from, to start thinking about his rock-solid background in acts of total self-compassion from walking in the shallows of his head, and shit, for it was all shallow, and there, only discovering his total immunity to morality, where his immorality weighed less than the slightest degree of fidelity to their one hundred per cent total world of Aboriginal Sovereignty. He had done what he had to do, while riding any government gift horse to get where he was in life. Who in hell cared if he maintained his own line in the sand on which side of his heart he kept his personal rights? He rode his own crazy horse. The horse was only a humble brand-new Toyota four-wheel drive, that could have been a Range Rover which was his preferred choice, or even a dream Mercedes-Benz G-Class which was also not cheap, but, by deliberately scraping the gloss off himself, just to show he was really one of the mob, he had chosen slightly less. This was his own genuine veracity of pretence, choosing a cheap tin bucket in the manufacturing of progress, to demonstrate his total humility to the common vision of his people in a challenging moment, rather than driving around in an expensive set of wheels, and by doing so, proving that he scarcely thought much of himself at all.

Headspace was everything, where it was at, and Ice Pick was not only obsessing about the funeral processions marching down to the cemetery on a daily basis for nothing. He was interested in seeing who was not supporting the local economy by not spending in Praiseworthy. Who was ordering elaborate flower wreaths and other fancy whatnot – holy statues, solar-light fripperies – in the recent online shopping blitz in the time of a global pandemic.

Most of all, Ice wanted his people to stop crying about losing things all the time, developing into a pack of emotional people. He thought, while looking at more truckloads of artificial flowers going to the cemetery, that his people were totally lost. They were only thinking of themselves, and not looking at the bigger picture of becoming normal, like colonised people. Join the rat-race. Get into mining and non-renewable resource extraction. Go and bugger the planet up like everyone else. Why were his people not thinking about how they were clogging up the important cargo ships in Shanghai, stalled bumper to bumper in the mouth of the Yangtze River? Didn't his people know anything about prioritising international cargo during a dive in the world economy from the pandemic? That international cargo needed to be prioritised. Carry more important stuff to keep the world tick-tocking along in a streamlined way, rather than this junk, all the plastic flowers in the world being piled up in thousands of shipping containers, held up on world wharves, instead of having stevedores cart important medicine and technology to get rid of the virus. He mandated his people to sit still for a half an hour and listen to the seven o'clock evening news to educate themselves in worldly matters. He did not care if they grumbled about being poverty people who could not afford batteries or electricity to run a TV or a radio, to hear about the backlog of containers on the world's busiest wharfs, where even Australian iron ore was sitting on the docks of God knows where, languishing when it should be feeding the world economy? He thought, you know, that every bit of worldly education counts in the world crisis, and that it was entirely up to the individual to stop the pressure on the liveability of the era, by not ordering online plastic flowers to be shipped thousands of miles across the sea to Praiseworthy. Yes, Ice was the main man who thought it was only admirable for his people still suffering multiple intergenerational effects of oppression, to help ease the pressure of the worldwide pandemic by not ordering more plastic flowers from overseas and crashing the global economy forever. What more does he want then? What about everybody living like Praiseworthy mob, what would the world be then? Ice formulated a lot of questions for everyone about their behaviour. Let them be busy with their conscience, about what was going on in the sub-conscience, and to leave his alone. How else was he to keep the model ark, a model?

There was only one trouble with his idea of excellence in accountancy, which did not match other people's excellent view of themselves on this matter. They thought his kind of accountability pedagogy made them feel sick in the stomach, and he should apply the same personal high standard of being accountable to the world, in the strictest pedagogy of who he was himself, which was much less than what they felt of themselves. This cheeky feedback found in the suggestion box made him hell-bent gung-ho mad, and drove him into becoming his own personal private detective on the lot – whatever it took, by setting stricter standards than a Canberra bureaucrat on auditing, accountancy, fact-finding, his own even higher standard of laws of thought, logic, probabilities, and possibilities for his people. There would be nothing fuzzy about who Ice Pick could become in a flash. He too could be the world champion fish-boner or butcher, fleshing out more crime in Praiseworthy than could be ticked off in all the episodes on ABC TV of *Midsomer Murders*. By now, while sick of the sight of plastic flowers in his hallway, he was using his own unique methods for suspecting who would commit a crime long before the actual crime was identifiable and committed, and he personally would be the decider, of who to chuck in gaol as murderers, child molesters, terrorists, drunks, radicals, liars, or in other words, all these violent types of crimes which he would sort out simply by intuition, by just having a feeling, a hunch, that he was right on the knocker about righteousness, to maintain the gold-standard credibility of self, the unmeasurable right to dwell in the model ark of Praiseworthy.

Whatever was happening about a burial on the prohibited beach where the plastic flowers and solar lights and statues were mounting up like the Himalayas, where you could hear the ghosts wailing in the gales roaring through imaginary chasms and mountainous valleys, while the mourners cried even more emotionally, carrying more plastic flowers to the grave of the t-shirt, you could say Ice had better things burdening his mind that he would rather deal with than all this fakery. His radar, in rocket-launch mode, pointed directly to what Widespread was doing about the feral donkey plague. Nothing! He would rather think about how this local plague was the worst thing on Earth staring him in the face at the moment, than about the criminal nature of his people ordering plastic flowers online in a time of crisis, and which all in all could have been easily imagined in his bed while fast asleep and dreaming about nothing. What joy could a political man like Ice get from doing what he liked, when he was able to read every single thought in Praiseworthy like a book he had owned forever? He had incorporated the lesser fortune of their world on the outskirts of his greater fortune real close, in a library of biographies written in shape-shifting lines and contours on the palm of his hand which resembled a live-wire act of balancing boredom, or falling into the chasm of his death.

Where was the surprise in life, if this beach was just a beach? If you asked Ice, he would tell you himself that it was hard to live in a world where there were no surprises. And he pursued potential surprises like there was no tomorrow. He already knew the composition of the daily procession of grievers heading to the beach. The mayoral business knew those who would be there on any given day, like the chief grievers of the multiple churches who thought they were better than the mayor of the place, who was not turning up to pay homage to the grave that was not a grave. He could tell you who would turn up with the showiest wreaths of roses by the truckload, or lilies, tulips, bird of paradise flowers whatever, or who was lugging more gifts chucked out of heaven – plastic giant-sized holy statues of guardian angels piling up to the rafters with everything else that had been stacked on top of the flowers over the imaginary grave. Ice hung around the beach while gawking at the thousands of golden Christmas beetles crawling over the mountain of plastic flowers now sanctified as a holy shrine. Then, because he was overwhelmed by the feast of colours, he mentally calculated, without requiring the use of adding up machines or computers, what conditions would be like for whatever had been buried underneath. Say? How long it would take for a body buried six foot under the sand, which was not the case anyway – but what if it was say – how long would it take for its spirit to escape from an eternity of entrapment under this pile of plastic that had been built over the grave and called a shrine? Did a spirit need a straight line to travel in a hundred-metre sprint, or would it become hopelessly lost while trying to work its way through a fathomless entangled maze of dumped plastic petals? Who could tell? But, all in all, Ice understood the logic of a spirit as enormous as Aboriginal Sovereignty having difficulty getting back to his clan land anytime in the near future under these circumstances of being enshrined in plastic, and so he thought, less havoc for himself, for this surely, was a good thing. Ice tried even harder to reconcile in his mind the prospect of the greatest spirit of all being lost in toxic waste for a very long time, by remembering some particular TV documentary among thousands he had watched in his lifetime in the hope of gaining a complete understanding of the world with a head full of vague snippets about all things foreign to Praiseworthy. But, the memory bank being what it was, now an overused and overwhelmed organ stuffed with a jumble of information ranging from purely useless idiocy to right pearlers of world wisdom, it took a moment for Ice to land upon what he had learnt about how long it took plastic to decompose, which was freaky but he had to know that it was going to take something like five hundred years for full decomposition, and possibly less in the era of increased global warming heating the haze dome quicker than anywhere else on the planet. Yep! With knowledge like this, you could not beat Ice. He nailed the logic flat in the face, for Ice knew immediately what destiny lay ahead for a spirit as huge as Aboriginal Sovereignty being buried in the sand as a t-shirt, instead of a body. He reckoned that it would take at least five hundred years to break out of the imaginary sand grave underneath shipping container loads of plastic flowers before the spirit of Aboriginal Sovereignty could travel back to its proper ancestral home and create some havoc. Like what? He thought of the transformation of the spirit of Aboriginal Sovereignty becoming something nice after stewing for five centuries. Again, he stared at the plastic mountain where the golden beetles were searching for its relevance to country, and in his mind's eye he saw plenty in its eventuality over time, of even becoming a priceless antique swan-like creature of pure sun-bleached white, limping back home over the seas – that was how it looked in his head.

What interested Ice Pick more in these circumstances of what he considered to be a dubious suicidal act in the sea, was how he was going to pin a murder charge on Widespread. He could always do the head work, using his brain in a densely insignificant way by calculating the cost of plastic flowers, but who cared if one plus one equals two, and why waste time chopping wood for practice? What was real here? How could you justify chasing small fry around the bush all of your life? If your whole point in life was being in the business end of proportioning blame upon others by continually wasting energy lifting your hand up in some totally bored way, just to point your finger of whiteness at the guilty for a crime of which you say you knew what the outcome was going to be in a total no-brainer nanosecond, knew simply by intuition, as a no-brainer, then like Ice, you would eventually have to think about what else could be of benefit for humanity? This was the reason that Ice knew you had to go for it, and bugger the consequences of the surrounding fallout.

Anyhow, mind job was the work description for a real man focused on being a Major Mayor of the world of Praiseworthy, and Ice now felt totally overloaded with sneaky eye-strain from continually watching what hundreds of feral donkeys were doing while shitting up the place by forever roaming here, there, and all over in a general donkey zigzag way instead of being locked up in proper pens and confined to walking up and down narrow grids, like an industry person would do in animal husbandry for a pack of useless feral animals. The man was going cross-eyed from watching packs of donkeys freely moving in the shire's no-go zone for feral animals that had been using the healthy Australian bushland to grow into the size of elephants, but he wasted no thought about other feral animals, such as pigs, and pigeons, which were holy, intra-family, connected spiritual relatives, and where Ice was told if he made a mistake and killed a feral pigeon instead of a donkey, he, himself, would be killed on the spot with a bullet. Ice ranged around every inch of Praiseworthy in his fuelled-up vent for vengeance, and he felt as though he had been caught up in the work of a full-time surveillance officer for removing illegal donkeys that would not leave, and he was not imagining it, their numbers were increasing the more he tried to drive them out of Praiseworthy. The whole surveillance thing was at risk of defeating Ice, for it was too much from a simple job description for a Major Mayor to expect him to endlessly have to conquer Widespread's spreading-diseases donkeys from overcoming the cemetery and taking over the homes of Praiseworthy. He could not legitimately spend his entire time herding feral donkeys with his four-wheel drive by cutting through rough scrub-like jungles from point A to point B all over Praiseworthy as if he had become some backwater proverbial shepherd. All Ice wanted was to work on the high ground, to find proof beyond reasonable doubt that the donkey herder was the real murderer of this so-called suicide of the t-shirt buried in the sand, and possibly, was also the head of the Canberra government's spies' rumoured paedophile ring operating in Praiseworthy, which had somehow in all truth led to the heinous murder.

Ice was confident that the criminal would sooner or later reveal a slither of incriminating evidence somewhere with Widespread following hundreds of feral donkeys by continuously retracing his steps in circles over the ground. Somewhere in all of those footsteps, evidence of what had really happened would appear. The evidence could be a piece of hair in plains of stumpy yellow grasses where even the animals that lived there were hard pushed to find some clump of dry roots that they called home. Or else a button. A bloodstain. A mysterious witness who still had not come forward to be interrogated to an inch of their life. He was not interested in the compromised t-shirt mumbo jumbo sand monument guarded by crabs on the beach. Ice wanted to be able to call the police office with real evidence like a hair strand, or a button, like you saw heroes catching villains in those crime series on television, and he wanted to say bluntly like a real endless suffering man of his world, that Cause Man Steel, @Widespread, @Planet, or @whatever, had murdered the suicide son. Ice did not know how he was going to prove it, but this did not seem to matter anyhow, because he knew beyond doubt that Widespread was the killer, and that was all one needed to know.

You would have laid a bucket of money on the table to prove he was right about this, and this idea appeared in Ice's everyday conversations of spreading the word, by naming Widespread whenever he spoke with one of the hashtag names as being the child murderer, and possibly as one of those child molesters from the rivers of grog that Canberra politicians were always talking about. For example, he would casually ask, what was the child murderer Widespread doing with those donkeys? Simple innuendos being placed in the thoughts of his general public on the road to make the ark pure again.

What turned up unexpectedly for Ice, and blew his mind right out of his head, was how the community kept rising up to grieve the death of Aboriginal Sovereignty, in the throes of an unusual amalgamation where the churches of steeples and observatory towers had combined in strength after lengthy discussion and compromise, and had decided to bury the false t-shirt. No one was buying the murder argument being floated by the Major Mayor. This constant denial of the facts created difficult moments for Ice, and the empty pit in his headspace felt catastrophically loaded with the nil and void devouring him from inside out.

Who knew why, but Ice always had to dig a hole for himself. This was the type of person who could not visualise perpetual pristine wilderness without seeing a hole dug in it. The man was a human pink underground mole, worm, snake, a wombat digging its way underneath the soil, only happy when looking at a big hole in the earth. He was another kind from the local ancestor, since becoming modern, he loved the sight of a man-made hole creating money and jobs for Australia, even if you never saw any of the treasure yourself. The iron-ore-silver-gold-lead-zinc-copper. The list of the holy country being endless. He was straight for the literal bolt hole. Yeah, he said you did not have to die in a ditch for the pristine land of your ancient beliefs just because a hole was being dug in it. Holes were normal. Everyone had to dig a hole. This was what humans do, he claimed. You had to think about the aesthetics of digging up stuff. You either dug, or you got dug into a hole. This was the modern world he had in mind for surviving the thing, where everyone faced up to being an excavator of dirt. Don't be frightened to dig a hole, he said. Open-cut holes, or deep holes created by blasting the surface to smithereens. This was the digging required to solve the mysteries of life, for whatever art was for, it was never about nothing, it was always about digging into the mind, boring into the heart, shovelling into the soul. He believed the art of excavation was the broken conscience, and the greater the hole to be dug, the greater the translucence. And equally grand in his mind, he saw the slagheap of a conscience unearthed as a beautiful thing to comb through for hidden treasure. Ice had dug that many grandiosely operatic holes in which to bury himself for the sake of the art of digging, he had created an underground ark from the depths, and it was this monstrosity he had brought to the surface to make a lot of money.

Ice, being this ark man and all, said the ark sprung from the depths was not all it was cracked up to be while hindered by the grief thing slung across the surface like a wet blanket. It burnt him out. One person could not carry all the ore for brightening the era. He needed some help from being overwhelmed by mad people's theories about stitching up holes from adversities. His life had become so terrible that he had not even noticed his golden beetle was prone, legs up on the dashboard of the brand-new mayor jeep, and was now totally silent, looked like it was dead. This did not matter. Ice was more into the tangibles, desperate to catch any murderer who owned feral donkeys, to bring closure to his trumped-up murder charge against Widespread as quickly as possible in the Australian courts, up to the High Court by throwing everything he had at digging holes to find evidence. He brought out the heavy equipment. The council's bobcat. Called up the road works. Bring in the bulldozers. Called the mining companies. Get the explosives. Rip the guts out. Dig the lot. Let's see some dirt flying around here rather than crawling around on the ground with a magnifying glass to see some grain of paydirt. A foul murderer still at large. Well! Holy smoke! Ice grew redder as he became madder. He was regularly seen by the total population hiding from the heat in their hidey-holes, watching him driving on the deserted streets, jump-starting in short fast spurts from one place and grinding to a halt in the next, to check for evidence about killers while leaving the not cheap latest mayoral buggy's siren ringing non-stop whistle and bells, and with the mayor sign brightly glowing in metallic gold with a string of red fluorescent show lights dancing in flickers around the roof of the cab. Ice looked everywhere for a slice of life to interrogate killers on the loose about, but all around was ghost-town dead. There was nothing happening. Only solemn ancestors spoke. They said they did not know who he was. There was a complete disappearing act, and Ice had been trying all day to find a handful of what he called his important 'pet black' people – the signatories to his various hole-digging ventures in thought, law or order, or in other words, in bringing convenient truths to the surface for personal gain.

Where everyone else was so immobilised with sorrow that only negativity flooded with fire and hatefulness, Ice's spirit remained full of movement, and he was way beyond any soul making a sound barrier of grief around him. He took the king hit, ignored the shit flying in the ether of his puff of smoke, and kept asking the bulldozer questions in the hole of denial about killers in Praiseworthy owning feral donkeys. He did not care how much it cost. If he had to, he would use up all the fuel left on Earth to find a bit of dirt. The signature people were nowhere to be found. It was a total disappearance act, and the eerie silence left behind, felt as though these people no longer existed.

Finally, Ice realised that he would not be able to finish off this business of catching a murderer without signatories to complete his statement of outing, by outlining the reasons he believed that Widespread was who they were looking for, and possibly, head of the government-created paedophile ring. But all was not lost. The hole was being dug deeper. It was simply not the end. Bedrock was still to be reached. So! Ice just forged the signatures. Not even really a forge. He had no idea how they signed their names. He just dashed something on the page like a cross, and wondered why he had not done this before, instead of wasting time and the cost of several tanks of petrol driving over and over on the same streets since after all Praiseworthy was not that huge. Ice took a screenshot of the document on his mobile, and sent the thing south, to the Affairs of Aboriginals Department.

A few minutes later, when he thought enough time had passed on Earth for heaven's sake, for his document to be delivered to the Minister for Aboriginal Affairs, he called her office in the Australian parliament situated some four thousand kilometres south from Praiseworthy, and again, asked to speak to her about how he had cracked the government's paedophile ring run by loose murderers. When he was told to hold on, the minister was in parliament, he ordered the bureaucrat to get her out straight away to speak to him.

He argued the toss with what he called *you belligerent bureaucrat*, but got nowhere, except the raw deal. *Listen! Cow*, he argued, *I am not asking you to personally tackle this emergency*. He further yelled into the mobile about the lack of common courtesy in the Government of Australia these days, and finally snapped he did not have all day so, *You tell her to call me*. Wham! He ended the call, while knowing she would get the message, knew that powerful Major Mayors like to be in the thick of the job in rich mineral provinces in the north, knew the traditional owner did not like to be kept waiting too long. Moving on now...fast. His list of urgent calls was long. Morally important. Media dogs, opposition politicians, local loudmouths, numerous hacks positioning and jockeying for whatever power was for sale, whoever else you see. Totally. Right up the guts of people like him to keep the country moving regardless, when times were tough.

18

Of course, Praiseworthy would be waiting another forever to get much help from Canberra. Some were feeling murderous about this too. The white government cried poor. It did not have enough money in the budget for sending riot police to some little Aboriginal place called Praiseworthy, just to arrest the most dangerous murderer in the world – the killer of Aboriginal Sovereignty – who was still right out of control. Sad thing to see. People running around who should be locked up. The havoc makers among all these peaceful people. The Major Mayor Ice Pick continued calling the nation's capital every day, just as he had done in his entire career of being the saviour of sometime in the future. Many forefathers had, and many future descendants would, sacrifice their entire lives on this thankless task of trying to preserve their sovereignty while it was being further eroded, and ripped from under their feet.

But this was the forever world enduring the greatest grief happening in their time. Goodness it was hot. Hotter than hell! The dogs were locked up. They did not bark. The birds had finished fleeing – all the skulking herons dressed in drab grey feathers, the angel gulls, the sea eagle watched no more, the snowy white pigeon, and those rails that hid in the mangroves – and, might never come back. Ants fell fast asleep in the ants' nest, the massive red mounds stacked all over country where soundless wind scurries slid like snakes over the soil, and destroyed all the wayfinding pilgrimage trails forever. The cicada could no longer drone, the morning breeze dropped, and no fragrance rose from the mangrove flowers to intoxicate the lizards, butterflies and bees. Nothing moved in this heat, not even a dust-covered leaf that used to be covered in lerp. The ancient serpent curled up, watching all this silence from its home under a clump of dry yellow dust-covered grass.

And from there, all remaining quiet, except for the swish-swash of fans waving across the faces of the respectable old ladies shimmering in the mirage, like the schools of mourning fish of silvery colours swimming the flows in the sea. The vigil ladies walked under the moon to the ocean, making their way through the grassy path to commence another day in their never-ending vigil of silence on the prohibited beach frontage. The place where they stood was where the ancestors' songs droned, and where the beating dukuduka clap sticks pulsed in heart beats reverberating across time, country, sea, sky, fire and wind. The fan-carrying ladies wore their church dresses – the worn long ago hand-me-downs from city ladies – now aged into the fading colours of the drab scaled moths of the local bush.

In the glare they saw a piece of the wrong vision coming towards them. The blur of the hazy mirage hit them in eyes, and they thought it was Jesus coming – *Oh! Glory Be* – but in the end, they saw only another human saviour, the main prowler after murderers – Ice Pick, heading towards them. He was acting scary like a stray dog, all hungry-looking, rabid-acting, jumping up and down in time with his mind, doing a bit of a brain twist and shout, while a person of his position ought to be guarding their proper oldest humanity in the world, should show off his ancient culture, by acting normal and sane at all times. They loved the popular interconnectivity more in powerful people who knew how to behave on country, rather than wasting precious eyesight on seeing mongrel dog behaviour in their old age.

This Ice was trying to jump out of his skin by screaming his white-type rage language into the dizziness of the mirage. The old women heard him angrily shouting about having something, was he saying he had gun power? You could hear him screaming his abusive violence all over the place – countlessly using his white language, ripping up the sacredness with his sacrilege heart. Then, as he drew closer, the old fanning ladies saw that the sinner man was trying to pull off the mobile phone superglued to his face. Again! More sacrilege happening. It did not occur to them to wonder who he was talking to while he was going off his head and creating so much sacrilegious offence as to call the spirit country up with his anger. Suddenly, those old ladies began to feel the great ancestor stirring in the ground, and because they were having heart attacks quick smart one, two, three on the spot from the panic of the earth quaking violently underfoot, it was difficult for those old ladies to firmly stand upright. They swayed back and forth in the rumbling, and with their mind full of anticipating, they knew that any moment now, the enormous ancestor would burst right out of country, and rise into the atmosphere to breathe in all of the oxygen in the world – for that was how these relatives breathed – and then, it would exhale a single enormous fiery breath of poisonous fumes, and everything would be destroyed in this one overpowering volcanic breath. This was not the first time that these old ladies had thought about the ancestral forward plan, and to be frank, they had always said that one day this would happen, knowing that such an eventuality was becoming clearer to them with people like Ice screaming on the hotline in the holiest law country, since how would it know about mobile phones?

Look! The whole earth shook. The stories of the ancestral world unfolded, of what happened long ago, of being remade. Everything moved. Was shocked. Shook. Country spoke its own language. Your soul heard every word. *Where's your Aboriginal Sovereignty for this place?* The old women gulped fear. They felt as though they were losing their mind, then when the mayhem passed as suddenly as it had appeared, as if they had returned from a dream, and thought that perhaps, Ice did not realise the terrible thing that had just happened, he did not realise that when they had lost their Aboriginal Sovereignty, their entire world had turned to silence, where even the dogs knew it was better not to bark, and even slugs had the sense to be silent and motionless, and birds were not singing anymore when there was now so much silent crying in the heart of life.

The grievers stood rock-solid on the side of the road while watching the mayoral jeep continuing on its way, driving a short distance, jerking to a stop. Ice jumping out to yell at yet another empty house where everyone had already taken off out the back door in an earnest walk to get away from him, while pretending not to hear a thing, which was the correct thing to do, since nobody should expect to hear a thing while all this grieving was going on.

ERRRRK! GET HERE! YOU! Finally, Ice decided that he could hear the old ladies gesturing to him in sign language. He expected to be hit for another ten-dollar loan. He stopped yelling into the mobile about not being able to contact anyone in the entire government of Australia ABOUT A MURDERER IN A REMOTE ABORIGINAL COMMUNITY, because they were either swanning about AT LUNCH AT A SWANKY CAFÉ DOWN IN CANBERRA, or crapping on about nothing in

PARLIAMENT. He caught his breath, and told the old women that he was in a hurry with no time to talk to anyone – GET THE DRIFT! *Catch me next time.*

These old women could not waste their life in being fobbed off either. They were ageing faster by the minute while waiting in a posse for him either here or there, and exhausting themselves by puffing up and down the street, or else, having to nearly break their necks by jumping out from around corners in front of the mayoral jeep while trying to catch up to him as quickly as possible, before he jump-started the motor, beeped the horn, and they were left listening to the engine roaring a couple of metres down the street to the house next door before they had a chance to catch up, to have a simple chance to whisper something into his ear like, SHUT THE FUCK UP, why did he have to keep thinking about the murderer business – this really bad thing that had never happened, where right at this moment, *the spirit ground was baba, moving through the air,* because country was looking for Aboriginal Sovereignty. *You can't hide anything from country.* They knew the long labour of life to achieve wisdom bore little fruit sometimes, but those elderly ladies were more or less satisfied that he had got their message by simply using the commonest language, of having chased him around with hearts thumping like teenage girls while they were ageing more prematurely with spider-web hair to catch up to the jeep to tell him to stop yelling ignorantly all over the sacred beach about the lack of the Australian parliament being in their presence. They did not want white government in their presence. These old women felt as though they were ghosts kidding themselves into believing that they saw actual comprehension when they had looked square into the blankness of Ice's pink eyeballs.

Gosh! Why do they do it? Anyone would feel disgusted for old mothy-dressed ladies acting like teenage girls mooning over some moron bringing them down, even while they knew the facts, that Ice Pick had not heard a single word of where they were coming from. After that, what else would they have left of dignity? They wondered what they had to do to make the idiot listen more, before all time ended in this place. You could tell just by feeling the air moving in circles that the lot could blow, everything destroyed in a single moment, and they were imagining themselves ripped off the ground, and involuntarily thrown through the air along with everything else: dogs, seagulls, butterflies, bees, snakes and lizards, the sacred mangrove trees, nothing spared from being thrown into the *frenzied-ing* vortex with the mad circling winds whipped up by the haze with all the dust coming off the ground, and spinning with the bushfires, embers pelting everywhere with lightning jumping, and thunder clapping, everything heading in a jet force fireball flight up into outer space. Then, while the haze was smashing their world and the entire universe was falling apart, the ladies claimed that whatever would be left of themselves, would be just a few ashes floating down into a crack in the earth which they called the gate to hell. Ice wondered why these ancient women were telling him these mad things. He had done enough. Hadn't he? And where was that fat-arse Minister for Aboriginal Affairs anyhow? He screamed her name again, and again, into the vibrating mobile phone – *You want to come and save us, or what?*

I have got something to tell you my boy. Listen! Ice Pick hated this side of Praiseworthy, where elderly women rushed him the split second anything went wrong. *I am not your old-woman magnet.* He thought about his magnetism to old women because it was happening a lot lately – this flirty haranguing confused his image of being the person holding the ultimate authority for the welfare of his people. That was how it works. One boss. He delegated power, not the old women delegating work for him to do.

Take youth suicide for instance. He thought this reoccurring problem should be a community issue that had nothing to do with him. People should be in charge of their own business. But he could hear these old grave women now, calling him from way down the street somewhere, shouting his name while heaving and puffing, running out of breath, having a heart attack from trying to run after him, the ladies he called the big units. Ice already knew the same negative story told from every possible angle of not coming back. In his mind, he could not recall when he was not endlessly tossing this question in his brain, DO I REALLY HAVE TO KEEP KNOWING THIS? He does not want to hear another word about suicide, and his blank eyes twitch uncontrollably. How would he know the answer to everything that happened in Praiseworthy? He felt quite uncomfortable to be put in this eternal predicament of having old ladies chasing him, which forced him to muster up some kind of extra inner energy to reassemble what was going on in his head about imprisoning the murderer of children forever, and to reflect on how this would transform him into a reasonably acceptable person to mainstream Australia. That was the goal. Get rid of the spookiness of being a snowy white other who gets abused by older women making up fairytales, while waving their fans tantalisingly in his face.

Such goings-on. Nobody helped. Ice had to tug every contorted feature of his face back into place, reset the nice man act while forcing himself to conduct his business with these women. He knew that a very smart part of his brain understood reputation even if he was not fussed what anyone thought of him, and there were eyes everywhere watching how he handled himself. What was the point in expecting remorse? It was hard to put yourself on top of people who saw themselves as being the true sovereigns of their own world. He hoped that these women felt satisfied for wasting his time. This was when he heard a thin squeaky voice continuously calling from the back of his head, trying to break through the other brain racket going on about Canberra. Someone was answering his calls about the murderer. When he listened more closely, Ice thought the weasel voice was trying to warn him that this was probably not the time to do some flirting business with these infatuated old women worshipping the ground on which he walked. But Ice could not believe that this mousy voice from the wasteland of his brain, the place where dead things lived, could just turn up when nobody asked it, and dare try and tell him what to do. In casting his eye over the dead fields of this vast wasteland, a junk field of the trivia which he rarely ever visited, he tried to pinpoint where this remnant idiot lived, where in all his past failures was its address, then, when he shoved the thing back where it belonged, he would return to the task in hand, which was catching real murderers. A task now to be undertaken single-handedly, it seemed to Ice, since the entire workforce of Praiseworthy employed by the municipal super shire had taken upon itself to endlessly grieve the funeral of a t-shirt.

The news sprung on him by some idiot in his brain crying of young people committing suicide, began to fog Ice Pick's wider vision of assimilating into the wide-angle white view of economic progress for Aboriginal people. As far as he was concerned, this was the only deal on the table, and now it felt tarnished by the brain idiot highlighting life-and-death matters that had nothing to do with the main narrative obsessing the rest of his brain of pursuing the forward plan of ultimate assimilation for achieving equity in the Australian world. When the Minister for Aboriginal Affairs finally called the ark man to find out why no one was working to close the gap in Praiseworthy, and sending in their daily progress reports in being trained in becoming white people, he mentioned to her that it was a very sensitive time culturally for Aboriginal Sovereignty. She told him that this never-ending argument about Aboriginal Sovereignty was annoying, but he told her, he would *not be committing treason by challenging the sovereignty of the Crown's ownership of Australia. Nope!* He sighed – why was it always about saying he was loyal to the Crown – and so he continued on answering her greater suspicions which were what her call was all about, that Praiseworthy was full of Aboriginal people trying to betray her government to China.

What makes you think Praiseworthy was promoting the Asia century? He could conduct an orchestra on paranoia as good as it gets. So! He did. The silences fell at will, the talk dance enjoying the civil argument of the western world, conducting a considered conversation as you would, while speaking with the majestical White Lady Mother of all Aboriginal people, particularly their children.

The thing was, Ice continued, after a suitably long pause to demonstrate that he was capable of carefully structuring his thoughts, *We are just trying to get rid of welfare dependency here, and never having to rely on the Australian government for any more hand-outs in the future (pause),* and he was only saying this, he said, instead of saying what the accused murderer Widespread would spruik to the world, *of never having to rely on people buggering themselves up completely in an overheated world,* and he was not saying like the old people were saying, of increasingly *noticing more twelve-year-old insurrectionaries roaming about the streets looking for trouble at half past two in the morning.*

You never want to lose a government minister on the phone call when you are still articulating your breathless point of view, so Ice quickly revved up the conversation into flooding word-rapids about the murderer. *Remember, I was telling you about that fake Native Title claimant Widespread, Cause Man Steel, the murderer at large?* He shot for goal. Bang! Bang! He told her flatly what she was after, what she could shoot up her pipeline in government, how to nail a black insurrectionist. It was a present. Thank you. No problem. Ice raced on, gave her, the Right Honourable, his personal best viper's score in his dash to beat the parliament of Australia's scarcity of time to speak to the lower-class, Aboriginal dignitaries from the regions, even those like himself from a super shire in the mineral-rich province of Praiseworthy. He spread lashings of syrup sweetly for there were no worries about that, and continued rocking, fear for fear. *Keep remembering Widespread as your biggest threat,* Ice slurped, almost licking the mobile, *Think of him as the only person up here in the north capable of spin-drying a pile of yuan like Rumpelstiltskin's gold.* He told her to forget all about suicide rumours buzzing in her *ear from the troublemakers, complainers, poseurs, do not fall for the wizardry of the shit-stirrers, fakery, scammers.* He picked up verbal speed, his racing tongue lying exponentially with a speeding heartbeat to reach the end of everything he had to say, with a bit of praise, like, *Your policy initiatives to prevent youth suicide are great.* Hmm! Hmm! *Really great! Believe me.* All Ice wanted now, before she hung up in his ear and cut him off mid-sentence, was to convince her that when the world went belly up with bugger-all fossil fuel left in the bucket – although he did not actually say this to her because he did not want to sound like an idiot, like Planet, but what he did say in a pushy way to get the last word was that – in Praiseworthy, it would be the likes of Cause Man Steel, the real live murderer on the loose, who was planning on becoming a Chinese yuan tycoon from shipping donkey loads of the collective Native Title iron ore reserves to China in a two to three degree increase in global warming reality post-2030, an irreversible situation which would not be long away now. It seemed like a good note on which to end the conversation, rather than being the other way around, with the Minister hanging up on him, like he was a tyrant. He felt on top of the world, far better of course than lying flat under the weight of a minister of government banging on about nothing. Ice came to the end. Said all he wanted to say about pushing the government in the right direction. He had kept control of the debate. Let her stew on that. With a moment to spare, he babbled on about how the murderer

Planet was already training tens of thousands of feral donkeys to cart all the remaining iron ore out of the country to China. With his fresh-air conspiracy theory firmly established in the mind of the Australian government, Ice hung up on the unarticulated gasp cut short at the other end of the line.

CARGO SHIFTER

Carpe diem
(Seize the day)

1

Oracle 6…Even though he speaks good English sometimes…

Yep! You can bring it on home right to where Aboriginal Sovereignty
had played like some big winner by being dead, in the era of viewing
through the lens the most economically souped-up and politically right,
left and centre, eye-fetching northern soils country. A wide-open vista
full with new-age internationally sophisticated thought, packaged for
fast-tracking exploitation from mineral wealth, exploding the bedrock,
and scraping the surface of country within inches of gouging the
eyes out of what living sacredness remained – the old wisdom men's
legal sovereign law that country knew protected the whole world, the
priceless solid, left like rubble, to rumble when it toppled over into a
miner's pit of the multinational. Yep! Watch out for the ancestor games
in these ancestral remains, the dust floating in the air, gathered in the
haze cell, the sepulchral permanently resting over Praiseworthy. This
was left of the sacred. Air laden with the betrayal. Thought Aboriginal
Sovereignty had been breathing into his lungs for his entire life.

Stolen! What did this word mean for something so priceless
that it could destroy the world, and the preciousness of Aboriginal
Sovereignty? Who steals thought? And what was the thing that had
gone completely wrong in Aboriginal Sovereignty's life? Was it so
simple, or great, that he had fallen in love? He got married. And that
was wrong, even though Aboriginal Sovereignty Steel was seventeen

years old, and knew he could be married in his law. It was not in white law, and so, he couldn't marry her.

A twenty-odd strong police contingent had been sent to Praiseworthy to hunt Aboriginal Sovereignty, and they chased him down like he was their slave, until he was savaged by the search dogs the police had with them when he was captured. While isolated from his community in a closed-off interrogation room, he was read the rape charges against a minor, and no one mentioned other matters in their mind plaguing the mood, of how offensive he was in the sight of decent people after they had been informed of the facts about him from the national race for racist rage spreading like lightning across the country, where he had been singularly named like a chosen one, the first paedophile caught for creating a rampant scourge on the white purity of Australian conscience. The boy was not a mind reader. His mind was locked into other thoughts in those moments, like, was he being brave enough to be a man to fight these creeps, or else, on the other hand, was he already dead? He chose death, and merely said that he really loved the girl whom he had been promised by traditional law, from the day she had been born.

Hey! Shithead? You can't do that type of thing here, not in this state, not in this country.

It was right way – we are married.

The first answer he received from the police presence behind him, was a volley of punches into his skinny back. *Hey! Shithead! Rapist! Who do you think you are talking to?* Aboriginal Sovereignty did not know. There were a lot of police crowding in the small room.

What's an arranged marriage?

What country do you think you are living in?

There are laws against what you call an arranged marriage.

What law, man, I don't know what you are talking about. This here, is one country – it's call Australia?

561

Thump!

The thumping with a baton was hard. His mind spun, he was unable to keep counting the times he fell, felt the boots hitting, being hauled up, and happening all over again.

Don't you answer us back, sonny – I will ask the questions, and you answer. Get it?

I am a man. These were the last words he was able to speak, but he went on speaking to the flow of country that took him on a long journey far into his ancestral world, and far away over the ocean covered with the whiteness of sky gulls and the storming of caper white butterflies journeying across the spray racing from the white caps.

Let me interpret for you on behalf of the Australian federal government that I represent as its law enforcer in Praiseworthy – what kind of man you are. You are a paedophile that's what, and fortunately, we now have laws for dealing with that kind of dirty thing happening since the emergency intervention by the government to take over the control of your black lives. You heard of it? It's called the National Emergency Response to intervene with what you blacks are doing. The Prime Minister himself made these laws with his own brain to change the slack black welfare attitudes of you people, to open up your so-called locked-up Aboriginal land, and to lock up men that prey on children. Came in law in 2007. Little Children Are Sacred! Remember those words? We now have laws to deal with all those allegations that were being made on the national ABC TV about rampant child sexual abuse, rivers of grog, and neglect in the Aboriginal community. You should have been watching the TV to see what kind of man you were likely to become, have become, are. The whole thing was on TV enough – even a moron wouldn't have missed it. You want to know something – know what these laws mean? Look! You are not listening. Kick some life into him will you constable? I mean, what I am saying is the real power I now have as a policeman intervening into your life. Well! I can't turn a blind eye anymore. The law is the law, and God damn it, I will enforce it.

Who knows why Aboriginal Sovereignty had to say, *Oh! You won't be hiding from us in your police station anymore.* It was the wrong thing to say under the circumstances while being kicked around the floor.

What the law means is that I have as much power as I fucking like with you black bastards now. What that word means – paedophile – is that what you wanted to know? It means that Aboriginal men like you, who tamper with young girls, won't get away with it. We can lock up scum of the earth like you forever, and throw away the key. Chuck the key into the sea. Just drive down there and do it. Just as good I suppose as bundling you into the police boat in the middle of the night and chucking shit like you in the ocean. It means you won't be causing any more trouble to women and children and that is a good news story as far as I am concerned. And the result is, you will want to know this too: women and children will be able to sleep at night without men like you bothering them. That is what this all means.

Rise your fists? Come on. Rise your fists?

Aboriginal Sovereignty never heard the police speech about him. Their voices were only within themselves, and seemed far beyond his hearing – a fade off, that could not be heard above the auditorium of the ancestral movement through land, skies and seas, where even in the slightest movement of air covering him, he was being enfolded by his family, the spirits of country. This was how it happened on the day of his arrest, when he had become tied into the chosen shame of a continent stolen from his people by a pack of racists, who had turned the argument against the people whose land they had stolen, and whose intergenerational lives have never recovered from so great a loss.

Rise your fists. You niggers like to fight. Rise them.

The chosen voices of the nation-state continued to be relayed to the unconscious youth in a haunting of all places across the ancestral domain. *You mean to tell us that a little Aboriginal girl was made to marry some dirty animal like you up there in Praiseworthy?* The self-appointed high lord commentators of the righteous speaking on the television, writing in the newspapers, trolling on social media, rolled the claptrap on for months about dirty old Aboriginal men like this Aboriginal Sovereignty seducing young girls who had been forced to marry them. It was riotous news for sanctioned rioters, an in for all media shouting slogans to whip up the public sentiment to demand the wiping out of the entire cultural world of Aboriginal people from the face of the planet, where all that would be left of millennia of ancient wisdom – so urgently relevant today in the Earth ruined by the colonial exploiters and thieves of Aboriginal lands – would be the law of white Australia. There would be no room for Aboriginal law in one law for all Australians, and no more barbaric cultural practices, except, except, what? Well! Their art if they behaved nicely for the tourists, and acted professionally while on public view with their 'lore stuff' in international festivities taking place on 'home' soil.

I am telling you, rise your fists, have the first shot, you bastard.

You can tell them I was not ever there. He was now so far away from being held up, and singled out like a demon of Satan that surpassed an uncontrollable virus pandemic, and major catastrophic unprecedented global warming disasters, when even the prime minister of the day made sudden dashes to the national news studios to strangle the microphone while telling the country to look out for Aboriginal people who weren't forgetting the grand theft of the total country. They needed to forget their culture. They needed to assimilate. What cool calmness came across to the nation from a voice romping with brutality, by being on show in this domestic crisis, showing how easy he controlled the black situation, which was sincerely educational too, training the populace that the only answer was for black to turn white. *Everything else had failed,* his voice was bleak, *and God knows we had tried.*

Look! The little black bastard has got those bony fists raised at last.
Let him swing the first shot.

Aboriginal Sovereignty never heard the Prime Minister talking about the years of failed government policies which was blamed on Aboriginal people by quoting an anthropologist who seemed to have only developed hate and spite in his heart from his years of building his reputation and career from studying Aboriginal people, which had made him more an expert on their lives than they knew themselves. He was relevant, someone to articulate the moment and explain Aboriginal culture to the white populace. The rioting media lauded it, when he said, *that they were racially wired back to front and hell-bent on being a failure.* Well! No worries! The frenzy of dishing black fellows travelled fast, and travelled everywhere with the so-called right to be simply crazed about hating Aboriginals, which was nothing new, since what have you got? Invaders! Plus! A bad spirit that had grown fat on negativity. Equals what in whose law? Brokenness. Poverty broken. Broken generators. Broken homes. Broken emotions. Broken ties. Broken culture. Broken land. Broken people. Broken love? Broken joy? Race broken. A broken state of affairs. Broken band-aids. Broken children. Broken thoughts. Links to all times broken? Broken deranged and emotive sick brains? While there was so much publicity about the love matter of Aboriginal Sovereignty happening in plain view with nowhere to hide, the haze people were becoming so utterly depressed that it felt as though the air they were breathing had a negative current circulating through it, carrying the spicks and the specks of ancestral dust, the only love from the heart of the ancestral people of country left from the brokenness that had somehow ignited the illegal nation-state into believing that Aboriginal children were so sacred, that their love-lacking black parents could not possibly love them in the way of the more superior white love.

Well! He took the first shot. It was amazing, mustering the strength to ask of his future, where was the girl he loved.

Afterwards, when Aboriginal Sovereignty had been accused countless times in the police station of being a hostile dirty old paedophile savage, he ceased to exist, he was no longer the sun, for he was being reimagined, his body parts cast into nothingness. He was dead to this world. Eyes sockets bloodied, pushed into the back of his head. Don't worry. He would not see you looking at him. And you do not really see a skinny kid crumpled on the floor for the blood, so much blood from skin and bones. What was left? Nothing except all this bloodiness? No. He was being personified by the imagination of the nation-state, the dull dirty lens of Australian folk law. Yep! He was the ethnological story. He fed the hunger. Fattened the mudslinger's narrative of racial vilification. He was the paedophile savage. You know what happens when you throw enough mud? Hallelujah! Well! Song at last. Some dirty old black paedophile had been captured. Oh! Rest in peace. Success and vindication at last. The national narrative strengthened at the total cost of billions of dollars to hold back the tide of black justice through a simple illusion of fear, the dreaded uprising of the soul, the spirit of black savages attacking Australian domesticity. Nothingness achieved again, and again. Where was the light? Where was the flame to see the way?

2

The haze felt new, transformed into a darkened disquiet hanging over Praiseworthy. All within slowly slid away, each hid in its own withering mind, each dug themselves into a pit, the lid covered with armfuls of storm clouds, and inside the gloom set about erasing memory. You would not know what it was like to take a step into the day without it becoming a momentous ambition of confronting failure, to override indecisiveness, to never know which of the improbable routes heavily drawn from one's hesitation could be transgressed, for it was a transgression too far, to be otherwise, to show face, while waiting there in the darkness, waiting for the next piece of news about the captured paedophile who was of them, equally them, equally family.

Look, but do not see who they are, who they felt themselves to be, becoming a bunch of paedophiles.

What sunk into the brain about being branded scum of the Earth, was how difficult it felt to claim what other people believed about who they were, which had made them hideously famous. Nothing much else was said after hearing the news of their paedophilia selves, for who cared about anything else happening in Praiseworthy anymore. Who cared about rampaging feral donkeys destroying their proof of being assimilable into the omnicidal bingeing Western world, just to maintain a trophy for a showcase tidy town of hate? They could grow fast-pace hate themselves. Give ground. Was this simply a retreating culture, having been moved back from the line in the ground many times already? A whispering hummed in the hemmed-in day talking to itself while trying to comprehend the news from afar. The Aboriginal Sovereignty people said they could not understand themselves, or who they were at all, in the new language of paedophiles. Some said: *Liar! That boy didn't have to be a paedophile. He had girls chasing him like anything. They were all after him. He was that handsome.* Some said: *He could have been anything. Anything at all. It doesn't make sense.* Some asked: *Then why did he rape that girl for? His wife? Well! Then! It means we didn't know him at all. Whose kid was he, anyway? He could have become the one. He could have.* Others said: *All these men here are supposed to be paedophiles, because of him. Where are those paedophile rings operating in Praiseworthy anyway, that these white people were talking about on the news? We don't know. Who were those white people anyhow, never seen them before, they never spoke to us.*

Did they come here and spoke to you because they never spoke to me, and how come I never seen any of them when I have lived here every day of my life? I am a churchgoer and no white people spoke to me. Some said: *Men are all the same! You can't trust any of them anymore.* Some said: *Yep! I always thought these were rotten men here, like white men. Nobody here treating their families properly.* Some said: *Who you talking about? You talking about my family? Might be your family, but you know nothing about mine, so shut your fat big mouth. Praise be to the Lord. Amen.* All else, and so forth. Some said: *Lay it on the table if you like, come on, show a bit of honesty, a bit of guts.* Someone said: *You know, my husband was always screaming at the kids – and he was a white man, so I divorced him over the matter. I could not trust him around our children. You couldn't turn your back on him for a minute, and trust leaving the kids alone with that type. So, I said to him, get out. I thought to myself, be rid of that mongrel.*

Anyone on Earth could feverishly dream about good things happening in their particular part of the world, and yearn for better days to come in their mind, but in the world of Praiseworthy imagination, they collectively longed to know what type of man Aboriginal Sovereignty would become, for he was already intimately known in a dreamlike state of mind as being of themselves, the you and me, the representation of truth in the ancestral creation of the collective family – before he had suddenly become the very opposite of the dreamt. And instead, what had now turned up, what came out of the haze of the era, was this vile old paedophile who had materialised the collective view of themselves. They too saw themselves transformed into the worst nightmare that was so frenzied and frightening that you would be too afraid to look and see what you had been told to see, what the white world of media and government saw – that a paedophile looked like Aboriginal people – and so you did not want to look from believing, that if you rose from the hole of eternal doubting you had dug yourself into, you would be destined only to see paedophilia in yourself, and in this old people's ancestral sovereign world, it felt like some unnatural force had destroyed the eternal flame of hopefulness always seen in a sixty thousand lightning flash thunderstorm's song.

3

Aboriginal Sovereignty Steel was now officially renamed paedophile by the nation-state – the only way to describe him under the circumstances, with the word popularised from top to bottom in the lexicon of the nation, the *lex talionis* spilling off the tip of the tongue, the buzz word for the war of the new millennium. This was the natural moment for the seeds of thought lurking in worldwide muck, the summer harvest, a paedophile dreamt into every Aboriginal man, woman and child.

Left alone in the detention room, Aboriginal Sovereignty was in another world. Where was life better? He could not grasp the thought of where life was better, and the more he failed to think where life was better, the more he freaked out, unable to breathe, unable to lodge the thought in his mind, the more panic-stricken he became as his throat tightened, constricted further, closed off the air, and he became overwhelmed.

In a delirious state of drowning in a world where there was no air, he might not have realised that he had already begun travelling somewhere that might have felt like hell in his descent into unconsciousness, a shifting into the fathomless, a fall to infinity, unreachable in unknown depths of shame, far from everything he had ever known. Then, on this journey of descending away from himself, Aboriginal Sovereignty might have realised he was dying, had forgotten the light of day, knew that he would never want to reach that place where he was falling, the place where life was better than anything he had ever known, or wished for, if he had wished it, for it meant nothing to him never to see it again.

Perhaps Aboriginal Sovereignty would never feel freedom in his senses, nor be reconciled to his deprivation of freedom, for he was never free, or freed.

Sometimes, in his moments of lucidity, he felt the touch of country pushing against his body, he could feel how the immeasurable hold of the world was catastrophically closing him in, he felt the shallows growing deeper from the incoming tide, while his head, hissing nothingness, was grabbing pockets of thought, realisations, knowledge that he could not be locked up, controlled, borrowed, not for a second, and he watched his future unfolding and ending, where repeatedly he could watch his suicide, and the smoothness of the tide travelling in, sliding past him, while walking deeper into the sea, to where far off on the horizon, he saw the infinite light burning from the ocean.

End of story, it ended just like that. Ask anyone you like who thought that they were well-accustomed to making speeches about the abundant twists of fate in everyday life, and of sucking it up big-time about what happened to Aboriginal Sovereignty. Myths were stacked to the proverbial rafters of the universe from the ice age to the white age, but, wait a minute, listen. The white law was just that, white law. There was a whole stack of laws in the world.

One of these laws said that you cannot have sex with a minor. He had raped an underage girl. Why did that girl want to get married to her promised one? She said it was the law, their law, the old true law. She said that other people had married same way, and all their families knew that too. She said stop being a pack of hypocrites, she insisted on being married, and went right out there, and claimed her man. There was no trouble about her doing that. Everyone knew. Said it was right. Those two loved each other since they were children. They said that they would spend the rest of their entire lives with each other. They were right for each other. This was law too. An old law, made before any white person ever set foot on the Aboriginal domain. Nobody would stop them. She saw how the older girls were already chasing after Aboriginal Sovereignty Steel, trying to take him away from her, threatening to get him married up, said that right to her face – marry him good and proper, whitefella way, so she married him anyway.

4

Far, far away, way out in the blue ocean where only the big fish lived with the old sea country ancestors, where in modern sea lanes the world's cargo moved in traffic flowing back and forth with international container ships, and people traffickers rolled in the wake, and the seagulls spun in angel flight, flurrying around the deep-sea fishing boats that passed by with trawling nets flung wide under the ghost moon as the travelling swallows rested on the decks in the tens of thousands, this was where Aboriginal Sovereignty Steel was drifting, sinking, and being pulled back to the surface again and again by the old sea lady, where she hurled him, eyes stage fright, back on the old sea turtle, another of his close relations, carrying him further into the open sea, the broken spirit of a praise inherited through the ages.

Of this ending, of a story almost complete in a wondrous ancestral sea country rolling and roaring in the eternal drift, nothing would be finished. His storm mouth, wide open but wordless, offering no defence, gurgling the turtle's air bubbles while the spirit creature moved on through the deafening sound of the sea, as his life was disappearing through waterlogged skin so translucent it was releasing whatever thought remained clinging worthlessly in memory, of being cooped up in a small, airless room at the police station. Of all the thoughts he could have contemplated in this widest of wild oceans, lost in the expanse of the sea, all that he had taken with him, was fear of confinement. But, even the ocean could feel like entrapment for a jellyfish in the bloom, or a shark off-loading life. He imagined his thoughts were sparks flying off in a hundred different directions through waters that felt alive, encasing him, and now tamed, of watching himself flowing in images, sliding into the depths.

The boiling waters continued to encase fish, seaweed, marine life and the dumped waste of humanity in its folds, capturing all in the massive roll, dragging below and bringing it all back up to the surface, while he goes on catching glimpses of himself through the sun-lit sparkle moving through the ancestral spirit world that surrounds him in the surf. The old boss woman was always there, big as the ocean, pushed his other relatives aside, pulled him back to herself where she spun the waters, then, snatching him from a sea serpent cousin that whisked him away, or the big fish brother, shook him from its jaws, while it ran off with him. He was stolen by thoughts he finds above the water, as he was thrown back to the surface, dumped again on the turtle's back as it swam for hours further out to sea to reach a star-laden night holding back distant storms, just like the night when he had disappeared from the beach at Praiseworthy and had barely thought of Tommyhawk standing in the whale skeleton, thinking he would not be seen, even though Aboriginal Sovereignty kept noticing the mobile phone lighting up, a mote of dull light in the dark night, seen from the corner of his eye. Stupid, he had thought at the time, as he turned his attention back to the sea from the chubby boy talking on his mobile to a message bank in Parliament House, while his thoughts flowed sharply with the acuity of seeing the closeness of the world to himself, how easily Tommyhawk believed that whale bones made him invisible.

While the world sang for lost sovereignty, the last thought that Aboriginal Sovereignty had on his mind as he drifted away in the vespertine glow of twilight falling over the currents flowing out to sea, was of her. She was the pain that clung to the terror inside his being, that was holding on, never letting him go, holding him back. Yet it was this vague scrap of thought left from the very first thing the sea had taken from his memory, that broke her grip, until she began fading from the epicentre of his thoughts, and he was forced to let her go. Their story manufactured no more fear, not when Aboriginal Sovereignty had always known fearfulness. He carried it like a dead weight, but now it felt lighter from being so far away, and driven by a malaise fiddling with his consciousness that overwhelmed him with a greater fearfulness that reached into his core, throttling all sense he had of being entrapped.

When another dawn arrived, that spoke of the beauty of the vast heaving blueness of the sea lady, he barely realised where he was. This dawn cried through the winds flowing off the waves that he should *look around*, but he was not able to open his eyes. There was no strength left in his arms or legs, and his sleep had settled into a sense of weightlessness. He could barely bring back the memory of being caged in the police station, and of where he had dreamt himself into an eternal closure, of becoming nothing, being in the better place of where he was now. In this state of passing through non-existence, he felt what closure was like. It felt like relief, of almost being able to reach into an incomprehensible distance, and sense faraway joy. He vaguely thought whether this was like waiting for a great moment, when he would again be lifted out of these spirit-loaded waters by a woman's arms both gentle and forceful, his whole body reaching out to another reality, like having a ceremony sung for him, the praying of great ancestors waiting to relinquish, or withhold from him, the most sacred thing, his desire to keep his memory of her. He might have known, while making the final decision of walking away from life, that when he reached this point, he would have achieved the one everlasting moment he had longed to feel just one more time, and that he would go on forever simply feeling this one thing, of keeping her close. He drifts further, while the turtle floats away, and far underneath in the great depths, enormous schools of fish split apart like an oil slick, spin, and regroup.

Way out where this inky darkness roared, too far to return if it had ever occurred to a boy taking his own life, he grew calmer, as though it felt the most natural place to be on his journey, he was almost in reach of taking in his own hand, the ancestral chosen hand from another time. If he still had any inkling of his suicide, or of any decision that had led him to this moment, he knew that once upon a time he had grabbed a moment, and run to this ending, where he would slip into eternity with her, only her, in his soul.

5

Only miracle makers, and the spirits of the sea, and the shifters moving cultural memories from one side of the world to the other – this was where the sea men lived in the vast watery world of oceans divided into sea lanes, moving the endless traffic of cargo ships as waves clapped over the decks when storm clouds blown from the ancestral realm of sky laws ran loose – wreaking great havoc. Now, so far away in these seas, a tiny dull light glowed from a kerosene lantern rocking from side to side, barely detectable in the open ocean from where it swayed on the deck of an ageing fishing boat slung low in the sea.

This was the kind of vessel that hid by day, camouflaging itself behind the swells, indistinguishable in the sea by the worn sea-blue paintwork of long-ago fishing men in love with deep ocean blue, and the mystical tales of far-off pale-blue skies, or its bleeding sores, sea salt corroding rust, worm-eaten rotting hulls smelling of centuries of salty seas and fish, memories locked with years of handling fish guts, the murmurings, splashes, and generations of sea algae stuck to the sides of boats.

This was the world of another kind of master cargo shifter, a ghost man of the ocean who was welded to the sway moving beneath his feet. On this journey far off the northern coastline, one taken no differently from others made routinely over many years on board this ailing junk boat that was not his, he was the type of man who hauled human cargo around by asking no questions, and giving no answers.

He left the talking to other more convincing sounds of invincibility – from what claimed to be neither ghost, nor spirit, but the real thing, still alive, Offenbach's operatic algae-tinctured parrot *Vert Vert*, the puke-green feathered oldest bird on Earth, and legal owner of the leaky boat. Let the fat reprobate parrot do the talking. Drum up the deal. Scam the scammers. Suss out dead weight. Be the liability dumper. Guarantee the profit margin. Sell a dud. In other words, organise the business end of their illegal trade in human flesh. Someone had to do it. And from beyond the swells, all you could hear all day long was the ancient parrot chucking about its shamble of psalms and pious hymn-singing like a medieval priest to its holy dove, while moaning and groaning, mostly in Latin, complaining about the growing cost of moving human cargo, that did nothing else but complain about the hardship of the trip. *I mean, any moron could see this was not a cruise ship docked in Venice*. The parrot was a creature of multiple personalities and did not act its age, nor did it bother to show a bit of respect for the political correctness of the era. It thought it was still back in the sixteenth century, where it was au fait to voice a shipwrecked sailor's blasphemy of the Earth's holiest verses, with its catalogue of what sea men composed on the job to save themselves in a wall of waves, words such as, *I fucking hate you, you cunt of a sea*. Let's just say this pious hymn-singer was of questionable alternating multi-identities, quote foul-mouth people-mover unquote, or, if you spoke like a doomed sixteenth-century slave, the parrot was what you would call a slave trader.

The cargo shifter knew there were already millions of faces like his in the sea, people who had long ago abandoned the homeland face, the father's face, the face of country, race, honour, love, or history. His was just another face of the worldliness coming hard on the heels of the era, a disposable humanity claimed only by oceans, and the sun above. His mind remembered not faces, not names, nor identity, but carried only the stories of untimely death written for someone else, to remember on the faces of those he pulls from the sea. And another thing. He remembers obedience. He runs to it, because he was told to run long ago, and he remembers to keep on running away from the living. You know what they say, best never to look back, the father's last words: *You live only for the family. Promise me this. Don't ever return here.*

Seas knew him, saw him living with people whose spirits he was moving, and while knowing they would never see land again, he simply watched as time went by, and as their weather-beaten faces darkened, then wearied into ghostly grey, were forged, lined, and shaped by the sea for the rest of their days.

In the vastness of where the seas and skies unified, his eyes squinted in the glare, but were totally adapted for staring into the sea for hours like birds hovering above the water, and while scanning the sea for days on end, he kept mingling eagle-like equalisations in his thoughts about what he had seen in the slightest disturbance of water, like a man who might have dragged into boats all sorts of creatures of the sea in his lifetime with the casual air of one who knew how to take care of whatever turned up from the ocean, and for reaching down into the depths, and dragging out without a thought what was caught in the net. It was what was in the net that had fed his mind in all these years of ocean-wandering around the world, just as there were many times when the old net had come in empty, or was full of great holes, and all he had to think about was starving, of eating only his thoughts in this hell. The swell was mild, and the current was running with the boat when he heard kites whistling, thousands caught up in an ancestor's net flung above the ocean. The kites were swirling above the sea in one spot, and for a while, he had watched their desperate flights to break free, their spinning off in the distance, and like bombs, snatching at the waves.

Once he had lived in an ancient low-lying fishing village beside the sea, and hell, what do you know, it too became a sacred relic under the sea. This new-era man, one of the last left standing, crept from the scene and would never again think of his people whose ancestry had been connected with ocean fish from forever in some small spot on Google Earth, now only a compass point in the ocean, with all else asunder. For all it was worth, he was the only living person who knew where the place was, since it was no longer registered on the rapidly changing map of the world. Initially, when they had walked bare-footed in tides running through their homes, they said you know what, let's move higher, and higher again with the sea continuing to rise, flew their flag SAVE US, and waved their banners to the world about being climate change refugees. Then, you know what happened? Those people moved even higher, and higher again, while clinging to the tops of poles cemented in the sea floor where their homes once stood, making a stand, to continue protecting their cultural heritage in complex weather systems, and while they were at it, evolving as some kind of aerial trapeze artists, but being people who liked saying *you got to keep having hope*, they were reaching for the skies on stilts and hoping for the sea to recede. This did not happen. He became the remains, what was left, and he would always remain floating on the sea as cargo, a carpetbagger – a highly skilled anticipator of the unexpected, second-guessing the unexplainable intruding on his world of self, and right now, he kept a steady gaze through the sun burning down in the haze radiating off a patch of water, before continuing to scan the distances, line by invisible line, catching the vowels together for describing what he had envisioned, before turning around to stare in the opposite direction, while ploughing the contours of the same open sea.

So! What if he had the ability to read changes in the movement of the ocean's terrain? What was remarkable about being able to read your surroundings as though your life depended on it? In the displacement era, when so many people of the sea were redefining themselves, the sea was full of people who had a planetary gaze seeded by the human spirit lost in the homeland. Did this make an exceptional human being? A triumph? Who knew what he felt? Did he even feel like a man? Or was he half fish? His was a steady gaze, more adapted to sea-mapping like fish, than looking at the structural geography of land, more accustomed to looking through the glare of the sun hitting the sea with narrowed eyes. He focused in to the dazzle of light shining on the water rippling and spreading in circles attracting the kites. He was wary, careful not to put the boat in more danger, for this man won his life by instinctively knowing the outcome of being led through many scenarios, prisms beyond his ability to control, from either fighting the force of nature, or the powerfulness of the spirit world, and as well as considering all the facts of scientific possibility in the changing world, he knew his limitations, and of his own capacity to contribute to man-made destruction. He had live cargo. They would survive only by his remembering that they had all come this far by believing in him, although he could not possibly say what amount of responsibility created success, for anything could slip into total disaster at the next possibility of tempting fate.

He knew, while searching through each of the imaginary grids of his endless surveillance of where to find easy fish, how many dead things wrapped around him. Stingrays. Octopus. Old whales. Cattle. Horses. Cats. Dogs. Pigs. Rats. A sea of dead fish once. The sea was a cemetery of seagulls. Men. Women. Children. Families. Many shrouds were wrapped around him, pulling the boat closer in this sea of death. He spoke just a few words, almost whispering to himself. *Do not panic.* No one felt there was a need to panic. A situation, whatever it was, would be dealt with. He would deal with it like he does, *and anyway,* his voice always low, felt calm to others close by who heard while wrapping themselves in his radiated strength, and felt the force of his determination on these high seas. But wasn't his language foreign in these waters? His from another continent, from the other side of the world. He gestured to the other sea men on board to watch the kites, looked to someone at the wheel guarding the little fuel left to finish the journey, only enough to bring the boat to the coast now, and their eyes locked, moved together, to bring the boat closer to where he was pointing to the kites. There were people on board who were like himself, who spoke this language of silence, and who were now leaning over the side of the boat, also staring at the birds, but they said nothing about the wastage of fuel. They left this fate to their God. Hoping. Good fate. More prayers, hoping to land safely one day.

The old sea slug crept through the crepuscular gloominess of the advancing night, while the ailing motor's chugging barely kept up the task of carrying its crowded human cargo, packed on the deck like sardines. All the desperate men on board looking towards the darkening horizon as it disappeared into the night. The parrot continued chanting holiness as the day's news, the peace dove cooed, but the sea men were not seeking unification with a starry night moving towards some faraway homeland that no longer existed for them, nor how they were going to fit into the growing realities of millions of others who found themselves homeless, somewhere on the heating planet.

There were some with families on board, some who were alone, but who together kept slinking away with luggage consisting of old wounds, hunger, and thirst, while habitually gathering in the night's darkness on a cramped deck, huddled in a sleepless mass of humanity's landless, left only with the light of sovereignty from the planet to guide feelings plagued with a sense of abandonment, self-scorn, and doom. There was no other way to look at it. Pre-heat. Post-heat. Call it what you liked. Those people were just a handful of the countless descendants of the once cooler world, who had become landless. They were over the sea. Those who were threatening other people's sovereign borders in the modern era. It was not safe to be in the same sea where incredible transformations were taking place down the decades as the sea gypsy world became a humanity never looking back over its shoulder to see land rights again, while simultaneously, never feeling that something significant had changed within them-selves, even while totally absorbed, with an overwhelming desire to be returned to the long-forgotten world of their sovereignty, never noticing how they were effortlessly evolving into a humanity capable of inhuman transformation, where in an instant, a click of the fingers, they became nothing more than a camouflaged breathing element on a rust-ridden leaky boat, and as though they too had lived their entire life under heatwaves radiating from a sun that was so fierce, it had burnt a horror story into the paint of the sea, and of the sky on its hull.

He had allowed the boat to drift south to save fuel, and it had taken weeks where they starved, went thirsty, drifted off course in the huge storms, when lightning struck the sea around them thousands of times before giving up trying to kill them, and the boat almost capsized, heaving itself into a murky grey soup. These people knew that the boat could not carry on much more. Not much more at all, and each secretly knew that the thing that was needed most of all, was to lighten the load. But how? What? There would not have been one person who would have complained if someone else died, if there had been an accident, someone had fallen overboard. It could have been anyone, anyone might have welcomed the boat sinking, and be done with it, for they wished to let go, the final lesson, letting go.

Some might have drifted off into dreams in the midnight hours, catching a few moments of sleep, one would never know who had been too tense to sleep, no one said, nor said who sat on the deck looking at the blackness, occasionally catching another's gaze in the dull glow of the lantern, the distant lightning, or the faraway light of a distant homeland abuzz in this moment of emptiness, and perhaps felt joy tinging throughout their senses for having captured in the ocean's placidity one, two, maybe three images of a faded long-ago time, of imagining what life might still have been, had there been a different course, or somewhere ahead, fate was finding a way now the storms had passed.

The boat continued bobbing where the kites were mobbing the sea, where each bird seemed to be throwing itself headfirst from the sky with great force, diving at the sea, returning to the sky and back again, as though locked in an invisible net. *There! There! Someone?* The cargo shifter spoke only to himself, *Must have fallen from one of the other boats.* Others asked: *Where?* Then, they broke the habit of refusing to see freely, and peered into the pitch-black sea, trying to catch a glimpse of the body adrift, but saw nothing, and falling back exhausted, gave themselves up to the night.

There! There! The waves poured, then churned, concealing the bounty hidden under its surface. *Go! Go!* It only took the smallest detection for his eyes to read this sea, to see a body falling into eternity, and this man from the other side of the world flew over to the side of the water-impregnated boat, drove the length of his arm into the sea among the diving birds, and dragged Aboriginal Sovereignty out of the broil.

Perhaps only mighty things happen in the vespertine hours, when in a momentary parting of the clouds, the moon shone brightest on the breaking waves' rhythm of nocturnal swellings signalling the sacred – a singular glowing on the disturbance of the ocean's night-time dance, a tablature creating a long flowing movement of tacit calmness in the gleam, which was enough for the eagle-eyed sea man, the one who never slept at night while keeping vigil for the slightest changes of light on the back of the ocean from breaks in the clouds, or else a falling star, enough to reach into the water, to pluck Aboriginal Sovereignty out of the sea, snatch him single-handed from its grip, and haul him over the side of the rickety boat.

The boat woke when sea spray shot upwards, stalled mid-air, and the weight of salty moisture clung in the air on this blackest of nights, as the body hit the deck, and the ocean shook as though being pulled apart by a volcanic eruption far below the surface. The boat owner, Vert Vert, woke startled by the shockwave trembling the vessel, from where it was twitching and scratching fleas in its century-old dreams with its head tucked under its salt-laden feathered wing while it slept standing upright in the corner of a pile of deck junk next to a strayed peace dove. The cocky jumped first up, then down, and carried on in a mad screaming tirade about killing the sea. A flash of distant lightning flowed along the deck, and picked up in a flash the wave of fear jerking through the mind-shifting nightmares jumping in the open air from bundle to bundle of sleeping people, reacting to the ocean water splashing onto their skin, which sent them skittling further down into the soul world where the terrible fearfulness of oceans had come to play tricks in their minds. The entire deck became a wave of people shifting out of the way of the touch of salty water that could be seen in patches of moonlight running in a torrent towards where they were lying in flits of sleep while waiting for the soft hour about two or three in the morning when the heat radiating off the flat sea dies and squashes from the mind all thoughts of the long days without relief from the relentless sun and windless days, when finally, it was possible until dawn, to drift off into deep sleep. Who noticed the rescue attempt? Bodies come. Bodies go. These people lived in a palace of death, not of divine faith, and they wondered why the man sailor with the eyes of a sea eagle was always searching for more people to rescue. Even, look now, rescuing the dead ones. It was not like they were living on an international cargo ship, or on one of the tens of thousands of dry-bulk cargo barges streaming up and down the Huangpu River.

You either breathed, or you stopped breathing, that was it really. There was only so much space no matter which way you looked at it, and to the people on that hot night's deck, spooked as they were by the world turning on its head when the body hit the deck, made room, moved accordingly as the boat rocked, to avoid being touched by the mystery in the water flowing from the body. You could call that a deficit. Something that added extra liability to the sum total of the scheme of things, when you realised that you were still breathing among the living, and perhaps, that you still cared about something, even though you could hide yourself in the darkness of nights like this, and had thought you were already dead. Then out of the blue, you were caught out by this dead person, he had shown you that you were still breathing. Who needed to ask questions? So many were asked already about whether saving anything was necessary. It was not about the money. Or being in another life. All this heady business to be weighed up. What a life was worth. The burning question of the era? All of humanity asking which life was worth saving, or how to risk death in any situation, like it was being asked right at this moment by that wet greyness, a ghost clinging to a body, that seemed to be asking these worldwide catastrophe-exhausted people on the overcrowded boat to decide if this dead person among all the dying, was worth sharing their space with, on this dangerous sea voyage, right now. This was the dilemma of dying in the ocean, when the spirit would not let go of a body not returned to the sacred homeland.

Ever since the lonely sea man in charge of this turnout was a child, helping his father pull dead people away from the arms of the sea, he knew by staring in the heaving surface water, how to read the message that the sea was asking of him. He knew how ocean waters behaved, how its ghosts carried a corpse of the Anthropocene in a roll, kept it floating on the surface while waiting to be found and taken from the sea. He had grown up with a deep sense of these old sea laws about bringing back the bodies to their families, the sacred people of country who had died in shock after being tossed into the sea like the waste of humanity. These people he had pulled limp from the sea always frightened him. He might have questioned once or twice, about whether he was out of date, that he had too much ancient thinking entrenched in his head, or whether he was out of touch with the modern reality of giving up what weighs too much, of travelling light without responsibilities for anyone else, for the era was too unprecedented, and unable to weigh up what it was that was expendable, or question what was worth saving. The trouble, and he knew it too, was that there were too many people to save, and you know what? There were not many people left doing the saving. Maybe humanity had become lost with having too much to save, and was now left saving for what remained of itself, more than worrying about the dying. Yet he knew that these people had died knowing that whatever was found in their watery remains, a god, ancestor, fish, or human eyes, or a guard bird in flight over the ocean, all would feel the story of horror written on the dead person's face, the last moment of being alive, their final act of writing a lasting testament. This was their legacy, the ending of a human law written in perpetuity, that would never be erased, nor forgotten, by eternal sacred laws of the Earth.

6

The chants of the sea will continue for all times, and sometimes, when you hear a rhapsody travelling in the winds across the water and far away in the flatlands, you will know it is the world rejoicing, and sometimes, it is the slow music of changing fate, like the way it was abruptly changing course in the time immemorial, for the here and now, sacred orders, renunciation, by intervening into a boy's suicide in those midnight hours. Sea spraying. The wind picking up the body in the spray, and pleading with the air to breathe life into his lungs, while guiding the boy towards an ailing people's boat in this seemingly ad hoc rendezvous through changing ocean currents so late on a weekday night.

You are my brother. The lonely sea man who rarely spoke two civil words to anyone, the same man who asked nothing of the ocean, who makes no lists of demands, or hopes for anything on Earth, such as any land giving him an identity, a temporary visa, or one inch of soil he could say belonged to him, was now oddly muttering over the unconscious broken body on the deck of the crowded boat. *Brother?* Ever heard anyone talking this broken kind of English before, *I, it was me, I found him alive*, and calling him his brother, yep, the very same man who had for years worked in the hospitality business of people smuggling, and barely acknowledged who was on board in this people-laden boat business that he kept afloat. He always faced the open sea – preferred it that way, with his view turned away from the sight of a damp, salt-encrusted huddled humanity hoping to be saved, and leaving parrot talk to the parrot. Let the bird handle the on-board entertainment, since it enjoyed the chitchat of its long cyclic chanting of avian sagas about the life and death of birds, the stories with many horrible bilingual mixed-up episodes which he stretched into decades before reaching the end. Who could say if the parrot's little dictatorial world found its equivalent in the world's major dictators of billions, or but a few scraps of life, but the parrot really liked indoctrinating its captured audience in this confined space like a detention camp with no escape, by screwing the brains of these boat people about the importance of brotherhood in times like these with the birds, trees, the flowers and the hills and on and on in its preaching through the complete catalogue of life on Earth, to teach the homeless seafaring what to say in an emergency on the high seas. *We are brothers. Brothers! Brothers!* Etc.! Et cetera?

Like always though, the world of this little boat-smuggling operation changed suddenly from time to time, and whenever change came, it was left to the sea man who preferred to be surrounded by silence, to answer the brute officialism of the next round of voices of border control people now headlighting the boat, demanding identification in some ungodly hour before dawn, and so he said something he had initially heard blurred through the static of life, sounding something like this, *Eh! Brothers*.

Only minutes earlier, when the military men had arrived suddenly, hovering in helicopters that roared above the ocean, and looking down through the beams of spotlights shining onto the heaving boat, they had abstractly noted the terrified faces staring up at them. The manoeuvre was quick. Before the boat people could raise themselves off the floor of the deck, the uniformed men were being lowered on board the stricken boat from the helicopter.

The custom patrol boats arrived soon after. Name? Name? A score of uniformed men demanded names of everyone through the fully uniformed interpreter who busily stumbled through a string of probable languages of these current boat people inside their sovereign border, the intergenerational sea-dwelling people whose mixed origins, it seemed, could be anywhere from the north or the south of the equator, including Middle East to Asia. Finally, with more orders barked into his ears to get the job done quicker, the interpreter started pointing to the unconscious man lying at his feet. The people-mover pointed to the deck, and thumped his chest: *He's my brother*. Name? Name? The other men on board nodded at the unconscious man lying on the deck. The people-mover thumped his chest, pointed to the deck: *Brother*. They thought Aboriginal Sovereignty had fallen from one of the other boats in the dispersed small fleet of moving homeless people, that were also in the act of being caught in this sweep of the Australian net of closed borders, and if you were boat people you would never set foot in the country.

Whatever followed the flashing strobe light circling the night ocean and back onto the deck in the questioning continuing forever, the life fantastic simply flew over the head of the sea man, who continued staring out into the night. He was more interested in expressing his idea of brotherhood, hissed by the wind now in the sea spray, *Brothers!* Without looking back, he casually gestured to the truth behind him – *brothers*, pointing to each bundle on the deck, where every man, woman and child on his boat was his actual brother, now caught in the passing strobe light. He shrugged his shoulders time and again while the border control interrogators, ignoring the parrot and the peace dove, were trying to get him to identify his boat people properly, to tell them the story of where these people really came from.

Who cares? He would not know. How could he know who any of these people were, when he had long forgotten what it meant to be identified as a person from somewhere. The border control officers reckoned that he was lying, because he was acting like a French man, the way he stalked through his human cargo without managing to stumble over anyone. They did not know that he had executed this stalk walk many times before through the crowded deck, for he knew how to stalk his way into oblivion. The sea man scoffed, and thought who cares if he becomes theatrical moody in a non-verbal kind of way by fully dramatising his indignation like a European, as though it had become utterly inconceivable to him to continue being forced to speak Australian in a cat bailing up a mouse kind of situation, when he was wasting his bilingual tongue on speaking ignorance, to match a version of the dismal English language plaguing the Earth.

Of course, while being restrained and forced to listen to this night raid invasion of sovereign border personnel questioning the authority of a master of vast oceanic voyages, you could imagine this sea man may well have felt rightfully loathe to respond, but how could a piece of the sea respond when its thoughts were habitually being used to communicate with his vessel about its problems of keeping afloat to move elsewhere on this oceanic planet, to speak back to the sea for its ways of persecuting him? What was the point of hearing the sound of any human language being spoken, when it was spoken without hope, as though the rising sun was unwelcome. This silent philosophising did not seem to be of interest to the parrot. The sea man often felt totally lost on understanding why the parrot was entranced with the sounds of its speech, as though it could never believe in the miracle of hearing itself speak like a man, but the parrot with ruffled feathered greenness did soak up every single word in sight, regardless of how worthless, or its stupidity. The bird shovelled the lot into its skull, the word churning hot as a burning coal-fired furnace firing up its foul-mouth shrills, or squeezing another word, phrase, please, any rendition in its fat brain to join the lulling hymns in its library of sagas thrumming to the captured audience. But now, the parrot was silent, and did not bother to say that it, actually a parrot, owned the people-smuggling operation.

While the sea man continued to act belligerent by not bothering to explain to another human being about carrying human cargo, or what lay behind the blankness of a human gaze closed and bordered up forever, he was no fool. He knew catastrophe, that there was no mind in the world that would be able to carry the full weight of lives silenced, nor feel the infinite weight of the betrayal that hung in the boat. It was all held there, locked by speechlessness, drowned in the sounds of the sea, and the sea birds wallowing in the twists and turns of the air braiding all knowledge inside out while following secret journeys across the world, all held by the weight of nothingness forever returning to the mountainous wishing, but failing, unable to wish in the private country of a sovereign world occupied only by the ghosts of an erased humanity, ghosts of country belonging to the vague long ago, which was nobody else's business except their own.

The easiest thing in the world would be to drown himself by jumping into the fathomless depths of their stories, but he felt it was not necessary to waste his breath where there was no respect for the sacredness of such knowledge. Why would he? He knew no language existed that was powerful enough to explain the world of one single person on the boat, nor was he sure if a comprehending language of man-made atrocities would ever be developed that discovered how to empathise with the depth of loss in the sum total of human endurance so far, nor the strength and survival of each of these people standing behind him, even though God knows a new form of language would be needed for a future world of exponential chaos, when someone of far greater compassion, will need to tell these stories of the broken world that even on this small boat he could not look at, and had turned his back on what these people saw, had known, and he was ashamed of being unable to reach the level of understanding required of him. It is a routine drill, he knows it, so he says next to nothing to the curt questioning of border control interrogation before again being sent on their way on the high seas of whatever ocean, and this will last, while air continued to pump in and out of their lungs.

Perhaps the continual flow of breath was just a question of looking at his situation in a certain way, by settling with short-term fate, rather than always searching for the longer view, but whatever was true, people felt foreign to the sea man. The world he views like the peace dove sleeping through the interrogation, perfectly simple. The only countries that existed, whether on land or sea, were occupied by blood brothers. You were either a blood brother, or you were not. *All the same! Well! We are the same. Everyone on the boat was a blood brother.* When asked what country they came from, he says – if he bothers to say anything – *Here, this boat. This country.* He flings his arm around in a gesture to protect the brothers behind him, and while indicating that the overloaded grossly submerged boat was the country of his blood brothers, snarls, *What was the difference? Humph! You are the invaders here. You think you own me. Think we are all the same.* It was simple to say they were brothers, while others on board say nothing.

The border control interpreter struggled to keep himself standing upright on the swaying refugee boat. He stood among the Australian Sovereign Border military men in mottled green and grey uniform, the colours of the ocean's floor, gloved, capped and navy-vested, light goggles hiding their eyes. Vert Vert's waterlogged cargo vessel, now swaying lopsidedly, tilting further sideways, was clearly unable to endure the extra weight. The hull drew in more water from the turbulence created by the helicopters, and was leaning dangerously, on the verge of sinking.

My brother! He needs medical attention, the sea man spoke in a style of voice that had been dragged through gravel, while he now crouched on the deck to cradle Aboriginal Sovereignty's head, to stop him swallowing more water spilling over the sides of the hull as it continued to pitch and roll. But in the speed of the operation to evacuate the boat and to destroy it, the people-carrier was pushed aside with a weapon, immediately ordered to stand with the others who were bumping into each other while they were being counted, as the panicky interpreter continued his futile attempts to question them randomly about their origins, where language had died long ago from wrecked weather systems, or had been killed by invaders. *Quick! Where are you from? Where are you from? Which country? Quick!* The boat was searched while Aboriginal Sovereignty rolled in the muck on the floor of the swaying boat, and somewhere in his unconsciousness, dreamt that he was touching eternal peace with his fingertips. The boat people were ordered to remove their clothes and identity, throw everything on the deck before leaving the pitching boat, and then roughly pulled on board the patrol boat, or dropped, pushed, or thrown into the sea, to be hauled up by ropes from a lifebuoy thrown at them.

Only one man among plenty spoke the wretched language of unwantedness, of what had been long lost in old sea burials. The sea man unfurled the world's broken and reassembled languages while gesturing pointlessness, throwing his arms above his head, and letting loose his mixed-up array of language while pretending he was fishing, and struggling to bring in the biggest fish in the world with a big smile on his face, which probably meant to the border patrol people that these people were lying about being only a bunch of poor fishermen. The language keeper assembled some more words of his unidentifiable language to the unidentifiable human beings camouflaged in army grey combat fatigues. Supposedly, he meant to say that they were not into the business of invading other people's countries, or wishing to be destroyers of traditional lands with global-warming consequences. They were not colonising destroyers. They were not the ecocidal people. Not army. No need to be frightened. They were not the ones murdering the planet of the broken homelands. He tried to indicate that they had run off course. They were out of fuel. They were intergenerational landless people, not invaders, not armed.

The vessel was searched for drugs, or anything else that could be seized in the illegal import trade. Rest assured, there was nothing worth money on this boat. No gold. No exotic parrots. No drugs. Ice. No rare monkeys. Smuggled orangutans. Endangered lizards. There was just an ageing millionaire parrot that was into the importing-exporting industry, the unstoppable verbaliser of bird saga, but now, strangely, silent. The green parrot was placed in a wooden box. The peace dove had probably flown off to continue its endless search throughout the world for peace. Then lastly, just moments before the fishing boat was doused with diesel and set alight, Aboriginal Sovereignty, now strapped onto a stretcher, was hauled up from the deck by one of those army helicopters while flames soared around him, and in his unconscious state he was only vaguely aware of floating through plumes of smoke he saw through slits in his heavily hooded eyes, and what he saw felt to him as though he was passing through the fog of forever. The boat people watching below thought the miraculous fish man, dragged dead from the ocean by the watcher of the sea, now appeared transcendently *aurea*, which was the word they used to describe a holy spectacle of deep memory, that felt like being in the greatness of a vast spirit-charged homeland, and they continued to stare upwards in awe at the corpse being lowered on board the ocean shield, the protector of sovereign borders from all forms of invasion, its Indigenous inhabitants, viruses, diseases, and other peoples in the rapidly increasing ocean population of the landless.

7

What was the gift of Aboriginal Sovereignty? Guts? A dazzling star-quality agility now handicapped, pinned down, like it was left shackled in the ocean, anchored to a reef? Someone would have to go out there, and find his spirit. This boy does not soar like an eagle anymore, or float above, like a thundercloud. Never mind! Just look at him instead! Leave his spirit out there, where over the sea the spirit healers flew, and back again to the mainland jundurr world of Praiseworthy. This dust fellow was not ordinary anymore. He could not remember how to recapture time everlasting in a heartbeat each and every time he breathes. He never knows how to cast an eye over the circus acts, fight them from tipping the life fantastic out of the blood stream, out of the force of his life. The less he sees somehow blinds the world too, through this business of diminishing the ordinary from everything. He was only capable of catching tiny glimpses, a snatch of what was going on around him through eyes that never fully recovered. The sea took it all.

The truth was, in the world where he was now living with his brother, the sea man, life was neatly folded and pushed away into the background. He does not mind becoming something else, of nothing that was vaguely recognisable to him. He would not know how to find what happened to the rest of his life, which his sea brother said was filtering time immemorial through the opaque depths of lonely oceans. He was no old dreamer, where he could have seen that the greatest spiritual ancestral beings were visiting him, because he no longer knows who they are, or how to feel their presence, he does not know to whose ancient worlds they belonged, nor that they were in his being. The old people came and walked along beside him, hobbling along, and finding it hard to keep up with this young spring-step fellow always walking too quickly, but look out, he was going nowhere except to catch up with the thoughts that kept running away from him.

Those thoughts were where the ancestral spirits of country, the ghostly serpents, were winding the rivers, and where the dingo dogs were sleeping in the mountain range in the distance, sitting with their huge backs to him, and with the mangrove forest along the coastline that looked like tribespeople dancing ceremonies in the storm winds singing the stories, rhythms that continued to stay in his mind for days, or months, and sometimes, with the fog women spread across flat country for kilometre after kilometre, lying there like something extraordinary in the red haze.

He continued to circle the thoughts of his traditional country, as though following the ancestors of changing seasons, but if you looked to see where he was looking, you would see his view kept shooting from this to that reality, hit by the glaring sunlight that blocked him from seeing anything clearly in the blurring mirage. The view was sweet, and became sweeter, as it moved through the years of his continual circling over the same piece of ground in the barren exercise yard of the detention centre while all the other prisoners watched, and thought he was really somewhere else, that perhaps his mind was safely away from imprisonment, and he was in the world for seafarers protected by the powerful gods that bring the tides, thunder, lightning, wind and the sea waves. He was protected by the goddess Mazu who protects sea travellers, sailors and fishermen. He was protected in the Irish sea world of Lir. He was watched over by Zhu Rong dwelling in the dragon's lair of the South China Sea, and other sea gods such as Long Wang the Dragon King, and in the Shinto Sea, by the sea god Watatsumi. So powerful became his influence of casting spells over others watching his travelling ceremony, shuffling over the same piece of ground creating country through the symbolism of circles, that even though the inmates of the detention centre, who had originated from all over the world, did not know where he was travelling in the ceremonial ground he was creating, they gifted him with the dreams of their destinations, their gods, and they willed him onwards, championed their proxy to be inside their desire to be elsewhere. Aboriginal Sovereignty generated peace of mind as the inmates who had illegally been incarcerated would calculate the distances he travelled through endlessly pacing the exercise yard in their inescapable barbwire-fenced detention camp, and they wanted to believe that he had reached the extraordinary distances of freedom, and had succeeded in passing through all obstacles, to reach the desired destinations that were otherwise impossible to reach, so that through him, they too could become closer to their gods in endless time. While they saw what they wanted to see of elsewhere in this impenetrable prison, only he could see the haze women roar down from the red sandstorm sky and dance across the arid baking flatlands while carrying their pandanus-palm fans, and see how they shimmered in their dancing mirage while weaving in and out of his brothers. And where you would find him pacing through one after another of his odyssean journeys, he was circling the haze lands, and watching the old wise people storming up from its sea of dust like silver fish chasing after swarms of those wandering white butterflies that colourblind his vision with cascades of whiteness, shielding him from forming real thoughts about any of his reality by changing the postcard scenery of freedom, and stopping his mind from leaving his sense of belonging elsewhere rather than falling into the entrapment of being locked inside a razor-wire prison surrounded by the sea, where he was marooned, and left to rot with his world of brothers speaking their disjointed languages.

What else was there to do? When he spoke in the language of the oldest ancestors, nobody understood a word of what he was saying. Nobody knew what his origins were, where he came from, and he could not tell them because he never left the dream place in his mind, and whatever homeland language he was speaking failed to succumb to the foreign interpretation of invasion.

The souls of the brotherhood sung from the same hymn sheet about the spirit boy shuffling up the shelly dust in a rhythm dance, rocking back and forth while continuing to pace in the compound. They were full of wonder about the sacredness of the boy coming into their stories, which they said were dreams falling from the stars at night. Their stories grew wilder in a garden blooming with dreams about how an actual spirit had fallen like a star from the sky, its glowing light plunging deep into the ocean like a gannet diving after a fish, and how the surrounding sea exploded into a silvery aura beside this falling star that became a sea wizard, leaning over the side of his country that he had shape-shifted by weaving and plaiting planks of timber to resemble a boat, and while leaning into the sea, had fished the sacred boy from the water. These people said it was as though another life had been created for them in their capsule of brotherhood. Where else would a true brother come from, one that puts his own life on the line for others? The way they saw it, it was as though they were heading towards the new world of an unmoored star, continuing these long journeys in redefining what freedom meant while reaching a haven built only in the mind. They said that when you were blessed like a shooting star travelling unmoored to anything, the language too needed to be redefined. And you know what? They felt you would not speak the languages of mankind while in the business of surviving, not when you finally understood, that a lodestar spoke another kind of language altogether.

What Aboriginal Sovereignty spoke was spirit language, the feel of dancing feet, pacing, shuffling through the pearly shells, dust rising, while travelling the ground in the compound. You could see in the trails of dust blowing from his footsteps, a divine presence speaking a language of its own coming up from the soil. Or perhaps, it was something else altogether, and he danced a language of forgetting, of not wanting to remember, not articulating anything, or knowing through a single word.

You might call them seasons, the wet or the dry that came and went as quickly as it had arrived, while rows upon rows of brothers gathered under the baking sun in bare feet on the edge of the oven-hot crushed-shell exercise ground to watch the ceremonial boy doing the sacred stuff. The weather was invariable, and did not change greatly from scorching heat when that mad typhoon fellow on steroids blew up the sand and shells into a storm, while the brothers held onto life in driving horizontal rain by clinging to the sand under their feet in flooding king tides, watching Aboriginal Sovereignty dancing, shuffling through the fish, circling the compound. These interned beseechers for life, the wide-eyed fishermen or the landless, cheered and spoke on and on about not being able to see the holy thing written in the broken shells through sandy blight eyes from weeks of sandstorms when hot winds blew howls from the earth. They howled too, but still, they wanted to watch that fallen holy boy shuffling the fragments of shells, and were giddied from his endless circling, as he rotated the backwards and forwards flow of his movements through the sand in a ceremonial on this small piece of earth, writing of journeys through the consciousness of all times. They could not read the stories being written in the pearly shell ground, but it felt as though something of life was being created, and you know something? It was not unusual to find some of these anguished brothers of the world rushing up to the boy too sacred to touch, acting as though they were unable to stop themselves from kneeling on the ground, or trembling like a leaf in front of the divine, and begging him never to stop making them see the reality of the betrayal of their time as fishermen, or as boat people left to die on this flooding atoll, this land forsaken, claimed by the rising sea, even though he seemed incapable of comprehending their presence.

Aboriginal Sovereignty remained unalive to the world around him. He barely noticed where he was living, or how he was joined to a league of brothers in a family that was so vast, their numbers formed a single place constituting neither land nor sea. They were a single soul of humanity trying to figure out what happens next, what was coming...their existence, clearly identifiable and interconnected through the map of human fate, enduring great circumstances of loss, eternally roaming oceans in the crisis of a ruined planet. Caught people. Stalked. Trapped. Silenced. Censored. Rejected. Captives of powerful planetary investors hiding from the plain view of world crisis in private gated sanctuaries throughout the world.

His life seemed to be caught in the quickness of a short breath of time, but this denied the agelessness of eternity bound together through his interconnection with the coming of the breeze, the clouds, the rain, the next storm, and continual growth. When he breathed, it was not to take the air from the atmosphere, but to inhale ancestry, the mighty creation spirits journeying through him, coursing their way in a regular pattern, slowly travelling to his lungs and returning through the moist air released back into the atmosphere. He wasted no breath on the plainsong of the brothers because he wished nothing from sacredness. He asked nothing of the sea that surrounded him. He made no list of demands to be saved, or hopes for survival, salvation, identity, new life, just as he asked no land to be his, for he was of country, and country was in him. It was as though his existence was enough while walking to his destination, the point of his endless navigation circling the compound like the hand of an implanted compass of ancestry that was always positioning homeland, always channelling the place of his belonging from any other place in the world.

Aboriginal Sovereignty might end up living this way forever, like some form of eternal life with his sea wizard brother, the restrained imprisoned lodestar, and beside the countless others, the hundreds of thousands, perhaps millions of people entombed alive, secretly hidden in the new lands being formed by the rattling of body parts all over the world, and by a frothing sea that vomited monstrous mudflats jutting from the ocean, which became covered by fine white sand from wave after wave crushing the pearly seashells in the surf. These places grew wilder in a world apart, where the planet unfolds merciless winds in an exorcism of wild arms, swiping at the sand it pushes back into the sea, and leaving no trace of hope for permanency in the bareness of the eroding mudflats, the peneplain it leaves behind in this cycle of waves delivering sand, and the winds blowing it away.

Makeshift shifting worlds were a total laissez-faire feature of modernity in the era of this burning planet, where the modern home was a weathered, stripped and mud-stained plastic sheet thrown over a couple of sticks. The collective broken from ancestral homelands existed in shelters resembling thousands of giant praying mantises dragged up onto the beach by frequent storms. If Aboriginal Sovereignty dreamt at all here, it was a beckoning dream of the dawn bringing glimmers of light over the sea, an awakening eternally revisiting the break of day. If this reality had any relationship to Praiseworthy, it was in the portrayal of the subliminal forces of colonisation, where he ate or drank what belonged to others, and he held his hand out without thinking, took what he was given as if by instinct, subconsciously begging for his life, knowing that his physical sustenance depended on one thing alone, which was called foreign aid. Aid workers. Aid workers' uniforms. Aid drops. Aid for world peace. Of being absorbed by a temporary landscape that will eventually be reclaimed by panicky waves throwing sand back into the sea.

Life flows through aid, aid that was only brief, selective, moves forward, and leaves him behind, circling the compound on that tiny spit disintegrating into the ocean. You know something though, there were millions of hands shooting up every day from inconsequential spits dotted across the world that were saying, *pick me from this rubble*. His hand automatically copied the arms of desperation – the brotherhood begging to be saved. Like their arms, his arm stayed upright in the air for hours while he continued shuffling the pearly shells in his dance. Gesturing! Look at his arm. See his empty plastic water bottle. That blue one. The one jiggling, bobbing so you will notice him in the throng. There were millions of people leaping, springing into the air in the ceremony to be saved, to be chosen, recognised as human beings among the damned. Look at this empty water bottle, it was waving far above all the others. See this hunger first. See this number one poverty situation. *Take me. Take me to the flowing river water. Take me to the pure ancestral lake water. Let me eat the food of the disappeared homeland.* Olives. Belacan. Coconut milk. Grapes. Wine. Chocolate. Eggs. Meat. Cheese. Rice. World food memory entwined in the sinew of the outstretched arm.

The sequestered sea brothers, the unwilling, imprisoned on this spit in the ocean will never have any idea where Aboriginal Sovereignty originally came from. How would they know that of the countryman? Main one? But, alas, and most unfortunately, what did anyone know about Aboriginal Sovereignty in a stressed out globally warming world?

Yo! Refugee man. You look here, and look yonder, while searching endlessly for the perfect dream world where streets are paved with gold, and diamonds and pearls grow quicker than flowers, and where nothing is cultivated other than for the consumption of a slovenly cravenness, nourished from the first to the last breath firing in every human heartbeat, thump, thumping in the midnight hours throughout the land. You want dream worlds that do not look like licks of mud vomited up by the sea? The paradise people who exist for the colour of ocean blue, the rising tide, were riding a wave.

Dreams were worth having for sure, and Aboriginal Sovereignty's dreams were big time. In these dreams, he frequently speaks in his traditional language, which could be heard from anywhere across the world by the ancestors. Dead people. Not the living mob carrying on all busyness in those Praiseworthy churches. Only a handful of living people of the ancestor country spoke this power wavelength, and you did not have to tell the mass brotherhood that it was a futile business to take words from the treasure chest in your heart where you kept dead homeland languages saved for the future. You could hear the iambic pentameter of refugee lingua franca constantly cultivated, overturned and reformed by the rhythmics of the sea – winds, storming waves, thunder rolls, fish too, screeching birds, the splashing, the sounds of nothingness, and the eternal creaking of rotting wooden boats while the old homelands accents either faded away, or were intermingled again, with the local spirits of the oceans.

When he dances with his feet shuffling quick through the crushed seashell sand, Aboriginal Sovereignty holds up his empty plastic water bottle amongst a sea of brown hands, hoping the aid workers that come and go will always see him, and when that happens, you know what, he really believed he was in paradise.

There were powerful governments right around the world who knew about the inmate whose strange behaviour stuck out like a sore amongst a million of the landless sequestered on some unnamed dot of mud in the middle of the ocean. Aboriginal Sovereignty had become a person of interest to the keepers of the big money of the world. Aerial surveillance from multiple locations in various parts of the safe bubbled world swung onto the target walking in circles on some rubbish-covered institution on one of the new uncharted mud formations which was a good place for dumping unwanted people. Although normally it would be pretty unusual for any big government to feel afraid of a beggar they had imprisoned on the other side of the world, it was the satellite analysis that was suffocating common sense by creating a disease, where the world had gone freak mad with horror shows running through the social media streets that pumped the blood faster through the mind. So, what was initially downplayed in online chat across the planet as being warm and fuzzy, friendly, perhaps a bit unusual, but harmless all the same to watch an idiot, soon turned virulent and nasty.

Like faith, it was not easy to break out of sudden full-scale addiction, and this was how it felt for all the government spies watching monitors aimed at the shelly atoll, and without realising what was happening, the spy world had become depressingly possessed with scrutinising the tiny existence of a prisoner causing troubles by walking around in a circle. They could not help themselves, these spy people sat all day in front of room-sized computer screens in their spying facilities across the world, while watching, drinking more and more coffee, eating stuff, and waiting for something to happen in that lonely exercise compound on an unnamed and unofficial pile of mud not listed on any map, and as time passed in the slow pace of watching nothing happening that was of interest but might become interesting, they could feel like they were actually right there on the scene, standing on razed mud covered with dusty pearly shells and a windstorm while blending in like a sore thumb among the forsaken standing around the compound in this razor-wired institution situation, and this was where their thoughts remained, even while flicking from one speck in the sea people storage facility world to the next anywhere else on the planet, and having to zoom back in on what felt kind of vaguely interesting or potentially dangerous, to see what happens when you keep watching nothing interesting, because obviously something was orienting the spy's mind to another bounty-hunter type of spying mind, to force them to stay in the hunt by becoming increasingly mesmerised to that point of madness, where you feel you must point out the indifferences of the haves and have nots because you need to prove you have a higher realm of imagination and more sophisticated thoughts, and this was just how it felt to be lured into watching this unidentified x male landless beggar constantly shuffling grids of slow clockwise circles for hours on end, to find out if it means nothing, or everything that you need to condemn, and put an end to this business wasting their time.

What swings in his head? Hell? Was he hostile to aid or something? Of being helped? Of being unappreciative of the well-oiled carousel of handouts being thrown into the air from the privileged to the beggar? Was he threatening their existence with some magic emanating from his shuffling feet? Spitting where he should not be spitting? Putting the privileged people protected from the viral load of worldwide pandemics at risk of being spat at while going about their normal lives? It was as though a fantasy was happening on the big worldwide surveillance screens, and becoming a nature documentary of human wildlife just by watching him shuffling grids slowly clockwise on an atoll not marked on a map. Yet, Aboriginal Sovereignty kept drawing in the crowd. He mesmerised the gallery of spy networks watching from the wealth-driven world. It was impossible for these powerful people with the satellite technology, to realise that they were being trapped by a beggar. They were already caught in a dream-web spun through the galaxies ignited by the dreamlike stamping of the ground with his feet, and in the end, they were being broken, unable to pull back, their resistance nothing more than twigs, a floating feather, against the rhythms of Aboriginal Sovereignty's feet waking the earth. The spies were incapable of grabbing a lifeline by closing down the computers that had woken a suicidal streak running in their brains. Instead, turned into binge-watchers, they were unable to stop staring at the computer screen where the rapid shuffling on the sun-struck shelly ground began quickening the heartbeat running hostile with their imaginings of what it would feel like to be removed from the rest of the world to a place where life shrank into nothingness, and where anything left in your soul was found in the single act of breathing that kept you realising you were where you would never be found.

Nothing broke the steel-like grip forcing the transfixed to keep watching a traumatised life abandoned forever, a life so far removed it meant nothing to them even if they felt a pang of conscience festering in the mind from watching the intimacy of despair. Nothing could break the glare of the spy world, eating bags of chips while having eyes glued to HOYTS-size cinema monitors relaying vision from orbiting spy satellites, until finally, Aboriginal Sovereignty released his hold. He let them go. It was hard to believe what you were seeing when the ceremonial boy began shape-shifting into gale-force winds from the sea that screamed through the air while bringing what looked like hordes of praying mantises changing into the shape of plastic sheeting thrown over sticks blowing in a cascade through the shells whipped from the ground, and flying away in a slithering serpentine haze that took with it the storied law Aboriginal Sovereignty had told through his feet writing grids comprising tens of thousands of ceremonial tracks. It was like watching a human galaxy cut through the magnificent sameness of creating a new time, place, or being, but spectacular storms creating havoc all looked the same when viewed from outer space.

ONE DONKEY AT A TIME

us mob all tru god
Yanyuwa Gem, *DIWURRUWURRU*
(Poetry from the Gulf of Carpentaria)

1
Oracle 7...Calling SOS at 1.57 a.m.

Tell you what...It was like this. Life was too short for some people to sit around crying their heart out about the era of loss, and this type of person, who already felt their feet were planted in the graveyard, decided to carry his grief privately. Cause Man Steel made the decision to move on with the Aboriginal Sovereignty idea. *Wake up on the bright side each day, look forward to it, and have something to do.* The rule-bending planet-fixer got on with being the heretic of Praiseworthy life.

2
Planet was on another of his long, arduous journeys attending to the needs of his fledgling donkey enterprise. He was travelling again in that 1980s red-dust-clogged Falcon that had long been battered into submission on as many bulldust bogged roads as he could find, the long dead tracks that stretched across the vast arid zone's driest drought-bleached country of the ancestral world, where it took more than sheer guts and stamina for a man to survive.

But the trip was a total mess. Cause Steel was a broken man. A man whose life had dealt with enough loss. It would have taken a miracle to know if he knew why he even existed, let alone if he had any sense of direction left to reach the simplest of humanly possible destinations, and to find another, but better, marvellously more platinum-coloured donkey. Yet, he had to go. The grey mass of the almond-shaped amygdala that said he must experience the emotion of finding an ultimate miracle, had made up his mind for him. So, while bouncing his emotional collapse back and forth across both cerebral hemispheres, weeping and complaining like an overgrown sookie, and chucking off the cruellest bantering like he was born stupid, he went on his latest adventure, for this was the gist of it: *Ya can't have a decrepit old donkey being the mask-head of a platinum transport conglomerate.* Well! Perhaps not! The quest in itself though, was more like a search for common sense in a world that had none, the stupid thing in his head telling him that nothing but the best would do. Even stupidity can be a relief, for Planet in any case, to finally realise that his world-class business would not go ahead in a total FedEX, COSCO, Allied Express, or Wridgways major transport aspirational fashion with any old donkey leading the way. You cannot have a quitter sitting up front as its mask-head. A big transport industry did not work like that. It barely mattered in any space of Widespread's god brain to think that his special old silver-coated donkey was the only donkey he had ever seen over the years of his feral-donkey pilgrimages to find such a mythical creature. He barely noticed this only donkey among five million that his dream believed was capable of generating a dollars and cents industry in the magnitude of millions required for running the future world's greatest sustainable, fossil-fuel-free transport conglomerate, nor did it matter that Planet had caught such a stubborn creature with his bare hands on a killer of a journey to hell on earth.

Who cared whether Cause Man Steel had emotional troubles for heaven's sake? He didn't. But men who steal *other* people's cemetery are like that. Widespread was not into cemetery ownership, or touchy-feely sentimentality. How somebody felt was not how you run a world-class conglomerate. Yet, he tried. In his heart, he had tried to make compromises with the conniving part of his brain's insistence for perfection, only to end up spitting through clenched teeth that his mind was already made up about the platinum donkey he had found to be the mask-head, and finally collapsing, defeated by the improbability of the whole exercise of staying true to his vision, by making whimsical excuses for the old silvery donkey to which he had become deeply attached. In the end, with the truth of failure not backing down an inch, he somehow found spare idle strength, spat the dummy, and agreed with himself, that the old platinum donkey in the back seat was wrong. No. You could not have a donkey on its last legs as a mask-head of an international transport conglomerate that needed to travel hundreds of thousands of kilometres crisscrossing the ancient epic highways and roads of the ancestral creation heroes of the entire sovereign country of the traditional owners. No. It did not matter if he had to continue arguing with his brain until he was blue in the face about nearly killing himself in his search to find an ugly old donkey in the first place, and having to cart the thing across the country, and all the way back to Praiseworthy on a long rough and dry journey of countless kilometres. He always knew it was going to take another journey even if it killed him, because he would not be able to start his dynamic business for the new era of global hardship with anything second-hand like a used donkey, and the old platinum donkey was exactly that, too old to be the mask-head of the conglomerate transport empire that stretched far, far beyond any dream now, for it was bigger than the dream itself, there was no doubt about that.

Cause left Praiseworthy like a done man of course, while he stewed on the loss of his Aboriginal Sovereignty, but on the other hand, he set out full of renewed determination, pleased to be on one more quest to find a younger donkey with an antique pewter coat of silver, more like the brilliantly platinum donkey he had once seen in what was an unreliable dream, since he could not truly see the colour grey he had seen in the long-ago dream. Yet what was a dream? What was the colour grey? He could make it up, or he could conjure the correct hue of platinum shown to him by an especially espial, acute, high-sensing night-time ghost claiming that whatever he was looking for, was exactly that, an oxymoron, and he did not believe the best-looking donkey in the world for creating a world-class transport conglomerate existed outside of a dream.

This poor old donkey, that had been gifted with the most exquisite coat of platinum in the world, lay prone across the back seat of the Falcon with fear shooting from its eyes, and far too petrified to move. Every primordial instinct in its being knew a couple of certainties: the lesser, that it was not good enough for the task as first donkey that it had never wanted in the first place; and the greater, that wild donkeys were survivalists. The animal barely eats, and at a guess, just lives on its enormous store of memories about the great herd left behind from its former life on the hard-plains country close to the ancestral world.

You do not get much out of kind regards and salutations while being a pet donkey to someone besotted in bridling your life with a dream for saving the world. Such thoughts had made the donkey feel like dying. A panic-prone creature in its inherited memories of man-made fantasy, the donkey had an acute sense that death stood nearby, in any close relationship with a man-made world crisis. The donkey played the game of being nonplussed for a while, while continuing to keep Widespread as the best company on his fantasy journey towards his unreachable horizon, and while being of no use for anything except itself, the donkey's brown watery eyes scanned every moment of the passing bushland with only one idea on its mind, of choosing the precise moment when it would jump straight through the windshield of Widespread's vehicle, which he was driving like a racing car on a wash-away desert road filled with bulldust. Deadly! Perhaps. Yet, you would not call this suicidal urge an act of fright, more the passing through one horizon, and into another.

While Widespread continued driving countless hours over the world's roughest and mostly non-existent roads, to follow his dream to save his culture, his every breath weighed the value of the rare donkey in the back seat of the Falcon in the same way that some would examine a distant galaxy. What could you know for sure about anything? The question he kept asking himself was whether he could afford to release this poor old good-for-nothing donkey in the bush somewhere, without having any alternative idea of how to find its replacement, and while having no plan B for another platinum donkey mask-head to bring good fortune to his visionary conglomeration. Put in a nutshell, the scale heavily weighed against keeping this donkey which in Praiseworthy never really looked like the colour of platinum at all, nowhere near the dream colour that he needed in his industry. Against the glaring light of sun-stoked silver-coloured spinifex, most grey donkeys would appear to be the colour of platinum, but not this one, not even close. His eyesight had been tricked by country. He had never cared to accept this fact, nor that the donkey had done nothing practical to contribute towards proving itself as having any magnificence, such as producing platinum-coloured foals, or a foal at all for a future possibility of striking it lucky. This donkey was devoid of eminence. Why could that be? How could Planet have been so mistaken? It had obviously been a supreme leader of the vast desert herd where he had captured it. Surely it understood the magnificence of the country from where it came, where it was only possible to live close to the ground of ancestral power to become a pure survivalist, excelling by executing visionary ideas. He resented the fact that the donkey had never shown this capacity of dreaming big, nor even to repay for his gesture of kindness in capturing it, to be incorporated into the dream of a lifetime, or many lifetimes, to save humanity. Cause often glanced back at the resentful donkey, and thought that since he would be in the vicinity of the spinifex country where he had captured it, he would release it there – back in the wild.

Only spirit country knew what the old platinum donkey most likely feared from hearing the braying of five million feral donkeys that the scientists of these vast herds of feral animals and toxic plants thought were occupying northern Australia, that if there were any truth in this reality, then the top half of the continent ought to be crawling with donkeys.

Widespread had already driven thousands of kilometres, stolen enormous amounts of petrol siphoned from mines dotted all over this vein-rich mineral-loaded country, or from wherever else he could steal stuff when a back was turned, in order to keep following the coordinates planted in his memory by the mapmakers. The Falcon charged forth, travelled like a zombie on autopilot up and down imaginary grid lines stretching across countless hectares of the spirit-charged country. Dry land. Drought stricken. Land that was supposed to be plagued by feral donkeys. Plenty of bones were seen. Skeletons. The land was littered with donkey carcasses like one big long senseless massacre field. All shot. *Bang! Bang!* Widespread pointed his index and middle fingers like a gun at the carcasses scattered like shells on a beach, while silently mouthing the sound of a firing bullet.

There was nobody to blame except the mapmakers. Days passed, and the killing field was endless. It would never end. His mind fled from the massacres, but then he became paranoid, beyond reason, unable to turn away, yet still maintaining his course. He kept driving. Up and down. Staring ahead. Searching for donkeys over countless grids that looked the same as the last, and the ones before that. He believed that the mapmakers were conspiring against him. He claimed these people were using drones to follow him through the bush. *You don't believe me?* What about those spy satellites he saw passing at night? *What do you think they were doing?* He complained to the old donkey that the New Age hippie scientists counting feral donkeys did not know what they were talking about. *They lived in some donkey dream of their own, counting ghost donkeys in their sleep,* misconstruing the facts, just to prevent Aboriginal people like himself from realising true self-determination. They too, like everyone else, were stopping him from building the world's first massive donkey enterprise of the likes never seen before on this continent, and why not? *They wanted people like me to remain pure, stuck back in the stone age, as though the future doesn't exist for Aboriginal people. The future always existed. We only got here from the time immemorial because we knew about the economics of feeding ourselves.* He told the donkey if it had been up to the job, it would have been like donkeys working in India. People making do. Or, like donkeys used by millions of the poorest people of the world for carrying, for transport, for self-reliance on their own terms like they had for centuries, and carrying their culture with them. *These New Agers think only about having the right to live in a first-world country. Yea, get that,* he laughs, while more or less saying to the less than perfect platinum patchy-fur donkey still pretending to be asleep in the back seat, that a bunch of land thieves had put fucked coordinates into his head, to prevent him from using donkeys to become a multi-millionaire in his own country, a billionaire if he wished it, but hey? What poor Aboriginal man like himself who wanted to be liked in a widespread, planetary way, would be mad enough to have inspirations of pure greed?

3

A day came when the wholesale esprit de corps of the magnificent-to-the-end-of-the-world souls of Praiseworthy heard something quite out of the ordinary pushing its weight through thin air. It was believed to be a dull pulse from the invisible ancestral colliding with its underneath-country lungs, and they thought that was very strange, and impossible for people like themselves who live the most ordinary lives where nothing great happened, to be caught up in such a sui generis moment. But, never mind they said, charging forth all the same, it was wonderful to hear the mighty ancestors awakened, and moving about in the air, and of course, this was to be expected in the unbraced era of planetary crisis created by humankind in the first place.

Life continued. Boom! Boom! Praiseworthy people said they country and did not mind at all if the ancestral was moving about doing their work, and they tried to sidestep, take a detour whenever detecting the presence of the mountainous huge, to stay out of the way of spirit work. You could live with anything they said, and they felt how nice it was to be listening to the repetitious slow pulse of country's ancestral heart thumping from sun-up, to sun-down. The old people said it was better to hear the country's heartbeat calming their nerves at last. The pulse gave them the right sense of being alive, rather than being overwrought traditional owners of land smothered by white colonisers. This was how the faraway droning played out, tolerated at first, from thinking that listening to a mighty ancestral heartbeat pulsing was something you put up with in life, like things that did not matter to the sovereign mind of traditional country, but after many months of hearing what became in the mind an amplified pulse – the greatest spiritual heart beating non-stop that now did not sound like a diamond dove cooing but had instead morphed in the most patient of minds into something else, like the continual sound of a motor car revving, and this was becoming very tiresome, to always be walking in an espial way over many miles to get around the ancestral invisible presence without bumping into it. Something nasty developed in the esprit de corps out of the inconvenience to all. Tolerance itself, once a terrific virtue to gloat about, jumped straight out of the soul and disappeared into thin air. Who knows where human tolerance went when it left? But wholesale tolerance leaving was another matter entirely, when a whole eternity of endurance went out the door, when the old people said they had no tolerance left in their brain anymore, it was all gone, and everyone should go out and look for where their tolerance might be hiding somewhere, maybe behind a stumpy saltbush plant out on the flat, for old people could not be expected to go around looking for tolerance in the haze.

There now seemed to be no sense in having to hear this monotonous monstrous heartbeat of country constantly going boom de the boom. It felt like being tortured with more dumbing down politics of the government, further enslaved, more than an eternal slave of racism, gaoled up by a pulse on their own land. Yet the distant pulse resembling non-stop cooing continued, and even though the young warriors went in search parties across the country and through the sea, tearing the whole thing apart to find where the eternal heartbeat was coming from, they could not find it, and the sound kept worsening until nothing seemed right anymore.

Things were intolerable enough for Praiseworthy people living under a perpetual dome of haze. It was the same as listening to pervasive racism and having no idea where to pin it down, or to find any sense of peace from listening to that malign sound eternally drumming in their ears. What could you do to stop it, except wish it would stop, or tell it to stop, but wishing something to stop, does not mean it would stop. You could feel your heartbeat quickening, beating faster and more rapidly, like a monkey's heart rate after eating a bag of Queensland sugar. Some said, rather than being a monkey, their own heart rate was more like the ant ancestor constantly moving which, if you were amplifying this sound, would be quicker than a monkey's, but the whole sense of hearing the increasingly rapid pace of the far-off droning had spawned a fear greater than racism, which was more like heart-attack fear, and the whole place crumbled in a sickness which was dialogised by many old wise people who had flown in from near and far in spiritual travelling, as well as in a jumbo jet. This community malaise they said, was a form of forlornness that came from a deep phobia related to hearing the country's sick pulse rate, and which in turn created a pathological obsession with many people checking their own pulse rate like they were the flying doctor ordered by the government to go every day to Praiseworthy to check the pulse of every man, woman and child queuing along Church Street.

It was sad to see pretty butterflies fainting all over the plains grass. Grasshoppers grew disoriented and saw the world upside down, by being unable to orientate their reflexes to jump upwards, instead of downwards. You had to push comatose snakes out of the way with a stick while trying to walk miles around the mountainous-sized invisible ancestor. Enough was enough. It felt as though life was near the end. Dance fainted when a rapid-pace thrumming quickened to a frequency that even she, the most tolerant of women, could not tolerate, and she felt nauseous, as though experiencing out-of-control jazz. This had to stop when brains now spun like a wringer rotating in a washing machine. *Stuff that*, the old people with disoriented brains said. They were finished with being brainwashed, and they tried to escape the sound by grabbing whatever they could to steady themselves, while walking away, and feeling wobbly, then fainting. There were people fainting on the ground all over the place. Look at those poor pretty pussycats, dozens of them that could sleep belly-up through an earthquake, and had now turned into fancy pets, and could do tricks like jumping off the ground with all that thrumming going on in their head. They were crazed-brained cats anyhow, like the dogs, and the cemetery donkeys, all trying to stay airborne, jumping off the pulsing ground. The sun felt harsher. No rest would come at night while so much heat radiated off the ground, and while dreams were about plagues. Some were only gentle plagues like unseasonal screaming locusts worming through the darkness of heat, along with clouds of drowsy mosquitoes that clung to the skin sucking blood until they burst, but others were not.

There was no good time to come from standing somewhere dangerous and getting killed in this place. You had to think quick, to get out of the way when tons of sand lifted off the beach each time the big ancestor spat from motion sickness. Electrical storms brewed, and lingered like sick dogs with sixty thousand lightning strikes over country. The unsettling weather seemed incapable of moving its great weight off Praiseworthy. The whole thing squatted in the sky for months with lightning strikes hitting a church spiral there, there, there in a random chain reaction. You needed to jump out of the way real quick when trees were knocked to the ground wherever you moved, with sand flying like a massive serpent soaring through the sky, then diving around in the turbulences, coming back down, and flying low along the ground, before soaring again, when all of a sudden, the gigantic serpent roared in and out of the haze storm. The country's old scientists said there was too much static electricity in the atmospheric pressure caused by the pulsing ancestral heartbeat that was driving everyone completely mad with its arrhythmic breathing bursting plenty of eardrums. The bird choirs sang off note while praying for all this stuff to stop.

Nothing stopped, the old wisdom people, the scientists of ancient knowledge, had to go out in the bush themselves with their racing hearts while having to hold on to whatever they could so they were not blown away, to search for the whereabouts of the beat affecting their heartbeat. The funny thing though, no one else around the country who was not a traditional owner of the land, cared if the country was falling apart, so the ancient people had to walk around all day long in the long grass, thrashing it to smithereens with their hunting sticks for all these lazy people too. The grasshoppers had to drag themselves out of the weird summer haziness to swarm into the sky around the thrashers while trying to escape being hit with a stick. The old people's dogs that had been told to stay on their feet if they knew what was good for them, started disappearing into the bush in search of the thumping sound, but came running back to their owners with their tails between their hind legs, and then refused to stop being the worst thing of all, a clingy belly-up dog. Then, some cats managed to set out in search of the sound which they had mistakenly identified as being the giant lickety-split rats attacking their imagination from the rooftops, or up in the church steeples, or where the rodents had taken over the abandoned sentry posts of the government minding other people's business. Other cats, the idiot tame ones, were maddened by the sound of rats scampering, pitapat, low-like, and very faintly heard, while being chased by mind-altered feral cats listening to irregular heartbeats in the internal speaker system in their brains. The whole pulse scenario grew worse, and felt more like techno music in the mind. Steel wire strands brushing flick-flack across a kettledrum! But the mysterious thumping did not stop, and there were terrible earaches that made listening no good in the hectic pace of the global emergency, where Praiseworthy had to keep abreast of the political climate for twenty-first millennium people left out in the cold in the rat-race to survive.

Some mothers of the time immemorial who claimed to be more expert in pacifying irritable sounds than anyone else, said the pulsing did not sound either ancestral or human to them at all. It was not a baby crying for instance, for they claimed to have the ability to hear any kind of baby crying in a thousand-kilometre radius, or even three thousand kilometres, and in fact, their hearing was so acute, they heard babies crying anywhere from coast to coast in a circumference of nearly twenty-six thousand kilometres of coastline stretching right around the whole country. These women had the capacity to order children to stop crying, so some of the special mothers who could hear where a big baby was crying, drove their minds right around Australia like racing drivers, and came back in a matter of days defeated. They were unable to find the sound, and said what the old people were already saying, it was coming from the country itself.

Thinking less magical, and more factual, it was easier to slip back into remembering one's obligations as brethren of any of the umpteen churches in Praiseworthy, where inside these holy places, while the drumming was interrupting the normality of sermons and choirs, Praiseworthy people began to believe the faraway thrumming was revelatory, that it came from heaven, and just perhaps, they were listening to God breathing, and now, no one spoke of the divine country, preferring instead to take an oath of silence about heaven stuff, to better hear the sound of the mysterious breathing holy one, when in total silence, listening to the God breathing in the atmosphere, they could decide if this was a miracle.

In this time of a heavy-breathing atmosphere, another remarkable thing occurred in a string of unnatural events. It was as though the world was throwing everything at the unprecedented stories it wanted to tell, to say it was changing, that a new story was being formed. There was a continuous hatching of ghost moths down in the cemetery. The spirit moths were everywhere. They crawled out of the sandy soil, from under the yellowing hummock grass, and from behind the peeling bark of drought-stricken gum trees. The world of Dance Steel became bedazzled. She clung tighter to her fascinated sense of the marvellous, seeing the haze land covered with fluttering ghosts, the smoke-filled sky becoming a glossy sea of whiteness. The sight overwhelmed her. What was the world saying? The moth-er fainted again and again with the sheer joy of the thing, of being in this space of wonderment, with the pulse continuing to create miracles in episode upon episode of fainting and then of revelation, awakened by the vibrating hum of the night moth's wings. As soon as something like this happened again, seeing herself even more alive, that she had not after all died, she would pull herself together, and eventually overcame the feeling of dying. She began believing that it was possible to be reborn from the mysterious power of the ancestral moths breathing in the atmosphere. Now she only dreamt of escaping death, and how the power of the moths breathing into the atmosphere that had once caused her to faint on the spot – sometimes on the top of a fallen concrete angel, at other times wrapped in a tangle of solar-power fairy lights – was the strangeness of country itself, that helped her to understand the true glory of her life.

With the realisation that she was on this planet for one thing, to be alive, and that she would endlessly be returned to life, no matter how many times she dropped dead like a moth that had fallen out of the sky, curled in its wings, and died. No. Death would not lie inside a person with a mission, and what was hers? She would never die. At least, not before making sure that only her sons inherited true Native Title over Praiseworthy, and not anyone else. White man's law electrified her mind. She was alive. Queen of the quest. She might need to be alive for a very long time. She might even be invincible, always alive, always dying and returning to life, heartbeat aligned with the urgency of the atmospheric breath even if it was oblivious to her. Her fainting episodes jumped out of her skin. The routine business of listening to air going in and out of her lungs, just to keep on living though the world's longest marathon court case to prove her Native Title over Praiseworthy was thrilling enough, though of a known war that was endless to her. She pulled the moth-sweetened pulsing air into her lungs, and like the world's greatest unconquerable, she was there, alive, just to continue proving her endurance for the impossible feat of proving that each of her forefathers from time immemorial had maintained unbroken occupancy to Praiseworthy through another racist piece of flawed white man's legislation. A paper structure aimed at non-recognition. A modern-day white man's law mess that did not recognise its own complicity in genocidal acts to steal a complete country.

4

While a faint sound seemed to be coming from a long way off, the actual location of the ever-present pulse could not be pinpointed in an instant, not in weeks, or months, or unless a miracle happened, or it would never be found in years to come. The irritating throb never stopped. The mysterious pulse continued beating with what was identifiable as being Buddy Holly's missing heartbeat, which you would hear in the rhythm – *thum thum…a thrum thrum,* and this musical sound of heart thumping missing a beat continued from the time you got up and put your thongs on in the morning, until you chucked them off again when you went back to the same bed at night. But even dreams change, and the sound of an eternity of a missing-beat pulse that never stopped, could become a monster so enlarged in the brain that the benign turned toxic, and the toxicity of the missing pulse would keep coming at you while you lay a long time in your bed like a semi-comatose cane toad that had been run over, and in this disturbed state, incapable of untying your tangled-up brain from the knot it made of itself from listening to this axe murderer chopping wood – chump-chumping, and missing a beat for the hell of it. Was this a living hell? Was this ancestral? The ancestral breathing heavier, choking in this polluted mess?

The pulsing sound with its missing beat grew into an even greater mystery, and sometimes, among other scenarios, the pulse felt as though your own heartbeat was out of sync, beating arrhythmically, that there was something wrong with your heart, as if you did not have enough heart. Or else, you felt that you were listening to the vibrating lungs of a fat bronzewing pigeon – *Phaps chalcoptera* you call it, with its non-stop oom-ing, a mantra in swells and thrums hummed to its disinterested mate while hanging around Praiseworthy, through another long summer of haze. The maddening sound never stopped, not for any tick of the clock. In the sermons under the multi-denominational church steeples, the church leaders shouted down to the sinners from the pulpit, that this cooing was exactly the type of interrogating sound that torturers used to drag up guilty feelings from the pit of the stomach in the middle of the night while they kept torturing, drilling for guilt, and until you were left wretched with the kind of emptiness felt in the middle of the day, and then? Then, you turned to your own true church without going down the street like a traitor, and joining your enemy church by switching the beat into reverse-action guilt, where the whole cycle of being guilty would only swing back to the starting point of existence: your innocence. Bite-sound. The soul tossed like salad.

Praiseworthy people felt tortured about being true believers of one faith. Why not swing around? It was the type of thing that made you feel mad from not knowing where this endless heart pulse skipping a beat was coming from, but that kept amplifying in the brain, which felt like a steel factory with the heavy machinery of your denominational boring drill holes in your head as though it were an underground mine with dumpsters pumping endless loads of raw sewerage into the river, into the country's heartbeat – and it had to be that, because what else would overtake the pure and glorious chants of the municipal mass choirs, the hallmark sound generally heard over all else in Praiseworthy?

But! The thumping heart had been thrumming from a place that was unimaginably far, far away. This was a place well known to the ancestral world in the windiest corner of one of the loneliest places of all in the Dreaming country – a power place that was dangerous and unloved, abandoned to pollution and decay, where worn grey soil lifted, and permanently floated thinly and useless in the sky, like spirit angels of enormous magnitude blowing their breath in puffs of wind that covered the atmosphere of flat-running ancestral fields with summer-dry thistles mixed with snapped off bits of dry grass, twigs mostly, pollen, fluff, dead spiders and flies, moth wings, pigeon feathers, and not much more. And there, among the soupiness of spirit scorn, the scrawny swallows danced in flight after flies, and minor sparrow birds bopped among grasshoppers, micro-organisms, frayed bits of plastic bags and other waste stuff of the continent's rubbish swimming amidst the thoughts of the old people back in Praiseworthy, and where strands of fur floated in the atmosphere from all sorts of semi-domesticated and undomesticated animals that were savages all the same, and the grey dirt smelt of donkey piss from a sea of donkeys running cheap and grown more feral in numbers. A changeling prospered in this place. A little boy was sleuthing himself away from his befuddlement from coming to terms with being dropped off by his father in this wreckage of an environment.

You could call this the result of blind political will enacted over several generations against the original inhabitants, accompanying the bewildering act of feral and gross neglect about the way that these first children of the land were being treated even by their own fathers, but in his seriously impacted child's mind, an enormous furnace hissed and spat fumes like a volcano amidst a high magnitude earthquake where savage camp dogs chasing one another – more than any person could conjure in a string of random thoughts over any lifetime – bowled each other over in dog fights. And above all of this, floated the

Minister of Aboriginal Affairs, the middle-aged blonde lady sitting on her office chair swivelling in the sky loaded with dust particles struck by the sun, who the child kept imagining was a golden angel, who in her gleaming yellow wattle suit and golden jewellery, could easily have unleashed through her outstretched hands missiles firing multi-tongues of fire that shot 'far out' across the land while singeing feral cats as they wandered the country in plague proportions. The boy went searching through his mind to find his parents who he seriously wanted to kill, and yelling his name was Tommyhawk Steel.

Well! That then, was actually that, thought L'uomo di ferro, the old donkey herder on the other side of the country, as he slipped away in the darkness while thinking about grassfires. His own hair of whiteness, perm-frizzled by hot winds and smoke, bounced this way and that, while he hobbled side-on as he went, and if you watched him departing through the simmering mirage of the heated earth, you would see him moving as though he had been permanently thrown off balance by the inextricable force of a twenty-first century world spinning askew on its axis.

The dumped boy Tommyhawk Steel stands alone in these chopped-up fields, that in their flatness stretch far away against every horizon meeting the sky. Behind him, the only dwelling that rose slightly higher than a donkey, was the herder's hut. A bare structure that had grown from limbs of ghost gum, and over time, was heaped with damp and rotting sheep skins and goat and donkey skins into a Tower of Babel in praise of living like a wild man. Ahead, the mirage shimmers deceptively over vast distances of flatlands that in the blink of an eye, becomes a shallow lake of great ancestral sacredness, a dangerous watery world stretching across hundreds of kilometres. The boy belts an old rusty forty-four-gallon drum with a stick, flogging the thing senseless on the head of an old flatland ancestral spirit sleeping beneath these lonely plains since the creation era, that preferred to be swayed by thousands of years of silence that was broken only by long-lasting droning ceremonies, the occasional low spurts and dreamlike chirruping of birdsong – the plague of feral pigeons cooing, the squealing of starlings, or the flocks of little diamond doves – or even, to be soothed by braying donkeys pasturing on the grey stubble grasses. But what is that? A land of silence does not care for someone banging monotonously on the side of a rusty drum dumped on its head like a crown, and missing every second beat.

5

This is how much I hate you. Tommyhawk's long-lived rage grew wilder. He never got over it, how he had been dumped, and he never stopped thinking about how his father had driven off and left him – months ago, after having *actually* kidnapped him from where he had been hanging out on the gravelly Praiseworthy airstrip waiting to be rescued by the Australian government from his parents. And then, without saying a single word to the fascist son throughout the long journey across the continent, had abandoned him thousands of miles away, in a place that looked like Mars. He stared at the dry lake's windswept moonscape, an empty mirage that had remained consistently the same from one monotonous day, to the next. He was ready to kill his father right there with the gidgee stick in his hand – if Cause Man Steel ever came back. The boy's skin was clammy and hot, even with the coolness of the early morning mist rising from the dry lake. Tommyhawk's blood boiled. He ripped his filthy t-shirt off, and bare-chested, and with a mind loaded with anger, he continued bashing the empty oil drum, sending secret messages in code to the White Mother with all the strength his bony left arm could muster.

With its eternal rest disturbed, from being rudely interrupted again and again by Tommyhawk's continuation of his racket, the mighty all times creation spirit whose being was all over this place, moved its enormity from deep inside the sacred country. The land shook, abandoned old beer cans rolled ting, ting, rattling against one another in the dirt rising into dust and heaps of marsupials – Macropodidae and whatnot feral cats and myxomatosis rabbits – jumped out of their holey abodes, and from under any bit of shade where they were resting on the lake bed, while sparrows and swallows leaped from the earth and shot to the skies. The donkey land scattered while leaping off the ground to escape the vibrations of an earthquake that was felt across the continent. The Dreamtime rumbled to life beneath the feet of the boy, and stretched its entire body across the land. But, just as suddenly, the lungs of the mighty ancestral paused, as Tommyhawk missed a beat, then continued rumbling as soon as the kid gathered more rage, and continued belting the drum with the stick.

Tommyhawk was not belting a rusty forty-four-gallon drum for nothing. He knew sound travelled a long way from this important place, and taking stock of what being rattled by an earthquake felt like, and utilising his knowledge about science, the boy thought he was being shaken by a 2.0 disturbance on the Richter scale. He gulped as the sequence of rumblings accumulated into another tremendous shake of the land, and this made him pause while he thought that the land might split open and swallow him before he got a chance to kill his father. Instead of running off in fear of his life, he knew there was nowhere to go. There was no escape, so he immediately started bashing the drum even harder than before.

Inside the land, the old ancestral spirit returned to its silence, perhaps to think, while trying to figure out what was wrong with this boy standing on its being. Perhaps it was calculating the weightlessness of a clan child's spirit against a fluffy breast feather of an owlet that had just dropped on the ground. This was not – *Fin! Fang! Foom!* The country's spirit spoke in its own language in the ancient sounds of the earth, but you knew what country meant when you heard it. The sound was enough. You jumped up immediately, rang the earthquake alarm, and jumped right out of the way for cover. Now, there was something right off skew around this place with the ground continuously rumbling, as though it was keeping up with Tommyhawk's heart beating as hard as he was beating the drum, and drumming now, with even greater strength. He wanted someone, anyone, to hear him. He wanted to be saved. He wanted his brother Aboriginal Sovereignty to come back from the sea, and save him. The ancestor groaned, feeling the kid's fear. Knew the real age of this heart. Where it had originally come from. Yep! Traced it. Identified the lot in an instant, just like the old wisdom people of country. So easy for an ancestral being! Pinned that kid Tommyhawk down. Had him pegged. Carrying too much weight on his mind. Some piece of work. A child slewed off course even before the moment he had fallen out of his mother's womb, and instead of breathing fresh air that contained the fullness of everything of country in which to nurture possibility, he had inhaled weight – the bushfire smoke generating off great summer heat, polluted soot, ash, radioactive waste particles and micro-organisms destroying life in the lands and seas, and the dust haze of extended drought micro-waving through the atmosphere that gave him *no time instead of it all.*

Sure, there was true country talking in the din that little Tommy-hawk Steel was bent on making – continuing his rat-a-tat through the night, the clickitty, clankitty-clank clank all through the next day, like the day before that, and then night again in the land of spirits. He had better watch out with this noise. The creation ancestor of the barren lake shook the big law governors of the creaking ground. It was unbelievable, seeing moonlit cracks widening in the old dry mud lake, while in the flurry, the hovering bosses skirted around the lake, and screamed at one another through the skies. It was hard to decipher what they were saying as the winds swung around and chewed up the dead stubble grass and sent it skywards. Seeing this made it easy to understand that even vapour, spirit ghosts, had more power than a piss-ant government in Canberra debating how to fix dirt-poor Aboriginal people, to keep them poor on their stolen resource rich lands. Old ghosts take it in turns to front up and loom in the skies directly above the boy, to look point blank into his motionless face, and then with worried expressions move aside for there were others behind. There were so many ghosts gathering, they formed low clouds, and mobbed the flatness of this country's heaven. Their breath fogged up the atmosphere. Mist falls, and settles over the dry, mud-cracked ground, and the shortened stock-chewed grass, animal droppings, a million rabbit holes, and the wetness lay over the backs of about a thousand multicoloured and grey-pelted donkeys stretching yonder to kingdom come over the dry lake.

Where does this bonny kid get so much energy? This was the question, the mysteries added to the low atmosphere rolling with thunder touching the earth, where the ground rumbles with the turmoil of worrying why he doesn't eat? Why he doesn't stop belting that drum to eat anything. Why doesn't he sleep? Maybe this boy is already dead? Huddling ghosts, the total ancestry about this place, have gathered on the land, the closest surround the child, looking at him, trying to figure him out, watching him bashing the drum, shocked to see their faces twisted, perplexed, traumatised, dark with anger, mirrored in his. They blow small gusts of wind in his face, hoping to cool his temper, but the wind gusts are tossed back from his nostrils, and fly off through the stillness to search for answers here, there and everywhere in this place where even strangers have been killed for lingering too long on the dangerous power of country.

6

A long way away, on a rainy night in Praiseworthy, the moth woman, the moth-er, studies the artistry of the mapmaking in the wing structure of a moth already a ghost paralysed against the glass of a lamp on the kitchen table, as though this creature had been trapped there, tricked by a positive phototaxis into believing in something else – reaching its zenith, already on the moon – and wasted its migration, taken off course from the ancestral map with only one day of life to reach the summit of its existence. Amen. Long thin strands of her grey hair, electrified by the dry storm hanging in the atmosphere of the haze, stand on end. This shimmering silvery mess, easily mistaken for wind in the grass, attracts disoriented moths left, right and centre that flutter around her head to scatter eggs. She sings in a preachy voice, *Amazing Grace*, taken from the Praiseworthy gospel's hymn sheet. She is no Aretha Franklin. The moth-er, though, is accustomed to studying her insects, either in the silence of an empty house like this, or to the sound of her own hymn songs, serenading moths in praise of their kingdom to come, but she still heard it, that sound of water leaking somewhere in the cemetery. Either a tap, or there was rust in the water-tank stand. Perhaps donkeys were pissing all night. She hears it drip more loudly on quiet nights like this, but now, she finds it almost impossible to concentrate on moth wings clinging to the glass globe of the lantern while there is a tap dripping arrhythmically into her ear. She cannot tolerate disorder, and wants to correct the rhythm of the drip, to go into the graveyard of deceased people in the middle of the night and fix the thing herself, but she knows that she cannot do this even if the constant out-of-rhythm dripping is taking over her mind. She is the prisoner of the ghosts and trapped inside her house. She would never leave the house at night.

Who cares where the blasted drip was coming from? She tried to concentrate on the lines of moths swimming haphazardly past her eyes, that then fall one by one plop, plop onto her dinner plate, their wings caught in the grease, and she sees others crash over teacups stacked in the sink and float in the dishwater. The more she listens to the perpetual unevenness of the drips falling from somewhere in the cemetery, the more she feels that the kitchen is growing quieter while the moths continue on their flight to the moon, and the only other sounds are the captured moths beating their frantic wings in an attempt to save themselves from drowning in the sink. The sound of the wings belting to stay afloat overtakes the sound of the disjunctive beating of drips hitting the ground from outside the house, and the more the moths fight to save themselves for the few hours left of their lives, the pounding in her ears grows louder, and there is nothing she can do to save a living soul, even from the kitchen sink, when she looks down and sees that the beat is coming from her own heart. She hurries to the sink and tries to stop this toneless rhapsody of wing beating from the drowning moths, that sounds like someone who does not know how to have a proper heartbeat, or know how to belt a drum, but nothing works, neither saving the beating wings of moths, or their silent screams growing louder in her mind.

Tommyhawk does not fit easily with living in this lonely faraway windswept landscape on the other side of the continent, nor does he tire easily for a child that was supposed to be malnourished because he refused to eat, and acts like what was officially described as a deranged Aboriginal child from a dysfunctional homeland community despised by the colonial weight of the country after these lesser black people had the nerve to win their rights back over their traditional land after years of hard graft and decades fighting racism through every court of Australia. He was at the pointy end of staring down the Aboriginal world by casting the spotlight on poorly kids according to the general thinking of the biggest outfit for casting blame in the burgeoning

Aboriginal industry, speculating on how all Aboriginal children were sacred, and unloved by their own parents, and wondering how you weigh Aboriginal parents not loving their children like white people loved their children? Deep in the pollution loomed the scales sitting out there in the bare earth-eroded paddock of the lonely brain where self-appointed judges weighed who loved children more than 'the other'. A chorus of old people filled everywhere with spirit laughter about this kind of stupidity, which normal people would never hear from the racket of that drum-belting Tommyhawk. The mad troll kid will continue belting that thing out there in the climate, while growing hot as hell, sweaty body, and never hearing his own noise. How was he going to survive?

The old spirit people keep gathering in greater numbers to watch that infernal waste-dumped diesel drum being belted, and tried to distract themselves from the noise echoing across the land. They have examined every single ant now, watching them dart along their ancestral spirit tracks in the dirt, and admired the manoeuvres taken across the hot earth from one clump of grass to the next. They stand directly in front of Tommyhawk, and stare into his eyes, but he looks straight past them. He stares into space, as though his brain had been permanently set on autopilot. They know he was starving himself, but his energy grows stronger, for he beats the drum even more loudly, and they notice that the hordes of donkeys have retreated to the back corner of the lake and with their long ears pinned back on their heads, acting as though they were trapped and cannot escape, they stamped the ground, and kicked up dust, trying to eradicate the noise.

You get back here, you hear me. Tommyhawk screams to the north, across the watery mirage of the lake reaching faraway into a distant flat horizon. He curses this cunt of a father. Hate can cast a long shadow, for it is now travelling across the ground and radiating over vast distances to where the ancestral pushed it back to Praiseworthy, and continues beyond even there on the other side of the continent, where the pulse travels and travels, until it reaches the hidden detention camp where captured boat people were languishing – where Aboriginal Sovereignty dances to the sound of his heartbeat along grids in the exercise yard that map his imagined journeys to Praiseworthy, where no one can pinpoint where this frightening pulse of the land's heart was beating from. And hate moves further on...

Into this vast sea of grey stubble-grass sameness, the boy frequently scans the landscape to see if his father is returning – that dumb bastard of a father Cause Man Steel – while the drum continues echoing SOS in code. Tommyhawk believes that the sound pounding in his head travels in another direction, to the east, travels interstate, all the way to the nation's capital – over a thousand kilometres away, all the way to his White Mother in the palace called Parliament House. He could see her walking around her vast mansion – staring at better butterflies than those in Praiseworthy – and he thought that if she had any sense at all – not that she had ever proven to him that she had no sense – she would be able to tell just by hearing him drum, that his SOS would give her world-class spy government the coordinates of where to find him. Occasionally, in tiny gaps of silence when Tommyhawk stops, pauses, brushes the sweat with all the dust picked up by the wind and blown into his face, and his dirt-engrained mop of brown hair falls back across his eyes, he flicks it with the back of his arm, listens, and the more intently he listens to the silence reigning over the landscape towards the lake's far distant horizons, the more he does not hear a vehicle coming, and the more certain he feels that his father will never return.

When the sun begins to set again in the west, the boy knows that if he keeps staring dead straight ahead into the haze over the flat barrenness, he is going to be fine. North, he must not become disorientated from seeing northwards, yet his eyes travel, and he stares at the back of his father's neck as he imagines him driving home without him. He willed the vehicle to roll on a straight stretch of lonely road. If he wishes his father to be killed in the rolling Falcon in a place where the out-of-control spinning vehicle will land, far off the road behind three-metre-high spinifex plains where he will never be found, he must keep looking north, to find his father heading home on the lonely road, because his own life depended on it. Will he give his father one last chance to turn around and come back to pick him up? He had not taken his eyes off this empty space for weeks now, then it will be months of seeing further, far beyond the donkey herds permanently stationed in the corner of the north fields to stay away from him. The north he sees does not include the sight of donkeys which have made tracks running off one another and over the lake bed in every direction. It is a total maze that becomes thicker each time his eyes blink, or whenever he brushes sweat off his face and squints to see further than the mirages shimmering in the stark sunlight. All that he knows is that he must navigate his sight through the maze of donkey tracks, and concentrate even harder on a single imaginary line which he now only thinks is the tracks of where his father was heading the day he left, but now, in this timeless forever, he returns to the maze of donkey tracks that appear to be covering the ground more thickly in a tangle of sun-glistened cobweb lines, and while Tommyhawk's mind becomes less focused, and absorbed into the tangle laid out before him, he becomes convinced that his father is the one lost, and he is not sure if he is looking at the right track in his imagination anymore.

All the lines know that Tommyhawk will never look to the south for refuge.

If you come from the north, look north, or you might become lost to the spirit winds singing through the she-oak forests where the ghost moths live.

7

When Tommyhawk's mongrel father had left him with the local Aboriginal donkey herder who called himself L'uomo di ferro, he had not hung around long. Widespread had driven day and night to get across the continent as quickly as he could to palm off Tommyhawk forever, and then he stood in the dust just long enough to get his business over and done with about dumping his fascist kid with the hermit, while mumbling about how the government was training Aboriginal children to kill their culture, and all the while looking elsewhere, fleetingly casting an eye over thousands of donkeys nuzzling dust to get their tongue around some tangled-up desiccated spirit grass root, tasting as sour as this over-pastoralised worn-out country itself. *That's all I've got for sale*, the herder growled. He did not speak much while looking at the kid. He would argue about the liability later on with his shadow. Cause said he did not want any donkeys anyway, although he never said that there was not one in these thousands of donkeys worth a second glace, since none had the right colour for a transport conglomeration, and then he left. Drove off. Hit the dust hard straight across the centre of the dry lake. Left bulldust rising off the ground at the rate of a hundred miles an hour, and forming grey clouds drifting high in the sky. All that took less than ten minutes. Arrived, did his business, and just drove off as he would whenever he left Praiseworthy, without bothering to think if anyone else was coming, or staying, or saying goodbye. Dumped the kid, and left. You could see the Falcon become a dot in the distance, and disappearing altogether.

The old hermit, his shadow's talker, often walked past the fascist kid while adoring the beauty of his donkeys, and he thought to himself – *fair enough*, the coloured kid could bash drums forever if he liked. He had probably bashed a few drums himself in his life for whatever worth it was, about nothing in the end. *Ya skin gets tough,* he might have mumbled. *Could make a drum out of it myself. You learn this.*

L'uomo di ferro casually looked in the direction of where the little fascist was staring across country, and saw neither rainbows, nor clouds, nor a chance of rain. All he saw was that Tommyhawk followed with his eyes, the increasing distance, the greater miles of travelling his father was putting between them. Real sad stuff. Tough on the kid though. At least he was not left with some little cry-baby. The old man sees what he knows, that the donkey tracks crisscross through miles of dense thorny brambles as tall as a man – that it grows thicker in the imagination each time you take a really hard look at the impracticality of cutting through it, to take a short-cut across this type of country. He knows this himself, knows how your mind can play many tricks on you when you try to follow any of these tracks through the escalating growth that looks deceptive, looks like dry stubble grass until you try to go through it. He knows what it feels like to be caught in the tow of its undergrowth which strangely, exponentially expands and covers all roads identically, until there is no road, no more maze of donkey tracks and you can neither go forward, nor backward, for in the scheme of this geography, his place easily becomes non-existent, his life is blotted out. He knows how you could drown in the endlessness of thinking about being lost, of suffocating underneath the groaning of this network of giant brambles changing its shape, deceptive, calling you to take the crossing across stubble grass, and it would be too late when you realised that this country was something more supernatural, like a wild spirit twisting you into tighter knots, for it does not want you on this country, strangling itself together to keep you out of its reach. He knew this was where the kid watched, this was what he saw, even willing his father's car to be squashed to a pulp and perhaps it had been, as he continues to drive blindly though its endless thorny thickets without sensing the danger that lurked so close to him, until it was too late, and the hermit wondered if the father would die without a thought for the son he had abandoned.

The thrill-maker in Tommyhawk's imagination was growing more murderous in one bang after another booming through the entire ancestral lines of the continent. All this went on one day after another, while he beats the drum harder through a pandemonium he sees in the oblivion of noise and blood spurting from the car in all directions, like it was shooting from a public fountain in a city such as Florence, where blood replaces water dripping from the thorns, and although the whole nasty spectacle makes him feel disorientated, and he feels dizzy from the sight of so much blood, still he refuses to stop looking ahead no matter what he imagines, refuses to stop beating the drum, and will not look at the emptiness behind him, because he has decided that he will not have anything to do with ghosts of the south. And, because he did not know what a ghost from the south looked like, who was he to believe that L'uomo di ferro was not a southern ghost, or what those donkeys were that were covered in grey dust, or what kind of spirit place he was in. All this, he instinctively knew, was a ghost land.

This could not go on. One day, Tommyhawk removed his wandering mind from its imagining, and he did this by continually reassuring himself that if he could only concentrate on what he really needed to see, if he kept looking north to save himself, then he would be okay, and by this he meant that he would keep faith alive by convincing himself that he will catch up with his father to kill him. But still this is hard work, since his mind cannot stop imagining the Falcon rolling over and squashing his father alive. He slams the drum with renewed strength – *I hope you rot in hell* – even while he hopes his father will come back as soon as possible and take him home so he can escape to his White Goddess Mother and live in the white palace of Parliament House in Canberra.

Even though there was nothing to see – neither spirits of animals changing pastures, nor a killing land – the sight of it created a stockpile of exploding imaginary mounds here, there and everywhere that could be flora or fauna seen as a mysterious landscape of storms in the mind of Tommyhawk Steel. The White Mother does not swivel on her office chair in this sky. He never sees her anymore. What he sees, mostly, are his own hard questions wrapping around his imagination for flight, that only tighten, render immobile, a stiffness that feels so suffocating while he belts the oil drum, he scarcely breathes. What could you do with any total disaster? The boy still wants to escape when his mind wanders off sometimes, but he is scarcely able to find a way to his former dreams, those old stunted mounds that have refused to grow higher, that explode as soon as they are touched. Sometimes he feels as though he is just in a bad dream, but soon enough, all the exploding bits of reality shatter in free air, then reassemble, and he realises over and over that the fantasy is real, and this was nowhere where he should be on his life's journey to happiness. He can no longer think of how any of this shit happened to him, or how he had been ripped off like this by his father, before his mind finds another banger to explode in his anger. Listen! This one is a double banger that sounds like it had exploded in a drum of gun powder, and all that was left in its wake of skyrockets shooting with long tails of crackling light was the dream smoke rising in the air that smelled of crackers and the singed fur of donkeys.

Sometimes in this possessed state of mind of wanting to kill everything, when he staggers through the heat of the day, or when he is unable to pull himself away from his addictive drumming through each night, Tommyhawk would ask himself the same question from every possible angle, about how he could have once been clever enough to read the sick circumstances of his life as plain as day, to plan his murderous trail into a dream life, yet then be tricked into giving it all up. What went wrong? He knows what any child knows, that it is the clever people who are not destined to end up in hell. They plan their lives by knowing how to latch onto all the good people, who were the most powerful people, like the people who ruled the country. He tried to retrace his thinking from ages ago when his child's mind was younger, to when he could jump straight into the moment where he had let his naïve guard down, the needy ice cream moment, a stupid desire that was not even worth it, but had ended up killing his vision of heaven on Earth, knowing that if he could go back in time he would and he would remain there to keep murdering that moment forever.

They left Praiseworthy together in the Falcon with that old donkey in the back seat. Perhaps the boy already knew the deal. The deal or no deal. If he had thought about it, he would have known that he would have to be exchanged for a donkey on the other side of the continent, otherwise, why would his father have bothered taking him on one of his journeys? Then, who would have known that when they had arrived in this backwater, his father said the old herder's donkeys were too scrappy, and left him for nothing, gave his own son away for free. Just drove off. How could you allow something like that to happen to you? Tommyhawk had felt like punching himself in the head a thousand times for being so stupid, of not trusting the White Mother to save him. He could have waited just a little bit longer because the White Lady Mother of all Aboriginal children would have turned up in the end, and saved him from the police tracking for murderers. Any smart police would have said they could see his guilty look all over his face and known how he had tricked Aboriginal Sovereignty to commit suicide. *Tricked all the other kids too, didn't you?* They would trick him into saying all their names. He tried not to think about how she might have sent her own personal Parliament House plane up to

Praiseworthy to save him, and found he never existed, that she had wasted the government's super jet fuel on nothing. Had she thought he was not interested in her adopting him anymore? But surely, no one need think of what could have been, of what it would have felt like if you were not adopted by the White Mother that represented what was right in Australia, and so he did not think of what could have been, if he had stayed at the airstrip for say, another five minutes, waited just a little bit longer, but a child does not really understand the workings of luck, who gets lucky for instance, or lucky enough to know when a federal government number one air force plane would arrive to rescue an Aboriginal child, to whisk him off his feet, and fly him to the White Palace in the capital of Australia, where he could now be living as the Golden Hair Lady's adopted son. The dream was lost, unreachable, for luck was just like catching a butterfly, or being rocketed to heaven – in fact, Tommyhawk wondered which part of the universe was heaven, and how you would find enough money for the flight if you were not a millionaire? All these dreams, so many thoughts about possibility, were only good enough for what? Mostly his mind was far too busy to be thinking about paradise lost. He had no time for wishful thinking about being a cute Aboriginal child of the White Mother of all Aboriginal children living in the White House in Canberra. Being in his reality, you could see he was not keeping up with the piles of lethal thoughts he had jumping all over the place in his head, escaping from the hidden box marked fireworks, next to broken imaginings, next to fumes, or the one marked ash-coated donkeys, or what was for murdering, and other such boxes stored in the back of his head. No matter, he would keep the main box, the biggest burgeoning colossal mountainous treasure trunk locked there forever if he had to, and drag it out when he saw his father again.

Look! Who cared where that kid Tommyhawk was in the world's problematic meltdown times, when all anyone could see was smoke rising tempo di menuetto in the atmosphere, and eventually after circumnavigating the world many times, evaporating in outer space? The whole land had become a very dangerous place in which to live, and you could not just pick up sticks whenever you felt like it, light a little fire, and let it go up in flames anywhere you liked as though you owned the place, as if you were some kind of sovereign-class citizen for the lot. When it got down to being on your own like Tommyhawk, either you thought about how the wicked father felt freaked, or he didn't, when he just shot off like fast freight with his dumb old platinum donkey, and had not cared less about dumping his kid with a stranger in a hellhole.

Tommyhawk senses only danger in this brittle grey country's hours of quietness, when a day wears itself out, and there is only the slightest change in the weather. Sometimes, he is surprised when an infrequent breeze gently sneaks up behind him and touches his skin with its finger. His immediate reaction is to think that someone is there, and initially, he feels that it is his father standing behind him, but he never turns around to see who it is, never reacts in haste, because he knows he must carefully plan the killing of his father.

Whenever the land feels offended in all points of its compass, its mood is altered, changed to no good. Perhaps when this happened, it had felt offended by man-made interferences with the atmosphere, or any sort of thing that wrecked its home like rubbish being left everywhere and other depredatory human activities, or perhaps, the country does not like hearing a perpetual arrhythmic heartbeat, something that feels unnatural. Gusts of wind travel swiftly over the grass from faraway places of who knows where and of which country's powers will strike Tommyhawk, but he will never look away from his thoughts. He never loses sight of the north even when clouds roll like monstrous ancestral spirits, and sooner or later, he would again be soaked with the muddy mist which covers the land. But the sun soon dries the dampness and returns the dust haze that becomes airborne through the slightest movement of a breeze, or the trampling of donkeys over the ground. Sometimes country crawls along the ground in places like this, and reaches up and grabs strangers to shake their brains loose, but the boy has hate-fists. Fists curled tight. He is in the groove with the strength of this place, with fists that stay clenched while he beats the oil drum. He pulled the filthy sweat-sodden t-shirt over his head. Threw it to the ground. His father's face frozen solid under his darkened sunburnt face, and he thrashes the drum, and screams. *I will fight you.* The drum rolls. *I can't wait to kill you off.* He was now covered in dirt. Sweaty hands. There was no difference between him and the ground. His blood boils. He looked like the old man that he might one day become.

The visibility of vast flat places disorients, and has the capacity to create a natural prison. The sun sinks quickly over these plains to entomb it in the darkness of heavy rolling clouds that frequently cross the night ground of the barren lake. Sometimes there is no moonlight at all, and not much visibility in the haze even during daylight, when the land becomes covered with hard fog. Wild winds come at other times to stir up blinding dust storms and Tommyhawk feels that another world has risen up from the dust and come alive, to bring back the stories of long-ago old people he sees over the lake covered in ash, and who are leading thousands of ash-coated spirit donkeys through an unseen landscape. He feels their slow movement of crossing the featureless lake, as he can see the endless parades that part to go around him, but the enormity of their presence touched him, and he felt as though the wind was trying to take his mind away, and was pulling him into these crossings of the spirits. He does not know where these winds go, but he feared his destination, of being inside the unknown, of becoming lost forever. Nobody should stand on sanctified ground where they do not belong, but this was just country to a fascist boy of Parliament House dreaming, even though he does believe in one thing, that he does not belong to the profound grief he feels in this place. If it was grief that this country wanted from him, there was no sorrow in his soul for this ghost country.

Tommyhawk beats the drum harder until the wind disappears into the darkness with the plethora of ash-coated ghost donkeys, tails dancing a cachucha while running off, and disappearing from sight on the surface of the dry lake covering these old lands governed by powerful atmospheric ancestral spirits. But he knew that even though he was trapped in this land prison, and confined inside of spirit country while waiting for the dumb dumper to return, that the sound of the beating drum would travel exponentially through space, through ghosts coloured grey, and into the consciousness of the guilty White Mother patron saint of Aboriginal children who had not answered any of the mobile calls that he had made to her. If Tommyhawk was anything, he was a law-and-order man. Had it all figured. While he beat the drum, he listened to the sound waves belting its arrhythmical pulse – travelling through open space that bewilders and bamboozles the spirits of country from knowing what was going on – spits the revolting sound off into the breeze, into the gale force winds, cyclonic storms, sixty thousand lightning strikes and thunderstorms, through unprecedented El Niño bushfires, global-warming droughts, then ten La Niña floods of inland sea proportions, all bouncing from the thrashing drumbeats, from off satellites, to his father – *wherever you are* – as the sound continues along highways, bitumen, and bulldust-clogged and washaway roads, hatching fish eggs that had fallen from the skies on moth wings, grasshoppers, sheep's backs, rats, spiders, the drumming charging his mobile phone, iPad and MacAir with flat batteries, and through the sky on the wings of migratory birds, or supersonic jets beyond the reach of the sound – doesn't matter – and travelling to its final destination from either the A1, or A20, B72, and B23, or B32, or the A25, to waft into Parliament House like swallows, or dark matter, delivered by a *Swan Lake* ballerina into the ears of the blonde-hair lady sitting in her office chair that swivels in the blue-sky dreaming of Canberra where all saints hover. Could he make enough noise for the whole world to hear his message? Listen! Clear as bells: *I tell her what you are really like, you are nothing but a dog – wait and see – the police will get you, they always get people like you. I will tell them how you abuse your children. I hate you. You should be locked up, you arsehole.* He wants to make his stupid father come back. *Then I am going to get you.*

So even if Tommyhawk remained imprisoned for an eternity, he would be king of a once-in-a-lifetime great escape that only a handful of the most exceptional people in the whole of humanity could ever dream of achieving, which would be almost like a time when whales walked on dry land and slept in your bed – imaginary things like that which you would call a bad miracle, or good miracles through one way or another of believing above all adversity created from the beliefs of others, that this little Aboriginal child from the bush, would or would not become a multi-millionaire dropkick like powerful white people.

That autopilot kid should have been called cancelled at birth.

The donkey herder wants the dumped kid off the place.

All! Clickitty! Clankitty! Day and night. Clankitty – clank! SOS-ing his coordinates, so he says, like he knows where he is, and yelling his name was Tommyhawk Steel. Good luck with that! I suppose I could have told him – look at this place. Do you really think anyone can hear anything coming from here? Echoing long distance that's what he reckons. What echoes? I don't hear any echoes I tell the genius. You could bomb the place and nobody would know. It doesn't exit. I tell him to his face that he is a prize fool just like his father. He had plenty of donkeys to look at here instead of wasting my time. I saw him standing there. Glaring, getting an eyeful. All full of disgust like he never smelt stench before. What do you expect with hundreds of donkeys hee-hawing at the fence, begging to be picked? Take me! Take me! Even that kid had about zero interest in looking at donkeys, and his father going on in his head: I don't know which one? Maybe that one. No, I think I better take that one. I don't know. Calls himself a donkey man – he doesn't know the arse end of a donkey. I gave that idiot at least a thousand donkeys here to choose from that all looked the bloody same to me, and I take it, of course it was a hard decision – not about leaving his idiot son behind – can see why nobody would want a rattlesnake like that. I am the prize fool for agreeing to keep him here. Haven't slept a wink since with an axe murderer running about the place, but of course it is hard to choose a good donkey. Like that big grey-pelage jenny over there. She's full of class, can't get better with the right kind of white gaze above its nostrils, long eyelashes around its dark eyes below that tatty Rastafarian fringe – can't help that. It's an infestation of prickles here. Knots in its ears! People get too spoiled for choice. Too specialised. What's a particular colour, going on about this colour, or that colour like he's colourblind, and can't see straight. But anyhow, how was he going to cart a donkey back in the type of vehicle he has with him? Where the boy sat probably. It did not even occur to that dumb kid that there would be no room in the car for him on the return journey.

The donkey herder decided that he felt out of place in his own home, and had to leave. He left, on foot, in the dead of night. He skirts in a wide radius around the belted drum, moving in a north-westerly direction, to avoid the boy staring north, whom he believed was too spaced out, and would not have noticed him leaving anyhow. The herder was, he believed, the only human being alive who knew the ancient knowledge for navigating across the now flooded muddy lake in the wintertime. This was a treacherous journey of spirits working on the surface of dangerous undertows, whirlpools and hidden crevices that exist beneath these grey waters, and could drown him if he was not careful. The old man relished hard country travels that were loaded with traps that threatened to imprison him, until the waters dry off in summer to expose his skeleton with what would look like his mouth gasping for its last breath. In this enclosed world of deadly threats devoid of a saviour, he slowly navigates by memory through kilometres of waist-high waters, for he wished only to be where the name of Tommyhawk Steel was neither recognised, nor wanted. Yet the pulse reaches everywhere, and the waters have grown choppy in the wind gusts, and the storms come with horizontal rain that creates sprays from the flapping grey waves that heap together into a tsunami of roaring tidal-like waves that, all together, drown the ringing sound resounding everywhere in this ancestral holy space.

Days before he left, the herder had given the boy a chance to go mustering for donkeys with him, mentioned the idea, but he had refused. He had too much SOS texting to do.

Might be gone a week, or two, don't know. The old man realised that he had never really thought about his sudden urge to count roaming feral donkeys on the ancestral lake at high-water mark in the middle of winter. Except? Well! It was just a niggling thought he had that he could not shake off, of not being sure whether Widespread had stolen his prized jenny, since he had not seen it around lately. It was a vast lake which stretched for hundreds of kilometres of isolation in every direction you looked, and the beauty of it was that you saw nothing except the spectacularly amazing changes of its hues, the multiple shades of greyness that remained the same through season after season, where in the sameness of the windswept stumpy grey vegetation, the same colour as marsupial mice, rabbits, and lizards, it would not matter too much if he stayed for days on end mustering thousands of his feral donkeys through the watery lake to find the missing jenny, but he told the boy if he died out there, nobody who tried walking off around this place by himself would find his body, not in a dozen winters, or summers.

Maybe it will take the police or somebody like that six or seven months to find a little fellow like you. Ya will be just a bit of grey skin, parched from the sun like a kangaroo hide.

Then he chucked the boy some bullets. The rifle fell in the dirt.

Fend for yourself. Kill something, if you want to eat.

8

Synemon wulwulam. You would find all nature of Latin names for the continent's endemic moths and butterflies while flicking through the shelves of the national libraries, encyclopedias, dictionaries, ABC news, social media, text messages, and whatever else was stored and archived in neat rows of boxes in Tommyhawk's head. In his urgency to find clues for navigating a safe route across the freaky lake before the crumbling platform of his mind altered irreversibly and fell apart, he began in an odd place, searching through the complete catalogue of the country's diurnal and nocturnal moths, and all was going well, until his mind was struck with another setback, and his tongue became twisted and got struck dumb on a chord, for no way in the world could he get his tongue around the musical sound of *Synemon wulwulam*, and the name of this moth remained locked in his head, stuck in a groove, paralysing his mind, as though the moth itself had terminated the moth count by conquering Tommyhawk's mind, and like a conqueror, was insisting its Latin name be repeated. Say it! Say it! *Synemon wulwulam*, while forsaking its own sovereign name which was unknown in Tommyhawk's assimilated head for Latin names.

Tommyhawk searched high and low to find where the Latin name had stubbornly attached itself inside his head, and how it had boarded up all the pathways in his brain world of home knowledge. He could not find the moth's real name to dislodge it from his head, and the creature's scaly shale-like greyness blurred his vision of how things should be, for he could not see the wished-for neon-lit A1 highway escape route through the monotonised greyness across this endless expanse of country, not while the colouring of *Synemon wulwulam* preferred not to be elsewhere, making a job of itself trying to cut a path for the mad boy through fifty-three point one degrees Celsius sitting across the vast surface of the lake, while caught in the updraughts of the air currents racing in the opposite direction.

Night moths wrote maps of journeying in the air as they flew through the canopies of stilled landscape. Sometimes, their stories were the waltz of mysteries that reached far away in the sea, gathered along the seawater lapping on the beach, or in flights further along the beach to the whale bone palace, broken wings falling through the flowering mangroves, down the streets of Praiseworthy, to the cemetery. Dance, the lepidoptera woman, was gone. Disappeared. Almost as though she had flown away with the moths one night, and left only the sweet smell of moths and butterflies that had feasted on gum-blossom lingering through the house.

In a world that does not change, the stories of all times continued to be told, and were serenading though the winds, and in the stillness across country, their fulness in truthfulness, never forgotten.

And also, in the airways these days, many static stories.

Put me through to the Minister. She knows me. She is my real mother.

What? The Minister for Aboriginal Affairs? Where did you get this number from?

The army gave a cup to us. It's got the hotline number on it. If Aboriginal children are being abused – then call this number. Well! I am an abused child, I'm Aboriginal, so come and get me. I want to live in Parliament House you dog.

HOLY DONKEY BUSINESS

At the end of these ten years, Chuang-tzu took up his brush and, in an instant, with a single stroke, he drew a crab, the most perfect crab ever seen.
Italo Calvino

1
Oracle 8...Speak like a business man...

It seemed from the word spreading around Praiseworthy, that technically, Aboriginal Sovereignty had only disappeared – just like that, like a spray spurting out of the neck of a bottle into multiple directions. He was all over the place. He was in the flow of hard stories, real stories, in the truth and lies continuously being constructed in the minds of the masses. The truth was that vulnerability had no place in stories constructed through long voyages into the deepest knowledge extracted from country's memories, not when the journeying grew harder, where to reach pieces of muted joy fetched from beneath the shadowy tessellated surfaces of life, one must first navigate the reckless knotted facts that formed the creepy doctrine orbiting illegally through the mind.

Let's believe that a sea serpent of the greatest spiritual significance had really taken him away on the rainbow iridescent scales of its back through waves rising higher than the tallest mountains? A thousandfold spirit had lifted him right through the atmosphere in the sea sprays flying with the winds across the ocean? Older and wiser people said differently, that Aboriginal Sovereignty was everywhere, he had not left, he was hidden in his own spirit. They believed he had gone away for the time being to somewhere in the future, but he would be coming back. You won't find him yet they said. It was too dangerous as long as Aboriginal Sovereignty was not recognised as the true owner of so much power country. He was a long way away now. Hidden in his conscience. You can't get in there. Nobody can. Not even powerful governments. The fish swirl about where they say he had disappeared in a strange-behaving sea. It would be hard to find him now. Some said that he was reconstructing himself but that he was still somewhere in Praiseworthy, always coming back, even though he was becoming something else. He was not dead. You could feel him. He was there. You could touch him just like that if you wanted. Some of the old ladies reached into the air and said they were touching him. They could feel him there. This was because his spirit was everywhere, like air, and you cannot kill the air. Fingers might reach around and through nothing. They let the air slip through their fingers and said that nobody could kill the atmosphere, and that would be what it was like to kill their Aboriginal Sovereignty, it was as though you could actually see him walking up the road, still feel his presence everywhere in the way of someone always just arriving, always making people feel glad when they thought about him coming home.

2

The Praiseworthy public broadcaster went to air as normal, at precisely three a.m. The *You-must-not-kill* show of the Major Mayor, the sometimes public-broadcaster expert Major Mayor, was again, and as usual, about the *thou shall not kill* mantra laconically stretched through fat lips in his half-dream, the thing about official government business requiring their Aboriginal clientele to not kill any more of their children. He repeated his words very slowly, sincerely, and with all of the conviction he could muster for a man with a plan for killing off all his enemies as soon as possible in order to make the vision work his way. So far, Ice had used his major-mayoral powers to relieve the sky of all blue-sky thinking, and lone operators etc. to be totally subservient to the super shire, which meant regularly firing all of his council workers for having lesser thoughts about what he was worth in the visionary future, and so he could, singlehandedly and without hindrance for a change, get a real job done properly. The total fact being, there was only one job for the chief human being of Praiseworthy, and it was not the construction of endless roads to be constantly maintained with truckloads of tar, nor for collecting the rubbish, nor fixing all the plumbing, leaky taps, and broken septic toilets in overcrowded public housing built cheap by mean-spirited government, nor for constructing a decent clean water supply so nobody had to drink polluted water and get sick, nor fixing the electricity everywhere so no one got electrocuted to a crisp, nor getting one hundred per cent employment instead of none, and ditto child welfare, proper schooling and vaccination, economic development and decent housing to decrease the amount of people living in overcrowded sweatboxes in a global warming and global virus catastrophe situation, or any normal thing you try to get a government to do while swapping all-encompassing treaty rights for a mayorship who advises, and fixes nothing. No. This was not the real work to be done here. Things like being an assimilator, or a sell-out was far too easy. No real excitement and passion here. The job of the Major Mayor of the super shire was simple. It was to get Cause. Get rid of the nuisance. Now Ice knew that he had the accused murderer pegged. Nailed the nemesis. It was not a matter of casual urgency that Ice was talking about here, more like every second in the world counted when you were out to kill off your enemy. This was the reason that he began his daily broadcast to the Praiseworthy super shire with the right feel, it was important to build up as much hate sentiment as he could muster for a brainwash with supreme loathing and things like that, and you could only do that by being totally believable.

The charm and personality for being believable in a world of believable people suffering a plethora of fools, was absolutely paramount in the way that Ice presented his public persona to the mob. The level of respect that he demanded from his mayoral constituents by insisting that they stop being roll-over pussies, and start feeling real honest hostility in their bones – things like that – was far beyond achievable by the run-of-the-mill ordinary people, which they were not. He thought that more would be achieved if they began thinking of themselves as a pixelated copy of himself, where the entire body was made up of layer upon layer of hostile fragments, for this he proudly asserted, was all he had inside himself, a compassion-free body, where you would be hell-bent finding a shard of decency when you were out to peg a killer on the job. It was a sad thought, that at the end of his advice-giving he always felt disappointed, because he knew that the roll-over pussies remained roll-over pussies with not a shard of hostility implanted in their soul by the miracle of listening to a godlike lecture. They remained without conviction, with no desire to get rid of their enemies. His hope of achieving a good emotional response from the community again was a failure, for there was no response. Even though Ice thought it was only logical to accept the logic of spite, it was beyond Praiseworthy to fathom what that entailed. Why did they not get it? The fact that you should not kill children. No one said a thing. All he wanted at first was total agreement on the logic of this one straight fact that you should not kill your children, that you should love your children like white people, but nothing, all he got was silence. He did not need any liberal-minded people to be on his side, or the country's 'lefties', which would be like the pot calling the kettle black, nor people who wore their hearts on their sleeves. He only wanted his people, his mayoral majority, the hard-face, hard-nose, hard-core never agreeable for once in their lives to accept one simple idea – his black opinion, that you must love your children, not kill them like the murderer Widespread. Just accept that Widespread was a child murderer was all he asked, and there was really no room for disagreement with this idea becoming dead fact, as far as Ice was concerned. You either believed in this fact because he said so, or else, you were part of the problem – and yes, AH! UN! AUSTRALIAN! – whatever that was, and in this case, if you did not believe him, then you were a child killer too, and this was the point of what he was trying to get into the combined thick skulls about what he called a child killer on the loose in the murdering zone, Cause Man Steel.

Ice never gave up on the *broadcastees*. He repeated the mantra for the hundredth, thousandth time about roll-over pussies living in the midst of children killers. He challenged: Where's your soul? Haven't any of you got a soul? The sound of his voice searching for a soul jarred the brain antennae radiating like flower stamens on repeat mode through the ears of the cultural, the people of the forward plan working to the bone on giving up the very existence of their soul, in preparedness for their adaptation into the Australian way of life by becoming more assimilable than the whitish whiteness. And this business of dumping the soul so you could be embedded in unsavoury messages about accusing a dreamer of being a child murderer at three a.m. was driving his wife Maureen completely out of her mind. She often stayed in bed these days while complaining of a permanent migraine, or some variation thereof, requiring a packet of paracetamols which hardly did the job of eradicating the pain of having her human rights violated by consistent and inconsistent mental torture from being imprisoned with the lies of a husband, and driven brain-dead from listening to the husband's monotonous voice sounding like a dripping tap, which she knew was exactly the same thing as having propaganda piped non-stop into the ears of political prisoners, which she seemingly had become, and the story was that all the paracetamols she swallowed only dulled her brain into believing its own looped-back whisperings jeered from the sidelines demanding where was her mental toughness, and why did she not run with the counterpunches, for to be truthful, *Wife! You have the right to remain silent*, but not to step in on a classical Major Mayor of the super shire's speech-making to his *broadcastees*.

3

Maureen's accumulated sleep-deprived head pain plateaued in an instant from being awakened in shock by Ice's heightened mantra extravagancies echoing through the house from where he sat in front of the computer screen, far earlier than his scheduled three a.m. broadcast. Unsuccessfully, she tried to smother herself with a pillow in her bed. She knows he will practise his broadcast of disillusionment-soaked reminiscences and bewilderments to perfection, so that the whole diatribe will appear seamless love-making with his backward *broadcastees*, as he showers them with umpteen agendas for dealing with their stupidity, in particular, their slow progress towards the march to assimilation. What he was especially aiming to accomplish, Maureen heard in her half-achieved asphyxiation, was how he felt sick of repeating the mantra about how killing children was a crime against humanity. He was not sure how many times one must say something that was completely logical to a moron to be physiologically effective, so his *broacastees* could get a grip about what was right or wrong. But, then he digressed by making big statements of comparison, by saying, *That even Australia has still not done anything in over two centuries about genocide and theft of Aboriginal country.* Maureen the scowler had had enough, and tramped up and down with her flip-flops on the loose wooden floorboards. Ice likes haters, and shouts at her:

Get breakfast. That was all he wanted her to do. And she paused on the spot right next to where he was sitting at his desk, and shouted at him to go and get whatever he wanted himself.

The story from her point of view, or a word or two about what you might call her *con spirito* view of her *con sordino* life. It was not something you would find being talked about in one of Ice Pick's broadcasts to the super shire on the state of their Indigenous world, nor what you would read in the newspapers by white experts milling in the distant view, trying to shadow box with the limelight that gives them plenty to write about how they saw the dying Aboriginal world, the rich art form that does not require mentioning a word about the self-defined sovereignty of the long suffering *Maureens* of this country. Nobody would want to know about Maureen, or how she felt about having a decent night's sleep gained from her own self-governing thoughts. No one said, let's ask Maureen, and asked Maureen about her mental injuries, by hearing her testimonials of what it was like living with a wobble-lip fabricator who had lost track of the truth, because if they did then everybody would know what it felt like to have a bunch of murdered ghost children being let into her house by the albino husband, and they would know what it was like to hear those little ghost children crying about their lost lives while they were running around her house in the middle of the night with their flip-flops creaking along the floorboard. Maureen knew about the powerful, and she could say how these children were the ones really speaking from inside the snow dome's head, and how they were orchestrating those pink lips to chip away at what he called changing the status quo about inappropriate parenthood in Praiseworthy. She would tell you herself, the fuckwit husband did not give two hoots about parenthood, or human rights, or sovereignty, or global warming, or global pandemics, because all that he cared about, was himself, of being white as...

The moonlit night dropped tree shadows on the walls, and leaf shiver from the sound of Ice's voice bouncing from wall to wall in the love-thy-children practice broadcast, while in some corner of the house, the half-deranged sleep-deprived Maureen whimpered in *andante con moto* mob style, which was a totally inaudible screaming pitch coming from nothing to the pink blob, *Haven't you had enough crucifyings yet?* Ice's ears must be razor sharp, for he heard this and stopped everything – to hell with his rehearsal, for he had to ask himself why she always wanted to attend her own crucifixion, and so he yelled, *fuck it,* he would have to start all over again. Quivery lips unzipped her self-imposed exile voice, ripped away the sellotape sealing her lips, chucked the sticky piece in the flip-lid bin, and let her mouth swing forth like a Top End river belting it out downstream to the sea in the wet season. The not short for tangled up wicked words in the head waters gushed forth staccato-like, bouncing from wall to wall right across the house. Saliva spuming everywhere, she continued slinging out her mad thoughts about being sick of Ice sitting at his computer in the middle of the night and killing her sleep. Hey! Snowball. Don't forget. He kills mouths. There was no room in this house for other people's soapboxes. Such a little thing could create a raging torrent from thinking only of herself, and Ice heard every word, but this did not worry him because he likes a hater, he understands Maureen, that she never knows when enough is enough while constantly looking back over her shoulder in her scurrying to get out of the house quick, without any idea of knowing where she was going after interfering with his broadcast, but hell, that was the story of his life. You can only try but you cannot help the circumstances.

The common people hanging about the world would say that Ice's people – like the black queens who stickhandled his balls – would usually call the nauseous looking Maureen, *a general cow.* Genteel snigger show talk amounting to how much the cow could make them feel sick in the guts. But who isn't living in a world full of sycophants like these queens waltzing into her house, as though they owned the place?

Now Maureen had almost become lost forever from her deadbeat, and increasingly sleep-deprived life, while tracing the thoughtless and directionless path of her late-night flight far into the world of spirit people. The roosters crowed and a house steeped in silence brought Maureen home where she scurried reverently, on tiptoes, in this dedicated sanctum of the sacrosanct, where sound was either cancelled, or blessed by Ice who knew how the divine lived, how they controlled sound, even mice whispering about where the cheese was, and mousy type of women were not required to speak about cheese at all, or have opinions. But of course, you could not stop the ghosts coming inside the house, and Maureen can hear them discussing Ice's broadcasts no matter how loudly he speaks, as she walks sideways along the walls, negotiating loose floorboards, each plank she knows intimately from the way it speaks, the subtle difference in the creakiness of each, while anticipating a face-to-face encounter with Ice's face centimetres from her own saying, *It's over,* and she saying, *What, the broadcast?* And he saying, *Get out of here. Nobody can afford idiots ruining their future.*

Let's end this stupidity. Let Ice continuously observe how fearful Maureen had become after she fled in the night and caused a night-bird to screech, for he has all the time in the world to help her build a high-security prison of herself. He likes piloting a few private test cases as a gauge, to see what works in how he utilises other people's ineptitude to further push fear into the populace. The more frightened she becomes, the stronger and more justified he feels in the growth of his strategic thinking to help save his people from murdering their children. She should not have caused the night-bird to screech, and there should not be dogs barking in the distance, nor wind rattling the leaves, and Ice does not want to hear a prowling cat screech at three a.m., and so, Maureen should sweat, should be frightened of hearing any sound that Ice must not hear when he was preparing his broadcast, for he would be forced to restart again and again, these broadcasts must be perfect, each a piece of art, and this cannot be done when she bumps into things, steps on the wrong floorboard, or touches anything that sends vibrations across the whole house that explode in the crackling of the sun-blistered tin roof cooling in the night air. There is nothing that can make a sound in Praiseworthy at three a.m., when Ice presents his broadcast.

In these nights when Maureen begins another epic journey of preventing forbidden sounds, she would finally muster the courage to cross the floorboards closest to the walls without creating any unwanted sound. She lived in the hope of being permitted to continue living in her home, and so, she reached the kitchen to silently prepare the 3.30 a.m. breakfast and hopes that not one of the hundreds of roosters would suddenly start crowing earlier, and she hopes no one left scraps of food on the ground, a fish head for a dog fight, but it was the kitchen that could not wait to dance with her fear. This was a noisemaking world of dropped plates, clanging pots and pans hiding from her in the back of a cupboard, and cross knives and forks hexing in the utensil drawer, banging as she clumsily tried to find whatever she wanted without wasting a kWh of electricity by turning on the light, while the hammering of Ice beating his words on his keyboard echoing in her brain ordered high-level invisibility. But this did not help at all, for Ice was wondering why she had not stopped the fly buzzing in the light of the computer screen. Nobody needed to hear a fly while reaching for higher levels of honest momentum in their work, and he did not know why she had not dealt with the plague of mosquitoes from the swamp that came into the house every night while he was trying to think straight, nor why she had not made insect-harbouring trees disappear to stop the cicadas screeching, and why owls were now roosting on the roof where he could hear rats chasing each other, and beetles belting over the wood floors that he could hear being eaten by termites every time that woman goes to the kitchen. His eyelids twitch. Where was his golden Christmas beetle that had deserted him until next summer? He wished it was summer again. His upper cheeks quiver. He was losing the purity of voice he had been perfecting for hours to keep a ring of authenticity to it, where even he could believe in himself. He had no idea why anyone could be so clumsy, and had asked himself this question so many times, it became a fucking billboard pinned to his head. He was lost for the life of him why he had chosen this of all women as a wife. No, he knows that was not true. She had chosen him. He had always been too preoccupied to be bothered thinking about marriage, but vaguely understands how he ended up with having such a stupid woman constantly in his life. He could barely resist the temptation to go into the kitchen to sort her out – again, trample her into the ground just by his presence – but he could not be bothered. He knows she expects him to react, to feel his presence. He paused, knowing he was able to capitalise on her sly neediness, by reassuring himself that she would always try to claim his attention, like everyone else, which he thought was a pathetic way of trying to get him to notice her.

Each night he goes through this rigmarole, restarting his broadcast, aiming for perfection: *Thou shall not kill your children. No! That's not right. You should not kill,* before diverging into, *Fuck you Cause. You should not kill, you arse-hole.* Then. Maureen. And forced to restart the public broadcast like he was incompetent. With no idea how to act like a professional Major Mayor of a super shire who cared about something. Stop! Start! The whole idea Ice had of surpassing moral relativity in Praiseworthy, of being released from the forces always gravitating to culture, to dismantle the apparatus of clingy old beliefs, for plucking his true glory from on high, was looking like a right balls-up. And in the midst of all Maureen's eternal interrupting noisiness of walking on floorboards like an elephant, he felt as though he had become dog meat, and was continuously being ordered to learn a new trick in how to dig its own hole at the bottom of the well to find some walnut-sized shrunken reserve of professional tolerance. *Was it too much to ask for a bit of quietness at three o'clock in the morning in this cunt shonky blackfella turnout I have ended up with*? Who knows? One could not say enough about the history to explain these things except to say it was *the kind* of thing that white people expect from Aboriginal people who cannot speak English properly, and just let the pots and pans being bashed around in the background do the talking of English for them.

Thou shall not kill.

The freak Ice took control of himself, even if he could not remember what his initial thoughts were for the broadcast to the *broadcastees*, because words had escaped him about who you should not kill, since he only wanted to kill Maureen now, while momentarily forgetting about how he wanted to kill Widespread, and why his people should not kill children, but he thought that some words always wanted to mock what was spoken, either blindly, or truthfully, or through a pack of lies.

4

The work problem Ice faced was that deep in his heart, he was in real deep trauma about his own fakery, of not really knowing how to be a proper collaborator to the multifaceted, the overall population of the continent. He was faking too much, he had forgotten what was real in how he was hell-bent on getting everyone to work together for the common good by reconciling themselves to the relatively short history of colonialism.

Though that was not where it was at all. Listen good now! What could you say about consciousness, if there was a conscience of the new era, and a conscience of inheriting more than one hundred thousand years of existence, and the conscience of all times? You would need to think about where your soul belonged, if it belonged in all three realms at once or none, or one, or the other. How would you know if you had made the right choice about which part of your conscience you should believe, that it wasn't a runaway train carriage falling into the abyss, or a conscience that attracts wild animals throwing themselves at your mind to tear it apart. This was what troubled Ice in a forked-lightning way of pelting bolts over and over the same brain, his brain in fact, as he worried about which of the three consciences would actually work for his soul, and of course it was hard enough for the best of his humanity to only choose being in the twenty-first-century conscience as a stand-alone-phenomenon for achieving greater whiteness, minus all other known realities rushing at the door. He just did not know. Was the ideology of preaching togetherness *a no-brainer of having no perimeter, no periphery, no boundary way of becoming fabulously a world of albinos like himself*, but he kept leaning towards togetherness by tying strong knots to get his people through the next century, alive, yep, breathing, hearts ticking, in this sick-in-gut worrying about how to shut the boundaries with an all-openness situation at the same time. When he thought more about his golden beetle, yes, he could see that it observed the boundaries of its conscience, but also moving without boundaries even if boundary bound, but his shadow thought *let's lock everything up anyhow* so there was only one way to move, his way to get through the forward plan.

The trouble with Ice was that he was always composting his shelf-bought mantras, and this made the ordinary people of Praiseworthy very sceptical, since they did not know what his forebodings were about except wasting their time. So, they prayed for him. They hoped down in the multi-denominational on Church Street, that he would find his conscience and see true light in the end. But buying disposable mantras for the masses was not a crowd-pleaser in their books. They thought having a vision to save culture should be second nature, that any of their superheroes should know how to successfully implement a vision for saving their culture from catastrophic destruction, and here they were, just with another ordinary visionary that nobody liked because he was as powerless as they were as far as they could see, for he had saved nothing, not even them. They wanted to see a killer, a visionary attitude – you see them all the time on TV so they knew what they were talking about when even they could imagine what it meant to take no prisoners, and they wanted to see that, to know thy enemy, instead of killing them off, making all of them his enemy, so what was it to them if he pledged himself to catch the child murderer Widespread, who had remained so far as they could see elusively hard to catch, and which begged the question, of who was the better man. Yet, why not linger a moment longer in the ruins of shelf-bought mantras, when the rules of limitation and common sense possibly applies to all cultures. Who was going to make the haze disappear? Bring the storks? The brolgas that bring the dance that lifts the dust?

If building a man of conscience involved an all-encompassing pain, how do you know when the work is done? How do you recognise this humanity, among others? Where were the eyes resembling a giant magnifying glass, that constantly scan the streets of Ice's brain to find the loose ends to stitch together into a conscience man with a better plan of how to capture this killer in their midst, for the sure thing was, he was still pursuing the same chase as they were, to be the best of who they were. But there was Ice with his infernal broadcasts, still not getting a Praiseworthy consensus about the hot topic of their killing children.

Say it was the worst of times that you were watching grow exponentially more catastrophic, when it was too bad for anyone wasting a single moment of their lives, but say, Ice was trying his best. He had built a single unblemished reputation. He was a Major Mayor of a super shire constantly kowtowing to a conga line of government politicians running up and down the country, by supplying them with a thriller of a story for the rave of the moment in changing the narrative of the nation-state getting too cosy with Aboriginal rights. And Ice was the man to do it, by accusing his constituents, his Aboriginal people, of being child-killer parents, and the way Ice told the story was an exhilaratingly pleasing way of indoctrinating the nation – built on fiction itself to excite the broader masses. But life happens, even to those who do not know the country's ancestral creators still lived in the land throughout the entire continent, but who regretted that old wisdom knowledge that makes survival happen in a planetary crisis, for they were rooting for the Aboriginal superhero to get his lethal culture people to toe the line of the majority who were not Aboriginal, by proving to the world that they were not killing their children, and by helping him to hunt down the accused Aboriginal child killer, the parent, Cause Man Steel. What was the problem with that? But why was there no progress? Were Praiseworthy people too dumb to be indoctrinated? It was just difficult to understand for the first world why a man who had them indoctrinated like a human God brayer, could not conquer his own people, to get them to see that you have to kill off a few of your enemies if you wanted to get to the end of time. This was what you saw at the end of the vision, and either Praiseworthy had to be left standing at the end of the century without feeling guilty for the fate of the rest of world humanity uninterested in saving itself, or it wasn't.

Well desperation was what it was, but Ice knew that he had a nose for something you might call predatory instinct, starving-dog affliction, of being a high-pressure steam cleaner for purifying the populace, and his secret weapon was not his Ice Queens, but the yardstick, the untrainable Maureen, the unconquerable itself.

It was only Cause Man Steel who was late to arrive at the theatre, to take his part on the stage, because he was always late, even for his own crucifixion.

Yep! Ice knew how hard it was to kill dreamers.

Can you believe it, the press, the bloggers, the Twitter feed – another zenith, Ice checked the blog, it was all fairytale, exponential 1000K +++ followers, tens of thousands of hits nationwide, each time he delivered a diatribe to the populace, and why stop there? Ice would pant and crawl over bare earth if he had to, if it meant he could convert one more opportunist to his way of thinking, for this man felt he was that ready for higher success by changing civilisation, as he called it, but what was the Australian population after all? A kindred spirit of a mere twenty-two and a half million people minus the Aboriginal world, which was not what you would call a planetary success. But why kill the dreams of a dream-killer? What was happening here was a dream run for an acceptable Aboriginal man of rare conscience that spoke to the populace – eased its conscience, spoke the right words, even though he had stolen less than a handful of hearts in Praiseworthy, but you know, who cared if you could feel a cold cleansing sensation coursing through your blood stream like Ice did by assuming it was his spirituality, even his ancestry sitting in the corpuscles and agreeing with him because this ultimately was what he would like to think his cultural humanity was about. And what a shame, Maureen thought, growing more and more astonished by how needy he was becoming with the white people, and seeing what he was holding back, stockpiling his brain with useless white political junk squirting out in his repetitious mantra broadcasts about his people needing to stop killing their children. But who knew what angle of changing the narrative Ice was using to spirit the mob from culture, and chuck them into a white future deprived of global emergency reality? Maureen knew. She heard the whispering house arguing – wanting him to prove there were people murdering children in Praiseworthy – and she saw that half-smile on Ice's face while staring at the computer screen, smirking there through the blankness, slyly gesturing in a modest way that even he was not conscious of, by emitting a low whistle instead of his usual wolf whistle when it came to self-congratulation, and in this twilight hour, it was as though he was in doubt, attempting to squash some of his own arrogance as he rechecked his bloggers' endless opinions about the fact-checked fact that the Aboriginal world of parents killing their own children should not be allowed to happen in the twenty-first century, but nothing as self-imposed as feedback on his own blog would stop Ice from feeling electrified in the end, of feeling the elation of a bullfighter beside the bloodied slain, that further convinced him, he had to be heard. So, of course, he was pumped! He was cornering the bastard Cause Man Steel, which was nothing personal as far as he was concerned, not as though he was running a vendetta about Native Title ownership like it was a war to be won. No – he was not bothered about any of that, or if the dreamer was keeping a pack of donkeys in Praiseworthy – no, not that, what mattered was that he knew his type. The type that kills his own people, like children, with dreams that do not work, and never would.

Like me Ice! Like me the most! The outraged Queens visited Ice more frequently now since he became popular with the government. They come to his place to speak about their hatred for Cause Man Steel at least a dozen times a day in this major moral crisis, after having already established themselves in the mayoral world as the keepers of all government policy for fixing Aboriginal abusive parents who hated their children. They needed to be referred to as the representatives of human exceptionalism above all others praised as praiseworthy in Praiseworthy. These are not ordinary women who sit at the high levee mark of loving Aboriginal children more than their parents, for this was where they looked down at the rest of their humanity wallowing in the murkiness of their doubt. How lonely it was to be on this mountaintop of specialisation, to hurtle hurt down on everyone else from where you were sitting in your abandoned sentry hut to meditate on ways to destroy more of others. Ah! But there goes Maureen sidestepping the creaky floorboards of the inner sanctum, her back against the wall, listening to Ice stewing about how you got to give somebody like Cause enough rope to hang himself, and he tells his audience of Queens while musing, scratching the red welts on his cheek where he slapped himself back into the real world often enough, *You want to know what, it looks like I am going to get away with it again.* And Maureen wondered to herself, what was he talking about.

ICE QUEENS

Glad All Over
Dave Clark Five (1963)

1

Oracle 9...You can either look up, or look down...

Hitting the high straps at precisely twenty past two in the morning before Ice's broadcast had begun, the real tempest in the midst, the main line-up of evil haters, his four black queens of storm clouds, havoc and wreck – *excluding one hundred per cent not a queen Maureen* – these four real movers and shakers, were firing up their wits for the day as the mayoral electoral committee of first things first. The new mantra again topped the agenda: baby-haters, the people not praiseworthy enough to share the same air as themselves. This so-called pick of the bunch of all the religious gospel singers of the inter-denominational from Churchy Street, his high-pitched raucous brain-drilling alarm clocks, were Ice's exclusive on-call, all-night dream choir for keeping the rivers of evil out of the place. At the ungodly hour, these four ladies were right with the day, angrily bashing pots and pans flung around their kitchens in fits of bad temper and pumping gospel-steam into their lungs for a day of singing the blues.

So! It was a normal day. The heavy heavers were lifting the load, and being shakers of souls with more spirit than the ancestral creators of the place, had enough electricity generators and gas combustion stored in their being, to charge up the spirit of the haze place while yoga-ing from bed to kitchen in their eBay not cheap nylon-pink China Doll shortie pyjamas like the high bidders they thought themselves to be. It was another perfect day for reaching across the ancestral breathing the good life for these four women fuming with jealousy of one another – Black Maudlin Able Mabel, Heavy Tytania the cat-talker fairy queen, big moaning Queen Meadow Lee, and the rivers of grog Miss Queen of the Outback. They knew how to let it rip behind your back while contemplating the bigger picture, which was how much ripping apart there was to be done in Praiseworthy.

Ice, on the other hand, felt satisfied with his conversation with the clientele, he told the Minister at 2.30 a.m. She was always a cinch. Easily won over. Totally convinced of his methodology of moving the Indigenous world into the twenty-first century of Australian life. *Call it assimilation. Call it what you like really.* He called it a piece of cake.

Maureen had not even bothered to stand in the backyard, as Ice had instructed, by scowling at her to go and kill those moths banging on the windows so he could have a bit of privacy from her endless pacing against the walls, while he was waiting for the Minister for Aboriginal Affairs to call him. *Who did that big pink flat-mouthed old salamander think he is?* She was not going to stand around out the back in gloomy twilight thinking about a salamander, for she had just come back inside after parading around the bush for hours – experiencing what it was like to feel homeless, while trying to figure out what to do with her life. What did the Minister for Aboriginal Affairs mean to her, or any of Ice's highfaluting politicians, journalists, or whoever else? They all talked about nothing. Instead, she hung behind the door of the lounge room where Ice had set up his office in the centre of the house, and tried not to go to sleep while listening to his conversation – the unchanging monologue of his dissertation to whoever he spoke to about his current philosophy and strategies to convince his listener on the other end of the line. But, as she stood leaning against the wall, daydreaming about once remarking to Ice matter-of-factually, although not entirely out of jealousy, *It's as though you and ya yard stick slack-arsed bitches are strapped to one another at the hip.* She thinks about this now, how these women monopolised him. Of course, he was infatuated with them, loved their attention and jealousy. She remembered how Ice had looked at her then, believing she was mad. An off-the-cuff man like Ice despised jealousy, and before she had finished speaking, he finished it for her: *Moron! Are you wired subconsciously to the same fuckin alarm system as everyone else here?* His face turned to rouge, like a man lolly who had seen snakes springing out of someone's mouth, and almost instinctively, to make sure she shut her mouth before more damage was done, he said, *If you were not so pathetic I would laugh*, and continued correcting what he called her utter stupid pathological jealousy, not to mention other plausible rebuffs – her moving maladroitly around the house and in his bed with something like, *You are more stupid than what I thought. Full stop. End of story.*

Everything else being strategy, not ecstasy, had now grown into a hard-edged stalactite face that was barely able to snipe dismissively in Maureen's direction, but it was enough to make her jump out from behind the door: *Haven't you got the breakfast going yet? Life's already started or hadn't you noticed, not at six o'clock, or ten o'clock, or when you feel like it.*

You're a fuckin jerk, Ice.

2

There was something else you should know about Lolly's preachy broadcasts booming from loudspeakers wired two point five metres apart throughout Praiseworthy when the jolting brethren woke electrocuted-startled. Nobody wanted to hear the high-tech black albino Shakespeare spinning their mind out – like their Praiseworthy was a puppetmaster's theatre of war for freaks at three in the morning. This was not the Sydney Opera House. Nor anything like it. No. Praiseworthy people did not want to be woken up at three a.m., and to feel that their bed had shifted in the night, moved backwards in time, and that they were actually sitting in the middle of a Roman colosseum bloodbath, instead of being in their own twenty-first-century home. Anyone would wonder, and they wondered, how many more years they would have to endure sleep deprivation which was so bad, that it would drive anyone to want to muffle the salamander.

Still, some good news. There was a mad wishing rush to be first in the long queue forming in front of the price-gouging supermarket-worrying people that wanted to hoard stuff. The brand-new supermarket of the new-era dreaming meant that you could buy anything at all, but it had sold out of toilet paper. Sold out of cotton wool. Glad Wrap. Disposable nappies. Cigarettes. People were hording the butts. Old fish-and-chip paper. They used whatever you could possibly roll up neatly like a plug to jam into their ears to not hear the three a.m. compulsory broadcast. Some people used pieces of rag, the old DOWN WITH WHITE RACIST GOVERNMENT t-shirts saved like treasure from the last federal election, now rolled like a smoke, to soak in cooking oil before plugging it in their ears. In the long suffering of hearing a rant instead of a lecture, about being child murderers and to stop it, what the people really wanted to know was how long they would have to listen to Ice talking about how they were all a pack of racists because of his albinism. The whole of Praiseworthy was sick to the guts of hearing the rant, and what came next, his line about being conceived by grog parents going at it hammer and tong in broad daylight like there was no tomorrow, by having unprotected sex in UV radiation right out there in the middle of the road for all to see, which he falsely claimed had robbed his skin pigmentation of melanin when a sudden dust storm lit up the country in raging bushfires that raced over the landscape and ascended in spinning flues far up in the skies, all of which created a fiery furnace spouting spikes of lighting spinning the dust haze with dry-grass turned into ash, and that included the spirit child with the colour of a ghost entering his mother's womb, and that was the reason why he was not black like everyone else. And the result of all this? Pink-skinned babies. Monstrosities. A grotesque, multi-pronged, catastrophe. A Trojan in the ancestral. A piece of malware junk. A worm-hacker, or a zombie in the network of ancestral lines. Then, some rare occurrence. A unique thing happened. People said they were not stupid. Beds were not burning. Beds were not in a Roman colosseum bloodbath. All the people with beds had to worry about was how to get down to the supermarket quick enough, gathering in safety under the security light, and scream about the lies, DID NOT HAPPEN ICE.

The night people had switched the brain off. Nobody was at home. They did not want to hear Lolly's graphic memories about what happens in broad daylight. They fled back into the sleeping world by bringing up the timeless infinity of themselves – the mangayi law, cod fish, eagle, dingo, march flies, devil people, barramundi, moth storylines going a long way off, letting it all run through their thoughts. They were long gone back into the ancient world of their sovereignty, and they never reached out their plugged ears for the story being broadcast again on those loudspeakers, of how *the angel-coloured foundling left in the atmosphere, the dumped one, swaddled in 'one love' reggae rags, had come floating through a dust-flooded desert in a cradle of spinifex, while all around the stationary rainless cyclone sitting low in the sky above, the most enormous lightning-and-thunder-carrying desert exploded, smashing the eardrums of sinners to smithereens.* Well! Could have, but they missed it all, this part about how *the baby had wailed exactly like the storm wind scattering all the bush tucker, where even the biggest fish flew out of the water, and everyone hit the grog, and their children went mad from the disaster that continued onwards in its vicious circle of what happens to sinners who murder their children's life expectancy in government statistics, and this was the reason that you lot should get straight out of bed, get dressed, stop running around in circles and look forward to the coming day, when you root out all the child murderers like Widespread living in your midst, and get them gaoled forever a long way from any children of Praiseworthy.*

Then he came along later to end with chastising after-words: *Can't you feel the pain? I can feel it. Can't you hear what I was saying?*

He asked for signs, and said he would like the signs to say something like this: *No! No! Sir Ice Pick, you – mayorship thing. Lolly. We are all deaf as a fence post. We are just plain people. Silly people. What would we know about anything? But do go on please. Tell us the truth again. About how that chorus of hundreds of deaf dingoes and starlings – more than anyone had realised were living in Praiseworthy – had joined in with everything else howling off-key in the mad storm from wherever, and how they cowered for shelter while turning their backs to the epic cyclonic wind thing swimming around in the blood that brought you here in that flood time – in the first place.*

The Minister for Aboriginal Affairs did not believe Ice Pick was any albino at all, balked at the fact because she said, he looked like a real Aboriginal to her, and not a far-fetched spirit wind that caused albinoness, because she knew what her Aboriginal people looked like.

3

Sometimes, when life seemed too much, Ice would try to disentangle himself from the urge to pursue extracurricular exhaustive vendettas. Lolly was after all a Major Mayor of a super shire. Mayors had major responsibilities now for saving the world, not just going around and killing it. A real man needed to be a higher jinx than a dust-world Shakespeare acquiring a better kind of black-man perspective than what you find in murderers of babies, like Cause Man Steel. At the very least, he thought, he wanted to ponder the moral consequences of how his all times black Shakespearian drama world would play out, such as whether he was being too dramatic and unbelievable, because when he appraised the matter through having a broader perspective, he knew that Praiseworthy was not theatre, would never grow into the Sydney Opera House, or be anything like it. There would be no fake skies to open and close at will for this was the real world with natural sky, where one could only hope that the sky would bring a natural calamity and sweep Cause up in a disaster so mighty it would finally kill him, and where unlike fakery skies, Ice would never have to lift a finger. Would the cost of real-life theatre, outweigh the cost of waiting for a fake fate to rid mankind of a piece of rubbish? But every one of these ton-of-bricks moments passed by, because in Ice's heart, he knew that the show must go on.

The phone rings, and Ice lets it ring several times before he reluctantly lets the philosophy go, and picks up the receiver on his desk – why doesn't Maureen answer it for God sake – it is only the thought that irritates him, and with the receiver to his ear, he continues to stare at the computer. *Yep*, he finally says. He already knows who it is. The special advisor to the Minister for Aboriginal Affairs who routinely called him seconds too late, after the broadcast. *How's it going Ice? What's the scoop? Continuing with the Cause Man Steel story? The Minister is eager to know. I need to prepare her press statement.*

Before he could answer this idiot, who did not know the time, his mobile rings. Ice sees it is the Minister herself, and he hangs up on the advisor. He always prefers to speak to the Minister in confidence. See if she agrees about his latest strategy to gaol Cause for murdering his children, or if again she has lost track of the main game, and had backed down when the hard decisions needed to be made about whether you could blow up a sacred site or not. He looked around to see where Maureen was hiding, saw her, and by the expression on his face, she knew he was telling her to fuck off right down to the furthest corner of the backyard. Ice noticed that she was still wearing her unfortunate choice of clothes – men's navy-blue shorts and the same old holey t-shirt she has been wearing for years. He wondered what lingerie the Minister was wearing, and flicks through a wishful-thinking wardrobe of gold foil disasters, and hisses at Maureen, *Give me some privacy can't you*.

4

Heaven, Queen Meadow Lee moments before, three a.m.

Queen Meadow Lee, Ice's reigning bully queen of moaners was a top dog of a woman, believing she was blacker than black, and far more ideologically richer in infinity thought. And there she was in heaven, *glad all over* – stomping up a pre-dawn thunderstorm to that old Dave Clark Five 1963 hit jammed on repeat on YouTube, prancing like a penned jaguar slipping across the creaky timber floors of her government-awarded, poorly designed, got-it-wrong-again house, never suited for the tropics. Her arms flung to the right, then to the left, arms up above the head, down flat on the kitchen floor, and so began her particular version of the salute to the sun in a pair of jazzy hot-pink tulip-patterned shortie-pyjarmie fusion with white nylon frills around the edges that became an electrified brilliant frizz of frenetic thrill-pink and shiny brown-skinned jerk movements, now with bum up in the air, and screaming baby *you will never be blue*, moments before

Ice's broadcast began blasting through the open breeze windows of the house. Shit!

Kill Cause Man Steel – left leg stretched out to the back, ditto motto, right leg stretched. What happened to the sound of night-vigil choirs singing softly *Leaving on a Freight Train* off in the distance, wafting on the beach front? Why could you no longer hear them from Meadow Lee's backyard? Even the caper butterflies could have told you, that the song people had fled from the hex radiating across a flat fifty-metre radius from that dead person's garden, the Methuselah molten in his manger like a baby snarling at them for the longevity of racism.

Now with eyes wide awake, and staring off into her personal nirvana space, the heaven of Queen Meadow Lee's hot furnace breathing quickened into short breaths, almost a pant, a breathing technique for her sombre mantra for dealing with another bad day in her life. The humidity was already high, and salty perspiration poured onto the floor and bounced off her sweat-soaked ringlets reaching to her waistline, while Ice's broadcast droned on. With enemies everywhere, a woman like Meadow Lee needed to know exactly where the next attack was coming from, and finally, she eye-balled the darkened backyard for enemies – so called spies, robbers, rabbits, ghosts – and saw nothing. The blank yard was just as empty and gloomy as the night before, and she looked disappointed, troubled even, that she could not see anything that could be flattened and spaced out on the ground, and to complain to Ice about having more enemies lurking around her backyard than Putin. The loudspeakers amplifying Ice's polyvocal colloquy included mimicries of those he wanted to belittle, and created a din of loop-back echoes as the haze grew warmer in the tepid humidity, but Meadow Lee only heard the crispness of Ice's voice that ran over the dew covering a dead lawn, and slid into her life through her open windows, under the cracks of doors, through the air vents, and nail holes, and more satisfactorily, into her brain.

This was her work, and she knew that her work cleared a path for his important message to all, to reach far into every ear blocked by DOWN WITH RACIST WHITE GOVERNMENT slogans throughout the entire population of Praiseworthy.

Wet from sweat, she was biting at the chuff to have her say too, desperate to echo Ice, when suddenly, almost accidentally, words burst forth from her mouth that were not in Ice's broadcasts and she shouted, *Kill the Salamander*. She flung her coffee mug down on the bench next to where the kettle had continued boiling in a frenzy of steam, and cutlery clattered in the drawer, and she saw in the darkness, that her dead-lawn yard was full of *Cenchrus ciliaris* ghost devils marching with placards lit by torchlight. The ghost protesters were like an Invasion Day demonstration, but instead of saying *Kill the Invasion*, the placards were written with the very same words she had just accidentally shouted out the window, *Kill the Salamander*.

Should I call Ice? The high priestess of anti-leniency for all, could sense the supernatural flaws of human nature from miles away, and felt she needed to pounce on the iPhone, to tell Ice of this very straying moment in the great revelatory scheme. Pardons were not an option in her idea of paving the assimilatory roadworks white, not even for her own momentary digression of seeing the wrong ghosts, but now, she could see even more placards about killing the salamander bobbing in the bushfire of the dead lawn in her backyard. Her mind was about to explode in an instant, which of course, was a zilch moment, since she was supposed to hate Cause Man Steel, but she did not know what the murderer looked like, and had never seen people whose main business venture in life was to work with donkeys like millions of other poor people do across the world. She needed to get back with the picture of a murderer of children living in the midst. But, how was she expected to wrap her head around such a low vision of self-determination to find this murderer? And, what about this hating baby thing? She knew plenty of people who never liked babies and that had never worried her before. She was not a big admirer of babies herself, and nor was Ice, but Meadow Lee never thought too much about what was in a full barrel of things to dislike. This was the high plateau, being with the best, where the sheer weight of scorn naturally flowed downwards. As the morning broadcast flowed on, she gave up thinking about low-life in her yoga moment of being elsewhere, where the rest could go to hell.

She decided to err more on the right side of caution, and decided not to disturb Ice's broadcast. Perhaps her sense that Ice's stance was weakening in the populace was just a glitch in her mind, more the fault of the PA system with haze dust muffling the microphone, making Ice sound like an imbecile, like he had gone soft in the guts. Everyone knew you had to dust, dust; dust everything, dust constantly, if you did not want to end up living underneath a dust dune in Praiseworthy. She blamed lazy Maureen for never dusting Ice's house for him. Had the woman not learnt anything, from the era of the missionaries to the government closing-the-gap assimilation measures of today, that native women are trained for nothing else, except how to be a domestic? Meadow Lee bypassed the beeping iPhone, and continued muscling the yoga around her kitchen – while intentionally making as much noise as was earthly possible to throw out a bit of pent-up anger on her family.

In the pre-dawn darkened streets of the three a.m. broadcast, there were many people calling out *why me Lord, what did I ever do wrong*, and tossing in time to Meadow Lee thumping bare feet on the floorboards while doing her yoga routine.

Michael Lee Senior, Meadow Lee's husband, though not a shrinking violet, and not king in this kitchen, sat down for breakfast anyway since it was no use trying to sleep. *You going okay my beloved*, he suggests, while she told him to shut up, which was breakfast – a pink lava dome flashing by – the mass of colour commonly known as his wife. She accused him of leering at her glamour, although she quickly convinced him with a cold stare that he had to be joking.

Their identical twin sons sleepwalked from their bedroom and stood at the kitchen door. Both were conveniently named Michael Lee Junior, because Meadow Lee was too busy saving other people's babies in the political world to be bothered about thinking of good names for her identical babies when they were born. Their co-wired brains warned them to halt at the door, wait, come no further, for though only ten in age, they had already experienced the decades of old men listening to their mother mouthing off about something they were doing wrong. Their eyes followed her moving amidst the subtle green-grey shadowy whiteness of the kitchen, and both agreed – stuff it, they would miss breakfast, school too, and they slunk off across the dead lawn and through the placard-waving ghosts of times past while promising each other: *We are not coming back neither*.

Honestly, stop your daydreaming and bloody whispering like a pair of wimps, you are not going anywhere unless I tell you to, the voice hits higher notes and continues, *You are not going to end up like your father, look at him*, and already, the boys were possessed, placed back under her spell by sheer alchemy which consisted of not lifting a finger, nor running off in the bush after them, but of knowing she was omnipresent in their lives, hovering wherever they went, in whatever they dreamt, and in whatever they thought. It will be school as usual for them. Homework, gospel readings and singing up and down their streets afterwards until late at night. She intended to grow them into decent men, even if it was the last thing she would do in life, just to make sure they did not end up either being murdered, or men who killed their own children.

Eat like normal people, she ordered, while inwardly asking herself why she bothered wasting her life.

The sunshine opulence of the two junior Michaels left Michael Lee Senior consistently nonplussed, for he was lost for words to describe how his spirit rose sometimes from a very darkened place, by looking upon the joy that swelled in his heart when in the presence of this whorl pool of Omo crispness, cleanliness, and brightness that overwhelmed him with such an unstoppable emotion of tears welling up in his eyes. He does not care if she sees him crying or not while he constantly probes his conscience for an answer as to where these two miracles had come from, and he smiles at every detail of his boys obediently eating their cereal in the wonderland of the dead plain lawn their mother kept watering with the sprinklers swirling full blast in the backyard to achieve a murder-free kingdom for the two Michaels, when, from all around, high five, they would be showered by red dust storms flown in from heaven. The sons smile knowingly at one another while their mother's back is turned, staring out the window to watch the placard-carrying ghosts trampling the high grass, flattening it to the ground, and the husband only thinks of Ice, and decides that he will go over to his place as soon as he has eaten – tell her that was what he would be doing, that would cheer her up – to bring some happiness into the house. Ice's private swimming pool, the only one in Praiseworthy, probably needs cleaning. Yes, that was it. Possibly, he would trim all the palm trees surrounding Ice's backyard pool at the same time. Get rid of the dead fronds. Have the place looking good – for Ice. Give her an excuse to go over to Ice's place too, to talk about parents who murder their children. She would like that.

5

Try me Lord!

Hit the bloody thing with the fly spray.

Maureen enters the lounge room thing looking like an ABC studio, all red lit signage, ENTER / EXIT / SILENT / ON AIR. She almost flies – soundless, in like an owl, then while hovering behind Lolly, sprays Mortein plus, the fastest knock 'em down multi-purpose flyspray you could buy, it was fail-proof, except for the totally uncoordinated who can never spray in the right place – directly where the mosquito fat with human blood sat on the wall. *Here! Here! Can't you see the bloody thing. It's just sitting there.* Maureen passes by, right behind Lolly, and she moves so silently by managing to avoid all the creaks in the floorboards that he cannot hear her. Then she pelts the room again like it was a mosquito-infested swampland, and with her finger jammed on the nozzle, continues to spray enough poisonous fumes to be left hanging in the air well into her next incarnation on earth. The flummoxed-face Lolly could not believe he had seen anything like her incompetence in the world, she had not even seen the red light beaming – ON AIR – but who was he to stop his compulsory broadcast heard uninterrupted throughout Praiseworthy in the hope that it might routinely stop his people from even thinking of being a killer anytime during the rest of the day, nor could he imagine any interruption going free to air across the world – the other leg of the journey of his three a.m. broadcast – which might make him look like he was too weak to stop himself being poisoned by his wife with a bit of flyspray. Hell no. He was never going to give any of those eight billion people the luxury of knowing his personal predicament was less than ideal, nor of even slightly imagining that some person named Ice Pick from God knows where, was less super-duper perfect than he thought himself to be in the high stakes

down into the underneath world like cannonballs whistling through a maze of trails, to where the old creation ancestors were listening to this thrilling of elaborative embroidered expletives pumping oxygen through the old corpuscles of country, and into the thumping heart of Praiseworthy – thump, thump, thump.

Nobody wanted to hear your bicarbonate singsong at this time of day, yah big fat moron.

The situation was high-verve out on the slippery slope of the dewy street, where the streetlights blazed. The Queen of the Outback called River was standing outside of Ice's house taking stock of heaven when a salacious reply from her sweet burgundy red lips sang out to the dark morning, *Ice isn't interested in you – you big fat cunt.* Then, the archetypical beauty queen jogged up and down the road full-drunk with dragon steam flaring out of her nostrils, pumping her fists at moths swarming in the floodlights while her newly peroxided dreadlocks wrapped in long aluminium foil flung this way and that – rat-a-tat-tat, mixing the dust in the air with particles of fluff and pet fur. *Fuck you, you fat moaning slag, Mabel. And you too Meadow. I'm not listening to you neither. And where's old moth-face Maudlin? Come out here you. Show your ugly face. No. Too scared Ice might see what you are really like? You can all fuck the hell off! Nobody wants to hear your slack-arsed voice around here.*

She was the one.

The breeze dropped. The rattling loudspeakers settled into reverb. So much silence created just like that, even the last of the gospel singers sang half asleep, then stopped altogether since you could not sing to God when eavesdropping on this sort of abuse, and so, one by one, the inter-denominationals all stalked off, to disappear into the echoes of Ice's broadcast looping in the stillness of the night.

Of course, most people just rolled over in their sleep in the compulsory state of listening to Ice whipping it around, and moaned, *that slut again.* River of Booze, Queen of the Outback, they said, *drinking like a sly dog all night,* while decent people standing on plastic milk crates had to keep a place like this holy by singing country-and-western gospel songs. Her party for one had now arrived at its destination – outside the very window of Ice's lounge room cum recording studio where she serenaded Maureen's roses, *Oh! let me go lover, let me sleep Lolly.* Maureen was furious, with Ice gesturing at her with his fat lips at the window while taking a pause to breathe in his rapid-fire address, then, pointing with his finger tattooed with a Casper the Ghost while trying to make sure she could see the window, and who was at the window, and that he wanted her to get rid of the person at the window while he was trying to speak about murderers. He expected her to get rid of all his idiot hot-to-trot women, cranked up by his ego. Maureen was not having any of that, and she hissed back at Ice about how sick she was of going outside in the middle of the night. She had already been out once because of him. But, anyhow, she ran out of the front door, drove River back to the street, and let off a bit of steam with highfaluting white mind-bending shit-talk, *Can't you see how sequaciously stupid you are behaving, have you got no shame, go home and get off the rivers of grog.*

Shockwave.

Who are you talking to, Tinfoil shook, *who you telling I am inconsequential or whatever you are talking about? Listen! Sweetie! I have far more consequence than you will ever have.*

Shut up, I am warning you River, Mabel Lee's voice suddenly rang down from far up the street, from its own cathedral lungs.

You git that piece of shit – Ice. You hear me – Ice. You get him how? Bring him out here so I can tell him how much I love him. Go on! Get Lolly for me!

You listening to me? Why don't you come out here and see me?

Maureen uncoiled, moved, twisted, ducked like a garden hose, rushing up and down the front fence like a watchdog on the loose while blocking River, pushing her back on the street each time she hurled herself at the cyclone fence to get back into the yard to find Ice. Maureen used these moments of conflict to have a good hard look at the Ice worshipper, and she wondered how anyone could spend so much time making themselves look this cheap for an idiot. Ghost mutton, she called it, looking like a tarted-up axolotl with squashed alfoil-encased dreadlocks around her rivers-of-grog white talcum-covered face, mascara streaking from her eyes down over smeared red lips, so that Maureen could not help thinking that Rivers of Grog must have spent some time in a creek a few hours ago pashing frogs, and she stared at this sight of Praiseworthy, worse for viewing forensically under a 250-watt streetlight at past three in the morning, and she tried not to cry, and felt sorry she had forgotten she was dealing with Ice's dirty work.

The streetlight mostly lit up a silver-sequined arse streaking up the street and back. It made Maureen want to puke from seeing Rivers of Grog, who had been crowned Queen of the Outback, make it white two decades ago with high-society cattle people – the bush millionaires, long-time family owners of blackfella traditional land they took for free, white Brahman bull kings of the white-over-black region, and now look at her? Queens do not look like roadkill. Not like a dead *Bos taurus* cow, belly-up on the highway, white runners hanging off legs in silver-sequin nylons shimmering from the reflection of the streetlight. Maureen scoffs loudly, knowing Ice would hear, and hoped his world audience would hear his preferable woman calling out for Lolly. Back in the house, she whispered in his ear, *That cow peroxided her hair. It's snow white. She looks like you. She'll be changing the colour of her skin next.* Ice ignored the sarcasm. Waved her away. Too busy finishing the broadcast.

Another queen, Cruella, from down the same street, thought she would open her big hostile trap from her face framed with fluoro sun-yellow plastic jumbo hair curlers, and ordered for things to happen in one big flat, monotone voice, *Hey! Meadow. Go out and kill that stupid, lazy, cheap trollop. Otherwise, I will kill her myself.*

The breathless River continued yodelling, yelling, and crying for anyone to hear how much she loved Ice Pick right in front of his house, disturbing the reverberations broadcast over the rattling loudspeakers. *Booze shit*, Maureen judiciously snapped at Ice's back like the seasoned wife forever trying to conserve a marriage as if it was a precious painting in an art gallery. It was a tough gig to be continually curating the circus of community queens on the make for a share of Ice's sphere of power, while navigating their excuses to come crawling into her house – in and out like it was an airport. And she quickly makes another mental count through the assets, to judge whether her sham marriage was worth saving anyhow, or worth continuing with the workload, considering the poor quality of the domicile. But then, while waiting like a cat counting the moments, eight, nine, ten, and like clockwork, she heard the knocking on the door. *Knew it. There she goes*. Maureen ignored the drunken woman leaning against the door, and Ice yelled for silence for Christ sake. *Missus! Missus! Can I have a can of Coke please.* Already picturing the scene of Coke guzzled beside Ice, the Queen of the Outback loved that Ice was killing the nemesis, Cause Man Steel, and urged him on with outback slang like, *You ride him cowboy*, while her clattering alfoil dreadlocks join in with the live-to-air broadcast, and she swings, *Yep! You got no respect murdering your children. And we have had enough of not being respected as elders*. Maureen decides to wait for the bingo moment of the rivals reacting to River's voice echoing alongside Lolly's through the reverb loudspeakers, and then, centre stage, she can almost see the explosions taking place one after the other, and reaching from afar, can hear the hot oil sizzling and splashing from cartons of eggs thrown from the fridge and into the frypan from across the room.

I love you doll, River's voice, tinny high with breathless spasms from squealing, *You get that piece of filth scourging on our Earth for me doll? Kill that Cause Man Steel for me Ice.*

Get away from Ice. Let him work, yelled the supernova Heavy Tytania from somewhere in the darkness, complaining about the unnecessary interference with the broadcast. She booted the fact home, that Ice needed to get his work done, and after seeing Meadow Lee fuming around across the road while kicking tufts of dead grass on the bare earth in her search for a big killing stick, she yelled at her to act like a real woman, and *go down there and finish that fat bitch off*. But Meadow Lee, who nobody tells what to do, retorts like a piece of wood speaking, about why it should be interested in being a stick doing another person's dirty work, and flatly returned the challenge in fumed snorts. *Why don't you go and do it yourself.* And, right then, there comes Maudlin, flinging herself onto the street with only her bare hands for a weapon, and saying that she would lay the fat Coca-Cola gut mole out flat once and for all. *No flippen worries about that.*

There were obvious benefits in having a husbandless house, and these were ping-ponging quicker in Maureen's alternative vision of herself, when she sees those loose fat lips of Ice smiling at River, while he sings under his breath, *Why me Lord?* What a smart-arse, she fumes, and walks straight up to him, whispers in his ear, *Get on with your extramarital affairs. Have a lot of pink babies.* And River, the archetype of the vision, continued to play the game, her far-fetched moaning heard through the tinny reverb speakers by all, eclipsing all the previous grog-laced Coke organisms accidentally overheard spilling out of her *radda-radda* mouth. She was like an industrial cement mixer that was forever anchoring her well-earned place as one of Ice's closest dilettantes, along with the moaner Meadow Lee, the seriously Maudlin Able Mabel, and Heavy Tytania. Maureen stomped off over the squeaking floorboards to the kitchen knowing that she was way out of her league when surrounded by the Ice Women, well, quite frankly, she was nothing to them, and she knew that these political monoliths were more in charge of what was thought soul deteriorating, or of what created debasement, of where to find the apex of terribleness, or what thought would be degraded, or disregarded, simply from where their fingers pointed the choir in the condemning and destruction of an increasing parade of people who they thought hated babies. These ladies, Ice's grand quad of governors, belonged to a preachy quasi-royal ruling class revolutionising right-sightedness in the brains of their people, and living evenly spaced in the same street as Ice, where their soliloquies could be forever in his range of hearing, and of course by default, also in the hearing range of Maureen, who knew wisely or not that it was only jealousy and hate that separated each from the other, and brought them together.

7

MAM, Queen Maudlin Able Mabel at four a.m.

All the night animals were scurrying home with the stories of the night, when insatiable hunger, more than ever witnessed in challengers for complete power – a humanly impossible destination to reach – was driving the complex mind of the third queen, locally known as Maudlin Able Mabel, or her royal highness MAM. What this woman longed for was to figure out how she would find real power by understanding what time immemorial meant, and how it would feel like she was really in touch with the ancestral power of the time of the great creation beings. Was this quest achievable, could it be found within herself, or would the ultimate power of country stay away, live under the waves of universal life, always only ready to attack, but failing to do so? Could she hold all the songs in her psyche that would bring her in touch with these ancestral powers? Or, was her total existence only that of a dead person walking, like a living ghost without power that would be born and would die forever in the line of her people's connection to spirit country blown up by a mine, or in other destruction of country throughout the Anthropocene? It was for these reasons that MAM wanted to try out what it felt to be a full relation to the ultimate power of ancestral life.

This was her trouble, to know how to find the way to stir up the power spirits, to make them move, or to placate their physical presence in the slow-moving phenomena of great floods and fires, and ride with the mighty Rainbow Serpent in cyclones, storms, lightning and thunder, by being able to rid the earth of plague of all kinds. There was no one more driven to yield unprecedented ancestral power inside the assimilated subtext of the Praiseworthy era, by being bent on achieving whiteness in black consciousness among her people. MAM felt very comfortable with the acquisition of knowledge – vast amounts of knowledge about wreckages from degrees, and increasing degrees of it. She had to deal with that. This was how she formed the ultimate question about whether ancestral power already resided within herself, if it was the toxicity in her bloodstream, the sense of what she felt inside, of what constitutes real power of country, like an after story similar to thunderstorm asthma. Well! Country is infinitely wise. Therefore, she thought it was the ultimate human quest to become wise like country, even if it was a hard act to follow.

Who knew where the itch came from for a woman like Able Mabel to want to achieve ultimate superiority over the future of the Indigenous world, for so many people have such a noble desire entrenched in their hearts whether they were themselves black or not, and were as equally afflicted as MAM, and bent with peddling their own better plan for saving the Indigenous mind. Such high-level games of desire to conquer the mighty powers of the ancestral world were like diving into a bottomless pit. This may have been what was driving MAM towards achieving ultimate superiority to satisfy her needs in life, for desire was a bottomless well, where at the bottom whatever truth lay there, you could safely say, it would never be reached. Yet MAM did not think so. A solid woman with the smarts like her was built for rougher times than falling into a bottomless pit. She knew her world well, and knew you had to be cruel even to yourself, to be kind to the bottomless pit. Yep! Spill the aces, this was how she was settling her questions.

It was not far from another thought, particularly about whether she should, or should not intervene in another woman declaring her love for Ice. She stormed with stiffly lacquered silver hair styled up in a 1960s Dusty Springfield beehive, and barefooted it out of her house like a cloud in a big blue terry-towelling dressing gown, looking just like the highly contemporary modern twenty-first-century woman should look – so she claimed – and she armed herself, not with rocks as though she was from the stone age, but with a stockpile of modern universalities – actual words, which were lethal weapons enough stacked on her iPad, and in no time at all she was in like Flynn, and had grabbed the bunch of ice-white dreadlocks wrapped in tinfoil sitting next to the Lolly broadcaster, and she recited from her iPad that she was holding in the other hand a piece-of-cake list of positive universalities of anti-Indigenousness from her own pedagogy in capital letters increased to 20-point font that read: GROG LEADS TO A BREAKDOWN IN ABORIGINAL RECONCILIATION. BREAKDOWN IN CLOSING THE GAP. DESTROYS THE GOOD INTENT OF FEDERAL GOVERNMENT INTERVENTION POLICIES TO TURN US BLACKS BETTER PEOPLE LIKE WHITE PEOPLE, AND FOR PREVENTING ALL THE PAEDOPHILIA, AND WHATNOT PEOPLE NOT CARING ENOUGH FOR BABIES.

With this done, the hefty MAM woman hauled her catch back onto the street, and swung the skinny-bean River, the forever Queen of the

Outback, around a number of times while she tried to jog away, then slammed an uppercut into her ribs, king-hit her victim several times with her bare fist in the face, clipped the Outback Queen under the chin and sent her flying. If she had noticed her victim's eyes roll as she went flying through the air like a rag doll, or heard her body drop, or saw the crumpled white icing, or the red dirt covering the white runners on the dew-covered street, it was hard to tell. Maudlin was already storming back up the road to her own house with an air of superior arrogance.

Her mobile phone beeped as she entered her kitchen to make a cup of coffee to settle her nerves. Noticing that she had received a text message, she flicked the gadget open and read the message from Ice. He said, *thanks*. She texted him back straight away, her fingers nervously running over the keys, punching in the words, *No worries*. He texted back, *Good. Catch u later.* They texted each other dozens of messages like this, in the course of the day.

Moaning Mabel reached for cheese from the fridge, and went for song – *you got to know when to hold them, and know when to run* – and she watched her need for creating good order, while chopping up a tomato into ever smaller, equal-sized pieces until nothing was left but puree, which was the same thing as strategically reducing a paddock of colossally huge white Brahman cattle to zero, or heaving upon herself the responsibility of devising strategies for putting Peroxide into a coma by brute force, to decrease the size of the monopolising pan-Lolly obsession by at least sixty per cent.

With so much worry inflaming her mind about whether the negativity in Ice's broadcast would be enough to change the world for better or worse, MAM dressed for work in a nice bright floral summer dress, checked the dirt stains on her pink flip-flops, half-chewed on a piece of tough topside with melted cheese and tomato puree, and sipped her fifth cup of strong coffee, while reserving most of the fire in her belly for the computer, to belt out a new ironclad social media Lolly document while the content of his broadcast was fresh in her mind. And a new thing was stirring, about analysing the dangerous lives of drunken women in communities like Praiseworthy, and anticipating the reaction in social media toxicity rising up for the day, after those who were overcome read her post to cancel old elders like Cause Man Steel – whoever he was.

It was quite possible that nobody else around Praiseworthy enjoyed listening to Ice's continuing saga to destroy Cause Man Steel more than Maudlin Able Mabel. It made eating tough topside an even more pleasurable chewing-the-fat experience, and old MAM sliced the meat on the plate into ever thinner slithers with her razor-sharp slaughtering knife, while thinking about the way that Ice could so naturally wield the explosives for upping the ante. She wondered how he did it while listening to him breaking the barriers to even greater thresholds of wonderment in his three a.m. broadcast, and it made her feel in a small part cold and shivery, because she felt sure that there was an evil snake coiled up in his stomach, and this spirit devil thing was breathing hot air up into his lungs, and it was really the snake, not Ice, saying those far-fetched things Cause Man Steel was – because she knew that Ice was too sweet, and a sweetie pie did not have enough guts to act alone. Casper the Ghost would always have to have a throng to help him cart himself along his road to hell, for Lolly was not capable of creating a campfire, let alone a firestorm. He was a dependency needing help, with no power in his guts without the devil snake to fire the way. Think about it. What would you do when you get someone bigger and more visionary like this Cause Man Steel going against the grain, breaking the rules, not being a team player, who was ballsing up all the work she – herself and Ice – had accomplished by pushing and shoving the Australian government into creating special laws to make their people assimilate? The rights pushers needed to be crushed in MAM's game so if you acted like some dumb-arse blackfella who couldn't speak English properly, you ought to be treated like a dog tied up to the fence post until you were trained and toed the line. Risk-taking business ventures hurt Aboriginal children and would not get her people to the end of the twenty-first century. MAM knew that they had Cause trapped now – you can't go around killing you own child. Can't do worse than that. MAM thought about the coiled snake – what it would do, and she knew there was no human being that would have enough energy for relentlessly blasting out Indigenous vice – what it had to be called, it had to be given its correct name. Would the snake make her think less of Ice? Probably not.

The far-fetched mistruths, sheer exaggeration, or unbalanced views were completely the art of manipulation, and MAM believed justifiable power for the cause, when you were in a war for survival – a small concession to achieve an overall outcome, of setting your own terms for keeping in place laws that made herds of her people by locking them up with government policies. She knew it in her heart – shove your own power in the only way you could to corral your family's safely. To lock them out of harm's way. If white government wanted you to teach your people how to be white parents, or gutless, or killers, well that was what you did, it was the weaker people's role – team players, not revolutionaries.

What MAM knew most of all was that the only way to preserve one's superiority over all aspects of Praiseworthy without breaking all of your fingers hauling baggage too heavy to carry, was that you did not carry the load. This was how she knew that Cause Man Steel's head was simply full of dreams too heavy to carry, and were only that, dreams, and dreamers weakened the Aboriginal world. These people were unable to play the game. The type of Praiseworthy she had in mind was continually being reshaped into a greater success story. What she wanted was a loose, flexible, never-entrenched, never-stagnant reaching, a forever reaching into infinity with a personal sense of jubilation. To MAM, the making of a world to your own liking was like eating the topside of an old bullock, in fact, it was a feeling of real heat radiating like baking sun spreading across country in a summer dawn, and she felt this good thing was already happening when she thought about how Ice would actually seek and burn out blights on the landscape just by using a piece of high-tech snake in the guts in his broadcast. And if she was relegated in the power game to second fiddle in Lolly's inner circle of wannabes – jockeying for the only available source of Aboriginal power in the cyber world bent on destroying Praiseworthy people like a pack of camp dogs – well, who cared? She knew what having a role was all about, and her role was to make sure that Ice was seen in the right light, by wrapping him in English words, as good as you could get, sourced from the first-class English-speaking world that you could use for playing in the dirt. Like! Rule number one, thou should not kill. Clever. What a fake weapon for storytelling in their era! She was searching for new angles all the time and feasted on any populist spiel of negativity and nastiness, knowing how she would be there to the end, still standing. Rock on MAM, as she thought, was this what power was really about? Thou shall not kill, keep it in mind.

And there was also River, at her own Praiseworthy super shire computer, crying her heart out for Ice, but managing to write another email of complaint to the Minister for Aboriginal Affairs about being bashed up in the street, which was not a street fight, but assault. Confidential emails like these that concerned Ice Pick, were kept in the Minister's private dossier of troublesome blacks throughout her continent, saved up for the rainy day that would certainly come, it was just a matter of time in the continuing colonialised world of governing Aboriginal people.

8

Praiseworthy at 4.30 a.m....

Ice enjoyed the silence of 4.30 a.m. in Praiseworthy where, except for the oasis of palm trees gently swaying in the wind in his backyard, the only other sounds were of his own volition, meeting his own needs with the sound of eating, yet another poor fare of a breakfast cooked by Maureen. While he ate his bacon and eggs, Ice cheered himself for another terrific performance – could not believe it – *I did it again* he yelled to Maureen, *did you listen to how I achieved just the absolute right level of sincerely in my voice throughout the broadcast.* He was especially pleased since his voice had travelled across the world via vast networks of social media. Yep! Nailed it, again, then pausing for about thirty seconds before announcing piously, more Pope-like than a priest, YOU SHALL NOT KILL. Any real god would have done the same, paused at the ultimate moment, after creating an edict for mankind about how to preserve the sanctity of another human life without killing them, without sounding phoney, or a bit ticky-tacky. You want to make others believe in you, and Ice knew he was exactly like God, hurling his law into the Sinai desert like a missile that would explode on impact at the feet of a prophet. Then Ice thought of his own personal satellite dish sitting in his backyard hurling the law worldwide, the cold metallic object that sung at the touch of a breeze – set like an abstract sculpture smack bang in the middle of a stunning garden in the semi-arid zone, with exotic palm trees, orchids, bromeliads, and an in-ground swimming pool shaped like a whale's belly, where gurgling crystal-clean waters were constantly being filtered and pumped of haze dust, in what he called a real cathedral, class, what being on the top was all about in Praiseworthy.

9

Heavy Tytania, the cat queen exploding at five a.m.

In the hour that rules the world, it was like reaching into the infinities of time immemorial thinking, where there was nothing to catch in the hand, which in any case would be like trying to grab an asteroid, or stop the unfathomable mind of the real Heavy Tytania, the cat queen troglodyte orbiting paradise in search of dirt. This cat queen was more myth in the sky. She was an elusive sense of aliveness from the all times, whose feet were the more planted on the ground, like life itself, since she possessed no mind. There was much talk about the phenomena of mindlessness on Churchy Street, where it was said that Heavy was no angel, nor believed to be a saint, even though who could say whether any heavenly phenomenon living in the company of a god would require a mind? All that they could truly say in the *preachings* was that she was not even human. Those astute life-watchers only said that the cat queen did not focus on herself, neither on the plentiful joys of life, nor on important stuff like saving the planet from burning itself to death, or on protecting the world today for the world tomorrow. More than having the agency that they preferred to have in long-time humanity, they could only say the cat queen was this/that, beyond belief. But what was useful about a true human weapon that sought only one thing, to cancel the oxygen that kept the life of the wicked alive, to stop them/they from breathing free air from the atmosphere? All these cat queen characteristics of desirability, and raw ambition, put Ice in the box seat of the major mayorship for the super shire forever, a powerful role indeed, that spared no one from the poisonous tentacles of this human jellyfish, shielded no one, or saved one from a brain that was multi-pronged like an octopus-arm assassin wielding a stack of Matrix deadly Desert Eagle pistols all at once, to wreak mayhem.

The cat queen was the biggest trophy in the Ice Queen arsenal.

Watch out if you did not love your children enough according to Australian law for how Aboriginal people living in bush communities should love their children. Better step out of the way, for when the cat queen cleans the place up, you needed to move it like a shivering leaf torn into threads by a right off the scale freight-train wind, for she was the fast wind in high velocity, not like moving a bit of dust around the ground with a broom. Heavy Tytania was mind-power blowing by just sitting there, spitting chips, with scalpel-sharp lightning ready for dissecting colonialism like a dead bullock, and bringing a killer over for tea even when you were not hungry for it. A woman essential to Ice's hate cartel, the frosting on top of a demolition party of insurrectionists guiding Praiseworthy's future.

Call! Call! Call! The cat queen hastened the pace, eagerly sits back, relaxed as, with the latest model iPhone planted on her ear, impatient for Ice to call with the day's killer of a plan. She was like the skinning man waiting for the door of the abattoir to open before sunrise, knowing that the only problem with the boss was his loose love problem, but all she wanted to know was who would be on today's list of cancelling, who embodied nothing worthy in the scheme of life in a world of happiness or sadness from anywhere on Church Street? What was another person's life worth was the question. What crossed the mind in making these decisions? Who decided? Like! Anyway! Who should be crucified extensively and permanently from being so cancelled out, that they would never rise from the ashes to live again? You decide. While she waited for the important phone call from Ice, the foul mouths she heard earlier in the street pounded harder in her head and she wanted to get those two women she hated equally with poor Maureen, and the horror show Meadow Lee. She continued to wait through the tick-tock seconds slipping away, while pistol-firing Maudlin Mabel and the Rivers of Grog from her head with mantras that repeatedly described the ugly cows as belonging to the rubbish dump of humankind. She quipped about how her work with Ice was far greater than the sum total of putting up with street fights resounding in her head. She scrolled through incoming emails. Fumed through numerous Twitter arguments, which were all similar idiotic solutions about what should happen to Aboriginal folk, and continued on, for the world wide web of Aboriginal haters was inexhaustible to her, and she knew anyhow, she had vastly more counterarguments flowing from her tank than the internet to deal with, more gas than the entire world's gas fields, because she could live on super-countering idiots.

She finished checking the chatter blogs of Ice's supporters of hate. Weighs the positives and negatives, shoots off all this information like she was running ASIO, and her brain flings everything into her hoarding abode, an extensive filing system in the cloud, and hell, she decides that she is better than Chinese surveillance, and smarter, for who else could cope with so many groupies of hate like the ones floating around in her sovereign stream of consciousness? Get the picture? It was huge. But she was wrong. These other Ice Queens were also made of the same gigantic statue stuff of coping with the worst, as she was. They were also high-voltage brain destroyers for the all times, who with each breath created minor earth tremors bouncing off the Richter scale.

Yet the feral cat ghost queen knew about being careful with her Ice Queen relationships. They also fiddled with locks. She knew this, and kept her brain empty at all times – just in case, which was not about the innocence of just pondering, but being dead certain that you could not be alert enough to what might be coming around the corner. You needed a clean desert-scape mind to see what was coming a mile off. This could not be done if you kept hoarding stuff in your brain. All the crap stuff. And, like herself, she knew how the other Ice Queens entered other people's brains – ether-like – and that once they got inside your head and began invading your thoughts with bile, none of them could easily be expelled. No key in the world would unlock the brain cupboard once they had installed themselves in what should have remained bare. No combination of numbers, nor key-opening words that break brain locks for exiling the unwanted, such as words like these, would do. *Who wants to listen to people slutting up the street in bare-bum shorts?* Nope! Never let the cheapness distract you.

You were not a queen for nothing. Tytania knew exactly how to measure the weight of travelling the battlefields. Shh! Listen, she speaks secretly, and more openly with the thousands of ghost-fairy feral cats that call her place home. These were her dead favourites amongst the roadkill cats from the highway, lounging throughout the premises. Curled on the table. Sitting about on the floor. Sprawled across the doorway. Their remains resembled not the clarity of seeing a real live cat, but more like a feeling of vapoury presence, an impression from her world in the bare-cupboard mind that could be opened at will. These cat ghosts watch her, stare, wait for their orders from the three a.m. broadcast too, and want the fairy queen to tell him to hurry up. *Look at his emails, the bloggers arguing. We need to know what he is thinking. Where he is heading with his infernal Cause Man Steel thing whoever he is,* and the cat ghosts wondered why she had never seen him in Praiseworthy, even though according to Ice, he had been living there for years, and the reason why she did not know him *was because he is not a team player, that's why. He hasn't got a team-playing bone with scruples in his body. Wouldn't know a single person here. He'd have us sliding backwards naked and poor into our graves if we let him. Don't ever feel sorry for somebody like that.* Not that a woman like Tytania would ever feel sorry, but she needs to know Ice's thoughts, even though she has already anticipated his every word, since he had made all of her ideas his own.

Rah! Rah! Rah! Emails, bloggers' tweets, were all pouring in thick and fast to point the metaphorical finger at the unsighted child killer

Cause Man Steel. The more brainy ghost cats, the ones with their feral instinct still intact, since their brain still looked like a brain after being smacked by a road train travelling two hundred clicks on the highway, had learnt how to act like Tytania's junior office assistants, and did a good job of finishing off a pile of tap-tapping indecipherable tweets to random whoever's tweets at the keyboard, and having scampered off invisibly, had actually gone over to Ice's house to speak to him in the ear in their mangled-body invisibleness on behalf of the fairy queen of roadkill cats. It seemed as though this worked, since a text message arrived from Ice telling her – *Read this*, his attached broadcast, *and weep*, he said, even though she had not long before listened to his entire live-air talk. Another text followed: *Was this the hour of the brilliant people, or not?* And as this text flew down the road from one house to another, all around the nation, in fact throughout the world, kangaroo courts were in session in the brains trust of thousands of households wallowing in disgust for the likes of Aboriginal people like Cause Man Steel. People like that, their very presence in the world was the pure logic of their hate. The reason why people like that should be allowed to exist was the issue, and the desire for toxicity was all the evidence that was needed, so thank you, thank you, the rant ruled the days beginning with the Minister for Aboriginal Affairs frothing at the mouth in her bed, for she was now dying to implement an even more severe legislation than she was having passed in parliament to protect Aboriginal children from their own families. Now, without any dead feral-cats spirits of her own to send as messengers over to Ice's place thousands of kilometres from the capital of the illegal Australian state, she had to keep tapping his number on her mobile, while being inconvenienced and hamstrung from enacting her legislation on the spot while still in bed, and unable to contact Ice to tell him she was pushing mountains, which was her aphorism for gutless politicians, to push the most punishing legislation through parliament to kill off any more murdering blacks. Well! Blast Ice. He never answered his cell phone when you needed to talk to him.

The fuming cat queen screamed back at the Minister who had called her as the last resort, to argue the toss with her about how Ice refused to answer her phone calls. *Don't call me then.* The cat queen fumed on about how busy she was herself, doing the government's job for them, *answering all of this hate mail*, and claimed she had no choice to do it, as well as manhandle the bitches on the street creating a scene. The Minister tells the cat queen she had no choice either, but to take her entire ministry to Praiseworthy to get some action done, to make Ice answer her phone calls. She said she would *bloody well fly up there right now if I have to in the RAAF Challenger 604.* Cat queen supposed that the Minister for Aboriginal Affairs could just fly around all week if she wished. Lucky for them. The cat queen let the Challenger 604 slide across her desert-scape mind, and she held her mobile up for the ghost cats springing into action left, right and centre for a kamikaze mission on the airstrip running through her mind, while the minister of government yelled, *Tell him I will have all Aboriginal men arrested by the end of the day in Praiseworthy if I have to, including the mayor. Tell him that when you see him, and then tell him to call me. Or better still, tell him to wait until I call him.*

Cause Man Steel was now known across the country of the *concerned*, as being the biggest *mamu* devil child-hating ogre amongst Aboriginal people. They call him number one murderer. The words slip easy off the tongue. In a way, he epitomised the entire child-hating Aboriginal world. The witch-hunt was on, and Tytania? The cat woman rearranged her jejune filaments of lacy droll layering by leading the spin in the pack-hunting of child-hating folk, of the likes of this Cause Man Steel.

Throughout the nine lives of the cat queen, it would never matter in Tytania's fairy land if she never laid eyes on this man since a predatory cat of any kind ultimately knows its prey, its instinct was its fortune, and that favours the brave. The prey dances in her mind. She taunts the hunted, twisted vision, but ultimately, she knew that somewhere in the barren drought-flat landscape of fairyland, the prey capture themselves in their own web of guilt. She was equal to a major ancestor, capable of sniffing out the law breakers. You were not a dead feral-cat woman for nothing, and she could only sneer at the absurd deformity embedded in Ice's mantra, of having child haters in her Aboriginal world. Her mind needed to shut down, flatten the mindscape to stop her roar, from yelling rather than saying she wanted to close the gap between the child lovers and the child haters. But, when she thinks of getting this Cause Man Steel who she had never laid eyes on, and had no idea what he looked like, though she assumed she knew, because of her superiorly barren brain, how to recognise anyone who murdered their children as much as Widespread had, all she really sees is a big black velvet curtain crashing down onto the stage in the empty theatre of her mind, that instantaneously obstructed the drama happening midstream. Yet, the show must go on, and the cat woman understands the heaviness of the pause, not to forsake the barren landscape in her mind, whilst being in the midst of a cyber war imploding into epodes of furies and ugliness about whether Aboriginal people have no more rights than any other Australian in terms of loving their children properly, in the endless scene that varies little, and barely changes from one generation to the next.

Now Cause Man Steel and his so-called crime of murdering a child in broad daylight became more heightened than normal in the mayhem. There were so many people in Praiseworthy asking questions about justice, about which was better, Australian justice or Aboriginal justice. Should that Cause Man Steel be made to stand trial? Should he be arrested by the police? Where was Aboriginal justice, and who were they now among themselves, who were they becoming, and who said they did not love their children, that Aboriginal people of this country don't know how to love their children on their own land better than a land robber?

Was there a manhunt out there looking to lynch up this bastard? No. Not at all. The stage was set but where were the players? Why were they not taking their part in the drama? Where was the Minister with the ministry, and the RAAF Challenger 604? The cat woman writes again, and again, another *cri de coeur* to the so-called ministry people in Canberra with more policy lines than a glutton to set things right in the Aboriginal world, to implore them to get rid of one single child murderer, to bring an entire police force to Praiseworthy to set an example for people who murder their children by hunting the criminal down like a mangy tick dog without mercy, like she would herself if she owned guns, and she would kill all feral donkeys standing in the way, while arresting the carcasses. All doyennes remain buoyant on king tide ideas.

A doyenne crippler of the impure; a hobbler of dreams and visions.

10

Cemetery at six a.m.

Cause Man Steel would not have heard the news. *Couldn't be fucked,* he said of *listening to Ice mimicking some dropkick Prime Minister slash Minister for Aboriginal Affairs slash invisible ministry people slash harping on about Aboriginal men killing their children.* He claimed that he was not into being a moron, and swore the mean language of the ancestral superpowers as he went about with a crowbar and tore apart the Falcon, and the loudspeakers broadcasting Ice Pick's middle-of-the-night chat show, then, he tore the speakers from every grave of Ice Pick's relatives in the cemetery, and any other speaker he could destroy from around Praiseworthy, so he would never have to hear either Ice Pick or the ABC news if all they did was bad-mouth Aboriginal menfolk. Then, what was left of the mangled speakers in the ashes from his bonfire, he threw in a heap over the fence of the cemetery, and out on the potholed dirt road, and simply said of the situation, *Why waste me time on that?*

Well! Ya shoulda listen. They mighta be talkin again, about you. Dance said she had a *finely tuned* second-sense for believing in premonitions and expectations at any of the moments of her déjà vu from being psychic, and from what her pet butterflies were forewarning her it was plain to see anyhow since no one else fitted his description, no one else kept a thousand feral donkeys in the cemetery, and many other particular descriptions which she summed up to her husband by simply stating, *Look! It's all about you.* She might have been able to give more precise details of his description, but thought it did not matter, Cause should know what he looks like, and she could not hear clearly from what was being said second- or third-hand through the weak reception she received on her precious radio that he had turned into a bucket of ash out on the street. He had said, *Forget about the expense of your precious batteries. Flat batteries were not the issue. You want to know how expensive batteries are these days? I for one am not wasting any money on things like that. Turn the thing off. It's full of static. Save the battery life for later on, in a real emergency, when it is a matter of life and death, like a tidal wave from rising seas, things like that, or if this overheated country was turning into an oven from global warming, and someone on the radio might say how you were going to save yourself.* What he meant to say was to save the batteries for radio programs that were not about the land or what city or country people had to say about the bush, he was not interested in listening to stories about grey nomads hiking it around Australia, or fishermen catching prawns in the Gulf of Carpentaria, or people telling him not to feed native birds, or not to encourage foxes into a garden, or hearing about the plight of endangered animals, or some adventurer or diehard living in a remote location in the world, or farmers talking about how they were doing it tough with the overseas natives and helping them to build schools, or wells, or roads etc., or climbing up some high mountain that was sacred and other people's law business for nothing, or swimming with whales which did not seem to have any reason that was plain or obvious to him for wanting people to swim with them. Cause did not want to know what any of these people did with their lives unless they were talking about donkeys, and that was what he thought listening to the radio was about mostly, and saving the batteries for the moment when some other fool would say that they had seen a rare platinum donkey. The key being what was worthwhile information that would bring plenitudes of cash in the end for the future of the culture in his people's minds to survive the global warming calamities, that was what you wanted the batteries in a radio to do.

Alas for today, and alas for yesterday and every day before that, woman, or any other day, Cause said rather sternly, even though his mind seemed to be thinking more remotely in thought, as though he was already elsewhere, and was thinking more about how his life was eternally reaching for something far more, for another vision, one which was way past the point of infinity far from the here and now mediocrities of destroying your neighbours, one that ran parallel to another strain of his shorthand explanation of not being interested in amplified noise manufactured by local clowns who had never achieved a worthwhile practical thing in their lives, or anyone else's life, and would never likely achieve anything of use in the future. *You don't need to listen to the black albino, or any other kind of rightful heritage country folk that are or aren't local preaching stupidity. These are the people you don't listen to, to find out about what it means to be culture here in the twenty-first century.* He called it *way down low thinking,* and Widespread knew in the lonely neglected backyard corner of his mind, a journey that might have taken a month of Sundays to reach in another time, that if Ice had cared to take his eyes off the glow of his own pointless vision, he might have thought about where he had buried the bodies of his enemies and visited the wastelands in the cemetery which was where, he said, *you keep people like Ice locked up gasping for air from his choked arteries. That's why I eat lots of fish and chips. So, my enemies can never get out because they are already buried inside me.*

You have got to stay here for once, and listen to what Ice is saying, Dance said to the belligerent husband. She knows what it feels like to wear the heavy burden of Cause on her shoulders. It was a load, of being there for somebody else's business, of carrying the fallout of Cause never being home when the police came knocking at the door looking for him, and any evidence, and tearing the house apart again and again because they know he lifts his head up to threaten officialism of state crime and corruption, and they warn her, if she knows anything, tell them where her boys are, *if they had come home yet,* and *why was she not worried about their whereabouts*? All these questions from the law enforcement people, the government's endless Aboriginal welfare ministry, and look, *another car load of police knocking on her door all day long* and wanting her to drop whatever she was doing as though she had no work to do in a time when she was fanning the hatching of rare lepidoptera, but no, no police wanted to hear about the birth of butterflies. *The racists wanted me to go out in the bush like a pet nigga,* like she was their own personal police tracker, *like I came from a pastoral scene in nineteenth-century colonialism,* or their pack donkey, to help them search for the boys. *You know how far that is, walking about all day in the climate-change prolonged-drought bush around here? They expected me of all people to go walking around for nothing in the heat of the day to find my own children, and then they wanted me to swim all over the ocean just to satisfy a bunch of half-smart police sitting back on the beach waiting to see whether they themselves were alive or not because they were so bored of watching me swimming in the sea with the man-eaters and you can be sure as day is day, they were not interested in what Aboriginal kids were doing. Of course, they are alive, just run off. I am their mother. So, I, myself, would be the first to know if they were dead because I would feel it in my spirit. Cause, you know what? I tell these police to get real, to stop looking for child murderers because there aren't any. What they needed to be looking for was mass murderers and they were looking at one right here, right in this doorway, and I am telling them I am ready to kill everybody, including those boys who do not think for one second that their parents want them to come home. I am the murderer in waiting, ready to kill police, government, gossipers, as well as those fuckin bitches with fat-lips Ice. That is what I feel like doing these days – just killing everybody.*

Widespread was already on the move, thoughts elsewhere, staying true to his vision of the transport conglomerate to save their world. He was not staying for this kind of trouble that lands you in a hard place where you are stymied, controlled by stupidity, in gaol, there was no future in that, not when you had a vision for overcoming even racism in a place like this, that will either end up being burnt to a crisp, or flooded with tidal waves, and a man had to stay optimistic, to cut the most brave and hopeful path to the future for the survival of the mob, before real disaster happened. So he decided to speak very calmly to Dance by saying what he wanted her to do, which was simple, to keep it real, keep to the vision, and he forewarns her of pending disaster if she fails to act, and not just act, but be full of guts, to stay full of compassion, and be courageous in the thick of hell times, for hell would become much worse and they better be ready and not distracted. And finally, he tells her this: *Hell! You want to get a grip of yourself Dance. Nobody is going to kill anybody.* He spoke while he looked her in the eye, staring straight into her face, and dished out the orders: *Settle down. Think about what you are hearing...All that talk about killing kids. That's Ice talking. Listen properly to pink-lips if you want to waste your time listening to rot, and you might really learn something about who is killing what. I am running a first-class business here. Schedules to keep. Deliveries to complete. Remember we are in the shipping business here. We are not the ABC, or any radio news network, television news, social media influencers rocking adult babies to sleep. I have no one rocking me to sleep with lullabies. I rock myself. This is what business is like. Business is where you move, and you keep moving. Where seconds count. Business is where you have a thousand pack donkeys to feed you know, shit to shovel, while other people sit around listening to shit.*

The hauling business stops for no one at a quarter past six in the morning, and a man like Cause knew he could counter bullshit with super bullshit any day of the week as he walked the fields at the slow measured pace of Joshua Bell playing Max Bruch's *Scottish Fantasy* with the Academy of St Martin in the Fields, and knowing he was nailing it, and would continue working through another hazy day over the ancestral spirit charged ground where the solemn blades of dead grass guessed the next movement in the spirit song of the breeze, and his thoughts never lost the single heartbeat of each donkey in the herd of a thousand he had accumulated across Praiseworthy in the platinum donkey conglomerate transport business.

THE GIANT KELP HAIR SEA LADY GULPED!

We are not asking for the moon here...
Alvin Yeung, Civic Party Leader, Hong Kong, 2019

1

Oracle 10...Speak of zero-sum clash...

Sometimes, Aboriginal Sovereignty lived inside Tommyhawk's thoughts as his smart elder brother who had disappeared one time into the ocean, and never returned. This was the Praiseworthy he remembered, an intangible unreachable place, one that could only belong in those faraway dreams. His world was about being stuck forever among hostile donkeys living in scabby, stubble grasslands covering the vast dry lake where forked lightning works the sky at night in supercell dry storms, and owls hunt rats over the stubble where wombats emerged from burrows and travelled along the mist-shrouded pathways through thickets of saltbush, and where the big waves could be heard pounding on hundreds of kilometres of coastline to the south. It's a good country in which to hide a fascist, and a country that had remained a mystery to him since the day, long ago, when he had been dumped there by his father and the screaming platinum donkey spread over his seat in the car.

The only voices he spoke to were in the wind speaking in these parts – whether it sang, or howled, as it travelled over the dead grass and saltbushes on the floor of the lake, and whistled through the she-oaks, or whether it was silent, and all you heard was the growing intensity of donkeys braying in starvation and thirst. He lived on his own now. The old man whom his father had left him with had quietly disappeared a long time ago and was not seen again. Whether he had died somewhere, Tommyhawk does not know, but he thinks the donkey herder had committed suicide. Not long after he realised the old man would not return, the boy had let the donkeys loose to fend for themselves, but they stayed, and frightened him. He had tried to shoo them off but they would always return, and stand and stare at him as though willing him to follow them further away on the lake bed, and when he followed them into the vast sameness of the flat featureless lake spread over a hundred kilometres, he would become disoriented, or lost in the haze or a sudden heavy mist. It was too dangerous, so he stopped following them out on the lake. There were times when he believed the donkeys were not only trying to lure him to follow them, but tempting him to go so far from the edge that he would not easily escape from their control, and they would one day trample him to death. But, if he was to escape, he must set off on the lake each day to pull bits of grass out of the hardened earth around its roots to stuff in a canvas bag to bring back to the donkeys. He has to feed himself too. He cannot live on nothing. Sometimes, he eats a donkey if one dies. He will not kill a donkey, tackle it to death and stab it with his knife. He constantly watches the ground, but rarely sees anything happening in the dry earth. Nothing grows higher than a few inches, yet he feels the wind blowing through the low-lying grasses and picking up the whirly dust, the uprooted clumps of dried grass rolling away over the ground, and leaving behind wider gaps of bare earth.

But sometimes, Aboriginal Sovereignty turns up in the constant haze, moist-laden by humidity, moving across the lake – a phenomenon that continues to come and go at the most unexpected moments. This happened when Tommyhawk felt someone was standing close behind him while breathing in his ear, staring at the dry lake with him, and even without turning around, he knows it is his brother for he knows his presence, and knew it was no use turning around to see what was invisible, or no longer there. His brother now stares into the back of his head, but does not speak, and he continues to stand there. It suits Tommyhawk's state of mind to know his brother looks exactly the same, has never aged, never grown older as he had himself in a land that barely alters in the way it looks, and where he had lost track of the time spent living by himself. Maybe he had become an old man in all this time, but he knows that Aboriginal Sovereignty was doing the same thing he had always done, just looking out for his little brother, coming by to see what he was doing, making sure he was okay, and looking back over his shoulder, the same as his spirit did that night when he had last seen him standing alone in the sea, for them both to see the same view. There was a sudden wonder of agelessness endlessly running with possibility in this isolated place, for in this infinite permanency days were lost in time, and Tommyhawk never knew for sure how much time had passed, or whether he and the lake had been welded together forever, and thousands of years had already passed.

Nobody found him, but occasionally, in the mirage shimmering just above the lake, or in the spooky travelling haze of the heat, or the fog in the mist, he can see the outline of a golden-hair angel swivelling in her throne in the sky, and occasionally, she appeared in a hole in the clouds, and he was almost blinded by the rays of sunlight shining off her immaculacy. Mostly, there was too much aura radiating from her being, so that he could not see her face clearly enough, though in time, she did not appear clearly at all, and had become just a vagueness, a slight tint of what she might have been, and in the end, a phenomenon, a weird shape formed and broken by winds travelling with fog, or mist, or a twist of how you might momentarily see the *spiritus sanctus* in a mirage while watching with Aboriginal Sovereignty at the same sky, and considering the vision as being another fleeting spiritual visitation, something Tommyhawk should bring up in his conversation with the spiritual of the ancestral lake, and which he claimed was not the same thing as having someone like Aboriginal Sovereignty suddenly turning up when he was not in the least thinking of having visitors.

As for himself, Tommyhawk was oblivious to the fact that the ancient lake thought he really looked to be at least thirty years old now, even though he thought he had only just arrived the other day, or maybe his looks were deceptive, and he was simply a vague outline of a shadow cast over the ground, and he really was a thousand years old like the empty lake, or like country where its infinity always was, and always will be. He could only read time from when it last rained, but these occasions happened so rarely, that such out of the ordinary memories become intertwined, interlocked, left him feeling confused, then were forgotten altogether. Sometimes, for a while, he might remember seeing a million water birds fly over the lake just metres above his head, and there was a time when a bird briefly landed. He remembered threats to his life over a very long time, from when the donkey chiefs tried to mesmerise him, out-staring him for hours, or days, while standing off in the distance, as though they were challenging him, and luring him to walk far into the interior of the dry lake where there was little hope of ever finding his way in any direction, and he would die. He did not think that the world was searching to find him, and if he thought for one moment of such a possibility in the darkness as he tried to sleep, his mind would become beset by the hell of swishing sounds of a swirling cyclone ripping land apart inside his head, which became a force so tremendous, the lake uprooted itself, and flew, scattering all the country for miles around – dirt, dead stubby grasses, saltbush, birds, insects, moths, rabbits and rats – and he would know this was how frantically country searched, when it went looking for something.

Tommyhawk always hid at night in this place, tried to curl up into a ball, hiding amongst some spooked donkeys that assembled around him after having come off the intemperate ghostly lake in the middle darkness when the wind reached its height. He would live in fear if he thought any spirit lake was searching to find where he slept, and there were times when even the spirit of Aboriginal Sovereignty arrived out of the blue and stood like a lamp behind him and the glow lit the donkeys, when Tommyhawk sensed the fullness of his brother's presence as being the total world of Praiseworthy reaching through the sky as a spectre for all to see, and he felt as though country itself was pinpointing him, and saying, *there he is, here is the murderer of Aboriginal Sovereignty.* It was these visitations of the night that really frightened Tommyhawk, and he curled tighter on the ground, embracing the infinite time of the Earth to hide himself.

2

A moth once took Dance on a big spirit journey into the world of butterflies and moths...And, this was what it ended up looking like in those long days when there was still plenty of daylight left for the humidity waltzing through the haze over the flatlands of Praiseworthy and the rabble plague of white cabbage butterflies, those *Pieris rapae* climbing the thermals with lazy wings barely afloat, began filtering down around the dust-stained cabbage leaves, and fussing about where to lay eggs, on a green *Brassica oleracea* leaf here, or there, for the caterpillars that ended up spoiling this un-belonging vegetation. It's a cycle, and they move on again, in another generation of snow clouds of streamers floating in wave after wave through the long mesmerising dance joining the caper white butterflies migrating through the country on hot December days in the arid-zone dryness where millions drabble through the swirling dust-storm winds along with plastic bags, cardboard cartons, chip packets, twigs and leaves, emotions, the wheezing of supermen and superwomen types pumping the engine house, fuelling up for something great, and stuff like that, all the rubbish, like a dappling panic jungle of brightness throughout the reddened haze, until falling into the sea and becoming the wrecked wash on the beach.

In this time of never-ending madness, this dizzying sight of rolling lines of leisurely floating ribbons of whiteness flying in the sky, the people of Praiseworthy suffered constantly from bouts of vertigo. Then, from out of these floating waves, from the here and there, single butterflies dropped from the sky. A butterfly briefly perching on a stem in dried-up patches of tough-rooted, impossible to eradicate exotic buffel grass, the cherished drought-resistant, teeth-breaking Brahman cattle *Cenchrus ciliaris* lawn – or else, butterflies were alighting on the cyclone-proof fencing, on or from a camp dog's bone left in the middle of the street, or were massing to sip from vile bacterial festering in open drains left there by the government bent on creating third-world conditions on traditional lands that had owned the people of its story since times ancient, or the butterflies rested on the pretty pink, orange and yellow zinnia flowers growing next to the open sewerage, or were landing on pieces of sludge from the mosquito-infested grey water pouring from old communal laundries, or rested on the wilting leaves on the top of frangipani trees that had been struggling to grow in this dry earth for years.

There were other butterflies too that flew through the open windows and doors of the stifling hot and airless homes and once inside, watched from the wall what Praiseworthy families were getting up to with their privacy, while the dance continued. Seeing in those invading butterflies the heart of those weak-from-hunger people who used every second of life to breathe in, and breathe out, and have enough strength to go on nursing their anger problem about the feral donkey business of Praiseworthy, there was plenty to take away from those stutter-flutter frayed butterfly wings about how Widespread was preventing these hungry poor people from becoming white-styled economically independent, in what was once a good assimilating to white type of town that had no donkey problem prancing around in its shit, on what should have remained another stifling hot day where only the heat stirred, and moved.

But now, all Praiseworthy heard was the sound of the transport conglomerate, and they were sick of hearing donkey bells moving the wheels of long, high-tech, lightweight, *all-terrain destroyer* semitrailer drays hauling and carting stuff around all day long, and half the night. There were donkey teams carting churches with Widespread yelling *Go! Go! Quicker! Faster!* Go along little donkey, go along. It all began with one church needing to be moved nearer to a palm tree for Pentecost, then Cause had to haul the thing called a cathedral back on the long dray to where it should have remained in the first place, at its permanent address on the street with all of the other churches. Now every church wanted to be moved on some holy day whim or fancy, which became too much business for the transport conglomerate. Then, that was not all. Cause needed more long teams of donkeys to move whole houses when everybody wanted to relocate, to get away from certain neighbours, gossipers, relations, or from being ordered to move your house somewhere else, and so forth. The demand to relocate was becoming too much. Everyone wanted to move something. Demountable offices had to be moved. There were businesses that required a transport industry that did not cost the earth. The supermarket chains wanted to relocate, bring their whole infrastructure holus-bolus to Praiseworthy. Coffee shops. Cafés. Offices. Building materials. The mining industry wanted donkeys to cart the iron ore. Every person with an idea about establishing themselves close to the only reliable transport system that did not require fossil-fuel resources, carbon, solar, or electricity or what have you, looked to the platinum transport conglomeration. It was hard yakka for the donkeys to deliver mail three times a week, as well as the fresh fruit and vegetables, then evacuate all the sick people to the nearest hospital, and transport the babies back from the birthing centres. Then, they were always queuing up to go on a donkey cart for visiting other people who only lived a few blocks away and they could have walked there, and taking the whole shebang to interstate ceremonies on the travelling lines because the donkeys could travel through the rough country. It did not matter about having a highway anymore, and Praiseworthy people were having big ceremonies all the time now, and preferred travelling further on the ancestral roads. It was too much, as other people in the country who were not the traditional owners wanted to become part of the ancestral roads too, and to be part of the ancient laws, and they could not make treaties that recognised Aboriginal sovereignty and Aboriginal government quick enough.

You want to know who paid for all this? Country. Country coughed it up. Coughed up the money. Chucked the cash of frivolity around like it was nothing but a trifle for the great ancestral powers governing the land in the all times. You saw it happen all the time. The powerful spirits of place washing the country out with those flash floods, or how those fat cyclones sat sulky for months lingering over country, or stirred up raging fires or prolonged droughts, or took a river away, or either gave or took the seasons away, it coughed money too. What couldn't a great ancestor of country do? So, it was exactly like what the old law people had always said would happen if *you look after country, country will look after you*. So, why not? The money kept pouring into Widespread's pockets from the ancestral government which had more riches than a government developed by colonialists. Old Widespread, he had bits of cash sticking out from all over him, and falling out of his trouser pockets.

The totality of his *fing fang* platinum donkey international transport conglomerate had finally become sensational. These days, he called his success as a hauler the result of his careful breeding program from day one, which initially came from one old platinum donkey that had given him a line of dozens of pure silver-coated donkeys from which to choose a lucky mask-head for each of his transporters. The search for the true colour of grey was a trifle to endure initially – to find the correct shade of platinum while hunting feral donkeys through the scrub from one end of the country to the other, but that was not his main concern now, for he was becoming fickle from being spoilt for choice, so that he was forever changing his mind about which platinum grey would lead the trucking business. Now, almost everyone in Praiseworthy wanted to have an integral part of the all times ancestral life in this particular age of new-world big businessman thinking sustainable and renewals while the ancestral was changing the climate. They thought you could not beat a phenomenon like this, where all you could see was money being thrown at Widespread's conglomerate. These days it was raining cash in Praiseworthy, and the ancestral mob called that the power of country pure and simple as proof of its age-old wisdom, where country was actually integrating feral donkeys as countrymen more than some other countrymen who were not true countrymen in the seasonal calendar of all family relationships...And, remnant wisdom was what it was, for those paying close attention to these things, seeing that feral donkeys had been keeping country company for a long time, more than the recent traditional owner. It was them donkeys talking more to country, staying with country, and more or less, it was only these donkeys incorporating themselves into the song cycles of the old laws.

Yep! Among the continual woo-woo-wooing, talk-talk of grey pigeons cooing everywhere, there were people wanting to talk too, when they wanted to complain as usual about how that Cause Man Steel transport business was the worst freight train conglomeration in the world by saying it was too slow, uncomfortable, and only had bare boards to sit on so it was not like air travel, or travelling with Qantas with an air hostess, and the transport system did not have any air-conditioning, nor any roof for passengers to get out of the sun on a long interstate journey. Why would anyone expect things to be like that, even if it was the modern age of renewables and sustainability? Yet there were people who wanted to remember the good times, the days of flying business class in a QF Qantas flagship over so many deserts thirty thousand feet below, while you looked down at a nice meal of fish served on a plate. Of course, you could not take memories like that away quickly, even if you were using feral donkeys for transport that were cheap as chips, cheaper even than using solar power in a worldwide energy crisis of dwindling oil supplies. Then, even Qantas got the wind up itself, of being forced into a hike war with other worldwide airlines that wanted part of the new world action, a merger with the donkey business. Poor old Planet was not a merger man, but said he supposed the big questions were: why fly, with no gas? Even in this new age, rock stars, film stars pushed sustainability on the country donkey thing, and agreed that they should be travelling like the billions of poor people across the world. Now, the big serious questions that were being put to Planet were about how donkeys could be converted into some kind of new jet fuel? Just saying, to make the thing go faster, quicker, when you know, the achieving people of the world worked in terms of terabyte speed, not taking forever trotting along like, take for instance, a rock concert on the road could not be expected to travel forever from A to B which was just a few miles down the street from one venue to another. Listen! Planet! How could you expedite these animals? It was fine enough that donkeys might be the great survivors of the global warming reality, but how could they be trained to generate a bit more oomph in themselves for the sake of humanity? Were there any other possibilities other than the slow crawl? How about having multiple donkeys with the equivalent mass weight of a semitrailer loaded with shipping containers – say, fifty tonnes hauling power, to extract residual puddles of crude oil from the Saudi Arabian deserts to fire up the fighter jets for war. Or else, imagine what it would be like not to concentrate on the magical powers of the colour platinum, and to think about breeding a swifter donkey where you do not care what colour it is, but get it to move quicker than a snail, like it was being fried by jet fuel?

Now, you name what the new world should look like, but the people of Praiseworthy regularly went down to the donkey graveyard depot turnout all dressed up in their fancy travelling clothes to travel like normal travellers in the new modern way, on Planet's conglomerate. No one was in love with what they had become – impatient people of the new time, having to wait for hours for the donkey bus that was never punctual, and they could not help what they saw in the heat and humidity, for everywhere they saw the failure of the conglomeration – the filthy surroundings which were not first class like themselves, while they were trying to wave off all the butterflies popping down from the ribbon of waves flying around the graveyard, and landing with filthy jointed legs for a few moments, here and there on the travellers in clean travelling clothes. Or else, having to swipe the germ-loaded feet of these white caper butterflies landing on their lips busy gasbagging about putrid donkey muck stinking in the air and filling their nostrils with pestilence. Everyone knew Widespread was loaded, and could easily have built them a modern and luxurious transport lounge terminal somewhere else while using one of those perpetual government trainee labour schemes to make Aboriginal people economically independent. The lack of facilities was seen as a disgrace, for Aboriginal people had rights, and should not be forced to have to wait for their bus at a stinking donkey depot. It was a human right to expect clean air in a modern world, where you do not have packs of butterflies extending their slender tube probosces along your skin to suck the salt from your sweat and taste the worth of your soul, before rising back into a polluted airborne rubbish dump of deadly viruses.

Far more butterflies began dropping down from the migrating waves in the sky, and would land dead or alive on the backs of puppy dogs lying around and sleeping on the street. Or the butterflies would be waving their exhausted wings while resting upon the mud-caked backs of domesticated wild pigs asleep in the open sewerage, then land on the arms of the travellers, and the bare backs of the little children rushing after the butterfly streamers rolling above them through the streets. Then, while lazily turning towards the sea, the butterfly waves circling the children had them corralled while they were still running and staring into the sky and did not notice where they were heading, and off they went with the butterflies fluttering over the tidal flats, and towards the sea.

Oh! Whose fault was that? You could ask for a full description of how the children were saved, and the whole town would tell you how good Praiseworthy eyes were for total wide-angle lens surveillances twenty-four seven from the plethora of steeples along Church Street, but in that heart-attack moment, fox screams, blood-curdling yelps in toto crashed into the tsunami wave, held it back, reached straight into the brains of those kids rushing into the sea, turned them around mid-step, and the whole thing was over in a moment. The children were nearly killed, but by some strange coincidence a mighty king tide rushed in at exactly the same time as the children were running over kilometres of mudflats towards the sea and carried them back to Praiseworthy. None were injured because of those inappropriate, murderous, crossbred butterflies who knew this would happen, and were thought to have been conniving this act of terrorism for years.

All hearts of the tempest people were blown apart, again, atoms busted. Praiseworthy people were not specialists in working with the atoms of the heart, putting the thing back together. So, let it be said, a shattered heart was of no use for anything when the precedent had already been long established in the era. Who was able to stop those children of the broken-hearted from listening to the hallucinations of butterfly terrorists invading the Dreaming, the Law? All this was because of that smart-arse fascist kid, that little expert on everything in the world Tommyhawk Steel, Cause Steel's son. That kid lulled you into believing his bullshit stories. Remember him? He even knew about classical music that no one in Praiseworthy liked because it was white music, and not the more relatable country-and-western broken-heart music. He opened a can of worms, created a cult kid following like a comic strip, the thing which continued to this day, where the school children would start to listen to the white butterflies while they were killing themselves in the sea, doing this, instead of listening to their white government schoolteachers. Opera, he called it. *Butterfly Coma*. Performed the thing, broke old law, in front of the white government school. The schoolteachers claimed it was brilliant. Kept the thing. Got the kids to perform it every year to the whole community. The kids narrate the whole dreadful scenario just like Tommyhawk had originally performed it with his sneaky little voice that was a strain to hear at the best of times. The whole thing was about how the influx of butterflies were singing the humming chorus from *Madame Butterfly* as they were joyfully ending their life while suiciding into the sea. What was brilliant about that? These kids did not want to be released from the butterfly's magical spell, they said, and wanted to feel the watery arms of the sea wrapped around their bellies while they were humming Puccini's *Un bel dì, vedremo, levarsi un fil di fumo sull'estremo, confin del mare*, and feeling beneath them the pull of the flow moving back over the sea meadows, pulling all back into the ocean, not listening to the ancestral spirits talking about the infinity of all times in the currents swiftly moving to another world, and believing somehow at the last moment, they would break into reality and run for their lives out of the water, away from a mass suicide pact, while watching until the last moment, the white ribbons like snakes dissolving into the storm clouds roaming the ocean.

Cabbage butterflies do not come out of nowhere like a miracle in the arid zone, and these insects were seen flying from Dance Steel's cabbages, her wilting brassica, the source of plague insects after she sowed her vegetable seeds everywhere, that mostly rotted in the ground, and what germinated encouraged plagues not only of butterflies, but moths, beetles, locusts, cicadas, aphids, mice, and rats, and further diminished the pristineness of the ancestral country. She left rotten watermelon vines growing all over the ground with butterflies and donkeys feeding on the stinking flesh, and whatever else she was cultivating for aphids festering up every green stem throughout the town, and leaving the entire region looking like a war zone.

In this time, the great spirit haze dome sitting over the pristine essence of Praiseworthy became a spectacle of colourful butterflies and iridescent winged insects in flight, which were chased by birds of great numbers like seagulls and starlings. It was another miracle with possible cultural tourism potential. Then, the haze became polluted. The whole thing turned sour. The dome transformed into an aerial cemetery when it became a slow-moving dust tomb that could not free itself from the sheer weight of dead, broken insects. This monstrous thing glistened from the sun shining on the floating dust-like scales from millions of dead butterfly wings suffocating the good dust of country.

Cause Steel's donkeys trampling cabbages was not right at all. It was the principle of the thing, in a place flowering with proper first-class Aboriginal Australians in a buggered-up swampland in the time of drought, becalmed oceans, stilled country. Where were the puppy dogs and the pleasant feral pussycats in these times, where had they rolled up into tight balls asleep at night, and were dreaming of a massive Hercules-like ancestral warrior carrying sixty thousand thunder and lightning storms on his back, and where were the billowing rising seas loaded with fish, and what of the days when clouds came down from the skies and sat on the ground and left lizards and frogs to hold up the atmosphere of dust, and the other days of being too frightened to go out in a fishing boat on the ocean of ancestral stories beneath, and then too, of having to carry the days as they grew sweeter? These thoughts were for the future traditional owner living on country-governed land, as it was and will always be from and to infinity, when poor eyesight in the era of global warming had become a highly prized asset, that had to be saved, and protected from what was seen too brightly, too fakery, like the polluted haze glistening brightly, where you had to wear fake Cartier square-framed sunglasses glued to your eyes to lessen the glare.

Sitting around on old plastic milk crates and so on while believing their imaginary churches were like all those churches that were once the pride of Praiseworthy, the old sophisticates of the all times laws of country said they were really more like political God fellas now, though they were not God hacks. That was very good. And having become more God than God, they used God words for renovating their Dreamtime cathedrals, which they claimed, was about being literate in government affirmative action jargon talk for arguing about where a true saviour might choose to live once Praiseworthy moved up on the global liveability index as being one of the most desirable places in the world to live through the era right now.

Well! Heck! Hacks! And that was that then. Who knows what could have been different for Cause Man Steel in life, if he could not help seeing nothing in what the rules were in the progression of things, or if he had become a masterful stooge sitting on life's fence – juggling the eventualities in the pantomime bouncing with impossibilities, intrigues, stuff-ups, of not being eaten alive by sharks and crocodiles massing in the local sea, or of not being bowled off the fence guarding the house full of moths that the moon lit up like heaven amidst the darkness, where Dance was waiting for the story people to come with their stories about moths on the cyber tribe, if he had not been left outside with the hazy fog spirit, grass plains ghost feral cats walking on the back road, where he could not bring himself to bring Tommyhawk home to run the business, not in this neck of the woods, for he knows the so-called dead brother keeps following the fascist around, and he was not having fascism in the platinum transport conglomerate, not until Aboriginal Sovereignty returned to head the business, he needed him in the donkey fields instead of seeing him as a puppet master of adversity in the conglomeration...Or, if he were elsewhere, where he watches his son working with pieces of wood, kindling, sticks he has found, making a collection of puppets spread over the ground, some he cannot bear to be parted from, while others he leaves in the bush, as he performs with these puppets that wobble around on top of a kerosene drum – ding, ding – where even Widespread loves hearing the monosyllable beat, hip-hop rap about life lived through puppets in a tidy town memory that Aboriginal Sovereignty performs to his night-time audience, where the nightjars sitting on the side of the road suddenly fly up to the light to catch insects attracted to the drying climate bushfires – starlings, swallows on the wind, grasses, wasteland. Odd, but sometimes Aboriginal Sovereignty likes being on a Chinese roller-coaster ride and wishes that Dance could go too, although Widespread noticed that Aboriginal Sovereignty always missed the lonely streaming banners of butterflies screaming *we want him back*, and of course he knows that Aboriginal Sovereignty is not dead, and could never die – just sometimes, seen differently, as though having sprouted from the ground, grown out of a multi-consciousness, wearing multiple ancestries with the same religiousness of country, atmosphere, cosmos, stars, heavens, lands, seas, flora and fauna, deep inside, where the law of silence in the bush reigned, or sometimes, storms rose with hazes of butterflies. Finished up? Fancy thinking it could be like that! Of course, the spirit of Aboriginal Sovereignty never dies, for you cannot destroy what was infinitely existing in the law of country that always is, and always will be governing itself.

A note on sources

Quotations embedded in the text are from the following sources: Jorge Luis Borges, *I Am Not Even Dust: Selected Poems*, ed. Alexander Coleman, Penguin, 2000; Waanyi language words and quotation on butterflies from the *Waanyi Dictionary*, Waanyi Nation Aboriginal Corporation, 2012 (p. 1); Winston L. Moore (Slim Willet) *Don't Let the Stars Get in Your Eyes*, 1952 (p. 164); David Auerbach, 'László Krasznahorkai's *Baron Wenckhelm's Homecoming*: The Spiderweb and the Abyss', *Music & Literature*, 2019 (p. 289); Jorge Luis Borges, from *The Suicide: Selected Poems* (p. 368); Henry Puna, Prime Minister of the Cook Islands, speaking at the Nansen Initiative on Disaster-induced Cross-border Displacement, 2013 (p. 455); Latin aphorism usually translated 'seize the day' (p. 560); Yanyuwa Gem, *DIWURRUWURRU: Poetry from the Gulf of Carpentaria*, by the Borroloola Poetry Club with Philip Hall, Rune Books, 2015 (p. 605); Italo Calvino, from 'Quickness', *Six Memos for the Next Millennium*, 1988 (p. 647); Dave Clark and Mike Smith, song recorded by The Dave Clark Five, Columbia/Epic, 1963 (p. 665); Alvin Yeung, Civic Party Leader, Hong Kong, 2019 (p. 707).